THE FALL
OF PARIS

The Fall of Paris

Ilya Ehrenburg

Simon Publications
2001

Library of Congress Control Number: 43006902

ISBN: 1-931541-78-7

Published by Simon Publications, P. O. Box 321, Safety
Harbor, FL 34695

NOTE

A few of the incidental characters and the general background of this work are historical, but most of the characters and the situations in which they are placed are wholly fictional and imaginary, and do not portray and are not intended to portray actual persons and situations.

THE FALL
OF PARIS

PART

1

CHAPTER 1

ANDRÉ's studio was in the rue Cherche-Midi — an old street with grimy houses, on whose fronts the shutters had left black streaks. It contained numerous antique-shops crowded with Directoire writing-tables, chubby-faced angels, ivory buttons, garnet neck-laces, Chinese coins, lockets with locks of hair, and lucky charms. The people who dealt in all this junk were sedate ladies or pink-faced, smooth-shaven little old men in black skull-caps. At the cor-ner of the street was a café and tobacconist's under the sign of the Smoking Dog, where the customers were amused by an old fox-terrier, which begged with a well-gnawed cigarette-holder clenched between its teeth. Almost opposite was the restaurant Henri et Josephine. Josephine excelled at baking string beans, goose, and sausages *en casserole*. Henri used to go down to the cellar for a dusty bottle of wine and tot up the bills on a slate. Invariably cheer-ful, he praised his wife's cooking, and chatted with everybody, shaking them by the hand with his broad paw. Next door was a cobbler. Although the cobbler was over sixty, he sang about "roguish love" as he hammered away at his shoes. A little farther on was a flower-shop full of anemones, carnations, and asters. The shop was run by a neat, desiccated old woman. Every morning she wrote up on the door the name of the saint whose feast was being celebrated that day. On the pavements were scrawled in chalk the words "Heaven," "Hell," "Italy," and "Ethiopia"; this was one of the children's games. In the morning old women hawkers with moustaches pushed their barrows along with loud, hoarse cries of "Oranges! Tomatoes!" An old-clothes man shuffled past, playing on a pipe in order to advertise himself; people brought out old jackets and worn-out bedspreads. Towards evening aged singers, violinists, and organ-grinders went the rounds, singing, scraping, and dancing. Coppers were thrown down to them from the upper windows.

Inside, however, the houses were quiet, gloomy, and rather stuffy, crowded with furniture and knick-knacks. Everything was old, and every scrap of junk was cherished. The covers on the armchairs were worn and patched and the cups on the sideboard broken and glued together. You had only to sneeze and you would immediately be offered lime-flower tea or punch; a mustard poultice would be prepared for you. At the chemist's they sold herbs for infusions, fomentations, embrocations, also cat-skins, said to relieve rheumatism. Cats are legion; fat and castrated, they purr in the shops and in the conciergeries, where the concierges stew mutton from morning till night. The street was peculiarly attractive towards evening, when everything seemed to swim in a bluish light.

André's studio was on the top floor. The view from it was remarkable: roof after roof, a sea of tiles rising and falling in waves. Slender trails of smoke rose above the roofs, and in the distance, amid the pale orange glow, loomed the Eiffel Tower.

The studio was so cluttered up that there was hardly room to move. There were picture-frames, rickety chairs, tubes of paint, worn-out shoes, dusty vases. It seemed as though the things were not merely lying there but had taken root. At times they reminded you of spring undergrowth, especially when the sunlight, overcoming all obstacles, filtered through into the studio, to the surprise of André, who greeted it by chanting absurd couplets. Sometimes the studio was like a fading forest: everything in it seemed to look rusty and decayed. André himself — big, slow, and taciturn — looked like a tree. He would start working in the morning, painting roofs or a still life of asters, cauliflowers, bottles. In the evening he would light his enormous pipe and go out for a walk round the streets. Sometimes he would turn into a cinema, smile at the antics of Mickey Mouse, and then go home to bed.

André worked slowly and lived slowly. At thirty-two he still looked at the world with the wonder of youth. He was already being spoken of as a clever painter, but to him it seemed as though he had only just begun to work. His father, a Norman peasant, knew well how slowly the apple-tree grows and how long it takes before the cow gives milk. With the same kind of patience André waited for things to take shape and colour.

That afternoon in the early, fickle Parisian spring André was painting a bunch of anemones. There was a tap on the door. He frowned. It was his old friend Pierre, who started chattering almost before he was inside the room. He always talked nineteen to the dozen. André smiled distractedly and glanced repeatedly at his canvas. He had only just noticed that the yellow tones were too dull.

Pierre looked tiny beside André. He was restless as a bird. His skin was of an olive shade. He had large staring eyes, and long arms. He spoke in a hoarse voice, fidgeting and hopping about among the picture-frames and vases.

A civil engineer by profession, Pierre took an interest in the theatre and had once tried to write poetry, even publishing a little book of poems under a pseudonym. He was always falling in love and when his love affairs went wrong he used to toy with the idea of suicide; but he was strongly attached to life and loved it in all its aspects. He was an impressionable man with a weak will; his friends sometimes induced him to do unexpected things. In a café he made the acquaintance of a pianist. At that time there was a movement in Paris against the French Parliament; many deputies were discovered to have been mixed up in the Stavisky affair. The conversations about "honour" greatly excited Pierre, and on the night of the disturbances he was among the rioters in the Place de la Concorde. Six months later, at an anti-Fascist meeting, where the Socialist Villard was making a speech, Pierre quarrelled with the pianist and began exposing militarism. He devoured dozens of newspapers and never missed a single demonstration.

The year 1935 was a turning-point in the life of France. The Popular Front, which came into being shortly after the Fascist riots, was the breath, the anger, and the hope of the country. On the 14th of July and the 7th of September — the day of the funeral of Barbusse — the streets of Paris were filled with a crowd of a million strong; the people were coming into action. They were told that the elections were drawing near and the ballot-boxes would settle everything, but they clenched their fists impatiently. For the first time the people glimpsed the spectre of war. Germany had sent troops into the Rhineland; the Italians had overrun Abyssinia. The fortunes of France were in the hands of insignificant men who were afraid of the neighbouring states and also of their own people. They considered themselves shrewd strategists: they spoke fair words to the British, who are not at all sentimental, and then egged Rome on against London. The wise men were simpletons. One after another the little states turned away from France. The period of isolation was approaching, but ministers were far more concerned with the forthcoming elections than with the fate of their country. They tried to split the Popular Front. The prefects bribed the waverers and intimidated the faint-hearted. Every day new Fascist organizations sprang up. Young men of good family were going about the rich quarters of the capital in the evening shouting: "Down with sanctions; Down with England! Long live Mussolini!" In the working-class suburbs there was talk of the approaching revolution. The frightened citizens were afraid of everything: civil war and a German invasion, spies and political refugees, the prolongation of the term of military service, and strikes. Everybody looked on the new year as a decisive one.

Gripped by these events, Pierre lived like a soldier on guard.

He had remained fond of André since their school days, but they seldom met. Pierre's life had been tempestuous and André had always remained aloof. Whenever they did meet, Pierre would always tell his friend about the latest craze: a new car, the poems of André Breton, the anti-Fascist writers' congress. André would listen and smile. Then they would go off to the Smoking Dog, drink beer or vermouth, then separate again. A year would go by. Then Pierre would suddenly remember André and come rushing into the studio, shouting: "I must tell you about yesterday . . ." just as if they had seen each other the day before.

It was the same this time:

"Have you read Villard's speech? He said: 'We must carry out general disarmament even in spite of German militarism. . . .'

Everybody is talking about war. Will there be a war or won't there?
The director of our factory has even been consulting the astrologers.
Aquarius, it appears, is for war, but Taurus is against it. You see
what rubbish it is! Of course Hitler's mad. But if the Popular Front
triumphs, there won't be any war. What do you think? "

" I don't know," André said. " I haven't thought about it."

Pierre suddenly darted towards the door.

" Where are you off to? "

" To the House of Culture. They're preparing some sort of surprise. Come on. Let's both go! It's impossible to live in this bear
garden. I often go there now. It's fascinating. There are workers and
engineers there, and your brothers, the artists. That's what I believe
in. I even told our director so — without a horoscope. He was livid
with rage. Of course it's going to come. . . ."

" What is? "

" Why, the revolution, of course. You should see what's happening in our factory. Come on, let's go! "

André gazed sadly at his canvas, but Pierre dragged him away.

They made their way with difficulty into the big room, dim with
tobacco smoke. The chandelier looked like an oily blur; faces
gleamed dimly as though touched up with paint. There were working men in caps, artists in broad-brimmed hats, students, clerks,
and girls. Here the people of Paris, notorious for their scepticism,
were experiencing a second youth, filled with enthusiasm, arguing
till they were hoarse, clapping their hands and vowing never to
yield. Here men of the most varied professions were shaking hands
with one another, the world-famous scientist and Nobel Prize-
winner and the young glazier who had just written a naïve poem on
the " new life." The words " *Le Front Populaire* " sounded here like
an " Open Sesame! " The Popular Front had only to win and the artist's brushes would immediately appear in the hands of the miner.
Even sluggish vegetable-growers would appreciate the paintings
of Picasso. Poetry would become the language of the day. Scholars
would acquire immortality, and a new Athens would spring up on
the banks of the Seine that had seen so many things.

André looked round at his neighbours. There was a working man
who listened as though he was drinking in every word. Another man
was yawning; no doubt he was a journalist. There were a lot of
women. Everybody was smoking.

On the platform a little old man was speaking. He was a famous physicist, but André did not know him. He spoke in a low voice and coughed a lot. André could only distinguish individual words: " Socialist culture . . . new Humanism. . . ."

André had never been to political meetings. Suddenly he felt a longing for his studio and the work he had forsaken. Then he glanced up at the platform and called out to Pierre: " Why, it's Lucien! "

So this was what they called a " surprise "! André recalled how at the lycée Lucien used to recite the poem " I love the rage of a virgin " and how he used to say he was an opium-smoker. And now he was with the workers. Yes, there was no doubt about it. People did change.

Lucien caught the attention of the audience immediately. He spoke abruptly in an inspired style: " The fate of the earth will be decided by those who are above the earth: the bomber crews. Or by those who are under the earth: the miners of Picardy, the Ruhr, Silesia. Six hundred deputies? I've been told by an entomologist that there are certain beetles in which flies lay their eggs. The maggots grow in the body of the beetle. The beetle moves, but it is dead. It is the maggots that move. . . ."

Lucien spoke about Hitler, war, and revolution. When he finished, there was silence. The charm of his voice still held sway. Then the applause broke out. Pierre clapped till his hands began to ache. A workman next to André struck up a song: " It's the young guard from the suburbs who is marching. . . ." André forgot all about flies, war, and Lucien. He wanted to paint the workman's portrait.

The little old man on the platform shook Lucien's hand for a long time. Suddenly a young man with a grey, emaciated face stood up. He was poorly but neatly dressed.

" I ask permission to speak," he shouted.

Distractedly the chairman reached for his little bell.

" Your name? "

" Grisnez. My name won't tell you much. The name of the last speaker is far more important. As far as I know, his father, Monsieur Paul Tessa, got eighty thousand from that swindler Stavisky. Evidently, with that money here . . ."

The rest was drowned in the uproar. Grisnez brandished a stick; his face became contorted with a nervous tic. A burly stalwart be-

side him hit somebody with a stool. It was all André could do to
make his way to the exit. In the street Pierre called out after him:
"Wait! We're going on to a café with Lucien."

"I don't think I'll come."

"Why not?" said Lucien who had come up behind them. "Let's
have some beer. It was pretty hot in there. I could hardly go on with
my speech. I was warned they were going to make a row."

Pierre smiled. "They've been taught a lesson," he said. "I remember that fellow Grisnez. I ran into him on the 6th of February. He
was like a man possessed. He was slashing the horses with a razor.
It's obvious why they picked a man like that. But you made a
remarkable speech! I can imagine what the papers will say. In the
first place, you've got a big literary name. And then the fact that
the son of Paul Tessa is with us! Of course, for you it's all a drama.
But how resounding it is! That's why they wanted to smash up the
meeting. It's plucky of you, you know. Honestly it is. André, why
are you so silent?"

"I don't know what to say, really."

"Why don't you?"

"One needs to think these things over. Especially me. You yourself said I was slow in the uptake."

A young woman with curly hair and no hat was walking with
them. She wore a look of perpetual astonishment, eyes like those
of a lunatic or a night bird. She walked on in silence. Suddenly she
stopped.

"Lucien, have you got the key? I'm going home before I go to
work."

Lucien turned round, aware of his neglect.

"So sorry. I forgot to introduce you. Jeannette Lambert, an
actress. These are two old school friends of mine: André Corneau,
Pierre Dubois. Let's go to a café. I'll take you to the studio afterwards."

The café was empty. Behind the partition they were playing
cards. "But I've got the queen, old boy!" André gulped his beer
thirstily. Then he glanced sideways at Jeannette and felt a stirring
inside him: what eyes she had! They tried to recollect their school
days, but the conversation failed to catch on. Even Pierre grew
silent. The noise and the stuffiness made them feel tired.

Two men, slightly tipsy, came up to the bar and ordered a couple
of beers. One of them, aged about forty and wearing a messenger's

cap, exclaimed loudly: "For instance, if they knock the feet away from under us, it's all up, eh?"

The younger man answered: "No, old cock. Two and two still make four."

The messenger dropped a coin in the mechanical piano. Everybody winced at the jangling roar.

Pierre began to hum: "'*Je cherche après Titine*' . . . Do you remember? We sang that after the war when we were boning up on gerunds. How absurd! What a lot of bunkum they talked in those days! 'Peace for ever!' And now you've heard what they say: 'Two and two makes four' . . . it's very simple! First of all they deprive the Germans of their milch cows. That's the first act. Then they hold conferences: are they going to pay or are they not going to pay? They announce 'Prosperity.' But every night there were men sleeping under the bridge near my house. Coffee was burnt; fish were thrown back into the sea; machinery was broken up. That was the second act. Then Hitler comes on the scene. To hell with treaties! They start rearming. We after them, they after us, we after them. . . . There's your third act. We can tell what the fourth will be. Hitler says: 'I want Strasbourg and Lille into the bargain.' They dole us out gas-masks and canned food. We're defending civilization. A bomb drops on this house, and so it goes on. Only I don't believe the people will allow it. Villard has made an enormous impression even on the bourgeois. The elections will return a majority of the Left."

Lucien smiled. André was not listening to Pierre, but Lucien's smile annoyed him. "Snob!" he thought. Nevertheless he could not help admiring him. Such an extraordinarily handsome face! A pale, sensitive face with light green eyes, and hair the colour of copper. He looked like an actor playing the role of a mediæval bandit.

"Splendid!" said Lucien. "And what then? Villard will rearm just like the others. Perhaps worse — he's a faint-hearted creature. But that's not the question. At present my father is in the majority of the Right. He'll be re-elected and he'll find himself on the Left, quite sincerely moreover. He's a bourgeois, but he's an honest man. Of course, tomorrow he'll do the same as he did yesterday. People of that sort don't change. There's only one way out. I know what you're going to tell me. But if it's the people who make the revolution, it's the organization that prepares the revolt. It's an art. Isn't that so, André?"

"Well, in my opinion, art is another matter altogether. It's an art to paint pictures and to grow trees. But revolution is a misfortune to which people have to be led. You clutch at everything on the wing. You want changes, but I like life when nothing particular is happening. Then you can gaze, you can really see things. Like Cézanne, for instance. He spent all his life looking at apples, and he saw something. That, in my opinion, is art."

Pierre sprang to his feet, " It's easy to say that when you're sitting in your own studio ' gazing.' But what about when they drive you around under the muzzle of a machine-gun? It's too late to think then. You simply must be capable of seeing it from the logical point of view, surely, André? "

André did not really want to answer, but suddenly he found himself speaking. Jeannette was looking at him with her almost absurdly large eyes, and under her gaze he changed and ceased to be himself.

" I don't understand either Lucien or you, Pierre," he said. " Look at the stars. They're a tremendous spectacle. Poems are written about them. They probably have an influence on philosophy. But not a single artist would take it into his head to paint the starry heavens. What is it artists have always pored over, from the primitives to ourselves? The body: its irregularities, its accidental features, its warmth and absolute concreteness. Or a landscape, which is also a body presented in a different way, the convexity of a hill, the tones of leaves, the blending of the sky with a fence. When you talk about revolution, it's an idea, mere words. But the people listening to Lucien this evening were living beings. I saw their faces and their suffering. . . ."

André broke off. He wondered why he had spoken. It was all to no purpose, not what he wanted to say at all. How did this woman live? Lucien had said she was an actress. She couldn't be! She was a child. Or mad. Lucien now, there was an actor for you. She had asked him for the key. That meant they were living together. . . . Without realizing it, André was jealous. He was making one blunder after another. When Jeannette asked for a glass of cognac, he said: " It's no good. The best thing is to go for a walk. Then you'll forget. . . ."

She made no answer, but Lucien screwed up his eyes ironically.

"A moral lecture? Jeannette, isn't it time you were getting along? "

She shook her head. André blushed with embarrassment.

They were all silent. The card-players behind the partition were getting abusive: "What the hell! Where are your trumps?" . . . A boy came in with the evening papers: "Latest edition! War inevitable!"

Jeannette was standing by the piano. She put a coin into the slot, and when the same old foxtrot resounded she turned to André: "Let's dance. After the last war everybody danced. I was a little girl then, but I remember. . . . We'll outwit them. We'll dance before, so as not to have any regrets afterwards."

André ought to have refused, as he could not dance. Moreover, in that quiet little café, where clerks and shopkeepers sat for hours playing cards and half-frozen chauffeurs came in for a quick drink, nobody had ever danced. But André blushed with pleasure. His enormous red hand trembled as it touched Jeannette's back. The proprietor looked reproachfully at them from the cash desk. They danced for hardly more than a minute. Suddenly Jeannette stopped.

"I must go," she said in a low, very tired voice. "Lucien, I'm going to walk."

When she was gone, Pierre asked: "What theatre is she in?"

Rather unwillingly Lucien answered: "She's working in radio now, at the Poste Parisien station. It's a small show — theatre and advertisements at intervals. They all say she's got a lot of talent, but you know how difficult it is to get on. . . ."

Lucien invited his friends to go to his place: "We can have another drink and talk." Pierre agreed at once, but André said: "No." Lucien insisted. "Oh, come on, nobody knows when we'll meet again. If war breaks out . . ."

André got up. "There won't be any war. But I'm off. I must take a walk after all this conversation. Don't be cross, Lucien. I'm the sort of chap that likes his own den. I'm a badger. I don't like meetings, or theatres, or . . ."

He was going to say "or actresses," but he waved his hand and went out.

CHAPTER 2

ANDRÉ walked with rapid strides. His way led right across the city. Shrieks of motor-horns rent the air. There were clusters of red, green, and purple lights. Swarms of people, strolling, selling newspapers and neckties, touting for cabarets. Prostitutes hoarsely repeated their tender invitations. In a little blind alley a loud-speaker announced: "The necessity of rearmament is dictated by . . ." André plunged into this din like a diver cleaving through thick black water. Then he stood a long while on a bridge. Below him the reflected lights seemed to live a second, dim life, but the water of the Seine was black as ink. A wind sprang up and it began to drizzle. André thought about Jeannette's eyes. What an extraordinary girl she was!

At the corner of the rue Cherche-Midi he went into the Smoking Dog to buy some tobacco. It was bright and noisy inside. Suddenly André sat down and ordered a glass of Calvados. The spirit warmed the roof of his mouth, and he smiled with satisfaction. He wanted to shake off the persistent thoughts that seemed to lead nowhere. This, for him, was a new and incomprehensible sensation. He drank three glasses of Calvados and was about to go when a thin-looking man with white eyebrows and eyelashes came up to him. He was wearing a wide overcoat.

"Excuse me," said the man. "My French is atrocious. I hesitated a long time before approaching you, although I see you almost every day. I live in the same house as you, at Madame Coad's on the third floor. I saw your pictures at the Salon. They impressed me immensely, especially the suburban landscapes and those grey tones. . . ."

André asked abruptly: "Are you a critic?"

"No. I'm an ichthyologist. Allow me to introduce myself: Erich Nieburg from Lübeck."

André looked with surprise at his bright, naïve eyes, close-cropped moustache, and starched collar.

"I don't understand. . . ."

"I'm a German."

"I didn't mean that. I meant the word ending in 'ologist.' You said it was your specialty."

"Fishes."

André laughed out loud. "Ah, fish! Now let's just get this straight: you like my landscapes of Fontenay-aux-Roses, especially the grey tones, and you're interested in fish in Lübeck. It still doesn't seem to make sense. But take a seat. Do you drink Calvados? That's fine! So Madame Coad is a lousy old hag. Did you have to leave Germany?"

"No. I was sent here for four months. I've been working at the Institute of Ichthyology. I'm going back to Lübeck tomorrow. That doesn't please you?"

"Me? It's all the same to me. Personally I know very little about fish. There are some very pretty ones, it's true, and some are good to eat. But as for the rest, that's your business. If you like Lübeck, then live in Lübeck. If you like Paris, you can live in Paris. . . ."

The German got a bit tipsy after the first glass. His bright eyes became slightly glazed. He took out a cigarette but did not light it. He was silent for a long time. Then he said: "It's not a question of what one likes. I've grown to love Paris. Perhaps I've even understood it. It's a question of where a man was born, although that too is outside his own conscious choice. For instance, I was born in Germany. That's why I love the German language, German trees, and even German sausages. You were born in France, and you . . ."

"You think I love France? Hardly. Nobody thinks about that here. Of course, at school they teach and at official ceremonies they talk about 'our beautiful France' and 'our native land in danger,' but we merely yawn. Or else we laugh. One man will tell you it's better in Moscow; another will tell you it's wonderful in your Lübeck; but they don't talk about Paris. They live in it, and that's all there is about it."

"Do you mean to say you don't love your country?"

"I've never thought about it. In the last war the people were hopelessly taken in, it seems. Now you hear them say: 'They stuffed our heads with nonsense.' I don't know. Maybe they weren't deceiving them. My grandfather used to talk about 1870. They shouted: 'Vive la France!' then. But that was under the German bayonets, when the Prussians were in Normandy. . . . Tonight I was with some very fine fellows, only they're too fond of philosophizing. It was they who put me into this mood. They talked about war the whole evening, the cranks! They're convinced there's going to be a war at any moment."

"Undoubtedly there is. I expected it last spring. . . . It's a good thing to have a year's grace. You and I have been very unlucky. First one war and then another, and a stunted life in between. Anyway I'm glad to have seen Paris while — "

"While what?"

"While Paris still exists."

André got up. "You're just another crank," he said. "You're not used to Calvados. That's why you imagine all these horrors. I wish you good luck with your fish."

André left because he had suddenly remembered Jeannette. Her voice seemed to float towards him from far away, imparting a deep significance to the most commonplace words. He ran up the dark winding stairs and rushed to his radio. A twangy, nasal tenor was singing: "The Baldoflorin Mixture cures headaches and the spleen. . . ."

He sat down on a stool and covered his face with his hands. He sat like that for a long time. Suddenly he started up. A familiar voice was coming over the air. He looked for Jeannette's eyes, but all he saw was the illuminated dial of the radio: "Leipzig," "Rome," "Poste Parisien." He heard the words: "The more I try to conceal all my feelings, the more I reveal my heart. . . ." Then Jeannette repeated twice the words: "Child's play." This was followed by a bass voice urging listeners to drink Martini vermouth before meals. It was so unexpected that André had to laugh. He paced to and fro in the studio, repeating to himself: "Very well. I'll drink Martini. I'll reveal my heart. Child's play. . . ." But the receiver threatened: "German air force. . . . Crisis of the League of Nations. . . . Anti-aircraft defence. . . ."

André went over to the open window. The March night was stormy. The boats in the Channel were heeling over, and the fishermen clutched fearfully at their religious medals. The wind from the sea reached Paris and battered against the houses. You could taste the salt in the wind. André had been brought up near the sea. Now the apple trees down there were being tormented. The sap was slowly rising in their trunks and the wind was driving the trees mad. What a nonsensical wind! "New Humanism, beetles, revolt, war." Could it possibly all be true? That German had said: "While

Paris still exists. . . ." And Jeannette? She might get run over or catch cold. How frail was the world! They had been arguing about ideas — the star-gazers, the lifeless stones! It was only possible to love apple trees — down there in Normandy, where the storms blew. Apple trees and Jeannette.

CHAPTER 3

LUCIEN brought Pierre to a cold, richly furnished, uncomfortable room. One felt that the occupants of this room were constantly changing, that nobody had any affection for the rococo cupboard or the sporting prints. Lucien lived with his parents. He had taken this room for Jeannette, although he talked of it as " My apartment." On the broad sofa lay a volume of Engels and a doll made of coloured silks.

Lucien brought out a number of bottles and began mixing a drink. Pierre began to talk about the theatre. He was an enthusiastic admirer of Shakespeare. Lucien interrupted him:

" It will all have to be put off for a hundred years. Yesterday Jeannette was declaiming: ' To be your fellow you may deny me; but I'll be your servant whether you will or no. . . .' Miranda would do better to hold her tongue. It's comrade Caliban's turn to speak."

He put out his unfinished cigarette and suddenly began speaking in a different, more simple strain: " I shall have to break with my father. It's not going to be easy. There's today's speech. . . . Besides, my new book is coming out in a few days. . . . I've got to make my choice! I can't understand people like André. You don't say ' no play ' when the stakes are high."

" André will be with us all right," said Pierre. " You don't know him. He's a good fellow, only he's slow in the uptake. You may think it absurd, but I sometimes think that everybody will be with us, positively everybody. I'm working at present in the Seine factory and I've come into collision with Desser. He's an exceptionally interesting man. If you argue along the ordinary lines, he's our enemy. He's one of the big-shot capitalists. Before the 6th of February he was backing the Croix de Feu. But I know from my own experience how easy it is to make a mistake. . . . Desser has understood a good many things. He's too clever to defend a rotten cause. In a year's time he too will be on our side. You'll see! Villard was right when he said: 'We Socialists will secure the co-operation of all Frenchmen.'"

Lucien fidgeted with the doll and yawned. "Of course. For that reason it will be necessary in the first place to shoot Desser and then hang Villard."

Pierre boiled up with anger and paced hurriedly to and fro in the long room. "That's the way to alienate everybody! People vary. They come to us in different ways. You've got to realize that! In our factory we've got a mechanic named Michaud. A remarkable chap, but he's a fanatic. To him Desser is a capitalist and nothing more. The Communists . . ."

"Personally I prefer the Communists to Villard," said Lucien. "They're courageous people. Only they too are poisoned with political cookery. What is the Popular Front? A troika dragging old Mother Marianne! The shaft-horse is Citizen Villard. The side horse on the left is your mechanic. On the right? Maybe they'll harness my father. The triumph of tolerance." Suddenly he began to laugh. "I've just remembered our history teacher and how he once said very solemnly: 'The great Revolution was ruined by intolerance.' And Freddie the fat boy raised his hand and said: 'I'm ruined by tolerance — houses of tolerance.' They wanted to expel him, you remember?"

They started reminiscing over their pranks of long ago. Lucien kept pouring out drinks. Pierre grew mellow. Unexpectedly, for him, he began to talk about his new girl.

"You must meet her. Talk about 'revolution.' Now there's a girl who will man the barricades. Her father's a working man. He knew Jaurès and he's been imprisoned. She's a teacher at Belleville. If you could see how they adore her there, both children and grown-ups! She has changed everything."

Lucien smiled. "Is this one of your regular attacks or have you decided to get married?"

"Don't fool. I'm dead serious. This is absolutely vital to me. But there's nothing between us. Agnès doesn't even suspect . . ."

"It was Jules Laforgue who said: 'Woman is a mysterious but necessary creature.'"

" Necessary to you, I suppose you mean," said Pierre indignantly, but he did not go on, for at that moment Jeannette came into the room.

She took off her hat and gloves, wriggled about in front of the mirror, and lit a cigarette, all the time without saying a word. Then she said: " Why didn't you ask André? "

Lucien was annoyed, but said nothing. Jeannette moved a glass aside and turned to Pierre.

" How has he been entertaining you? Has he been telling you all about his father's money? Or was he brewing a revolution in the cocktail shaker? "

Lucien looked at her in amazement.

" What's the matter with you? " he said. " Why all this irony? "

" Irony? That's not irony. I'm just bored."

Pierre began to fidget. " I ought to be going. I've got to get up at six."

CHAPTER 4

MICHAUD said enthusiastically to Pierre: " Now this is a proper bench! "

Then they began to talk politics. As usual, Pierre spoke highly of Villard. Michaud listened in silence. He was a stocky man of thirty with grey, sceptical eyes. A spent cigarette end stuck to his lower lip. He wore a cap and a short-sleeved shirt that showed an anchor and a heart tattooed on his arm. He had served in the Navy. He was a good worker, but he had a sharp tongue. In the factory they respected but were also rather afraid of him.

Pierre addressed him as if Michaud were his senior. He was anxious to know whether he approved of Villard's latest speech. Michaud did not answer.

" Perhaps you don't agree with the slogans? "

" Why not? They're the slogans of the Popular Front, and Villard is a master at making speeches."

" Then you don't trust him? "

" It's the Popular Front now. That's the official side of it. As an individual I might trust him with my watch or my wallet, but I wouldn't trust him with our cause! "

" I don't understand you, Michaud. This bench isn't yours. It isn't ours. It belongs to the Seine, to Desser. We're making engines for bombers, that's to say for war. You can find a kind word for your bench, but you talk of a man who has devoted the whole of his life to our cause as though he were an enemy."

" The bench is not merely Desser's property," said Michaud. " It's a tool and a good one. At present it doesn't belong to us, but to-morrow it may. That's why it's worth looking after. The bombers are a shady business. Whom are they going to fight against? Whom and how? As regards Villard, everything is quite clear. At present we're together. It's to his advantage and to ours. Afterwards, either we'll send him to the devil or he'll send us. I don't know who'll be first. One thing is certain: if we don't put him up against the wall in time, he'll shoot the lot of us. And how! Well, I've talked enough. I've got to test the hydraulic press."

Pierre thought about this conversation on his way to Agnès after work. It was that twilight hour when everything seems imponderable and fantastic. Old houses, that in the daytime are covered with stains like a rash, look like blue hills. Faces, jaded and deformed by age and sorrow or coarsely painted with cosmetics, take on the semblance of beauty. The visible world is touched with the enchantment of art.

To Pierre, Michaud's words seemed intolerably harsh. Perhaps he was right, but in that case everything would be dull — both the struggle and the victory. Pierre immediately felt that Michaud was wrong. It was enough to remember Villard's record, how he had refused the rosette of the Legion of Honour and how the chauvinists had attacked him. He was not the sort of man to go in for compromise.

Pierre did not understand Michaud and his way of thinking, which was tortuous and at the same time direct, like a mountain stream that bores through rocks. Michaud was a Parisian, sceptical and stern. Pierre, on the other hand, was born in the south among the vineyards of Roussillon. His father was a composing-room foreman in a printing firm at Perpignan. There the earth was reddish, the light was glaring, and the sea so blue that it looked like molten enamel. Pierre himself liked loud laughter, vehement gestures, tempestuous tears, Victor Hugo's verse, the Jacobin tradition of passionate speeches from the scaffold, and all the external, expressive beauty of life.

As he looked at the chestnut trees of the boulevard, scarcely visible in the blue haze, but already stirring with the beginnings of spring, he said to himself: "We'll win, because people want happiness, the warmth of hands, friendship and trust!" He recalled his half-childish verses: "The wind and the fight — black bread and life. . . ." His thoughts turned involuntarily to Agnès. How would she greet him?

Pierre, who lived aloud and was inclined to exaggerate all his emotions, found himself at a loss when faced with the concentrated silence of this girl. He said to himself: "I can't live without her!" He had even told Lucien about his love. But never once had he dared to express his feelings to Agnès. He often went to see her, telling her about his meetings, books, and cars and asking her questions about her school and the children. Suddenly they would both become silent and hear the rain beating against the window of the villa.

Once he ventured to ask her: "Have you ever experienced that?" He had just been telling her about a novel by Knut Hamsun. Secretly he hoped she would say: "Yes. Now." But she turned away and said gruffly: "I have had a lover." From that day Pierre's yearnings were tinged with jealousy. He interpreted Agnès's sadness and aloofness to mean that she was pining for his unknown rival.

The street lamps were lighting up as Pierre walked along the rue Belleville. Pigs' heads, adorned with paper roses and bathed in a violet-coloured light, lay like stones in the windows of the pork-butchers'. On a poster at the entrance to a cinema a painted beauty, clasping the hand of a sailor, wept gigantic tears. In dozens of cafés the glasses jingled pleasantly and the balls flitted about the green surface of the billiard tables. In the evening this street had a pathetic tinsel glitter. Branching off it were dark narrow side-streets like canals heavy with smells of margarine, onions, and urine. Urchins played at pitch and toss. Old women screeched abuse at one another. Children and cats howled. This was one of the poorest quarters of Paris. No romance in poverty here. It was a matter of sewing patches on patches, finding something for a miserable stew, and carefully calculating every mouldy copper.

In one of the wretched side-streets a new house had recently been built for shopkeepers, employees, and officials. The tiny flats were adorned with bright wallpaper and cluttered up with fantastic armchairs — a humble luxury. The seventh storey at the top had been set aside for the servants' rooms, as in expensive houses, but the shopkeepers and the office workers' wives did their own cooking, so the attic rooms were let to solitary poor people. Here lived an out-of-work book-keeper, an aged masseuse, an unsuccessful travelling salesman; and here too lived Agnès Legendre, who had conquered the heart of Pierre.

Her room contained a narrow folding bed, a table with a pile of school exercise-books, two straw-bottomed chairs, and a washstand. The walls were bare, with neither pictures nor photographs. On the book-shelf were school-books, a dictionary, *Madame Bovary*, and a life of Louise Michel. Through the window at the end of the room you could see a hazy, almost theatrical moon floating in the sky.

Agnès could hardly be called beautiful. She had a bulging forehead, short-sighted grey eyes, and a turned-up nose. Her hands were reddened with work. Nevertheless, there was about her the attraction of hidden feelings, perseverance, the will to work and, maybe, to sacrifice herself. Whenever she smiled, her face at once became simple and pleasing, like a girl's who likes morning in the forest and berries, a girl's who could easily be deceived and offended. Agnès seldom smiled, and when she did, it was not from merriment but from a profound inner peace. In moments of great joy she cried.

Pierre had never before seen Agnès in such a sullen mood. When he told her about Lucien's speech, she said morosely: " Disgusting! They're playing on his father's name."

Pierre tried to argue. He talked about Lucien's sincerity, the conflict between the two generations, and the necessity of propaganda; but Agnès said obstinately: " Politics are sordid. It's all a game. Yet people are starving."

Pierre thought: " She's probably in love with an artist." He would have to find out once for all who his rival was.

" Tell me," he said, " who's that man you once mentioned? You know the one I mean. Is he a poet? "

" No. A druggist. Why drag that up? And today of all days, too. I've trouble enough without that."

" Are you thinking about him? "

Agnès did not answer. She looked at Pierre, and her eyes, which usually had a look of helplessness as with all short-sighted people, became hard, almost malignant. Her voice was cold. "I heard today that I'm being dismissed from the school. One could scarcely have a more prosaic subject for one's thoughts than that."

"Dismissing you?" said Pierre indignantly. He felt stifled in the little room.

"Who's dismissing you?" he cried. "How dare they? It's not possible!"

Agnès told him there had been a circular sent round by the Ministry, and then one of the children's parents, the proprietor of a drug store, had reported that his son at school had been obliged to write a "revolting composition."

"Here you are. Read it. The boy is aged eight."

Pierre read it aloud: "*We had six puppies. Mummy drowned five. She said there was not enough milk. René says that he is soon going to have a sister. René says they have not enough milk. I think they will drown René's sister too. When I was little, we had a lot of milk. Mamma says that when I am grown up, they will kill me in the war. I like playing at ball and riding on the merry-go-round.*"

"I told the children: 'Write about how you live.' There were some remarkable pieces. Have a look at them. In the letter from the Ministry they talk about 'anti-patriotic spirit.' Today I was told to go and see the inspector. He said to me: 'Change the character of the education and then we'll intercede for a modification of the censure on you.' I refused."

"And yet you reproach me for politics!"

"This is not politics. This is the truth. I don't like politics. In politics everything is like rubber. You can compress it or you can stretch it. You don't know what's good or what's bad. It's all talk, talk, but the people don't change."

"What are you going to do now?"

"I can sew. I'll go into a workroom." Then she added quietly: "The worst of it is I like teaching. I was a girl at the time, but I remember how my father suffered. He was working at Renaud's. The men went on strike. It lasted a long time. Mother moaned that she had nothing to feed us on. But Father didn't lose heart. He pawned his watch, treated us to sausage, and joked and sang. There was a song at the time about a hippopotamus who became a senator. All the same the men gave in. Father was not taken on again.

He was one of the 'ringleaders.' He was out of work the whole winter. He got odd jobs from time to time, mending a sewing-machine or something. He kept going to the guild, telling them that if they'd let him come back he'd work for nothing. And he used to tell us that he missed his machine."

They were silent for a while. On a piano down below somebody was playing that popular romance, *Tout va bien, Madame la Marquise,* picking out the notes with one finger. Pierre was standing by the table, looking at a child's exercise-book in which a youngster had drawn the dream of man: a blue sea and a little ship. Pierre suddenly took the girl's hand.

"Agnès!" . . .

He had been trying to make up his mind for months. He had imagined how he would have to talk, convince, and prove. But now all he could say was her name. All other words failed him. But Agnès understood everything. Her hand answered his.

"Darling! . . . You know, I've been through such torments!" Pierre said. "I didn't know how to say it."

"And I thought it was all on my side and you didn't care. It seemed to me I was merely an incident in your life and that you had someone else. I couldn't understand why you kept on coming to see me."

The piano had long ceased playing. All seven floors of the building were asleep. The wretched side-streets were quiet. The people who had laughed and cried in the cinemas had returned to their homes. The last bus rattled by. Only the moon still hung above the roofs like a forgotten lantern, and the cats lifted up their voices. Suddenly Pierre remembered: "She's had another lover! She said he was a druggist. It was the proprietor of a druggist's shop who reported her. Coincidence? No, that's the man! He wanted to have his revenge. What a terrible man! He probably whips his little boy. He's got a clipped, slightly greying moustache and wears striped trousers. He probably went straight to the police station with a high moral purpose. And she lived with a man like that!" Pierre became all hunched up and quiet, as though suffering from a headache.

"Pierre, what are you thinking about?"

"About him. You said he was a druggist. . . ."

"Yes, Duval. He informed the inspector."

"I don't mean that. I mean your lover."

"You goose! You believed it? I said the first thing that came into my head. I was thinking about the man who reported me, so I said: 'A druggist.'"

"But who is he?"

"You. And before you there was nobody."

He put his arms around her and suddenly felt tears against his cheek.

"Agnès, are you crying?"

"Silly! I'm all right."

CHAPTER 5

THE windows of the big room looked out on a dark yard. It was often necessary to have the light on in the early morning. The large table was littered with files, newspaper clippings, and letters. Anything might turn up under the papers; an ash-tray full of cigarette ends, a detective story, a stray glove. The owner did not like his desk to be tidied. The furniture was a jumble of styles: an Empire cupboard, a modern armchair with metal tubing, unmatched chairs. On the wall hung a Marquet landscape: greenish-grey water and an old boat. Next to it was a map scored all over with red pencil, the circles representing the oil and the triangles coal. Here worked the financier Jules Desser, one of the real rulers of France.

Desser was a somewhat bloated man of about fifty, with sharp eyes underneath thick, beetling brows. Sometimes he looked much older. One could not help noticing the dropsical puffiness, the morbid greyness of his skin, and the stoop of his shoulders. At other times he hardly looked more than forty. He had the movements of a young man, and his eyes were amazingly lively. He dressed in a careless manner, drank a good deal, and was never without a short, blackened pipe in his mouth.

Unlike other representatives of the financial oligarchy, Desser did not like ostentation. He never allowed reporters or photographers to come near him, stubbornly refused to make any political speeches, and denied having any influence on affairs of state, although no government could have existed even for a month without his approval. Desser preferred to remain behind the scenes. Unseen, with the help of people whom he richly rewarded and who were devoted to him, he dictated laws, directed foreign policy, selected ministers, and brought about their downfall.

Desser's power was derived from figures, their combination and their contradictions. It was connected with capital invested in Polish railways, with American oil, Indo-Chinese rubber, with owners of aircraft factories interested in the growth of armaments, stockbrokers who reacted to every warlike speech by Hitler with a joyous bout of stock-jobbing, bauxite kings who sold raw material to Germany, the shoe-manufacturers' trust, which dreamed of humbling the shoe emperor Bata, and Beneš into the bargain; liberal textile manufacturers who were prepared to grant civic rights to Negroes, provided the Negroes clad themselves in imported pants; intransigent directors of the Comité des Forges who appealed to the authority of the Pope in order to keep down wages. It was also connected with the war between the road transport and the railway companies, with empty trains and the failure of motorbus companies, with millers who grew rich on Canadian wheat, and with the chauvinism of landowners of the Beauce district who demanded protective tariffs. Here was a ball of various interests that beat like a human heart.

Desser knew the last-minute prices of cotton and zinc. He knew how much had to be paid to this or that minister. His head was filled with figures like the buzzing of flies. Yet he never reckoned up his profits: he worked in money as a sculptor works in stone. He was modest in his personal life. He had no family and took no interest in charities. He could have lived on the wages of one of his employees. Rubber and copper were abstract ideas to him. He once asked where Saigon was. No doubt he would have been unable to distinguish wheat from oats.

Desser had taken his degree at the Polytechnical School. He had worked for two years as an engineer, and in his heart he considered that money had ruined him. He had betrayed his profession for the sake of lucre. With a morbid apprehension he waited to see how Pierre and the other engineers received his remarks. Being a conceited man, he would say: "Don't pay any attention to what I say. I'm a dilettante."

Desser was by nature a passionate man in love with danger. He might have become a test-pilot, an explorer, or a demagogue plotter of revolutions. Indeed, even in his own business he appreciated risks: the unexpected fluctuations of the London or New York Stock Exchange like the whims of a flighty coquette; the alliance of yesterday's enemies behind the back of yesterday's friend; the breakdown of a diplomatic conference; in a word, everything in which it was easy to miscalculate.

Such a man seemed bound to take a fancy to Fascism with its philosophy of fatalism, its worship of rank, its inclination towards adventure, and its doubly tragic insignia. Actually, until the 6th of February Desser had been giving fairly large subsidies to the leaders of the Croix de Feu. This, however, was a gambler's move; he wanted to overthrow the Cabinet. Having achieved his purpose, he calmly told his recent friend Breteuil: "From now on you'd better forget my address." Desser was now inclining towards the Left. This was the latest sensation in the parliamentary lobbies, where it was even said that he was hobnobbing with Villard. In fact Desser's real favourites were the Radical Socialists, that enormous ramshackle party of the "average Frenchman," uniting big traders and small wine-growers, famous professors and semi-literate shopkeepers. It was a party that teemed with orators, who played Danton or Gambetta in out-of-the-way places. It was a radical party that feared radical enterprises more than anything else. Neither his position nor his ability made Desser an average Frenchman, but he loved, like the very soil and air of France, the chatter of these tame Jacobins which was always followed by sober, painstaking work. He used to say he was a cynic. Nevertheless, he had a political ideal. He wanted to preserve the France he had known from childhood; its wealth and continuity; the unshakable foundations of the family with its intimate dramas, its jealousy stronger than love, and its epic lawsuits over inheritances; the pleasant tedium of French provincial towns; the unconcern and at the same time the thriftiness, even stinginess of the housewives; the industriousness which obliged well-to-do old men to dig their vegetable plots or mend fishing nets; the flower-beds of the rentiers with sweet peas and green peas that have no equal in the world; the passion for fishing in any and every piece of water without hope of landing even a minnow; the world intrigue in the refreshment-room of the Chamber and the academic disputes as to which apéritif is most beneficial to the stomach; the rights of patronage, the mutual guarantee of the Masonic lodges, the clannishness that gave to high politics an atmosphere of comfort and intimacy; and the iron that spared neither God, medicine, nor France, nor even a man's own wife.

No doubt Desser's origins had much to do with his attitude. Known in New York, even in Melbourne, he was the son of a man who kept a little café in Angers, Le Rendez-vous des Amis. It was there that parliamentary candidates canvassed electors before polling day. Oldest inhabitants would talk about the troubles of the last century — the floods, the tiger that escaped from a menagerie, and the war — and loving couples, appreciating the dim light of the gas jet, would hug one another in passionate embraces. Jules Desser's father never lived to see his son's grandeur; he died of typhus in the last war. Having made his millions, Desser remained faithful to the habits of his childhood. He found peace of mind over a game of chess with his old gardener. At meals he mopped up the gravy on his plate with a piece of bread. Sometimes he managed to get away into the country on a Sunday. The little cafés along the Marne and the Seine reminded him of the Rendez-vous des Amis; taking off his coat, he would dance with the sweating, made-up seamstresses.

Desser lived on a small estate near Paris. He would rise early, go into the kitchen, and breakfast off a tomato and a piece of cheese, washed down with a glass of white wine. After reading the newspapers he left for Paris. He would smile at schoolchildren and dogs on the way, but figures soon blotted out everything. He worked at his morning's mail, letters, cables, private reports, until ten, after which he was ready to receive visitors. The ministers, diplomats, and financiers of Paris were well acquainted with his uncomfortable, ornate reception-room like a dentist's waiting-room.

When Pierre came in that morning, two bankers and the counsellor of the Rumanian Embassy were waiting to be received. Pierre nervously unfolded a newspaper and pretended to be engrossed in an article on the Geneva sanctions. He felt as if the other visitors knew why he had come.

The manservant announced in a solemn whisper: "Monsieur Pierre Dubois." Desser was seeing Pierre first. He liked Pierre; he liked his appearance of an impulsive southerner, his naïve chatter, and especially his poverty. As a capable engineer, scarcely able to make ends meet, he reminded Desser of his own youth. Moreover, Desser wanted to show the bankers and the diplomat that they were not in his reception-room as guests but as petitioners.

He greeted Pierre in a kindly manner. The young man hesitated, not knowing how to begin. In a disjointed, rambling fashion, he told Desser how the Minister had dismissed Agnès.

"It isn't a question of her being a friend of mine. Of course, I don't pretend not to be interested in what becomes of her. But, you see, it's such a howling injustice!"

Desser smiled. "There is no justice, my friend," he said. "However, we'll settle the affair of this young woman of yours right away."

He reached for the telephone and dialled a number.

"I want to speak to Monsieur Tessa. This is Desser here. How are you, my dear chap? How's your wife? All right, thanks. Look here, I want you to do me a favour. You'll be seeing the Minister today at the committee meeting, won't you? Yes, yes. Well, this has to do with a young teacher called Agnès Legendre. She has been dismissed for 'unpatriotic teaching.' It's all nonsense! You realize, of course, this isn't the time for that sort of thing, on the eve of the elections! Besides, it's all very complicated. . . . At this rate they'll be saying tomorrow that we're anarchists too. Or traitors from Coblenz. Marvellous! Tell me, are you free for lunch today? There's a whole heap of things we must have a talk about. Splendid! I'll come and fetch you sharp at one."

Turning to Pierre, he said: "It's settled. Mademoiselle Legendre may educate the children as she likes — as Communists, Tolstoyans, or savages. Well, have you decided to get married?"

"No. Well, er, yes. I don't know. But what makes you think so?"

"You're not doing anything this evening? Come and call for me. I'm spending the night in town. We'll go for a stroll and have a chat. Now I've got to receive three idiots. The director of the Bank and Castellion have come about the Polish loan. I shall have to tell them: 'You're backing the wrong horse!' In the first place Danzig isn't worth a Frenchman's little finger, and in the second place the Poles will steal everything. Did you see that diplomat? There's your Little Entente. The 'Macaronis' have already gobbled up the Negus. We shall probably give them the Balkans as well. There's nothing to be done: we want peace. See you this evening!"

CHAPTER 6

DEPUTY PAUL TESSA was known to be a gourmet, and Desser took him to the Dogarno, near the Halles. It was an unassuming-looking restaurant with the best steaks in Paris and a first-class cellar. The big cattle-dealers, who were expert judges of meat, came here for lunch. On the wall was a board on which the proprietor chalked up how many head of cattle had been sold in the market and at what price. The Dogarno was also frequented by fastidious gourmets, the members of gastronomic clubs and snobs who were intrigued by the high prices and the coarse manners of the cattle-dealers.

Desser studied the menu attentively. He ordered oysters, eel soup, *coq au vin,* and of course a steak. Tessa smacked his lips and asked the head waiter: "We get some of that brain sauce of yours with the steaks, don't we?"

"Certainly, Monsieur Tessa."

Despite his appetite, Paul Tessa was thin, with a long pale face, prominent chin, and sharp nose. He looked like a sick man or an ascetic. In fact he was vigorous, even frisky. If you heard whispering accompanied by peals of laughter in the dining-room of the Chamber, you could be fairly certain that some indiscreet colleague was telling a story about the amorous adventures of fifty-eight-year-old Tessa. At the same time, Tessa was an excellent family man. He was devoted to his fat wife and his two children: Lucien, who gave him no end of trouble, and Denise, a shy, pretty student. Tessa worshipped his daughter. With an extraordinary lightheartedness he would flit from an opera singer's boudoir to the family bedroom, where the double bed, adorned with bronze cupids, stood like an altar beneath the crucifix.

Not a strong character, but the voice was resonant and attractive; Tessa was considered one of the finest orators in France. He had entered the political arena comparatively late, after having established his reputation as a famous counsel. Pointing to an avaricious, dull-witted murderer, he was capable of exclaiming in moving tones: "Look, gentlemen! There stands before you a tortured dreamer! " The jury blew their noses and brought in a verdict of not guilty.

Tessa was put up for election by the Radicals of one of the departments in the west. He won his seat without much difficulty. He was opposed by a Communist, a locksmith in a railway yard with a stutter and a disinclination to make big promises, and by a retired general who demanded the birching of minors. Tessa seldom spoke in the Chamber. Twice he refused a post in the Cabinet; being uncertain of the future of the Radical Party, he preferred to look around him and bide his time. There was some talk in the lobbies of his wanting to break with the Radicals and go over to one of the groups of the Right.

His deputy's seat provided Tessa with a new source of income. He took money from concessionaires and contractors. For substantial fees he accepted directorships in corporations and lent his name to shield various shady undertakings such as mines in Venezuela, plantations in Martinique. He was not greedy, but he liked to live on a grand scale. He never refused anything to his family or mistresses and easily ran into debt.

Tessa knew " all Paris." He was on a ' tu ' footing with thousands of people. He entertained ambassadors and attorneys, gave bribes to journalists, and willingly carried out the requests of his constituents, obtaining from the ministers a decoration for a local inspector of finances, a tobacconist's license for the widow of a brave gendarme, or the cancellation of legal proceedings against an over-slick blackmailer.

Tessa swallowed an oyster and drank a little wine. " Is that young teacher you spoke to me about a Communist? " he said.

" I don't know. But she hardly constitutes a direct threat to the Third Republic."

" You're a cynic. The Chablis here is marvellous! So you feel there's no danger? You're wrong. I consider the elections will be catastrophic. The Radicals are committing suicide. If the Popular Front wins, they'll be swallowed up — like this," and he swallowed an oyster. " Even in parliamentary France they've succumbed to this fashion. Personally, I'm against it. I'm standing as a National Radical, but I'm afraid. . . ." He squeezed lemon over another oyster and gave a mournful sigh: " I'm very much afraid they won't elect me."

" Have you started your campaign yet? " Desser asked.

"The first meeting is on Saturday. I'm going down tonight."

"Then everything's all right."

"What do you mean — all right?"

"Very simple. You must declare your support for the Popular Front."

Indignantly Tessa flung his napkin aside and roared, as though he were on a platform: "Never! Better collapse, ruin, anything you like, but not treason! These gentlemen are the sworn enemies of France. Look at them — Blum, a man who hasn't even got a French name, cunning and bloodthirsty; Dormoy, the intriguer; Moch, with his eagerness to ruin transport; Monnet, the enemy of agriculture; and, finally, Villard, who even appeals for disarmament in face of Hitler; Villard, who . . ."

"Villard's simply a babbler. Make him a minister and he'll come to his senses at once."

"But the Communists?"

"France," said Desser, "is a country of individualists: rentiers, shopkeepers, farmers. Why does Jean or Jacques vote for the Communists? Because Jean was taxed six hundred francs more than he should have been, and Jacques's son was refused admission to the Veterinary Institute. It's their way of grouching and nothing more."

Tessa was silent, absorbed in the eel soup.

"Is it possible," Desser went on, "is it possible for the Communists to rely on you? Of course it's not. But they are prepared to support your candidature. That's strategical cunning. Why should we be simpletons? They've arranged the Popular Front with the calculation that they'll first of all destroy the Right and then devour us. But we'll outwit them. We'll smash the Right in the elections and we'll be quits with the Communists on the strength of it."

"This soup is absolutely delicious! But tell me, Jules, why do we need to smash the Right?"

"Because, for one thing, they'll be smashed even without us, if we're going to be obstinate. You see, politics are like a pendulum. They swing to the left, to the right, and then to the left again. Our business is to see that the pendulum doesn't swing too far. In 1924 the Left won. The result was the 'Cartel,' the transfer of the body of Jaurès to the Pantheon, red flags. Two years later the Radicals swung to the Right, and Poincaré came into power. In 1932 the elections were ineffectual. Not a single Cabinet was able to remain

in power. But in the country there was a swing to the Right. That
was at the end of 1933. Every evening there were demonstrations
in the rue Saint-Germain. 'Down with the deputies!' Who was
being baited from the Right? The Radicals? Didn't they try to
implicate you in the Stavisky affair? Finally there was the 6th of
February. Blood flowed. Abroad they were convinced that France
was on the eve of a dictatorship. But the pendulum unexpectedly
changed its direction, and on the 9th of February the Communists
came out. A middle way had to be found. Old man Doumergue
popped up and the pendulum was steadied. But the process is still
going on in the country. This time it's deeper, and therefore slower.
It still hasn't reached the end of the swing. The Popular Front must
win and it will win. If it wins with our help, then in a year or so the
Radicals will swing to the Right and everything will be quiet for
three or four years. Let me pour you out some Bordeaux. It's
Mouton-Rothschild."

"It comes to this, then," said Tessa. "I've got to help my enemies
to triumph?"

"You know the proverb: 'When the wine is poured out, it has
to be drunk.' Sometimes the wine has to be diluted with water. Of
course, not Mouton-Rothschild. . . ."

The *coq au vin* was served. Tessa forgot the sorrows of politics
for a few minutes and gave himself up to gastronomy.

"Do you know why the *coq au vin* is better here than anywhere
else?" asked Desser. "A cock is a misfortune, but we Frenchmen
have learned how to turn a tough old rooster into an exquisite dish
by stewing him in wine. Anyway, a hen is far more tender and
that's the secret of the Dogarno. You're not eating a cock, but a hen.
Why do they call a hen a cock? It's modesty. Or maybe pride. In
any case, it's culinary strategy." He laughed. "All you've got to do
is to follow this example. You're a National Radical, but we'll
serve you up as a supporter of the National Front. That's modesty,
or pride. . . ."

"But this is all in the air," said Tessa. "In any case they won't
elect me. I've neither the time nor the means for a proper campaign."

"You'll manage to find the time all right, all the more so as you're
anxious to serve France. As for the means, you needn't worry about
that. I'll stand all the expenses of the campaign. . . ."

Tessa did not approve of Desser's strategy, but the proposition attracted him. For a moment his face lit up. Then just as suddenly it darkened again: after all, one had to maintain one's dignity! But the appearance of the steaks with the famous brain sauce cheered him up again. And then came the Burgundy. Tessa's usually pallid cheeks became flushed with a rosy glow. He felt he wanted to talk about something pleasant, such as his little actress, Paulette, but in order to conceal his joy from Desser he began talking about his family troubles:

"My son," he said with tears in his voice, so that it was almost impossible to know whether he was acting or whether he was really distressed, "my son Lucien has made a most improper speech. My name is now being torn to shreds in all the newspapers. I tried to have a talk with him about it and do you know what he said? He said: 'This is the class war.' It's terrible: my son an enemy!"

"You've no need to worry. Lucien is sowing his wild oats. How can it be the class war if he's still living on your money? You'll see he'll be a deputy yet, a 'National Radical' even. I met him a short while ago at Maxim's with the most charming girl."

"Lucien at Maxim's? What a ne'er-do-well he is! He's thirty and not earning a penny. He writes some sort of rubbish for a puppet show. I tell you, a man like that may become an anarchist, a gangster. He's got no morals! My only consolation is Denise. There's a worker for you! She's studying some very dull subject. Romanesque architecture I think it is. She's a very serious-minded girl. Have you tasted this cheese? Almost mediæval. It's got the most remarkable smell. If only they let us have ten years' peace! I'm afraid everything may collapse. If the Popular Front wins there'll be war."

"Hardly. We can't fight without allies. We want to frighten the Germans and we're playing up to the Italians. The British are applying sanctions to Mussolini, but they're sparing Hitler. In general, we'll have to make concessions."

"That's impossible! What Frenchman will agree to give up Alsace?"

"Why Alsace? There is the Little Entente. Have we been feeding them for nothing? If anything happens we'll sacrifice the Czechs. And Poland. Poland too can be used as a ransom."

"For how long? Five years, ten at the most."

"Why look ahead? At present we've got to preserve France, peace, and the wealth of the country."

"It's all right for you. You haven't got any children. I dread to think of what's going to happen to Denise and Lucien." Tessa said this merely for effect. He smiled to himself as he drank his coffee. Desser was going to pay for his election campaign, which meant that he would be a deputy again. As for his thoughts on the future, these were just a little light melancholy, suitable accompaniment to the end of an excellent lunch.

Desser glanced at him. Tessa's eyes were clouded. His sharp nose was covered with beads of perspiration, his face wore a self-satisfied smile. Desser felt a desire to tease him. "You want to know what's in store for your children?" he said. "Maybe a paradise — peacocks *au vin*, airplane trips to Guadeloupe. Or maybe the usual war, labour camps, penal servitude, death. Most likely the latter. But you mustn't be down-hearted now you're a Popular Front candidate. It will be interesting to see you giving the sign of the clenched fist at meetings." Desser laughed out loud; then wishing to mitigate the effect of this rather crude joke, he patted Tessa on the back. "Enough of these damned politics! I saw Paulette yesterday. You're in luck. She really is the most beautiful girl in Paris."

CHAPTER 7

AFTER lunch Desser summoned Joliot, the editor-publisher of the big newspaper *La Voie Nouvelle*. Fat Joliot trotted in, panting and out of breath. He realized at once that he was in for a serious talk.

Joliot's career had been a stormy one. He had been before the courts a number of times, sometimes for extortion, sometimes for libel, but never failed to get off; he was said to know too much about the pasts of various politicians.

Joliot was a southerner. His father was a fishmonger in Marseille who had managed to get in with the big live-stock dealers. Joliot grew up in an atmosphere of speculation. He despised morality, but was very superstitious, far more afraid of black cats than of the public prosecutor. Arriving in Paris as a young man, he became tout for a small insurance company, which existed by the simple process of never paying out on its policies. Later he dabbled in journalism, writing articles for the gutter press about the private lives of senators and financiers. His income as a journalist came not so much from what he wrote as from what he didn't write: people bought him off. Then he started a Stock Exchange newspaper, *Les Finances*. One day he brought it out with an enormous advertisement: "Deposit your savings in the savings-bank of the Crédit d'Alger." Next day the director of the bank telephoned to Joliot: "Why the devil are you running that advertisement? We never ordered it." "I know you didn't," said Joliot, "but it's my duty to recommend sound banks to my readers." "For heaven's sake! Our depositors are withdrawing their deposits." "Can't help that," said Joliot. "My duty to my readers comes before everything." An hour later the director handed Joliot fifty thousand francs, and the advertisement was killed. After this Joliot began to make his way in earnest. The *Voie Nouvelle* appeared. At first the paper struggled on the point of death. Joliot wrote all the articles himself while the printer clamoured for payment. Then things started looking up. Articles appeared bearing the signatures of famous writers; there were sensational reportage features and columns of advertisements. The paper alternately supported the Radicals with enthusiasm and denounced them as "criminal Freemasons." At the beginning of the Abyssinian campaign Joliot sympathized with the Negus. Suddenly one morning the *Voie Nouvelle* came out with a eulogistic article entitled: "Italy's Civilizing Mission."

Joliot lived like a bird, never knowing in the morning how the day would end, whether with a sumptuous dinner or yet another summons from the public prosecutor. He would thrust a hundred-franc note into the hand of a poor woman and pay his staff with dud cheques. He bought pictures by Matisse at fabulous prices, pawned and re-pawned his wife's family plate, and all alone late at night sat up twanging selections from *Carmen* on the guitar.

He was a somewhat florid dresser, with a taste for orange silk shirts, cornflower-blue ties, and a tie-pin in the shape of a golden lizard. Despite his fat, he was very agile. He talked with a southern accent, gabbling his words in an Italianate fashion; and the shadier the substance of his conversation, the loftier became the style in which he expressed himself.

No sooner did Joliot arrive in Desser's office than he began extolling the merits of *La Voie Nouvelle* in the hope of wheedling another ten thousand francs out of him. "In the midst of this general lunacy," he said, "we're standing up for the principles of law and order. Did you read Lebœuf's article on the corrosive influence of Marxism? I've got a surprise ready for the elections. I've commissioned Fontenoy to write a series of articles describing the ruinous conditions in Soviet Russia. We're going to publish them in the form of cabled dispatches, as though Fontenoy was in Moscow. I've had to pay the expenses of his trip to Warsaw. Then I've got hold of a document about Villard. A house-owner has agreed to give evidence that Villard raped a postman's daughter in the days of his youth. It's going to cost ten thousand, but you can imagine the sensation it will create! Duchesne can wield a really daring pen. . . ."

"Well, he'll have to turn it round the other way," said Desser abruptly. "These new fountain-pens have very remarkable reversible nibs. They write more thickly, but they don't scratch. Now then, let's get down to it. *La Voie Nouvelle* must come out on the side of the Popular Front."

Joliot rose and held out his hand in a theatrical gesture.

"That's impossible!" he said in a voice that was almost stifled with agitation. "I know what politics are like. I've had recourse to some manœuvres in my time, more than once, but I've never betrayed France! You hear me, Monsieur Desser? Never!"

"Shut up. You're not at a meeting! I'm talking business. If you can't do without that highfalutin talk, listen to this! The victory of the Popular Front in the interests of France! There's a smell of revolution in the air. If we don't open the safety valve the boiler will burst. I don't care whether Villard raped a postman's daughter or not. Personally I doubt it. I doubt if he's even lived with his own wife. The man's a eunuch. But Villard is dangerous in opposition. He roars like a lion. Give him a ministerial portfolio and he'll immediately start bleating like a lamb."

"But this is disastrous! It means putting France into the hands of people who only yesterday were betraying their country."

"Now wait a moment," said Desser. "You've touched on an important question there. Strictly speaking, that's what I really wanted to see you about. Have a cigar. I haven't the slightest doubt that *La Voie Nouvelle* will support the Popular Front. You're quite experienced and far-sighted enough for that. Besides, I'm willing to give the paper a helping hand."

" But . . ."

" Now for the main thing. These people are seized with patriotic fever. They hate Fascism. That's perfectly understandable, but it's dangerous. Your paper must become the organ of the pacifists: the brotherhood of nations, the economic unity of Europe, the lives of the little ones that must be protected from danger, the tears of the mothers — anything you like if only we have peace! Peace at any price! "

" But what about the rôle of France? . . ."

" Better to be happy little Andorra or peaceful Monaco than the ruins of Carthage. I don't believe in the victory of France. We're tired. We're tired of falling in love, of being jealous and picking quarrels. It's the law of nature. It's only your Tessas who are capable of carrying on like a tom-cat in the spring at the age of sixty. You'll say that the French are a courageous people? Certainly! Once they went all over Europe with the *Marseillaise*. The children are taught about it at school. But now we've grown flabby. We live too well. We're afraid of risks. Who's going to fight for prestige or justice? Laval? Maurice Chevalier? You? To cut it short, if Remarque writes another novel, buy up the rights, wire for them. You won't have to wait for your money."

Joliot thought for a while. Then he exclaimed: " There's no doubt about it, you're a genius! Heaven knows where it will lead to, but the idea of peace, peace at any price, attracts me enormously. To turn the swords into ploughshares. . . ."

Desser smiled. " You seem to forget that I've got some connection with the armaments industry," he said. " It provides hundreds of thousands of Frenchmen with a livelihood. Besides, if we weaken the production of armaments we shall be attacked. The main thing is to lower the temperature. I repeat: they've got the fever of liberty. Write about how the cannon-merchants, the ' Two Hundred Families,' are anxious to have a war."

Joliot calmly slipped the cheque into his pocketbook.

" I'll write a remarkable article. I'll call it: ' Desser against the Two Hundred Families.' "

" Foolish and improbable. Better write: ' Desser, like the rest of the representatives of the Two Hundred Families, is eager to drown the people in blood.' That's much more convincing." He smiled. " And perhaps it's nearer the truth."

Racing upstairs into his office, Joliot called out to the typist:
"Lucille, from today I'm raising your salary to three hundred — no,
five hundred francs!" He wanted everybody around him to share
his joy. All day long he was giving orders: "Get some Left writers
with a name! A caricature of Mussolini! Something pathetic about
the workers! War memoirs — the horrors of Verdun! Tell Fontenoy
he needn't trouble. . . . No, wait a bit, you needn't tell him! Let
him do his stuff. It'll come in handy — not now, but in a year's
time."

That evening he dined in Montmartre, came home late, and woke
up his wife. He gave her some roses which he had bought in a
night club. They were half-wilted and gave out a sickly smell.
Joliot whispered into his wife's ear: "Four hundred thousand! My
God, what a stroke of luck!"

Then he took off his shoes, put on his bedroom slippers, gulped
down a glass of mineral water, and suddenly exclaimed with a sadness which he scarcely understood himself: "But it's all up with
France! It'll soon be the end now. No wonder I met two priests
today. That's a sure sign of disaster."

CHAPTER 8

EARLIER that evening the all-powerful Desser and the humble engineer Pierre Dubois strolled in silence along the embankment of
the Seine. Those grey tones peculiar to Paris, the quiet of the Seine
with its rare barge lights, the forest of stone of the cathedral of
Notre Dame, all contributed to their silent mood. As they passed
the Halles-aux-vins a sour smell of wine was wafted on the fresh
breeze. From the darkness beyond the enclosure of the Jardin des
Plantes came the screams of the wild animals, restless with the urge
of spring. Cars with flashing headlights raced across the bridge
towards the Gare de Lyon; then the calm bluish-grey haze settled
down again.

The harmony between houses and river, the names of the old
narrow streets: The Street of the Wooden Sword, The Street of the

Little Monk, The Street of the Two Escutcheons, all the mystery of
the city that had seen so much life, affected them both in different
ways. Desser, who had spent the day with Tessa, Joliot, figures and
falsehood, slouched along gloomily. The resting city reminded him
of that moment before setting out on a journey when friends sit
around the strapped trunks, at a loss to find words capable of overcoming the sense of futility in separation. Pierre, on the other hand,
rejoiced in the evening and the stones, in the same way that he
rejoiced in the clouded, mysterious beauty of Agnès. Throwing
open his overcoat, he sniffed eagerly at the fresh breeze. He felt
as if he were experiencing spring for the first time. Never before
had he known a happiness so acute and yet so simple. He could
have turned into one of the side-streets and spent the whole night
telling the animals in the Zoo or the street lamps about Agnès, her
charm, sweet nature, and intelligence.

But it was not only love that had set Pierre's head in a whirl.
Like so many others, he believed that this spring would be a season
of regeneration for his country. Pierre's father had been a Socialist.
His mother used to tell him how Villard came to speak at Perpignan
and had supper with them after the meeting. One day his father
came home covered with blood; an attempt had been made to
rescue a Spaniard named Ferrer from being shot; the gendarmes
had beaten the demonstrators. Pierre was seven years old at the
time. He woke up in the night and, seeing the blood on his father's
cheek, began to cry. His father was killed in the war. Shortly before
his death he wrote to his wife: " They're going to pay for all this —
there'll be a revolution! "

The word " revolution," like the sun on a foggy day, filled Pierre's
contemporaries with yearning. When the last war broke out they
were still in their childhood. They had joined in the crowd which
burned the Maggi dairies, shouted: " To Berlin! " and been delighted with the baggy trousers of the Zouaves and the high, clumsy
taxis taking the troops up to the Marne. Later on they saw the
wounded — legless, mutilated, gassed. France behind the lines
reeked of carbolic and was dark with widows' weeds. When their
fathers came home on leave, they talked of the lice and mud of the
trenches and the bodies rotting on the wire, and obstinately repeated: " There'll be a revolution! " Mutinies began to break out
among the troops: the voice of the " Aurora " had reached Champagne.

There was a short spell of happiness when the trumpets announced the news of the Armistice. Youngsters and grown-ups danced all night long in the squares. They were told: "Now you're going to be happy." When the soldiers came home, they found nothing but indifference and meanness. Strikes broke out. The terrified bourgeois hunted down the revolution like a wild animal. Every weapon was brought into service: slander and tear-gas, demagogy and imprisonment. The Communist with a knife between his teeth was the bogy-man with which Poincaré terrified the habitués of the Café de Commerce and the farmers.

The revolution withdrew into the party cells, behind the closed doors of working-class families, amid the bitter reflections of the disappointed poor. From time to time it reminded the world of its existence with a miners' strike or a demonstration in the streets. One summer day in 1927 startled the capital; the great heart of the people expressed its indignation at the execution of Sacco and Vanzetti. Cobblestones flew through the air; once again the streets of Paris ran with the working man's blood.

Life became more and more difficult. The depression stopped the weavers' shuttles and at night filled the boulevards with ghostly lodgers. Fifteen years had passed since the day of the Armistice, and again the revolution looked out on the streets of Paris. "Are they going to drive us into war?" asked the young men of Pierre's age, who had been starved of life and grown prematurely old.

Pierre's grasp of politics was weak. He was inclined to put his trust in phrases. Two years ago, in 1934, he had nearly given his life for a cause that was not his own. On that dark February night he had mistaken falsehood for truth. Whenever he remembered this he would blush uncomfortably and say to himself: "I'm the son of a working man." Now he was afraid of not keeping up with Michaud, but something in his blood frightened him as it had done before. The mechanic's words seemed to him excessively severe. He wanted the revolution to be gay and noisy, like rain in May.

A girl was standing outside a Metro station as they passed. She kept looking anxiously at the doors and the clock as though she was waiting for someone. Her expression was like that of an offended child.

Suddenly Desser said to Pierre: "So you're going to marry a teacher?"

This time Pierre did not evade the question, nor did he ask how

Desser had guessed. He felt he would like to shout her name until it filled the quiet street. "Yes," he said. "Agnès."

Desser stopped and gazed at Pierre, at his dark eyes with their large whites and at his blissful half-smile. "I envy you," he said quietly.

"But why . . ." stammered Pierre. He was on the point of asking: "Why don't you get married yourself?" but he checked himself in time.

"It's all very banal," Desser said, "but nothing can be done about it. They've loved me to the point of tears; they've threatened to commit suicide. But it's never me they love, only my money. What do you advise me to do? Conceal my identity? Wear an invisible cloak?"

"You can get rid of your money. You're not a speculator. You're an engineer. If it's an encumbrance to you . . ."

"No, I like money. Why? Probably because money is power. Not just distinction or fame, but real power, the possibility of deciding everything for others. Why do I need it? That's what I'm trying to make out myself. It's a burden? Yes, but a pleasant one. Besides it's a slow poison like cocaine, only it gets into your blood like syphilis."

They were now walking down a dark street. The lamp of a police station glowed red like an inflamed eye. A woman was rummaging in an ash-can. Some drops of rain began to fall.

"Everybody's poisoned with it," Desser went on. "It's a universal disease. Nobody wants to give it up, neither the 'Two Hundred Families' nor the twenty million. They'll fight. Not for France, but for their money — to their last gasp. War? There won't be any war. Nor any revolution either. People are afraid of losing what they've got. Now, that woman over there has got nothing. She isn't afraid. But how many are there like that? They'll terrorize them and if necessary they'll shoot them. However, it won't be necessary. Our people are well broken in. They're not stupid; they know what's what all right."

"I simply don't understand how you can exist with such contempt for people," said Pierre. "In the past they were fooled, but now they're beginning to understand. What are they hoping for? Only revolution! In our factory there are thousands of grand people. They're not tramps, who've got nothing to lose. They've got their work, their families and homes, and a good many of them have small savings put by. But they'd give up everything to put an end to that. . . . He pointed to the woman at the ash-can. "Sometimes I think people are like clay. In the past men shaped gods and animals. Now we're trying to shape man."

"Not clay," said Desser. "Not clay, but chewing-gum. That's why everything changes and everything remains the same. After all, what is it that changes? Only the names. The real change is death. Now, that really does change everything. That's why I'm afraid of it. I don't understand suicides. However, this isn't what I wanted to say. You keep on talking about 'revolution,' but that means death not only for me, but for millions."

Both were silent for a moment. Warm light oozed through the closed shutters of the little street. They passed a house where the shutters on the ground floor were open, and caught a glimpse of people having dinner at a round table with a lamp in the middle; the light fell on a woman's face, tired and pretty.

"I dread to think of what may be destroyed," said Desser. "Not so much buildings — Notre Dame, the Louvre. They're glorious and beautiful. But there's something else that grieves me even more. It's what is in these houses, the happiness, maybe the illusion of happiness, in any case the cosiness and that stillness when you can hear them breathing in the next room. I grieve for the christenings with the sugared almonds, the weddings where they strew flowers under the feet of the happy couple, even for the funerals when the mourners return from the cemetery to have a snack and a glass of wine over their sorrow. At present all this exists. But it can disappear in a flash — as the result of a bomb, the first shooting in the streets, Hitler's hysteria, clenched fists, or some other hazard. Of course in a hundred years' time they'll say it was all 'historical necessity.' . . . Well, I must leave you now."

Desser gave Pierre his hand in its damp leather glove and strode quickly away along the embankment. The conversation had irked him. He reproached himself for having said too much — chattering with a love-sick engineer about the fortunes of humanity indeed!

He made his way back to the centre of the city, where the boulevards were bright as day. All kinds of brightly coloured articles lay glittering in the shop windows. Across the faces of the buildings scurried bluish-purple dwarfs and snakes, advertisements for apéritifs, invitations to visit sunny Morocco. Throngs of people jostled one another as though they had nowhere else to go, weaving aimlessly back and forth like fish in an aquarium. The kiosks were stuck all over with newspapers in twenty languages. Desser stopped and glanced at the headlines: "DEMAND FOR THE POPULAR FRONT . . . DANGER OF ARMED CLASH. . . ." He yawned wearily. Everything here seemed to talk his language: he knew the price of the houses, advertisements, and stocks, the dividends paid on Moroccan railways and the famous bitter-sweet drinks. And everything here belonged to him — the building sites, motor cars, newspapers, even the smiles. In this kingdom of his he was a passing visitor who needed nothing, a conjuror who had turned himself into one of his own puppets for an hour. . . . Wasn't it worth while preserving all this? Certainly it was, but, my God, what a depth of weariness! . . .

CHAPTER 9

PROFESSOR MALET's lecture that evening was on the Romanesque architecture of Poitou. His lectures were open to the public, and among the students in the auditorium sat quite a number of older people — lovers of architecture, self-educated individuals who attended every lecture with bulging notebooks in which Sanscrit roots jostled the binomial theorem. There was also a sprinkling of down-and-outs who came in to get warm and have a nap. Some took down every word that Malet uttered. Others yawned or whispered among themselves. One old woman who had climbed up to the top bench was knitting a sock.

Michaud, the mechanic, regularly attended Malet's lectures. He had been interested in architecture ever since he was a child, and was familiar with proportions, computation, and building materials. He knew a lot, but whenever he looked at buildings he admired, he felt that, besides the clarity and harmony of construction which fascinated him as an engineer, there were other qualities in architecture, qualities that affected him like the features of the human face or like a forest. By studying the history of architecture he hoped to discover the secret of this fascination.

Michaud's thirst for knowledge was insatiable. He would have liked to pull the world apart, even as a child takes a toy to pieces. He had left his elementary school with only the three R's and a few moral phrases learned by heart. Then he was put into the school of life. Luc Michaud's father was a hatter. There was a crisis in the hat trade after the war. People gave up wearing hats, and Luc was not even taken on as an apprentice. He delivered condensed milk on a tricycle. Later he worked in a tannery amid the powerful stench of hides. He was a voracious reader, but his knowledge was casual and disjointed. He served his time in the Navy, in a torpedo-boat, where he became friendly with a draughtsman named Quérier, who afterwards stood as a Communist candidate in the elections. Quérier quickly recruited Michaud. Both of them went to work in the Seine aircraft factory. Michaud began to attend meetings. He read books on political economy and the history of the workers' movement. At the same time he poured over mathematics. He became a skilled mechanic and earned a decent wage. But he still felt that he knew nothing. It was a painful, frustrating feeling, as though he had somehow missed the bus. But he had so very little time; he had to go now to a party conference, now to a meeting. He longed to go to the theatre and visit the museums. And at times there hovered in front of his mind vague glimpses of distant countries — the ruins of Rome, the Turkestan-Siberian railway.

Michaud was fond of roaming about the town in the foggy November evenings, warming his fingers with hot chestnuts. To him, Paris with its misty lights looked like a ship; he felt as if the gangway was just about to be drawn up. Now and then he went to the cinema, sat amid cuddling lovers and a smell of oranges, and sighed aloud as he watched some dumb but fetching American actress. For three years he was in love with the daughter of a comrade, a pretty girl called Mimi, with a fascinating lock of hair that hung down over her forehead. For her sake he learned to dance; he brought her presents of flowers and chocolates, even tried to write verses. But it was all in vain. Mimi married a book-keeper. She wanted a quiet life. Michaud's ideas and his stormy temper frightened her.

Michaud was twenty-nine. He was powerfully built, but somewhat out of proportion. His head was too large and too heavy. His face, even in winter, was covered with freckles. He had attractive grey, mocking eyes and prominent white teeth. He seemed to be always smiling. He was constantly waving his arms and punctuating his words with the exclamation " And how! "

Michaud followed Malet's lecture closely, from time to time making notes in a well-worn notebook. Sitting next him was an exceedingly pretty girl. Michaud had noticed her at the beginning of the lecture, especially her long black eyelashes, like a film star's. Then he had forgotten about her, absorbed in the beauty of the cathedrals of Poitiers.

But when Malet, discoursing about pillars, made use of an unusual word which Michaud failed to catch, he turned to the girl and whispered: " What ornament did he say? "

" Fretted," the girl said.

The lecture came to an end. They were sitting on the bench at the back of the hall and had to wait while the others went out. Michaud turned to the girl and said: " I hope you weren't annoyed with me for asking you a question during the lecture. You're probably a student, but I'm only a layman in architecture. My subject is engineering."

" Well, I know nothing about engineering, not a thing."

" Oh, it's just a special subject," Michaud said. " But when you don't understand art you feel you're missing something. And is it hard to understand! I'll say it is, and how! You know I used to try to interpret one art in terms of another. For instance, whenever I listened to music I kept trying to translate it into words: did it mean ' being in love,' was it about ' a military victory ' or ' a storm at sea '? Hopeless, of course. The wrong language altogether. And it's the same with architecture. You know that better than I do."

Together they went out of the hall. After two days of wind and rain the face of the city had changed. Spring was creeping out on all sides. The chestnut buds were swelling. The bluish tarmac reflected a new light. Winter overcoats were giving place to light mackintoshes. People were migrating from inside the cafés to the terraces. Street musicians made their appearance and little boys sold green, half-open lilies of the valley.

They crossed the bright noisy boulevard Saint-Michel, where youth was heaving sighs and making declarations of love, drinking café crème or grenadine, and getting anxious about the approaching examinations. In the romantic semi-darkness of the boulevard Saint-Germain housemaids were taking little dogs for their night walks; lovers clung together in the shadows. A clock struck ten. Michaud was telling her about his adventures climbing the glaciers in the mountains near Grenoble. He was pleased to see she was laughing.

"It's nice to see you so cheerful," he said.

"I'm not always cheerful. At home they scold me for being gloomy. My brother has even nicknamed me 'the marmot.'"

"You're not in the least like a marmot. I caught a marmot once when I was staying with my uncle in Savoy. We taught it to stand on its hind legs. It's interesting to observe wild life. I've just been reading about the ants. What clever creatures! The way they organize everything! And eels, do you know about them? It appears they travel from all over the place to the Sargasso Sea. It's love that drives them on. They swim five thousand miles. They even leave the rivers and wriggle overland. Millions die on the way, but that doesn't matter. That's passion for you! Human beings aren't like that." He wanted to tell her about Mimi, who had preferred the book-keeper's salary to love, but he managed to refrain. "There are so many interesting things." He sighed. "But I don't know anything, apart from engineering and politics perhaps."

"I'm sick of politics," said the girl. "At home they talk of nothing else. You see, my father —"

She hesitated. How absurd this was. Why was she talking like this to a perfect stranger? She had always held aloof from people, and now, for some reason, she was talking quite freely with a man, about whom she knew nothing except that he was an engineer. It was ridiculous, childish. At the same time she felt a twinge of sadness as she realized that their casual meeting must soon come to an end together with the temptation of the spring evening. In a minute she would have to get a bus. Dryly she said:

"My father's a deputy. You've probably heard of him. His name's Tessa."

Michaud laughed out loud. "That's a surprise. I'll say it is. And how! But what's your father got to do with it? I'm not talking to him. I'm talking to you. Do you think I can make head or tail of what they cook up? It's a miserable business. I'm talking about something else. I say, where are you going to? Let's walk a little farther — as far as the next bus stop. It's a lovely evening. . . ."

Denise agreed. Again she felt surprised at herself. Why was she going with him; why was she listening; and, above all, why did she suddenly feel so simple and cheerful?

"I understand politics in a different way altogether," Michaud went on. "It means reconstructing the world. There is so much that is casual and evil. Somehow I kind of feel ashamed of people. And yet a gay, harmonious, full-blooded life is possible, it really is. For me revolution is a sort of architecture. If you're fond of art, you're bound to sympathize."

"Are you a Communist?"

"How can I be anything else?"

"My brother talks like you, but I don't believe him. I don't trust words."

"That's because your father is a lawyer," said Michaud. "I'm also suspicious when people talk too beautifully. But it's different with us. Look here, there's a pre-election meeting tonight. Let's drop in for half an hour. You'll see the difference! It's quite near — in the school in the rue Falguière. If it bores you, you can go. But it's worth while having a look. Come on, it's the duty of man to be inquiring. How about it?"

Denise shook her head, but she knew she would go all the same. She even said to herself: "I'll think it over later when I get home. Then I shall understand. Now I feel gay and that's all that matters."

At the meeting there were many people who were not on the roll of electors, girls and youths. It was one of the thousands of meetings held that astonishing spring when Paris repeated the words "The Popular Front" with tenderness and passion. It was hot in the hall. A lot of the men had taken off their coats. They sat smoking, their caps pushed back on their heads. Denise looked at the faces around her. What a world of sorrow, sickness, and want! A woman was nursing a sleeping baby — obviously she had no one at home to leave it with. Water trickled from an old man's inflamed eyes as if he were crying. None of these people knew each other. They had come here from the grimy back streets of the vast city, drawn together by a new brotherhood. When the speaker talked of the struggle for justice, their fists shot up in the air and hundreds of voices answered as one. Their oratory was totally unlike Tessa's. They spoke abruptly and with difficulty, as though seeking for the right word; and the words sounded different. Now and again their tired faces lit up with a smile. The weariness of childbearing, the mystery of growth, filled the smoke-dimmed hall. A woman shook her dried-up, wrinkled fist as though, after bearing and burying her children, she was grasping a little air, warmth, and welcome or clutching at a word that had escaped her.

Half an hour went by, then an hour, and then another hour, but Denise did not go. She listened attentively. She would scarcely have been able to repeat what these people were talking about. It was as if she was listening to the dull throb of their hearts and to a world that was strange and new to her, as she had listened as a child to the sea in Brittany for the first time.

The meeting finished at twelve o'clock. Denise suddenly realized that she too was singing the words of the *Internationale,* mixing them up and not knowing why or what she was singing.

A tall elderly workman with dark, sunken eyes and a gash on his cheek came up to Michaud and said: " We've enrolled four men from your factory today. Tell Charles it would be better to distribute the leaflets according to the shops in the factories. The fences can be used for placards." He turned to Denise: " What district are you from, comrade? "

Denise blushed. Michaud answered for her: " This comrade is a student."

Denise thought: " So he has taken me for one of his own." And for some reason this pleased her.

They went out into the street, and again the blue-grey, warm, restless air of Paris reminded them of spring.

" Did you like it? " asked Michaud.

" I don't know what to say. ' Like ' isn't the right word. It thrilled me."

" That's understandable. You know why — it's like this evening, like what's in the air. There's only one word for it — hope, the hope of changing everything."

" I didn't believe my brother, but I believe the one who came up to you. It must be true. I don't know whether it is for the others, but it is for him. But I must think it over. It's very difficult to take in all at once."

Michaud talked again about hope, his own and that of the others. Now she was barely listening — there were too many words — but his voice continued to please her. When they parted she smiled at his grey mocking eyes. " And how! " he said enthusiastically.

Denise smiled. " We'll be seeing each other again. At Malet's lecture, or if there's another meeting write and let me know and I'll come. O.K.? "

She was home at last. On the walls of the hallway hung photographs of famous trials — murderers and criminals standing between two gendarmes, and in the foreground, raising his bony hands to heaven, Tessa, in his counsel's gown.

The apartment was like a stagnant pool, dark and tranquil on the surface, but with seething passions underneath. Denise's father was not yet home. He was probably seeking oblivion from Desser's craftiness on the bosom of Paulette. Her mother was in her bedroom, playing patience and waiting for her husband. Mme Tessa suffered from nephritis. She was terrified of death and especially of hell. She had always been a believer. Formerly her life had been taken up with running the house, clothes, and gossip, but when she became ill she found herself face to face with God. She remembered the days of her childhood at the convent. Now the Day of Judgment was drawing near. She would be called to account for everything: for Tessa's anti-clerical speeches in the Chamber, for his affairs with *demi-mondaines*, and for the blasphemy and corruptness of her son Lucien. Who was there to shield her? Denise? But Denise hardly ever spoke, never went to church, and never answered her mother. Perhaps she too was taking after her father? . . .

" Denise, is that you? I thought it was Papa. Come here. Where have you been? "

" I've been sitting in a café on the Boul' Mich. It was a wonderful night." Denise said the first thing that came into her head. She was anxious not to upset her mother by telling her about the meeting.

But Mme Tessa burst into tears.

" On the Boul' Mich? Oh, you're taking after your father! "

Denise tried to console her, telling her that she had been with girl friends and had brought back the vervain water which her mother took at night. But the tears kept dropping on the kings and queens.

Lucien tapped at his mother's door and said good-night. Denise went with him into the library. He was back from an evening with the Surrealists. "They've got an amusing new trick," he said. " They determine the sex of everything — ideas, colours, and words. You can imagine how indignant everybody got — especially the Communists, who writhe at the very name of Freud. Have you ever heard the way an orthodox Communist argues? "

Denise shook her head. Lucien started telling her about a new Balinese dancer.

" Seeing her makes one appreciate Gauguin," he said. " One feels that for her the only reality is animal passion."

" Why tell me that? "

" Because you're twenty-two, not seventeen. It's time you stopped playing the *ingénue!* Or are you going to be like Mother — read the lives of the saints and use pessaries? " Then, noticing her sullen look, he said soothingly: " Don't be angry, Marmot! I didn't mean to offend you. Good night! "

Denise went to her room, undressed, got into bed, and switched off the light, but she couldn't sleep. The clock struck two, half past three. She heard steps in the passage. Her father had come home and was humming quietly: " *Tout va bien, Madame la Marquise.*" Then all was quiet.

Denise felt the house was like a tomb. She began thinking about her school days in Brittany and the childish pranks they used to play. The sea was always there. The fishermen lounging in the street, looking, in their red tarpaulin trousers, like huge lobsters. When there was a storm the whole house shook; the big clock creaked in its glass case and the plates danced on the walls; but the girls' hearts throbbed with joy.

When Denise left school and came home, she immediately felt she was being suffocated. The family all lived together in such stifling intimacy. Denise knew all about her father's affairs and about Lucien and Jeannette. On the surface the family appeared to be devoted to each other. Their regular meetings at meals and the outward semblance of unity began to have a cloying effect, like ooze.

Denise had a genuine interest in the history of architecture. In the past, people had believed passionately, out of the fullness of their hearts, not like her mother. They built square churches like barns. It seemed as if the grains of faith still lingered in them. Denise took refuge in the past from her father's futility, her mother's sanctimoniousness, and her brother's aimless effervescence.

But today something of infinite importance had happened. She had promised herself that she would try to get to the bottom of it. She kept twisting and turning and asking herself what it all meant. She remembered many things: the old charwoman's fist, the workman with a gash on his cheek who had addressed her as " Comrade," Michaud's smiling grey eyes. All this was blended with the spring air and the dampness and quiet of the night streets. Her heart was throbbing. And the cold dawn crept through the curtains into the room, filling it with greyish quivering half-light and the vague shapes of dimly perceived objects. Denise remembered the words " And how! " smiled, and with that smile fell asleep.

CHAPTER 10

AFTER reading a review of his book in a Communist newspaper, Lucien was annoyed. He particularly disliked the concluding sentence: " Some excessively ' revolutionary ' passages arouse distrust." The blockhead! And so were they all! They weren't capable of social surgery; they could only patch up! The Rightist newspapers were only too pleased to discuss the book; being anxious to blacken Paul Tessa, they hailed it as a dreadful example of the results of a Radical upbringing. But in the people's newspaper, which ought to have welcomed Lucien as their champion, a new Valles, there was only scant praise: " the author is well acquainted with his milieu " — and finally: " distrust."

Suddenly Lucien smiled: perhaps they were right. Only a short time ago he had wanted to join the Communist Party and had been trying to prove to his friends that party discipline was the highest form of self-restraint, such as Goethe attributed to the Creator. That was Lucien all over, blow hot and blow cold.

His father's wealth relieved Lucien of the necessity of earning a living. After leaving the *lycée,* he began to look round. First he became a medical student at the university, after a year got bored with anatomy and took up international law. Then he developed a sudden interest in the cinema and became assistant to a film director. He wanted to make an unusual film about the collapse of the machine age, but was obliged to work on an idiotic farce in which the heroine kept mixing up her husband and her lover, who were doubles. Lucien tired of films and began to haunt the literary cafés, affecting the pose of a disillusioned genius.

Lucien was twenty-six when he first met Henri Lagrange, the explorer, who was setting out for the Antarctic. He had long been dreaming of adventure and persuaded Lagrange to take him along. Lucien wrote in his diary: " The penguin resembles Mistinguette. I'm sick of canned food. In general, it's beautiful but boring." A few pages farther on there was a brief note: " Henri died at four o'clock in the morning." Lagrange died in Lucien's arms — from gangrene.

Back in Paris, Lucien resumed his former life. He attended Surrealist exhibitions and soirées but often sat silent amid the chatter of his friends. Death· had become an obsession with him.

Such was the origin of his novel *Face to Face*, which had a resounding success. It was a rambling, uneven book with pretentious harangues and brilliant patches that rose to genuine heights of feeling. The novel dealt with the last days and death amid the ice of a man who loved mathematics and his four-year-old daughter more than anything else in the world. Lucien's reputation as a novelist was made overnight. When interviewed about his future literary plans, he said he was writing a big novel about the disintegration of family life. In fact, he was writing nothing, and felt like a squeezed-out lemon.

The years went by and people began to forget that Lucien had ever been a writer. Paul Tessa, who had started off by believing in his son's literary career, once more began to nag him for his idleness and extravagance. Lucien was incapable of living without money and he had the knack of squandering tens of thousands of francs without noticing it. He entertained his friends in restaurants that were unpretentious outside but very expensive in, ordering the rarest vintages on the list and saying with an air of apology: " An unassuming little wine." He gave expensive presents to any woman who took his fancy. He had a mania for cards, and high play seemed to him to be the only thing that mattered. With his pale, handsome face and chestnut hair, he was a familiar figure in every gambling-house. Lucien would lose from twenty to thirty thousand francs in a night with a smile. The inevitable day arrived when he was obliged to visit the money-lenders. Lucien borrowed from one to pay back another. That same boredom which four years ago had driven him to the Antarctic, only to attack him with renewed intensity at the sight of a penguin looking like an ancient actress, and the stale taste of canned food, took hold of him once more.

In the summer he went to the Soviet Union with a party of tourists. This came about quite by accident: he had planned to go to Egypt with a friend, but they quarrelled on the eve of departure. Lucien stayed a week in Moscow. They did the usual round of sightseeing, antiquities, museums, children's nurseries, and so on. All this had no effect on Lucien. What stirred him was the will-power and spiritual youthfulness of the people. One day, watching a group of workers on an underground railway construction job, he noticed among them a girl in heavy boots with a thin, pale face and a look of burning determination in her eyes. He suddenly real-ized that she was building something more than an underground railway. He felt mentally stimulated, as he had felt after Lagrange's death. Once again he returned to Paris a changed man.

Marx took the place of Lautréamont. For the first time Lucien thought about the lives of the people around him. Everywhere he saw lies, hypocrisy, and boredom. His personal drama was the drama of society. It inspired him to write a superficial, satirical pamphlet ridiculing the philosophy, morals, and æsthetic taste of the bourgeoisie. His father saw red and threatened to break with him. But the young people who frequented the Maison de Culture listened enthusiastically to Lucien's speeches on the coming revolu-tion. He even forgot gambling: the game he was playing now was far more fascinating.

After six months he began to have doubts. The Communists now seemed to him to be just an ordinary political party. They liked their home comforts and even hummed the romantic songs of Maurice Chevalier! Lucien, who always thought himself more dar-ing and more clever than anyone else, said to himself: " I've made a fool of myself again! This card may win, but it's not my card."

His next phase was the love affair with Jeannette. He did not exaggerate his feelings, but openly told his friends about his new affair, hoping to belittle love with irony. But love refused to yield, and the very tone in which he spoke her name gave him away completely.

In character Lucien and Jeannette were utterly unlike, but in ex-perience they had much in common. Both had knocked about the world. Jeannette was thirty, but often felt like an old woman. She was the daughter of a Lyon lawyer. The dull puritanical town and her harsh, narrow parents had warped her childhood. From morn-ing till night they talked of nothing but money — how one mustn't waste money; " suitable " marriages; the outrageous behaviour of wives who spent a fortune on their backs and flirted with other men or ("Jeannette, leave the room") were unfaithful. She remembered one rather lean man with a white spot in his eye whom her parents always spoke of with great respect. He was the owner of a big factory and had shot his wife's lover with a shotgun and got off scot free owing to influence.. The dead man was declared to be a burglar who had broken into the house at night. In the home of Jeannette's parents the furniture was never uncovered the whole year round, and her mother was always in a panic lest her husband should spill a drop of wine on the clean tablecloth.

Jeannette was eighteen when she had her first affair, with the doctor who had attended her when she had measles. He was married; in reality Jeannette felt profoundly indifferent towards him. Her father found out about the sordid liaison and turned her out of the house, shouting: "Your place is in a brothel!" The doctor sighed and gave Jeannette four hundred francs for her fare to Paris. That night in the train she kept on asking herself: "Why did I do it?" but she could find no answer. The doctor was no Adonis; he had a gigantic Adam's apple and was always telling dirty stories. Perhaps she went to the fatal rendezvous merely because that day her mother had whined at the cook for three hours on end: "This isn't mutton you've bought. It's nothing but bone!"

Jeannette got a job as a salesgirl in a department store. She used to arrive in the morning with dark rings under her eyes. The other girls whispered that she was leading a fast life, but actually she spent all her spare time reading for nights on end. She started with the moderns in the hope of finding out about herself. Then she developed an enthusiasm for Stendhal, Dostoievsky and Shakespeare. The passions of the people around her began to appear to her not as disconnected incidents but as dramatic and significant episodes. Everything which before had seemed unintelligible and therefore hostile — narrowmindedness, casual behaviour — now became clearly defined and subject to strict laws. Although she lacked worldly experience and held aloof from people, she acquired from these great artists a deeper understanding of many things and a more mature outlook on life.

She did not brood over literature and art as she did over her own destiny: they were the breath of life to her, whether she was poring over a book or sitting in a gallery. When there were no customers in the store, she would play, murmuring under her breath, the role of one of Racine's heroines or of a stupid provincial dreamer.

In the restaurant where she usually ate she met a middle-aged actor named Figet. They started living together; they were not in the least in love with each other, but both were lonely and unhappy. Figet was attracted by Jeannette's physical appearance; indeed, she attracted attention wherever she went. The enormous wild eyes in her quiet face made one think she was possessed. She looked as though she had just received some shattering piece of news, as though she were racked by love, or filled with the joy that comes only once in a lifetime. Moreover, Figet appreciated the way Jeannette looked after him. This crack-brained creature had a kind heart. She looked after the unsuccessful, grumbling, slovenly actor as though he were a child instead of being nearly old enough to be her father. She didn't love him, but then, it never even entered her head that she could love anyone. She never related her personal life to what she read in books or saw on the stage. Racine's heroine peacefully darned socks. A few months later she gave up her job at the store. Figet had arranged for her to be taken on at the Gymnase Theatre. She was given tiny character parts — frightened maidservants or village nit-wits. She did not aspire to be a great actress, but the smell of the theatre made her feel gay and she was grateful to Figet for this change in her life.

A year later Figet dropped her. He had started an affair with a successful musical-comedy actress. He took a long time making up his mind to tell Jeannette as he was afraid of jealousy, reproaches, and tears. But Jeannette listened to his confession with such indifference that he exclaimed in an injured tone: "I don't believe you've ever loved me!" Jeannette said she didn't think she ever had.

One of the managers of the Maison de Culture, Maréchal by name, had taken it into his head to organize a "Revolutionary Theatre," and was looking round for a cast. Professional actors were unwilling to come to him, as they thought the project would be a flop. Maréchal met Jeannette on the theatre stairs and was struck by her possibilities. He asked her to come and see him and tried to persuade her that she had the makings of a great tragedienne: "What eyes! And what a voice! If you could only hear yourself!" Maréchal was staging *The Sheep-Spring*. He offered Jeannette the leading part. Everyone at the first rehearsals raved about her acting and said she had such extraordinary simplicity and passion. Unfortunately, the well-known actress Javogue chose this moment to have a row with the manager of the Odéon and rushed round in a fit of rage to Maréchal. She was a thoroughly second-rate actress, but her name guaranteed a good deal of publicity. She was given Jeannette's part. Jeannette took this set-back quietly, and immediately agreed to take a minor part. Back in her own little room after the first night she repeated the speeches which she had never had the chance to deliver on the stage.

The Revolutionary Theatre soon collapsed. Jeannette went on tour, playing the lead in a stock company, and spent two summer months in the provinces. Then, worn out and half-starved, she got a job at the radio station Poste Parisien.

Lucien had met her at one of the rehearsals at the Revolutionary Theatre and fallen in love with her at once. This was during the height of his revolutionary phase. The words of *The Sheep-Spring* sounded like the ravings of excited Paris, and Jeannette's voice gave them that fullness and weight which Lucien failed to find in political speeches and articles.

Jeannette was quite amazed by Lucien. It was the first time she had met a man who talked like the hero of a novel. His denunciations of the baseness of society and the cleansing storm to come were linked in her mind with the fiery colour of his hair, his pale face and jerky gestures. She believed every word he said, and when he declared his love for her, she gave herself to him, if not with love, at least with a quickening of the spirit.

Love might have been awakened in her, but Lucien did everything to repel it. In her presence he became affected and fatuous. She was too young to laugh at his self-conceit. Listening to his pathetic tirades day after day, she began to doubt whether he really loved her, but Lucien, for his part, grew more and more devoted to her. His feelings towards her were complex. He did love her after his own fashion, but rather as a phenomenon — a lyric or a sea-bird. If he had been asked to face death for her sake, he would have done so, but when Jeannette was ill and begged him to stay with her till morning, he began to make excuses, saying they were waiting up for him at home and his mother would be anxious. Whereas the truth was he simply wanted to have a good sleep.

Jeannette said to herself: "He'll drop me, the same as Figet did. . . ." She thought she ought to leave him, but by nature she was too passive; such women never leave men unless they are led away. Perhaps she still had vague hopes of happiness with Lucien, a quiet grey content like that of all the women around her.

Lucien had not seen Jeannette since the evening she had first met André and Pierre. He rang her up and she told him she was not feeling well. A few minutes later she rang him back and said she wanted to have a talk with him. She sounded excited. The thought flashed through Lucien's mind: "André!" At once he was on his guard. He told Jeannette he would call for her at the studio and they would have supper at Fouquette's.

Jeannette didn't want to go out. She said she didn't feel well enough and must have a talk with him in private. Lucien insisted. Actors and writers forgathered at Fouquette's in the evening, and it flattered Lucien to see people looking enviously at Jeannette.

He was in a good humour, in spite of the review of his book, and gaily ordered oysters and white wine. Jeannette was silent. He told her about the review. "'Distrust' — I ask you," he said.

Jeannette said nothing. It was obvious that she was thinking intensely about something. Lucien forgot all about the suspicions of the Communists and the admiring stares of the men at the other tables. He was seized with jealousy, and was so positive that Jeannette was in love with André that he decided to precipitate a showdown.

"André's exhibition opens on Monday," he said. "They say his landscapes are beautiful. Do you want to go to the private showing?"

"I don't think I'll go. I'm not in the mood."

She said this so naturally and with such indifference that Lucien was baffled: perhaps it had nothing to do with André after all. Having drunk a bottle of Chablis, he cheered up, forgot all about his fears, and returned to the subject that he had been harping on all day.

"You know," he said, "on the whole I can understand why they talk about 'distrust.' The other day I went to see a Communist who's on the staff of *L'Humanité*. His apartment is thoroughly bourgeois. Conventional reproductions on the walls: Rodin's *Thinker* and that sort of thing. His wife served up the usual stew and he boasted that she was a good cook. There were four children; the eldest was doing his home-work and Daddy was helping him. You see the picture? Of course, a man like that can vote, but that's all. But when such middle-class people — "

Jeannette was not in the habit of arguing, but now she showed unexpected animation.

"Is it a crime for a man to have a wife and family? I've told you that's what I'm always thinking about. It's a woman's whole happiness. Don't you understand? . . . I sometimes think it's what you want too, only you don't dare say so. . . . Life is impossible without it, Lucien. It's so bleak, so lonely."

"It's entirely a question of temperament," Lucien said, "and of the times we live in. If I were asked to surround myself with a family, I'd shoot myself. I live for other things, things I may have to die for tomorrow. It's ridiculous to chatter about a family. What's the matter with you?"

"Nothing. I told you on the phone I wasn't feeling well. My head aches. Ask for a glass of water. I'll take an aspirin."

Lucien went on talking: the times demanded renunciation, solitude, and courage. Family snuggery was treason. Jeannette made no comment. Her spirit of animation had subsided.

They left Fouquette's in silence and turned off from the Champs-Élysées into a narrow, badly lit street. Suddenly Jeannette stopped on the corner near a druggist's. A large green globe showed in the lighted window. Jeannette's face looked like a corpse in the emerald light. She said quietly:

"I'm pregnant. Now I'll have to find a doctor. . . ."

Lucien was filled with pity, acute as pain. "Perhaps it isn't necessary," he stammered.

Jeannette gave a shrill laugh. "No, you've explained everything and convinced me — these are not the times."

Lucien quickly regained his calm, which enraged Jeannette. In the same artificially bright voice she said:

"Don't excite yourself. It's not yours."

"What do you mean? I don't understand."

"When I was on tour. At Vichy. An actor was sleeping in the next room. The door to my room wouldn't fasten. The lock was broken. And that's all there was to it. Now do you understand?"

She ran into the street and hailed a passing taxi. Lucien shouted after her: "Wait! I'll come with you."

"There's no need. Solitude and courage — that's what you said, didn't you? Good night!"

Lucien's immediate reaction was that Jeannette had lied to him. An actor? The lock broken? It was altogether too fantastic! But could it have been André, perhaps? She hadn't been able to take her eyes off him in the café and André had kept staring at her.

Besides, she had asked him why he hadn't invited André back to the apartment. Of course it must be André!

After the rain the Place de la Concorde gleamed like the polished floor of a state apartment. The cars left orange and purple stains coiling on the wet blue asphalt. The great street lamps glowed like tropical plants, and from the Tuileries gardens floated the smell of wet earth, trees, and spring. Everything seemed to have been made for a carnival, but the atmosphere was tainted with an undercurrent of uncertainty and alarm. An old prostitute, plastered with rouge, accosted Lucien. He quickened his pace. On the embankment he suddenly stopped, remembering Jeannette's eyes outside the druggist's. Lagrange's eyes had looked like that when he said to Lucien: "Don't argue. I know it's gangrene." Lucien hurried back to the square and took a taxi to Jeannette's.

She was lying with her head buried in the pillow. She was crying. The doll lay beside her. She was crying because she felt hurt: how could Lucien believe her ridiculous story? She was crying because of his unfeeling attitude and because she was lonely. She carried an even greater grief inside her, but she could not cry on that account. It was a grief that surpassed all words and gave her eyes that expression of fatality which had frightened Lucien outside the druggist's. Only that morning she had still believed in the possibility of happiness.

When Lucien entered the room, she stopped crying. She sat up and powdered her face.

"You know, Lucien," she said, "the most dreadful thing of all is that I don't love you."

CHAPTER 11

THE SLEEPY old town, whose antiquities were described to Denise and Michaud in Professor Malet's lecture, was changed out of all recognition. People were now arguing and gesticulating in the streets, where usually aristocratic old ladies gossiped sedately, abbés waddled along with open breviaries, and children played at knuckle-bone. The words "Popular Front," "Fascism," "Law and

Order," "War," rang in the air. The ancient walls, as wrinkled as the cheeks of the elderly dowagers, had broken out into a violent rash of election posters of the various parties. All day long, people gathered round the screens of the urinals, reading the mutual recriminations of the candidates. And near by, in the porches of the ancient churches, the long-faced saints blessed the sinners, and tremulous swallows alighted on their stone fingers.

Three rival candidates were contesting with Paul Tessa for the honour of being made deputy for Poitiers. Two of them had stood against Tessa four years ago: the Communist, Didier, and the retired General Grandmaison, the candidate put up by the Conservative circles of the town, the aristocracy and the clergy, who described himself as a "Nationalist." On that occasion Tessa had easily defeated his rivals. Now he was far from being sure of victory, although Desser had kept his promise. *La Voie Nouvelle* had given Tessa a tremendous write-up, and two of the three local newspapers had been bought up by the Radicals. In the last few years the Communists had gained ground. Though Didier was not a brilliant speaker, he collected a huge audience. Moreover, a new competitor had appeared on the scene. This was Dugard, a young agriculturist connected with the Croix de Feu. He was an energetic fellow, canvassing house after house and everywhere exposing " the machinations of the financiers, Masons, and Jews." Shopkeepers hit by the spread of chain stores with fixed prices, artisans overburdened with taxes, professional men obsessed with the idea that they were being squeezed out of existence by foreigners, rentiers perturbed by the Stavisky scandal, in which Tessa had been involved — all these warmly applauded Dugard.

The meetings were stormy, and Tessa, who, when prosecuting, had been accustomed to jeering at prisoners in the dock, often felt as though he was on trial himself. Dugard mentioned, with cunning casualness, a certain cheque drawn by Stavisky. Tessa had long forgotten how he had spent those ill-gotten eighty thousand francs, but he banged the table with his fist and roared: " That money was set aside for disabled soldiers! " Grandmaison harped on Tessa's immorality and quoted extensively from Lucien's book: "Here is what this young writer saw in the house of his own father! " Didier was not concerned with Tessa's private life. He spoke about the bribery of the press and the role of the " Two Hundred Families." Tessa, however, thought that the Communist locksmith was referring to him personally, and the shouts from the audience confirmed his suspicions. Didier had only to mention how the press could be bought, and voices would immediately call out: " *La Voie Nouvelle!* " and his tirades against the " Two Hundred Families " would be interrupted with shouts of " Desser! Desser! "

Tessa worked like a galley-slave. He chatted with thousands of electors, inquiring after the health of their wives, whether their sons had passed their examinations, when their daughters were getting married. He promised the town a new bridge and a couple of squares, and its citizens pensions, honours, and Government jobs. In the bars he drank toasts with the red-nosed partisans of Daladier and Herriot: " To the Republic! To victory! " He roared himself hoarse at meetings, wrote pamphlets, edited the newspaper reports, and thought out ideas for cartoons. He went short of sleep for sixteen nights, wrecked his digestion at banquets, and forgot all about the tender embraces of Paulette. One of the biggest cafés put up a notice: " Open all night because of the candidature of Paul Tessa." Here Tessa distributed various presents to his supporters — a watch, a fountain-pen, a hundred-franc note. He got a couple of senators to come down from Paris and make speeches for him. A local music-hall singer sang the following topical couplets:

> *We don't want the brawlers and minions of hell,*
> *A moderate policy suits us quite well.*
> *With coffee for breakfast and love after dark,*
> *When Tessa gets in we'll be safe as Noah's Ark.*

Tessa kept his best ace up his sleeve until the last moment. This was a widow named Mme Antoine, whose son, a minor official, had been sentenced to ten years' imprisonment for embezzlement. Antoine had been unjustly condemned and Tessa secured a reinvestigation of his case. At the great meeting at which the announcement was made, the widow Antoine exclaimed, with tears in her eyes: " Paul Tessa is a saint! "

In the evening, when the votes were being counted, Tessa could hardly stand on his feet. He even had difficulty in drinking an orange-flower infusion to calm his nerves. The strain was too much for him and he went over to the window. The square was packed with gaping people waiting for the result of the ballot to be declared. Tessa noticed a girl who had a look of Denise. A wave of depression swept over him. Why had he bothered himself with these damned politics? What did it matter who won: Dugard or the Popular Front? It was all bunkum anyway! It would have been better to stay at home with his wife, look at Denise, dash off to snatch an hour with his beautiful Paulette. That was life! All these speeches and slogans were boring drudgery.

The crowd was disappointed. None of the candidates got an absolute majority; the vote had to be taken again in a week. Tessa had dropped nearly three thousand votes as compared with the last election. Grandmaison had also lost. The Communists had increased their poll. Dugard was ahead of all.

People began to speculate: if the general withdrew his candidature in favour of the Croix de Feu, Dugard stood a chance of winning. Would Didier withdraw in favour of Tessa? Who would the moderates vote for? They sat in the cafés calculating and calculating.

Tessa yawned irritably. He had thought everything would be over by today, and tomorrow he would be back home. Now he would have to stay another week in the town. He sent his wife a telegram: " Second ballot arrive Wednesday one o'clock love you Denise Lucien." A week of torment lay ahead of him. Even if the Communists agreed to vote for him the poll would be even — six thousand each way. Everything depended on a mere chance. And the Communists were hardly likely to agree: they hated Tessa.

That evening a meeting was held. The Radicals had invited the Communists and the hall buzzed with impatience: what would Didier say?

Tessa himself opened the meeting. " Citizens, I thank you for your confidence. I call upon all who cherish the Republic, all who are devoted to the cause of peace and social justice, all who are opposed to clericalism, to vote for me as the only candidate — " He paused for a moment and then roared: " *of the Popular Front!* "

Didier spoke next. " The Communist Party neither bribe nor seduce," he said. " They appeal to reason and conscience. At the last elections we polled six hundred votes. And now two thousand three hundred and seventy. You see how our strength is growing. We must bar the way to the Fascists, Dugard and Grandmaison. Tessa promises to be loyal to the Popular Front. France is going through a difficult time. The danger from without is increasing and there are traitors within. It has always been so. The Chouans joined hands with the English or the Austrians; the Prussians helped Versailles.

Only the Popular Front can save France. Long live the Popular
Front! Long live France!"

Clenched fists were raised in reply.

Tessa stood up and made an actor's bow. He didn't know whether
to be glad or sorry. He hated both Dugard and Didier. Upstarts!
Nincompoops! The Communists had decided to vote for him. That
was undoubtedly a success. But who could tell whether the workers would obey? Hadn't he heard one of them say: "What! Vote for
that swindler!" Besides, even if Didier's supporters did vote for
him, Dugard might get two or three hundred votes more. It was
impossible to count on the moderates. They would be saying he
was openly fraternizing with the Communists. That scoundrel
Desser! What scheme was he hatching? What was he trying to
make money out of? The ruin of France? And he, Tessa, had
stepped into the bog.

Without waiting for the end of the meeting, Tessa went back
to his hotel. His forehead was contracted with a headache. The
hall porter stopped him.

"There's a gentleman to see you, Monsieur Tessa," he said.
"He's in the smoking-room."

Tessa sighed. Just another pension-seeker, he thought, but when
he opened the door, there was the deputy Louis Breteuil.

Tessa was astonished. What was the meaning of this visit? Tessa
was on friendly terms with all the deputies, Right and Left. He
was also friendly with Breteuil. At any other time he would have
exclaimed with exaggerated pleasure: "My dear chap! How delightful to see you! And how's your wife?" But now he felt as
though he was on a battlefield. He could still hear Dugard's insults: "What about that cheque?" To think that his seat in the
Palais Bourbon might be occupied by that impudent clodhopper.
It would have been much better if Breteuil hadn't turned up.

People were rather afraid of Breteuil. He had the reputation of
being a fanatic. His outward appearance was that of an elderly
sportsman. He was over six feet, with a poker-straight back, red
sunburnt face, grey hair, and a short clipped moustache. He had
been wounded in the war; two fingers of his right hand were
missing, and somehow this mutilation was reflected in the expression of his face. He spoke tersely, snapping out the words as though
he were giving orders. Whenever a Communist mounted the platform, Breteuil left the hall. He said he couldn't listen to such

people. He was not on the board of any company, had nothing to do with financial speculation, and lived modestly. He was said to spend part of his salary on propaganda. His favourite hobby was the training of youth. He formed boys' brigades, drilled the lads, and spoke to them in glowing terms about the Chouans, the National Guards, and the gendarmes. He made the mothers' darlings march in the rain and raise their arms at the word of command. Late in life he married an ugly woman with no money and fussed like a nurse-maid over his puny, capricious five-year-old son. This seemed to be his only weakness.

Tessa stood in the doorway, not knowing what to say. Breteuil rose from his chair.

" How do you do, Paul? You don't look well. Expect you're tired."

" I am, very. But what are you doing here? Passing through? "

" No, I've come down from Paris. You know, don't you, that Dugard is a pupil of mine? He's young, but he's not stupid. He needs encouraging."

Tessa was furious. Breteuil had come to help Dugard. Well, that was his affair. But it was most tactless of him to come to Tessa, still more so to condole with him for looking tired.

" Forgive me," he said, " but I must really go to bed. I'm done in."

" Wait a bit. We must have a talk. Only not here. I'll come up to your room."

Tessa went up to his room, undid his tie, took off his shoes, and lay down on the bed. When Breteuil knocked on the door he called out to him: " I think we'd really better postpone this conversation. I'm absolutely exhausted. After the elections — "

Breteuil marched into the room. " Out of the question," he snapped. " I know you're tired. I won't take up more than five minutes of your time. We've got to come to a decision. You know yourself that Dugard has every chance of winning. He ought to get a majority of five or six hundred votes. But I'm against — "

" Against what? " asked Tessa.

" I want you to be elected. Dugard is a clever fellow. He'll come in handy to us later on. But in the Chamber he'll only be a dumb performer. Can't compare him to you. You're an experienced politician, a man of enormous experience, and a wonderful speaker. Moreover, you've got a name. Your defeat would be a misfortune for the country."

"Look here, Louis," said Tessa, "I don't understand what you're driving at. Why all these compliments? Haven't you been supporting Dugard? Well, he's been slinging mud at me day after day."

"Why attach any importance to words, especially at election meetings? Damn it, you've been boosting the Popular Front, haven't you? Oh, yes, I know what you think about the Communists. It still remains to be seen who loves them most — you or I. Now listen, Paul, I want you to be elected to the Chamber. Let them think you're for the Popular Front. It's the man that matters, not the label. You need only say one word. . . ."

"An hour ago I stated that I agreed to support the Popular Front."

"It isn't a question of public statements. I repeat: one word from you is enough. I mean what I say, and you can trust me. You must realize, Paul, the country has no time for parties now. The nation has got to be saved! Very well, Dugard must withdraw. Of course, he can't call on people to vote for you, but it will be enough if he withdraws. Two or three thousand votes will go to you."

"But Dugard's followers will prefer Grandmaison," said Tessa.

"What, the old general? Oh, I know him. He's a fool, but quite a decent chap. I'll have a word with him tomorrow. All right, then, Grandmaison will also withdraw and you'll be the only candidate. There you have the symbol of unity that can save France!"

The temptation was so strong and the whole thing was so unexpected that Tessa began to mutter incoherently: "Symbol! But you've come from Paris, haven't you? Is it as hot there? I can't stand the heat. . . ."

Breteuil was silent. Tessa tried to think, but failed. His thoughts were cloudy and confused, like fish in muddy water. He realized one thing: he would be a deputy again! He drank a glass of water and rubbed his forehead with a wet towel. Consciousness gradually returned to him. "France is in danger," he said to himself. "The enemy is on the watch. . . . And there is treason within. I'll be the symbol of national unity. It isn't a question of labels, but of men!" Without realizing it, he was repeating now the words of Breteuil, now of Didier. At last, like a child who has been promised a wonderful toy, he stammered timidly:

"But look here, what can I say?"

"Only one thing — that you agree."

"Well, I suppose it's all right, then. After all, I've no right to refuse."

Breteuil shook Tessa warmly by the hand. "I knew you were an honest man," he said. "Well, now you have a good sleep. Good night."

Next morning Tessa woke late. The sun was streaming through the shutters and the old green velvet armchairs looked like little grass plots. Outside the hotel Tessa saw a poster which had been newly pasted up: "Jacques Dugard thanks his electors and, submitting to his duty as a patriot, withdraws his candidature. Long live France!" Tessa was unable to suppress a smile. He even winked at a young flower-seller; and now that he looked at her, he was reminded of Paulette's neck and shoulders. Once again life was good. That morning everything gave him pleasure: the Romanesque churches, the vacuum cleaners in the shop windows, the old market women. He was ready to kiss them all. No doubt Dugard was a fine young fellow. It would be a good idea to ask him to lunch, have a chat, and crack a few jokes with him. Tessa was sorry he had no estate or he would have given Dugard a job. And Didier was a decent fellow too, just an old locksmith with a kind heart and a big moustache. A man like that could mend a lock. . . . It wasn't the label that mattered, it was the man! Tessa stopped at every poster. People were discussing the announcement. A taxi-driver climbed out of his cab, read it aloud, and spat. "What a damned swindle!" But even this failed to damp Tessa's joy. He was positively beaming with pleasure. He decided to run up to Paris for a day or so. He wanted to spend a whole evening with Paulette. He went into a confectioner's and bought a box of chocolates for Denise. Then he sat down in a little café and ordered a brandy. At the next table was a man who, even at that hour in the morning, was already slightly tipsy. He was feeding the sparrows with crumbs from a piece of bread wrapped up in a newspaper. He turned to Tessa. "It's a pleasure to talk to the birds. It's been nothing but elections and elections. . . ."

"Whom are you for?" asked Tessa instinctively.

"Me? I'm for myself. That's who I'm for! And for the birds. But I'm not going to vote. It's all humbug!"

Tessa laughed. "Quite right!" he said. "What will you have to drink? This is on me."

Tessa caught the four o'clock train to Paris. An hour later

Breteuil set out for the house of the Marquise de Nior. It was here that the bigwigs of Poitiers forgathered every Tuesday. They were mostly impoverished landowners, who lived modestly but maintained all the forms of etiquette. Their clique included a couple of factory-owners, a professor of the Archæological Institute and a handful of clerical gentlemen. A manservant handed round weak tea and tiny sandwiches — the Marquise was noted for her stinginess. Usually, after devoting five minutes to foreign politics and the excavations (the town was noted for its antiquities, and all the local aristocrats adored archæology), the visitors settled down to a good gossip. But this afternoon the conversation revolved round one subject — the second ballot. Grandmaison felt like a hero. He was a testy but inoffensive old man with the skull of a new-born baby and a gouty foot in a felt slipper. Whenever he got angry he would stick out his gouty foot and shout: " Never! "

Breteuil stirred his cup vigorously and said: " My friend, in the situation that has been created the noblest thing to do is to withdraw."

" Never! I'm not Dugard. I know Tessa will get in, but there are some defeats that are more honourable than victory."

"There's no need to get angry," said Breteuil. " The two thousand votes given to you will throw Tessa into the camp of our enemies, but remember he's one of the right sort."

This provoked a general outburst of indignation.

" He's a friend of Chautemps! Remember the Stavisky affair! "

" The man's a Mason! He's a member of the Grand Orient Lodge! "

" And what about Desser's money? "

" The right sort? " roared Grandmaison. " Do you know his writings? The man's an atheist. Worse than that — a cynic! ' The lay school,' indeed! It produces nothing but a pack of loafers, who want to divide up everything. Never! "

Breteuil began speaking with a passion unusual for him. " Now let's get this straight," he said. " Our country is on the verge of revolution. The Popular Front may drag France into war. And even if we're victorious as a country, the victory will be a defeat for us. Tessa is against religious education? Granted. But what's the sense of worrying about a cold when a man's got galloping consumption. Tessa is emphatically not a Communist. I talked to him yesterday and he gave me his assurance of everything. The Popular Front will be in power tomorrow. If we can't stop it by frontal assault, we must blow it up from within. A dozen Tessas will do the job. In order to save France, I'm willing to unite not only with Tessa but even with the Germans. Yes, yes, let me finish! If I'm told tomorrow that revolution is inevitable, I shall answer: call in Hitler."

There was a general silence. The Marquise de Nior whispered: "You talk in a very remarkable way, Monsieur Breteuil! But it's depressing! Lord, how depressing it is!" She dropped the sugar-tongs on the floor.

CHAPTER 12

TESSA decided to tell his family all about his success while they were having lunch. He liked talking politics with a tasty dish steaming in front of him.

"The situation was absolutely critical," he said. "Dugard was slandering me — Stavisky again! By the way, Lucien, you ought to be pleased: your little book is selling like hot cakes down there — all on account of me, of course. Grandmaison quoted it every day: 'Just look at his son!' *Maman*, where did you get such a deliciously tender duck? I had the most wonderful lobster *à l'Américaine* in Poitiers. Where was I? Oh, yes. Well, the Communists didn't lag behind either. They blazed away at me with 'Freedom and Peace,' the usual, irresponsible demagogy. The result was — a second ballot. I thought I was going to collapse from exhaustion. And the headaches I had! . . . Denise, why are you looking so pale? You ought to take a trip to Poitiers. The Romanesque churches there are in a class by themselves. You ought to see Sainte Rédégonde. I calculated: if the Communists withdraw their candidate, the chances are equal. But there was a rumour the Reds were going to vote for Didier again. You see, I'm not exactly popular with Lucien's friends. Anyway, I got up and announced that I was the Popular Front candidate. Terrific applause. They even raised their fists. To tell the truth, I can't bear that gesture. I say, this duck is really superb! Well, we had cleared the first fence; the Communists declared they would vote for me. But then the Rights raised an outcry:

they wanted to mobilize everybody. So the chances were equal:
Red and Black. . . ."

He paused to gnaw the flesh off a wing.

"Anyhow, you'll beat the Fascist," said Lucien. "The feeling of
the country . . ."

"Ah, but wait a minute! You've no idea what happened. Have a
guess! It was just like a play. *Maman,* give me some salad. What
about you? . . . Aren't you even allowed to eat salad? This diet-
ing's a frightful business! Well, can't you guess, Lucien? Dugard
withdrew, and now I'm the only candidate. That's national unity."

Lucien was unable to restrain himself: "And you agreed to
that!" he said. "How sordid!"

Tessa was offended. "I don't see anything sordid about it," he
said. "All the parties have agreed on me. I think it's something to
be proud of. Is national unity sordid? Even your Red locksmith
kept saying 'France! France!' all the time. You are behind the
times, my friend."

The lunch was ruined. Tessa's own family did not understand
him. His wife sighed. Denise wasn't listening. She was playing with
the kitten. And that infernal loafer Lucien was probably thinking
up a new lampoon. Tessa drank his coffee and left the table, saying
he must work. Everybody knew that he slept after lunch, but he
always called it "work."

Lucien reproached himself for his lack of restraint. He had been
waiting for his father to come back in order to ask him for five
thousand francs. Jeannette was obliged to have an operation and
there was nobody he could borrow from. Why had he been such a
fool as to upset his father? He would probably refuse now. Lucien
remembered Jeannette's eyes and, forgetting everything else, went
into the study.

He plunged in right away.

"I need five thousand," he said. "I need it very badly."

Tessa was silent.

"I didn't mean to upset you," said Lucien suddenly. "There's no
need to get in a rage."

Tessa lay on the sofa. Resentment had sharpened the lines of his
birdlike face. There were beads of perspiration on his forehead.
Lying there so slight and pale, he looked like a corpse.

"What do you want five thousand for? Another infernal lampoon?"

Lucien did not answer. Tessa glanced at him and turned his head away. A fellow like that was capable of anything! Tessa's uncle had had exactly the same chestnut hair. Nobody in the family ever mentioned him; he had forged a cheque and got seven years.

He got up and wrote out the cheque. Lucien took it and went out.

Tessa lay down again. He decided to take a nap in order to calm his nerves, but his thoughts prevented him. He experienced a feeling of disgust, as on the evening when Breteuil arrived in Poitiers. Didn't Lucien realize how it sickened him to accept a favour from the hands of Breteuil? Of course it was disgusting. It was also disgusting to hobnob with Communists. In order to get a lock mended if you like, but not to decide the fortunes of the country with them! That was an abomination! Just like life. What a dirty game it all was! Heads or tails? In the Chamber when they voted on the question of confidence in the Government — a few votes for or against decided the fate of a man. And the juries? Would they cut off a man's head or not? That, too, depended on a trifle. Had Tessa's speech touched the feelings of some shopkeeper? If not, they would wake the man up at four in the morning, give him a glass of rum, and slice his head off. A lottery! Everybody knew that the Popular Front was a loathsome thing. It wouldn't even last a year. Nothing would last, anyway. Everything was rotten! Muck! Everything would fall to pieces. And who cared a damn if it did! In the evening he would go to Paulette. And Paulette would die. Everybody would die.

Tessa's thoughts about the inevitable ruin of existence had a soothing effect. Soon a light snore was heard coming from the study. Presently it changed to a long-drawn-out whistle.

Lucien was talking to Denise.

" Say what you like, but it is a sordid business all the same. He's with the Communists and the Croix de Feu at the same time. There's nothing honourable or honest in that."

" I feel sorry for him," Denise said. " He's grown so old in the last year."

" Not surprising! Paulette's enough to ruin a man at his age."

" Lucien! "

As he glanced at her, her eyes reminded him of Jeannette's. Ah, these quiet girls were . . . But Jeannette didn't love him. She had said so herself. And why indeed should she?

"You can be sorry for me as well," he said. "Maybe Father will die, but I shan't. I shall just wither away."

That evening Tessa indulged in a little old-fashioned amusement. He went to Paulette's apartment, and afterwards they had supper at Maxim's. Lazily he watched the legs of the girls alternately rising and falling in the cancan. "This is the life," he said to himself. He drank glass after glass of champagne, but it had little effect on him. The brooding mood which had taken hold of him earlier in the day still remained with him.

He got home at two o'clock. His wife was playing patience as usual, sitting up with a hot-water bottle on her stomach. When she saw Tessa she burst into tears:

"Thank goodness you're back! I've got such pains!"

"It'll pass, Amalie. The doctor said it'll soon pass."

"No. I know it won't pass. I shall soon die now."

"Why do you talk such nonsense? The doctor says it can be put right. I've spoken to him. You'll survive everybody yet."

"What have I got to live for? I'm no longer good for anything. I got up today on account of you, and you see, it's worse again. I'm not afraid of death. It's something else I'm afraid of. I know you don't believe in anything. . . . But there must be a Judgment. . . . I didn't want to say anything in front of the children. . . . Getting mixed up with the Communists! How *can* you? I read what they're doing in the paper yesterday. They've burned down eight churches in Malaga. What savages! And to think of you, my own husband, in with them!"

Tessa undressed and got into bed. Then he said: "You seem to think I don't find it disgusting myself, but I do. Politics is a dirty game. Even speculation is better. But what is it you're worrying about? It isn't as if we were in need of money. We'll manage to exist somehow. Of course the children are a problem. Lucien took another five thousand off me today. If he doesn't get what he wants, he's capable of cutting someone's throat. And then there's Denise; she may fall in love some day. I don't want her to be dependent upon her husband. She's as proud as the devil. She won't be able to get along without money. You know, Amalie, there's no need to finish me off. I'm in a bad enough way as it is."

His wife kissed him on the forehead and turned out the light.

Tessa lay on his back, gazing into the darkness. He knew he wasn't going to be able to sleep. Little bright specks like cham-

pagne bubbles kept floating in front of his eyes. His wife groaned
at his side. He whispered: " Amalie! " She did not answer; she was
groaning in her sleep. Tessa began to feel afraid. Amalie would
soon die and he would die too. . . . Then nothing! He remembered how they cut off the head of Laroche, who had killed a
policeman. It was autumn. The leaves rustled under your feet on
the boulevard, and there was a huge red sun. Laroche drank the
rum, smacked his lips, and said: " Good! " They thought he would
die quietly, but when they led him to the guillotine he struggled
so they had to drag him to the knife, and he howled like a prairie
dog. Tessa shuddered; even now he could hear that howling. And
still the little bright specks kept floating up to the ceiling. . . . It
was all right for Amalie! She believed in hell. That too was a way
of escape, if you could only believe! . . . But there was no hell:
only the grave, and cold nothingness. Unable to bear the thought,
Tessa cried out. His wife woke up:

" Paul, what's the matter with you? "

" I was dreaming," he said guiltily.

CHAPTER 13

AUGUSTE VILLARD, the subject of Joliot's cock-and-bull stories and
the object of Pierre's worship, looked like an absent-minded, good-
natured professor. Everything about him suggested a bygone
world: the eye-glasses, the broad-brimmed black hat, the penchant
for psychological analysis, and the oratorical style.

Villard was born at Châlons in what was known as the " Terrible " year; the Prussians' bullets whistled round his cradle. His
father was a convinced Republican who had served a sentence of
two years' imprisonment for attacking the " Little Napoleon." From
his earliest years Auguste was accustomed to hearing the names
of Marat, Blanqui, Delécluze, and heated arguments about Socialism.

In Paris, Villard studied for his degree in history. He wanted to
devote himself to the political struggle, but like so many young men
of the period he became preoccupied with art and literature. As a

young student in the Latin Quarter, sometimes in a café, he met old Verlaine, who in the midst of his drunken mutterings would let fall exquisite lines that were like the cry of a migrant bird broken on the telegraph wires. Villard published a book of his own poems. They were imitative but not without talent. He wrote notices of art exhibitions for the press and aspired to become a critic. But then he got engrossed in the Dreyfus affair, and became a disciple of Jaurès. Being a modest man by nature, he performed any kind of work; he wrote articles for tiny newspapers, unmasked the clericals, and travelled about the countryside making speeches against militarism and demanding equal rights for women in a trembling voice. He read a good deal in his leisure moments and continued to take an interest in art; his friends jokingly called him "our Athenian." Shortly before the war he was elected to Parliament. About the same time he married a woman doctor. In the Chamber he was not entrusted with the task of making responsible speeches, but he worked on various committees and was considered a specialist in cultural matters. He attended international congresses and made the acquaintance of Lenin, Bebel, and Plekhanov. He was firmly convinced that when the Socialists got a majority in the elections they would bring about great changes.

Instead the war broke out. It was a great blow to Villard, and spelt the ruin of all his dreams. Nevertheless, he refused to take part in the Zimmerwald Conference, declaring that it was "impossible to set the working class against the nation." The talk about a "Holy Alliance" both annoyed and at the same time attracted him. He confined himself to making protests against the censorship and against shootings without trial.

Then came the stormy years after the war. Villard welcomed the Russian Revolution, but condemned the Communists: "We must go our own way!" The war had strengthened his horror of bloodshed. He was convinced that humanity would tread the path of peaceful progress.

He became one of the leaders of the Socialist Party, being helped in this by his age and erudition. Mentally he had grown old and dried-up. His wife had died. His children were married. He lived alone in a spacious, uncomfortable flat that was like a picture gallery: he was still as fond of paintings as ever. More and more frequently he felt the need for solitude. He had a country cottage, covered in wistaria, at Avalon. There he would sit on a cracked garden seat and listen to the crowing of the cocks and the croaking of the frogs. On returning from the sessions in the Chamber he would sit in front of his daughter's portrait, painted by Renoir, and admire the rosy tones, which were warm and sweet like the froth on top of newly made jam. The fear of anything that might disturb the even tenor of his life influenced his political calculations. The man whom the Right caricaturists represented with a knife between his teeth was a mild domesticated individual who repeated old revolutionary monologues from force of habit.

Suddenly, like a wind at sea, the storm arose. Finding no place in the world for themselves, the young people turned to the extreme parties. The February riots frightened Villard. He hated the disciples of Breteuil: they disturbed the peace of the country. Villard became a partisan of the Popular Front. He even overcame his old hostility to the Communists: he was defending his house at Avalon, his pictures, and his seat in the Chamber.

At a big meeting on the eve of the elections he appeared on the platform together with the Communists, and ten thousand people cheered him enthusiastically. He began by talking about democracy, vacations with pay, and civil peace, but, being a born orator, he sensed the feeling of the crowd. Living sounds broke through the sands of eloquence. The cracked voice grew strong. Villard began to speak about Spain, where the Popular Front had won the elections:

"The peasants of Estramadura have ploughed up the land of the landowners. In the monasteries the globe and compass have taken the place of relics. The workers are learning to shoot with rifles in order to defend their liberty. . . ."

And ten thousand voices shouted in answer: "Long live the Popular Front!"

Michaud and Denise were sitting in the top row of the gallery. Michaud clapped his hands and shouted. Then he whispered to Denise with a smile: "Not him. The Spaniards. . . ."

The speaker after Villard was a Communist, Legrais. Denise cried out: "I know him!" It was the workman with a gash on his cheek who had asked her what district she came from.

"Comrades," he said, "it's not only a question of voting. We shall have to defend the Popular Front Government with our own breasts. It's not a question of words, but of deeds, and it's not going to be an easy job. We must conquer, without fail! . . ."

Villard shook Legrais's hand. Everyone was delighted at the gesture. It seemed as though the bygone age, the utopians and dreamers, were greeting the people who were capable not only of sacrificing themselves, but also of winning the victory.

Denise and Michaud went out. It was hot and sultry in the street. A storm was coming on. On the café terraces people were drinking beer and lazily mopping their sweating faces.

Only six weeks had passed since the election meeting in the rue Falguière, but Denise and Michaud were talking like old friends.

"Villard speaks well," said Denise, "but there's something lacking in him somewhere."

"He doesn't believe in what he says."

"I think he believes, but only half. I can understand that. It happens to me as well. I say something with assurance and then I begin to have doubts." She smiled. "Only I don't speak at meetings. I like Legrais. He's in earnest in everything he says."

"Words should be backed up with actions," said Michaud.

"Is that possible?"

"It's possible. With blood. . . ."

There was a clap of thunder and the rain came pouring down. They took shelter under an awning. They stood close to each other in the rain and lightning and talked in low voices although there was nobody near them.

Denise told him about her life: "There is so much falseness. I don't want to talk to you about my father. That wouldn't be fair. But I can't go on living like this. I sometimes feel like a fish out of water. Something has got to be done. I'm not asking you for advice. I'm simply telling you."

"The way out is simple."

"Not for me it isn't. It's simple for you. You see, you're used to that life. Perhaps you've even inherited it. Anyway, it's what you've known since childhood. But I've been cut out to a different pattern. When I'm with you I don't feel it, but at meetings I always do. I need to go over things in my head about seven times; otherwise I'd be just like my brother. Lucien isn't bad, he is just flighty, that's all. He falls in love, and afterwards he doesn't even remember her name. It's the same with his convictions. But I'm a dull thinker."

"Denise, you are extraordinary! What nonsense you talk! Can you explain to me how it is that when I begin to talk to you about this sort of thing, nothing makes sense? How does it happen? Tell me, please! All right, let's quit fooling! I want to tell you something, only don't go and take it to mean something else. Now when I listen to you, I sit up and take notice and I begin to understand something. It's the same as with art. I kept trying to find out why it affected me. There are poems and poems. You read some and forget them, but others move you to the depths of your being. Now I seem to have understood architecture also. Without Malet. With you. And how! "

He waved his arms comically, but Denise did not laugh.

" Michaud, there's no need to talk about that. I'm thinking about something else at present. . . . I'm learning from you — how to live, to breathe, and to talk. Perhaps I'll learn the other as well. What was it you said about action? But look here, this rain isn't going to stop."

They ran out under the rattling downpour. People glanced at them with astonishment: they were getting soaked through and smiling. Denise was hatless, with her hair twisted up at the back, and wearing a grey coat and skirt. Her beauty was severe and rather old-fashioned. Michaud's eyes were brighter than usual. They walked in silence to Denise's house and gaily took leave of each other. The rain continued to pour down, and huge shining bubbles flecked the pavements. There was a smell of grass and the countryside.

When Villard got back to his flat, his recent enthusiasm on the platform seemed to him overdone: he felt the kind of shame that accompanies a hang-over. Why had he made that speech? The State would have to suffer on his account tomorrow. Every word of it would be weighed. It was impossible to become a minister with the manners of a provincial actor!

He tried to divert his thoughts a little and sank into a deep armchair. On the wall facing him hung a landscape by Bonnard: through a mass of green foliage the spots of pale sunlight were like honey. All the stillness of a hot day seemed to stream from the canvas. Villard began to enter into that world of immobility and torpor in which he spent his best hours.

His enchantment was disturbed by the manservant, who brought in the evening mail on a salver. Reluctantly Villard opened the first letter, and his face immediately changed. It was a typewritten note:

*If you dare to govern France, we will burn you like an old
rat. Death to the Popular Front! — A French Patriot.*

Villard was frightened by this anonymous note. He was not afraid
of death, but he feared responsibility. Within a few days he would
have to make decisions, give orders, and perhaps punish. And he
was incapable of doing it. He was accustomed to analyse, to criti-
cize, and to maintain his own personal opinion. At sixty-five he
felt the shudder of a girl on the verge of her first affair. Once upon
a time everything had seemed quite simple to him: they would get
a majority at the elections and then announce the era of Socialism.
Perhaps it really was simple in those days. Before the war people
were softer and more pliant. They knew neither pogroms nor burn-
ings of books nor Fascist concentration camps. Now this man had
written: " We'll burn you like an old rat. . . ." Yes, they would in-
cite and instigate and shoot from behind corners — the same as in
Madrid. They wanted to drown the Popular Front in blood. And
who were Villard's allies? To the Communists he was a " traitor."
The Communists would begin to demand and insist on firm measures and appeal to the masses. And the Radicals? For Tessa, Villard
and Legrais were one and the same gang: it was enough to hear the
disgust with which he pronounced the word " Marxist." Villard
was alone. If they applauded him today, it was merely because he
had spoken like Legrais. When he began to act, the very same people would boo him.

What was the good of it all? How much longer had he got to live?
Five years? Perhaps less. He could gaze at Bonnard's landscapes,
read good books, and go away to his cottage at Avalon among the
goldfinches and carnations. . . . How incomprehensible and boring
everything was! And how cold the room felt! For some reason he
recalled his youthful verses:

> *A musty frost*
> *And lamps at night.*
> *A gad-fly thought:*
> *" Thy end's in sight."*

On that warm May evening he felt a chill creep over him. He
rang the bell.

" Robert, bring me my rug."

The manservant said to the cook with a smile: "Results of the election campaign — there's not a breath of air, but he's feeling cold!"

CHAPTER 14

On the Sunday evening Pierre went to see Agnès:

"Let's go down to the Boulevards," he said. "They're going to announce the election results."

Excited by the thought of the results, he was shouting and waving his arms. Agnès had no desire to go out; she was not feeling well. Besides, she wasn't interested in the elections. However, she gave way.

A stream of people was flowing from the dark narrow streets down towards the centre of the city. The fever which had gripped Pierre shook the whole population. Questions, guesses, rumours, and expressions of alarm or hope were heard on all sides. The main boulevard seethed with workers' caps. The ordinary public had disappeared; only foreigners and prostitutes sat on the terraces of the smart cafés.

Pierre and Agnès stood in front of the office of an evening paper. The crowd in the large triangular square buzzed with impatience like an audience in the theatre before the curtain goes up. Presently the names and figures on the white screen would announce the fate of France. Maybe the Right would win? . . . Superstitious anxiety gave birth to rumours: the peasants were frightened of the Popular Front; the provinces had voted for the Fascists; even the Red suburbs of Paris had deserted the Left. Several names appeared on the screen. They were the first deputies for Paris. People were eagerly buying the evening papers, although they knew they did not yet contain the election results. The square looked like a crowded fair. In order to kill time, someone started to sing *Madame la Marquise*. People were chewing peanuts, and Arabs were singing the praises of their little goat-hair carpets. It was warm evening and the neighbouring bars were doing a brisk trade in beer and lemonade.

Suddenly the loud-speaker boomed out:

"Thorez, Maurice. Elected. . . ."

A storm of voices took up the answer. Thorez was popular. Shouts rolled round the square: "Long live our Maurice!" Although nobody had doubted that Thorez would be elected, this first success filled the crowd with enthusiasm. They started singing the *Internationale*. All the neighbouring streets were now filled with people. The gendarmes tried in vain to clear a way for the cars. They were not very insistent. Being uncertain which side would win, they tried to be tactful.

"Flandin, Pierre. Elected. . . ."

"Down with the Fascists!"

"Shoot the traitors!"

"Blum, Léon. Elected. . . ."

"Long live the Popular Front!"

The cheering and clapping alternated with whistling and booing. But the shouts of joy became more and more frequent; the howls of disapproval became less. By ten o'clock it was already clear that the Popular Front had won. The smile remained on the people's faces. The announcements of Right victories were greeted with a lazy whistle. The easy victory of the Popular Front seemed magical, almost miraculous: everybody had won five millions in an extraordinary lottery. It was not guns, but tiny leaflets that had saved the people. For decades past, voting had been a tedious ritual: what difference did it make who got in — a Radical Socialist or a Left Republican? But these elections were something special. They had been born in the street, amid the stones and blood of the 6th of February and amid the Red flags of the demonstrations. That night in May everyone was filled with the hope of a change not only in the Government but in his own little life as well. In other Paris squares and farther away — in smoke-begrimed Lille, in jovial Marseille, in taciturn, hard-hearted Lyon, on the shores of the Atlantic and at the foot of the Alps — millions of hearts were beating excitedly.

"Villard, Auguste. Elected. . . ."

Pierre shouted so loudly that Agnès laughingly covered her ears. His shout was taken up by other people, but Pierre did not think it was enough. "When a Communist gets in they'll shout for all they're worth," he said jealously.

"Tessa, Paul. Elected. . . ."

This was greeted by a few half-hearted shouts of: " Long live the Popular Front! "

" Let's go," said Agnès. " I can hardly stand on my legs."

They went back to the Boulevards and sat on the terrace of a small café. All around them people were clinking glasses and congratulating one another.

" You don't seem very exhilarated," Pierre said. " Why aren't you celebrating? "

" What about? Because they've elected Tessa? Yes, I dare say that scoundrel did put in a word for me. But I'm not celebrating."

" It isn't a question of Tessa. That's a detail. The important thing is that the Popular Front has won."

" You know how I feel about that," said Agnès. " For me life is what you call ' details.' "

" Tessa? "

" No. Straightforwardness. Honesty."

Pierre was too much exhausted by the events of the day to argue. He merely shook his head and gave himself up to the noisy merriment of the passers-by.

Some soldiers were sitting at the next table. They were slightly tipsy, shouting:

" The colonel will fill his trousers. . . ."

" Yes, now they'll keep a tight hold on them. . . ."

" Are you off to Strasbourg tomorrow? "

" The day after. It's the season there now, old boy. The Germans are constructing something all the time. It's as plain as a pikestaff. . . . They've put guns right opposite the town. . . ."

News-venders hurried past: " Special edition! Complete victory of the Popular Front! "

" Pierre," said Agnès, " do you think we could possibly take a taxi? I'm feeling all in."

As soon as they got home she lay down.

" What's the matter with you? " said Pierre. " Have you caught a cold? "

She smiled very faintly. " No. But don't you worry, I'm not ill. It's often like this. Don't you understand? . . . What a dolt you are! "

Pierre understood at last. He began to skip about the tiny little room.

" It's marvellous! And to be told about it on a day like this! . . .

He'll be a wonderful little fellow, you'll see! Of course, it's going to be a boy! Can I get you anything? Medicine? Oranges? "

She smiled at him. " I don't want anything. Sit down here. Like that."

She took his face between her hands, gazed into his eyes, then shielded them from the light with her fingers.

" So we're all alone," she said. She was smiling, she felt so light and peaceful.

Through the window came the voice of someone singing the *Internationale* — " For the last fight let us . . ." The poor people of Belleville were mounting the humpy streets to their homes in the dark, evil-smelling houses. That day the people had seen a fairy-tale — not the love of an American beauty, nor a ready-made daydream on the screen of a third-rate suburban cinema, but a fairy-tale about themselves. Someone had fought for Belleville and had won, and now they would be happy!

" Unite the human race . . ."

Agnès suddenly remembered the soldiers in the café. The one who had talked about Strasbourg had pink downy cheeks like a child's. She frowned. Her short-sighted eyes looked more helpless than ever.

" Tell me, Pierre, will there be a war? "

No."

" Later on? "

" Neither now nor later on. Never! "

CHAPTER 15

THE VICTORY of the Popular Front filled some people with anxiety. They talked about the prospect of strikes, a crisis, and disorders. Ladies nervously whispered to one another: " My maid has started to be impertinent already! " Shopkeepers hid their wares. Official bigwigs condescendingly explained that they would not submit to the new ministers: " They're only caliphs for an hour! " Breteuil called on " all honest Frenchmen " to adorn their houses with the national flag as a protest against the Popular Front. In some streets some houses were decorated with the Tricolour while others hung out the red flag, and one got the impression that not only the people but even the stones were ready to attack one another. In financial circles confusion reigned. There was talk of a big tax on capital and even of nationalizing the banks. Capitalists hastily transferred their money to America.

Only Desser remained calm. When one of his banker friends asked: "How can you work at a time like this?" he answered: "Tell me, what's the difference between Blum and Sarraut? I'm too coarse by nature to distinguish such fine shades."

Hearing that Villard had been given a ministry, Desser decided to have a good talk with him; after all, these people were children and might do something silly. He rang him up and said that he had always been wanting to have a look at Villard's pictures.

When addressing meetings, Villard had mentioned Desser's name more than once, referring to him as a typical, unscrupulous business man. But after Desser had said he was coming to see him, he proudly reflected: "After all, it was Desser who elected me!" He quite forgot what he had said about him in his speeches. Villard was now living like a young man, to whom everything is new. Hardly a week had passed since he had been made a minister, but he already had a different way of thinking, smiling, and crossing his legs. All his thoughts, gestures, and words were brought into line with his new position.

Desser had not forgotten, but he was quite indifferent to insults as well as to praises. He despised words. "My dear friend," he said, congratulating Villard, "may I say how glad I am to see you in this position?"

His stiffness disappeared when they came to look at the pictures. Villard realized at once that Desser was a good judge of painting. They chatted pleasantly about Picasso's blue period and Matisse's drawing. Looking at some drawings by Modigliani, so full of anxious foreboding, Desser remarked: "It's amazing how extremes, even excesses, express themselves in static art."

"That's what I like in the old masters, in El Greco, Zurbaran. . . ."

Desser took his pipe out of his mouth and puffed out a cloud of pungent smoke — he smoked cheap black tobacco.

"Now you'll have to give it all up," he said. "There's nothing to be done. You chose this *métier* yourself. I, for instance, can afford to be a gambler. I put my stakes on you, but it was a risk. But you

haven't the right to take risks. Each art has its own laws. In politics
it's big speeches and little deeds. I backed you up in the elections
and I'm ready to help you in the future. But how many are there
like me? The Stock Exchange hates you. To Wendel you're a bandit. To the gentlemen of the Crédit Lyonnais you're a burglar.
You've only to take one rash step and they'll tear you to pieces.
There's no need for conspiracies or parliamentary intrigues: it'll
be quite sufficient to rig the fall of the franc. Then you'll see what
tune the workers will strike up — to say nothing of the rentiers!
They'll start shouting: 'Hang Villard!' That's a beautiful Braque.
I don't much care for him myself. He's rather dry. But this still
life is one of his best. It was Braque who said: 'The artist must
verify his inspiration with a ruler.' You'll have to verify Socialist
projects by the exchange rate of the franc. . . ."

Villard was indignant. He wanted to answer: "We'll forbid the
export of capital. We'll fix a firm rate for the franc, and we'll pop
you into prison!" But his anger lasted only a moment. He remembered his responsibility.

"There's no need to put spokes into our wheel," he said. "The
stability of the Government is the only chance of a peaceful solution of the conflict."

"Incontestably. And that applies to the international situation
as well. By the way, I hope that in this respect you'll avail yourself of the experience of our friend Tessa."

Villard frowned slightly; he regarded Tessa as an enemy. But
Desser did not notice anything and went on: "I'm convinced you'll
be able to preserve peace. Of course Hitler's intolerable, but any
concessions are better than war."

Villard beamed. He had feared that with the danger to the country as a pretext Desser would begin rattling the sword. And now
even Desser was for peace! Villard shook him warmly by the hand.
"You can have confidence in me," he said. "As long as I'm in power
there'll be no adventures! I won't allow French peasants to die for
the Abyssinians or the Czechs."

When he had shown his visitor out, Villard sighed with relief
like a schoolboy after a difficult examination. Of course, Desser was
defending his own interests. But now everything was all mixed up
together; the interests of Desser coincided with the interests of the
workers. He was a sincere pacifist. It was obvious therefore that
Desser represented neither a party nor a class, but the nation.

A secretary came in for Villard's signature to an order for the removal of an official who had played a leading part in Breteuil's organization. Villard put the paper aside.

" Why set everybody against us? " he asked. Then, in jest, he said: " My friend, one has to learn how to govern forty millions. In Marx's day the workers had nothing to lose but their chains, and the world to win. Now we have peace to lose and nothing to win but chains."

Out in the street Desser disdainfully shrugged his shoulders. It had been only too easy! And yet Pierre believed in a man like Villard! And not only Pierre, but millions! God, how stupid people were! Probably that was their salvation.

Desser was to have gone on to a conference of financial experts, but he changed his mind. Villard's cowardice nauseated him. He strode down the long rue de Rivoli. On reaching the Place de la Bastille, he turned into a little side-street and saw the illuminated sign of a dance-hall. Without hesitating he went in; he wanted to forget for a while. . . .

The accordion-players were giving a skilful rendering of an old fox-trot. The paper lanterns and cotton garlands gave the place the air of a stage set. Sailors, workmen, little modistes, and waitresses were dancing vigorously.

Desser slipped the musicians five sous and took hold of a plump freckled girl. She smelt of cheap powder and rolled her eyes blissfully as she danced. After the dance Desser treated her to a cherry brandy.

" Are you fond of dancing? "

The girl turned out to be talkative. " Oh, very! Only I don't often get the chance. I work till six o'clock in the evening. And then I have to take work home with me. Do you know how much they pay me? Five hundred and fifty a month! How can you live on that? They say everything's going to be different now. Our dressmakers have told them that if they don't pay us more, we're going on strike. We've got the Popular Front now and nobody wants to live in the old way; isn't that so? "

Desser knocked out his pipe and knit his unnaturally large eyebrows.

" Of course," he said. " Everything will be different. For instance, the blondes have been dancing with the brunettes, but Villard will order the brunettes to dance with the blondes. *Au revoir, chère mademoiselle!* It's time for me to go home."

CHAPTER 16

THE STRIKE at the Seine aircraft works began on the Saturday. All through the week the workers had tried to come to terms with the management. Desser agreed to an increase of wages, but firmly rejected the men's other demands. He was particularly adamant on the questions of collective bargaining and vacations with pay, and said curtly: " There can be no discussion."

Desser realized that strikes were unavoidable from time to time. These little wars ended now with the victory of the workers, now with the victory of Desser. At the same time the losing side never for a moment gave up the idea of revenge. The strikers' demands always boiled down to one thing: shorter hours and more pay. And Desser found this quite natural. He had hundreds of ways of making money. The workers could only increase their wages by striking. The rest depended on the particular situation and the power to hold out. If the factory was overwhelmed with urgent orders and it was difficult to find skilled men among the unemployed, Desser made concessions. If orders were few and scabs were plentiful, Desser would hold out. After a week or two the strikers would get tired of starving and come cap in hand, or he would pay them off and take on new ones. Desser regarded this perpetual warfare as the law of life and felt neither sympathy nor malice towards his opponents.

The Popular Front had won a victory in the elections and Desser had helped to bring it about. He believed in the adroitness of the Radicals. Some of the new ministers were old friends of his. His talk with Villard had definitely set his fears at rest. That old agitator would turn out to be a good fireman! Fiery speeches did not perturb Desser: no sense in mistaking fireworks for a conflagration. He expected strikes: the workers were sure to take advantage of a favourable situation. He was prepared to meet them and to raise the stakes. But the demands put forward by Michaud filled him with indignation. Desser was not the State, but a plain business man. If Villard wanted to send the workers to the seaside, well and good, let the Exchequer pay for it. But collective bargaining was quite a different pair of shoes.

"No, Monsieur Michaud!" he said. "I stand by freedom! You're free to stay in my factory or to go away. That's your business. I can keep you on or dismiss you. That's my business."

That Saturday the men did not start work. Eighteen thousand of them assembled in the yard in front of the smelting shop. Legrais called out: "Those against, hold up their hands."

Among the workers were some timid souls, who were trying to persuade the others not to strike. They were afraid of reproaches at home, of hunger and defeat. But now that they would have to acknowledge their cowardice in front of everybody, they gloomily held their tongues. Not a single hand was raised.

They moved towards the gates. Then Michaud's voice rang out: "Comrades, stop! . . . Don't go away! . . ."

Standing on a truck, with his mouth to a loud-speaker, he shouted: "Don't go away!" and like an echo voices answered from all sides: "Don't go away!"

"Comrades," said Michaud, "if we go away, they'll take on scabs. We must stay in the works, spend the night here, live here — a day, a week, a month — till we win."

Shouts of astonishment. Nobody yet understood what Michaud was getting at.

"We're on strike!"

"But what are we going to eat?"

"Anyhow, the police will chuck us out!"

Michaud went on shouting into the loud-speaker: "The question of food will be settled by the committee. We'll get the money from our union. Nobody will drive us out of here: they'll have a job if they try! We must place pickets. And don't let in any spies. The gentlemen of the management can go home, but we won't let them come back. It's true, comrades, there has never been a strike like this before. But we'll show them. . . ."

A friend of Michaud's, a young turner called Jeannot, climbed up on the roof of the management building and hoisted the red flag. He shouted down: "The flag over the fortress!"

So began this unusual strike which shook the country.

All day throngs of people stood on the quay and in the streets leading to the works. Three thousand gendarmes in tin hats and with gas-masks slung at their sides prepared to storm the factory. The Government, however, was undecided, and the gendarmes vented their feelings on the wives of the strikers who tried to get through to the gates or on casual passers-by. By evening the women were still getting through to the factory, bringing bread, sausage, cheese, cherries, and wine. Some even brought footballs, chess-boards, books, and guitars. Jeannot's mother brought him some eggs and a pillow. He climbed up on the fence with the others, and his mother shouted up to him from below: " What crazy idea have you got into your head, you shameless scamp! Come home to bed! " Jeannot gave an embarrassed smile.

Pierre was the only one of the managing engineers to join the strikers. " Be careful," said the works manager. " Nobody likes deserters, you know."

" I'd have you know, m'sieu, that my father was a working-class man."

Jeannot was delighted when he saw Pierre. It gave him the assurance of victory. Jeannot was nineteen and dreamed of barricades, bullets, and flags. Even Pierre was not immune from romanticism.

At night the factory was transformed into a military camp, with sentries everywhere. Pierre and Jeannot stood near the main gates. Pierre felt as though he were at war and that the enemy would attack at any moment.

" What if they attack? " Jeannot whispered. " Have you got a revolver? "

" I've got one, but I mustn't use it. I'll have to ask Michaud."

It so happened that Michaud, who had so far been known only to the Communists and his workshop mates, had immediately become the leader. Everybody said: " Ask Michaud. . . . Michaud has given orders. . . . Michaud doesn't approve. . . ."

Michaud worked untiringly. He organized a soup kitchen, got together a band, established contact with the district committee, and dictated reports for *L'Humanité*. He cheered up the fainthearted: " We'll win! And how! " He inspected the machinery: you had to be on your guard against sabotage.

In the evening the band played the *Internationale* and thousands of voices took up the words of the song. It floated out of the factory over the heads of the gendarmes and trailed away over the river and the darkened houses of the excited suburb. The women tossed in their beds as they listened to the distant singing. What would tomorrow bring? Hunger? Bloodshed? Happiness? The strikers did not sleep, either. Under the clustered stars of the summer night they dreamed silently of victory.

Fearing a clash during the night, the Government decided to remove the police. On Sunday the people were free to pass along the quay to the gates; but the factory continued to look like a besieged fortress. Who was besieging it? Desser? The ghosts of the scabs? The phantom of hunger? It was essential to hold on till victory.

On the Monday evening Michaud opened the evening paper, cried out: "The others too! All of them! And how! . . ."

He was too excited to speak. *La Voie Nouvelle* stated that the unusual strike which had begun at the Seine works had spread all over Paris. All the big factories had gone on strike and hundreds of thousands of workers had locked themselves in. The department stores were on strike. They were brilliantly lighted at night and the salesgirls had locked themselves in there too. The waiters in the cafés and restaurants were holding a sit-down strike. The minor employees of one of the Government offices had also declared a strike and refused to leave the building. The account of the sensational strike was written by Joliot himself with his own special brand of pathos: "The plebs of Paris has retired to the Aventine hill. . . ." The report stated that the working-class quarters of Paris were empty. Only women and children were to be seen in the streets. Joliot concluded his story on a poetic note: "One is reminded of the years of the war, when the men were also far from their homes — at the front. . . ."

Desser spent a couple of days on his estate. On learning of the strike, he cancelled all his business engagements, cut off the telephone, and sat down to read Ovid. He intended to wait. The seizure of the factory seemed to him so absurd that he foresaw a speedy dénouement: either the strikers would come to their senses and go back to their homes or there would be a revolt. On the Monday, Desser was informed that the strike had spread to other concerns. The following morning he went to Paris, and it was not yet nine o'clock when his car stopped outside the factory gates. The young worker who was acting as sentry barred the way:

"No admission to outsiders."

"I'm no outsider. I'm president of the council of administration, Desser."

The worker smiled: "The name seems familiar. But you see, Monsieur Desser, if we let you in, you won't be able to go away again. You'll have to stay here until — "

"Until what?"

"Until Monsieur Desser gives way."

They both laughed. But in his heart Desser was furious. What a racket! A fine idea of liberty! What would messieurs the strikers say if they were not allowed to go home? Desser did not show his indignation. With the same benignant smile he said:

"You're a witty fellow, but you'll have to let me in."

The worker sent a comrade to Michaud for instructions, and five minutes later he announced:

"You may come in. You can leave whenever you like. But you mustn't go into the workshops — in order to avoid incidents."

Desser clapped the worker on the back.

"So you're learning how to run the show? Remarkable!"

Desser went through the deserted offices of the management. The old messenger who followed him sighed apologetically.

"Is there nobody here?" said Desser.

"They all left last Saturday. Only Monsieur Dubois has stayed on, and, begging your pardon, sir, he's with the workers."

"Is he looking after the machinery?"

"I beg your pardon, but Monsieur Dubois is on strike."

Desser burst into laughter; so Pierre too had decided to seize the factory! "Fetch Monsieur Dubois," he said.

Desser asked Pierre to sit down and offered him a cigarette. "Sorry to bother you," he said, "but I want to ask you a question. It's purely personal. Have you decided to seize the factory for good or only for a while? I'd like to know, so that I can plan how to dispose of my time."

"Nobody has seized the factory," said Pierre. "This is a strike. And in my opinion the workers' demands are justified."

"Very interesting! In your opinion this is a strike? No, my friend, this is violence. Don't think I'm trembling for my property. My fear is for France; one act of violence breeds another."

"You said yourself that you value the happiness of others. These people want to live, and to live better, more freely and happily. How can you object?"

"I've told you," said Desser, "I've told you that our country can be ruined by a mere chance: the equilibrium is unstable. Everything's rushing downhill now."

"But it depends on you. You've only to sign the agreement and the workers will clear out of the factory."

"You mean I should capitulate? That's not my trade. And it's not in my nature. I prefer to wait. And I'm not calling for the police. I'm not asking the Government to protect my rights. Why? Maybe because I voted for the Popular Front. But what are you doing? You're ruining everything. You're not giving Villard a chance to carry out reforms."

"On the contrary," said Pierre, "we're helping him. Now he can rely on the movement of the masses. There's no doubt that he approves of us. He . . ."

Desser recalled the old man in eye-glasses, surrounded by his pictures and sumptuous furniture. He smiled and said placidly: "Are you convinced of that? If so, then so much the better for you. I wish you success. Oh, I forgot to ask you how your wife is getting on. . . . That's fine. Now I can leave your factory, can't I? *Au revoir.*"

Pierre informed the foremen's committee of all that had passed between him and Desser. To Michaud he said: "I would never have thought he'd turn out to be like that." Words failed him.

Michaud smiled.

"You mean you never thought Desser would turn out to be Desser," he said.

In the evening they decided to get up a concert to entertain the strikers. Michaud rang up the Maison de Culture to ask if they could help. Maréchal tried to round up his actors. Some of them said they were busy, but Jeannette agreed at once, although she had not yet fully recovered from her operation.

They set up the stage in the little garden in front of the management offices. There was a smell of jasmine in the air. Chinese lanterns were placed over the light-bulbs. The orchestra started tuning up their instruments. The factory yard took on the aspect of a square in a provincial town on the local fête-day.

The program was made up of various items. Maréchal recited Rimbaud's elegy on a dead soldier. The magic of the words entranced the audience. There was dead silence everywhere. Then a woman singer sang one of Ravel's romances. She gave encore after encore, smiling against the background of red flags and sheets of corrugated iron. A factory stoker sang one of Maurice Chevalier's songs: *Paris Is Still Paris.* Everyone joined in the chorus and laughed: no, Paris was no longer the same! Then Jeannette's turn came.

Never before had she felt so uplifted. After the long months of dumbness, during which she had repeated the soulless words of the advertisements in front of the microphone, it seemed to her as though she had been given back the gift of speech. Her enormous eyes glowed among the little lanterns and her voice was moving to the point of tears. She declaimed a speech from *The Sheep-Spring.* When she came to the end she was greeted with a storm of applause. Shouts resounded above the clapping: they were the shouts of the people of Fuente Ovejuna, who were being led to victory not by her, the poor actress Jeannette, but by the heroine of Andalusia. Jeannot ran up to the foot of the stage and shouted: "Let's go!"

He didn't know what had made him call out, or why; he was only answering Jeannette's eyes. She smiled quietly, tired and happy. Pierre went up to her and took her by the hand.

"You recited beautifully," he said. "What a good thing you came! You see how they understand you. This isn't a theatre audience. These people are alive. It's a pity Lucien didn't come. Is he busy?"

"I don't know. I don't see him now. We've separated."

For a moment Jeannette felt sad. She remembered her loneliness, the little untidy room in the hotel into which she had recently moved, the quiet of the radio studio and the banal words of the advertisements. Suddenly a chorus rang out. The workers were singing *It's the Young Guard.* Thousands of arms were raised like the straining branches of a forest or the masts in a harbour. Carried away by the sound and by her own tears, Jeannette too raised her little fist. Then she gave a sigh and, without looking at anybody, went to the gates.

All night the lights in the factory buildings showed as Michaud went the rounds of the sentries.

CHAPTER 17

ON the night when Jeannette made her appearance at the Seine works, Lucien lost fourteen thousand francs at baccarat. He had such a run of bad luck that people began looking round at him. The Artistic Club was a low gambling-house. Sharpers, money-lenders, and prostitutes mixed with the players, who were jaded by the excitement and the heat. After changing his last thousand-franc note, Lucien suddenly felt suffocated. He went over to the open window.

Someone whispered to him: " Admiring the stars? "

Lucien didn't answer. Below him stretched the hot street, with a urinal, the turret of which bore the illuminated sign: "The best cheese — The Cow That Laughs." Lucien caught a sickly whiff of ether, reminding him of an operating-room. He looked round and saw the drivelling face of Berger. He knew at once he was going to talk about the promissory note.

" I shall have to see your father," Berger said angrily.

Then Lucien realized he would have to go right away — leave the country. Lately he had been feeling all the misery of the disappointed man. Ambition consumed him like a hidden disease. He had become acutely conscious of death. Sounds were deadened and the contours of objects were blurred; the smell of ether was always in his nostrils. At night he would suddenly run after an unknown woman in the street, thinking that it was Jeannette. He saw her eyes in the dark and stupidly repeated over and over again: " It's not my fault," as though the ghost of Jeannette were reproaching him with something. He was convinced that Jeannette was living with André, and he hated the dull-witted painter. His decision to go away came to him in a flash and seemed like salvation. At one stroke he would rid himself of a dead love, the tiresome people of the Maison de Culture, and his creditors.

However, to go abroad he would need money — a lot of money. He decided to try his luck. This time he was not banking on cards, but on the condescension of his father. He carefully thought over the best way to touch his father's heart, but when it came to the point, he forgot everything and gave free vent to his feelings.

"You know you crouch over your money like a dog with a bone," he said.

Tessa looked at him with his little birdlike eyes and said nothing.

"I want to go away," Lucien said. "There's nothing for me to do here. Maybe I'll get fixed up in America. But I need money for that, fifty thousand francs at least."

Tessa yawned. "Let's go to Maxim's," he said suddenly.

They found themselves in a regular flower-garden of women: pretty faces, cool bodies, elegant evening dresses, expensive perfumes. Tessa took a fancy to a dusky girl who looked like a creole, with huge whites to her eyes.

"A knock-out, eh?" he whispered.

Lucien nodded his head, and this brought them closer together at once; they felt like comrades. The champagne helped to increase the intimacy. Then, remembering his son's request, Tessa said: "What do you want to go away for? Now's the very time for you. I believe we're on the verge of revolution."

"No, it'll all end in yet another ministerial crisis. For revolution you need people, but there aren't any. I know now what the French public is like. When I went to the Communists, I was counting on something different."

"So that's it, eh! But I thought you were a Communist. Bravo, Lucien!"

"What have you got to be glad about? I hate your world even more than the Communists do, and I don't want to compromise."

Tessa had been suffering all day from heartburn. He drank a glass of soda water and said in a gentle voice: "You're thirty-two, but you talk like a child. I was an anarchist when I was eighteen. Anyhow, that was more forgivable."

"So you condemn me for . . ."

"I'm not condemning you. When I told you about my election you said: 'How sordid!' Yet you consider I ought to support the family — your mother, Denise, and yourself? I'd like to know who pays for your intransigence?"

Lucien burst out laughing. "You do," he said.

"You don't like our form of government? Nobody does. But what do you propose to put in its place? Any other will be far worse. Believe me, an old well-worn bed is better than a prison plank, however new. You say 'your world,' but you're bathing in it. You have the talent of a pamphleteer, but you attack our society from within. The Communists may applaud you, but you've no common language with them. You admitted that yourself. Well, there's only one conclusion. It's time for you to take up something."

"I've taken up rather a disagreeable position."

"That's all to the good. We like a man to begin with eccentricity. During the war Laval was a Red. He wouldn't speak to me. You want to go abroad? Not a bad idea. But I haven't any money. All that Desser put up went on the elections. I don't know when anything will turn up now. I'm talking frankly to you. But I can suggest something else. Writers love small diplomatic posts. Look at Claudel, Giraudoux, Morand. . . . I can fix that up in two seconds."

"To represent Blum and Villard?"

"Why not? . . . You won't betray your ideas. You'll be able to write anything you like. And you'll free yourself from financial worries right away."

Lucien made a wry face as though he had swallowed something bitter. It was repulsive to him — like everything else in life. Was he to blame? He wanted to be with the revolution, but they didn't understand him. Neither did Jeannette. When Lagrange was dying, he had said: "Lucien, I'm cold." How cold it was in the world, how very cold! It was impossible to live without cynicism. Anyway, it was better to become a diplomat than to have to debase himself begging his father for money. When he had a position in society, they would all treat him with respect, even the blockhead on the staff of L'Humanité. And happiness? Well, happiness didn't exist. Jeannette was with André. . . .

"All right," said Lucien sulkily. "I agree."

"I thought you would. After all, you're my son. At present I feel all this very keenly."

Tessa wiped his damp face with a table napkin and whispered to Lucien: "What about asking that creole over to our table?"

All next day Lucien stayed in his room, swallowing headache pills and gazing gloomily at the wallpaper. He did not want to live.

At dinner Tessa said to his wife:

"Maman, I congratulate you. Your son has been appointed vice-consul at Salamanca. You'll be able to observe revolution at first hand, eh, Lucien? You can do that far more pleasantly in a foreign country and with a diplomatic passport. . . . The women of Spain — " He glanced sideways at Denise and shut up.

"You've been quick," said Lucien wearily.

"I rang up Villard. He wants to get on the right side of me now. It's all such a farce."

Next day Lucien ran into André near the Opéra. He wanted to pass him without saying anything, but André stopped him. "What a state of affairs!" he said. "Literally everyone is on strike. Tell me, what's going to be the end of it all? You probably know."

"I'm going off to Spain in three days."

"Really? Well, they've got a little trouble there too, according to the papers."

Lucien did not tell him about his consular post. Why should he confide in this lout? He held out his hand in silence.

"Is Jeannette going with you?" André asked in an embarrassed voice.

Lucien could hardly conceal his amazement. So Jeannette wasn't living with him? For a moment he felt glad: That's good! Let her be nobody's! But immediately a cloud of melancholy descended over everything. He remembered that evening at Jeannette's, the rag doll, the empty eyes, the loneliness. He had let happiness fly like a bird from the hand, like a card he had failed to back. And looking distractedly at André, he muttered between his teeth: "Excuse me, I'm afraid I'll have to be getting along. I've got a headache. Jeannette, you said? I don't know. Really, I don't know."

CHAPTER 18

BRETEUIL stood at the bedside of his five-year-old son. The child was hoarse and his face was flushed with heat. Breteuil's wife was whimpering.

"Stop it," said Breteuil. "He'll get better, with God's help."

"I said he wasn't to take a cold shower. He was running about just before. He was in a sweat."

"Stop it, I tell you. The boy must be toughened."

It was getting dark, and Mme Breteuil could not see her husband's eyes. He stood there, tall and lean, with the tears trickling down his hollow cheeks.

Breteuil was a native of Lorraine, the son of a poor and pious family. The frontier was only twelve miles away from his native town. From his earliest years he had heard stories of the siege of Belfort, the ruthless brutality of some German officer, and of the lost provinces. He had crammed up on the dream of revenge like a catechism. He was twice wounded in the war. He was in the advance column that entered Metz, where an aunt of his fainted when she saw the first French flag. Temperamentally Breteuil was unlike a Frenchman: he couldn't bear a joke, disliked pathos, and never drank wine. Tidy almost to the verge of mania, dry and pedantic, in the salons of Paris he was taken for a German. Politics taught him a certain elasticity: he was obliged to hobnob with people of Tessa's cut. In his heart he despised his parliamentary colleagues. His friends were army men, small landowners, and learned theologians. After the war he had believed in the " renaissance of France," which his countryman Poincaré had talked about. But the years went by and nothing was changed. The country was ruled by Freemasons — Briand, Herriot, Painlevé. Now even those days seemed to him a lost paradise. Where would Blum, Cot, and Villard lead France? Two years ago Breteuil had decided that the only way out was by a violent change. The " March on Rome " had saved Italy. Hitler had stamped out Marxism with iron. Breteuil set to work to organize secret detachments. Each detachment was composed of fifty men, who were called " the Faithful." The leader was known as " the Ironclad."

The people who joined Breteuil were a mixed bunch: romantics and blockheads, ambitious adventurers and exasperated seekers of revenge. The rich saw him as their defender. Shopkeepers and artisans believed that he would save them from ruin. Small brokers, clerks, and reporters dreamed of getting on in the world with his help.

And who was there not among the " Faithful"? The maître d'hôtel of the Versailles restaurant joined Breteuil because he worshipped rank. Life seemed to him like a pyramid of customers and lackeys, goblets and wines. Florio was a specialist in venereal disease who hated Jews because he thought they enticed his patients away and deprived him of his livelihood. He had joined because Breteuil promised to clear the Rothschilds and all doctors of Jewish origin out of France. The son of the big miller Bombard wanted to restore France to her former prestige and become an ambassador into the bargain. Dinet, an ex-agent of the Intelligence Department, who had been dismissed from the intelligence service for embezzling the funds entrusted to him, considered himself a victim of the Freemasons; he yearned to break up Parliament and hang Herriot. Grimaud, the proprietor of a stud farm, went about with a horsewhip, was crazy about coloured girls, and despised mechanical progress; he considered that to belong to a detachment of the "Faithful" was a sign of good form. Godet, the owner of a china-shop, was afraid the Communists would get hold of his business and take away his savings. He was a big man with red cheeks and broad shoulders. He did exercises every morning and was prepared to do battle in earnest. Aubry, a subway employee, was exceedingly ugly and poor as a church mouse. He was said to have been jilted by a girl. He hated the people and smiled at the sight of Breteuil, saying: "Now there's a man who'll restore order! . . ."

There were a good many policemen among the "Faithful," and the "secret detachments" were no secret to the Chief of Police; but the authorities turned a blind eye. In order to camouflage his movements, Breteuil formed sports clubs and friendly societies for people from the provinces. The business required financial backing. Breteuil applied more than once to the big capitalists, but was rebuked. He talked about arms instead of propaganda, and frightened everybody with his boldness. The events of the last few weeks had lent wings to his ambition. The directors of various trusts, who had previously thought only of ministerial combinations but were now frightened by the strikes, began to look hopefully towards Breteuil's intransigence.

Breteuil made the sign of the cross over his child and set out for the Metz Countrymen's Union, where he was to meet General Picard. The shop windows on the Grands Boulevards were lighted up, showing the strikers' placards decorated with red ribbons. Girls stood on the pavement with collection boxes: "For the children of the strikers." Some of the passers-by frowned and hurried on. Others tossed a coin into the box. When a girl held out a collection box to Breteuil, he stopped and asked sternly:

"Do they teach you to work at the camp?"

General Picard was already waiting for him — a lean-looking man of sixty-five, with the bow legs of the cavalry officer, a row of medal ribbons, and a contemptuous smile. He despised everybody: Daladier and Gamelin, the King of England, his own wife, the

theatre, the press, and the elections. The only one he trusted was
Breteuil, who he thought could save France and the Army.

"Well," said Breteuil, "how goes it?"

"They're fools. And cowards. They're afraid Blum will begin to
clear out the Staff."

"What's the feeling among the troops?"

"Bad. The Communists are working their hardest. The most we
can count on is the Army's neutrality. I'm not talking, of course,
about the colonial units. By the bye, I've managed to transfer two
Moroccan regiments to Vincennes."

"The Moors alone won't be enough. I'm relying only on the
'Faithful.' There are two possibilities: either you provide us with
arms, or we'll take what they offer us."

"Who?"

Breteuil glared at him.

"It's not 'who' that matters," he snapped, "but what. Sixty
thousand rifles, four hundred machine-guns, and ammunition.
From Düsseldorf. At the same time we're not taking on any obligations, apart from those that spring from our program: order and
peace."

Picard thought this over for a while.

"Not bad," he said. "Personally I prefer automatics for an operation of that sort. Anyhow, take them. The one won't hinder the
other. I'll also scrape up some in the arsenals. . . ."

"We must begin with local actions in order to discredit the Government. Villard wants to give a nuance of legality to the seizure
of the factories. We must mix a little blood with his speeches. . . ."

They went on talking for a long time. In the next room, dimly
lighted, the "Ironclad" Grisnez, who was waiting for Breteuil,
yawned and sharpened his nails with a file. Grisnez, who had once
started a row at the Maison de Culture, had a blind faith in
Breteuil. He was an orphan who had been brought up in a children's
home. He had toured the provinces as a travelling salesman in
orthopædic instruments. He was a miserable fop, who took hours
to make up his mind which tie to wear with his threadbare but
carefully pressed suit, an ugly fellow who dreamed of the love of
a beauty, a hysterical bawler and an acrimonious failure. He became the "Ironclad" of the first detachment of the "Faithful,"
and Breteuil picked him out for military espionage.

"The day after tomorrow," said Breteuil, "the 'Faithful' will go to the Seine factory in the guise of unemployed. You must get close to the gates without attracting attention. You're to pick a quarrel with the pickets. Try to provoke them. If they don't begin it, shoot. I'll try to arrange for the police to be near by. It's necessary to bring about a real clash, you understand. All the 'Faithful' will be given tickets of the Christian Workers' Union. They mustn't know about the nature of the operation. I've chosen you because you haven't any children."

" Everything will be carried out, Leader."

Grisnez raised his arm and was about to go away, but Breteuil warmly embraced him. " Thank you," he said.

Breteuil got home at two o'clock in the morning. His wife met him in the hall. " It's pneumonia," she said.

Breteuil sat by the sick boy's bedside till morning. All next day he worked. He tried to see Desser; the best way would be if the management of the Seine factory announced that a new staff of workers was to be taken on. But Desser refused to see him; he was afraid of some underhand scheme. On the other hand, Breteuil succeeded in persuading the Chief of Police. They decided that the gendarmes were to stand on the quay near the factory. If any disorders broke out, they would intervene. In the evening Breteuil had another talk with Grisnez and went over the details of the operation. Then he sat up again with his child all through the night. The doctor had told him there was no hope of recovery, but Breteuil believed in God. His lips moved as he repeated the words of a prayer.

It was a beautiful summer morning. The birds were singing in the gardens. The noise of the city had not yet drowned their voices. From time to time the market gardeners' trucks rattled past. Baker women went by carrying long loaves, and the smell of freshly baked bread hung in the air. The upper windows of the houses shone with a warm, rosy light, as though from within. One after another the " Faithful " approached the Javelle Bridge. Grisnez called the roll: four had failed to turn up. Forty-six men, divided into small groups, moved towards the factory by various routes.

That morning, the eleventh morning of the strike, began peacefully in the factory. New sentries relieved the old. Michaud had slept during the night and was now washing himself and snorting in a soapy froth. Near the main gates Jeannot was singing the songs he had heard at the concert. Pierre was up and was munching a roll. For some reason he remembered Verlaine's lines: "The pale star of the dawn." But the sun was already shining brightly. Some of the older workers were thinking gloomily: "Eleven days already! When's it going to end?" There was a rumour that the Government were going to clear the factory by force, but Michaud only laughed: "Nonsense!"

"Come on, Jeannot, show us how Mistinguette walks downstairs."

Jeannot made a comical face in imitation of an old woman trying to look young and, holding out his trousers like a skirt with the tips of his fingers, started to pirouette down the fire-escape. Suddenly he called out:

"Who's there?"

There was a crowd of people in front of the gates.

"Open the gates! . . ."

"We're being taken on. Clear out of here, you loafers!"

"Red swindlers!"

Jeannot was not behindhand: "You dirty swine! Scabs! Fascists! We'll tar and feather you!"

Now hundreds of people were shouting. It was difficult to make out what they were saying. Grisnez was particularly hotheaded. He kept running up to the workers and shouted something very rapidly. His face was twitching convulsively; he looked like an epileptic. Michaud tried in vain to get his comrades to listen to reason, but the insolence of the Fascists stung everybody to madness.

Throughout the last few days Michaud had been expecting an attack. He had placed firemen with hoses near the gates. The main thing was to prevent a clash. He laughed when he saw Grisnez: "Fifty ugly devils! Our chaps will shout them down!" The other workers also took it calmly. In vain the "Faithful" stormed and scolded. The strikers answered them with mild and even good-natured abuse. Jeannot began teasing Grisnez:

"Look over there, comrades. There's a mad turkey full of macaroni. . . ."

A shot rang out. Jeannot fell to the ground. Michaud knocked the revolver out of Pierre's hand and shouted above the roar of the crowd:

"Don't dare to shoot! Turn on the hoses!"

The firemen squirted the water at the "Faithful." They scattered.

Only Grisnez still remained, hopping about as though he felt nothing. Then the police appeared and Grisnez vanished.

Michaud bent over Jeannot and saw that he was smiling. But there was blood on the stones.

"Jeannot!" he said.

The death of this cheerful young man seemed so unintelligible that Michaud suddenly cried out: "They've killed him!"

He looked round at the others, as though wondering if they would say "No." The workers were standing with their caps in their hands, and through the mist that dimmed his eyes Michaud caught sight of the pain-racked face of Pierre.

Having lowered himself into the river, Grisnez hid under a bridge. He was trembling with cold and indignation. A tramp said to him:

"What you up to? Having a bath?"

Grisnez spat at him. He sat in the sun a long while; it wouldn't do to go about looking soaked through. Then he went to a hairdresser's. They shaved him, squirted eau-de-Cologne over him, and rubbed his hair with oil, but still he asked for more. He was doctoring himself with semi-oblivion, and the noise of the scissors sounded to him like the chirping of cicadas in a sweet-smelling garden. It was eleven o'clock in the morning when he reported to Breteuil. He was taken into the study. Breteuil was kneeling before a crucifix. His son was dead. On seeing Grisnez, he got up.

"Are there any killed?"

"I brought down one."

"But among the 'Faithful'?"

"None. They used hoses."

"Not one? What the devil have you been up to? Everything's ruined now!"

Grisnez did not understand. He gaped foolishly at Breteuil in a dull-witted way and said: "As an 'Ironclad,' I'm responsible for the lives of the 'Faithful.'"

"You're not an 'Ironclad.' You're a fool."

Breteuil went down on his knees again. Grisnez quietly left the room. The maid was weeping in the hall. He said to her:

"Your master is a great man. But I expect it will soon be the end of me."

CHAPTER 19

ALL the Paris papers were full of Jeannot's murder. Those of the Left accused Breteuil and demanded strong measures against the Fascist secret organizations. The newspapers of the Right made out that Jeannot had been killed by the Communists because he wanted the strike to end. *Le Matin* published a maudlin article on "this unfortunate lad who adored his old mother and whom the Communists had condemned to death." Only *La Voie Nouvelle* attempted to gloss over the whole affair. Joliot wrote: "Whoever the murderer may be, we deprecate violence and appeal to all Frenchmen to maintain the peace." This was high-sounding and imposed no obligation on anyone.

Two days later Jeannot's murder was the subject of a debate in the Chamber. It was Breteuil himself who raised the question. Everyone expected a row, and the public galleries were crowded. Even before the session began, the noise in the Chamber was indescribable; deputies shouted furious abuse at one another. The Speaker, Herriot, rapped on the table with a ruler like a distracted schoolmaster. Then he shook his little bell violently and bellowed: "Silence!"

For a moment quiet was restored, but when Breteuil mounted the rostrum, there was a roar from the Left of "Assassin!"

The deputies banged on their desks and shouted. The sergeant-at-arms stood ready, expecting a fight to start at any moment. Herriot kept on trying his utmost to restore order.

At last the hubbub died down, and Breteuil began: "Who's calling me an assassin? The assassins of this innocent worker are the Communists, who have shed blood. . . ."

A roar of shouting drowned his voice. He went on speaking, but only a word could be caught here and there: "poor mother" . . . "reign of anarchy" . . . "Blum's helplessness" . . . "Villard's connivance." . . .

On the Government bench Villard was distractedly drawing little ships. Breteuil's speech did not frighten him: it was a clumsy attack on the Parliamentary majority. He was thinking of something else: how could the strike be liquidated? Some of the Radicals were already beginning to grumble. The workers were standing fast, but the owners would not even hear of concessions. Desser had thought of something. . . .

Applause and booing broke out. Gathering up his papers, Breteuil left the rostrum.

The Socialists had already arranged for a Radical to speak in defence of the Government; this would be more diplomatic. When the Speaker called on Tessa, there was a burst of friendly applause from the Left. The Right were silent. Tessa began his speech in a low, tense voice. He deplored the loss of a young life, condemned those who were aiming to plunge the country into civil war, praised the defenders of Verdun, and quoted Victor Hugo. The deputies glared at one another in perplexity. Suddenly Tessa turned to Villard and said:

" To my regret I am obliged to admit that in tolerating the seizure of the factories the Government are giving their approval to violence. I say this as a supporter of social justice, as a deputy of the Popular Front. . . ."

This was so unexpected that for a moment nobody spoke. Then Breteuil got up and shouted: " Bravo! " with all the power of his lungs. A storm of cheering and clapping shook the Chamber: the Right and a section of the Radicals applauded furiously. In vain Herriot tried to restrain the deputies; resentment at defeat, hatred of the Popular Front, the alarm of the last few weeks — all this was expressed in the applause. Villard's face lengthened: a good half of the Radicals were applauding! What would become of the Popular Front? Tessa went on to speak of his confidence in the Government, but everybody realized this was merely gilding the pill.

Tessa was followed by a Communist deputy from one of the northern constituencies, a foundry-worker with purple veins standing out on his face.

" We demand that the Government put a stop to the activities of the Fascist assassins," he said. " There must be an investigation of the activities of the deputy Breteuil. . . ."

The Right began to clamour. Breteuil had left the hall, but his friends went on shouting: " Good! He's right! " The Socialists sat motionless, as though they were not concerned with what was going on. They thought the Communist's language was too harsh. At last Herriot donned the tall hat that signified adjournment. Like a lot of schoolboys let out of class, the deputies rushed joyfully into the lobbies and the bar.

The Radical deputies met for a private conference. Some of them approved of Tessa's speech. Others talked of the "country's disappointed hopes" — the first rift in the Popular Front, and the intrigues of the Right. Modestly Tessa explained: "I wanted to save the Popular Front and our party." After a long dispute the Radicals decided to fall into line with the Socialists, pointing out the desirability of clearing the factories. The Socialists delayed their reply: Villard wanted to negotiate with Desser. There was disappointment among the public in the galleries when Herriot proposed to postpone the discussion of Breteuil's question till the evening session, and to deal with the bill on the prevention of foot-and-mouth disease. Breteuil shouted: "The Radicals have got cold feet, and Villard's waiting for instructions from Moscow."

A Socialist rushed at Breteuil swinging his fists. Breteuil gave him a slap on the face. A scuffle broke out. A sergeant-at-arms got trampled underfoot by the deputies, and Herriot went on ringing and ringing his little bell. Then the deputies went off to the bar: everybody was tortured with thirst. Only some thirty deputies were present at the session, and even they paid little attention to the monotonous voice of the speaker and sat reading newspapers or writing letters to their electors.

It was with a heavy heart that Villard went off to see Desser. He had hesitated a long time, debating with himself whether the visit would lower his dignity. To think that he, a Minister of the Popular Front, was truckling to a mysterious financier who not so very long ago had been supporting Breteuil's gangsters! But what was to be done? The strikes were spreading like ripples in a pond. All France seemed to be on strike. The movement had spread from Paris to the provinces. Buses were stopping. Ships were remaining in port. Every day brought new surprises. Actors were taking over the theatres; cashiers were closing the wickets of the cash-desks and grave-diggers were refusing to dig graves. But the owners stood firm. Some of them were saying: "All the better! Let everything go to the devil!" The life of the country was paralysed. At any rate, thought Villard, Desser was the best type of representative of capitalism. It was essential to try to reach some sort of agreement with him and understand his game.

Desser began by inquiring sympathetically after his health. Villard answered that he felt very tired.

"That's understandable," said Desser. "Carrying out a strike like this. . . ."

"We're suffering from it just the same as you are," said Villard. "That's what I've come to talk to you about. Tell me, what do you suggest?"

"My friend, you're a Minister, and I'm only a private individual. I await your decisions."

Villard wanted to get up and go away, but again the consciousness of his responsibility overcame his resentment. He said mildly:

"I don't understand your irony."

"It's not irony, it's self-defence. Judge for yourself. If I start asking for stern measures against the strikers, you'll say that we 'Two Hundred Families' have prevented you from establishing paradise on earth. I prefer to wait. Maybe you really are magicians. And maybe you aren't. Then the workers will see for themselves that you haven't changed anything and that in fact you couldn't. So I'm not insisting upon anything."

"But today Tessa demanded that the factories should be cleared."

"I know. Our friend Tessa is what I call young in mind. But I prefer to wait. I'm not against police measures, but everything in its own time. How do you like my Marquet? Of course, it isn't as good as yours, but this green tone . . ."

Desser switched the conversation to the subject of painting. Villard was not in the mood for pictures and refused to play up.

What was he to do? Desser's game seemed to be a complicated one. Apparently his intention was to split the Government majority. Today half the Radicals had supported Tessa. Therefore the factories would have to be cleared? But in that case the workers would go with the Communists. That meant revolution. It was a disgusting game and it meant losing either way. Villard thought it over a long time. A voice that seemed to come from his feeling of fatigue suggested: "Why not wait?" The waiting game was something he had known from childhood, cosy and close to his heart. Had he not waited all his life? He had waited for victory in the elections, for the triumph of progress, and for universal appeasement. And in his personal life he had waited for happiness, recognition, and quiet. Desser was right to wait. Of course it was necessary to wait! They would all come to their senses. The main thing was not to make any drastic move.

Before the evening session Villard received a report from the secret police. The agents stated that a split was beginning to show itself among the strikers. Many were advocating ending the strike. At the Seine works the number of those in favour of an agreement was growing. Villard smiled with satisfaction. Then he thought to himself: " The total collapse of the strike must be prevented, otherwise the Right Radicals will take advantage of it. Moreover, Desser is in a conciliatory mood. It should be possible to find a compromise. Time is working for us. . . ."

The Radicals failed to obtain anything. At the session the Government in the person of Villard gave a vague reply: it was necessary on the one hand to defend the interests of the workers, and on the other hand to uphold law and order. The Right protested, the Socialists applauded, and the Radicals kept quiet. From his seat in the Chamber Tessa shouted: " If you don't clear the factories, you'll be swept away by a flood of public indignation."

Again there was a burst of clapping and cheering. Villard smiled mournfully; he was tired, oh, so tired.

But Tessa was the hero of the day. They shook him by the hand and compared him to Mirabeau, Lafayette, and Gambetta. He was still flushed with the success of his speech in the Chamber. He felt himself to be a fearless champion, a fighter for the truth. He said: " I'm swimming against the tide."

When he got home he felt weak but happy. His wife was lying down as usual with a hot-water bottle. Lucien was out — enjoying himself before his departure. But Tessa wanted to tell somebody about his triumph, so he went to Denise.

He repeated his speech to her with all the gestures, and put on a different voice for asides such as " Here they applauded like mad."

He was so carried away that he did not look at Denise. She was sitting in a kind of coma. For the last few days she had been thinking about her father. Back in the winter she had known very little about politics; she thought her father was engaged in a boring, but honourable profession. Now that she was going to meetings and reading the papers, her father's talk at the dinner-table had become unbearable. He was revealing himself to her more and more as a slovenly dabbler in politics, who was ready to strike any bargain that suited him.

The fever of the Paris streets took hold of Denise. She read in the papers that Michaud was leading the strikers in the Seine works.

She believed in him and looked on the strike as a battle for justice. When she heard of the young worker's assassination, she remembered Michaud's words that the only way to unite words and actions was with blood. She asked herself what she ought to do. She was reserved by nature and fought shy of gestures and loud words. She wanted to do something to strike out her past at one blow. She wished she could ask Michaud's advice, but Michaud was busy with something else. And now her father had come to her and was boasting about his behaviour and repeating that those damned "grabbers" were to blame for everything. Suddenly she interrupted him:

"That's quite enough!"

Tessa looked at his daughter in astonishment. What on earth was the matter with her? She stood there tall and slender. Her beauty had taken on a look of austerity; her angry eyes stared at him.

"What's the matter with you?" Tessa said.

"I can't listen to that sort of thing! I don't want to offend you, but what you're saying seems to me to be unworthy. Perhaps I feel as they do. . . . Probably one has got to live differently. I don't know. . . . But what agony this is! . . ." She ran out of the room.

Tessa felt annoyed and went up to his wife's room. "Your daughter takes after you," he said. "She's got some sort of religious fanaticism. Heaven. Hell. The deuce knows what!"

"Paul, why must you make fun of me?"

"I'm not making fun of you. You're all off your heads. But I'm a free-thinking man and I prefer purgatory."

He went off to Paulette's, where he sat gloomily drinking brandy. In vain Paulette tried to distract him. When she said: "Kiss me, little chicken!" he didn't budge and only muttered wearily: "Everything's going to the devil, absolutely everything."

CHAPTER 20

JEANNOT's mother, Clémence Duval, was a rather querulous but good-hearted woman with rheumatic hands, grey hair turning yellowish, and the still sparkling eyes of a former beauty. She went out to work, did young bachelors' rooms, washed floors, ironed and darned, and managed to scrape up a living. At one time things had been more difficult — her husband was killed just before the Armistice and she was left with two small children on her hands. Many bitter complaints were heard in the poky little room on the sixth storey with its stone floor, smoky stove, and enormous bedsteads which Clémence had inherited from her grandmother. At times there was not enough money for a bucket of coal and the children froze; or else Jeannot's trousers were worn out or an exercise-book had to be bought for Annette. But she managed to set the children on their feet. Annette married an assembler in an engineering works and went away to Lyon. Jeannot managed to get taken on at the Seine works. What a piece of luck that was! That day Clémence even bought a bottle of wine with a label on it. This was not surprising. So many lads of Jeannot's age were wandering about the long streets of the Paris suburbs and going from factory to factory in the hope of being taken on. But the same notice was on all the gates: "No help wanted." Even apprentices were not being taken. Her women neighbours were complaining that their grown-up sons were "a burden to us all," and Clémence could scarcely believe her eyes when Jeannot brought home his first pay-envelope.

She was proud of her lively young son, but was always afraid something might happen to him; he was given to playing tricks on people and was always the first to pick a quarrel. How many times had she told him he might easily come to grief! She still regarded him as a boy, whom she could justly clout for any silly prank. When he started to go to labour meetings, she grew alarmed. Her heart warned her there was danger. She told him to give it up and tried to frighten him, but he passed it off with a joke. On May Day that year she had seen him march past carrying a red flag. Clémence was not a church-goer. She held that if God existed, there was no way of getting at Him. Nevertheless, when she saw Jeannot with that flag she crossed herself. She was afraid he was on the road to ruin.

Then the strike broke out. And what a strike! In the past the workers had gone on strike quietly. They sat at home and waited. Now they had invented the sit-down strike. They might be arrested for that. Clémence tried to put Jeannot to shame and urged him to return home, but he refused to listen. Each evening she took him eggs, cheese, and sausage. She did not complain of being short of money. She wasn't afraid on her own account.

Then came the terrible news. From that moment she seemed to be struck dumb. Neither her neighbours nor her relations nor Jeannot's comrades heard her speak a single word. At the funeral she walked at the head of the mourners, weeping silently. Behind her walked Jeannot's aunt with her children, some of the neighbours, and a delegation of workers from the Seine factory with Michaud at their head.

It had been decided that the workers would not leave the factory till victory was achieved, and for this reason the funeral was on a small scale. They buried Jeannot in the suburban cemetery among the most crowded graves with their iron crosses and bead-woven wreaths. It was a sultry summer morning. There was a smell of mignonette, and the birds were warbling. No speeches were made. Jeannot's comrades silently shook Clémence by the hand, one after the other; only the red ribbons on the wreath held by Michaud told of the terrible tragedy.

As the delegates were on their way back to the factory, a turner named Sylvain suddenly cried out angrily: "They make speeches and kill other people!"

The police had not deceived Villard. The situation at the Seine works was difficult. Two weeks of the strike had broken many of the men's will to hold out. Wives were now coming to the gates with complaints instead of provisions; their money was all spent and the shopkeepers refused to give credit. For a few hours Jeannot's murder had roused everybody; they wanted to get back at the murderers, and Michaud had difficulty in restraining his comrades. But by evening they were once again in the grip of pessimism; their families were starving, the strike had gone on so long, and it was all for nothing! People who were in touch with the management spread all kinds of rumours: the works would be closed until January for want of orders; the police had presented an ultimatum to evacuate the factory — otherwise they would use gas.

The discontented elements among the strikers grouped themselves around Sylvain, a man of violent impulses and no balance. At the beginning of the strike he proposed starting up the factory and replacing the management with an elected committee. When they laughed at him, he lost his temper. "Then it's all up with us," he shouted. "Desser can easily wait, but we can't." When his wife told him she hadn't even a franc left for milk, he flared up again: "It's time we wound up this idiotic strike!" He spoke hysterically, with tears in his voice. Each day the men listened to him more willingly. He proposed they should arrange a secret ballot: he was convinced that ten thousand of the eighteen thousand workers would vote for calling off the strike. Michaud objected that it was a question of honour and the voting should be held openly. He was far from being sure that the comrades would hold out. The day of defeat seemed close at hand.

Desser, of course, was well informed of everything that was going on at the factory, and he decided to try and break the strike. He again sent for Pierre.

" How do you do, my dear enthusiast! Incarceration has done you good. You're looking fine. I want to transmit my views to the strike committee. I've been told you're a member of it. I accept the points regarding wages and working hours. I categorically reject collective bargaining and paid vacations. That belongs to the realm of miracles. Do you still believe in Villard? Maybe he'll work a miracle. As far as I'm concerned, if the strike isn't called off, I'll shut down the factory."

" I don't think your proposition will be accepted."

Usually impulsive and enthusiastic, Pierre was now curt. Desser at once sensed his hostility.

" Why get angry? " he said. " I'm a capitalist. That tells you everything. The workers are right in their way. But you, you're neither fish, fowl, nor good red herring, yet you want to be a beefsteak, and a bloody one at that! Dreams! What's collective bargaining to you? You're breaking your neck, but people remain people just the same."

" I believe in them," Pierre said.

" No, you don't. Maybe you like them. But you don't believe in them. You're leading the people to the most bloodthirsty despotism. How sad it all is! "

Pierre went away. Desser looked out of the window at the clear blue sky, the red flag, the lounging lad on guard outside the management offices, and Desser envied Pierre: he was stupid, but happy. He believed in something. Did it matter in what? Desser experienced a wave of loneliness. How terrible it was to wake up in the morning and to start the busy day that was empty as a wilderness!

Pierre told Michaud of Desser's proposition. Immediately Michaud said: " Not a word till morning. Tomorrow we'll get all the men together and take the vote."

Pierre himself thought it was necessary to act cautiously and explain to everyone what it was all about. Above all, Sylvain must not be allowed to know about Desser's offer. They discussed the matter for a long time. Suddenly Michaud embraced Pierre, and Pierre realized how much this gesture meant. He was so worked up himself that he was unable to utter a word.

Michaud had formerly regarded Pierre with some distrust. In moments of anger he even called him a milk-sop because of his softness; he couldn't forgive him for admiring the Socialists, especially Villard. Since the strike, however, Michaud had got to know and like Pierre. The fact that he, one of the best engineers of the Seine works, had thrown in his lot with the workers was evidence of his courage and disinterestedness. Pierre had the gift of attracting people in everyday life. He was fantastically romantic, always thinking out some impossible plan, but whenever Michaud told him it wouldn't work he never argued or took offence, but promptly started to think out something else. He was a gay southerner and could always make people laugh even when things were at their worst: he would tell Marseille stories, hop about and play the fool. Although Pierre was two years older than himself, Michaud thought of him kindly as " a child."

Sometimes they had vigorous arguments. As the result either of his education or of his kindly, carefree disposition, Pierre steadfastly maintained the ideas of the last century. He would have cultivated people like flowers — with a watering-can in his hand. He believed it was possible to win people over by persuasion, and Villard's professorial tones sounded to him like wisdom. When Michaud chaffed him, Pierre would smile sadly, like a child being deprived of his favourite toy.

Now Michaud said to him: " You must explain your conversation with Desser at the meeting. You can do that quite well. I felt at once that all was not well with Desser."

" All right," Pierre said. " But do you know what's the funniest thing of all? Desser's in a bad way all round. His millions are millions all right, but his life isn't worth two sous to him. He went for a walk with me once and told me so. Apparently he's just drifting along."

" You talk like an intellectual," Michaud said. " But I know that if they do beat us you won't fail. You'll go to the same wall. And I'll answer for you if we win. But you've got one pound of faith to ten pounds of pity. There's a girl I know, a student. Sometimes it seems to me that weakness is greater than strength to her. I'm damned if I know! . . . But she herself is strong. I'll say she is. And how! "

He smiled dreamily and bashfully. Pierre beamed with pleasure; so Michaud too could understand that! But Michaud was already on his way round the factory, talking and persuading.

Sylvain got to know about Desser's offer: the management's spies made sure of that. And Sylvain himself lost no time. The word " agreement " passed round the yard and the workshops, exciting the men who were weary of their long spell of idleness and separation from their families and alarmed at their plight. The agreement had only to be signed and this dog's life would end right away! Sylvain whispered to them: " They're keeping it secret. What for? Politics! But our people can die of hunger."

Towards evening the situation became threatening. Pierre tried to warn them of Desser's cunning, but Sylvain's followers spurned him: " Engineer! How much have you got in the savings bank? " It was said that Sylvain had organized a meeting for ten o'clock that evening and the voting would be in favour of agreement. Pierre was in low spirits and thought that all was lost. And not only Pierre; Michaud tried to keep calm and even joked, but it cost him a great effort. In his heart he felt that only a miracle could save them. He would have to make up his mind to do something; the fate of his comrades and maybe of the whole Paris strike now depended on him.

When it was getting dark, he said to Pierre: " Listen. I'm going out for an hour. Don't tell anyone. They'll say I've run away."

" Where are you going? To the committee? "

Michaud didn't answer.

Clémence was sitting at the dusty window, motionless as a dead shrub. Michaud came into the room and gently took hold of her flabby red hand. He wanted to speak, but couldn't. He had come to this woman for help, but her grief enveloped him like a warm mist. He forgot everything he had meant to say. He forgot about the strike, Sylvain, and the question of agreement. His only thought was for the mother of his comrade. He began to talk about Jeannot, about the way he had joked a few minutes before his death and about his cheerfulness and courage. He talked passionately in broken snatches. Never before had he spoken with so much anguish.

It grew dark. Clémence did not turn on the light. In the dark room Jeannot seemed to come to life again. It was here that he had grown up, played with his blocks on the floor, told his mother about his comrades, the demonstrations, and the clashes with the police. Clémence felt that his short but crowded life filled everything; and out there in the factory his life was going on. So strong was her perception of the ties and kinship between her dead Jeannot and this man, a stranger to her, that she thought with fear in her heart: "And they'll kill him too! They're all madmen!"

Suddenly Michaud stopped talking: he remembered the factory, Legrais, and Pierre. He stood up.

"We need your help," he said.

Then without a thought Clémence followed him out.

The workers had all collected in the factory yard as on the first day of the strike. Sylvain was taking advantage of Michaud's absence. He declared that the management had accepted the workers' demands, but the strike committee was concealing the fact. When Michaud came up to the crowd the vote was being taken. On all sides men were shouting that the majority were in favour of agreement. It was difficult to tell whether this was true or not, as hands kept being raised and lowered. Many had no idea what they were voting for. People were shouting and swearing at one another. All was excitement and confusion.

Michaud mounted a truck and called out: "Comrades, wait a minute!"

Sylvain cut him short: "That's enough! They've already voted!"

Michaud refused to give in: "All may have their say and vote. But there's one who is silent: Jeannot. Have you forgotten about him? Jeannot's here. With us. Jeannot's mother will speak for him."

A deep silence came over the crowd. Jeannot's loss was still fresh, and the mother's grief hovered over everybody. The old woman with her red, tear-stained eyes and locks of grey hair climbed up on the truck. In silence she raised her fist — that was what Jeannot did when he went with his comrades to the meeting. Clémence wanted to say something. Her lips moved, but she was unable to utter a word. But her fist shook above the crowd, and all their fists were raised in response. When Michaud said: "Those in favour of agreement, lower your hands," not a single hand went down. Even Sylvain voted for the strike; Clémence's eyes were fixed on him.

Then Clémence said: "Now I'm going to stay here. Instead of

Jeannot." She glanced tenderly at Michaud. "Don't you go to the gates. They'll kill you."

It was the fifteenth day of the strike. That night Pierre danced around Michaud rejoicing like a child and kept shouting: "We've won! We've won!"

Three days later Desser telephoned to Villard: "I've decided to accept their terms. We've got some very urgent orders on hand. And besides, the winner is he who knows how to retreat. But I've no need to tell you that. You, my friend, know how to retreat — like Napoleon."

Desser wanted to distract himself a little with this rather tactless joke. Capitulation filled him with resentment and wounded his self-esteem. Now Pierre was probably grinning. But how could one go on losing half a million a day? Politics were a game like the Stock Exchange. Today the workers were going to the seaside. Tomorrow they might be going to the concentration camp. The famous pendulum was beginning to play tricks. It was swinging too abruptly. So was Desser's heart: he was not feeling well; his doctor had forbidden alcohol, tobacco, and coffee. But he was not obeying his doctor: his heart needed a stimulant; if not love, then some substitute.

At seven o'clock in the evening of the nineteenth day of the strike the agreement was signed. The original demands of the workers were only slightly modified. Everybody realized that it was a victory.

The Seine works had opened the battle and had been followed by the others. Their victory meant a victory for all. In the course of the day, news of the capitulation of other owners began to pour in. Joliot wrote in a lyrical strain: "The armistice has been signed. Now, Frenchmen, back to work! The wounds must be healed!"

At eight o'clock in the evening the workers of the Seine factory lined up in columns and, after their three weeks' voluntary incarceration, left the building with bands playing and flags flying. At their head walked Clémence and Michaud. Thousands of people joyfully greeted the victors. Among them were the families of the strikers, the residents of the factory district, and the delegates of the various unions. The summer twilight was falling and the first stars were coming out in the still bright sky. Their blue sparkling seemed mysterious above the gold of the sunset. The festive crowd filled the streets and the terraces of the cafés. The people welcomed the workers, handing them flowers and treating them to beer.

Michaud was supporting Clémence. The events of the past few days had so exhausted her that she could hardly stand on her feet. She had got used to Michaud and kept her eye on him like a mother. Now they would soon have to part. He would go about his business, hurry off to the meetings like Jeannot, and shout till he got killed. And she would go back to her empty room with its stone floor and the big bedstead.

Suddenly Clémence said: " Why don't you get married? Anyway, it's better than being single. Otherwise you'll be all alone. You'll get killed and there'll be nobody to weep for you. That's not nice! "

Michaud smiled bashfully. The trees were etched black against the sky. A light blue haze hovered over the Seine. Everywhere Michaud seemed to catch the gleaming of a familiar face: it was Denise coming to meet him, smiling and stealthily squeezing his hand.

CHAPTER 21

HAVING persuaded himself that the studio was unbearably stuffy, André turned the easel to the wall and went out. Of late he had been unable to settle down to work. He had not been giving himself airs when he told his old school friends that he did not understand politics. That was three months ago. Since then there had been great changes. Politics had forced their way into his studio without asking. He now picked up the paper the first thing in the morning, and listened to the conversations in the streets. Everybody was talking about the strikes, the battle of the political parties, and war. The movement which had taken hold of the city roused a new set of feelings in André. He was too closely connected with the people and too integrated a character not to feel the strength of solidarity and the fever of their hopes. Yes, that's how it all was! But how could he get on with still life?

At some time or other André had read an article about the scientific treatment of the cultivation of wheat in the Soviet Union. As a man of peasant origin, he was fond of everything connected with the life of the soil, and the article interested him particularly. When he was roaming about the streets he began to think about what he had read, and decided that painting was in a bad way. There were trees that only began to blossom in the eighth or ninth decade of growth. The gardener planted the seed, knowing that it was his son, perhaps his grandson, who would see the fruit. But over there a few days in the life of a one-year-old plant had changed the face of a whole region. Obviously, it was all a question of the age. The painter needed quiet; he lived by immobility. He portrayed a mature world, with a wealth of established forms and fixed colours. In periods of decline or upheaval there was nothing for him to do. Lucien had said at the Maison de Culture that a revolutionary without good taste was unthinkable. Nonsense. There were times when "good taste" became a painful vice like that "blue blood" for which they cut off people's heads in 1793. The rehabilitation of history referred rather to epochs than to individuals One epoch produced Robespierre; another, Delacroix; yet Robespierre was not responsible for David's painting, any more than Delacroix was responsible for the parsimony of Louis-Philippe. Lucien wanted to introduce a correction, a rectification, into historical events as into a theatrical *mise en scène*. But he was not a stage-manager; he was a supernumerary. Anyway, that still life had got to be finished while there was still time, a studio and paints! André forced himself to work, but it was no use; an hour later he again threw his brushes aside.

Soon it would be the evening hour, which he had been waiting for so eagerly, when he would sit by the radio. Jeannette was still working at the Poste Parisien studio, and the contrast of her deep, nervous voice with the banal words of the advertisements seemed to André as painful as his own thoughts. He recalled Laforgue's poetry and Pascin's water-colours: what childish and morbid irony!

He often asked himself: "What is Jeannette to me?" The word "love" never entered his head. He thought how little he knew her; perhaps they had nothing in common and it was all just a caprice. André was made for great and enduring sentiments; affection was slow to develop in him, striking deep roots and requiring patience and careful attention. Since his last meeting with Lucien he had been feeling rather like somebody who had fallen into the water: he felt guilty of having made a tactless admission. Lucien had been right to imply: "What's it got to do with you?" André told himself that he ought to give up this caprice, but when evening came he again rushed over to the radio set.

How could he work? The red flags of the stone-masons on strike fluttered on the scaffolding in the neighbouring streets. On the radio Jeannette's voice alternately recommended love and patent medicines. It was July and the weather was sultry. The thunder-storms at night failed to clear the air. André was beginning to feel exhausted.

At the beginning of July the well-to-do quarters of Paris were deserted. In previous years many people put off their departure for the seaside or the spas until the end of the month, fearing the roads and trains would be crowded. But the events of the past few weeks had caused the Parisian bourgeoisie to disperse earlier than usual. They were going farther afield, to the south, declaring that the centre of France would be overrun by the workers, who were now having vacations with pay. Respectable business men were horrified at the prospect of finding stokers and stone-masons sitting next to them on the beach. The gossip columnists whined that the watering-places were "befouled." The lucky ones went off to Switzerland or Italy. Nobody who was "anybody" wanted to stay in Paris: they were frightened at the thought of the big demonstra-tion which was to take place on the Fourteenth of July. Once upon a time everybody celebrated that day; but now the national holiday represented the triumph of the Popular Front, and Breteuil's friends who remained in the capital made haste to remove the flags from their houses in order not to participate in the general celebrations.

In the working-class quarters a joyful atmosphere prevailed. The vacations with pay, which had given Desser so much to think about, immediately became part of life and led to long conversations as to where the most picturesque places were to be found and which river had the most fish. When gossiping in the working-class cafés, Desser would say: "What a marvellous country! They expected a revolution and what they're going to have is a gigantic angling competition!" After the stormy June days July seemed a month of bucolic calm. True, the Communists talked of a counter-offensive by the employers and of Breteuil's conspiracy, but their talk was soon forgotten over maps and railway guides, new bicycles, new bathing-suits. Most of the vacations with pay were to take place

in August, and the Paris workers got ready to celebrate the Fourteenth of July at home. To some people this meant a military parade,
to others a political demonstration, and to many more it meant
dancing in the streets.

On the evening of the 13th of July dancing was already in full
swing. There seemed to be hardly a single unemployed musician
left in Paris. On all sides people were shouting, trumpeting, whistling, and generally letting themselves go. Stands were set up in
all the squares for the orchestras; trumpeters with faces coppery
and the veins bursting out on their foreheads thirstily gulped beer.
Processions bearing multi-coloured Chinese lanterns swung through
the streets. The cafés set out all the tables they could find: dining-
tables, kitchen tables, card-tables. The weather was hot, and everybody took off his coat as though he were in the country. Men
danced away in their shirt-sleeves, the metal plates on their suspenders flashing in the light. Little children squealed or slumbered
in their mothers' arms. Conjurers swallowed fire, and produced
chickens from battered top-hats. Hawkers went about selling crys-
tallized fruits, flowers, and paper fans. There were booths everywhere with fortune-tellers, roulette wheels, and shooting-galleries.
Boys shot down the ping-pong balls tossed up by a jet of water,
shattered the whirling clay pipes. And over all roared the merry-
go-rounds with their traditional dappled horses or more up-to-date
aeroplanes.

Nothing showed more clearly the provincial character of Paris,
made up of hundreds of little towns, each of which has its own main
street, its own movies, its own heroes, and its own local gossip. The
central districts that in the daytime teemed with unknown passers-
by were empty. But there were no passers-by in the squares of the
working-class quarters: here everyone knew everyone else and the
dancing was a family affair.

All the evening André strolled about the streets. He loved the
people's holidays for their picturesqueness and boisterous, unaf-
fected gaiety. He loved the stands with gingerbread pigs on whose
backs you could have your sweetheart's name written in sugar icing.
He loved the accordions and hand-organs and the traditional sadness of that blaring music. But now he felt lonely, especially when
he found himself in the Place de la Bastille. There on that sultry
evening the people were dancing lightheartedly on their ancient
battle-ground. From the distance the sound of the thousands of

couples whirling round and round was like the surge of the sea. André turned back towards the Seine and then walked up to his favourite square, the Contrescarpes. Here all the poor people of the neighbourhood were making merry amid the fantastic signs and dark-green chestnut trees. It was after midnight. André was sitting drinking warm beer when he suddenly caught sight of Jeannette. She had arrived with the actors. He was so delighted that he cried out. Then, after fidgeting in his chair and cursing himself for a fool, he went up to her.

"Will you dance?"

She looked at him with her astonished eyes, and they started to dance in silence. Both were so surprised at this wonderful meeting that they frowned and looked stiff. It was a chaste passion, and somehow André was unaware that his hand was touching Jeannette's body and that he could feel her breathing. The square was crowded and they were constantly bumping into other couples, but to them it seemed as though they had escaped to some remote plain or desert.

Then André suggested they go for a stroll. Jeannette said:

"I'm with some people. . . . Oh, never mind, I'll tell them to wait for me."

They went down a narrow, dim-lit street, holding each other's hands, like children in the dark. Jeannette talked about the evening at the Seine works.

"I don't understand much about it," she said. "You see, I hardly ever read the papers. But that was the real thing. How they listened! They moved me so much that afterwards I went home and howled. I don't know what for. Perhaps because it was so good."

"All these weeks," said André, "I've been going about, listening and looking. I don't know what's going to come out of it all, but it's extraordinary! Everything with them is simple and deep. I feel they have roots. But you and I are used to something different, to other people altogether. Maybe, they have a lot of taste, but they're light. It's easy to blow them away. There are plants like that in the fields. They're torn up and they sail away, heaven knows where. And it's all arbitrary, accidental. . . ."

Jeannette stopped and said sadly: "André, that's us."

They came out into the brightly lit Place d'Italie, where there was music, fireworks, laughter.

"You know," said Jeannette, "the frailty amazes me. . . ."

"Frailty of what?"

"Of everything. One ought to be able to get used to the idea. It isn't as if I were a young girl. But no. . . ."

André was deeply moved: she was expressing his own thoughts. "Why is it we think exactly alike?" he said.

"I dare say in a sense it's the result of art. When I was at the factory, I had this feeling. I thought: 'They may consider us to be on their side, they may like us and spoil us, but there'll come a moment when we'll find ourselves left out.' I can't explain it. Have you noticed how people pronounce the word 'art'? Sometimes like the beginning of a prayer, but more often like the name of a disease, the plague or cholera. No doubt they'll soon invent some kind of inoculation. André, do you like riding on merry-go-rounds?"

Grotesque animals, green and orange, dragons, unicorns, and centaurs rushed round, rising and falling. The enormous organ roared: "You'll never know how much I loved you. . . ." André and Jeannette climbed up on a shiny blue elephant. A sudden fresh breeze drove away the stifling atmosphere.

They came down with their arms round each other. They were silent. At moments like this you were afraid to say a word, afraid even to look round or move your hand — in case happiness might slip away.

Jeannette was the first to recover her senses. She began to be afraid there might be trouble in store for her if she didn't go away at once. This was no passing fit of passion, it was something strong and devouring. They couldn't live together. They were infected with the same disquiet; they were of the same breed. . . . What was it he said? Yes, a plant that drifted from field to field. With him? No, it would be like incest!

"André, I must go," she said, "they're waiting for me."

At the dark corner of the square, under a chestnut tree where a stray lantern gleamed among the leaves, she kissed him tenderly — with a kind of renunciation, as if he were not a man so much as a gift. He put his arms round her timidly. She moved away. "You needn't. . . ."

He did not ask why. They walked back in silence to the Place Contrescarpes and parted without a word.

The other actors began chaffing Jeannette about her "secret admirer." She did not answer. She felt terribly thirsty and drank sour wine like water. The wine made her feel even hotter; her temples

began to throb. And the hand-organ went on roaring out its complaint about unsuccessful love, and Jeannette thought vaguely:
" That's probably how an elephant declares its love." The blue elephant. . . . What had she done? She wanted to talk a lot, loud
and fast.

" How funny it all is! " she said. " They kept her underground all
her life. In the Metro. No, deeper than that — in a mine. Deeper
still — in hell. Then they brought her out and said to her: ' Run,
laugh, breathe! ' But she said: ' No.' Why? Because she couldn't run,
couldn't laugh, couldn't breathe. No, no! "

" What on earth are you talking about? Who said that? "

" The goddess in the text-book. Somebody I know asked her. You
needn't be afraid, Maréchal. It wasn't you; it wasn't any actor. It
was a brewer. Or myself. Does it matter who? "

" You're tight, that's what you are! "

" I don't know. I feel I want to talk, but I can't. Tell me, Maréchal,
have you ever thought about happiness? "

" Course not. Nobody thinks about happiness."

" Now, you know that isn't true. I'm always thinking about it. I
look at people and I think: you see how they take care of their
happiness — under a glass case, like cheese under a baize cloth. And
they dance and dance. Today they can still dance. You remember
the lines: ' Lisbon has perished, but in Paris they dance.' There was
an earthquake then. Well, there may be another one here. Or a new
volcano may erupt. Or the plague will break out. Or bombs will
begin to drop from the sky. I don't know. . . . But this happiness,
how frail it is! Be careful, Maréchal, don't breathe! "

The tears ran down her face as she talked. The dawn was breaking. The people were going back to their homes. Somebody next
to her kept saying:

" Never mind, darling, tomorrow we'll be dancing again."

The faces of the people looked ghostly in the daylight. The deserted square was littered with trampled flowers, orange-peel,
cigarette ends, corks, and crackers.

When André got back to his studio, the huge rosy sun was rising
over the sea of roofs. Everything shone and quivered. André sat at
the window. Sadness was slowly spreading in his heart. He remembered everything; far away in the darkness of the crack-brained
night the Chinese lanterns still glowed among the artificial leaves —
like the sun over there. The merry-go-round was spinning too fast.

Yes, everything was spinning like that — it was impossible to understand or to see it. Storms and trees live according to different calendars.

André recalled the words of Cézanne, which he had often reflected over: "One must observe nature a long time. Then what is seen is liberated from the influence of the light and everything accidental, and reflection breeds understanding." How pleasant it was for him in quiet Aix! Those days were different. But Jeannette had said: "You needn't." Needn't what? Desire? Hope? Understand?

The sun was already high in the sky. The city was sleeping dead-tired under the gorgeous light; and the light was devouring all the colours. André gazed like a blind man at the world he failed to understand. He dozed off as he sat, bathed in the golden July sun.

General Picard cut a splendid figure on his light bay charger. At the head of the Moroccan infantry he looked like some old military painting come to life.

Every year there was a military parade on the Fourteenth of July. Usually it attracted the middle-class section of the population, also modistes who adored uniforms, and swarms of little boys. But this year the parade drew other spectators. The habitués of the Champs-Élysées were far away at the seaside or the spas, and the fashionable quarter was invaded by the inhabitants of the suburbs. Workmen's caps were seen everywhere. Only at the corners of the streets stood elegantly dressed, arrogant young men in berets — the followers of Breteuil. They shouted: "Long live the Army!" The workers answered with: "Long live the Army of the Republic!" and although the Republic was already in its seventh decade, this cry had a challenging ring and frequently led to scuffles.

Lately the press had been writing a lot about the danger of war, and the ominous activity beyond the Rhine and the Alps. The people looked hopefully at the soldiers' helmets, the gunners, and the cheerful-looking airmen. Military marches — *Lorraine* and *Sambre* — resounded continuously. People marched in step along the pavements, holding themselves erect, with a spirited look on their faces. There was something about the Army that captured the hearts of the crowd: the soldiers were all different heights, giants stalking beside little undersized fellows. They swung along easily, as though on the march, and the spectators recognized them as their own people.

The young men in berets greeted Picard with enthusiasm and their shouts were taken up by the crowd. Picard was a general with a great past. He was twice wounded in the war and had the bearing of a brave man. But today Picard wore a smile of contempt, and on this occasion the mask corresponded exactly to his state of mind. The unusual public that attended the parade filled him with indignation. What pleasure it would give him to turn his Moroccans loose on such rabble! He looked straight in front of him in order to avoid the objectionable scene; and the spectacle of the Arc de Triomphe, that monument of past glory, seemed to him incompatible with a city that was in the hands of the riff-raff, where red flags were hanging out on all sides, and where he, a fighting general, had to carry out the orders of upstarts and Masons.

A crowd of workers were standing near the Arc de Triomphe. When Picard came level with them, Michaud's voice rang out: " Long live the — " Immediately Breteuil's young men rushed at the workers. Police whistles shrilled. Picard's horse pricked up its ears; but the general did not even glance at the pavement. Only his sneer became still more pronounced and again the word " Rabble! " passed through his mind.

For the last two years the Champs-Élysées had been the sacred preserve of the Fascists. Every day they beat up the sellers of Left newspapers, workers suspected of being in sympathy with the Popular Front, and Jews. The chic public on the café terraces was quite accustomed to these goings-on of Gilded Youth.

Today, however, the Champs-Élysées was occupied by newcomers from other quarters, and a regular battle broke out near the Arc de Triomphe. The Fascists were armed with rubber clubs, bludgeons, and knives. One of the workers fell to the ground with blood all over his face. Michaud tried to fight his way out of a ring. Suddenly he felt a sharp pain, as though he had been slashed across the back with a cane. He gripped a door-key in his fist and began to punch away at his attackers. The gendarmes energetically shielded the Fascists. They weren't thinking about Blum or Villard: though sheer force of habit they struck anyone who was not well dressed, and protected the habitués of the Champs-Élysées. Michaud's comrades hurried to his rescue. A Fascist tried to knock him down, but Michaud laid him out.

The soldiers glanced at the tussle as they marched past.

Michaud sighed as he examined his coat, which had been slashed with a knife. He did not feel any pain, although there was a bright red mark on his back like a burn. His comrades took him to a druggist's. He made them all laugh, repeating over and over again: " Oh, the bastards! My best suit, too! "

After the parade Picard took a hasty lunch. An hour later he left in civilian clothes for the country. In every village his car was held up by young people dancing in the streets. The general gaiety drove him nearly frantic. He closed his eyes; he would have given anything to silence those accordions and saxophones!

Breteuil was waiting for him in a small house near Ferté. It was an exquisite neighbourhood and suggested a love idyll rather than a meeting-place for conspirators. The house stood on the steep bank of the Marne. From the veranda you could see the river, the islands overgrown with rushes, and the meadows with the dappled cows that seemed to drowse with their muzzles dipping into the bright green grass. Wistaria twined itself over the veranda, filling the air with a sweet languor.

Stern and gloomy as ever, Breteuil related in a metallic voice the events of the past few days.

" Tessa has collected a considerable group," he said, " but I don't think the matter will be decided in Parliament. The Spaniards are going to make a move very soon. If they succeed in liquidating the Popular Front, we're going to move too — this autumn."

Picard remembered the crowd in the Champs-Élysées.

" The poison has penetrated deep," he said. " It will be necessary to destroy hundreds of thousands. And it's difficult to tell how the Army's going to behave. What are officers without soldiers? Romanticism. I don't know. What are you reckoning on? "

" Too early to talk about that," Breteuil said. " The arms from Düsseldorf have been supplied. Of course, they're only a snack. But compared with what your colonel gave us, it's quite a lot. Now there's something else I want. Can you get the plan of mobilization? You see, one must expect anything with these blockheads. I don't want to see us caught unawares in the event of war. . . . "

Picard looked away. Though intensely devoted to Breteuil, for the first time he was seized with doubt: ought he to carry out this request? Picard came of a military family. To him everything connected with the Army was sacred. It was linked up with remembrances of battles, the traditions of his whole milieu and all the resounding names from Jena and Austerlitz to the Marne and Verdun. Cool-headed though he was, he suddenly began to talk excitedly, like a young lad:

"I thought that in the event of war we'd forget all our dissensions."

Breteuil paced the veranda. Then he came and stood very close to Picard.

"I thought so, too," he said. "I hope you're not going to doubt my patriotism. We were both of us at the front and we left our best friends there. But believe me, it's no longer a nation, it's a gang that has seized power. I'll go against it even with the Germans. I pray God it may not happen! It's hard to say this and it's even harder to do it. It requires strength of character, an almost superhuman willpower. But nevertheless that's how it stands. Their victory won't be a victory for France; it will be a victory for revolution."

"But the Army?" said Picard. "What will happen to the Army?"

"The Army can regenerate France. And if not? Well, then her song is over. For a hundred years. . . ."

Picard stood silent. He stared at the distant fields. He seemed to be contemplating something, but he saw nothing except the intolerably bright light. His mind was in a state of bewilderment. He even wanted to shout, to smash the glass jug of water and go away. But the wistaria spread its sweet smell everywhere and the bumblebees droned in the air. Then Picard remembered the crowd in the Champs-Élysées. That rabble! No, that wasn't France! Breteuil was right, then. Even Hitler was better. At last Picard spoke. He hardly recognized his own voice; it seemed stifled and dead.

"If you are right," he said, "you've taken upon yourself a terrible cross. But if you're mistaken — No, I don't want to think about it! I'm accustomed to obey orders. I am now giving up everything: not only life, but honour. . . ."

Breteuil offered to accompany him back to town, but Picard refused. He wanted to be alone. In the car he again closed his eyes and sank back into an anxious daze. The steam organs of the merry-go-rounds were roaring as irritatingly as ever. In the suburbs of Paris the car was held up by demonstrators returning from the Place de la Bastille. Seeing some soldiers on the terrace of a café, the workers shouted merrily: "Long live the Republican Army!" Picard put his hand over his eyes, scowled, and said to the chauffeur: "Try another way, any way you like, but drive as quickly as you can. I've no time. . . ."

CHAPTER 22

THE DEMONSTRATION went on all day. Over a million Parisians took part in it. The procession seemed endless. They marched and marched: through the Place de la Bastille, de la République, de la Nation, along the winding narrow streets and wide boulevards. Just when the spectators thought it was all over, a fresh column came in sight.

The general amiability of the victors gave the demonstration a somewhat unexpected character. That same day a year ago columns had marched along those same streets ready to give battle. Today the procession reminded one of a carnival. Few were thinking about the struggle that lay ahead. All were lulled by a sense of power: " Eight hundred thousand have gone by! A million! A million and a half! . . ."

Half the city was left without police. They had been withdrawn in order to avoid clashes. The workers were maintaining order by themselves; there were no fights, no quarrels, no shouts of abuse: holiday Paris sang songs and joked without malice.

Delegates had come from all over France. The miners of Picardy marched by in their coal-begrimed working clothes, swinging their safety-lamps. The vineyard workers of the south carried clusters of paper grapes swinging on long poles. The women of Alsace in their traditional dresses sang their national songs. Bretons blew their enigmatic bagpipes; the mountaineers of Savoy danced along the streets.

Ex-servicemen were also in the procession. The legless ones were drawn along in little carts, and the blind were led by guides. A hundred thousand men who had been mutilated by it repeated hopefully: " Down with war! "

The procession was headed by some twenty or thirty bent old men — a handful of veterans who had taken part in the Commune. Once upon a time, as young lads, they had helped to build the last barricades in the humpbacked streets of Montmartre and Belleville. Now they were looking on at the triumph of their grandsons, and their shrivelled, faded lips were smiling.

The Young Communists were very proud of their new silk banners streaming into battle on the light breeze. They carried several portraits of Maxim Gorky, who had died a short time before; that typically Russian face swayed over the heads of the procession.

One after another the columns went by. After the metal-workers came the leather-dressers. Then came the writers, then the students. Then followed the employees of the gas company wearing their regulation caps, then the actors, firemen, hospital nurses, then more metal-workers and leather-dressers.

Paris was like a vast raft on to which the shipwrecked people of various countries had clambered. The refugees who had settled in the capital marched side by side with the Frenchmen. Foreign voices were heard at frequent intervals, and foreign words stood out on the flags and banners. There were builders from Naples and Sicily, heroes of the Asturias, Austrian tailors and confectioners, Jews from the Polish and Rumanian ghettoes — polishers, cobblers, sign-painters — students from Shanghai, Annamese, Arabs, Negroes. And all of them were singing the *Internationale*.

The hatters carried an enormous cap, the classic headwear of the French workman, underneath which was written: " Thy Crown, Proletarian! "

The steel-workers carried bunches of flowers, pinks and pansies. But behind them marched laughing young flower-girls with a huge silver hammer.

All along the route from the Place de la Bastille to the Porte de Vincennes the grey dingy houses were decorated with réd. Red curtains, red carpets, red cloths hung from every window. Women in red blouses stood on the balconies, and it seemed as though that day all the red flowers of France, poppies, pinks, and tulips, were gathered together in the streets of Paris.

Swarms of merry-faced cheeky little boys perched in the trees like sparrows. There was plenty of amusement. They burned a straw effigy of the traitor Doriot. A bloated Mussolini dangled from a gallows alongside a rag dummy of Hitler; a man on stilts represented an elongated caricature of Flandin.

The Seine workers were greeted with special enthusiasm. They carried a model of the Bastille prison, over which was written: " Remember the Bastille that was taken! Remember the Bastille that has yet to be taken! " At the head of their column marched Michaud, Legrais, and Pierre.

On the reviewing stand were ministers and trade-union delegates, writers and workers, Communists and Radicals. Blum wore
a mournful smile. Daladier, stocky and with obstinate creases round
his mouth, kept his fist in the air. Villard quietly repeated: "The
last fight let us face. . . ."

As the Seine column was passing the platform, someone called
out to Pierre: "Dubois, Villard wants to meet you."

Villard had been told about the talented young engineer who
was a member of the Socialist Party and had taken an active part
in the recent strike, and Villard even in the midst of affairs of State
remembered his party obligations. He shook hands with Pierre in
a friendly way.

"Bravo!" he said. "The Communists say we've lost the revolutionary spirit. You're the best answer to that."

Pierre was so embarrassed that he could only answer: "Thanks."

"I think I knew your father," Villard said. "You're from Perpignan, aren't you?"

Villard might not recognize a deputy to whom he had been talking the day before, but he remembered everything connected with
his youth — his school-fellows, the towns where he had lectured,
the delegates of long-past congresses.

"He and I organized a demonstration against the execution of a
Spaniard, Ferrero. That name won't convey anything to you, but
in those days the whole country was in a turmoil. Our people are
amazing! The feeling of international solidarity! The responsive-
ness! . . . Well, I wish you every success!"

Villard was moved by these reminiscences. He felt young and
uncompromising, like this engineer. Now he looked with different
eyes at the demonstrators; he felt as though he was marching with
them, advancing with them to meet the foe. He waved his hat gaily
to the Scouts.

It was the Radical deputy Piroux who brought him back to
reality. Nobody could make out why Piroux had come to the demonstration: it was well known that he hated the Popular Front. Possibly he wanted to check up on the popularity of this or that
minister. He stood on the platform like a graven image, neither
joining in the singing nor replying to the greetings. Finding himself
next to Villard, he decided to talk business; he had only just arrived in Paris from his constituency in the Pyrénées Orientales.

Piroux said: "The Prefect told me that in some places they've

actually gone so far as to seize the land. They're imitating the Spaniards. And everywhere the ringleaders come from among these foreign elements. We have a lot of Catalonian workers down our way.
They used to be taught that foreigners had no right to interfere in
the political life of the country. But it's different now the Communists are organizing this mob. The situation is dangerous. . . ."

Villard knew that Piroux was a friend of Tessa's and he treated
him with exceptional deference.

"I'm having a talk with Dormoy today," he said. "It goes without
saying that foreigners must be forbidden to take part in political
demonstrations. I assure you, my dear colleague, that we will not
depart from tradition. A little confidence and everything will be
all right. . . ."

Piroux thanked him and stepped aside. Villard whispered to one
of the Communists: "If we don't check Tessa's gang, they'll destroy us."

Villard thought that this was real statesmanship and that this
sort of manœuvre would set him well on the way to victory.

A delegation from the small town of Lans marched past the platform. The delegates consisted of one old man in a velvet jacket
with a cigarette butt clinging to his lower lip, and four young workers in their Sunday suits. They carried a banner on which was
written: "Lans will not permit the victory of the Fascists." Villard
thought: "There are probably three hundred workers in Lans, not
more. . . ." And he half-murmured, half-sighed: "Children!"

Excited and happy, Pierre caught up with his column. He said
nothing about his conversation with Villard; he was afraid
Michaud's irony would break the charm.

Michaud had long forgotten about the morning scuffle and his
ruined coat. His back ached, but he was cheerful. The demonstration had been a roaring success. It was only when he arrived at the
gates of the suburb that he became silent. It was getting dark and
the lights were beginning to glow, signals, show-signs, green, yellow, and red — like an immense suburban flower-garden.

"What's up, Michaud? Feeling low?"

"No. It's hot!"

He wiped his forehead with his sleeve. Suddenly he said: "I've
just been reading a life of Blanqui. You know it made me feel kind
of envious. It was a fine life and, what is the main thing, a simple
one. The barricades for a few days, and prison all the rest of the

time. He even wrote about the stars. In those days the only thing you had to do was to die. Now you've got to live — whatever happens. That's a much tougher job, but it's got to be tackled."

Pierre listened to him with amazement. He suddenly realized that despite Michaud's complicated way of thinking, his precise formulas hid — like an animal's fur or the grass on the earth's surface — a passionate nature, and deep, tortuous suffering that was vital and responsive like an animal's fur or wind-swept grass.

"You've grown up, Michaud," Pierre said. "I used to think of you as just a comrade. But now — well, you're able to lead."

Michaud made a childish grimace and whistled like a finch. He was a marvellous whistler.

And the demonstrators marched and marched, and there was no end to "The last fight let us face."

CHAPTER 23

THE NEXT morning Pierre went away for a month's vacation. A vacation always appeared to him as something blue and gold, like the posters in the travel agencies.

Agnès had left a week earlier. She had taken a fisherman's cottage on the cliffs near Concarneau. The house was like a little white box. Down below, women mended the blue nets, and the red sails flapped in the wind. The place lay open to the sea. There was a perpetual breeze; the tides ran strong, and day and night the Atlantic moaned ceaselessly.

Pierre inspected the clean whitewashed room with its chromos. Everything smelled of fish: the bed-linen, curtains, and even the walls.

He arrived full of the events in Paris. He proudly told Agnès about his conversation with Villard, gave her a detailed description of the demonstration, and talked about the intrigues of the Fascists. Agnès said nothing. This annoyed Pierre; he wondered if he would ever be able to convince her of the importance and righteousness of his cause.

"But it's the only thing that makes life worth living," he said. "Can't you understand?"

"No. And I don't want to. It's a game, and a bad game at that. I can feel the falsehood of it all. Nobody wants to give up anything. Villard? . . . He'll betray, like all the rest. Don't you see that the people are always just the same? . . ."

"We'll re-educate them."

"No, you won't. You're doing something quite different: you're painting them over. That's easier, but Lord, how dull it is! And besides, it's dishonest!"

So they argued on the day of Pierre's arrival. Then he gave himself up to his holiday. For three days he did nothing, thought about nothing, bathed, lay on the sand, climbed up the cliffs, and watched for hours on end the ever increasing waves of the incoming tide. He had often been to the Mediterranean and was familiar with its gentle, lazy charm. But the Atlantic amazed him. At first everything seemed to him almost unbearably disturbing, as though Nature herself lived in expectation of an imminent catastrophe. But he soon began to realize that the ever present thundering roar corresponded to his own state of mind. He took pleasure in the strength of the wind, which made it impossible to open the door, tried to blow a man off his feet, and bent and twisted the low, sturdy trees.

Three days passed like this. Pierre's face got sunburnt and his whole being was thoroughly ventilated. Hundreds of things that had seemed important in Paris now only provoked a careless smile. On the other hand, new worlds revealed themselves: the strange life of the sardines with their own strictly defined sea-routes, the smell of seaweed, and at night the clustered stars.

The papers arrived so late that the news was already stale. One day Pierre turned on the little portable radio which he had brought with him, and listened to the news: Stock Exchange prices, a Chinese-Japanese incident, a speech by Tessa at a commercial banquet — Pierre waved his hand and went to catch crabs.

Agnès brightened up. Her happiness was now complete. In Paris she had felt uneasy about Pierre and been jealous of his interest in events. Her origins and her hard life, so closely bound up with the life of Belleville, might have inclined her to take an interest in what was happening, but she was repelled by the general, abstract talk, the political squabbles, and language of newspapers and meetings.

She indignantly dismissed it all as "politics." The only thing that
troubled her was the fate of individual people. For this reason she
was quite indifferent about the strikes, although when Pierre told
her about Clémence, she turned away so that he shouldn't notice
her tears. Pierre's enthusiasm for the Popular Front seemed to her
like whirling round on one spot, a kind of verbal cyclone. She said
to herself: "People don't die for that sort of thing!" Mixed up with
this was a strain of unconscious egotism. For the first time in her
life she was experiencing security and quiet and she was afraid
it might suddenly all come to an end. Her pregnancy — the fact that
she now had two lives to defend — gave substance and tenacity to
this feeling; and the fact that Pierre did not listen to the radio
seemed to her an omen of salvation.

On the evening of the fourth day a storm broke out. It came on
very suddenly. Pierre was sitting on the beach with Agnès. Suddenly the wind whirled a column of sand into the air. Agnès screwed
up her eyes. A few minutes later everything around was in an
uproar. The sea tossed the boats on to the shore. The wind shrieked
past the houses. It was all Pierre and Agnès could do to get back.

Agnès sat down by the window with her sewing. It was getting
dark, but they did not light the lamp. The seething, dark-violet
ocean was wonderfully beautiful. Amid the raging elements they
were hidden away as if in a shell. They were keenly aware of the
warmth of love and all its vital tenacity.

Pierre idly turned on the radio. The little green eye lit up, and another familiar noise mingled with the roar of the sea: shrill howlings
and the crackling of Morse.

An English announcer's voice: "The general tendency on the
Stock Exchange is upward. Royal Dutch was today quoted at two
points higher. . . ."

Jazz.

A German song: "You were the sweetest blonde. . . ."

"This is Paris calling. Radio station Île de France. Maurice
Chevalier will sing: 'Paris remains Paris.' . . ."

"Buy Luxe vacuum cleaners. The Luxe Company has pleasure
in presenting to the attention of listeners a sketch entitled: 'The
Invisible Speck of Dust.'"

Italy. The speech of the secretary of the Fascist Party: "We are
educating the young legionaries in the spirit of bravery. . . ." More
dance music.

Bicycle races: "On the Pau-Carcassone stretch the Belgian Grenet has covered a distance of — "

" Listen to the exact time! At the fourth stroke it will be nineteen o'clock Greenwich time. Events of the day. . . ."

"Two thousand killed. . . ."

Agnès laid down her sewing. Pierre clutched the radio as though he wanted to strangle it.

But the announcer continued calmly: " In Barcelona the Hotel Columbus was bombarded with cannon-fire. In Madrid the troops loyal to the Government, together with the workers, have driven the rebels from the La Montaña barracks. In Seville fighting is going on for the possession of the Triana quarter, inhabited by the poorer classes. General Aranda has captured Oviedo. At Burgos mass executions have begun. . . ."

Pierre ran out of the house. The storm had everything in its grip. The lighthouse beam flickered over the huge waves that stormed against the cliffs like columns of soldiers. Down below, the red lights flickered. The roar of the ocean was like a mighty siren. Pierre turned back to the cottage; his face was wet with spray. Agnès was standing in the doorway. She said quietly:

" I've looked up the trains. There's one at six o'clock in the morning that gets to Paris in the evening."

She kissed him in the darkness and they sat together in silence until the dawn. The storm raged on all through the night and showed no signs of abating.

Tens of thousands of people were unable to get into the hall. The shots on the other side of the Pyrenees had roused all Paris. Excited people stood in the aisles, clung to the galleries, and climbed on to the platform. When Cachin spoke of the shootings at Badajoz, his voice shook. And from outside in the street came the singing of the *Internationale,* now solemn as a vow, now quick and spirited.

An old man mounted the platform. His dry, clean-shaven face had those deep furrows that give such a tragic cast to Spanish faces. This was Muñez, a teacher, one of the leaders of the Madrid unions. A hush came over the audience: a man who had come from there was about to speak! But Muñez stood silent; his mouth was half-open with pain. Someone on the platform said loudly:

" They've killed his son. . . ."

Then the Spaniard cried out:

" Arms! . . ."

And the entire hall shouted: " Arms! " And from the street came the reply: " Arms! Arms! "

Then a professor spoke. He was counted as a Radical, an old crank, who in the course of his life had warmly defended the wine-growers of Aude in their struggle for the right to name their wine " champagne," Dreyfus, the English suffragettes, and the Negus. The professor spoke about the " knight without fear and reproach " and offered the Spaniards " moral support."

Michaud spoke last. He said: " One of the Italian bombers which Mussolini is sending to Franco has come down on French territory. We've got the details: the Fifty-seventh and the Fifty-eighth Italian squadrons. Hitler has sent his Junkers to the rebels. But our comrades only have shotguns. We must demand of the Popular Front Government planes for Spain! "

Again the hall roared: " Planes for Spain! " And the words: " Planes for Spain " were taken up outside on the boulevard Wagram, in the Place de l'Étoile, and in the twelve boulevards radiating from it. And when the great human sea was silent for a moment, somebody's thin, hoarse voice began again: " Planes. . . ." And once again these words from the heart of Paris swelled above the noise of the city, invaded the houses and the tunnels of the Metro, and, issuing from thence, aroused the sleepy outskirts.

When the meeting was over, Michaud took Pierre to one side:

" Muñez has come specially about planes. As a specialist you ought to be able to help them."

Muñez had been sent to Paris to buy twenty bombers. He spent three days going round the Government offices, where he was given a friendly handshake and told: " The matter will have to be considered." He called on Meuger, the big industrialist. Meuger listened to what he had to say, offered him a cigarette, then smiled politely and said: " The sooner Franco wins, the better."

" Try to have a talk with Desser," said Michaud. " You see, it's a business proposition. Maybe he'll bite."

Muñez went out with Pierre. He told him what was happening in Spain.

" They're fighting with revolvers, shotguns, and clasp-knives. It's ludicrous and it's terrible! The peasants have only got antediluvian blunderbusses. But everything may be all over in a couple of weeks; the others are advancing rapidly. They've got Savoias and Junkers.

All we've got is ten commercial planes. They had to make holes in them to drop the bombs. Old galoshes! They can bring them down with a pot-shot. I told them here: 'If we go down it will be the end of you as well.' But they don't understand."

All around them the shouting was still going on: "Planes for Spain!"

Muñez smiled. "These people would give them all right," he said, "but the planes are not in their hands."

Next morning Pierre went to see Desser. Desser received him at once. Pierre decided to talk plainly.

"When the strike was on," he said, "we were on different sides of the barricade. But this isn't a matter that concerns your factories. It's not the Communists who are in power in Spain, but your fellow thinkers, Giral, Azaña. They need bombers. They ask you to sell them twenty A 68's for cash down."

Desser smiled. " I particularly like ' for cash down '! You seem to think that Desser can be seduced with money. By the way, Meuger told me yesterday that the Spaniards had been to him. He told me proudly: 'I showed them out. I don't betray my class.' You can't object; the man reasons as you do — in the Marxist way."

" I didn't come to see Meuger. Meuger's a Fascist. But you . . ."

" I'm a Frenchman first of all. Peace is more important to me than Spain."

"Who can forbid you to sell aircraft to the Government of a neighboring country?"

"Don't pretend to be naïve! If I let them have twenty A 68's, the Italians will send another forty Savoias within a week. And so it goes on. . . . Of course I prefer Azaña to General Franco. I'll give you a hundred thousand francs for the Spaniards; only please don't say you got them from me. But I won't sell you any planes. I don't want to risk the peace of France. One's own skin is dearer than another man's shirt, as they say."

" Then we've got to look on while they go down? That's the depth of meanness! I can understand Meuger, but you! . . . You remember that talk we had one night? How am I going to tell Muñez that you've refused?"

Pierre paced up and down the room, shouting and banging his fist. Desser looked at him with his tired, mocking eyes; in his heart he liked Pierre. Pierre was on the point of going, but Desser stopped him.

"Look here," he said, "eleven A 68's are on order for the
Argentine. A certain Manu is to receive them. Offer to buy them
from him and he'll let you have them. As you see, I shan't make
any money out of it. If you think it can save them, well and good.
I guarantee that Manu will undertake it. And with a combination
like that there won't be any complications with regard to delivery.
You see, I'm convinced that Blum won't let a single plane through."

"Impossible! In that case I'll go and see Villard."

"I shouldn't like to be in Villard's shoes just now! Ah, you roman-
ticists. Here are the licences for Manu. Now are you satisfied?"

Pierre took leave distractedly and hurried off to see Manu.

According to his passport, Manu was a citizen of Honduras, of
Rumanian origin. He had settled in Paris a long time ago and considered himself a Frenchman. He was engaged in various shady
transactions and was now quite bursting with hope. Spanish affairs
were a positive source of inspiration to all go-betweens, agents, and
speculators. Every day delegations were arriving from Madrid and
Barcelona with cash and instructions to procure war material. They
included representatives of various ministries and trade unions,
military men and journalists — Republicans, Communists, and
Anarchists. The delegates were often unknown to one another and
found themselves approaching the same business men at different
times; they got taken in and fleeced all round. The Burgos agents
were also busy; they too were looking for arms. Every day the
speculators put up their prices.

When Manu heard about the A 68's, he asked for treble. "I'm
afraid it may lead to unpleasantness in Buenos Aires," he said.
"Besides, you can rest absolutely assured in dealing with me; the
goods will be released. You see, I've got the licences."

"Oh, no," said Pierre. "I've got the licences myself."

Manu reflected that he was not talking to a Spaniard whom he
could humbug, but to an expert, an engineer of the Seine works,
and a man who was a friend of Desser's into the bargain. A man
like that could get planes even without coming to him. Yes, but
all the same he had come to him. So Manu said he would let Pierre
have a definite price tomorrow.

When Muñez heard about "tomorrow" he gave a mournful sigh.
Nearly a week had gone by already! . . . To him it seemed that the
fate of Madrid and the Republic depended on those planes. He
kept buying the same newspapers several times a day and was al-

ways listening to the news. He talked excitedly when he met Pierre:
" Alto de León. . . . Two armoured cars. . . . They've beaten
them off at Irún. . . . Estremadura is the chief danger; they're approaching Medina. But Medina . . . Medina. . . ."

He couldn't understand how the people around him could joke
and dine, stroll about and go to the theatres. Paris stirred him to
anger with its indifference, and but for Pierre he would have hated
the French. But Pierre lived as he did — from one edition of the
evening papers to the next.

On the third day Manu yielded and gave up the planes with an
increase of twenty per cent on the original price. The bombers
were at an aerodrome near Toulouse. Muñez reported the purchase
to Madrid in code. He had arranged to leave for Toulouse with
Pierre that evening, but at the last moment a telegram arrived
through the Embassy: the bombers were not enough. A further
twenty must be obtained, and also thirty fighters of the Dewoitine
type. It was impossible to obtain such a large quantity of aeroplanes without the help of the French Government: the aircraft
factories belonged either to Desser or to Fascists. Pierre wanted to
stay on in Paris to have a talk with Villard, but Muñez was on
tenterhooks; he was afraid of losing the eleven A 68's. Eventually
they decided that Pierre should go to Toulouse and Muñez should
go alone to see Villard.

" I know him," Muñez said. " We used to meet at the international
congresses."

At the station Pierre sent a postcard to Agnès: " Am going away
for a week." He took his seat in the stifling, crowded train. The
sultry August weather was driving the belated Parisians to the seaside or the mountains. The conversations were all about bathing,
holiday excursions, yachts; and Pierre felt like a foreigner. He
opened the paper and without reading it kept repeating to himself:
" Medina, Medina," as Muñez had done. If only he could get to
Toulouse quickly. He wanted to jump out and give the train a push
from behind; the stops were special torture to him. Suddenly Pierre
remembered the kind, honest face of Villard and what he had said
about solidarity; and nodding with drowsiness amid the smoke and
stuffiness and conversations about bathing and excursions to the
peaks of the Pyrenees, he vaguely thought: " Villard will give everything. He won't forsake the Spaniards." Then he fell asleep.

CHAPTER 24

WHEN Muñez saw Villard, the distant past rose up before him. He remembered the Basel Congress, old Bebel's speech in the cathedral, the car with girls, the allegories, oaths, and tears. Then, just after the war, he had met Villard in Bern. They tried to stick together the Second International as if it were a porcelain cup. There were debates on the responsibility for the war, on reparations and colonies. Sixteen years had gone by. . . . In those days Villard had dark hair and a ringing voice. Now he had grown old. Like Muñez. . . .

Villard also had his memories. The two old comrades called up from semi-oblivion the shades of their youth: Plekhanov, Jaurès, Iglesias. Villard said: "When you get to a certain age, all paths lead to the cemetery. No matter where you look, there are graves."

The word "graves" roused him and he remembered why Muñez had come to see him. He had been preparing for this meeting since morning. He could not receive Muñez as the official delegate of the Government or party. Muñez was an old comrade; it was impossible to ignore that. And how was it possible to forget that he had now been overtaken by misfortune?

"They told me about your sorrow," Villard said.

Muñez turned away. He hid his suffering from everybody. In his sleepless nights he saw his beloved laughing son, Pepe. It was in the middle of the day. White walls, white dust. People were staggering with heat and fatigue. They found him in an attic, took him out and shot him.

Muñez felt as though Villard had torn the skin from his body and looked inside, and this gave a sharper edge to his suffering. He was silent. Again it was Villard who spoke:

"My friend, I understand how you feel. Three years ago I lost my wife. It's terrible to survive those you love! Very terrible! Sometimes you ask yourself: what's the good of going on? . . ."

Muñez still failed to understand what exactly it was in Villard's words that filled him with indignation, but he got up, walked the length of the room and suddenly began to speak out loud as at a meeting:

"I've come about aeroplanes. You know our situation. If you don't help us they'll crush us. The Popular Front is Socialism's final throw. Is it possible you'll betray us body and soul? I'm talking now as one Socialist to another. You see, there's still something left from those days! Yes, they've killed my son. I don't want to talk about that. But they're killing every day. Today I was informed of the shootings at Cordova. They're Jesuits, fanatics! They've brought over the Moors, the most uncivilized barbarians, with dervishes. They're burning and outraging. Comrade Villard! . . ."

"But of course we're with you with all our hearts," said Villard. "Personally I haven't had a single night's rest since the rebellion broke out. I feel your suffering as though it were my own. But you must understand: we're responsible for the life of the country. France desires peace. It's such a tragedy! After all, what has the average Frenchman got to do with the political regime of another country?"

"We don't need people," said Muñez. "We need planes. You can sell us war material in accordance with former agreements. . . ."

"If it was a war with a third power, I shouldn't have any doubt about it," said Villard. "But this is a civil war."

"Then you haven't the right to support a legitimate government against rebels?"

"Not quite that. You see everything is complicated by the international situation. Hitler and Mussolini are behind Franco. If we give you aeroplanes, this affair may end in a world war."

"And you prefer to betray us?"

"Why put it like that? You yourself realize that we want the Republic to win. But we're bound hand and foot. We can't sell you aeroplanes. Why don't you apply direct to the industrialists? You know I'll take any risk. All that's necessary is to maintain discreetness. We'll declare that we won't give anything. You'll buy and take the goods. We'll close our eyes and pretend we don't see."

"Either you don't know how matters stand or you don't want to know. I've been here a week already. The results? Eleven A 68's. And with what difficulty! It was a good thing they put us in touch with Dubois. Our comrade. . . ."

"The engineer? So you see! And yet you attack us. I know him, an excellent comrade! The A 68's are excellent bombers. What prevents your getting any more?"

"They won't sell us any. Not at any price."

" But what can we do? After all, it's their right."

" You can give us the Army planes."

" And weaken our own Air Force? No, my dear comrade, that's impossible! What will the Radicals say? The Cabinet may fall on account of a dozen aeroplanes or so. And then it will be worse for you as well. I repeat: we'll turn a blind eye to all the deliveries. We can organize help for the refugees, ambulance corps, and so on, and send bread and condensed milk for the children. But risk war? No! "

After shouting " No " several times, Villard calmed down; he wiped his forehead with his handkerchief and rang the bell.

" What can I offer you? Tea? Lemonade? "

Muñez got up.

" You realize they've occupied Medina? " he said. " They've now united with Mola's army. I'm not a diplomat. Besides, I'm sixty-four. . . . Comrade Villard, I'd better go: I'm afraid I might tell you everything, but they haven't empowered me to do that. . . . They sent me for planes."

Muñez went. Villard's lower lip trembled with resentment. The conversation had been even more difficult than he had expected. The Spaniards' cause was lost; even a child could understand that. Twenty aeroplanes would make no difference. The Popular Front had to be saved in France. One incautious move and everything would crash. Then Franco would find followers in France. And who would come to the rescue? The three hundred workers from Lans? Madness! They were pushing us into the abyss. Not the Communists, but people of our own party! Of course, it was easy to understand Muñez: it was no joke to lose a son. But so had others.

" Aeroplanes! " Villard would be cursed. And yet how was he to blame? It was impossible to govern the country and keep all your principles. With a load like that you'd soon stick in the mud. But why had he taken all this on? It was all right to be the ordinary citizen — he just voted, walked in processions, and then " sat in the bower and listened; the birds are singing." Yes, but somebody must govern. There was more than one loathsome profession: sewermen, slaughter-house butchers, prison warders. Villard began to pity himself. He was sitting hunchbacked and oppressed with this pity when his secretary came in:

" Tessa is on the telephone. He asks to speak to you on urgent business."

Tessa insisted on seeing him at once. Villard had to agree. The abominable day dragged on.

Tessa embraced Villard with his usual familiarity and immediately began to wail:

"Beware! Spain is a hornets' nest. It was there that Napoleon met disaster. And in the seventies? . . . 'The Spanish succession'!"

"I don't see the connection. . . ."

"You don't see it? You're wrong! If you give planes to the Reds, war is inevitable. Hitler won't climb down, let alone Mussolini."

"In the first place, why do you call Azaña and Giral 'Reds'? In what respect are they more 'Red' than yourself?"

"It isn't a question of Azaña," said Tessa. "Who has got the guns? The workers. And what does it matter what I call them? To the whole of Europe they're Reds. I repeat: it smacks of war."

"The conclusion to be drawn is that we're unable to maintain trade relations with a legitimate Government?" Villard said. Without realizing it he was repeating Muñez's conclusions.

"That's casuistry!" said Tessa. "You'd drive the people into slaughter on account of your political sympathies. Fine rulers! We've got to separate Rome from Berlin, but you want to weld them together."

"How is it possible to separate them, when they're working hand in hand in Spain?"

"We must pretend we don't see anything. We must go out to meet Mussolini. Then Italy will remember her Latin nature. At a time like this France needs diplomats, not party fanatics. We must be doubly cautious over the Spanish question. The Duke of Alba has been at work in London. The British are in favour of restoration. Alfonso or Franco — that's a detail. In any case the City prefers the general to the anarchists of Barcelona. In the long run France will find herself alone. You know that I'm defending the Popular Front. . . ."

"I haven't noticed it!" said Villard. "Your speech in connection with the strikes . . ."

"I saved the Cabinet! Of course I criticized your policy, otherwise I shouldn't have been able to do anything; they were all up in arms. But I moved a vote of confidence in the Government. And you know what happened then in the Radical faction? Malvy, Marchandot, Meyer, all shouted together: 'Resign!' The strike question is a matter of the past. But now the situation is far more dangerous. Malvy raves and shouts; you see, he's a friend of all these Spanish grandees. Listen, Auguste, I too prefer Azaña to General Franco. In general I'm a devoted Republican and a democrat. But nobody's asking me. And, in fact, they're not asking you either. All they ask of us is to sit still and not to interfere."

"But the others are interfering."

"In that case my reply is: what is permissible to a bull is not permissible to Jupiter. The Italians are on the rampage and so are the Germans. There's only one thing for us to do if we don't want war, and that is to keep quiet. No matter if you do give Madrid a hundred aeroplanes; they'll send Franco five hundred. It's folly to play with fire!"

"We can't forbid individual business men to sell aeroplanes to Spain."

"More casuistry? Auguste, this is not a matter of parliamentary combinations. Take care, it smells of blood! I speak with absolute assurance, you understand? With absolute assurance. They'll stop at nothing. It's no good trying to be crafty. If you let through even one aircraft, war will break out. I know you sincerely detest war, and it's for that very reason that I came to see you. It's a cry from my heart. It's the cry of all French mothers. It's the cry of France!"

"Of course I'll do everything to preserve peace," said Villard.

"I know that, but your enemies are at work. There's an uproar going on among the Radicals. Malvy is crying out that you don't wish to abide by the national interests. And they'd listen to him. I'm not even mentioning the Right. Of course Breteuil is a fool and a madman. We're not Spaniards. We're a highly civilized people. A regime like that is impossible with us. But Breteuil has enormous influence. Yesterday he declared he was going to put you in the dock as one of the warmongers. I'm convinced you'll frustrate their game. And for that reason I answer: 'Villard is the guarantee of non-intervention.' You must set me at ease; I want to hear a decisive 'yes' from you."

Tessa waved his hands, paced to a distant corner of the room, and repeated his tirades from there like adjurations. Then he went close up to Villard and spluttered over him. Villard retained his calm, and even smiled. Firmness unexpectedly revived in him. The spirit of Muñez seemed to be present in the room. An hour ago Muñez, overwhelmed by fate but proud, had stood on that very spot where

Tessa was now playing the buffoon. And Villard, who had spoken to his old comrade like a soulless diplomat, now tried to maintain his dignity in the face of Tessa's threats. He even forgot about strategy. When Tessa demanded a clear answer, he said: "I'll carry out my duty." And Tessa got nothing further out of him.

When Tessa left, Villard lay down exhausted on the sofa and began to think anxiously: "What's to be done?" His thoughts were hampered by a severe headache and a feeling of nausea. How abominable Tessa was with his shrieking and spluttering. How was it possible for women to love him? . . . Yes, but somebody had sent Tessa. The Right Radicals. Breteuil, perhaps. Maybe the Italians from the Embassy. A complicated game! . . . It was true they were on the rampage. Did it mean war? But what would the people say? For forty years he had been denouncing war and now he would send millions of people to their death. In Spain they were already killing. . . .

Closing his eyes, he saw the fly-infested corpses, the mangled bodies, the shattered houses. What was to be done? Tessa had said: "Not a single aeroplane!" Yes, the Radicals might leave the Cabinet. And forgetting about the miseries of war, Villard became absorbed in his usual political arithmetic — calculating how many votes the Government would collect on the question of Spain. A minority of course! Then the Radicals would come to an agreement with the Right — a bloc stretching from Tessa to Breteuil. That would be the beginning of the end: a Cabinet of that sort would be a short step for Breteuil, who was dreaming of a dictatorship. It was far more dangerous than the 6th of February. The shopkeepers and farmers were frightened by the strikes and would follow Breteuil. The Socialist Party would be dissolved. The Supreme Court. They'd put Villard on trial: "He tried to provoke war." It was only necessary to shoot down one aeroplane to find out everything. The Public Prosecutor would say: "A 68's with the co-operation of Villard. . . ." No, such things were not to be played with!

Until ten o'clock in the evening Villard racked his brains, not knowing what to decide. At last, frowning with headache and weariness, he sent for the Chief of the Secret Police:

"I'm told that an engineer named Pierre Dubois is trying to transfer eleven A 68 bombers to Barcelona. This may give rise to international complications. The aeroplanes must be held back. Do you think it can be done?"

"Quite simple. They must be either at one of the Seine aero-dromes here or at Toulouse. I'll see to it at once."

When the Chief of the Police had gone, Villard lay down on the sofa again. He took two headache powders. The medicine induced a state of coma in him. He could hardly move his arms; he felt an ache in the pit of his stomach, and his feet were cold. He tried not to think about anything. He had done all he could for the time being, and now he must wait. Nevertheless, the word "betrayal" kept on coming into his head and refused to be dismissed. "Non-sense!" he said to himself. "I'm not betraying anyone! The Span-iards' cause is lost, in any case. Eleven aeroplanes against two hun-dred! . . . Children! Like the workers of Lans. This way I shall save the Popular Front. And our party. And peace. I've done my duty. That's all." He reassured himself as a mother reassures a frightened child. But again from out of the surrounding gloom — he had put out the light — the same harsh word came floating back like a black slippery fish.

Suddenly he remembered the little frontier town of Cerbère, where he had often been in days gone by — on one occasion with Pierre's father. He remembered the pink houses in the foothills of the Pyrenees, the fishermen's boats, the vineyards, the big noisy rail-way station. And the sweet wine like muscatel. Now they would bless him at Cerbère. They were next door to war; you had only to climb up the little hill or go through the short tunnel. Across the frontier there were shattered houses and wailing women in tears. But at Cerbère the mothers would say: "Villard has saved peace. Villard has saved our children. Villard . . ." He fell asleep re-peating his own name.

CHAPTER 25

"It's impossible!" Pierre exclaimed. "I'll ring up Villard."

They were standing beside a lamp in the pouring rain. An un-ceasing deluge seemed to be determined to drown everything. The boards underfoot were floating. Streams of water poured off the police superintendent's cape.

"Orders from Paris. No doubt they're acting in agreement with the Minister. . . ."

And in Madrid they were waiting! Today the radio had said the Fascists were advancing. Pierre tried to get into touch with Paris. He waited for a long time at the telephone. A well-fed cat was sleeping on the desk. The rain rattled down. At last Pierre got Villard's secretary on the wire. The secretary was polite and cold: "I'll give your message to Monsieur le Ministre. . . . Monsieur le Ministre is engaged. . . . I don't think Monsieur le Ministre would wish to interfere in police matters. . . ." Pierre realized the conversation was useless and put down the receiver. He vaguely thought: "The secretary's a Socialist too!" Out loud he said: "I'll leave for Paris by the first train."

The superintendent did not answer.

Pierre went into a little café near the station. People shook their clothes as they came in; inside there was the snugness peculiar to any shelter in bad weather.

Pierre was so busy with his own thoughts that when the proprietress asked him what he was going to have he failed at first to understand. At that moment all his thoughts were centred on Madrid. He saw a circle on the map with four arrows directed towards it. Muñez had reported that the eleven A 68's would arrive in Barcelona tomorrow. The people there had taken heart and were waiting. And now everything had miscarried! Could it possibly be Villard? The very suspicion horrified Pierre; he was indignant at his own baseness. Suspect Villard! He drank a glass of cognac, smoked cigarette after cigarette, and tried to listen to the talk at the next table — about a certain Marie who had poisoned the neighbours' rabbits. He listened to the rain and remembered the eyes of Agnès, and the dim lamp under the deluge of water. But it was no use: his thoughts kept returning to Villard. His suspicions were painful and heavy, like the first symptoms of a serious illness. He remembered Michaud's caustic words and Muñez's stories of how the Socialists had received him. No, it was all a concoction. Perhaps he really was going to be ill. He was feeling chilly despite the warm damp air of the café. There were still two hours to go before the train left. He tried to doze, read the advertisements in the local paper about the sale of mules and calves, recalled disjointed scraps of poetry. And again Villard's face appeared to him — he was smiling on the platform under the red flag. But what had happened? It must be simply that the secretary was a nonentity, a petty jack-in-office. But the police were obstructing. Why hadn't Villard cleaned up the police? They were Fascists, as if they had been picked for that very reason. The superintendent had called the Spanish Government "the Reds" and laughed disdainfully. He must be a member of Breteuil's gang! No doubt they'd remove him. Only it was a pity that a whole day had been lost. And in Spain they were waiting and waiting. . . . What a weary thought!

All was now quiet in the café. Some of the people had left; others were dozing while waiting for the night train. The plump, podgy proprietress was also dozing with her ball of green wool pressed to her belly. A workman in the corner was proving something to one of his mates as he dipped his bread in red wine. Pierre listened.

"The whole affair is in Spain now. I'm going there. You see if I don't. We've got to help them; otherwise it'll be the end of us as well."

Pierre had to restrain himself; he wanted to go up and shake the man by the hand or shout out: "Quite right!" He merely smiled; the workman understood and winked cunningly in reply.

On arriving in Paris, Pierre went at once to the Ministry. He was told that the Minister was engaged. For two hours Pierre sat in the waiting-room among the callers, most of whom were Socialists who wanted to wheedle out of Villard either the Legion of Honour or some sinecure. A nervous little lady twittered: "You see, I knew him when he was an agitator. He won't refuse me." Villard received her; he received the other applicants also, but Pierre still waited. At last they told him: "The Minister has gone to lunch. He'll be back at three o'clock."

Pierre sat on a bench in the boulevard till three. Life went on as usual around him. Dressmakers were lunching on rolls and a piece of chocolate. Ladies rummaged in the bolts of silk outside a shop. Taxi-drivers hurled abuse at one another. Old men fed the sparrows. Guides pointed out the sights to phlegmatic English visitors. Middlemen passed one another the latest Stock Exchange quotations. Nobody was concerned about Madrid. But Pierre anxiously wondered: "Will they take Talavera? . . ." The hands of the clock seemed to have gone to sleep. It seemed to Pierre as though he had sat there all day. But it was not yet three o'clock.

After lunch Villard returned to the Ministry. Pierre sat in the waiting-room as before. This time he was alone; the reception was over. At last a secretary came out to him.

"Monsieur le Ministre begs you to excuse him: he's engaged on urgent work. He has asked me to discuss the matter with you."

Pierre began to tell about the superintendent's arbitrary action. The secretary interrupted him.

"Monsieur le Ministre is fully acquainted with the matter," he said. "We are Socialists and can talk frankly. . . . The situation is very grave. We must make a choice. If we go to the aid of the Spaniards, we may lose everything. There will be war, and at home the triumph of Fascism."

"But Franco is in Madrid. It's Breteuil here!"

"I don't think that's quite the correct point of view. Spain is a backward, semi-feudal country, the borderland of Europe. Which is more important? To defend the Spanish Republic, which has been artificially created and has no roots, or to save the cause of Socialism in an advanced country which happens, moreover, to be our own country? Monsieur le Ministre has decided to adopt a policy of strict non-intervention."

Then Pierre lost his head. The anguish of the last few weeks — from the storm in the Breton village to the bench on the boulevard and people's indifferent laughter, the sleepless night with his poignant trust in Villard's honesty, the anxiety over Madrid — all this poured itself out in a single cry:

"Monsieur le Ministre? Judas, you mean!"

It was so unexpected that the secretary said:

"Excuse me, I don't think I quite understand."

But Pierre was already running down the purple-carpeted stairway, under the mocking looks of the flunkeys: "So you didn't get your soft job!"

In vain Pierre rushed along the streets in the hope of recovering his senses. The anguish was too keen; nothing could assuage it. He no longer tried to make out how his idol could have fallen so low. He only felt the horror of loss, the emptiness that prevented him from breathing. So Agnès was right, and all he had lived for was an illusion, crafty nets spread for the simple-minded, a mutual-benefit society of deception? He had been cheated like a simpleton. An hour ago he still believed in the goodness of people, in the sentiment of comradeship, and in the cause that was the breath of his life. How would he appear in the eyes of Muñez? Talavera. . . .

The recollection of Spain brought him to his senses. No, there was still a great deal in the world that hadn't changed in that wretched hour! The men of Madrid were still fighting. They had no A 68's, only shotguns. Pierre would go there, and die there. The thought of death appeared to him as the way out.

He jumped on a bus; he would go at once to Michaud! Michaud would tell him how to get to Madrid.

Michaud understood everything at once.

" They've held them up, eh? "

" Yes. All of them. You know who? Villard. You understand? I think I shall go mad. Look here. I want to go to Madrid; you must help me. But I don't even want to talk about him. What's the good of talking? "

Michaud realized how deeply Pierre was suffering; he shook his hand in silence. They were standing by the window. Outside, the children were playing leap-frog.

After a long silence, Michaud said: " Muñez has got an offer of three Potez planes. He doesn't understand anything about it. You're the only expert we've got. I realize how you feel. We're recruiting volunteers. Maybe I'll go myself. But you mustn't. Everything will miscarry without you here. . . . "

Pierre did not object. All right. Tomorrow he would go to the aerodrome. All right, he would stay. The last loophole of escape was now closed.

Out in the street again, Pierre looked around him in perplexity. Where was he to go? Afterwards he himself could never understand why he dragged himself right across Paris to André, or what he thought to find in the uncomfortable, untidy studio in the rue Cherche-Midi.

Six months had passed since their last meeting; to Pierre it seemed like decades. He was still a greenhorn then. . . .

" How are you getting on, André? "

What could André say? Was he to tell Pierre how he had been stirred by the events of the terrible summer, how he had found and lost Jeannette?

" I've started on a still life, but I can't get on with it."

Pierre looked at him in amazement:

" You're still just the same, André. Remember how I dragged you along to the Maison de Culture? "

André whistled. "Did you know that Lucien was in Spain? he said.

"It was in the papers. He's got a diplomatic job."

"Really? But I thought he was fighting. . . ."

Pierre smiled. "He's a child," he thought, "like the Pierre that used to be!" He began to tell André about Villard. As always, he lived aloud. He felt as though he wanted even the canvases on the walls to expose the traitor. But André was silent. Impulsively Pierre asked: "What do you think? Can you understand it?"

"I suppose it's possible."

"To understand such deceit? They used to tell me how he once worked with my father to save a certain Spaniard. And now he's handing them all over. Is it possible to understand that, to understand betrayal?"

"Remember Goya's portraits. . . ."

Quite beside himself, Pierre cried out:

"There you go with your art! But are you really human beings? You find delight in everything: blood, misery, tainted meat. Like dung beetles!" He ran out on the landing and shouted from there: "I'm sorry. I'll come another time."

And it was only after he had gone that André felt offended. He went out on the stairs, but Pierre was nowhere to be seen. André puffed mournfully at his pipe. Why had Pierre insulted him? He had only said it was possible to understand. Of course it was. He could see right through a man like Villard. But Lucien? A wag-tail! Better to live with dogs! No doubt they scrapped among themselves and tore one another's fur out, but they did it without fine phrases, and that was something to be thankful for! But Pierre was wrong to offend him; he didn't like treachery.

Pierre had a difficult time. He hated working at the factory: what was the good of putting your heart into it when these engines would go to Franco, or Breteuil? The three Potez planes were successfully transferred to Spain. A month later a couple of fighters were delivered; but all this was only a drop in the ocean. Madrid kept sending telegrams in despair. The French police never took their eyes off the planes. And Villard's dignified features were seen everywhere on the newspaper kiosks. He spoke of non-intervention as though it were a noble exploit: "We have saved peace!" He donated five thousand francs to buy milk for the Spanish children, stipulating that it should be "for all children."

That day Pierre said to Agnès: " However much I love children, I feel that if Villard had a child, I'd strangle it. . . ."

Day after day German bombs were shattering the houses of Madrid. The walls of Paris were covered with placards showing the photographs of bombed and mutilated children. Agnès said it was torture to look at them. Pierre said nothing; he had been tortured for so long. Franco had taken Toledo and was advancing on Madrid. Some of the papers glorified the Fascists who had defended the Alcázar. Others reported that the Moors had slaughtered hundreds of wounded in Toledo. Joliot wrote: " Our ancient French wisdom preserves us from such misfortunes." Breteuil's women friends made preparations for parties to celebrate the fall of Madrid. But the Spanish people did not yield.

Pierre felt Villard's betrayal as an all-round betrayal: his own, that of Agnès, and that of France. And the betrayal became like a persistent stench, a bad taste in the mouth which it was impossible to overcome. Pierre hated Paris because it went on living without giving up a single one of its customary ways: there were the same cafés crowded with people at the apéritif hour, the same political discussions and card-playing — bridge or poker — the same music halls with naked actresses. There were no sirens, no bombs, not even a stingy tear, nothing.

The schools opened. Children shouted as they scampered along with their new satchels and pencil-cases. Pierre knew how their carefree laughter was being paid for: they were fighting in the suburbs of Madrid. The late gold of the chestnut trees glowed on the boulevards of Paris. It was the shooting season. Tessa had been invited to Marquise de Chambrun's house-party; after shooting a pheasant he had disappeared with a young housemaid. This story was going round the lobbies of the Chamber. But Villard disliked blood sports; he couldn't bear the sight of blood; he was a pacifist. And Pierre said angrily: " Why isn't he a vegetarian? . . ."

Only Michaud did not lose heart. He was soon going to Spain with the first detachment of volunteers. Pierre looked at Michaud with admiration and envy. There was a man for you! What was it he said? — " It's harder to conquer. . . ." And Pierre, too, seemed to be on the way to understanding it. Once upon a time they used to represent victory as winged. But her feet were heavy and blistered, covered with blood and dust.

CHAPTER 26

LUCIEN disliked his life as a diplomat. The office work did not take up much of his time, but he didn't know what to do with his leisure hours. He looked with indifference at the sumptuous Renaissance façades, the students and mules. He couldn't live without the Paris cafés with their aimless discussions, without the gossip and dramas that were as familiar to him as his own bed or cigarette-holder. So Lucien was on the point of giving up a decent salary when the events in Spain suddenly caught him in their grip. Once again this man, who was like those roadside signs which light up in the glare of headlights, decided that he had found the truth.

The rebellion aroused Lucien's enthusiasm above all by its outward effects. At times he thought he was assisting at the staging of some old mystery play. People with elongated ascetic faces killed and burned the unbelievers. Some, brandishing crosses, took death for their bride. Cripples, whose number in Spain is legion, hunchbacks, the blind, and monsters crept out of their hovels everywhere. Women in mantillas embraced the machine-gunners, and lace fans fluttered over the hand-grenades. All this was something out of the ordinary for Lucien and it fascinated him by its theatrical variety, lack of taste, and violently accentuated tone.

He got to know one of the Falangist leaders, a dry, dismal major named José Guarnez, a cold fanatic who shot people by day and preached at night. Lucien was amazed to find that this Spanish officer repeated his own secret thoughts. José talked of the sacredness of social rank, the splendour of inequality, the subjection of the mob to reason, talent, and will. And Lucien recalled his humiliation in Paris, that blockhead on *L'Humanité*, the mediocrity of Pierre and of all Pierres, the arithmetic of elections, and his own superiority, which nobody appreciated. The Falangists had obtained recognition with fire. José wrote pamphlets without bothering about the opinions of tailors or coal-miners. Lucien had always said that the old world could only be overthrown by the daring of the few, by a conspiracy. The Communists had laughed at him for this; they talked about educating the people and rousing the masses to action. They were living in the past: Marx, the Commune, de-

mocracy, progress — it was all rubbish! How could they fail to see
that Marxism was linked up with the " Declaration of Rights," the
Encyclopædists, belief in science, and with the horrible idea of the
positive principle of man? Society was not a square building like
this house, but a pyramid! Fascism would bring new standards:
instead of books, enthusiasm for physical strength and athletic
records; instead of parliamentary reports and debates, the armed
seizure of Government buildings; instead of elections, tommy-guns.

There was something else in this Spaniard's conversation that inspired Lucien — the cult of death. Since Henri's death Lucien had
long realized the significance of non-existence, its power over all
the reactions of the young and fiery heart. He had written a novel
on the subject. His enthusiasm for Communism was a slip of the
pen. He had been momentarily infected with other people's gaiety,
the childish hubbub, the fawning attitude towards youth. To José,
as well as to Lucien, death was not only a subject for reflection, but
an absolute value, a corrective to accidental and therefore precari-
ous life.

Lucien gave himself up to his new enthusiasm; and when the
major suggested he should go to Paris and put the Falangists in
touch with Breteuil, he agreed at once.

He did not even ask Paris or the Embassy. He didn't want to
think about his job; it humiliated him. He made the journey via
Jaca. The car rushed along the winding roads among the red-
brown, sun-scorched hills. Not a villager, not a soul! The landscape
matched Lucien's feelings; death appeared to him as a sister — red-
brown and burning.

After the magic atmosphere of Spain how trivial seemed the
fields of France, her peaceful occupations, and the talk about vacations with pay, and taxes! Everything was flourishing, and on the
very first day he heard that cursed epilogue: " Everything is settling
down."

His father greeted him with open arms. Lucien was no longer
the prodigal son, but a diplomat (Lucien wisely refrained from
telling his father why he had come). Tessa didn't ask his son about
the situation in Spain. He considered that Franco's victory was a
foregone conclusion; the rest didn't interest him. On the other hand,
he told Lucien about his own plans. He had been appointed chairman of the Foreign Affairs Commission. He was also studying the
secret reports of the Foreign Office; at the necessary moment he

would make a thundering speech and bring down the Cabinet. Lucien yawned; parliamentary cookery again!

Breteuil knew how to deal with a variety of people: he was rough with the " Faithful " of the Grisnez type, and could charm and even flatter the deputies. He treated Lucien as an equal, and Lucien opened out — at last he was appreciated. At first they talked about propaganda: Franco's rebellion must be held up as an example. Breteuil was collecting money for a gold sword, which he wanted to present to the defender of the Alcázar, Colonel Moscardo. Then Breteuil began to discuss active measures — the shipment of arms, the dispatch of pilots to Burgos, and liaison work, for instance — the material of the Intelligence Service in Barcelona was going through Paris.

" When are you leaving? " Breteuil asked.

" I don't know."

Breteuil laid his dry, parchment-like hand on Lucien's arm.

" I'm older than you, but life is not to be measured by the years of the calendar. You know what real hatred is. Why go back to Spain? Everything is going to be decided here."

" A conspiracy? "

" Yes."

Breteuil told Lucien about the brigades of the " Faithful."

" You're going to play an important role in this," he said. " Your father — "

" I've got nothing in common with my father! "

" I understand. But your father is now chairman of the Parliamentary Commission. They're hiding a good deal from me. Thanks to you, we'll be in a position to carry on the game, while having had a look at our opponent's hand. Of course, it's not quite so romantic as the battle for Madrid. But everything has its time. . . ."

Lucien nodded. As he was leaving he said to Breteuil:

" Do you know why I'm willing to do everything — even this? Each generation has its destiny. You can call it historical fatalism if you like. We accept death not as the decay of the cells, nor as the aimless rotation of matter, nor as a passing over to the other world, but as a higher individual creative power."

Breteuil glanced at the handsome young man with the chestnut hair.

" Perhaps you're right," he said mournfully, " but I can't give up my faith in personal immortality. My son died. . . ."

Lucien very nearly had a serious quarrel with his father. When Tessa learned that his son had neglected his diplomatic career, he stamped his foot and wailed. Lucien was unable to explain his reasons to him; and moreover he was obliged to ask his father for several thousand francs.

Gradually the Spanish impressions began to fade from Lucien's mind. The conspiracy seemed to him to be little more than a game: there was no plan, no definite date. Breteuil kept on saying: "We must wait." But José's friends were already approaching Madrid. Lucien carefully acquainted himself with the contents of the various documents on his father's desk and gave reports to Breteuil. But this took up comparatively little of his time, and boredom lay in wait for him in the corridor of his father's house, in Breteuil's waiting-room, and in the evening streets.

In his efforts to kill time, Lucien accepted every invitation, danced, told fantastic stories, and flirted with young society girls. The daughter of a big industrialist named Montigny fell in love with him. Josephine was a plump, giggling girl; she was fascinated by Lucien's romantic face, his stories of Spanish fanaticism and the fact that in the middle of polite conversation he would suddenly turn silent, gaze fixedly at one spot, and smile vaguely. When Tessa was told about his son's flirtation, he beamed with pleasure; Lucien couldn't be such a fool after all, if he was exchanging a vice-consul's job for a rich bride!

Josephine was expecting a proposal and made dates with Lucien in empty tea-rooms or in the Bois de Boulogne. But Lucien did not seem to notice her feelings. One day she could bear it no longer and took hold of Lucien's hand. It was a bright autumn day; they were walking along a red and copper avenue in the Bois. In the distance a woman on horseback was cracking a whip. Josephine blushed all over and turned away. Lucien cautiously released his hand.

"Let's be frank," he said. "I like you. Besides, you're rich. And yesterday I had to pawn my watch. . . . All the same, I couldn't touch you with a finger. You're twenty-three. You're always laughing. And me? I'm like my friend José, I've taken death for my bride."

CHAPTER 27

WHEN Tessa heard that Lucien had stopped seeing Josephine, he had a fit of the dumps: nothing good would ever come out of that loafer! But another blow awaited him. He was dozing over a report from the Ambassador in Rome when Denise came into his study. He was delighted; all this time he had scarcely seen anything of his beloved daughter. Amalie had told him that Denise was not feeling well, out of sorts. Tessa had realized that Denise was angry with him ever since the evening when he had told her about his success in Parliament. Oh, these politics! They had ruined the whole summer for him. Amalie didn't go to take the waters, declaring that she didn't want to share her beloved Vittel "with the rabble." Lucien had returned unexpectedly from Spain. And Denise — well, perhaps she really was ill; she looked very pale and there were rings under her eyes. He wanted to ask her about her health, but he wasn't given an opportunity.

"I'm leaving," Denise said. "I'm going to live by myself."

Tessa even wailed with displeasure:

"Well, I'll be damned. With some young man?"

"No, alone."

Tessa looked at his daughter in amazement. No doubt about it, she was ill. He tried to restrain himself; he became polite, concealing his feelings with irony:

"Perhaps you'll be so kind as to explain your reasons to me?"

"I thought you'd understand yourself — after that conversation. There's nothing else I can do. I don't want to live at your expense."

Tessa was beside himself. "You prefer to go and be kept by some parasite like your infernal brother?"

"I knew it was impossible to explain to you. Perhaps that's your justification. Lucien is to blame all round, because he could live differently if he wanted to. But you do everything naturally, as a matter of course: you take money, you shield blackguards, you harass the Spaniards. And now it's just as natural for you to insult me. We'd better not talk."

"Wait! Where are you going?"

"I've got a place of my own. I've taken a room."

"With your mother's money, I suppose, which means to say with mine?"

"No. I'm working in an office."

"And how much do they pay you for your learned labours?"

"Eight hundred francs a month."

Tessa smiled artificially:

"Very luxurious! It was worth while having you educated! Wait!"

He took her distractedly by the hand, like a child. Pity took the place of anger. Poor little thing! This was nothing but nerves. Time the girl was married. He told Amalie so long ago. . . .

"Denise, don't be silly. You need a rest and medical treatment. It's just common or garden neurasthenia. I had attacks like that when I was young. Wait!"

But Denise went out. Tessa overtook her in the hall and began to thrust money into her hand:

"Take it, you crazy girl! . . . Please take it! For my sake! . . ."

Denise went off without the money. Tessa went back to his study, lay down on the sofa, and suddenly began to cry. He was surprised at his own tears and wondered if he had ever cried before. The silly girl! She would ruin herself. How was it possible to live on eight hundred francs! She wouldn't be able to stand a month of it; she'd probably go with somebody for a pair of stockings and then be done for. And all on account of those damned politics! Why did he ever take up the cursed business?

As soon as she was outside the odious house, Denise experienced a feeling of relief. Although she was reputed to be unsociable, a "marmot," she never stopped smiling. The respectable poverty with which she was now obliged to become acquainted failed to diminish her cheerfulness. The grumbling book-keeper mockingly called her "our little bird." In the dark office, where the lights had to be turned on all day, she smiled over the correspondence about tons of English anthracite. She also smiled at home: she had taken an attic room in a small hotel. The dark, spiral staircase smelled of damp and cheap powder. There was hardly space for the bed in the tiny room with its dirty wallpaper. But even this little hole seemed beautiful to Denise, and for the first time the dim mirror hanging on the wall reflected a cheerful face.

Her decision had taken a long time to mature. It was on one of
the early spring evenings after she had first met Michaud that she
vaguely felt the beginning of her emancipation. And now the
autumn rain pattered all through the night on the little attic
window. It had needed all the events of the summer, the conversations with Michaud, and long solitary reflections to help Denise
to find herself at last. But her forehead with its frown of amusement
and her smile indicated that her decision was irrevocable. So it was
that when she met Michaud one evening after a long interval, she
said simply:

"And now about action. . . . I want to do something for Spain.
My evenings are free."

They were walking along the boulevard Sébastopol. There was
a thick fog in the streets, the first fog of autumn in Paris. The street
lamps seemed to float in the billowing yellow clouds. It was impossible to make out anything, and the passers-by kept on bumping
into one another. Mingled with the rolling moisture were the smells
of roasted chestnuts, perfumes, and smoke. And the red letters of
the shop-signs: "Frégate," "Lippe," "Flowers," alternately appeared and disappeared through the wreaths of fog.

"I wanted to ring you up," Michaud said.

"I've no telephone now. I've left home."

He understood everything and squeezed her hand. She began to
laugh; her merry eyes gleamed through the fog like the letters of
the shop-signs.

They arrived at the committee rooms. One word was on everybody's lips: "Madrid." It was being repeated on all sides: by young
lads who yearned to fight, women with children at their breasts
who brought their scanty savings for the mothers of Madrid, workers, artists, waiters, students, foreigners. All the harassed but live
conscience of Paris concentrated in those two crowded rooms that
were decorated with a plan of Madrid and a paper flag of the Spanish Republic. There was anxiety in their voices as they said:
"They're advancing on Madrid." They consoled themselves with
the hope: "They'll throw them back!" They offered their money,
their services, their lives.

Denise arranged to come there every evening. Michaud smiled
as he noticed her simple way of calling everybody "Comrade" —
as though she had talked like that all her life.

Michaud saw her home through the fog. On the way he bought

some roasted chestnuts; Denise warmed her frozen fingers with them and told him about her new life.

"The book-keeper is an awful grouch. He's always saying 'There! You've made me make another blot!' And the manager is a Fascist and a frightful creature. He says Madrid has already been taken. He asked me to go to the movies with him and hinted that it was in his power to raise my salary or fire me. I told him I had a jealous lover who was a dead shot and he laid off at once."

They laughed. They were both feeling gay. In this fog where no one knew where they were going, they found their happiness.

Later on Michaud said: "I'm leaving the day after tomorrow."

"You're going to Spain?"

He nodded.

"Michaud, you'll come back?"

He was silent.

"I know you'll come back."

Michaud did not answer; he suddenly felt sad. Why had it all turned out so awkwardly? They had met and were talking, but there was something they hadn't mentioned. Now he was going away. . . .

"Michaud, I want you to come back."

Michaud cheered up again.

"Of course I'll come back," he said. "We'll win, and I'll come back. And then . . ."

They had reached the hotel. Its dim light was scarcely visible; they nearly walked past it. They said good-bye in a simple way, as always. But Denise suddenly looked back, rushed to Michaud, and kissed him awkwardly on the cheek. When he had recovered from his surprise, she had vanished. For a long time he stood alone smiling to himself. Luminous wreaths of fog went floating past.

CHAPTER 28

ON the evening when the workers of the Seine factory were gathered together to celebrate the departure of their comrades for Spain, the newspapers reported the statement made by the Soviet representative to the London Non-Intervention Committee. The few lines of the brief telegram stirred the workers of Paris. In the streets, in the Metro, and in the cafés people were saying: "Now the Spaniards are not alone!"

Michaud felt as though he was celebrating his birthday. Another joy had been added to that of departure — the triumph of the idea to which he had devoted his life. He was excited when he began his speech:

"For how long was this only a dream! What was the dream of Babeuf, who inspired the sans-culottes of Saint-Antoine? Before his execution he said to his judges: 'Our revolution is only the forerunner of another, greater, and more beautiful!' In 1848 the blue-bloused workers died under the fusillades of the Guards: Work or death! Communism was to them a vague dream, magic bread, workshops as in a fairy-tale; and as the fathers died, they said to their children: 'The era of the social revolution will come!' Out of superstition, they did not call it by its name. But their children raised the flag of the Commune. The forts of Paris defended themselves, as Madrid is now doing. The Versailles rulers shot tens of thousands of the best; and waiting for the bullet, the prisoners in the orange-houses of Versailles shouted: 'It will come!' It was a dream. The strikers of Fourmies died for it. Jaurès died for it. The soldiers in the casemates of Verdun and in the trenches of Champagne dreamed about it. That dream has become living reality, a country, an enormous State. And nothing can hide it away or wipe it out. We are going to fight not for what may be, but for what already exists."

By order of Blum and Villard the frontier was closed. Nevertheless hundreds of volunteers crossed the Pyrenees every day. Some went by train with papers proving them to be travelling salesmen or journalists; others went on foot by mountain paths.

Michaud was accompanied by eight other workers, for whom the appropriate papers had been obtained. Michaud went as the special correspondent of *La Voie Nouvelle*; Pierre had got the necessary papers for him. The batch of ninety-four volunteers was leaving for Perpignan; from there they were to be sent on to Catalonia.

The train was to leave at eight o'clock in the evening. A large crowd gathered in the Quai d'Orsay station to see the volunteers off. Several people stood near the first- and second-class cars; young married couples were laughing; an old man bought a magazine with a naked woman on the cover; a lady at a window was nervously fussing with a bunch of flowers. Porters were hoisting up suitcases plastered with hotel labels of various colours. Among the passengers were business men, ladies of Paris seeking refuge in the south from the autumn fogs, and officials going to Algiers. One or two mentioned the events in Spain: " Madrid will be taken either today or tomorrow. And then everything will quiet down. . . ."

But it was a different crowd which collected round the third-class cars. Red roses and carnations were conspicuous, looking like tiny flags amid the smoke and bustle. The friends, comrades, mothers, and wives of the volunteers had come to see them off. Their whispered words of love and loyalty were mingled with a joyful buzz — " Now they won't get Madrid! " — shouts and songs. Denise was lost in the crowd and it was only when the guard shouted: " All aboard! " that she pushed forward and caught Michaud by the coat-sleeve, saying quietly: " I shall wait."

The whistle blew. Fists were raised on the platform, and fists appeared at the windows of the four third-class cars. A woman standing by one of the first-class cars exclaimed: " What a disgrace! " Denise waved her handkerchief. Through the fog she saw Michaud lean out of the window; he shouted: " And how! " The old mother of one of the volunteers was weeping and sobbing; the red lights gleamed in the darkness of the tunnel, and the song of the new war floated back through the fog.

Michaud was so tired after all the excitement of the last few days that he fell asleep at once. In his sleep he heard the rumbling of the wheels, the arguments, and the names of the stations. He woke up at dawn somewhere near Narbonne. The train was passing by the side of grey lakes with deserted, reedy shores. Birds flitted low over the still water. Farther on, the water became flushed with the rosy light of the sun. In these moments Michaud's thoughts were of Denise, the warmth of her hand, and her last words. He did not feel sadness, but a great tranquillity.

Then came the sea. How peaceful it all was! Everything about it seemed to have been created for happiness — the vineyards, the southern sun, the light nets of the fishermen. But war was close by, just over those mountains. Everybody in the car woke up. They looked eagerly at the mountains, now purple, now brick-red; beyond them was destiny.

The Spanish frontier guards who met the train, which was now almost empty except for the volunteers, raised their clenched fists.

Near the first ruins children were whistling the *Riego March* with its sad careless notes.

Six months later Lieutenant Michaud of the Paris Commune Battalion, with a hundred Frenchmen, was defending a small half-demolished village near Madrid. They arrived there an hour before dawn. All around was the Castilian sierra, like a petrified sea. How little these people resembled the surrounding landscape! Everything about them was different — their cheerful lively faces, their jokes, and their fluid speech. They were unable to blend with this cruel and beautiful land or with its inhabitants, so full of dignity, sternness, and hidden passion. The children of mocking and playful Paris felt they were strangers in the land; only their faith in the common cause and the cordiality of the Spaniards eased their nostalgia.

The Fascists began to advance about seven o'clock in the morning after a short artillery preparation. Four machine-gunners were killed by a shell. Michaud and his comrades lay in some hastily dug trenches on the top of a hill. They saw the Fascists creeping forward by the rocky escarpments. Machine-gun fire held up the enemy, but a second wave followed the first. Michaud gave the order: " Use the grenades! "

It lasted only a few minutes, but it seemed to him like a whole day. They beat off the attack. Michaud's comrade, the locksmith Genteuil, died at noon; he was tortured with anxious thoughts and kept on saying: "Tell —" but Michaud failed to make out the words.

In the evening a Spanish battalion relieved the French. Out of their original hundred only forty-two remained alive; seventeen were sent to hospital.

The French lit a fire, warmed their swollen feet, and made soup. Somebody heaved a sigh: there was nothing to put in the soup! Usually when they were resting they joked and sang. Today, in spite of their military success, they were all sad; they had left so many friends among the rocks and prickly shrubs on the hill. And the evening was cold, with an icy wind blowing. The men were poorly clad and hunched their backs in the cold. One of them swore all the time; it was obvious his curses helped to relieve him. He swore at everything: the soup, the wind, the Fascists, the war.

The village was empty: the inhabitants had fled. Only two or three little houses showed faint gleams of light. An old woman came up like a ghost out of the darkness and approached the fire. She was an ordinary peasant woman in a black dress with a black kerchief on her head. She said something to Michaud which he did not understand — with great difficulty he had learned a few words of Spanish. The old woman went away and came back with a ham and began pointing at it with her fingers: " Eat! " Michaud remembered Jeannot's mother; this woman was like Clémence. He heard her sigh. No doubt, she was saying: " They'll kill you, too! " How small was the world and how quickly everything could be understood!

Michaud said to the comrade sitting next to him: " They say to us: ' You're fighting for us.' No, we're fighting for Paris, for France. Genteuil died for Paris today. I went to his place once. He used to live at Montrouge. A little square, and down below a café. . . ."

And the comrade quietly began to sing: " Ah, Paris, my village! "

CHAPTER 29

PARIS went on with its usual life: theatrical first nights, the autumn session of the Chamber, new fashions, the inevitable bank crash, the sensational kidnapping of a rich American woman, a few romances, a few suicides. Tessa still hoped to overthrow Blum; but in the lobbies they were saying that the Government had grown stronger: the policy of non-intervention had pacified the Radicals. Both the red and the tricolour flags had disappeared. Desser was triumphant: he had rightly banked on the good sense of the people. In other countries people were killing one another, tightening their belts, and piling up armaments, building fortresses and prisons, and hailing their leaders and generals; but Paris went on applauding Maurice Chevalier, who sang without a blush for the thousandth time: " Paris is still Paris. . . ."

Nevertheless, under the surface of this peaceful life a struggle was going on, stifled passions were seething like whirlpools. Families had broken up and Tessa was not the only one to lose his domestic calm these days. The arguments in the cafés sometimes ended in shooting, more often in a silent rupture. Everything was determined by foreign geographical terms and by the struggle in a neighbouring but infinitely far-off country. Paris was split into two camps. All who had been infuriated by the strikes in the summer, and, fearing for their property, had closed their shutters when the demonstrators passed their houses, now hopefully stuck little red and yellow flags into the map. And in the workers' quarters the people looked at the same map and said: " Madrid is holding out! "

By the middle of November even Breteuil's newspapers had to admit that General Franco's troops had been held at the very gates of Madrid. The working-class suburbs of Paris repeated the miraculous words that had come from the banks of the Manzanares: " They shall not pass! "

Legends were circulating about the heroism of the workers of Madrid. People related the deeds of the international brigades as though they were the exploits of Roland; and more than once the metal-workers or textile-workers added with pride: " Our men are there too! Duval . . . Jacques . . . Henri. . . ."

After reading the morning papers Villard smiled. Madrid was holding out. Sour grapes! Since the day when he became a Minister, he no longer thought about the war of ideologies, the class struggle, or the life of the world. For him politics had now become a matter of concessions to one side or the other, a daily and at times an hourly calculation, of the Government's majority, appointments, rewards, and transfers. The world became as narrow as a room crowded with precious and fragile bric-à-brac: there was no space to turn round or move a hand. And now, telling himself that Madrid was holding out, Villard broke out of this crowded room for a moment and gave a gasp of joy: they were fine fellows after all! He even thought: " Our people are there too! There are Socialist workmen among them."

To his secretary he said: " Have you seen the news? Breteuil celebrated victory too soon. The workers are not like his ' Faithful,' who run away like rabbits at the least thing."

Shortly afterwards, Villard devoted himself to the tedious tasks of the day. The reception began. He was obliged to give evasive replies, refuse with a pleasant smile, promise the impossible. One of his callers was Piroux, the deputy who had pestered him during the July demonstration. Piroux, of course, was full of complaints:

" Every day dozens of people are secretly crossing the frontier.

We're turning Franco against us. And tomorrow he'll be master of the whole of Spain. My constituents are particularly interested in the maintenance of good relations with Spain, quite independently of who governs it."

Villard answered with a gentle smile: "My dear colleague, it's still unknown who's going to win. You've probably read the latest telegrams? However, I have no objection. . . . We promised not to let any volunteers go to Spain, and we'll carry out our promise."

When Piroux had left, Villard said to his secretary: "It will be necessary to instruct the Prefect of Pyrénées-Orientales to increase the frontier guard."

Fortunately there were no official invitations; after the gorgeous lunches which had so overburdened Villard's stomach, he was glad to eat a soft-boiled egg and spinach. He had a delightful afternoon before him — pure æsthetic emotions instead of a parliamentary session. He had long been meaning to look at the work of the young artist André Corneau, who had exhibited a wonderful landscape at the last Salon — a spreading chestnut tree, with a merry-go-round on the left and a tiny figure against the wall on the right. No doubt his other pictures would be interesting. Corneau was being much talked about. . . . Villard would buy that landscape. He was not stingy, but neither was he fond of flinging money about. He thought with satisfaction: "They asked three thousand for it at the Salon. That means they'll let it go for two."

André, hearing of Villard's intended visit, remembered what Pierre had told him and frowned. The devil take him! What about putting the studio in order? No, it wasn't worth it.

Villard gazed lingeringly at each canvas and made remarks: "What delicate tones! You can feel the air under that chair. The asters are a little harsh. This landscape is reminiscent of Utrillo at his best period." André wasn't listening. At first he had looked attentively at Villard and thought: "It wouldn't be interesting to paint his portrait. His face is a mass of flabbiness, all blurred." Then he lit up his pipe and obediently presented the canvases for Villard's inspection and shook the dust off his clothes. No doubt he wanted to buy, but this prospect had little effect on André, one way or the other. He was indifferent to money; when it came in he spent it; when there was none he ate bread and sausage instead of dining. At one time he used to take a fervent interest in the fate of his pictures and wondered whose hands they would fall into. But it was nearly always the dealers who took them, and André got used to the idea that when his canvases left the studio they disappeared.

Villard said: "I liked that landscape you exhibited at the salon very much. You know, the one with the tree. . . ."

In silence André put another canvas on the easel. This one was his favourite. After the night he met Jeannette, he had gone to the Place d'Italie and painted it. It was a gloomy day. A girl at the corner was waiting for someone, and the horses of the merry-go-round were resting.

"I should like to have this landscape," Villard said.

André's face darkened. He knocked out his pipe against the table-leg. Then he took up the canvas and turned its face to the wall.

Villard looked surprised. "Is it sold?" he asked.

André answered with the rudeness of a child, neither reflecting nor choosing his words: "I don't want it to hang in your house. Can't you understand? There's a limit to everything. I'm not going to have you looking at it!"

Whenever Villard took offence, his whole face trembled — the eye-glasses, the ends of his moustache, his lower lip, and his chin. He said politely: "As you please," thanked André for the pleasure of seeing his pictures, and ceremoniously left the studio. André watched him go and exclaimed: "The humbug!" And yet Pierre believed in a dummy like that. Was there any limit to what people would do? And good people too, like Pierre. André waved his hand and settled down to the work that Villard had interrupted. He couldn't get on with it, but he refused to leave the canvas: he was afraid of his own angry and weary thoughts.

When it got dark, he lay down on the sofa without turning on the light and waited again for the hour when Jeannette's voice would echo in the dead-silent studio. It was like a drug for which he had developed a craving. Wherever he might be at that hour, he always looked around for a radio. And today the chestnut tree and the merry-go-round reawakened memories of her with a new sharpness. The hours passed slowly by. At last it was time. He turned the switch and the little green eye lit up; someone sang a song, the violins did a bit of scraping, and then Jeannette's voice came through. She began with a talk about the bed of the ocean, about sea-shells and their everlasting murmur; this was an advertisement for artificial pearls. Then she recited a poem — André didn't catch whom it was by:

Deceived, I go to meet my death,
And like the sand, the brass of midnight battle. . . .

Again the violins scraped and people sang. André automatically
turned the knob. A woman's light voice said something in French:
" This is Madrid calling. Today our units, composed of La Mancha
fighters, together with men of the International Brigade, repelled
attacks in University City. By a counter-attack we drove the
Fascists from the building of the Medical School. German aircraft
carried out two attacks on the northern quarters of the city. The
population suffered casualties in killed and injured. . . ."

André looked out of the window. The old rue Cherche-Midi was
asleep. So were the antique-dealers, the merry cobbler, and the
flower-shop woman. The clientèle of the Smoking Dog were
asleep; so were the cats. Occasionally a few belated pedestrians
walked past. A truck rattled along. Then stillness reigned once
more. The grey houses seemed to be deserted. And a great sadness
came over André. He thought of Madrid. He had never seen that
city and he was always trying to picture what it was like — white,
dark, noisy, quiet — he didn't know. But now at night all the sky
over Madrid was lit up, and down below a woman was crying out.
And it was like that every night. That was worse than death. It was
enough to make you go mad. Not because of the bombs or the solitary cry. But what could you do? . . . And here they had closed
the shutters, pulled the quilts over themselves, and were sleeping.
They felt warm and cosy, because it was damp and cold outside
and the houses were burning in far-away Madrid. Cosy! And then
perhaps this very sky of Paris would be filled with a drone; the night,
black and hostile, would come alive. The eyes of the searchlights
would peer helplessly into the sky: no, can't find it! Then — crash.
One, two, three. . . . Someone would announce on the radio:
" Many were killed and injured." And at night a woman would cry
out. Maybe Jeannette. Why did they deceive her with this quiet,
why didn't they wake her up and say: " Hurry away into the country, to the sea, does it matter where? " They were deceiving all of
them — the cobbler and the cats, everyone. Jeannette had said:
" Deceived, I go to meet my death." It was simple and terrible.

PART

2

CHAPTER 1

THE MONTIGNYS received on Tuesdays. In the spacious library Breteuil's friends discussed current political questions amid the smoke of their cigars over a cup of coffee and white rum from Martinique. Meanwhile in the drawing-room the ladies drank tea and gossiped. Montigny's daughter Josephine waited impatiently for the men to come into the drawing-room: she still retained her affection for Lucien, who came to the Montignys' every Tuesday.

Nearly two years had passed since the victory of the Popular Front. As Desser said, everything had settled down. Villard boasted: " I've learned how to govern — they don't notice me now." Business was good. The factories were overwhelmed with orders. The shops were scarcely able to cope with the demand for goods. The notices " To let," disappeared; there were no longer any empty premises. Economists wrote about the end of the crisis and prophesied a long period of prosperity.

However, the mantle of appeasement cloaked a general discontent. The bourgeoisie remembered the June strikes; they could not forgive the Popular Front for their fright. The forty-hour week and vacations with pay were the cause of all the trouble. This was the attitude not only of the Montignys' visitors but also of people of small means who read the newspaper articles. The shopkeeper who told his customers that soap had gone up another four sous shrugged his shoulders and said: " There's nothing to be done. You see, the gentlemen workers are going to the watering-places." The farmer filling up his income-tax form grumbled: " Parasites! " By " parasites " he meant the schoolteacher, the two post-office employees, and the workers in the neighbouring town. The workers were also discontented. The cost of living went up every day, and the wage increase which they had obtained a couple of years ago was of no benefit. Strikes kept breaking out. The owners refused to yield. Villard appealed for moderation. The Fascists were openly forming military detachments, and the workers were asking: " Who's going to protect us? Not the police; they're only waiting for the hour to get even with us." Fighting was still going on in Spain, but the Fascists had cut off Catalonia from Madrid, and the workers murmured angrily: " They've been betrayed." The betrayal, like rust, corroded the spirit of the people. The press was writing about the danger of war. German divisions marched through the streets of Vienna. Everybody tried to guess Hitler's next move. They got hot under the collar, argued in the cafés, and then went peacefully to sleep. The unusually cold spring of 1938 found Paris peaceful and distracted, well fed and discontented.

Meanwhile Breteuil had been up to a number of things. The friends he met at the Montignys' were unaware of his many-sided activities. Holding the view that the root of the evil lay in what he called the " appeasement " of the working classes, Breteuil had devoted a whole year to the organization of terrorist acts. The most responsible affairs he delegated to Grisnez. It was Grisnez who set fire to six military aeroplanes and planted a time-bomb in a railway tunnel. Wishing to frighten the capitalists, Breteuil entrusted Grisnez with the task of blowing up the house belonging to the Employers' Confederation. The bomb damaged the front of the house and killed the watchman.

The newspapers of the Right accused the Communists of having perpetrated these outrages. Evasively Villard told the press: " The nature of these outrages has not yet been elucidated." The partisans of the Popular Front demanded vigorous measures. In order to pacify them Villard " discovered a plot." Of course, he did not seriously touch either Breteuil or the arms dumps of the " Faithful "; but the police extracted a few machine-guns from various cellars and arrested about fifty of the " Faithful." Villard made out the plot was a piece of childishness: at his suggestion the papers nicknamed the conspirators the " Cagoulards," stating that they wore mediæval hoods and masks. In the Chamber Breteuil indignantly declared that the Government was persecuting " true patriots," and the arrested men were soon released.

Breteuil now decided to change his tactics. He passed from bombs to parliamentary intrigues in the hope that international complications would help him to split the Government majority. All the walls were covered with appeals: " The Popular Front is dragging France into war! " Breteuil's friends went about the country persuading the peasants " to save the cause of peace." The usual Cabinet crisis was in the offing. The Radicals were tired of the Socialists. The levy on capital — ah, that was where cautious Blum was likely to meet disaster! In that case Tessa might come to the fore. So Breteuil made up to the old lawyer, praised his speeches, and entertained him with duck à la Rouen and pheasant ragout. Tessa appreciated the food, but was on his guard; he even stressed his good relations with Villard and said that the Socialists had turned out to be good Frenchmen. Perhaps he realized his triumph was imminent and wished to make sure of the votes of the Socialists; perhaps he was trying to pacify the Left Radicals, in particular the vehement deputy Fouget, who frankly called Breteuil a Hitlerite.

Of course it was a tougher proposition to overthrow the Cabinet than to blow up a house. Breteuil was obliged to enlist the aid of new forces. Grisnez and the other " Ironsides " were now sitting around kicking their heels. Breteuil became friends with Ducane and Grandel, a couple of prominent deputies who frequented the Montignys'. They were a pair of contrasting types. Ducane was the son of a vet in the provinces. He had known poverty in his youth, but kept aloof from the Socialist movement. His ideal was a chivalrous, æsthetic France; he fed his fancy on the exploits of Joan of Arc, the work of the unknown builders of the cathedrals of Chartres and Reims, and on the nation considered as a whole. He had served as an airman during the war and was severely wounded; he was decorated twice. Then he took up politics and preached what he called " integral nationalism." He was elected to Parliament by one of the Alpine constituencies. In the Chamber he took his seat on the extreme Right, but he often upset his neighbours by his unexpected statements. For instance, in one speech he said: " If we're faced with the horrors of a new Commune, I prefer the post of a defender of Paris to the double-faced role of a Thiers." He was a reserved, ugly man of about fifty, with a stutter. When he got excited he spoke so indistinctly that even his relations failed to understand him. Although he seldom made a speech in the Chamber, he exercised great influence; he was respected for his personal decency and his knowledge — he was the finest aircraft specialist in France and directed the work of the Air Force Commission. He joined up with Breteuil because he considered that the Popular Front was leading France to ruin. Breteuil tried to keep on good terms with him and never uttered a word in his presence regarding co-operation with Germany.

If Ducane was well known in parliamentary and military circles, Grandel was known throughout the whole country. Grandel was young and very attractive: he had a fine face, a Roman nose, and dreamy blue eyes; he looked like the portraits of Saint-Just. He was an excellent speaker, and even his opponents listened to him enchanted as if by a nightingale. He had been something of an infant prodigy and had played the violin marvellously. His father had made a fortune in Stock Exchange speculations after the Armistice, but soon went bankrupt, and Grandel himself had to go out into the world; he wrote essays on " the mysticism of poverty," " cosmic storms," and sociological dramas with allegorical personages. A few years back he had joined the Socialists and addressed meetings with great success. He was elected to the Chamber. There he suddenly announced that he was disgusted with the internationalism of Blum and Villard and that he was a Frenchman and the representative of the French workers who cared for Proudhon, not for Marx, and refused to live at other people's bidding. Grandel became the hero of the day. He was courted by the Radicals, the Republican Socialists, and the Democrats. He called himself an " Independent Socialist," but in the divisions in the Chamber he supported the Right opposition and became friends with Breteuil. Grandel had a good many enemies; any gossip likely to damage his reputation as a rising young deputy found willing listeners in the parliamentary lobbies. It was said that he was meeting one of the attachés at the German Embassy a little too often; it was even declared that the Radical Fouget had got hold of documents which severely compromised Grandel. In the face of these insinuations, Grandel himself merely raised his thin eyebrows. "An old trick," he would say, "blacken your opponent and at the same time jumble up the cards! When the time comes, I'll prove Fouget is an agent of Moscow."

Some three years before, Grandel had married a very pretty creole girl. Her name was Marie, but everybody called her Mouche. Grandel went about with her everywhere; they were spoken of as "the Inseparables." Mouche went with him to the Montignys'. She did not take part in the general conversation and used to sit looking at old albums. Josephine felt in her heart that Mouche was a rival: she would often glance at the door of the library, and the expression on her face changed when she caught sight of Lucien.

Montigny, who was subsidizing Breteuil's political campaign, had a heavy, stern manner and a bulldog face. It was not surprising that Josephine longed for the day when she would leave her father's house at last; Montigny would plague her for hours on account of a book by Paul Morand or because he thought she put on too much lipstick. He was an obstinate, dull-witted man. He believed that Breteuil would keep the workers in their place. The past year's dividends gave him no cause for complaint, but he considered himself to be humiliated: "A forty-hour week indeed! The rabble! Do I count how many hours I work? And yet I take risks, I may have to suffer losses. All they have to do is draw their wages. Parasites! " To Montigny the workers were not opponents, as Desser regarded them, but dreadful insects ready to devour everything. He could go on talking forever about their laziness and greed.

This particular evening he never gave anyone else a chance to open his mouth, but went on jawing for the hundredth time about the truculence of the workers, who were demanding separate wash-basins.

"They'll be demanding baths next. You see if they don't. Just think of it — while the Germans are working twenty-four hours a day, our workers are going away to the seashore."

He broke into a fit of angry coughing. Breteuil, who wanted to

talk about the impending battle in Parliament, not about wash-
basins, took advantage of this interruption. In order to make sure
of Ducane's support, Breteuil based his arguments on the Nazi
peril, as Montigny had done.

"I think that in May the Germans will begin to put pressure on
Czechoslovakia," he said. "Before then we must create a genuine
national Government. Personally I've no objection to Tessa, provided, of course, that he declines the votes of the Communists."

Lucien frowned. He had long suspected that Breteuil was busy
with parliamentary intrigues, not with a conspiracy. Anyway, he
didn't expect that his father would be put up as the saviour of the
country. It was a fat lot of good putting a fence round the orchard!
And stifling a yawn, Lucien thought: "If only they'd dry up
quickly!" He wanted to talk to Mouche.

Grandel supported Breteuil. "Tessa is the lesser evil. Only he
must be got away from the Fouget gang. I was told yesterday that
Fouget had passed that forged document on to Tessa. Of course I
went to see Tessa at once and said: 'Will you kindly tell me what
it is they accuse me of?' He was extremely pleasant, but declined
to give any explanations. But it's quite clear what their plan is.
They want to make a row in the Foreign Affairs Commission. It's
a classic way of diverting attention. In order to save Blum they trot
out the latest sensation."

Ducane was indignant. "I didn't think Fouget was capable of
such baseness. He gave me the impression of being a decent fellow.
He fought at Verdun. And now he blackguards a political opponent! But you must expose them, Grandel. With your talent as a
speaker . . ."

"I'm only sorry I have to wait. The trouble is I can't even prepare myself properly. I don't know the contents of the forgery."

Breteuil explained:

"I, too, tried to have an explanation with Tessa, but he wriggled
out; he's staking on both cards. But we're old friends. After all, he
owes his victory in the elections to me. Besides, he doesn't believe
in an atom of these insinuations. But what can you expect? The man
is bound by party discipline. He's afraid of incurring the wrath of
the Freemasons and Herriot."

Lucien smiled vaguely. Then he said abruptly: "My father's an
honest man, but he's a bungler."

The deputies started reckoning up the votes. About seventy Radicals would vote against Blum. The Government's majority was melting, but it was melting too slowly. And there was no time to wait; in a month Germany would move.

"The senators will come to the rescue. Caillaux has sworn to flay Blum alive."

Ducane muttered: "Caillaux is a fox and a defeatist."

They discussed the program of the future Government. The first condition: Tessa must break with the Communists. A firm policy over the Sudeten question, but there must not be too much of the big stick, and everything must be done to find a compromise acceptable to both sides. The immediate recognition of General Franco. Laval to be sent to Rome; it was vital to come to an agreement with Mussolini before it was too late. Control of the press. Credits for the aircraft industry — Ducane insisted on this. A seventy-hour working week.

Breteuil added: "Armed force to be used in the case of factories being seized."

For the benefit of Montigny.

But on this point Montigny begged to differ.

"No," he said. "Use gas! Gas and nothing else! Smoke them out like rats! And you must add: accelerated shipbuilding. The death penalty for acts of terrorism. We'll get that villain yet who threw the bomb into the Confederation. The guillotine's too good for him!"

Breteuil looked at Montigny's heavy face: anything could be expected from a fool like that! Breteuil said he had urgent business to attend to, and left.

The rest went into the drawing-room. Josephine looked at Lucien, but he did not even glance at her. He sat down next to Mouche and started a drawing-room conversation about Giraudoux's new play: *The Trojan War Will Not Take Place.*

"It's a very good title," he said; "people go to have their fears set at rest."

Mouche whispered: "On Thursday. He won't be there. I'll let you in myself."

Ducane was heatedly proving to Grandel that it was time to adopt an active policy. "Whether with or against Italy it's all the same. It's not the Sudetens I'm worried about, but the Czech Maginot Line. . . ."

"Of course. But you mustn't forget that the Sudetens are Germans. And Hitler has declared that he has no further claims in the west. . . ."

Ducane became excited. He shouted out something, but it was impossible to make out the words; he seemed to be chewing rubber.

Grandel smiled: "You're absolutely right," he said.

Josephine overtook Lucien in the hall. Without looking at him, she said rapidly:

"Lucien, if anything happens to you, don't forget — I'm always ready to do anything for you."

Lucien was touched, but restrained himself. "Thank you. It's chilly out here. You'll catch a cold."

Tears came into Josephine's eyes. "Oh, how I hate you!"

Outside, a cold east wind was blowing. Lucien turned up the collar of his coat. Everything disgusted him — Breteuil, Josephine's stupid tenderness, and Mouche.

In one of his "local associations" Breteuil sought out Aubry, a ticket-inspector on the Metro, a repulsive-looking individual bursting with malice, and with no family ties.

"Listen, Aubry. There is a traitor who must be got rid of."

Aubry brightened up with pleasure. He had long been waiting for an opportunity to show his courage. Only once had he been given a job to do, and a very nasty one at that. He had beaten up a girl who was selling *L'Humanité* in the avenue Wagram.

"I'm at your orders, Leader."

"You must do away with 'Ironside' Grisnez. And without anything being found out. Then you'll plant this near him. . . ."

Breteuil opened his pocketbook and took out a Communist party card.

"It shall be done, Leader," lisped Aubry.

When he got home Breteuil didn't open his letters or answer his wife's questions. Scarcely moving his thin lips, he said his prayers. He was sorry for Grisnez. But what else could be done? A new chapter had to be written on a clean page. A man like Grisnez was likely to blurt out everything after a couple of drinks. . . . Of course, he was an honest fellow, but a fool. "I'm an 'Ironside'" — paradise was ready for people like that. But what was in store for him — Breteuil? He had taken a great deal on himself. He would have a lot to answer for. And after reciting the prayer for the dead once again, he said to his wife:

"I never knew anyone called Grisnez, understand?"

Mme Breteuil wiped her hands on her apron — she had been making Breteuil's favourite macaroons — looked at her husband, and exclaimed:

"Monster!"

Breteuil said nothing.

CHAPTER 2

GRISNEZ plodded along the muddy path from the station of Verneuil towards the old hunting-lodge. It was the first warm day after a long spell of bad weather, and Grisnez thought: "It will soon be Easter." Coming out into an open glade, he felt hot and unbuttoned his overcoat. Under the trees the pointed leaves of the lilies of the valley glowed with a greenish light; in a month the Parisians would be coming here for picnics. Peaceful scenes of everyday life usually irritated Grisnez. Although he did not realize it, he envied other people's carefree attitude. But now the sunshine and the stir of spring in the forest inclined him to a gentler mood, and he thought of the couples who would come to this glade to pick the lilies of the valley.

Where would Breteuil send him to now — the Spanish frontier? Brittany? From his early youth Grisnez had been used to wandering about France. He was used to the stuffiness of smoky railway cars, the chilly dreariness of railway junctions, to taking his meals at the common table in third-rate hotels where travelling salesmen told each other threadbare anecdotes, to spending the night in unheated rooms with greasy quilts and chromos on the tarnished walls. He had no liking for moving about, but he could hardly imagine himself in a settled life. His former profession helped him to carry out the risky tasks with which Breteuil entrusted him. When he disappeared from his hotel for a week, his landlady showed no surprise. Grisnez knew France from end to end. Everywhere he had his favourite places of call, his boozing companions, and connections with the local police. For the last four months he had been idle. The letter from Aubry neither overjoyed nor saddened him. Carelessly he slung a few things into a suitcase, put a flask of brandy on top, and slipped a revolver into his hip pocket.

He told his landlady: " I'm going to Annecy with the instruments."
Then he thought to himself: " Instruments or bombs — what does
it matter? " What had seemed to him two years ago to be an exciting romantic gamble had now become merely routine work; he
carried it out efficiently, but without any enthusiasm.

The April noon, the gleaming sunlight, the riotous twittering of
the birds mellowed his feelings. He was not thinking about the
" Faithful," but about curly-haired Lulu, the daughter of the hotel
proprietor at Annecy. It was no accident that he had told his landlady he was going to Annecy: he was daydreaming and had made
a slip of the tongue. How nice it would be to chuck it all, marry
Lulu, and take a café or a little hotel! Dreams! Grisnez was incapable of saving; all the money he got from Breteuil went on new
suits and presents for Lulu.

Aubry was already waiting for him. The hunting-lodge was a
half-ruined building among alder trees. Lovers had scratched their
names and dates on its white walls. Aubry sat down on the little
stone seat, turning first one side of himself and then the other to
the sun. He, too, felt the softening influence of spring. After the
long months spent in the stuffy Metro with its stale smells of soap
and acid it was like being in paradise to sit beside a tiny stream,
under the trees that were covered with a pale green down. He had
forgotten why he was waiting. When he caught sight of Grisnez,
smartly dressed and freshly shaved, he sighed; the fairy-tale was
over.

They shook hands. " Sit down," Aubry said. " Ironside Delmasse
is coming. He has all the instructions."

Grisnez spread out a newspaper: he didn't want to dirty his new
trousers.

" It's not damp," Aubry said. " The sun's shining. Still, it's as well
to be careful. It isn't worth while catching cold."

They gazed in silence at the silver ripples of the tiny stream, and
little by little a pleasant drowsiness came over them.

" Isn't the Leader coming? " Grisnez said.

" No. He's not very well. He's getting on, you know."

" How old would you say he is? "

" Over sixty."

" He's aged a lot since his son's death. That was two years ago. I
remember it quite well. There was a strike on. His wife was crying.
And when I arrived he was praying. . . ."

"Yes, that was a bad show. . . . What about you? Are you married?"

"No. Are you?"

For a moment Aubry's ugly face lit up with a bashful smile. "Not yet," he said.

"Then you're thinking of it? It's better that way. I'm getting married soon. I've found a nice girl at Annecy. A regular peach. Her father's a lawyer. They've got an estate there. I want to go and live there myself. I shall buy a hotel. The English will come. They bring in the money. I've already saved up the cash. And she's a stunning girl. Sings beautifully, a real coloratura. . . ."

Lulu had never sung a note in her life, but having begun to tell lies, Grisnez couldn't stop. Perhaps he was not merely lying, but expressing his dreams. All around them in the forest the birds were warbling passionately.

Aubry glanced at his companion's fashionable light-brown shoes and thought with a touch of sadness: "It's easy for a fellow like that to get married. But who'll have me? Some old trollop, perhaps. . . ."

"I say," Grisnez said, "where is this chap what's-his-name, Delmasse? He must have got lost."

"Oh, he'll come," Aubry said.

Aubry wasn't waiting for anybody. He had thought it all out beforehand, but now for some reason he was going slow. Grisnez took out his flask. Then Aubry produced some bread and sausage which he had brought with him, foreseeing a strenuous day. The sausage was supple as rubber. Grisnez ate it with relish: the walk had given him quite an appetite. Aubry took a drink from Grisnez's flask. "Here's to you," he said.

Grisnez grew even mellower under the effect of the brandy. He felt sleepy and yawned. As he gazed at the water he said dreamily:

"I like fishing. At Annecy the trout are as big as this — look!"

Then he fell asleep. His hat slipped on one side. His mouth was half-open. His pale face, which was usually contorted with twitching, became restful and even rosy in the sun. There was even something childlike about him as he lay there asleep. Aubry still delayed. He was no longer thinking of his loneliness; no longer daydreaming. He kept repeating to himself: "Come on!" A feeling of disgust came over him; his former snugness gave way to a state of semi-drowsiness. He frowned savagely. Damn that brandy! And there was that swine, asleep! " Wants to open a hotel, does he! The Victoria or Mon Repos. Like hell he will! " But maybe he wasn't a traitor, after all. The chap simply wanted to settle down. Of course, it was pleasanter to go fishing. Anybody could understand that. Only why was he, Aubry, any worse than Grisnez? Why did he never have any peace? Beating up and killing. The bastards! Whoever this outburst was supposed to refer to, it put heart into Aubry. He felt a wave of malignant rancour, as though acid was rising in his throat. Then he pulled out his dagger.

Two minutes later, having made certain that Ironside Grisnez was quite dead, Aubry slipped the card which Breteuil had given him under the seat. It was made out in the name of Jacques Delmasse. Having carefully examined his hands, overcoat, and trousers, Aubry strode quickly along the path. All his enthusiasm for the spring day had left him. Only the feeling of disgust remained. He recalled the sausage with loathing — like rubber! He wanted to spit, but his mouth was dry.

It was getting dark. Two girls were standing by the bus stop on the main road. When they caught sight of Aubry, they started to laugh, and one of them said: " Looks as if he's had a pleasant walk! "

Aubry glared furiously at them. " Lousy tarts," he muttered.

Late that evening he reported to Breteuil at the Wounded Soldiers' Union.

" It's done," he said.

Breteuil thanked him and made him sit down next to him on the sofa. " This is your fighting baptism," he said.

" Was he really a traitor? "

Breteuil stood up.

" Yes," he said. " You may go."

As he watched Aubry go out, he thought vaguely: " We'll have to get rid of him, too."

Next morning there were pictures of Grisnez in all the newspapers. The reports stated the murdered man was known for his Right convictions and had taken part in the demonstration of the 6th of February. He hadn't left a penny. He was a poor man; the crime could not have been perpetrated for motives of gain. Of course the Communists declared they had no knowledge of Jacques Delmasse, but it was obvious they had bumped off Grisnez in order to get rid of a political opponent, who had a lot of influence in the Catholic Travelling Salesmen's Association.

Aubry didn't read the newspapers; he never mentioned the mysterious affair in the Verneuil forest to a soul. He went on as usual with his job, punching tickets and yawning convulsively. After knocking off work he went into an unknown café and ordered a Pernod. The strong drink made him dizzy. Another glass. A third. . . .

Some men in caps were drinking at the next table. Aubry didn't want to listen to what they were saying, but the repetition of Grisnez's name infuriated him. Grisnez no longer existed, and he didn't want to hear about him. The fools never stopped talking about him.

"Well, one dog less. . . ."

" Yes, but when a man like that goes over to the Fascists, it means they bought him. . . ."

Aubry got up, walked over to them, and said sternly: "You lie! He wanted to buy a hotel. He was killed by the Communists, the sans-culottes, like you. Understand, you bastard?"

One of the men at the table got up and hit Aubry in the face. There was a clatter of glasses. Aubry fell to the floor. The café quickly emptied. The old waiter was a long time picking up the heavy dishes, spoons, and scattered dominoes.

CHAPTER 3

THE DAY before, Tessa had celebrated his sixtieth birthday. The number sixty figured in countless telegrams and letters. The young lawyers gave him a huge cake with sixty wax candles. In the evening the candles were lighted, and Tessa gazed a long while at the little blue flickering flames. He tried to feel sad and forced himself to think of the road he had covered and of the approaching end, but these thoughts were in the abstract; actually he had never felt so young before. He looked upon the figure sixty as a beautiful monogram. His life was only just beginning. Of course, he was a famous lawyer, but tomorrow he would be one of the leaders of the country; his name would pass from the fifth column of *Le Temps*, which gave the law-court reports, to the first. The days of extremism

were over. The country wanted peace. It was tired of the clenched
fists of the Popular Front and of Breteuil's Roman salutes. It preferred a good friendly handshake and looked hopefully towards
the jovial gourmet, the good family man, the eloquent, but thrice
cautious Tessa.

Yes, it had been a wonderful day, although overshadowed by
family sorrows. In vain the best specialists had held consultations;
in vain Mme Tessa underwent a course of treatment at Vittel; her
disease continued to progress and the attacks became more frequent. Yesterday Amalie got excited and exhausted herself, and in
the evening, as Tessa gazed at the sixty candles and thought of
France's delight in him, she lay in her darkened bedroom, which
smelt of medicine, and could hardly keep back her groans.

But Tessa had other cares besides the illness of his wife. Lucien
was incorrigible. Amalie still went on calling him a boy, although
this "boy" had just turned thirty-four. The hopes of a diplomatic
career had crashed long ago. The wretched ne'er-do-well had discovered a peculiar way of earning money: he was acting as racing
tipster for Joliot's paper. It was rumoured that he used information
given him by the jockeys in order to lead people astray, and split
his own winnings with Joliot. This was hardly a desirable occupation for a minister's son. For the sake of his own health, Tessa never
spoke to his son; the pair of them sat at the dinner-table in silence.
Whenever Lucien opened his mouth, Tessa fidgeted anxiously, expecting a scandal.

Denise was a source of even greater sorrow. Tessa now realized
there was no justice in the sphere of affection. When he thought
of Lucien, he was afraid on his own account: his son might disgrace
him. If Lucien died, Tessa would shed tears and feel relieved. Not
so with Denise. The fact that she had left his house, disgraced her
father by becoming a packer in the Gnome factory, and, according
to the information of the Chief of the Secret Police, become a member of some Communist committee, seemed to Tessa a trivial matter
compared with his anxiety about her health. She was having a difficult life; she wasn't fit for heavy work, and she might be killed in
one of those idiotic demonstrations. Tessa only heard about Denise
through the police or a private detective agency. He tried to write
to her, but she didn't answer; she didn't want to have anything to
do with him. This thought brought him to the verge of tears. Over
the sixty candles he thought of Denise and remembered how as a

child she used to send him rhymed congratulations on pink paper. He was on the point of breaking down; but just at that moment a telegram arrived from the president of the Senate. Tessa smiled: he was the only hope of wise and honest France. His sharp nose exuded tiny beads of perspiration; this always happened in moments of excitement. Forgetting about Denise, he thought over the beginning of the Cabinet declaration.

Next morning there was an unpleasant incident. When Tessa sat down to read the report of the French Ambassador in Prague, he discovered that the document handed to him by Fouget had disappeared. The whole Grandel affair irritated Tessa. He disliked exposures. Politics were a subtle business; loud speeches were only a part of it. There were also the whispers in the lobbies, the intimate conversation at lunch " between the cheese and the pear," the fine shades of meaning, the hints. Exposures had no part whatever in the game. What a disgraceful rumpus Breteuil's gang had provoked over the unfortunate Stavisky affair! They even wanted to implicate him, Tessa. Fouget wouldn't have got in without the Communists' votes. Of course he was a supporter of the Popular Front. But even without him Tessa knew that Grandel was an upstart. It was necessary to beware of Grandel. What an orator! Only the late Aristide Briand was capable of such spellbinding eloquence. But what had this sensational exposure to do with it? Already last autumn Fouget had told Tessa that Grandel was connected with the German secret service. Tessa had cut him short: he didn't believe in the young deputy's treason. And in fact the very word " treason " seemed to him like something from another world. The people who were likely to be connected with a foreign secret service were seedy majors who had been ruined by gambling or good-for-nothings like Lucien — in a word, people with their backs to the wall. Tessa understood any laxity — shady dealings with speculators, defending swindlers. You had to draw a line between a perfectly legal participation in a corporation and the Stavisky or Oustric affair. But treason. . . . Tessa thought of Victor Hugo's poems, Devil's Island, the sword hanging over the head of the pale deputy. No, the deputy wouldn't do a thing like that!

Only three days ago the indefatigable Fouget had given Tessa that damned scrap of paper. Tessa read the letter and put it in a file with the documents of the Foreign Affairs Commission. The note mentioned two million francs allocated for the purpose of boost-

ing the mineral waters of Kissingen and Baden-Baden. Tessa was
annoyed. All right, Grandel was making money on German spas,
but that wasn't treason. True, Fouget said that Grandel was unable
to produce any documents in justification, but Tessa was against
any interference in the private lives of deputies, and he had told
Fouget so. But Fouget had insisted that "the members of the Foreign Affairs Commission must be acquainted with the letter." It
was all so silly; especially now, when it was necessary to overthrow
Blum with the help of the Right and at the same time make sure
of the support of the Left. Tessa was unable to refuse Fouget, for
this would mean that all of the Left Radicals would vote against
the new Government. But if Tessa divulged the contents of the
document to the Commission, Breteuil would fly into a passion; the
Right would go for the Radicals, and the Radicals would again go
to the rescue of Blum against their will. After thinking the matter
over, Tessa decided to postpone it for a week or two: he hoped
that the Cabinet crisis would come to a head in the next few days.

But who could have stolen the document? Nothing of the sort
had ever happened to him before. The file lay on his writing-table.
He remembered locking the drawer before he went away yesterday.
All the papers were in their place. If he told Amalie, she'd probably
say the thief was Beelzebub.

In the Chamber Tessa forgot all about the loss. The bill under
discussion related to the opening of two veterinary institutes. Only
the deputies of the constituencies concerned were present in the
Chamber. The others were crowding the lobbies and the smoking-
room. They were all talking of the approaching crisis, and from
the attentive way in which they asked Tessa about his health it
was obvious that Blum's days were numbered.

Villard came up to Tessa. After congratulating him on his sixti-
eth birthday, he said with a melancholy sigh: "When I was sixty
I never even dreamed I should ever get a minister's portfolio.
You're starting early. That's the way!"

"A sixty-year-old virgin," sniggered Tessa. "Not bad, eh? By the
way have you heard the one about . . ."

Villard blushed and moved away. Suddenly Fouget loomed up at
him through the haze of tobacco smoke. When Tessa saw his spectacles and little beard — Fouget aspired to be in every way like the
Radicals of the past century, the "devourers of curés" — he immediately remembered about the stolen document.

"When are you going to acquaint the Commission with the Grandel affair?" asked Fouget bluntly.

Tessa waved his hands. "Don't you think this affair ought to be handled rather carefully?" he said. "The whole matter needs thorough consideration. I'll have a talk with Herriot. It's necessary to be doubly cautious at present; otherwise all the intermediary groups will be against us."

Fouget was not to be restrained. "The Rights hate us anyway. But we've no enemies on the Left. Besides, this isn't a party matter. It concerns the State. Do you understand? The State! If Breteuil is an honest man, he should be the first to fling Grandel out. Grandel is simply a German spy. Have you read *Paris Midi?* Berlin is saying that these 'oppressions of the poor Sudeten Germans' may end in an advance on Strasbourg. In a time like this I won't tolerate a representative of the fifth column. . . ."

"Why get so excited?" said Tessa. "We're not in Spain. Arguments here don't end in slaughter. Calm yourself. I'm older and more experienced. When the time comes, I'll produce the document myself. You'll excuse me, I've got to have a talk with Daladier. . . ."

Tessa made haste to escape from the tiresome Fouget, but he could not escape from thinking about the lost document. Of course, the matter could be quashed. He could tell Fouget that he had sent the document to be examined by the experts, and then he could put all the responsibility on the experts or the Intelligence Department; Tessa had friends there and they would shield him. He could simply refuse to give Fouget any explanation or declare the document to be a forgery and raise the question of confidence at the party meeting. It was a trivial affair. What did it matter if Grandel did do a bit of commercial boosting on the side? Enough of puritanism — it was time to attend to serious politics.

But Tessa could not stop thinking about that wretched paper. He couldn't make out what was behind its mysterious disappearance. Was he being watched by Villard's agents or, still worse, by Denise's friends? He shuddered. He looked upon the Communists as shameless criminals who would stick at nothing. They might decoy him and take him to Moscow. . . . Could it really be the Communists?

At home he tried to calm himself and settle down to work. Once again he looked carefully through the contents of the file: there still remained the hope of a second miracle — the document might suddenly turn up. But there was no sign of it. He began to study the reports from the Ambassador in Prague. He had long ago decided that it was possible to reach an agreement with Hitler regarding the Sudeten Germans. To his friends he said: "Of course, Karlsbad is a beautiful spa, but what interests me is the fate of Vichy."

A groan came from the bedroom. Tessa tore himself away from his work and went in to his wife.

Amalie whispered: "Forgive me. It's so terrible for me now. I'm going to die soon. What's going to become of Lucien?"

Tessa looked at her white, bloodless face and tried to soothe her: "You'll get better. Of course you'll get better. All the doctors say so. We'll soon go to Vittel together. Without fail."

Amalie wasn't thinking about herself. She was thinking about her love: her chestnut-haired wayward son. "Tell me," she whispered again, "what's to become of Lucien?"

"He'll manage all right," said Tessá. "It isn't as if he was a boy. You've no need to worry."

When he went back to his study Lucien was just coming out and they collided in the doorway. Immediately it dawned on Tessa: Lucien had stolen the document. This was not the first time that he had found his son in the study. Lucien had always explained in an embarrassed manner that he was looking for matches or the evening paper. Now everything was clear. Yes, a creature like that was capable of anything.

Tessa hurried along the passage. On the table in Lucien's room lay some photographs of horses, a lady's long glove, and a revolver. Tessa sat down on the sofa, wiped his sweating face with the palm of his hand.

"Lucien," he whispered, "it was you who took the Grandel letter?"

Lucien looked at the floor and didn't say a word.

Then Tessa, beside himself, shouted:

"Are you working for the Germans?"

Lucien rushed at him with his hand upraised. Then he stopped abruptly and muttered: "Blackguard!"

"Get out!" spluttered Tessa.

He went back to his study. He heard Lucien saying good-bye to his mother; Amalie was sobbing. Now everything was finished. What good was a cabinet minister's post to him now? His daughter had left him. He had driven his son out of the house. His son — a spy! Tessa began to pity himself; he kept blowing his nose sadly for a long while. And from the bedroom came the sound of Amalie weeping. He went into her room and sat on the bed.

"Mother" — this was what he called her whenever he was particularly moved — "now we're all alone."

"Why have you turned him out of the house? He's proud. He won't come back now for anything."

"I won't let him, either. Do you know what he's doing? He's a spy. He's working for the Germans."

Tessa, who had always thought of his wife as both foolish and ignorant, was astonished when he heard her say:

"I always told you politics was a nasty business. Lucien learned it from you. Didn't you say at the top of your voice that it was possible to come to an agreement with the Germans and that Hitler was better than Thorez?"

"Oh, be quiet," he said. "I don't want to hear it. Lucien is not a diplomat but a spy. Don't you understand the difference?"

Tessa was already upset enough without this; he banged the door and went back to his study. For a long time he paced up and down the room, muttering: "Spy. Mercenary. Good-for-nothing." When he was tired out he sat down in an armchair. He must think the matter over. If Lucien was being used to get hold of documents, then it was a serious matter. It meant that Grandel really was implicated. But now the document had disappeared. The evidence was missing. Should he report the theft? But that would mean sending Lucien to prison. Amalie wouldn't survive the shock. And what advantage would Tessa get from it? A fine saviour of France with a spy for a son! No, not a word about the theft. Fouget would have to be told that the document was a forgery. But what about Grandel? A spy in the Chamber of Deputies — it was absolutely unheard of. But there was no proof. If he gave Fouget's version, he would merely raise a crop of enemies among the Rights. Besides, to take a sober view of the matter, even if Grandel was a German agent what harm could he do to France? He wasn't a member of the War Committee. The Germans probably had thousands of spies. What did one more matter? . . . On the whole, it was the business of the Intelligence Department people to deal with it, not his. Having carefully weighed everything, Tessa decided to bury the affair; he had got rid of Lucien as a lazybones and incorrigible rake.

He went in again to Amalie. "Don't say anything to anyone about espionage. It's all nonsense. I was in a rage. He brought me another of his blasted bills. Besides, he insulted me. You may send him money, but he mustn't come here again. Good night, my dear."

He lay down on the sofa in the study. He put out the light and lay with his eyes open, thinking about his unsuccessful life. As always, his thoughts went back to Denise. For the first time he began to think: "Perhaps she's right." She had gone away from a cursed house. What was her father to her? She reasoned in a child's way, she didn't understand the legal system. He defended murderers, faked alibis, and directed the affairs of notorious scoundrels. That was the sacred right of his profession. But Denise looked on him as a liar, a man with an unclean conscience. Her understanding of politics was no better. He was playing a complicated game; he was on friendly terms with Breteuil and smiled at Villard. That was necessary in order to save France. But of course it was a nasty business. And so Denise was full of indignation. She had left her father with his incomprehensible shady life, her superstitious mother, and her brother, who turned out to be a spy. Denise was honest, uncompromising.

Tessa vividly recalled his daughter's stern face. He began to fall asleep, and the familiar features merged with the pictures and statues. Now she was holding up a sword, like Joan of Arc; now she was grasping a blood-stained dagger; now the sullen gaze of Louise Michel appeared to him, and he repeated: "Mischief-monger!" He knew that the Communists were murderers. Now he blessed his daughter, who was to kill him. Here she came. Her face was like plaster of Paris; there were holes instead of her eyes. She seized Tessa by the throat.

Tessa began to cry out in his sleep. He was wakened by Amalie. Hearing his cry, she tried to get up, but failed and fell down on the floor. Then she crawled from the bedroom to the study and grasped Tessa's head in her hands.

"Paul, what's the matter?"

It was some time before he recovered his senses.

"I was dreaming of Denise. . . . Mother, now we're all alone. . . ."

The telephone bell rang. Tessa shuddered. Who on earth could be ringing him up at this time of night? Had something awful happened to Lucien?

He took up the receiver. It was Marchandot. He wanted to tell him that the voting in the Senate had come to an end ten minutes ago. Blum demanded emergency powers; the voting resulted in forty-seven in favour and over two hundred against.

Stammering with excitement, Tessa said to his wife: "Tomorrow I shall be a minister. This is a victory."

He wanted to say something cheerful to revive Amalie's hopes and to soothe her. But his nerves were unable to bear the strain. Sitting in his blue pyjamas at his writing-table, he wept and wiped his nose with his sleeve.

CHAPTER 4

WHILE the senators, coughing angrily and revealing their indignation by the purple flush of their apoplectic necks, were listening to Blum, at the other end of the town the workers of the Seine factory, who had already been on strike for more than two weeks, were holding a meeting to discuss the management's reply. This time Desser bluntly refused to enter into negotiations until the workers quit the factory buildings. He had given up playing the philosopher or the wit: times were different. Moreover, the workers no longer had that fiery energy which had helped them to win their victory two years before. The Seine factory followed the example of the others. The strike affected the entire war industry. There were no flags, no concerts, no cheerful back-chat with the police. They were on strike because their conditions of life were impossible; but only a few of them believed in victory.

Michaud was away; he was still fighting in Spain. His comrades didn't know whether he was alive or dead. The Paris Commune brigade was said to have suffered grave losses in the February fighting. Pierre sided with the strikers; but the last two years had made a difference in him. He had grown grey and taciturn and had become very unlike the former naïve Pierre who took an interest in everything. Villard's betrayal had crushed him. He continued to fight, and neither self-interest nor Agnès's mournful short-sighted eyes nor his one-year-old Doudou could hold him back from risky flights to Barcelona and Cartagena. Only now he no longer fought with hope, but with the bitterness of despair.

Legrais was leading the strike. If Michaud's enthusiasm expressed the spirit of the June strike, Legrais's sullen determination fitted in with the stern battle of this cold and backward spring.

There was silence when Legrais announced the management's curt reply. When he proposed that they should carry on with the strike, there was neither applause nor protest. All the men looked down-hearted.

"Who wants to speak?"

The silence was oppressive; defeat seemed to hover behind it. Suddenly a weak voice came from the depth of the long, dim hangar:

"I wish to speak."

An old man named Duchesne climbed up on the platform. At one time he used to work in the foundry, but had long since been acting as a night watchman. He found it difficult to bend his back and could scarcely hobble about the yard, but he didn't want to retire and said: "It's boring at home." Everybody knew Duchesne. He seemed to have worked there since the beginning of the world. The engineers paid attention to his remarks, and Desser shook hands when he passed the time of day with him, and said: "This is our pride." Now the men pricked up their ears. What was Duchesne going to say? He was no loud-mouthed young spark who didn't care a damn about anything. What was the use of talking about low wages and the increasing cost of living? Everyone knew about that. But this wasn't 1936. Desser was sticking to his guns. And their families were starving. There was no sense in this strike — not a chance of winning it. What would Duchesne say? He had seen everything in his time.

Duchesne stood up on the platform and for what seemed a long time he said nothing. At last he opened his mouth and began to sing in a cracked, aged voice the first words of the *Internationale:*

"Arise, ye prisoners of starvation."

All stood up and raised their clenched fists in silence.

It was decided to go on with the strike. While they were discussing the question of appealing to other factories, Legrais was called away. A message had come from the committee saying that the Government was going to fall.

Denise at once recognized the worker with the gashed cheek, who had spoken to her that evening when she met Michaud. Perhaps Legrais would have heard something. She often got letters;

Michaud wrote about the fighting, the difficulties of the Spanish language, his comrades in the brigade, the cold and heat of Aragon, the bravery of the peasants. Sometimes they were notes scrawled on a scrap of paper, sometimes long screeds. At times he recalled Paris and the evenings they had spent together. Other times he wrote about the military operations, the casemates of Teruel, the work of the fighter planes which they nicknamed " snub-noses." In his last letter, after an enthusiastic description of the battle for the out-skirts of Teruel, he wrote in pencil: " I love you, and how! " Denise carried the letter about with her; during the day she looked to make sure it was still there. She knew every word of it by heart, but she read it over and over again.

Outwardly her life was unattractive: work, then a meeting or a lecture with names and figures scribbled in an exercise-book. But she realized that this was a war and that she was side by side with Michaud. His letters that read like military communiqués, and the boyish words of love which were suddenly slipped into them, helped to sustain her in moments of spiritual fatigue. But no letters had come from Michaud since February. Denise struggled against her growing anxiety. She kept on saying to herself: " He's alive," and repeated his favourite exclamation: " And how! " But as the days went by, her anxiety increased. When she saw Legrais, she felt a wave of excitement: perhaps he would have heard some-thing. . . .

At the committee meeting they talked about the Cabinet crisis. The Senate wanted Blum to resign. The Socialists were trying to ingratiate themselves — they were afraid of alienating Tessa and being left with the Communists. The strikes in Paris were on the increase. But there was no enthusiasm. And the efforts to set the peasantry against the workers had succeeded. In comparison with last year the situation had deteriorated.

Somebody said: " We missed the right moment."

He was met with a chorus of disapproval: stick to the business in hand! Paris could be made to rise in defence of the Popular Front. If Blum refused to resign, who would come out against him? — Breteuil's friends, the Cagoulards, and perhaps the police. The Army wouldn't support the Fascists. Blum and Villard had only to take up the fight. . . .

They elaborated a draft declaration. The Government to remain in power. Villard to arrest the Cagoulards, with General Picard at their head. Aid to Spain: it was time to open the frontier!

There was no need to write it down; they knew it all by heart. The words sounded trite, as though they had lost their meaning, like "How do you do?" and "*Au revoir.*" They decided that Ducloud should negotiate with Blum, and Legrais should go to Villard, as he had supported him at the elections. Besides, it would be better to send a worker rather than a deputy; that way Villard would know what the people were saying.

They went on to discuss the question of the strike. They must hold on! Much depended on how the crisis ended. They asked Denise about the situation at the Gnome factory.

"They all say that the strike ought to be called off, but they all realize it's necessary to strike," she said. "While the others are holding on, our Communists aren't taking the lead."

Legrais smiled. "Same as in our factory."

Out in the street Denise caught up with him. "Have you heard anything from Spain? . . . How is Michaud?"

Denise's voice betrayed her agitation. Legrais frowned. It was three months already since he had had any news from Spain, but he said quietly: "Everything's all right. A comrade has just arrived. He saw Michaud a short while ago. . . ."

Denise was unable to conceal her joy. And a vague smile, like a spring day somewhere in Billancourt amid the slag and smell of burning, lit up Legrais's gloomy face.

"I'll come and see you at the factory tomorrow," he said. "We must put some heart into the boys. We're in a bad way in our factory, too. It was an old man who came to the rescue today: he started singing the *Internationale.* It's only because they're afraid of one another's contempt that they hold on at all."

After saying good-bye to Denise, Legrais walked along the embankment. It was a different Paris here: the houses were new and unusually white; factories everywhere, and the sirens were hooting as in a port. It was a curious spring. It was April, but very cold. People went about hunching up their shoulders, snarling, and sneezing. The chestnut trees were already beginning to sprout; their green buds seemed out of place in the keen wintry wind. Legrais thought of Denise's joyful face. What if something happened to Michaud? What frightful bad luck if it did! She loved him, you could see that at once. A fine girl. Michaud said she was a student. Anyway, it was a good thing to have somebody you were fond of in the world. They said she was a quiet girl, but she wasn't; she was rather excitable. All the better: more life.

Legrais had been a lonely man for as long as he could remember. He had never known his father. His mother died when he was still in long clothes, and he was brought up by his uncle, a pork butcher and a mean skinflint. Legrais had to carry the tubs of pigs' blood, light the stove, and wash the floors. Later on he went into a factory.

The war broke out just at the wrong moment for Legrais — just when he had taken a fancy to laughing, chattering Anne-Marie. He used to think about her when he was in the trenches of the Argonne Forest, where the war went on underground with each side undermining the other. Legrais was wounded in the face by a shell splinter; the scar remained. When he came back from the war, Anne-Marie had disappeared without leaving any trace; he was told she had gone off with an American airman.

From then on, Legrais frowned on all women. He led a dull life in those days. He used to go to the movies a lot and from time to time he got tight. Then he began to take an interest in politics. Again he fell in love and again he missed his chance. He didn't know how to pop the question to Margot: he thought she despised him. That summer was a period of disturbance — Sacco and Vanzetti. . . . Legrais spoke at meetings every day. In the autumn Margot married Dubon. Legrais thought: " She'll find it more interesting with him." On New Year's Day Dubon gave a party in his little house near the fortifications. Everyone stayed late, drank a good deal, and filled the place with smoke. Margot went out into the garden to get a breath of fresh air. Legrais was leaving. She called to him from the garden. She began to talk about the movies and asked him if he had seen a film called *The Island of Sorrow.* Legrais was silent. Suddenly Margot said quickly: " I loved you then . . ." and went back to the guests. Legrais was furious with himself. He decided that he wasn't made for happiness and became still more taciturn.

Why did he remember all this now? And now there was Josette. She was the daughter of a comrade. Sometimes Legrais thought that Josette looked at him tenderly. But she was twenty-four, and he was forty-two. He said to her: " I'm too old for you." Why did she lose her temper? He ought to have a talk with her. He kept putting it off; it wasn't the right time. Now he was excited by his conversation with Denise and thought about what he had missed.

He wrapped his scarf round his neck. It was neither raining nor snowing. . . . What a queer spring! He must ring up Villard. If Blum resigned, Desser wouldn't yield for anything. Then maybe the factories would be cleared by force. And yet only a short time ago the workers seemed to have had everything in their grasp. Tomorrow Breteuil would be in command. They had relied too much on their strength: majority, elections, Popular Front, demonstrations. But the others had gone on undermining, undermining. And now the chance had been missed! It was like himself and Margot. . . . Ugh, what filthy weather!

Legrais went along to the room where the strike committee was in session. They crowded round him and asked: "What's the news?"

"Three points. The first is about the strike. They must hold on. The other factories are in a fighting mood. There were delegates there. At the Gnome factory they won't yield for anything. And Desser's in a bad fix. They want aircraft now more than anything. Hitler's up to something again. That means they'll put pressure on Desser: he has got to deliver the orders. Point two: regarding the Cabinet. Our people have decided to appeal to the Government. They must not resign. The Chamber has expressed its confidence. As for the Senate, it's an almshouse! Those old fogies ought to have been retired long ago. I'm going to Villard. We offer him our support. If necessary, we'll come out in the streets."

Somebody said: "Villard's a pretty fine turd."

"I don't deny that," Legrais said. "But even turds aren't all alike. And we've got to make a choice: it's not a question of choosing between two roses. With Tessa it will be even worse."

"That's true. But what's the third?"

"Third what?"

"You said there were three points."

Legrais smiled.

"Yes. I forgot. The third point concerns the weather. Is this what you call spring, comrades? This isn't spring. This is a disgrace!"

CHAPTER 5

SINCE early morning crowds of gapers had been gathering outside the palace of the President of the French Republic in the smart rue Saint-Honoré. Reporters stood ready with their notebooks and cameras. Bets were laid as to who the President would summon. In the neighbouring bars the inquisitive warmed themselves with coffee or grog. At nine o'clock a large car drove up to the gates. Tessa, freshly shaved and perfumed, got out and walked forward with a jaunty step. He allowed himself to be photographed, but jokingly wagged his finger at the reporters:

"The President has summoned me for a consultation. That's all I can say. The buds are opening. Why pull them open prematurely? Patience, my friends, patience!"

The loss of the document, the anxiety over Denise, his wife's illness — all this was forgotten. Tessa was beaming. One of the reporters muttered enviously: "And to think that he's already getting on for seventy!"

The photographers took pictures of Herriot, Daladier, and Bonnet. The deputies and senators had had their morning upset. None of them had been able to breakfast in time. They crowded the lobbies of the Chamber, exchanging gossip about how the President of the Republic wept with excitement when he thanked the president of the Senate; Daladier forgot to drink his apéritif; Tessa embraced Breteuil, in front of everybody. In vain the actresses of the Comédie Française, the ballerinas, chorus-girls, and mere lovely women waited for their influential lovers at the appointed hour: the representatives of the nation had no time for love.

Only Villard began the day with unusual calm. The reporters did not bother him; he did not go to the Chamber; he was out of the game. During the winter he had already realized that the Radicals were ripe for their next customary betrayal, and now he felt no resentment. He gave all his attention to his domestic affairs, watched the workers pack up his pictures — he was moving without delay to his private flat — and wrote to his housekeeper at

Avignon to have the repairs finished by July. This year he was going to enjoy his holiday at last.

A few days before the Cabinet crisis he was visited by his younger daughter, Violette, who had been living at Nancy, where her husband ran a moving firm. Violette had found her father very worried; he was reckoning up the votes, grumbling at the senators, and complaining that nobody understood him. But now Violette was unable to contain her joy; her father was radiant. He drank coffee out of a big cup, blew off the scum, and smiled craftily. Anyone who didn't know about the latest events would have thought he was celebrating a triumph.

"From today on I'm as free as a bird," he said. "I'll take you to see some pictures in the rue de la Boëtie. There's the most delightful exhibition of Derain's."

He went along to his study. His secretary was waiting for him: there were several urgent matters. The Prefect of Charente-Inférieure had reported a flood; emergency measures must be taken to help the victims. Even yesterday the news had perturbed Villard; he knew how easy it was to make use of a natural misfortune for the purpose of political agitation. But now he shrugged his shoulders:

"My successor will deal with that. Incidentally, I don't envy him. The Prefect of Charente-Inférieure is a friend of Breteuil. Anyway, the whole department is a hornets' nest. You say the Charente has risen a great deal?"

And without listening to the secretary's answer, Villard gave himself up to his thoughts. He saw the great dark, silent river. Half-drowned trees jutted out here and there. Crows' nests. To Villard, set free from the cares of State, the flood was a mere phenomenon of nature, a poetic picture. An uninvited visitor brought him back to reality. It was Legrais.

"The Communists ask you not to give in," he said. "The Popular Front won the elections and only the Chamber expresses the will of the country."

"But the Constitution. . . ."

"The Constitution doesn't oblige you to submit to the vote of the Senate. You want juridical justification? Very well! When the Senate declared itself against the Radical Cabinet, Léon Bourgeois didn't resign. That's a case in point. If you resign, you'll open the way to the Fascists. At first Daladier, Bonnet, Tessa. Then Breteuil."

"My friend, why exaggerate the danger? Daladier is the organizer of the Popular Front. And Tessa isn't so terrible either. If I'm not mistaken, the Communists also voted for him. He's a typical Radical, a bit unstable, but honest. . . ."

Legrais was incapable of pretence. He stood up and raised his voice:

"You once said in my presence that you'd bound up your fate with the fate of the working class. The workers want you to remain. I'm not going to deceive you. We've often condemned your policy, as you know. But this is not the time for quarrels. The Fascists are longing for the opportunity to break up the workers' organizations. And we are ready to defend you. You're obliged to remain. There's going to be a big demonstration tomorrow in front of the Senate house. We'll show those old codgers which side the strength is on."

Villard gave a scarcely perceptible smile. "I'm very grateful to you and your party for your confidence," he said. "But all this bears rather a retrospective character now. This morning Blum handed his collective resignation to the President."

Legrais sat down and covered his eyes with his hand.

"All this will end badly," he said. "To start with they'll break up the workers. And then? Then it will be the same as in Austria — the Germans will come. Spain is going through her last days. The Czechs will be betrayed. Breteuil will join up with anybody, with Mussolini, with Hitler, so long as he can 'restore order.'"

Villard nodded his head in sympathy. He was only a Left deputy now; he could express his sentiments freely.

"You're perfectly right. They've behaved abominably with regard to Spain. Frankly speaking, the Non-intervention Committee is a shameful farce. The Italians do what they like. . . . I fully share your pessimism."

Legrais wanted to ask: "And who's to blame?" But he held his tongue; he realized the futility of the conversation. Villard waved his hands pathetically. Legrais remembered how Villard had embraced him at the meeting two years ago. He repeated Villard's words:

"A shameful farce. . . . *Au revoir*. There's no need for me to bother you."

When he was gone, Villard thought: "He's not without delicacy. He realized I was dead tired. But the others don't. They keep pestering. . . . Ah, yes, I wanted to say something to the secretary. . . ."

The secretary was already standing with his notebook open.

"Tomorrow," said Villard, "there's going to be a demonstration outside the Senate. Inform the Prefect of Police that the demonstration is prohibited. I don't want to give them the opportunity to reproach me with blackmail. We're beaten and we're resigning; those are the rules of an honest parliamentary game."

He rang for his manservant. "It's very cold in here. Light the fire. And bring my slippers."

What a consolation it was! The logs crackled merrily. Villard took off his heavy boots and, sitting alone in his warm, fur-lined slippers, enjoyed freedom at eleven o'clock in the morning. There was no need to go anywhere. His thoughts were lazy and comfortable. Legrais exaggerated. France was an enigmatic country; she went to ruin every ten years and yet she was never ruined. And she wouldn't be ruined this time. Perhaps the senators were right. The international situation had become acute. Tessa, Daladier, Sarraut, even Laval. . . . They were home-made slippers. France was used to them; they were worn out, but you wouldn't notice it. But the Popular Front could be put away in the cupboard for the time being. . . .

Violette came in and he cheered up; now he could have a talk with her. He asked her about her husband, the business, and her flat.

"I was hoping you'd have a boy. I'd like to dandle a grandson." (Villard's elder daughter had two girls.)

"Maurice says it's not the time now. Everybody in Nancy is expecting war."

Violette wanted to ask her father about politics. Maurice would pester her afterwards with the question: "But what did he say?"

"You know, Papa, these last two years have been very difficult ones for me. They don't understand you down our way. Of course they don't say anything in front of me, but I get to hear about it all the same through Maurice and Jeanne. For some reason or other they're all up in arms against you. Some say you've corrupted the workers. That's what I heard. They even sang about it in the cabaret. But others are furious with you for letting the Cagoulards out of prison. I give it up. . . . But I hear it everywhere. I've often cried over it."

Villard's chin trembled with resentment. What could he say to his daughter? That great men were always condemned during their lifetime? That for two years he had saved France from bloodshed? But he himself felt that these resounding words were out of place. He drew himself up closer to the fireside.

" I know they all hate me," he said. " I've nobody left since Mother died."

Then he got up and carefully measured twenty drops of medicine into a glass.

" I nearly forgot about it. I have to take it one hour before meals for my digestion."

CHAPTER 6

WHY had Mouche become so attached to Lucien? He didn't love her and he never said he loved her. She was just another conquest to be jotted down in his stud-book: a pretty girl with the reputation of being inaccessible. It was only now that he realized how strong had been his feeling for Jeannette; he used to be tortured with jealousy, waiting impatiently for each rendezvous and fearing coldness and aloofness. With Mouche he was just having a bit of fun. But in order to liven up her embraces, which had begun to pall, he suddenly took to reproaching her for living with her husband. With tears in her eyes Mouche said: " Do you want me to leave him? " She thought it would be ecstasy to go and live with Lucien in his dirty furnished room, where he had been staying since his quarrel with his father — to starve, darn her lover's socks, and take his articles to the newspaper office. But having had his little game of jealousy, Lucien said: " No, I don't need you, but he loves you." Mouche cried all the more. He frowned with impatience, and controlling her feelings, she joked and sang Hawaiian songs.

Mouche had met Grandel three years ago at a little seaside place in Brittany. He had taken a fancy to her at once. He roamed about the cliffs with her and talked about " cosmic storms"; he was a budding author then. In the winter they got married. Both of them were young, handsome, and witty. Grandel was also in luck; he became a deputy and came into a fortune. They took an expensive flat at Auteuil and entertained a good deal. Mouche bought her clothes at the most expensive dressmakers' and drove about in a huge Cadillac, which the chauffeur never forgot to adorn with her favourite Parma violets.

Everything, it seemed, should have contributed to their domestic happiness, but in her fourth year of married life Mouche met Lucien and lost her head completely. She was struck first of all by Lucien's physical appearance. Grandel was handsome in a cold, unfeeling way that reminded one of an engraving. But everything about Lucien was impulsive: his crisp chestnut hair and bright eyes, his vague, barely perceptible smile and long, slender hands. After she had got to know him a little, Mouche felt he was quite unlike anyone she had ever met before. He blazed up at a single word and then sank into an unaccountable silent melancholy. He often gambled, as she noticed, but even when gambling he remained himself, was rude and reviled himself and was ready for anything noble or base. What the future held for him was an enigma both to others and to himself. Mouche was also attracted by his reputation of fickleness, unfaithfulness, and profound cynicism. She had grown up in the well-behaved, well-regulated family of a minor colonial official where everything was measured out — her father's love affairs, her mother's prayers, the bribes, and the few coins given to the old servant. Mouche gave herself to Grandel because he seemed to her like the hero of a novel; but after living with him for three years, she realized that he was a callous careerist. He himself once admitted to her that he had been unfaithful to her with an actress merely in order to get in with an influential deputy. Grandel's only real passion was gambling. Formerly he used to go quite often to the casinos at Monte Carlo and Biarritz, but when he became a deputy he settled down; he told Mouche that politics were the same to him as roulette. She didn't believe him. She despised him. She admitted to Lucien: " I have a sort of feeling as though he's bought me." Lucien sometimes replied by railing at her; once he even struck her, but more often he just laughed: " I love prostitutes. They're decent women."

Lucien's break with his father and the fact that he was half starving strengthened her attachment to him still more. But she couldn't understand why he took it into his head to save Grandel's reputation. She took no interest in her husband's affairs; she never asked him about anything. One day she had an idea that her husband suspected her liaison; she was afraid for Lucien, being convinced that Grandel was capable of any villainy. But when Grandel met Lucien at the Montignys', he was just as affable to him as ever.

Lucien never told anyone about his unpleasant family affairs, as he was afraid it might reach Joliot's ears, and then he would be deprived of his only source of income. Tessa likewise preferred to say nothing about his quarrel with his son. Only Mouche knew everything. Grandel now talked to her about Lucien almost every day. She held her tongue. At last he said: " I know you're friendly with him. You needn't drop him. I'm not jealous. I only want you to get him to come here. We've got something to talk about in private."

She went off to Lucien in a state of considerable anxiety. She didn't know how to give him her husband's message. In her heart she sensed there was danger. Lucien, as if out of spite, was in a merry mood and made fun of her. And for the first time his embrace aroused no feeling in her except fear; it was as though she felt chilled. Then she released herself from his arms and said:

" He wants to see you. Oh, Lucien, I'm afraid for you."

" Nonsense! Grandel isn't Othello."

" You don't understand. It isn't a question of jealousy. He's a terrible man. He's going to get you into trouble. I know that little smile of his. What can he want you for? "

" He probably doesn't know that I've fallen out with my father and wants to get into his confidence. He's just a careerist. But enough of that." He kissed Mouche. She turned away and said suddenly:

" Who was that letter from? "

Lucien shrugged his shoulders.

" A stupid forgery. The usual story about money. It was signed by Kilmann."

Mouche buried her head in the pillow. Lucien shook her by the shoulder. " Do you know anything? Tell me! "

" He'll kill you."

" Tell me! Do you know anything about the letter? "

" No. I don't know anything about the letter. But I know Kilmann. Only, for God's sake, don't say so! He'll kill you. It was at a hotel in Lucerne. He left me alone with him for a few minutes. We had rooms next door to each other. He was a horrible man. He went in at the waist as if he wore corsets, and the back of his head was shaved bare. . . . He talked French in a funny way. He said " t " instead of " d." He was a real Boche. But don't tell anyone!

Grandel told me not to say anything. He was very excited. . . .
And you know how quiet he is usually. You mustn't have anything
to do with him."

Lucien was no longer listening to her. He hurriedly put on his
clothes. Then he shouted:

"Get dressed!"

Mouche couldn't make out what was driving him; she tried to
put her lips to his hand.

"Darling Lucien, don't be angry! It's not my fault."

She cried. Wishing to please him, she took out her compact and
started to make up her face. He snatched the powder puff out of
her hand. "Oh, do come on."

They went out together. She whispered:

"Lucien. Oh, darling, I feel so frightened!"

She noticed that her blouse was undone and rushed into the first
doorway. When she came out, Lucien was nowhere to be seen. She
sat down on a seat. It was a bus-stop and people were crowding
around her. But she didn't notice anybody. A news-vender frightened her by bawling right into her ear: "The danger has not
passed!" Mouche cried out hysterically, and tears flowed from her
eyes. A woman went up to her and said in a gentle voice: "Don't
worry! My husband says there won't be any war."

CHAPTER 7

IT was eight o'clock in the evening when Lucien arrived at Breteuil's. The servant showed him into the drawing-room and asked
him to wait; Breteuil was dining.

The leader of the "Faithful" lived like an average middle-class
citizen. There was an upright piano in the drawing-room which
nobody ever played; the furniture had covers to prevent the red
satin from fading. On the round table were albums of family photographs and an enormous book, *The Châteaux of the Loire*. The
walls were adorned with landscapes — sunset at sea and an orchard
in blossom.

The door leading into the dining-room was ajar. One caught a glimpse of a sideboard with antique cut glass. Breteuil was sitting opposite his wife and eating stewed prunes. In the corner was a baby's high chair: his wife refused to have it taken away. After carefully folding his napkin, Breteuil came out to his visitor.

He frowned when he saw Lucien's excited face; he didn't like people to drop in on him uninvited. But Lucien was too excited to make any excuses. It was still less than an hour since he had left Mouche.

He said at once:

"The letter isn't a forgery."

Breteuil smiled. "Did your worthy father tell you that?"

"No, I wouldn't have believed him. But I know now that Kilmann does exist and that Grandel had a meeting with him."

Breteuil paced up and down the long, gloomy drawing-room. Lucien watched him out of the corner of his eye; he wanted to see whether he would show anger, amazement, or distress. But Breteuil's stern, bony face remained unmoved.

"Who told you that?" Breteuil said.

"Does it matter? I can't tell you the name, but I give you my word . . ."

Breteuil switched on the light. Lucien winced at the glare of the chandelier. Breteuil stood over him, resting his arm on the back of a high chair.

"I advise you to forget what you've just said. You've become a pawn in other people's hands. You give me your word about a man whom you don't even wish to name. But I give you my word about Grandel."

Lucien got up and went out into the hall without saying good-bye. He was a long time groping for his hat in the darkness. Then he suddenly went back to the drawing-room. Breteuil was still standing in the same position.

Lucien said with unusual calm, almost as if he were thinking to himself: "I've been having dealings with you for a year and a half. And now there's something interesting. . . . But are you blind? Or do you also know this Kilmann?"

He expected Breteuil to strike him or shout out: "Scoundrel!" But Breteuil's face was unchanged.

"You're too insignificant to insult me," said Breteuil. "My advice to you is don't meddle with politics. They're not for you. By nature you're a petty crook or a pimp. Get out!"

Lucien clenched his fists, but he did not go for Breteuil; he went out submissively. It was only outside in the street that he said to himself: "Why didn't I go for him?" And he was so disgusted with himself that he forgot about the insult. He walked about the streets in spite of the cold wind. It was the end of May, but the winter still held on.

Once again Lucien experienced the shipwreck of everything that he lived for, and now he knew that it was irremediable. He had been working for a certain Kilmann with a shaven nape. Disgusting! And Mouche was living with Grandel. Lucien quite forgot that Mouche had often wanted to leave Grandel. He now looked on her as an accomplice in crime. Who knows? She might even have lived with Kilmann. They were all one gang! His father was right: "You're working for the Germans." But he wouldn't go back to his father. And he wouldn't go back to those fools at the Maison de Culture either. The way back was closed. And in front there was nothing. Tomorrow Joliot would know that his father had turned him out. Then good-bye to his income; why should Joliot go shares with anyone? Breteuil thought to insult him. And it was true — tomorrow he would take to stealing, or become a pimp. Anyway, it was better than their politics!

Suddenly he stopped in amazement: decorated carnival cars were coming along the street. Half-clad girls, shivering in the cold wind, tried to smile at the few onlookers. Everything was bathed in a pale caustic light that seemed to increase the cold. Lucien remembered the polar ice and Henri's death. What were they doing — the white car, the enormous plaster swans, the girls in starched headdresses with thickly powdered faces — why was there a carnival today? Lucien tried hard to remember; oh, yes, it was in the papers. Paul Tessa was amusing the good French people. Enough of clenched fists, red flags, soulless politics! Long live mirth and trade! Tessa had decided to show the whole world that Paris was not afraid of either revolution or war. The carnival procession was to open the spring season: first nights at the theatres, sweepstake prizes at the Hippodrome, balls, fashion displays. Hurry up, you British and Americans! Bring your money with you! All the cabarets, all the dressmakers, all the perfume-sellers, all the whores await you. The saviour of France, Paul Tessa, awaits you.

Another decorated car swayed past. A plump woman with a tricolour scarf across her shoulder held aloft an electric torch: this

was France. She was cold; her eyes were sad and her lips purple.
Lucien stood and stared at the woman; suddenly, like a street
urchin, he stuck out his tongue at her.

CHAPTER 8

UNTIL quite recently the word "war" was associated with memories. Fifty-year-old people, peaceful wine-growers or accountants,
were fond of reminiscing in the long winter evenings over the
stormy days of their youth. They began their stories: "In those days
the war was on. . . ." Some of them did not spare their listeners.
They exaggerated the dangers they had been through and tried by
imitation and gesture to convey the thunder of shells and the groans
of the dying. Others looked on the war years as a time of fascinating adventure that was followed by a grey, humdrum life. Forgetting about the mud of the trenches, the lice, and the terror, they
enthusiastically described their heroic reconnaissances, army revels,
and amorous adventures. The children had long grown tired of
the miseries and daring of their fathers' youth. War to them was
something that had gone out of use like horse-cabs and oil lamps.
And now the familiar word had turned up again. It had become a
presentiment, an oppression; it stood across the path of the morrow.
People said: "If there isn't a war, we'll get married in the autumn,"
or "I'll pass my exams in July, if only there isn't a war."

That spring a good deal was written about the Sudetens, of whom
nobody had ever heard before. Looking at the map of Czechoslovakia, people squirmed timorously; they remembered 1914, the
Serbs, and that hot day when the little white notices and the muffled rolling of the drums announced general mobilization.

The May scare turned out to be a false alarm; yet everybody was
afraid to peer into the dim haze of the sultry summer. Those Sudetens again! What would you say to your friend when he asked
you about a vacation? The answer was always the same: "If there
isn't a war. . . ."

But the holidays drew near. And brushing aside their fear, the
Parisians set about choosing a fishing hamlet or a mountain village.

They weren't going to stay in the scorching city on account of those damned Sudetens.

Tessa had a firm belief in his own lucky star and in that of France. "Our country is an oasis of peace!" he declared. And immediately the press and the radio began to boost the peacefulness of France like a patent medicine or a superior brand of mineral water. Where could the Americans go? Wiesbaden? Good heavens! It was full of Storm Troopers, military manœuvres, concentration camps, and ersatz. Certainly not to Karlsbad: it was there that these very Sudetens lived. In Italy the hospitals were full of wounded soldiers from Spain, and there was a general hubbub — the Black Shirts were getting ready for new campaigns. But Vichy, Cannes, Biarritz were waiting for visitors. These were oases of peace indeed. And every evening Jeannette repeated at the microphone: "Oases of peace. Reserve your rooms in good time. . . . The Emerald Coast. . . . Don't forget the beauties of the Mâcon country, celebrated by Lamartine. . . . 'Oh, evening bells and fragrant smell of thyme!' . . . Superior white wine and 'fat pullet in mourning' stuffed with truffles. . . ."

Jeannette's holiday began on the 15th of August. She drove through the empty streets to the Gare de Lyon. As in former years, Paris seemed a dead city. A few provincials, a bus with English tourists. The vacated town was alive and snug; it resembled the country. Fat men on the café terraces unbuttoned their collars without more ado. Slippered concierges sat with their knitting outside the doorways. There was a pleasant atmosphere everywhere. People smiled benevolently, and the taxi-driver wished Jeannette a pleasant vacation.

The conversations in the train were again about the Sudetens, Hitler, and war. Jeannette paid no attention to them; they seemed to her remote and detached from life. And here was Fleury.

What made her choose this sultry, white village nestling among the vineyards and known only to wine-merchants? Perhaps she had remembered the pretty name from her childhood: Fleury.

It was a long time since she had been out of Paris. Her head felt dizzy with the air, the green, and the quiet. When she breathed, she really felt she was breathing; she relished the freshness of the blue morning, ran about the meadows, and climbed the hills. Everything here was peaceful and undisturbed. She remembered having seen little houses and vineyards like these when she was a girl;

and laughing, she repeated: "An oasis of peace. . . ." For once at least she was not telling a lie.

The wine-growers sprayed the bunches of grapes with sulphur. Everything about them was blue: their blouses, their hands. They examined every bunch affectionately; they glanced up with satisfaction at the cloudless sky and said to Jeannette: "It'll be a good wine this year." They remembered their life year by year according to what the summer had been: whether there was plenty of sun and if the vintage was successful. The good years were shown on the labels of old bottles and lived in the wine-growers' memory in association with the brooding solemn sultriness of August. And now the bunches of grapes were already beginning to darken.

Down below in the valleys were trees. Each one lived its own life; the elms, oaks, and ash trees were older than the people. And the people respected the trees, cherished their shade, and came to them in their hours of weariness or love. They ate their food, slept, and kissed under a tree. One of these trees was a favourite with Jeannette; it was a tall ash standing on the bank of a small muddy stream. Its dark leaves seemed to be etched against the white sky. It stood up straight, it did not yield to the wind, and Jeannette often thought of it as standing on guard at the entrance to the village, protecting its peace.

The talk of war reached Fleury also. In the dim café, where it was always cool and where the peasants slowly sipped a heavy wine from thick glasses, there suddenly resounded the voice of that unfriendly bumptious townsman the radio announcer. He spoke about the Sudetens and a certain Henlein. The wine-growers frowned: the war was creeping up to their houses. Then Eugène, the local rake, came in. He had red cheeks and a big moustache, and for some unknown reason was nicknamed "the Austrian," although he was born in a neighbouring village. He announced with enthusiasm: "Today I've eaten forty crayfish." Forgetting all about Henlein, the people in the café crowded round "the Austrian" and tried to worm out of him the whereabouts of the river where he had found the crayfish, but the rascal silently grinned. There were other incidents: some people came from Lyon to buy wine for a workers' beanfeast; old Baugé sold some tourists a stopper made of twigs; the café proprietor's goat ran away. All this was life, but the newspapers and the radio talked monotonously of death, and the living tried not to listen to this obscure talk.

Jeannette became part of the landscape and the little world of the village. The peasants gave her wine and joked with her. Among themselves they said: "She's a droll girl"; that meant "nice and pleasant." She immediately forgot Paris, where she had left nothing but loneliness and dull, exhausting work. The cars with smart Parisiennes that passed along the highway reminded her of that hostile world; she thought with a twinge of dread: "Soon it will come to an end."

And then on one of the hottest days, when the flaming August sun drove the people into the cool café, a Parisian spoke to her. He was dressed informally: without a collar and in sneakers. With his merry disposition, battered old pipe, saucy freckled face, and lively eyes, he looked like a wine-merchant from Mâcon or Dijon. He drank wine with gusto, smacking his lips and puffing out his cheeks. That day everybody was feeling drowsy with the heat. The landlady of the café was even snoring. But the man with the pipe was cheerful. He made Jeannette laugh when he teased the landlady and the "Austrian." Then he told a Marseille anecdote: "Olivier was excited. He said: 'I was going along the Cannebière when I caught sight of Marius. I called out to him: "Hello, Marius!" But he didn't turn round. And just imagine! It turned out that he wasn't him and I wasn't me!'" Jeannette laughed: "How ridiculous! He wasn't him and I wasn't me. . . ." She laughed so infectiously that the landlady woke up and smiled, and then dropped off again.

Jeannette liked the stranger, although he was neither young nor handsome. She was attracted by his simplicity, sauciness, and a certain vitality. Jeannette lived in the world of the stage where everyone's gestures and intonations were artificial. This man whom she took for a wine-merchant had something that appealed to her heart. They chatted amiably. And when the heat abated, they went out together and Jeannette led him to her favourite tree. He sat down on the grass, took off his hat, wiped his brow with a big silk handkerchief, and said: "It's amazingly good." Then he looked sad. Jeannette was likewise looking gloomy.

"You don't seem so cheerful," he said. "I've got that sort of talent: I put a chill on everybody. In fairy-stories there are people who pick up a handful of sand and find it's turned into gold. With me it's just the opposite: instead of gold I find sand."

"I can understand that," she replied.

Jeannette mournfully recalled another tree that stood drowsy and dusty near a merry-go-round in a Paris square. She could have been happy. Why had she refused happiness? She was like him. Sand instead of gold. And the strange man became doubly dear to her. She said to him in a surprised tone:

"It's queer how we've become friends. And yet I don't even know who you are. I'm an actress. Only don't think my name will mean anything to you. I'm an actress in a small way. I work in radio. Jeanne Lambert. Jeannette. And what do they call you?"

"Desser. There are probably a hundred thousand Dessers in France."

"There are more Duponts. I've heard about a certain Desser. A millionaire. They say he's a crank, but he's a horrible creature like all of them. . . ."

Desser smiled. "Of course," he said. "Let's finish the introductions; let's say, like the wise Olivier: you're not you and I'm not me. Good? It ought to be easy for you as an actress. What sort of parts do you play — ingénues? Disappointed girls in love? Country maids? Marguerite Gautier?"

"I advertise Cinzano vermouth and National beds. And also the prosperity of France. You see what an insignificant person I am! Once I was to have played a leading part. But they gave it to somebody else; it was a question of name — that is to say, money. I've got a friend who's a stage-manager. His name is Maréchal. You've probably never heard of him. He's very clever. He's always thinking about staging plays, but he never produces them; he hasn't the money. He has a revolutionary theatre, but it's not the fashion now. He had a wonderful idea for the production of a play and I was to take the leading part. But these are all dreams. I shall go on boosting artificial pearls or a new laxative. It doesn't matter. I'm only sorry I've got to go back to Paris so soon. . . ."

It suddenly occurred to her that she didn't even know what her companion did for a living or where he was from. Was he from Mâcon near by, or from Paris? Timidly she asked: "Have you come here on a vacation?"

"Yes. I've taken a little house not far from here on the way to Julien. I'm staying till October."

"Is your family with you?"

He burst out laughing. "I'm always alone! I don't know why — whether people run away from me or I from them. But I haven't run away from you."

"And I haven't run away either. I'm alone too. I mean, I once had near relations; no, that isn't true, they were distant ones. I lived with them, that's all. But that's all the external side, the role I was given to play. Sometimes it was even less: a room in a hotel. Does it matter which?"

The evening came, cool and fresh; the leaves of the ash trembled in the breeze. The frogs began to croak. The little cow-bells jingled in the distance. Jeannette was quiet. All at once Desser's face looked old and lean. In silence they returned to the village. When saying good-bye, Desser asked if he could come again the next day. He said rather bitterly: "I'm begging like a schoolboy for a romantic rendezvous under a shady lime tree."

"This isn't a lime. It's an ash. Don't talk like that. You mustn't be depressed! Till tomorrow!"

The next day he told her that she had the eyes of an owl, the hair and good nature of a poodle, and the speech of a Paris urchin. Also that he despised everything and was ready to dance with the girls of Fleury till he dropped, that the tires of his car were worn down and his coat was worn out, and that he liked the poetry of Laforgue, but for some reason he was interested in statistics.

A few days later and they were both waiting with impatience for the hour of their rendezvous. They were both of them naïve and conceited and neither of them had admitted any feelings of sentiment to the other. Jeannette thought: "He treats this as a banal holiday adventure." Desser said to himself: "I'm old and ugly, but money will buy anything."

The beginning of September was sultry and the peasants rejoiced. The grapes were swelling. Soon the vintage would be here. But Jeannette would not be there to see it; in a week her vacation would be over.

It was their last rendezvous but one. Awkwardly Desser put his arms round her. In affairs of love he was no more than a schoolboy. Jeannette sensed his sincerity and emotion. She freed herself from his arms.

"You mustn't," she said sadly.

He submitted at once. For some time they walked along a woodland path without speaking. Presently Jeannette said: "There've

been a lot of strawberries here. Look at the leaves. Don't be angry.
If I should have nothing for you. . . . You see, I'm not a virgin.
I've had affairs; just like that. I don't know why. I was lonely. Or
I couldn't refuse. But with you it's different! "

Desser said nothing.

After this conversation Jeannette reproached herself all night:
again she was refusing happiness. True she didn't know herself
whether this was a caprice or a genuine sentiment. Sometimes she
thought she only liked talking to him because he himself talked like
an echo answering her thoughts. They were both of them tired and
desolate. They had both run to seed for lack of kindness. They were
both beggars. What could they give each other? Desser sometimes
found pleasure in talking to the wine-growers, in resting, and in the
simple jokes in the village café. But now Jeannette felt that she
loved him. She was angry with herself for the scene in the forest:
why had she adopted that ridiculous touch-me-not attitude? Then
she was angry with him: why had he listened to her? Finally she
decided: " Tomorrow I'll kiss him." And with that she fell asleep.

Next day Desser came dressed in town clothes. His face was full
of anxiety. He didn't listen to Jeannette's chatter.

" I'm leaving for Paris in an hour," he said.

She cried out:

" Oh, no! "

" Thanks," Desser said quietly.

He waved a flimsy piece of blue paper.

" Telegram," he said. " They're calling me back. The situation
has unexpectedly become acute. . . ."

And Jeannette suddenly heard familiar names; as though a radio
announcer had begun to speak — Hitler, Henlein, Chamberlain.

" Surely there's not going to be a war? "

" I don't think so. But peace has got to be saved. At any cost. . . .
You've seen how happy these people are here. This is what we've
got to preserve. . . ."

" Yes," said Jeannette in a dull voice.

A moment later she said in surprise:

" But why you? No, I don't understand anything. You see, I still
don't know who you are. At first I thought you were a wine-
merchant. But now you talk as though you were a deputy or a minister."

For a moment he cheered up: " No, no, not a minister! God

forbid! I'm a business man. Only I don't deal in wine. As a matter of fact, I'm that same Desser who is a horrible creature. You remember you said that the first day? Now, I suppose, you'll tell me to go to the devil."

Jeannette looked at him in astonishment as though she hadn't seen him before. A millionaire. She recalled the rich people of Lyon, stuck-up and haughty. But Desser drank with the peasants, went about in an alpaca jacket, and spent his days with a third-rate actress. The fact of her being attracted to him made it all the more incomprehensible. What a pity he was going away! They said good-bye under the ash tree. Jeannette wanted to kiss him, but suddenly turned away.

" I decided during the night that I'd kiss you," she said. " But now it's impossible — you'll think I've got an eye on your millions."

Tears came into his eyes and, annoyed with himself at his emotion, he muttered: " It's always the same."

She kissed him quickly and, running up the little hill, called out to him: " My telephone number is Soufrênes 0826."

And a little farther up she called out: " *Au revoir!* We'll see each other in Paris? All right? "

He had already succeeded in becoming himself again, ordinary and slightly ironical.

" Of course," he said, " provided there isn't a war."

CHAPTER 9

TESSA had been telling everybody about the security of France for so long that now he believed in it himself. When anyone said in his presence: " If there isn't a war," he answered with assurance: " There won't be! " Whoever it was would then smile and feel more cheerful — Tessa knew something! But Tessa knew nothing. Like everybody else, he could sit and wonder: " Will there or won't there be war? " But he remained calm. This calm was inexplicable and unshakable; it came from the spectacle of people peacefully drinking their apéritifs, from Paulette's chatter and from the usual parliamentary gossip. Everything in the world seemed to him to be comprehensible and preordained. Was it possible for this well-ordered life to be disrupted merely on account of some infernal Sudetens?

Then came September. The cables from Berlin spoke of an early dénouement. It was impossible to get away with optimistic phrases. Tessa was about to go and stay with some friends at their country house on the banks of the Loire, when the storm blew up. Few people realized the gravity of the situation. Nobody believed the papers; they remembered how the press had croaked in May. They said: "It will blow over." The vacations continued; people basked on the beaches, climbed up the glaciers, and angled for fish. In the warm peace of the vacation resorts the newspaper reports seemed quite unrelated to reality; it was hard to imagine that the dispatches of ambassadors could interfere with bathing or walks.

Responsibility frightened Tessa. Was it worth while to have intrigued, undermined, and flattered in order to get into authority at an execrable time like this? He sometimes sighed for the past: it was far easier to defend an honest murderer, who without high-sounding phrases had cut the throat of a rich sister-in-law! But not for anything would Tessa give up his Minister's portfolio. There was something exhilarating in the sense of power. He had become ten years younger; even Paulette noticed it. He was on the move all the time, alert and excited. He said to himself: "What a moment this is! There have been many ministers. They are forgotten, but our great-great-grandchildren will read about me. If only I can save France and peace!"

The situation grew tenser each day. Something must be done to restrain the Germans. But the British endured in silence. And France was disunited. Tessa took Flandin aside. "Peace is hanging by a thread," he told him, and kept repeating the words over and over again in a melancholy voice. Tessa thought that all the trouble was due to the Czechs. Then bearded Fouget came up. He shouted about freedom, quoted Clemenceau, and kept exclaiming: "France! France!" Tessa in alarm said to him: "What are you fuming for? We won't let the Czechs down. I guaranteed . . ." And escaping from this bearded fury, he sighed: "Apparently we shall have to fight."

A telegram from Prague had just been handed to him. The Sudetens were going to rise in the next few days; German troops would cross the frontier to "protect their brothers"; Beneš insisted on

joint action by the powers who had guaranteed the inviolability
of Czechoslovakia. Tessa began to think. Was it possible to save
the Czechs when France was on the verge of collapse? The Right
was threatening to revolt. Daladier was drinking absinthe and saying: "I won't send the peasants of France to be slaughtered."
Lebrun was weeping. And Denise's friends were passing bellicose
resolutions and fomenting strikes. Yes, it was certainly more difficult than defending the most terrible murderer.

When Breteuil entered his study, Tessa mournfully blew his
nose: another unpleasant conversation awaited him. As if the
Sudetens were not enough for him to cope with, he had also to take
the opposition into account and to humour Breteuil. Tessa suddenly
remembered Lucien and the stolen document. He bristled all over.
His birdlike nose stuck out like the beak of a bird of prey.

"Apparently we shall have to fight," he said.

"Not at all," said Breteuil quietly. "You know that we must not
and will not fight. Pacify the country. This panic is affecting our
whole economic life. On the Bourse today . . ."

"But have you heard that the Sudetens are expected to carry
out a putsch this week? Everything has been arranged; the Germans
will cross the frontier. We shan't be able to wriggle out of it."

"If you announce mobilization, civil war will break out. The
defeat of France is certain. Of course, Germany is our natural
enemy. But it's necessary to be in a position to fight, and France
is divided. Some think that the Sudetens should be handed over:
to God that which is God's, to Hitler that which is Hitler's. That's
how the deputies of my group reason. Who are against concessions?
The Communists. The Popular Front. That admirer of Moscow,
Fouget. They don't care a damn for the Czechs. They want to
strengthen their own positions. Out of every hundred Frenchmen,
ten are for a compromise, five are for Beneš, and the rest are simply
fed up with the whole thing. Surely you're not going to follow the
Communists?"

"What have the Communists got to do with it? It's a question
of the Czechs."

"Yes, but the Czechs are the allies of Moscow."

"And of ourselves. It wasn't Cachin who signed the treaty with
Prague; it was Laval. In questions of foreign policy one mustn't
be guided by party interests."

"We're not sitting on Olympus," Breteuil said. "You said yourself that Frenchmen didn't want to die for the anarchists of Barcelona. No, wait! Did you or did you not say that? Quite so. And now Frenchmen don't want to die for an artificial state, which, moreover, is governed by the creatures of the Kremlin. You realize, Paul, Czechoslovakia is Moscow's advance post. It's quite understandable that Hitler wants to climb over the wall."

Tessa looked at Breteuil's stern, bony face and wondered all the time whether he knew that the Fouget document had been stolen. At last he blurted out:

"What is your attitude towards Grandel?"

Breteuil shrugged his shoulders: "I'm talking to you about serious matters, and yet you ask me about some infernal small fry. It isn't done, you know, Paul!"

When Breteuil had gone, Tessa began to reckon up: the Rights had broken away from the chain — that meant two hundred and forty votes against. Breteuil was right about one thing: the country was divided. Ought he to bring up the Grandel affair? But he would merely be making a fool of himself; what evidence had he? How about intimidating Berlin? But what if Hitler refused to be intimidated? It was a dangerous game. General Gamelin had talked for three hours on end about the "Czech Maginot Line," but when Daladier put the question bluntly, Gamelin preferred to withdraw: "The Army will carry out the Government's orders." It was easy to obey, but not so easy to give orders.

Before dinner Tessa summoned his own friend, General Picard, whom he trusted. Picard was looking young and calm; somehow he seemed to be the personification of the invincible Army of France. He did not rush at Tessa with tirades, as Fouget or Breteuil had done, nor did he try to make evasions; instead he expounded his views in a cold-blooded manner.

"I'm not considering the political side of the problem," Picard said. "I'm a soldier. Of course the loss of the Czechoslovak fortified line will be a heavy blow to us. But the truth must be faced. I don't think we would succeed in carrying out mobilization. You know the attitude of the country. The people don't understand why they should have to fight on account of the Sudetens. The idea of a preventive war isn't popular. As regards Germany — "

"But the Czechs will hold them up."

"Good! Perhaps for a week. It's a pincer movement; the main thrust will be from the direction of Austria. The Hungarians will

march. And the Poles. The Germans will be able to attack us immediately. Of course, we've got the Maginot Line. But — "

" But what? "

" We've got precious few planes. Our airmen are poorly trained.
Our anti-aircraft guns are far from being up to the mark. And
experience in Spain has shown — "

Tessa interrupted him. " Then it's impossible? "

Picard smiled politely. " For a soldier that word doesn't exist.
But everything must be weighed in the balance. The loss of Czechoslovakia is better than a military defeat."

Tessa had felt rather relieved when Picard arrived. Now he was
depressed. Picard painted an alarming picture of the devastation
of Paris. If Picard knew, the Germans would know too. It was impossible to bluff. What was to be done? Submit? But the role of
France? Her prestige? . . . Tessa felt keenly resentful; he was
being reduced to the level of a minister of Belgium or Portugal.
His patriotism was roused. Sitting alone in the twilit study, he
thought of the days of Verdun, the comrades who had fallen in the
war, and the unavailing victory of 1918. Yes, the statue in the
Louvre was full of significance: Victory had wings, but she was
without a head.

He was dining with Desser; and although Desser always knew
how to delight his friend with exquisite food, the dinner did not
promise to be a gay one. Tessa did not even look at the menu. It was
a Marseille restaurant; this was evident from the smell of garlic
and the vine leaves on which the fish was grilled. Another time
Tessa would have made an inspired speech on the wonderful gifts
of the fertile south. But now he was feeling the bitterness of a fall.

Desser smiled. " We're not asking if they've got crayfish in white
wine? Well, well, what a statesman we've become! "

Desser, however, was gloomy also. He had one extraordinary
peculiarity: in a single day he could look twenty years older or
younger. Jeannette would scarcely have recognized in this flabby,
gloomy man the lovesick romantic who used to come to the shady
ash.

Desser had been going downhill in the last few years. At the best
of times there was little enough that he believed in, but he had a
passion; he would build up and overthrow powerful trusts, rig
Stock Exchange crises, and change ministers like gloves. He devoted
all his powers to the task of preserving a fossilized society, its com-

fort, stuffiness, and modest joys. The events of the last few years, the strikes, the terrorism of the Fascists, the Spanish drama, Hitler's seizure of Austria, and the prospect of further and greater trials had deprived his life of its meaning. The whole climate of the world had changed; it was impossible to hope that old-fashioned France, with its enthusiastic anglers, country dances, and Radical Socialists, would be miraculously saved. Desser continued to work, but it was with a species of inertia. Like an obstinate gambler, he had staked everything on one number, and the roulette ball made fun of him. The situation was urgent; people put questions to him and he had to give an answer, and every word he said was looked on as a command.

It was the same with Tessa. He had not come to the restaurant for the sake of the crayfish. Desser tried to distract him with gastronomic surprises, but Tessa's thoughts were preoccupied with the devastation of Paris, the votes of the Right.

" What's going to happen? " he asked wearily.

" We'll have to give way. Haven't you spoken to Breteuil? "

" Yes. They're storming and raging. To them Beneš is a ' Bolshevik.' "

Desser roared with laughter. " Of course. The first Bolshevik was Azaña. It would be interesting to know who'll be the third. You or Chamberlain? It's all very amusing. But the conclusion is clear: we'll have to give way. You realize they've jumbled up all the cards. An honest plain-sailing war is impossible now; any war will turn into a civil war. Once upon a time the danger was only in the underground movement, unrest among the people, or revolts among the troops. It was positively idyllic! But now there exists an enormous state with its diplomats and, what's worse, with an air force. It's natural that everybody should look askance at the east. If the Russians go with us, Breteuil's friends will become defeatists. If the Russians go against us, the workers will become defeatists. And if the Russians keep out and prefer to wait and see, then everybody will become defeatist. Our middle class is afraid of defeat and afraid of victory. What they fear most of all is that Moscow should become strong. Just try to make war in a situation like that! I can understand the workers singing the *Marseillaise*. But don't pay any attention to that. Songs are songs, but we've got to give way."

Tessa sat silent over a plate of crayfish. He was paler than usual, complained of the heat, and wiped his forehead with his napkin.

"I'm very tired," he said. " But something has got to be decided.
You know what Daladier is like — he bangs his fists and shouts:
'I, I, I . . .' Napoleon . . . but in reality he's a bungler. He wants
to bluff. But what if the Germans reply by sending over five hundred or a thousand bombers? Picard says our air force is no good.
I feel that a terrible responsibility rests with me. Prague is waiting
for an answer. You see, we promised them . . ."

" I had lunch with Chamberlain recently," Desser said. " A crafty
business man. Malignant, but all honey! He showed me his grandfather's watch, a large bulbous one with an engraved motto: ' Never
promise what you cannot fulfil.' A remarkable motto that, for a
merchant. But don't be down-hearted. You didn't promise anything;
it was your predecessors. And even if you did, it doesn't matter.
Politics are not business, and it's impossible to be honest in
politics."

" But we've got to decide on something."

" Others will decide for us. . . . An hour ago I had a telephone
call from London. The honourable Chamberlain has decided to
come to terms with Hitler. I tell you, he's a crafty old fellow. So
you've nothing to worry about. For the time being we're a British
dominion. Maybe we'll become a province of the Reich. Breteuil
will be *Gauleiter*. Atrocious! But you can't do anything. The French
have gone flabby. I repeat: we'll have to give way."

Desser became even more gloomy. But now Tessa was smiling.
The news of Chamberlain's intentions cheered him up no end: the
Government was relieved of responsibility. If the British gave way,
even Fouget's tail would be between his legs. Then both the Right
and the Left would vote for the Cabinet. It would be possible to
make a beautiful speech: " In these tragic moments national unity
is a necessity. . . ."

If the crayfish passed unnoticed, Tessa appreciated the ox-tail
ragout. He ate greedily, smacking his lips and belching; then he
leaned back wearily with a faint smile and asked in a surprised
tone: "Why aren't you eating anything? "

" No appetite."

Only then did Tessa notice that Desser was not looking well.
Patronizingly he clapped the all-powerful financier on the back.

" We'll get our own back in a year or two. The main thing now
is to delay. You're wrong not to eat anything. We must hold up
the sacred torch. Well, I've had a remarkably good dinner. I didn't

even suspect I was so hungry. I'll have some more cheese."

He ate and ate. Desser smiled.

"When my aunt died," he said, "my uncle ate two ducks at one go and said: 'That's from grief.' . . ."

When Tessa got home he was in a cheerful mood.

"Have you been drinking?" Amalie asked.

"No. But I've dined well, exceedingly well. Besides, there was important political news. You wouldn't understand — its devilish complicated. The conclusion is clear: we'll have to give way."

And as he pulled off his trousers, he muttered playfully: "Give way — way — way."

CHAPTER 10

JOLIOT complained: "However much they starved me at the spas, I never got any thinner, but now I've probably lost seventy pounds." The editor's office was like an army headquarters. Joliot behaved like a general in command; he received mysterious packets, gave yet more mysterious orders, and hung up an enormous map of Czechoslovakia. In reality he didn't understand anything and grew thin with worry. He was afraid of incurring the anger of Desser, who continued to back *La Voie Nouvelle*. But it was impossible to get anything out of Desser; he only kept saying: "Support the Government." But whom? The ministers were unable to agree; Daladier was working against Mandel; Tessa was undermining Reynaud. And they all expected Joliot to render them services.

Thanks to Desser, *La Voie Nouvelle* had become one of the most influential newspapers. Joliot betrayed his patron right and left; he took money from the secret fund of the Ministry of Foreign Affairs, and did not despise the bribes of the various political parties. Sometimes he reproached himself for his levity: what if Desser suddenly got to know? But he soon appeased his conscience with the thought that he had many sources of income, that his wife needed a sable coat, that his collaborators were greedy, and finally that he was taking money from honest Frenchmen, Desser's friends, and therefore was deceiving nobody. Now, however, the poor fellow was in a quandary: the communiqués were like a Scottish shower-bath — alternate hot and cold water. It was difficult to guess the Government's intentions; were they preparing for war or were they going to capitulate? Joliot said to his wife: "This isn't politics. It's a brothel. I hope to God they don't do something silly!" But in the presence of his collaborators he pretended to know everything and to be full of diplomatic secrets. Whenever a question was put to him he always answered: "We're playing a very complicated game, very, very complicated. . . ."

The country was perplexed. Some newspapers said that Hitler was preparing to attack Strasbourg; others declared that the Czechs were persecuting the Sudetens and that France was in no way concerned. After reading a dozen articles, people anxiously asked one another: "What on earth does it mean? And, above all, how is it going to end?" Meanwhile everyday life went on as usual. The wine-growers got ready to gather the grapes, the theatres prepared for first nights, and the schoolchildren awaited the beginning of the school term. Women getting in supplies of sugar and rice said: "If only there isn't a war!" And everywhere there were people who answered: "There won't be any war. What have we got to do with the Czechs? It's only the Marxists and Jews who want war. But we'll soon make short work of them. . . ." The bourgeois were in love with Chamberlain, who was christened "the Angel of Peace"; poets wrote lines in his honour; the papers collected money in order to present him with a valuable gift; and the streets of French towns were named "rue Chamberlain." In the luxurious watering-places, in the casinos, on the country estates, and in the rich quarters of Paris — prematurely awakened after their summer sleep — people cursed the Czechs; they swore they were the cause of all the trouble and worse than the Bulgarians, something between Bolsheviks and bashi-bazouks. But in the working-class suburbs the people abused Daladier, remembered Spain and "non-intervention," and shouted: "No more capitulations!"

In the evening came alarming news: Chamberlain's second trip had ended in failure. Joliot waved his arms. He had been just about to devote a couple of columns to the bloodless victory of the "Angel of Peace," who, at his advanced age, was not afraid of making another journey by air. And now there were complications once more! Joliot was pacing up and down the office, not knowing what to do, when Desser unexpectedly telephoned to him: "Come and see me."

The streets in the Invalides quarter were dark. Joliot shuddered superstitiously; the little blue lamps looked to him like the little lamps on graves. Nor was he soothed by Desser's appearance — the flabby face, the dull eyes with purplish bags under them. Even Desser's writing-table, which was usually littered with papers, induced a feeling of sadness; it was quite bare except for a glass of water and some headache pills.

The moment Joliot came in, Desser said: " The situation is serious. Of course, nobody wants war, but they're all bluffing. It's not the people, it's the rifles that may start it! However, as always, I'm an optimist. Now listen to me, my friend. Your paper is read by the people who matter and not by half-wits. They don't trust Maurice Déat. He's a man with a tarnished reputation. They're making fun of Maurice Rostand's poetry. It's impossible! Look at their names: Kérillis, Ducane, Fouget, Cachin. And whom do you put up against them? Nincompoops. Or sob-sisters."

Joliot was breathless with agitation. He rummaged in his pockets, which were stuffed full of letters, accounts, and amulets; he was looking for a manuscript. No, he wasn't being paid for nothing! Proudly he handed Desser a sheet of thin crinkly paper. " There! "

It was an article by a famous author, headed " Slavery Rather than Death." Desser read it through and laid the paper aside. Why did his face wear that disdainful grin? He himself had more than once expressed the same idea, defended concessions, suggested that France should accept the position of a second-rate power, and ridiculed the last-ditchers. He was afraid of death, hated going to funerals, and often thought: " Anything to keep alive! " And now it was written on this thin sheet of paper: " Slavery Rather than Death." The word was unpleasant and harsh; it didn't fit in with his recollections of his childhood — the eager lads, the grumbling old men, the cabaret singers, the wind off the sea — or his favourite authors.

Desser handed the manuscript back in silence and took another headache pill. Then he said: " It would be a good thing for you to publish an article by Villard. Or an interview. Of course he's got somewhat tarnished since he entered the Government, but so far as a considerable section of the workers are concerned he remains an honest man. If he expresses himself in favour of compromise, nobody will suspect that he's grinding his own axe. They'll say:

'An internationalist, a pacifist. . . .' As regards this article, the ideas are right, but all the same, I'd alter the word 'slavery.'"

For some reason or other Desser remembered Jeannette, the woodland path, and her sad voice when she said to him: "You mustn't."

"I'd use a different word altogether: 'Humility,' or 'Suffering.'"

Next day Villard received Joliot. The tubby little man at once explained what he had come for.

Villard answered in a tired voice: "I know. Desser has already told me. We'll talk about it later on. You'll excuse me, but I didn't know that Hitler was going to speak on the radio. We'll listen to him presently. A good deal depends on what he's going to say."

"Do you know German?"

"Of course. At the international congresses I heard all the old Social Democrats: Bebel, Liebknecht, Kautski. I remember Bebel making a speech in Basel just before the war. Those were good times! Not like now. Yes, my friend, the situation is very grave. We Socialists said that it was necessary to preserve the Weimar Republic in Germany. It was easier to come to an agreement with Stresemann. They didn't listen to us. And this is the result! But we can't make war. And we mustn't. Democracies are not made for war. That's an axiom. War either destroys them or leads to their decline. Clemenceau very nearly devoured Parliament. Look at what's happened in Italy; and the fate of Kerensky! If we're defeated, a revolution is inevitable. Everybody realizes that. And what awaits us in the event of victory? Some general will seize power. Of course, we've got an honest general or two even if it's only old Pétain. But there will be plenty of adventurers. The other day I was at a meeting of the War Commission. There was a Colonel de Gaulle there, cocksure, ambitious fellow. He declared that we were wasting time, that it was necessary to revise the budget, set about mechanizing the army, and so on. A swashbuckler like that might declare a dictatorship in a couple of seconds. As a general rule, my opinion is that military men must be kept out of it. It's folly to take their advice. And Daladier also . . ."

He did not finish the sentence, but rushed over to the radio set. There was a rumbling noise.

"Now he's going to speak. To think that at this moment the whole world is waiting with bated breath at their loud-speakers."

When he asked Joliot what languages he could speak, he proudly replied: "French and Marseillais." He didn't, in fact, know a word of German. All the same, he listened attentively to the loud jerky speech. Hitler opened in a quiet manner, but soon started uttering threats in a hoarse voice. The loud-speaker spat out the unintelligible words that sounded for this very reason all the more terrible. Hitler barked like an old wolf. Joliot felt very uneasy. He gripped the back of the chair with his hand; he had a great respect for all omens and believed in touching wood to ward off evil.

At times Villard nodded his head as though approving the speech of the invisible orator. Other times he shrugged his shoulders resentfully; his chin, nose, and eye-glasses all trembled. Joliot eagerly watched Villard's face in an effort to understand the meaning of the unintelligible speech. From time to time the room was filled with the roar of the crowd: "Sieg heil!" and Joliot would clutch the chair convulsively. So it went on for a good hour. At last a roar of enthusiasm resounded. Villard wiped his brow with his handkerchief. Joliot asked timidly: "Well, what?"

"Oh, nothing particular. I foresaw all this. On the whole I'm rather optimistic. He repeated his assurance that he has renounced any claim to Alsace. And that's the most essential thing for us."

"The Czechs?"

"On that question he's absolutely intransigent. But as he renounces all claims in the west, I consider agreement is quite possible. In the end, the position of Prague depends upon us. A compromise is indicated. It must be explained. I'll dictate an article at once."

He rang the bell. A curly-haired, heavily powdered typist came in. Villard began to dictate. He walked to and fro about the room, stopping from time to time and declaiming instead of dictating; he imagined he was on the platform. His voice trembled with emotion.

"The Gorgon's glassy eyes are known to all mothers. We know what the soil of Verdun is! We note with joy that Hitler, as a soldier of the World War, has not forgotten all the horrors of that terrible carnage. The hand held out by him we, the representatives of French democracy . . ."

He held out his hand and began to think.

"Period after 'democracy'?" asked the typist.

"No, comma. The sons of a peace-loving nation, the disciples of Jaurès . . ."

Afterwards he checked it over and signed it. As Joliot was leaving, he said to him:

"Put at the end that all rights are reserved by the Atlantic Agency — that's for the Americans. One's got to think about one's daily bread, you know — can't get away from it. You see, I've returned to the profession of journalist. We're colleagues now."

When he was alone, Villard recalled the speech and sighed. No, it certainly wasn't Bebel! What a good thing the Cabinet crisis had taken place in the spring. A dirty business! It was even worse than with the Spaniards. France would have to ransom herself at the expense of others. Besides, it would be far better for the Czechs to yield; otherwise they would be crushed immediately. At a time like this it was much pleasanter to be a journalist; less responsibility. Well, the Radicals were determined to throw the Socialists out of the Cabinet. Now let them clear up the mess!

He dozed off, sitting in the armchair. He was roused by a feminine voice: his elder daughter, Louise, had unexpectedly arrived from Périgueux. She embraced her father and whimpered:

"Gaston was called up yesterday evening. He's in the anti-aircraft artillery. Papa, what's going to happen?"

Villard became benevolent and important; his face took on the same expression as when he used to give presents to his daughters.

"I'll tell you later. Wait, don't cry. It'll turn out all right. We're not going to allow war, you understand, we won't allow it."

Joliot arrived home in a gloomy mood. Of course Desser knew what he was doing, but all the same the little blue lamps and Hitler's speech. . . . Brrr! Joliot felt uneasy. His wife fussed over him, brought him his slippers, and brewed his favourite vervain infusion.

"I got an article out of Villard," he said. "Three hundred lines. We've put it on the front page together with his photograph. Desser will be pleased. But if you'd only seen them, my little kitten! They talk about optimism, but they look like drowned dogs. I believe Desser is ill. He certainly looks as if he was. I wonder if it's cancer. That would be another surprise! It would mean the end of the paper."

His wife poured out the vervain infusion. "Is there going to be war?" she said quietly.

Joliot smiled. "What war? They'll give up Prague, you'll see!

Hitler has been shouting and shouting. I heard the whole of his speech. He's a raving maniac. Villard went as white as a sheet. Do you know what I'm afraid of? I'm afraid they may even give up Marseille! Then there won't be anywhere to run away to, damned if there will! "

CHAPTER 11

ALL day André wandered about the streets of excited Paris and listened to the feverish conversations: " Will it? . . . Won't it? . . ." Towards evening he arrived back, tired out, in his own rue Cherche-Midi. But even there it was not quiet. The cobbler was shouting: " If they're not headed off, they'll come here. They're hungry rats! " The wife of Boileau, the old antiquarian, a grey-haired lady in ample corsets, complained: " No! Tell me, what has France got to do with it? Have you ever seen a live Czechoslovakian? " In the café of the Smoking Dog one of the customers tried to prove that the Germans were in need of more space: " For instance, take the cafés on Sundays. They often put the tables out farther than they should. That's in the natural order of things." The landlord frowned. " But they get fined for it," he said. A plumber began shouting: " The Germans want more room? What about me? What sort of Frenchman are you? You're a Fascist and a scoundrel! " They came to blows.

André looked at the objects in the window of old Boileau's shop; the sight of them soothed his mind. What an extraordinary jumble of things there were! A Negro idol majestically and shamelessly showed his divine essence to the world. The plates gleamed with dull lights: Delft ware, white and blue like frozen canals — Rouen ware, warm and rosy — Quimper ware with cockerels and Bretons. Ivory Chinese buttons. Snuff-boxes with the Phrygian cap and the intransigent motto: " Equality or Death." Necklaces of heavy amber, garnet bracelets, Persian turquoises. Valenciennes, Bruges, and Venetian lace. Blue glass. English sporting prints — jockeys in pastel-coloured jackets, pale, shy horses. A hookah, sumptuous and enigmatic, like an alchemist's retort. Angels, coins, locks of hair, wax roses. How much labour had gone into them all!

Next door to the antique shop was a dairy. André gazed entranced at the cheeses as though he was in the presence of canvases by the great masters. There were red globes of Dutch cheese; a weeping mound of Swiss cheese; dry, wax-like Parmesan; Roquefort like marble with blue veins; golden Brie oozing languidly; goat's-milk cheeses on green leaves; and many other sorts of all shapes and colours.

Farther on was a wine-merchant's; well-shaped, tall-shouldered bottles for Bordeaux of a quiet family type favoured by senators, savants, and academicians; bulging bottles of comfortable dimensions, like aunts, for Burgundy, the wine of maturity; but for *vin d'Alsace*, which is favoured by lovers, the bottles were romantic, slender and green. On the labels were the names of little villages that have gone round the world: Chambertin, Chablis, Barsac, Beaune, Vouvray, Châteauneuf-du-Pape. A bottle of cognac was so thick with dust that it might have figured in the antiquary's shop. André thought: " It's a lot older than I am."

Next came his favourite shop window. He often stopped there to gaze at the pipes: there were long pipes and nose-warmers, straight pipes, curved pipes that looked like mountain ram's horns, tiny pipes for snobs, and massive pipes for sailors, black, brown, and light red pipes. The owner of the shop once explained to André how pipes were made from brier roots; the roots had to lie in the ground for at least half a century, otherwise they would not taste good. Now André wanted to have another chat about the dead roots, but the tobacconist stuttered with emotion and asked: " W-w-what's your opinion? Do you think there will be war? " André strolled back to his studio. Pierre came in. He was in a hurry to explain everything; there was to be a meeting at the factory that evening and the workers were excited. Although Pierre had aged he still retained his southern impetuosity. He was alarmed by the situation and unable to finish what he was saying; he kept switching the radio on and off all the time. " There's a limit to everything! " he shouted. " They can't give way now. They're on the verge of a precipice. And yet they're afraid! . . . Have you read Villard's article? What a disgrace! But the working class . . ."

André interrupted him: " Dreamer! But on the whole I don't understand anything. As usual. What do you think? Do you want war? War's a filthy business. In the pictures in the Versailles gallery it's all generals, flags, and clouds. But in reality it's mud and lice. Honestly, I simply don't know how I'm going to live. It's all right for you. In the first place you've got — " he bent back his huge knobbly thumb — " Agnès. Secondly, you've got a son. And thirdly, you've got what are called ideals. But I've got nothing. Nothing at all! "

" But you've got your art."

" Art? That's all talk, Pierre. The weather isn't suitable. I had a letter from my father yesterday; he wanted to know about the prospects of war. On account of his apples. Well, I want to know too, on account of my pictures. But I've no one to ask. If it all blows over now, it'll start again in a year or two. And you want me to live for art! Everything is stagnant. It will take a good deal of time to get going again. I saw a wonderful pipe today. Do you know what it's made of? Dead brier root. Understand? But it lay in the ground for a hundred years. And what have we got here? Strikes, demonstrations, howling Hitler, some Sudetens or other, and you expect me to sit down and paint masterpieces! I say to you — muck! "

This time it was not Pierre but André who rushed to the radio. Pierre stopped him. " It's too early yet. The news isn't for another half-hour."

André couldn't admit that he was indifferent to the reactions of Rome and Washington to Chamberlain's flight and that he was waiting for something quite different. He had cherished this passion for two long weary years now and listened to Jeannette every evening. He had not seen her again and knew nothing of her sorrows, but for him she was still the same. Yes, she was the only one who had not changed in this mad world.

" I don't want to miss it," he said. " They give advertisements first, but they don't last long."

The radio was silent. There was no Jeannette. To André this seemed to be the most terrible omen. " They haven't come to an agreement," he said.

" I'm only afraid that Daladier will back out."

They were thinking of different things and fearing different things. Instead of the usual broadcast, instead of Jeannette's deep voice, the beats of the metronome resounded hard and merciless. Suddenly an indifferent voice announced:

" Men liable for military service with names beginning with the letters A and B . . ."

André cheered up; a weight had fallen from his shoulders. Now others would do his thinking for him.

"This is a nice how-do-you-do," he said. "It means we're going to fight."

He did not listen to Pierre's arguments, conclusions, and admissions. The old familiar street was still the same — a pot of flowers on the balcony opposite, a pale, impotent moon in the bright sky. André realized that for him all this time had been only a tormenting pause, from the June days with the red flags and the night with the whirling merry-go-round to the ticking of the metronome, the tramp of feet below the window, and now — mobilization. He did not want to know, to remember, or to think. For a moment he felt a wrench at his heart: what had become of Jeannette? . . . But even this longing was impotent; everything was falling, whirling, and disappearing. He went out with Pierre. Outside the street door a woman was weeping. Some reservists went by, carrying their suitcases; they sang the *Marseillaise* and then the *Internationale*. It was a warm summer night. "A paradise for lovers," thought André, and once again he saw the Place Contrescarpes on that July night. The lights were burning everywhere. . . .

"I must catch the Metro," Pierre said. "I'm afraid I shall be late. *Au revoir*, André."

Pierre said this, but he did not go away. The words "*Au revoir*" troubled both of them. André did not see Pierre the father, Pierre the engineer, with all the talk about Desser, the Socialists, and war. Before him stood his school companion, the mischievous and dreamy boy who once, as a boy of twelve, suggested to André that they should go on a trip to Greenland.

André said: "You remember how you wanted to go to Greenland? Whale-hunting. How funny that was! And they'll probably call you up too. We'll get killed off like flies, that's a certainty. It'll be like Verdun, only from the sky as well. But it doesn't matter. The one good thing is that we know where we are; we couldn't have gone on living like that. Now it's a sort of showdown. There's a poem, I forgot who it's by: 'Deceived, I go to meet my death. . . .' But do you realize what the funniest thing of all is? It was a long time ago; a German sat down next to me in our café. He was a typical German with blue eyes and the back of his head close-cropped. I thought he was a refugee, but he turned out to be a German of the Germans. He was interested in fish. He liked my

landscapes. He got tight and said there was sure to be war and the
Germans would devastate Paris. A funny fellow! What amuses me
is that he has probably been called up too. That means he'll be
fighting me. Well, isn't it muck? But I'm glad, Pierre, the uncertainty has come to an end. If it's war, then it's war."

They said good-bye.

CHAPTER 12

BRETEUIL could hardly stand; his eyes were red from sleepless
nights. Only his iron constitution and will kept him going. A compromise had to be reached at any cost. It was possible to come to
terms with Germany. The main thing was to tear up the pact with
Moscow. But events followed one another in rapid succession. Hitler would not wait; in vain the "Angel of Peace" flew over bewildered Europe; in France the Mohicans of the Popular Front urged
resistance. Breteuil wrote articles and pamphlets, conferred with
diplomats, instructed the "Faithful," and directed the Army staffs,
through General Picard.

Paris was blacked out. And Breteuil's agents operated in the
darkness exhorting or inciting: "The Czechs have only themselves
to blame. It's the wealthy Jews that want war."

"Mandel is in favour of war. His real name is Rothschild. Beneš
has bribed him. But it's our children who are being driven to the
slaughter! "

"The Germans have got a hundred thousand planes. They'll
smash Paris to pieces the very first day. . . ."

The Gare de l'Est was full of commotion; trains loaded with
reservists were leaving every few minutes. Some of the men raised
their fists, sang songs and said: "We must show the Germans that
we're not all crawling on our bellies." Others muttered sullenly:
"Why should we have to crawl?" Women were in tears. There was
plenty of scope for the Fascists; they said that mobilization had
been declared illegally, that the Czechs had broken the treaty themselves and that the French ought to let them go to the devil.

As at the start of the Spanish war, Paris was divided into two camps. In the Champs-Élysées "pacifism" was triumphant; people cursed the horrors of war and appealed to humanitarian sentiments, even that of "brotherhood." They easily forgot not only their own recent words but also their mode of life, the traditions of their class, and the myths of caste. Their blind hatred of the "sluggards" — as the Fascists continued to call the workers — proved stronger than anything else. Colonial officers who had been through the Riff campaign, high-handed martinets who had soldiers shot for some trifling offence, now swore that nothing could justify the shedding of blood. Academicians who only yesterday were boasting of the "invincibility of France" and lived on quotations from Marshal Foch maintained that it was impossible to go to war: the Germans had only to blow and the whole Maginot Line would collapse like a house of cards. And Breteuil, the native of Lorraine, who had said that the finest moment of his life was when the French troops entered Metz, now declared: "The frontier question recedes into the background in comparison with the defence of our Western civilization against the Bolsheviks."

The rich quarters were now rapidly emptying. The watering-places had been on the point of closing down; alarmed by the newspaper reports, the holiday-makers had gone back to the capital. But when mobilization began and the blackout was introduced, the bourgeoisie started leaving Paris and sent their families farther afield. So at this unusual season of the year the seaside resorts and mountain villages livened up again. The leaves were already falling from the trees; autumn gales were raging in the Channel. The holiday-makers were nipped with the cold and grumbled with resentment: "Anyway, it's time those damned Czechs were curbed!" — Nobody thought any more about the Sudetens.

In the working-class suburbs, however, there was a different kind of talk. Nobody there was pleased at the prospect of war, but the men went off in silence to defend their country. They knew that it had its back to the wall and they told themselves that it was impossible to go on living like this. The word "aggressor" was understood and became part of everyday speech. And the reservists often went off accompanied by the singing of the *Internationale*. They looked into the future with hope: they were going to fight the Fascist aggressors and their French friends — the followers of Breteuil and Doriot. At times it seemed as though June 1936 was coming to life again. Aubry, who dared to praise Chamberlain at

Billancourt, was roughly handled. When the police carried him
away, the street urchins called out merrily: "The war's begun!"

At a meeting of the "national-minded deputies" Breteuil said:
"There won't be any war. And there mustn't be. The Czechs have
a treaty with Moscow. In other words, we're asked to fight for Communism. A compromise is essential. Let us reason soberly. We're
undermined by Bolshevism. In Spain the national war is still going
on. England on her island is protected against infection. The English may play the hypocrite, bluff and flirt with liberal ideas. But
who in reality is capable of defending Europe against Communism?
Only Hitler. Consequently our allies are our enemies, and our
enemies are our friends."

This was the first time that Breteuil ventured to express his ideas
in the presence of Ducane. He expected controversy and patriotic
tirades. He was unaware of Ducane's attitude; he had not seen him
since the beginning of the September scare and had avoided meeting him. Ducane was nearly at his wits' end. This man, who though
slow and obstinate was by no means stupid, now seemed to wake
up. He had joined the Right wing because he thought they stood
for "Great France." And now he saw that Breteuil's friends, his
own friends of yesterday, were disrupting mobilization, advocating
desertion and treason. And who really wanted to defend France?
The workers. It was a terrible thought — the Communists! This was
a heavy blow for Ducane. He was a long time bringing himself to
believe the truth. He had consoled himself with the thought that
the class egotism which blinded thousands of people was alien to
Breteuil. Of late he had been trying to have a talk with Breteuil
but had not succeeded in getting hold of him. Now doubts assailed
him. Had Ducane been younger, he would have found relief in a
military job; but at fifty-six it was hard to think about air combats.
He had done his best to oppose the propaganda of the defeatists.
They shunned him; sometimes they shrugged condescendingly:
"A dreamer"; or else they angrily cut him short with: "Moscow's
instructions." Now for the first time he heard from Breteuil's own
lips the very things that had filled him with indignation. He wanted
to expose his former teacher and the enemies of France, but he was
so excited that he was unable to speak. His defect of speech increased to such an extent that he was tongue-tied. He made a sound
like a painful moaning. At last he shouted in a loud, unnatural
voice:

"So that's what you are! Hitler's admirer! You were wounded in the war. That's a badge of honour, but you're unworthy of it!"

There were tears in his eyes. Snatching up his papers that lay scattered about the table, he rushed out of the room. The deputies shrugged their shoulders. "He's mad!" Some said Ducane mustn't be judged too severely: he had been trepanned in the last war; it had probably affected his mental condition. Only Grandel grinned ironically:

"He pretends to be mad, but his behaviour is perfectly logical. I met him with Fouget yesterday. It isn't so much patriotism as Moscow bread and butter. . . ."

Breteuil suggested they ought not to waste valuable time; the Ducane incident could be postponed until a more peaceful period, but at present they had to attend to the international situation — any hour might bring a dénouement.

"We must rely on Mussolini. He will get us a rapprochement with Hitler. Chamberlain is anxious for it too. The Radicals must realize by hook or by crook what we have been dreaming of all along — a four-power pact."

They adopted a resolution stating: "The national-minded deputies hope that the Government will do its utmost to preserve peace and refrain from taking any hasty steps whatsoever."

When the deputies had left, Grandel went up to Breteuil and said in a friendly way: "You were amazingly restrained! If I'd been in your place, I'd have lost my temper. That talk about your wound — what low-down villainy!"

Breteuil glanced about him. There was nobody in the room. "I don't like being taken for a simpleton," he said in a low voice. "Ducane is a fool and a psychopathic subject. As far as you and I are concerned, well, I've now been informed of the motive forces of your patriotism. I hope you understand me?"

Grandel blinked, nonplussed. "No, I don't," he said.

"In that case I'll be more precise. I know that a certain Kilmann —"

"That forgery again!"

"Excuse me, but I've had confirmation that you really did have a meeting with him."

Grandel went white as a sheet: if Breteuil came out against him, he was done for. He said nothing.

"It's a good thing you don't object," Breteuil went on. "I haven't told anyone about it. And I don't intend to. But I don't want you to take me for a mug. Your Berlin masters think they're making use of me. That's their business. Personally I'm convinced that I'm making use of them. I serve, Monsieur Grandel, not Kilmann but national France."

Grandel recovered his composure and even became cheerful. " It's a question of shades of meaning, my dear sir," he said. " Why argue about them? "

Outside, the same anxious hubbub filled the streets; people kept coming and going, gathering in knots, discussing the rumours, snatching the latest editions of the papers from the news-venders, saying good-bye, arguing and singing. Breteuil was in a hurry. He had an appointment with the correspondent of a Rome newspaper, but on the way he went into the Church of St. Germain-des-Prés. He dipped his yellow finger in the holy water in the marble shell, crossed himself, and then went to the altar on the right, where a swarm of tapers flickered around the stone image of the Mother of God. He went down on one knee and recited a prayer. All around were women praying for their husbands and sons.

After the gloom of the church the sun seemed unbearable. Breteuil screwed up his eyes and for a moment everything began to swim in front of him: the sleepless nights were taking their toll. But the newspaper-sellers were rushing along. A vested priest came out of the church at the same time as Breteuil. A choir-boy in a surplice was ringing a little bell. Somebody was dying and the priest was hurrying with the Sacrament. In the churchyard the birds were singing. And on the terrace of the café opposite the church the Parisians sat drinking their apéritifs flavoured with wormwood, aniseed, arrowroot, eucalyptus, orange, and lily of the valley and pretended that nothing was happening in the world.

CHAPTER 13

THE MEETING at the Seine works ended early: the men were no longer in the mood for words. They all knew that the country was in the hands of insignificant, mean-spirited people who were capable of any treachery. The workers were ready to fight, but there was neither gaiety nor passion in their resolve. They decided to send a delegation to the Czechoslovak Legation to express their solidarity.

On the following morning Legrais and Pierre crossed the Champs-de-Mars on their way to the Legation. Tanks rumbled past. Girls were playing with hoops. A prosperous-looking middle-aged man was holding forth: "They say the Czechs have got good beer. But I don't like beer. Now I ask you — what have we got to do with the matter?"

Legrais said to Pierre: "You were saying yesterday that France will soon find herself isolated. That's true. But we're isolated too in the middle of France. We still talk about the Popular Front, but it doesn't exist. I prefer Ducane to all the Socialists; he's an honest man. The workers are behaving splendidly, showing great maturity. But what about the peasants? If Daladier capitulates, they'll be pleased."

Pierre smiled. "Not only the peasants," he said. "My Agnès will be pleased too — and she's a workman's daughter. She ought to understand. It's a terrible mix-up. She keeps on saying to me: 'But look at what you wrote before.' Personally I trust my feelings. It was the same with Spain. . . . I saw Azaña in Barcelona. He's a typical radical, like our Sarraut. Do you think he didn't let the workers down? Of course he let them down. But it wasn't a question of him. It's the same with the Czechs. But Agnès doesn't understand; she lumps everything together."

"Maybe she does understand, only she's afraid they'll send you to the front. She's got a child. That's understandable. . . ." Legrais sighed: he was alone in the world; nobody would worry on account of him.

It was a cloudy day, but you could feel the sun behind the white film.

"They'll give way," Pierre muttered. "It's a sort of enchanted circle. . . ."

All these last few weeks Pierre had been living in a state of expectation. Even Spain receded into the background. Years seemed to have passed between Chamberlain's two flights to Hitler. It was impossible to work or think or sleep. Pierre had none of the enthusiasm of the Popular Front days. All that was left was the bitterness of disillusion, a feeling of dejection even. This was hardly in keeping with his temperament, and he thought: "I'm at a dead end."

He had occasion to carry on diplomatic negotiations with dealers in armaments. The few short trips he had made to Spain now seemed to him like wonderful dreams. He was awaiting a showdown, departure and war. But the child that still lived in him, the dreamer from lazy Perpignan, demanded happiness. And now when he heard the notes of a piano coming through the open window, he stopped and screwed up his eyes with pleasure.

"The same old scherzo. . . . Wonderful!"

At the Czechoslovak Legation they were received by Vanek, the first secretary. He was a stocky, sluggish man with the broad hands of a peasant and a thick neck constricted by a starched collar.

Constantly throughout the last few days workers' delegations had been arriving at the Legation, and yet Vanek frowned every time. Hearing the words "the solidarity of the proletariat," he asked himself: "What's happened?" Who were these people who shook his hand and talked of anger and hope? The Communists! And to the Minister he admitted: "I no longer understand anything!"

Nine years before, Vanek, who was a philologist by training and a liberal by conviction, had a post at Ostrav in Moravia. Disorders broke out there: the Communists demonstrated against the new military laws. They were arrested. At the trial Vanek appeared as a witness for the prosecution. He was delighted with the sentence: the ringleaders were given four years' imprisonment. And now he was being encouraged by the Communists in Paris! But the people with whom he had been friends, the people whom he had entertained at luncheon and with whom he had chatted about the Maginot Line, Titulescu's speeches, and Smetana's operas, these cultured and sympathetic people had disappeared from the scene. How Vanek had rejoiced in the spring on hearing that Tessa had been appointed Minister! Was it not Tessa who wrote, on the occasion of Masaryk's jubilee: "Czechoslovakia is the bulwark of our Western civilization in the very centre of Europe; it is the land of humanism. . . ." And now it was impossible to get anywhere near Tessa. Vanek was anxious about the fate of his country. The articles in the French press filled him with rage. When he read Breteuil's speech, which called the Czechs "barbarians," Vanek lost his temper and smashed the coffee cups. In addition to all this, there was his personal grief; he was born in a small Moravian town not far from the frontier. His old parents and sister lived there. He stubbornly repeated a hundred times a day: "Surely the French won't

betray us?" He went to the Ministry of Foreign Affairs. He button-
holed the deputies whom he knew, but either they had nothing to
say or else they sighed funereally. Delegations kept arriving at the
Legation; but Vanek waited in vain for the representatives of the
French press, the professors, the lawyers, the Radicals, or even
the Socialists. It was the workers who came and repeated the same
words. Vanek thanked them, shook them by the hand, and thought:
" The Communists again! "

At the Legation Legrais was silent all the time. Pierre did all the
talking. And Vanek was struck by Pierre's spirited tone and unusual
vocabulary. He realized that this man was neither a worker nor
a Communist, but a free-thinker, a man of the same sort of background and ideas as himself.

" What you say gives me great pleasure," said Vanek. "It's a good
thing that people of varying convictions come to us. Otherwise the
impression might be created that only the Communists are for us."

" I am a Communist," said Pierre stiffly.

Vanek smiled politely. They were standing by the open window
of the balcony. The alarming cries of the news-venders came to
their ears. Vanek blinked at the light and wondered whether Tessa
would receive him today.

When they got outside, Legrais said to Pierre:

" Listen, Pierre, of course this isn't the time to talk about it, but
I've been wanting to ask you for some time. Why don't you join
the party? "

Pierre did not answer at once. Then he said: "I don't know — I
suppose it would be more honest."

Tessa received Vanek at long last. Wanting to avoid any reproaches, the Minister began to shout at once:

" How don't you understand? The fate of the small nations depends on the fate of the big. We're unable to go to war at present.
But when we've rearmed we'll return these provinces to you. One
must know how to wait. When the Prussians took Schleswig, we
didn't interfere. But half a century later we gave the Danes back
their property. That's the A B C of diplomacy."

Vanek, who was normally very reserved, committed an indiscre-
tion. He said: " By permitting the seizure of Schleswig and then the
defeat of Austria, France paved the way for Sedan. . . ."

" That analogy does not apply," snapped Tessa. " The Second
Empire was in a state of disintegration, whereas France in 1938 is

in the flower of her strength. You needn't worry: Sedan will not be repeated. But one has got to wait. On the Sudeten question France is divided."

Vanek was silent. His weather-beaten face became still ruddier. The veins stood out on his forehead. But Tessa calmed down. He passed from anger to amiability. He came close up to Vanek and whispered:

"Believe me, your sorrow is ours. I well remember the time when the statue of Strasbourg in the Place de la Concorde was swathed with mourning crape. You're mounting the stake like a propitiatory offering. You're sacrificing what you hold most precious in order that peace may be saved. The women of France will never forget it. . . ."

Vanek recalled his mother's wrinkled face under her black kerchief — his mother dressed like a peasant woman. An absurd, childlike hope awakened in him; perhaps after all they wouldn't betray the Czechs.

"You said France is divided on the Sudeten question," he said, "but in the territory in dispute there are many districts with a Czech population. There are no Germans there. I know that very well. I come from there. It is essential to insist on retaining those districts at least."

Tessa yawned: he was bored by the conversation. "Daladier informed me an hour ago that he was flying to Munich," he said. "There they will settle everything. The representative of your Government will be informed, of course. So it's hardly worth while bothering about geography at present."

Vanek's blue eyes became misty; but he quickly recovered himself and, after thanking Tessa, went out. And Tessa thought to himself: "Well, what a job I've got! Far better to accompany murderers to the guillotine. That Czech's a good fellow, but how naïve he is! How is it they don't understand that we can't risk everything? Enough of philanthropy! France needs to think about herself for a change."

He rang up Paulette:

"May I come round? I'm in need of a little consolation. No, no. The news is good, very good even. There won't be any war. But I'm in an abominable mood. What was it that Verlaine said? 'The soul is sad for no reason.' Good! I'm coming now. I'll be round right away."

CHAPTER 14

JOLIOT had taken off his coat and was fluttering about the printing-room. The front page of the special edition was being made up. Joliot was particularly proud of the story of Chamberlain's childhood; at the age of four the British Prime Minister had acted as peacemaker among the other children, and his mother had prophesied he would have a brilliant future.

"How shall we dish it up?" asked one of the sub-editors. "'Agreement at Munich'?"

Joliot frowned. "Colourless," he said, "inexpressive. Doesn't correspond to the mood."

"What about 'The Victory of Peace'?"

But this also failed to satisfy Joliot. Tossing back his head and screwing up his eyes, he whispered:

"'The victory of France,' and splash it right across the front page. . . ."

On arriving back in Paris, Daladier went to the Arc de Triomphe to lay a wreath on the tomb of the Unknown Soldier. All businesses, offices, and shops were closed. The broad pavements of the Champs-Élysées were crowded. People were full of joy; they were not going to be driven in to the trenches. Women were specially numerous. Flags were hung out everywhere. The florists were selling roses and geraniums. The day before there had been a sad whispering, sobbing, and hoarse singing in the darkened streets. And now everything had suddenly given place to a holiday bustle.

In a second-rate restaurant not far from the Champs-Élysées Desser was sitting at a dark corner table. He had just finished lunch and was drinking his coffee. He had chosen this little-frequented restaurant in order to avoid meeting people. He bought a copy of La Voie Nouvelle from the newsboy, skipped the front page, and began reading the reports, tucked away in small print, of robberies and fires. He was in a gloomy mood and his gloom increased all the more when he looked up and saw Fouget.

"You here?"

"As you see. . . ."

At any other time Desser would have been pleased to see Fouget.

Their acquaintance was of long standing; both of them had studied at the Polytechnic and dreamed of becoming engineers. Later on, Desser had devoted himself to financial operations, while Fouget took up history and politics. They seldom met, but when they did they talked in a friendly way without stiffness or pretence. When Desser was told that his favourites, the Radicals, were corrupt, sponging on the Republic and hand in glove with Stavisky, he said: "What about Fouget?" For him that bearded enthusiast was the personification of the virtues of old France.

Fouget was a conscientious historian. His books about the Jacobin clubs in Picardy and the struggle against the Chouans had merited general recognition. He lived not only for scholarship but also for the clichés of the French Revolution. Patriotism for him was synonymous with simplicity of manners. He would exclaim with absolute naturalness: "The fatherland is in danger!" Taking in his arms the new-born son of one of his constituents, he would say to the happy father: "A good citizen!" Fouget considered himself the heir of the Jacobins.

He was blinded by his love for the past. He was perpetually convinced that someone or other was sure to be threatening the Republic. He suspected any general of Bonapartism and turned away indignantly whenever he met an abbé in the street. For him the world was limited to France; what happened in other countries was of no interest to him. Instead of "Soviet, Chamberlain, Duce," he said "Sovié, Shongberlang, Deuce." He not only garbled the words; he also called the Croat Ustashi "the nihilists of the Balkans," and Gandhi "the Hindu Danton."

The son of an engraver who was in love with his craft, he knew from his childhood that work was happiness. He had had good luck and always found congenial work. He failed to see that all around him were millions of people who hated the drudgery of ill-paid labour. He looked on the Socialist movement as the fantasy of well-meaning but abstract minds. "Above all," he used to exhort the French trade-unionists, "above all, don't overlook the machinations of the Vatican!"

His pockets were stuffed with material relating to the victims of injustice. He took up the cause of some widow who had been turned out of her flat, and intervened on behalf of Senegalese and anarchists. Naturally, he was one of the most zealous workers of the League for the Defence of the Rights of Man and the Citizen.

His wife referred to him jokingly as "our busybody." She was a plump, quiet woman — always busy about the house, making lamp-shades, hanging pictures, and embroidering cushions. Fouget jok-ingly complained: "I married a snail with a house on her back." His sons grew up to be ne'er-do-wells, who had no desire to do anything whatsoever and wheedled money out of him, reminding him that he stood for "tolerance."

In the Chamber Fouget was considered a Radical, but to Tessa he was a Bolshevik. Tessa shouted: "Good heavens! That man says the Radicals have no enemies on the Left! What about the Com-munists?" Fouget once said of the Communists: "They express themselves in an abstract manner, but they're good patriots." He was only fifty-two, but everything about him was old-fashioned and in the Chamber he was nicknamed "the last cabman of Paris."

Desser was depressed. He had no desire to talk, but he knew he wouldn't be able to escape from Fouget's conversation. And sure enough, Fouget, who was aware of Desser's activities behind the scenes, began to ask questions:

"Why aren't you in the Champs-Élysées? Why aren't you drink-ing champagne? You ought to be delighted. After all, to some extent this is your victory."

"What can I say? You see it's not exactly very pleasant to gain such an easy and such a noisy victory."

Fouget failed to understand and got annoyed. His beard began to quiver.

"Words, Desser, words! It's what you wanted, don't try to wrig-gle out of it! You even mobilized that mummy Villard. I know all about it. You may celebrate your triumph!"

"No," said Desser, "I didn't want it. I knew we weren't ready for war and that we couldn't fight. I was in favour of a compromise. But in the first place, the terms are much heavier than we expected. And secondly, and this is the most important, I turned out to be only too right. You understand? Too right! Today has shown us that neither Maginot Lines nor armaments will be of any avail. Some-thing has gone wrong. I took refuge here after seeing the crowds in the Champs-Élysées. Making a triumph out of a diplomatic Sedan! Daladier was afraid to show his face at the aerodrome. He thought they were going to pelt him with rotten eggs. But they greeted him like a ballerina — with bouquets of flowers. A people like that won't be capable of defending itself."

"Why do you accuse the people? You others are to blame for it. And you, Desser. I told you so at the beginning of the Spanish affair. You can't hold up cowardice as a civic virtue and then be surprised if the people rejoice at capitulation. You're backing newspapers that glorify desertion. You're supporting the enemies of France. What you want is to — "

Desser interrupted him. "I don't know what I want myself," he said. "My card is beaten. So is the card of our country, probably. I know what I wanted. I wanted to preserve the equilibrium and maintain a happy France, among the young, hungry, and pugnacious nations. But it didn't come off. The rest is not interesting. If I could, I'd go away to Tahiti. But I'm tied by business. I don't care a fig for it, but I can't chuck it up. For a poet neurasthenia is a regular condition. It appears the Muses like that. The Stock Exchange doesn't."

He paid the bill. They turned, as though under a spell, into the Champs-Élysées and stood watching.

Daladier drove past in an open car. The crowd greeted him with enthusiasm. Behind him drove Tessa. He looked on it all as his own feast-day and was unwilling to let Daladier take all the applause. When Tessa bowed in reply to the cheers, his sharp nose quivered; he smiled bashfully and with dignity, like a tragedian who had just ended a pathetic monologue. A lady threw him a rose; he pressed it to his breast.

"A merry funeral," said Fouget. "And, by the way, they're burying France."

Desser smiled unexpectedly. "Tessa was particularly good. Why the rose? He ought to be wearing laurels."

"This is not the time for poking, Desser," growled Fouget. "The fatherland is in danger! I'm afraid that in a year's time the Germans will be marching down the Champs-Élysées. The trollops will find roses for them too."

"The fatherland is in danger, eh? You're an honest man and an incorrigible spouter. But maybe the fatherland already no longer exists. *Au revoir*, Fouget!"

CHAPTER 15

THE WALLS were thin. People were listening to the radio in all the apartments, and the announcer's voice seemed to be repeated like an echo.

Pierre had moved here shortly before the birth of his son. It was an enormous building consisting of ten blocks built by the municipality on a wild tract of land. Until recently the place was pitted with fortification trenches and covered with coarse grass and dockweeds. It was here that Pierre used once upon a time to make romantic appointments, declaim poetry, and vow everlasting love. Now there were enormous houses everywhere, and at night the lights glowed in thousands of windows. The tenants were employees, technicians, and workmen. Each flat consisted of two tiny rooms, and the same kind of life went on in all of them: the people rose early and ran to the Metro; at nine o'clock in the morning the women hung the mattresses out of the windows for an airing and shook the mats. At twelve o'clock the children came home from school in their pinafores, with ink-stained fingers. The smells of margarine, onions, and coffee hovered in the air. Towards evening the radio began to blare; at half past seven the people ate soup; at eleven o'clock they put out the light and went to sleep.

The last few days the radio had gone on blaring until midnight; people expected dreadful news. But now the announcer set everybody's fears at rest: there would be no war.

Pierre and Agnès were having dinner. On hearing the news Pierre sat gazing blankly with the fork in his hand. Then he jumped up, threw down his napkin, and swore. Agnès experienced a whirl of conflicting emotions. She was glad because Pierre wouldn't have to go to war and also because there wouldn't be any war, ruined houses, killed and mutilated children; and yet she felt an unaccountable sadness — she did not share her husband's ideas, but his sorrow imparted itself to her and worried her.

How unlike each other they were! Pierre was bustling and noisy, showed everything in his face, and swung from elation to despair. Agnès was reserved, secretive even, intransigent, always seeking

the sole, absolute truth, healthy and full of the joy of motherhood
and simple physical passion. They lived as friends, with occasional
stormy but shortlived disagreements and with a constant sense of
their oneness, which lay outside their own understanding and voli-
tion. Both of them had their own life, activities, and enthusiasms.
Agnès put a real inspiration into her work; every baby was to her
a mysterious frail plant that was capable of perishing or flourishing. She said to herself: "They're all for me, like Doudou." This
was untrue; she loved her son blindly and jealously and was proud
of his first lisping and his pale gold hair. She had no stronger feeling than this except her love for Pierre, which she hid not only
from him but from herself as well. There dwelt in her a maidenly
resistance; she gave herself to him as though for the first time, with
a light gasp of amazement and joy.

Her little nook was bare and clean; she didn't like a lot of things
about the place. But on Pierre's table there was an accumulation
of geological specimens; a little rummaging would have brought
to light the relics of all the various hobbies he had discarded.

They might have been happy in their stuffy little apartment on
the boulevard Brune, among the school-books and the drawings
and together with chubby pink Doudou. But they were not happy;
there was something extraneous that interfered with their life.
Agnès had realized it long ago — in the café on the Grands Boulevards when the soldiers joked about the coming war. For two years
the strain of waiting had gone on. It seemed to them as though this
life was temporary and that they were hiring it as a traveller hires
a room in a hotel — by the day. Once Agnès said: "Well, they've
given us another day." To Pierre it seemed to be part of the struggle
and linked with his ideas and his fever of hope and despair. But
Agnès tried in vain to understand with her heart his excited talk.
The last few weeks had been particularly bewildering. In the Spanish war there was something human. Agnès was indignant when
she saw the photographs of the ruins of Madrid and involuntarily admired the heroism of the international brigades. She said to Pierre:
"It isn't my cause, but it's a clean one." Coming from her, the word
"clean" was an admission. But now, when everything was mixed
up — diplomacy and sentiment, pacifism and cowardice, the *Internationale* and the corps of generals — she withdrew into herself
and was dumb. Weeping mothers came to the school. The evil day
was drawing near. But now there was the short communiqué on

the Munich agreement. There was not going to be any war!

"Pierre, how many people are rejoicing at this moment! And among the Germans. Do you think their feelings are different? Do forget your politics, at any rate for a minute!"

"You reason like André," Pierre said.

"Why André? Like millions! You call them ' the ordinary people.' There's no doubt about it, it's your time now. . . ."

"I don't understand."

"Formerly we used to live, work and bring up children. But you — that is, people like you — tolerate that, barely tolerate it even. In those days they used to write long books, build roads, discover serums. But now we've got to put up with the will of people like you. I'm not talking about ideas, but about character. Now everything is subjected to one thing. . . . And it's horrible. . . ."

He did not attempt to argue: he took up the newspapers and read how what had been life in the morning was now past history. But Agnès was worrying. She realized that nothing had been solved. How long would the postponement last this time? A week? A year? And how could one dole out life in drops?

She went over to Doudou. He was sleeping peacefully. She thought: "He ought to have a long life, a very long life." His teeth would grow and fall out, but that was only because they were milk teeth. How would Doudou be able to live? From one mobilization to another. She wanted to kiss him, but refrained. She set about correcting the school exercise-books. The stillness was oppressive. Far better if the radio was blaring, but it was shut off. For a week? For a year? She tried in vain to concentrate her thoughts and to enter into the meaning of the simple childish phrases. She read over a dozen times: "My uncle at Fontenay has some rabbits and a calf." She was seized with a longing for trees, the warmth of byres, and an unhurried existence — neither hurrying, nor waiting, nor thinking.

Pierre fell asleep, tired out with weeks of excitement, night work, and meetings. His dark head with its prematurely grey hair sank on the grey newspaper. His even breathing had a soothing effect on Agnès: now at least life was coming into its own. Then, having broken her pencil, she got up and cried out at the look on Pierre's face — like that of a corpse, boldless and taut, as though frozen. He woke up at her cry, said drowsily: "Aha," and dropped off to sleep again.

CHAPTER 16

To Lucien, mobilization appeared as a welcome relief; since the summer his life had been ghastly. The very thing he had been fearing happened: the rumours of his break with his father came to Joliot's ears; and the tubby little editor, who had long taken a dislike to Lucien's superciliousness, gave the racing column to his nephew. Lucien had no other source of income. He became acquainted with hunger, dirty collars, and evenings without cigarettes. He left the hotel at meal-times so that the landlord, who looked askance at him for not paying his bills regularly, might not guess that he had no money. He wandered about the warm streets; people were eating on the terraces. The sight of them annoyed Lucien; they scanned the menus to see what they would have, savouring, fussily choosing, and smiling; the smells made him feel giddy. Then he would run into some friend or other — a literary man or a frequenter of the Maison de Culture, a partisan of Breteuil or someone he had met in the gambling-dens. Lucien quickly invented a story: he had left his wallet at home or it was not a good day for changing Egyptian pounds — and boldly smiling, he would beg for five hundred francs, which he promptly blew.

One day he got a letter from his mother; she said her health had become worse, and begged him to make it up with his father. For a moment he felt a wave of pity for his mother; he remembered his childhood and how he had been ill with scarlet fever, and promptly felt pity for himself. Perhaps after all it would be a good thing if he followed his mother's advice. He'd had enough of starving and borrowing! He even took up a sheet of paper in order to answer the letter, but screwed it up into a ball. No, no! Of course, there was a clean bed there and a three-course dinner, but he wasn't going to humiliate himself for the sake of that. His confidence in Breteuil was a mistake, but the mistake of an honest man. But his father was a schemer, devoid of conscience. Besides, what boredom! And to have to listen again to those lectures: "Work and you'll get everything. I didn't become a Minister all at once either."

Lucien sometimes remembered Mouche and her emotional state

on the evening of their last meeting. He felt rather repentant towards her, although he didn't admit it and dismissed such feelings as "sentimentality." Mouche wrote to him several times: she implored him to forgive her and said she was disgusted with life. He frowned painfully and tore the violet-coloured sheets of notepaper into tiny pieces. Then he gave up opening her letters; what was the point of reading them? He couldn't help her. He was unhappy enough himself. And there was no pity in the world. Henri had died, Jeannette had forsaken him, and Breteuil had turned out to be a low intriguer.

After his break with Breteuil, Lucien lost all interest in politics: he didn't even look at the newspapers. The historical events in the world seemed to him to be wearisome and dirty, like his father's files, Breteuil's home, or the nape of some Kilmann's neck. Hearing conversations in streets or cafés about Hitler and war, Lucien yawned; obviously, his father was playing up to Fouget. Then all of a sudden he was called up. Remembering Salamanca, the feverish mustering of the troops, and the Falangists' drinking-bouts on their return from the front, he felt glad.

A couple of days later, however, the Munich agreement was announced. Lucien mocked at himself; they had made a fool of him again. Together with millions of other mugs he had been taken in by the blackout, the tanks in the streets of Paris, and the mobilization. But his father was making votes out of it in the Chamber. Lucien yawned convulsively: now he would have to go begging for money again, his landlord would grumble about his bill not being paid, and his own angry, unshaven face would be reflected in the windows of the shops.

Fate took pity on him. Near the Madeleine he ran across his former publisher, Gautier. At any other time Gautier would have made haste to get away from Lucien, but today he was in a state of nerves; that morning he had been sobbing over the cot of his three-year-old daughter, thinking he was going to his death, and all of a sudden a special edition of La Voie Nouvelle seemed to give him back his lost life. Gautier was ready to kiss not only Lucien, but the newsboy and the gendarmes as well. He didn't even notice how Lucien had let himself go, but took the thin unshaven face, the shabby suit, to be the natural accompaniments of the days of turmoil.

"I can hardly bring myself to believe it," he shouted. "Do you realize what a stroke of luck it is? I was to have gone to Colmar yesterday — sergeant in the artillery. And now —" He paused to recover his breath: "What about you?" he asked.

"Me? Infantry. Soldier of the second rank."

"What! Aren't you pleased, you idiot?"

"To be quite frank, it's all the same to me."

"Snob! No, wait a bit, you've had a nervous shock. . . ."

Lucien remembered: money! Smiling mysteriously, he said:

"Besides, something decidedly unpleasant has happened to me. I was at Trouville with an actress when all this fuss started. Somehow I knew there wouldn't be any war, but then came this surprise: mobilization; and I was obliged to leave her there. Now I've got to go to Trouville to bring her back. They've given me leave, but it's all very stupid. All the banks are shut. I don't want to put it off till tomorrow. If you could help me out, I shall be most grateful to you, but if it's inconvenient to you —"

"But of course not! . . ."

Gautier opened his wallet and took out a thousand-franc note. Lucien grinned; he knew how stingy Gautier was. He used to have difficulty in getting his royalties out of him. And now he was getting a thousand — Lucien had reckoned on two hundred at the outside. Gautier shouted: "Wait! I'm not going to let you go like that. When's your train? You'll have time."

They went into a bar and drank a couple of cocktails. Lucien had a feeling of warmth and satisfaction. After saying good-bye to Gautier, he hailed a taxi and drove to Montparnasse. He entered a large restaurant and went up to the second floor. Catching sight of his reflection in a mirror, he nodded back at it affably; nowadays one might be unshaven and shabby, but beauty remained beauty. Sure enough, the woman cloak-room attendant was admiring him.

He ordered an elaborate dinner; he took delight in his own ingenuity and capricious mood. Actually he was ravenous and longed at once to gobble up the bread lying on the table; instead he indolently said to the maître d'hôtel: "After that, if you please, pullet with truffles, of course, if it's Bresse pullet. . . ."

People were celebrating all around him. The heroes were men of military age; they looked tired and weary, as though they had just returned from the front. Some were in uniform, almost all were unshaven. It reminded one of life in the trenches; they deliberately used coarse language and swore. Their women fussed over them;

they were fairy godmothers, sisters of mercy, faithful sweethearts, who had been waiting many years for their knights. The table-lamps with their pastel shades shed a soft light that coloured everything. The tango spoke of paradise regained. Champagne corks were popping; the wineglasses clinked as the revellers drank: "To peace!" Some who had already emptied several bottles and recalled Joliot's enthusiastic outpourings shouted: "To victory!"

Lucien drank a bottle of vintage Chambertin; his face wore an absurd smile. He no longer thought about Kilmann or the hotel-keeper or his shameful existence. Once more he was a famous writer, the friend of the Surrealists, the son of a fashionable lawyer, the lover of a beautiful actress; he was living again.

He was not the only one to be set free from the sense of time by the day's events and by the night's drunkenness; all the people around him sensed the exceptional nature of the evening and its detachment from the round of humdrum days. Lucien was not surprised when Guillot, the proprietor of a picture gallery whom he had not seen for three years, came up to him and shouted gaily:

"Why don't you ever drop in at the gallery? My dear fellow, I've found a pearl, a real pearl."

Guillot staggered. His round red face was lit up. In his buttonhole was a white wax camellia with broken petals. He hauled Lucien off to his own table. Lucien was quite ready to go with him, for he had seen a woman who attracted him at once. She was slim and very dark, with a neat head, an impish, turned-up nose, thick half-open lips, and green eyes that looked like porcelain. Guillot hiccuped: "Get together. This is the pearl herself — Jenny. She's an artist. And this is one of our best writers — Lucien Tessa. Please don't mix him up with his father."

Lucien burst out laughing: "What are you chattering about? I'm not a writer at all. I'm a specialist in horse-breeding."

Jenny stared at him; her eyes livened up and darkened.

"I've read your book. The one about death. I've waited for you, as death waited for the Persian gardener in Bagdad."

Her English accent imparted a childlike effect to her conversation. Lucien thought to himself: "She's had a drink or two, but what a beauty!" He sat down and drank a glass of champagne. Then he said:

"I've been waiting for you as well. But more prosaically: as a pretty girl. Now we've got to know each other. Let's have a drink."

"All right. But I can only drink whisky."

Jenny was born and grew up in one of the dullest little towns of Kentucky. Her father was a Methodist and dealt in plywood. She was highly strung from childhood; she read with enthusiasm the poetry of Shelley and Keats, wanted to become a Roman Catholic, wrote stories about the sufferings of the Negroes, and ran away to greet President Wilson when he returned from Europe. She was then sixteen. At eighteen she married an itinerant photographer who had promised to take her to Hollywood. She soon divorced the photographer, but got to Hollywood all the same; she wanted to become a movie star. There she knew poverty and insults. Assistant directors and studio executives had a business-like way of saying: "Let's have supper together and afterwards . . ." She rejected all these proposals indignantly. She took up painting; on an empty stomach she painted landscapes — the reddish-brown earth, cactuses, the many-coloured houses. She was capable, but had no taste; indeed, she liked everything that was crude and loud in nature. All of a sudden she had a stroke of luck: a Los Angeles engineer, an aircraft engineer, fell in love with her. She also liked him, and they got married. Jenny passed from poverty to riches. In his home life the engineer was kind and gentle, if rather dull. She said to herself: "I didn't know real love was like this." Two years later her husband was killed in a crash. She swallowed two tubes of veronal; the doctors saved her. She threw herself into a lake; they fished her out. For months she lived almost entirely in a darkened room. Later on she livened up. She found she had been left with plenty of money. She sailed for Europe and wandered from one country to another, visiting museums and night-life. She had affairs with adventurers — she yearned to know "real love." She attended various art schools with the regularity of a schoolgirl. Then she settled in Paris, in Montparnasse, where disgruntled Americans drank whisky and made fun of both Old and New Worlds. She too made fun and drank.

She was only a year older than Lucien, but she took him for not much more than a boy. He made another conquest; his feverish eyes, chestnut hair, and the melancholy cynicism of his conversation affected her so strongly that she could do nothing but look at him and paid no attention to Guillot's chatter. Nor did she want to dance. It was a powerful feeling. Lucien responded to it — he thought he was in love.

Guillot tapped his glass with a knife. " I'm going to propose a toast. Lucien is in the infantry, I'm in the ack-ack, Charles is an airman, Dumont is a captain, also in the infantry. So all of us might have been fertilizing the fields of Alsace a month from now. But we're alive and we're going to live. It's a real victory of ours, the victory of our diplomats and writers, the victory of Paul Valéry, Derain, the victory of the wine-growers, tailors, and concierges. I beg you not to despise the concierges; they too are angels of peace. I propose we drink to the most beautiful of French victories! "

Jenny clapped her hands. Then she said to Lucien: " I don't like Valéry. I prefer Eluard. And you? Guillot talked like Wilson just now, but the French were against Wilson at the time. Don't be cross. I don't understand politics. But I'm so happy. It's terrible to think they might have killed you! . . ."

Lucien laughed.

" It's much simpler than that: we might not have met."

Guillot called out: " The bill! " Lucien insisted that he would pay. He tossed the old waiter a hundred-franc tip. The old man smiled: " Thank you, monsieur major."

" An error: monsieur soldier of the second rank."

To Jenny he said softly: " A last drink to you. The Persian gardener was afraid of death and fled to Bagdad. There he met a beautiful girl. He'd never seen anyone like her before. . . . And he drove death away."

She squeezed his hand.

They went out; they drove as far as Passy. Jenny lived in a quiet street. A large tree quivered vaguely in the light of the street lamp near the house. She wanted to say good-bye, but he came into the hall. She felt embarrassed and begged in a childish way: " You mustn't. . . ."

It seemed to her that this was real love. She was afraid of losing everything all of a sudden. He sat down in a deep armchair without taking off his overcoat and closed his eyes. His face was tired and weary. Jenny suddenly became calm.

" I'll make some coffee. O.K.? "

She got the coffee-machine and lit the little blue flame under the glass globe. Opening his eyes slightly, Lucien said:

" Alchemy. . . ."

He felt at rest; there was nothing he wanted; the strong, sweet coffee seemed to him the limit of happiness. Jenny chattered on without stopping; she instinctively dreaded silence. Though she had had a by no means inconsiderable number of love affairs, she was behaving like an inexperienced girl.

"There's nothing I adore so much as yellow roses — not tea roses, but yellow ones. They've got a whole heap of them at Bauman's in Montparnasse. They've got the most wonderful scent. If you really wanted to please me you could bring me some. . . ."

"I doubt it," said Lucien from the armchair. "I haven't even got my fare for the Metro. . . ."

He was ashamed of his poverty, and this admission even surprised him. He had come here knowing perfectly well what he was after. Then everything had got mixed up — the coffee, Jenny's stately pose, the conversation about painting, Greece, and flowers. Besides, he had drunk a good deal and was tired. His voice seemed to be coming from a long way off. Jenny thought he was joking: hadn't he just paid for the lot of them?

"Now, now," she laughed, "that's what comes of going on a spree."

Lucien opened his eyes; the jesting reproach irritated him.

"I went on the spree at the expense of a man called Gautier," he said. "Such opportunities occur very rarely. Usually I borrow small sums — not for roses, but for bread and sausage. You can't understand that. You're a rich American. I'm just an ordinary down-and-out. We belong to different classes."

He even felt for Jenny the hatred of the destitute man. He did not look at her. He did not see that she was crying.

Jenny knew well what poverty was like; she had not forgotten those two years in Hollywood, when she used to tell her friends she didn't eat because she was afraid of getting fat, although she was fainting with hunger. She ran into the next room and came back with a wad of notes. She tried to poke the money into Lucien's pocket.

"Please please, take it. I implore you to."

A really ugly grimace distorted Lucien's face. He screwed the notes into a ball and flung it on the table.

"I didn't come for that," he said.

He gripped her shoulders painfully. He felt neither desire nor passion; he was proving the purity of his intentions. Jenny thought he had forgiven her for being rich; he was in love, he didn't want to wait, he couldn't. . . . And she gave herself to him without regret or hesitation; she plunged into the emerald depths of the sea.

She fell asleep exhausted but happy. Lucien did not sleep. He reviewed in his mind the course of his life during the last few months. What was he to do? Work for some blackmailing little newspaper? Eat humble pie before his father? Rob somebody? He glanced at Jenny and felt quite surprised; he had nearly forgotten all about her. Then he fastidiously made a wry face. The warm odour of animal satisfaction came from her. Tried to be stand-offish at first, had she, with all that intellectual conversation about Valéry, painting, yellow roses? And how many adventures of this sort had she had? He wanted to wake her up, abuse her, and strike her. But he lay there without moving. He looked round the room at the imitation Louis-Seize furniture, a copy of a Watteau picture, a vase full of lilies. Jenny had taken the flat furnished; all the things belonged to other people, but to Lucien they represented her own middle-class surroundings. He looked at her again. The keen morning light revealed wrinkles; her skin was too tender and creased like a flower that was beginning to wither. He yawned; he began to count the number of women he had loved. He got up to twenty and then became mixed up — there were two Margots. He hadn't counted in the second, or had he? She was a blonde, or rather dyed, the daughter of a music-teacher. He interrupted himself: what intolerable baseness! He felt disgusted. He dressed quietly and was just creeping out when Jenny woke up; she was still smiling, dreamy. Then she saw Lucien.

" Why have you dressed? " she said in a nervous voice.

" Time I was off."

" Lucien — "

He laughed in an affected manner. " Guillot drank to victory. In reality it's the Germans who have won. Even children can understand that. But when you drink you have to tell lies. We're not drinking now. Yesterday you were a beautiful girl, weren't you? But now you're an aunt from America. No chicken, either. I'm not a Persian gardener, but a ' tom-cat.' Maybe, you don't know what a ' tom-cat ' is. In the language of Paul Valéry — a *souteneur*."

She didn't understand anything; she burst into tears and clung to his legs.

" You must come back this evening! Promise me! "

Something in him broke down — his last pride, the remnants of his spiritual purity. He glanced at the crumpled notes lying on the table: pale-purple thousand-franc notes. At least ten thousand. He thrust the money into his hip pocket and said indifferently:

"All right, I'll come. Perhaps not today, tomorrow or the day after."

It was a wonderful morning, clear and warm. Lucien walked as far as the Luxembourg Gardens. He looked at the leaves of the trees, copper, gold, and red — the scattered treasure of a ruined kingdom. In the gardens life went on as usual. Despite the early hour, mothers and nurses had already brought their perambulators there; little children were playing about in the pale brown sand; boys were sailing toy boats on the pond. Elderly rentiers and re-tired officials were warming themselves in the sun and reading the newspapers. Blackbirds were hopping about the grass. Lucien saw above him the head of Verlaine; the poet looked like an old faun; there were black streaks on the marble — Verlaine was weeping. Lucien automatically repeated a line of poetry: "A simple and quiet life. . . ." Why was it impossible for him? Simply and quietly — take a job, eat soup, fondle children, walk in these gardens.

Near by, people were talking: "Chamberlain promises peace for twenty years."

"Well, I'm not dreaming of twenty. Even if it's only ten. . . ."

Lucien looked at the speaker; he was a man of at least seventy. What did he want ten years of peace for? He muttered: "Not at all!" The old man blinked with annoyance. Lucien got up and yawned. What was he to do? And suddenly he remembered the money. The night seemed unreal. Doubting, he felt his pocket; the notes crackled. . . . Then he drove to an English tailor in the rue Pyramide; he was going to order a suit of green Scotch tweed.

CHAPTER 17

AFTER a long interval Denise got a letter from Michaud.

Denise, dear:

I've written to you twice from here, but I'm afraid the letters didn't arrive — on one occasion they burned the truck with the mail, and the other letter I sent through a Serb comrade who was leaving. They say he was caught at Cerbère. And we've been having a pretty hot time. No chance to write letters! Now we're having a rest ten miles from the front. This morning they brought us some water. We had a good wash and are enjoying ourselves. Only we're hard up for tobacco. Sometimes at night you nearly go out of your head for want of a smoke. Send whatever you can. It's all for our people.

Yesterday we again beat off the Fascists' attack — that's the eighth on our score. Since we crossed the Ebro they've never stopped. They're anxious about their lines of communication. Some day I'll tell you how we got across the river. The current is very swift and there are whirlpools everywhere. I've never seen any rivers like it at home. We marched during the night. The Spaniards are plucky chaps. When we arrived we found them short of everything. They used to leave the positions in order to go and get their meals. The disorder was indescribable. There were traitors everywhere. Now it's a real army. And the spirit remains the same. When we took Flis, we started singing the *Internationale*. The Spanish lads took it up in Spanish and attacked on the left. They're all young peasants.

The Fascists have tried their utmost to wipe us out. Their aviators are German. They've killed all the fish in the Ebro. The pontoon builders go on working while the bombs are dropping. And we've been defending Height 544 for seven weeks. Their bombers have been flying over every day. We call them "turkeys." They've dropped tons of bombs. Then there's the artillery. Yesterday they came to the conclusion that none of us were left alive, whereas in reality we only lost four men. I'm sorry about Carpino. He was a fine fellow, an assembler from Toulouse, and a good sport. Once when we got up an evening entertainment for the Spanish people, he imitated a prima donna singing an air from *Lakmé* and made everybody roar with laughter. He was a plucky chap. When he went out on a reconnaissance, he brought back three Italians.

The Fascists attacked towards the end of the day. The sun was already setting. The landscape here is peculiar. It looks like a picture of the moon with craters. There isn't a tree to be seen. They've turned the earth inside out. They bombarded us for two hours before attacking. It would be interesting to know how many batteries they've got. We let them come up to about a hundred

yards and then we let them have it with the machine-guns. They
rolled back, and how! They wounded Peletier, a Belgian. I bandaged him up and he shouted: " Have we beaten them off? Bravo! "

As you see, our morale is not at all bad. Although everybody is dead tired, of course. And as I've already told you, there's
no tobacco for a smoke. But that doesn't matter. The main thing is
we're holding on. That's one reason why they didn't go for Valencia.
They've got strong forces. Their air force is ten to our one. We know
from our own experience what " non-intervention " means. Our
men see through Blum and Villard and even swear at them: " Ah,
you —— Villard! " The Fascists have plenty of infantry, and good
infantry too, not like the Macaronis at Guadalajara, but Moors and
Navarrese troops. But all the same I think we'll hold out. Only of
late our men are getting rather depressed. That's on account of the
people at home. It's terrible to pick up a paper and read about
another capitulation. The Spaniards look down on us and wonder
what sort of people we are. And in my opinion they're right. But
I think everything will change now. It's impossible to retreat any
farther. Today the radio announced partial mobilization. Our men
cheered up at the news. Even the Radicals will have to admit that
it's France we're fighting for out here.

This letter will be brought to you by a good comrade.
Cheer him up. He's got no family and no country. He'll tell you all
about our life and the military operations. And you'll understand
for yourself the things he doesn't say. You know what I mean? I
always remember and often picture to myself how you walked back
to your place that night when it was foggy. Well, you know what
I mean. I didn't even think it could be so strong. But it's hard to say
what I want to say, especially in a letter. All I can say is that I
hope we'll soon meet again. With a warm embrace, yours ever,

Luc Michaud

Denise answered the same evening:

Paris, October 4

Dear Michaud:

How pleased I was to get your letter! I won't hide the fact
that I've been very worried about you lately. My comfort has been
some sort of vague belief in your lucky star — your own and mine.
The comrade who brought the letter told me a good deal about

you. He realized at once how much store I set on every detail. He is sympathetic and courageous.

I will tell you frankly, Michaud, I envy you. What happiness it is to fight in a straightforward, open way, risking your life every moment, and to be surrounded by honest brave people and to feel all the warmth of their friendship! People here often say that the fate of Spain has already been decided and that there is no sense in continuing the struggle. It isn't true. So long as there's at least one man with a gun in his hand, nothing is as yet either decided or lost.

I find it difficult to write to you about the things that are happening here. We're gasping for breath in the midst of vileness, cowardice and falsehood. Before the Munich agreement our people believed in resistance. There was a strike of the Paris building workers. It was called off four days before Munich for patriotic reasons. But it all turned out to be just a move in the game of Daladier, my father, and the whole gang. If you'd only seen how they scared the people and organized the panic!

In the last two days everything has changed. Now, even if they want to fight, nothing will come out of it. They're delighted at the collapse of the Popular Front, but in reality it's France that has collapsed. They're jubilant, celebrating victory, arranging balls and even triumphant processions. Yesterday I saw the German swastika flag on the Grands Boulevards. It's horrible! Flandin has sent a telegram of congratulation to Hitler. When I read your letter I remembered an amusing detail. You wrote about a comrade who gave an imitation of *Lakmé*. Our engineer told me he went to see *Lakmé* at the Opéra Comique. The singer put in a line of her own: " Oh, how I'd love to kiss Chamberlain! " and she got a storm of applause. Don't you feel how vulgar and stupid it all is?

The workers are furious. The influence of the party has grown in the last week. We had a meeting at our factory today. They decided not to work overtime. The proposal was put forward by our group. There's enough unemployment in the country as it is. In view of the fact that our factory was working on armaments, we hadn't made any protest before. But now it's obvious that it's no longer a question of the defence of France. Articles about the Ukraine, and maps even, have appeared in the papers. I shouldn't be surprised to hear that they're preparing with the Germans for a campaign against the Soviet Union. All the pacifists here have suddenly become militants!

At the same time the persecution of the party has begun. There are rumours that my father is in favour of suppressing it. We're ready for it. We've got a skeleton organization that will be able to carry on underground.

And now for the final villainy. Legrais told me yesterday that they're going to post up the men of the international brigade as deserters on the pretext that you failed to present yourselves for mobilization. This is the limit of cynicism. Imagine deserters accusing the men who have been fighting for two years at the front of desertion!

What can I tell you about my life? I'm still working at the Gnome. Quite honestly, I only live for party work. All the rest leaves me cold. The other day I had a talk with an engineer, a cultured man and a Leftist, something between the Anarchists and Blum. He said to me: "You're blind. You ought to have been born in the days of the Inquisition when fanaticism was in fashion." It's all nonsense! But I'm really sorry I lost so many years studying ancient architecture. Not because it isn't necessary. Of course it is. I know that beautiful things outlive this or that political situation. You see, I'm not blind. But it doesn't concern me. The struggle against Fascism will decide everything for a hundred years, not only our personal fate but that of our civilization as well. In comparison with this, everything else pales and fades into the background.

This letter is rather bare, but I've grown out of the habit of using other forms of language. You've got war and that's something vital. Whereas we're digging and digging like moles. . . . Now a word about our own affair. My dear Michaud, don't think I haven't understood. I'm waiting for you every day. Sometimes I have a feeling that you've arrived or are just about to and that you're bustling around and exclaiming: "And how!" I'm always with you even when I'm thinking about something else. I'm like that. I don't want to write about it in order not to upset myself. You'll understand without words.

Your Denise

CHAPTER 18

A MONTH had passed since the day when Tessa pressed the roses to his breast as he bowed to the applause of the crowd. But he had forgotten about those beautiful moments; every day brought him new alarms.

The country was experiencing the aftermath of intoxication. The brightly lit streets ceased to be a cause for rejoicing. People soon forgot about the September alarm. Mobilization became a question of finance; it had to be paid for. Every day the Government imposed new taxes. The price of bread was raised. Riding in a bus became a luxury. Strikes broke out. The employers demanded drastic measures. The papers went on writing about prosperity, but nobody believed them any longer. In Breteuil's " county associations " feverish preparations were being made to organize a putsch. Aubry declared: " We'll restore order by New Year's." Daladier wailed hysterically about his " iron will " and was held in suspicion. The Government seemed to be on its last legs, and Tessa rushed about frantically in the lobbies of the Chamber.

Tessa didn't believe that the Fascists would revolt, nor was he afraid of strikes. He looked on disorders in the streets as the usual accompaniment of the debates in the Chamber. He was afraid of something else: would the Chamber suddenly express its lack of confidence in the Government? How many times he had said to Daladier: " Be careful! Don't raise the question of confidence. You never know what they'll do! " When Villard said one day: " Do we know what the country is thinking? " Tessa waved his hands and answered: " Worse still — I don't even know what the deputies are thinking! "

Realizing the instability of the Government, Breteuil now began to talk to Tessa as if he was an inferior. He demanded the suppression of the Communist Party. Advice of this sort made Tessa shudder. It was no joke to dissolve a political party. There would be an outcry. Of course the Socialists would be delighted, but even so, there was certain to be a score or so of malcontents among them. They would carry the Left Radicals with them, and Tessa would be left at the mercy of Breteuil. And who could guarantee that

Breteuil would not say: "Tessa has done his job; now let him make way for Laval"?

Grandel was busy all the time behind Breteuil's back. His reputation had increased. People said that he had saved France from a catastrophe in September. The wives of the reservists in the town of La Flèche presented him with a desk set. The paperweight was adorned with a marble dove holding an olive branch in its beak. His speeches became more and more aggressive. At one meeting he declared: "It's time we rid France of the Communists and the servants of the international plutocracy — all the Tessas!" How bitterly did Tessa now regret the loss of that unfortunate document! If only he had that letter, he could crush Grandel and get rid of Breteuil into the bargain! And who had landed him in this awkward positon? Lucien! Whenever he thought about it, Tessa became beside himself with rage. His own family had betrayed him: Denise was egging on the workers against her father, and Lucien was working with Grandel.

Tessa found enemies springing up all around him. Breteuil's hostility was natural; he was a representative of the opposition and it was in accordance with the rules of the parliamentary game. But voices were also being raised against Tessa in the Radical Party. It was the same fanatical Fouget who was at the head of the gang. Tessa was filled with indignation. People ought to know how to live and let live. He had never intrigued against Fouget; they had different constituencies, different professions and different interests. Fouget was a bookworm, while he, Tessa, was a live man. And now Fouget had dared to throw doubt on his patriotic sentiments; at the party meeting he had said: "Tessa defends Munich. He has the right to do so. But why did he shield that German agent Grandel and destroy the document I passed on to him?" In reply Tessa made an ardent but obscure speech and hinted at the higher interests of France and diplomatic secrets. He was applauded. Nevertheless, a number of deputies believed Fouget, and the story got about that Tessa was in secret contact with Grandel. Tessa was furious, but he kept mum on the subject of the document. How could he explain the affair if Lucien was involved in it? Fouget, however, refused to abate his efforts.

Daladier proposed to dissolve Parliament and announce a general election right away. The deputies got alarmed. Tessa realized that it was an idiotic idea. It would lead to the strengthening of the

Communists and the Right. The Radicals would lose at least fifty seats. It would mean they were digging their own grave. Besides, the Chamber wouldn't agree to it; nobody was attracted by the prospect of suicide. All would unite on that point against the Government — both Right and Left; was there anyone who didn't care about keeping his seat? Daladier said that the elections in 1940 would be a catastrophe. Of course. But there was a long time to go yet before the elections. The worst of it was, the deputies were already beginning to play up to their constituents; they either opposed the new taxation or were anxious not to annoy the workers. What was to be done? Tessa thought it over for a long time and at last he had an idea: the emergency powers of the Chamber would have to be prolonged for two years. It was a bait which everybody was sure to snap at. Who wouldn't be flattered at the prospect of sitting an extra couple of years in the Palais Bourbon? It was a measure that would secure a firm majority for the Cabinet for a year. It was foolish to look beyond that. Who knew what would happen in a year's time?

If only Fouget could be gagged! Tessa was counting on the Radical Party Conference, where he would put a curb on the recalcitrants. In preparation for the conference he wrote an inspired and crafty speech. It was full of quotations from Plutarch and Gambetta and referred to the defects in the country's aircraft industry together with pathetic reminiscences of the heroes of the Marne. Nor was Tessa averse to doing less elegant work; he gave instructions to the provincial committees, paid the travelling expenses of suitable delegates, and promised sinecures and decorations.

When Amalie said to him: "It's dreadful to look at you. How can you work so hard?" he answered meekly: "What can you expect, Mother? The children have left us. I've only got France now." Amalie had grown very thin during the past year. She couldn't eat and slept very badly. She had become like a little grey child. Tessa turned away; he was sorry for his wife. When he was preparing his speech and writing out a quotation from Jeremiah, he came across the story of Job. He read a couple of pages and felt as if it had been written about himself. Like Job, he had lost everything. His house had become a house of discord. His children had left him. Amalie was sick unto death. And all men were speaking ill of him. Nobody realized that he was a lonely and unhappy man. Job had a

God, but Tessa was an enlightened man. He did not want to live in superstitious fear, like Amalie. He had no hope of compensation in the next world. What was it that supported him? Thinking this over, he told himself that he was sustained by his pride and the consciousness of human dignity.

Among others who were preparing for the party conference was Fouget. He was loath to oppose the Government in the Chamber, as it was composed of his own party colleagues. He was devoted to his party and believed that the Radicals were the spiritual heirs of the Jacobins and that Tessa had got among them by accident. The conference would bring together the best people of the party, the industrious and honest men of the provinces who were ready to die in defence of the Republic. At the conference Fouget intended to reveal Grandel's treachery, expose Tessa's duplicity, and demand that Daladier should draw his inspiration from Robespierre and not from the Prince de Condé.

Fouget firmly believed that the word " liberty," if uttered from the tribune, was fully capable of raising a storm and overthrowing the Government. He declared: "Either the Radicals will abandon the shameful policy of capitulation and lead France to victory or they will be swept away by a wave of general indignation." When he was asked how he thought this outburst of popular feeling would manifest itself, he replied without hesitation: "Barricades, my friend, barricades!"

The conference was to take place at Marseille. The day before he set out for the south, Fouget attended a meeting of the Society for the Study of the Revolution. He came away in a state of agitation. The Dantonists denied the authenticity of a number of documents and continued to accuse Robespierre of having worked a "frame-up." Fouget lost his temper and called one venerable historian a "wishful thinker." On arriving home he roared out in the hall: " Never could I have imagined such confounded blindness! "

His wife, after listening to a long lecture on the immorality of Danton, murmured sadly: " I've got something more important on my mind."

Fouget grinned amiably. "I suppose you mean moths have got into the curtains?"

He knew that his plump wife, Marie-Louise, had only one care, which was to look after the comfort and cleanliness of the house. But she replied angrily: " You live in the clouds, but I have to clear up everything. Louis has got entangled with some girl or other. She's the daughter of an official. A Catholic family. She has decided to procure an abortion and she's demanding money. She threatens to tell her parents."

Fouget began to shout indignantly: "I'm against it! Absolutely against it! What a disgrace! Let him get married or live without benefit of clergy. Anything you like, only not that!"

"But he doesn't want to get married. He says he doesn't love her and it was all a casual affair."

Louis came running out of the next room. He was a pimply youth in a blue blazer. He piped in a falsetto voice: "I hate her! She's a sanctimonious humbug and a skunk. And her father's a Catholic, a terrible scandalmonger. Where is this 'tolerance' of yours?"

Fouget was adamant and kept repeating: "I'm against it!" He went on shouting in the empty room, quite unaware that Marie-Louise and his son had gone out some time ago.

At last he gave it up and sat down to work. He wanted to revise the notes for his Marseille speech. Marie-Louise came cautiously into the room, glanced at her husband as he sat engrossed in his work, and said timidly: "Two thousand. Not for Louis, but for me. I've found a very cheap fur coat."

"Why didn't you say so before?" muttered Fouget distractedly. "I've just given three thousand for the Czech refugees. You'll have to wait till the 20th of the month."

Marie-Louise was a thrifty woman. She knew how to remodel old clothes, bought her husband's socks at sales, and visited dozens of shops looking for cheap tablecloths or chairs. She never chided her husband for not giving her more money. But now she was indignant at his obstinacy. She had been obliged to invent the story of the fur coat in order to get the two thousand francs for Louis.

"It isn't as if I often ask you for money!" she cried out. "Why don't you go into business if you've got to support these refugees? Everybody says to me: 'You're a deputy's wife. You must have a lot of money.' And here am I working like a scrubwoman. Other deputies make plenty of money. But how much have you made out of your book on Robespierre?"

Wild with anger, Fouget stamped his foot. "Shut up! Do you realize what you're driving me to? I'm not Tessa! I'd rather go and wash windows!"

Marie-Louise flicked her fingers and went out of the room. She

told her son she was going to pawn the silver the next day. It was
her marriage dowry and this was the first time she was parting with
it. Sitting in the kitchen, she polished up the sugar-bowls, milk-
pitchers, tongs, and spoons.

Fouget paced up and down the room till daybreak, hurling accu-
sations at everybody — at his dissolute son Louis, at Tessa, at the
historian who had slandered "incorruptible Maximilian," and at
himself — one ought to live more simply, more strictly, more
cleanly! Then, after splashing his face with a little water and comb-
ing his dishevelled beard, he drove to the railway station.

Tessa was to have left the same morning, but Daladier had called
a meeting of the Cabinet: the banks were opposed to Marchandot's
bill. During the meeting Tessa yawned wearily and reckoned up
how many mandates were likely to be on Fouget's side. When the
meeting was over, he went home to pick up his luggage. An unknown man was waiting for him in the hall.

"I've no time!" Tessa shouted.

"It won't take more than five minutes, Monsieur le Ministre.
It's a very important matter."

Tessa did not want to listen. He thought the man was some official with a grudge.

"Then may I trouble you at Marseille, Monsieur le Ministre?"

Realizing that the man was a delegate and the matter concerned
the conference, Tessa changed his tune. Affably he led his visitor
to the study. The man took out his delegate's credentials and introduced himself: "Weiss, delegate of the Colmar group of the Department of Haut-Rhin."

Weiss was a pleasant-looking man with pathetic blue eyes and
fair curly hair. His appearance was that of a provincial: he wore a
high collar, striped trousers, and a gold chain on his waistcoat.
He talked with an Alsatian accent.

"The Radicals of Colmar have always been opposed to the
Popular Front, and we look upon you, sir, as the real leader of
our party. We were indignant when we heard that Fouget was
going to make trouble at the conference."

"But Fouget is an old member of the party," said Tessa. "He
has a perfect right to defend his point of view, however erroneous
it may be."

"The Radicals of Colmar consider Fouget to be a secret Communist working under the orders of Moscow. With his excessive

attacks on the Church he is working to separate Alsace from the mother country. More than once he has taken the part of deserters. He hindered the police from clearing the sit-down strikers from the armament factory at Besançon; that is, he sabotaged the defensive power of France. He has given letters of recommendation to German refugees in order to embroil us with Germany. Finally he procured the release of Larichot, who was accused of corrupting minors."

Weiss talked on in a dull, monotonous way as though he was reading out an indictment. His blue eyes expressed a childish indignation at the baseness of the world. Hearing the name of Larichot, Tessa smiled. He knew all about that affair. Larichot's mother had appealed to Fouget. Fouget had gone to the lawyer for advice, but on discovering that it was a very shady business, he began to scream: "Why do you defend people like that? Guillotining isn't good enough for him!" However, Larichot managed to buy himself off. The girl's mother was bribed to give evidence that she had instigated her daughter to slander an innocent man. Tessa refrained from discussing the matter with Weiss. He merely asked: "What do you intend to do?"

"To prevent Fouget from speaking."

"But that is against the traditions of our party. The liberty of opinion —"

"Not for criminals!"

Tessa was silent for a while. Then he said with a smile: "I understand your feelings. You young people are the hope of our country. But why be so intransigent? However, I've no right to dissuade you. You're fulfilling your duty as a citizen. We'll meet again at Marseille. Look up my friend Billet when you're there. He's nearly sixty, but he's a young man at heart and thinks as you do. He'll help you."

When Weiss had gone, Tessa told the maid to carry his luggage out. Then he went to say good-bye to Amalie. She was lying in bed looking ghastly pale and moving her lips as she told her beads. He kissed her gently.

"Au revoir, Mother," he said. "You'll get better! I hope to come back with a shield. If he only dares to open his mouth."

Marseille was known as the "French Chicago." Its port was a hotbed of gangsters, white-slave traffickers, pimps, smugglers, opium- and cocaine-dealers. It was also infested with people who bought and sold all kinds of weapons from revolvers to bombers,

Breteuil's agents and racketeers who were making money out of Spain's agony. Corpses were found lying about the town from time to time; the gangsters did away with traitors and people who couldn't hold their tongues. The narrow streets of the Old Harbour housed innumerable brothels. Half-naked women lay in wait for travellers, clerks, business men, and sailors. If the passer-by refused to be lured and tried to get away, they snatched off his hat or dowsed him with slops. The souteneurs and pimps prepared the election campaigns, broke up strikes, and shielded or gave away spies.

On the eve of the elections the gangsters gathered rich windfalls. The candidates had to be generous, otherwise the gangsters would beat up the speakers, tear the election appeals off the walls, and drive the electors away. The gangsters were divided into two clans. The first was under the leadership of a one-eyed man named Lepetit, who was in the service of the local municipality, or, more precisely, the Socialist majority. Although until recently his only interest had been cocaine. Lepetit condescendingly explained: " I stand for disarmament." The second clan worked for Breteuil and was headed by Lebroc, who had begun his career with the murder of a Brazilian merchant. The gangsters passed easily from one clan to the other. Unless their co-operation was guaranteed, it was equally dangerous to stand as a candidate for the Chamber or to open a café on the Cannebière.

The gangsters of Marseille were all set to make as much as possible out of the Radical conference. And in fact, after weighing up everything, Tessa's friend Billet applied personally to Lebroc. Billet had been a wholesale coffee-dealer and knew that Lebroc was a reliable man. He had sometimes availed himself of Lebroc's services in order to put a check on the pilfering of coffee. He now requested Lebroc to maintain order at the meetings of the conference. Two hundred pimps and smugglers were given invitation cards, some as guests, others as newspaper correspondents. Everything was done to prevent Fouget upsetting the arrangement.

When Fouget entered the vast hall, he was amazed. At these conferences he was accustomed to meeting middle-aged provincials with beards and thick heavy necks, shopkeepers, lawyers, farmers, teachers, travelling salesmen, craftsmen; in a word, the middle classes of France. Of course, on this occasion, as usual, he saw a number of the beards of which he was so fond, but they were lost among the crowd of young people of the sporting type, who were proud of their biceps and flat glossy hair. Some of these were "guests" who had been collected by Lebroc. Others had come as delegates and called themselves Young Radicals. They were sent by groups in which Tessa had found supporters or by people with a liking for money. Many of the Young Radicals had formerly belonged to the Fascist detachments, having been lured by the prospect of the Fascists shortly getting into power. But following Breteuil meant waiting for a change of regime, whereas here it was easy to pick up a soft job, the red ribbon of the Legion of Honour, or at least a few thousand francs. The Young Radicals abused the workers and the Jews, demanded an "authoritarian republic," and displayed a boisterous enthusiasm for Mussolini's "realism" and Hitler's "daring." They strolled about the hall, exchanging witticisms, yawning, and squabbling, and the meetings of the conference reminded one of the crowds at a football game.

Daladier was given a tremendous ovation; the bearded old-timers, the Young Radicals, and the pimps all shouted: "Long live peace!" Nobody wanted to fight. The young men of military age candidly thanked the dull-eyed little man who had saved them from the trenches. The older delegates were flattered that the hero of France was one of their party colleagues, a Radical of long standing, Citizen Édouard Daladier. Tessa was secretly annoyed; Daladier was stealing all the limelight again. But he realized that Daladier was only a symbol, and thinking to himself: "They're cheering me as well," he joined in the applause.

Daladier spoke in a loud voice which often rose to a shriek. Like a good many weak-willed people, he wanted to convey an impression of unshakable strength. He kept returning to the idea of his strength, shouting out: "I said . . . I want . . . I won't allow . . . !" At times his voice seemed to echo the tearful whinings of a little schoolteacher whom everybody teased but who was obliged by fate to play the role of a Napoleon. Daladier cried out: "I forbid anyone to talk of capitulation! Munich was not a capitulation!" He stood on the tips of his toes, thrust a couple of fingers into the opening of his waistcoat, and bowed his head; perhaps he was indeed a Napoleon who had won a bloodless victory. The hall replied with a roar of applause. For a moment they were all carried away by the illusion: this was a contest not only with Fouget but with history as well.

When Daladier left the platform, the delegates experienced a feeling of mental exhaustion. They all began to joke and shout and roam about the hall. In vain the chairman rang his bell. Nobody listened to the next speaker, who was giving a report on the defence of France. Military problems were of little interest to these intensely civilian-minded people. They had come there to give their approval to the policy of peace, to bury the Popular Front and demand drastic measures against the "loafers." What was all this about the defence of France? What for? Who was threatening France after Munich, except the Communists? Only a couple of bearded wine-growers paid any attention to the speaker and tried to understand the meaning of the unfamiliar words and figures. Afterwards one of them said to the other: "It's all very obscure, but as we've got the Maginot Line we can sleep in peace. Of course it cost a great deal of money, but on the other hand, as he pointed out, it's once and for all. . . ."

The delegates left the hall. They filled all the cafés and bars of the town. They drank their apéritifs, dined, and then broke up into small groups. They streamed into the Old Harbour, where all sorts of people awaited them: brothel-keepers, girls, pianists, bouncers, and a guard of honour in the form of the young bloods of the Lebroc gang. The "out-of-bounds quarter" had long been excited by the news of the conference, as a change from their ordinary customers and the shiploads of American tourists. For the provincial delegates the conference was not only a matter of fulfilling their civic duty; it was also a fascinating adventure. For five days they were let loose from their family ties and turned into bachelors who had arrived in gay Marseille from their dreamy little townships. No wonder the proprietresses of some of the houses hung out notices on the doors of their establishments: "Open only for messieurs the delegates."

While the delegates enjoyed the illusion of love, however, they did not forget about politics. The salacious matings were interrupted by political squabbles. The few opponents of the Government were quickly snubbed. The propaganda of the Fascists, and subsequently that of Tessa also, had penetrated into the depths of the country. Shopkeepers were indignant at the Popular Front: "We joined up with them, thinking we were defending the Republic from the Fascists, but they took us in. They've corrupted the workers, connived at the strikes, and ruined the country!" The

peasants defended the Munich agreement: "Who are they driving
into war? Us. The workers will remain in the factories. It's a
swindle!" After drinking a few bottles of champagne, the delegates
became bellicose, shouting and threatening to shoot the strikers,
Thorez, and even Blum. The pimps promptly took up the cry and
shouted: "Bump off the whole lot!" But the girls whispered: "Give
me a little present, dear boy!" and the bearded "boy" grunted
and took an enormous wallet out of his pocket.

The second day of the conference brought matters to a head.
When Fouget mounted the platform a hush descended on the hall
as though everyone was expecting something unusual. Fouget
spread out his papers in front of him. He had spent the whole night
working on his speech. In view of the delegates' attitude, he had
softened the tone of a number of passages and decided to be
cautious in his references to Daladier. He was ready to make any
concessions provided he could bring about a crisis. He said to himself: "The most important thing is to show the conference, and
thereby the country, that the traitors are driving France towards
the precipice. One can argue against ideas. But what will the delegates say when they get to know about the letter to Grandel, which
Tessa has hidden away?"

Fouget began his speech quietly:

"Children don't quarrel at the bedside of their sick mother, and
France is seriously ill. . . ."

He was interrupted by a shout. A tall man stood up in the second
row. It was Weiss.

"We can't allow an agent of the Communists to speak here. . . ."

"Who are you?" asked Fouget distractedly.

"The delegate for Colmar."

Immediately, as though at the word of command, the Young
Radicals and Lebroc's boys began to howl: "Down with him! Go
back to Moscow!" "Long live Alsace! Shoot the Communists!"
"Bandit! What have you done with Larichot's money?" "Besançon!" "He raped a girl! Shoot him!"

In vain Fouget tried to speak. His words were drowned in the
uproar. The chairman rang his bell furiously and banged on the
table. Then he said quietly to Fouget: "I think it would be better
not to insist."

Some of the delegates who were in favour of Fouget were furiously indignant, but they were scattered about the hall and sur-

rounded by Lebroc's friends. Here and there they came to blows. Herriot heaved a mournful sigh and went off to the refreshment-room. At last Fouget gathered up his papers and came down from the platform. The chairman announced that it was the turn of the next speaker. Everybody rushed towards the doors. Suddenly Fouget's voice rang out again: "When I gave Tessa the document about Grandel — "

It was impossible to make out anything more. The hubbub broke out again. Then the chairman announced a recess.

Weiss was the hero of the day. Delegates came up to him, shook his hand, and congratulated him. Billet, the president of the Marseille group, who had rigged up the whole thing at Tessa's suggestion, invited Weiss to dine with him at the Lucullus restaurant. Billet knew how to entertain to perfection. The pride of Marseille, the famous bouillabaisse, was beautifully done and seasoned with red pepper and saffron. Weiss said with a dreamy air: " I love everything piquant."

Fouget went off to dine with an old friend who lived somewhere in the centre of the town, in the neighbourhood of the Zoological Park. He went on foot in order to calm down. He had decided that the next day he would send an open letter to the party committee. If the Radical papers refused to print it, he would send the letter to *L'Humanité*. He would relate the facts about Kilmann. Then the country would decide who was the true patriot — himself or Tessa.

He was walking along, deep in thought, when he was overtaken by two men in plus-fours and brown sports jackets. They stopped and stood in front of him in the middle of the pavement. Fouget tried to get past. "Excuse me," he said.

"Take that, you swine," one of the men said.

The blow stunned Fouget and he fell to the ground. The dark street was almost deserted. A cat mewed mournfully. There was a smell of rotting leaves; the late southern autumn was dying.

In the evening Tessa was sitting with other delegates in the lounge of his hotel. He was drinking lime-flower tea. His youngish secretary hurried across to him:

"Fouget has been attacked by ruffians. He's in the hospital. The police say his wallet was stolen."

"What a terrible thing! " Tessa exclaimed.

He was deeply moved and saddened; he felt sorry for Fouget.

What if he were to die of internal hæmorrhage? Alone. In the hospital. Tessa turned to Marchandot.

"Of course, Fouget was no use as a politician," he said, "but he was an enthusiast. . . ."

"Atrocious morals! I say, when will they clear the gangsters out of Marseille?"

"It's time they did! I hope they'll catch the gang who've done this."

He wiped his face with his handkerchief and pushed the cup aside. It was very warm. But Marchandot, with his usual want of tact, asked: "What letter was that he mentioned? What have you got to do with it?"

Tessa shrugged his shoulders. "Anyone would think you didn't know Fouget," he said. "He's fantastic! He lives in a world of books, like Don Quixote. Probably his head is full of documents about Danton and he's mixing it all up with Grandel. But I'm exceedingly sorry for him."

Next day Tessa himself made a speech. Although he was no longer facing any risk, he was very nervous. He spoke beautifully. The connoisseurs glanced at one another and whispered: "He's in top form!" He spoke of his humble love for the fatherland, love which was devoid of any ambition. He quoted Lamartine and then talked about the Continent, which was soaked in the blood and sweat of centuries:

"We must defend Europe against the ant-heap barbarism of Asia and the ready-made nostrums of America. Like the builders of the ancient cathedrals, the people of the various countries add their mite to the work of creating a new and a better Europe. What separates us from Germany? A river and prejudices. The frontiers of Europe are not here. They are far away in the east, where Christian and chivalrous Poland gives place to a semi-Oriental socialistic community."

The Young Radicals clapped like blazes. And when Tessa exclaimed: "The Communists have broken the pact of the Popular Front; they are outside the nation," they gave him another burst of applause. The delegates were tired of half-measures and followed Tessa's lead. At the luncheon arranged in his honour by the Radicals of Haute-Marne, he said with pride:

"The climate of Europe has changed. With all my heart I'm with the young. It's no use clinging to out-of-date maxims. The Radicals have always been a live party. Breteuil is hoping to bring about a change of regime and to impose an imported one upon us. No, we ourselves will abolish the diseases of parliamentarism. We will create an authoritarian republic without parting with either the genius of our nation or the traditions of our freedom-loving party."

He was digesting a wonderful lunch when he was told that a large fire had broken out in the centre of the town. Tessa did not like anything in the nature of a catastrophe. As a child he always got angry when other children ran to look at a fire or a flood. The spectacle of the raging elements filled him with gloom. But now he thought it was his duty to go to the scene of the disaster in order to express his sympathy for the unfortunate town.

The Universal Stores was burning like a match-box. The mistral was blowing, and the fire rapidly spread to the other side of the street, where the best hotels were. The Cannebière was roped off. When the police saw Tessa, they began to bow and scrape. Tessa was coughing with the smoke. He caught sight of fat Herriot, who shouted: "This is a devil of a mess! There are no fire-escapes in the town! I've summoned the fire brigade from Lyon. But Lord knows when they'll get here." In the street people were saying that several shopgirls had perished in the fire, as there wasn't a single emergency exit. Lebroc's boys forgot all about the conference. They slipped into the hotels and filled their pockets with everything they could lay hands on. The indignant crowd kept grumbling: "No ladders! No hoses!" The Fascists took the opportunity to carry on a little propaganda: "The regime's rotten. Could anything like this happen in Italy?"

For a moment Tessa admired the scene. The flames were leaping up from the tall building into the smoke-darkened sky. Despite his horror of disasters, he thought it was like a fireworks display and not very terrible. Then he recollected himself and frowned severely — this was a national misfortune. Of course, Breteuil would take advantage of the fire. And what a coincidence — at the very time of the conference! It was a good thing the Socialists and not the Radicals were in power on the town council. What would Villard say when they informed him there was not even one fire-escape in a town with a million inhabitants? Loafers! It was a pity it brought grist to Herriot's mill; he'd got everything in order in Lyon. And besides, those poor shopgirls! What a terrible thing! How dreadful!

The hotel where Tessa was staying was half burned out. The ministers were given rooms in the Prefecture, and their luggage was taken over there. Many of the delegates found that their documents had disappeared. Tessa proudly hugged his portfolio; he had grown wary since the Lucien affair. He had got off lightly. All they stole from him was his dressing-case, but a very good one with tortoise-shell fittings.

A fire was lighted in the reception-room at the Prefecture. Tessa glanced at the cheerful flames and recalled the Cannebière. Anyhow, it was beautiful. Smiling, he said to Daladier:

" The losses are very small. Only a dressing-case. . . ."

Daladier was upset. He saw in the conflagration a "bad omen." But Tessa was quite cheerful; he was thinking again of his triumph at the conference. What, after all, was a fire? — quite a trivial event. In a week it would all be forgotten. But the policy of France was now settled for a good number of years. A new era was about to begin. One more crisis and Paul Tessa would be at the head of the country.

He was sitting with closed eyes in a deep armchair when a telegram was brought to him. It was from the family doctor telling him that Amalie had suddenly got worse.

Tessa felt the salty taste of tears in his mouth. But he preserved his calm. He handed the blue form to Daladier.

" I must go back to Paris at once. But it doesn't matter. Tomorrow's meeting is purely a business one. But you were right. It appears that the fire was a sign of bad luck. No, no, I'm not losing heart. I'm quite calm."

CHAPTER 19

Two candles were burning in the dim room. There was a sickly smell of lilies. Amalie's face was peaceful, even happy, as though she felt a sense of liberation from physical suffering and anxiety. Tessa sat beside the bed. He was still unable to realize what had happened. Thirty-six years he had lived with his wife. He knew that she was always close at hand, breathing, worrying, and groaning. Dead, she still continued to live. When he said to himself:

"She's no more," it was just a formula. She lived. Her face, lit up in the twilight, among the flowers and flickering candle-flames, took Tessa back into the past. For some reason he remembered his pranks as a student. Everything floated up in the bright haze. He thought to himself: "This isn't right." He felt that his sorrow was melting away, and wanted to devote it only to Amalie. It was a long time since he had brought her any flowers. Once he used to bring them. She was fond of pansies and anemones. He remembered how they had first met.

It was in the spring — the year after he had taken his degree. At that time he was living in the Latin Quarter, wore a wide-brimmed hat and loose bow tie, admired the speeches of Jaurès and the sculptures of Rodin, believed in a one and only love, but ran after all the midinettes shouting: "Let the proletarians freshen our blood!" and, having drunk a couple of absinthes, he would recite to some enraptured little seamstress Rémy de Gourmont's lines:

> Que tes seins soient bénis, car ils sont sacrilèges!
> Ils se sont mis tout nus, comme un printanier florilège.

He also read these verses to Amalie, not long after she arrived in Paris from the Ursuline convent where she was educated. When she heard the verses she was embarrassed and began to cry. She stammered: "You know, Paul — " She said no more, and crumpled her tiny lace handkerchief into a ball. He took her out to the theatre. That night they were playing Œdipe. The famous tragedian Mounet-Sully exclaimed: "How terrible is life!" In those days there were cabs with little windows hung with dark-blue curtains; the driver sat in front wearing a tall hat. As they drove down a dark avenue in the Bois de Boulogne, Tessa kissed her. She was wearing a hat like a hood with long ribbons. She embraced him and said: "What happiness!" And then: "But this is a sin!" And hugged him all the more. Her lips were swollen, like Paulette's. . . .

Tessa was angry with himself. All this was out of place. He knew that his grief was deeper than these incoherent memories. He repeated to himself: "She's dead. She's dead." Perhaps the word would convey his sorrow. But the word was empty and official. How many times had he said the same thing about others! And if he called Amalie, she wouldn't hear him. Was it possible? She was a light sleeper. No, now he could only say: "She was." He couldn't tell her all about Marseille, Fouget, and the fire. He'd never be able

to tell her anything again. There lay her knitting. She hadn't finished the scarf for him. There lay her knitting-needles and the wool.
He began to count the stitches. Then he dozed off. His anxiety had
prevented him from sleeping on the journey.

He did not hear Denise come into the room. She had read about
her mother's death in the papers and hurried to the house. When
she saw her mother she was surprised. She had never seen her like
that before. There was so much wisdom in her face that Denise
thought to herself: " I never knew her!" And now it was too late.
She looked at her father. He was asleep with a skein of green wool
on his knees. And there were lilies as in a church. It was all quite
unbearable, like a bad dream. Everything seemed alien. Only her
mother's hand was familiar. For the first time Denise saw her childhood from afar. She pressed her warm lips to her mother's thin cold
hand and realized she was crying. Her tears made everything
simple, but they neither assuaged her grief nor restored her calm.
And having wept, Denise tiptoed out of the room. She went along
the familiar long corridor. Tessa in his lawyer's robes still looked
out of the photographs on the walls. Outside in the streets there
was a festive atmosphere. There had been a shower of rain and the
lights glittered on the asphalt. Everything gleamed — black, dark
violet, and silver.

Amalie had received the sacrament before her death, but Tessa
made arrangements for a non-religious funeral. Why annoy the
Left, especially right on top of the Marseille conference? The
cemetery bell began to toll. The funeral procession moved slowly.
Tessa walked at the head. Then came the men, after them the
women. The funeral of a minister's wife was an event, and " all
Paris " was there. Hundreds of cars were parked in the neighbouring street — the same cars that stood outside the Palais Bourbon
on the days of big debates, or outside the theatres on first nights.
The deputies of the various groups were anxious to express their
condolence with Tessa. Conspicuous among them were that old
fox Marin, and Villard, Marchandot, and Breteuil. There were also
lawyers, representatives of the companies with which Tessa was
connected, attorneys, and business men — Baron Rothschild, Desser,
Meuger, journalists with Joliot at their head, Paul Morand, theatrical producers, and diplomats. They said that the presence of the
counsellor of the German Embassy was a " good sign." The wreaths
were brought in a separate truck. Flourishing a malacca cane with

a gigantic knob, Joliot was saying to journalists: "Fouget? Him!
I know Marseille. . . ." Tessa walked calmly, but frequently took
out his handkerchief and sadly wiped his nose.

They buried Amalie in the cemetery of Père-Lachaise. This was
the most luxurious burial-ground in Paris. Tessa had spared no
expense. He selected a beautiful plot and immediately bought a
place for himself as well. It was just one of the ordinary details
of life. Everybody did the same. The conversation had been all
about plots and so much per square yard, and Tessa did not connect it with the idea of death. He signed the contract "for use in
perpetuity." It was proper to have a place among respectable
graves. On the left of Amalie was the grave of an admiral and on
the right lay the wife of a senator.

Tessa had often been to cemeteries. It was part of his duties to
attend the funerals of ministers and deputies. But now he looked at
the cemetery with a possessive eye and was astonished. It was a
regular town! There were streets with names, and houses with numbers. No, not houses, but graves. And all so clean. The gardener
was cutting off the dead branches of the bushes. Of course, it was
rather crowded. But when people died, they somehow kept close
together. On the other hand, it was a nice quarter. And the fact
that the cemetery was a town and formed part of life comforted
Tessa's heart.

He stood alone at the open grave. He caught sight of Lucien's
reddish-brown head in the distance and turned away. How much
Lucien resembled his Uncle Robert! Robert was a crook. . . . But
Lucien disappeared behind a monument. He had come there without thinking of anything except to bid farewell to his mother — he
hadn't been able to make up his mind to go home. When he saw
the coffin adorned with silver leaves, the draped hats of the under-
taker's men, the lean face of Breteuil, and Joliot's cornflower-blue
tie, he realized that his mother was not there. And looking about
him like an unsuccessful thief, he hurried away.

All the mourners lined up and, passing the grave-digger one by
one, took a few grains of earth from the plate he held and scattered
them in the open grave. Then they shook Tessa by the hand.

How often had Tessa taken a pinch of earth and shaken the hand
of widows and widowers! But now it all seemed to him so strange.
A bitterly cold wind was blowing. It made the eyes smart. Tessa
screwed up his eyes. Suddenly it occurred to him: "Perhaps it's me

they're burying. Two places." He began to sway on his feet. Someone's hand sustained him. He looked round and saw Dormoy's
beard. He thought to himself: " And yet they told me that Dormoy
hated me."

Now Tessa began looking round at the faces to see which deputies had come. It reminded him of the voting in the Chamber and
he was glad to think that he was alive. He had simply been tired.

In the evening he went to see Paulette. He was a long time making up his mind whether this would be showing disrespect to
Amalie's memory. But in the end he went; he was in need of sympathy and tenderness. The place was too empty at home. And every
little knick-knack reminded him of Amalie.

Paulette was a full-bodied, fine-looking girl. She had a pleasant
average voice and sang songs in the music-halls. Sometimes they
were sentimental ones about the wife of a sailor, or the death of a
soldier in the desert, and sometimes they were highly improper.
She did not really like the salacious side of life. She was good-
natured and created for comfort; she was fond of children, gardens,
and handiwork. She went on the stage by accident, after a silly
affair in her youth. Her intimacy with Tessa had begun three years
ago. It was a liaison that flattered her. It pleased her to think that
a brilliant lawyer, a deputy of the Chamber, and now a Minister,
was coming to her, a little actress. The daughter of a provincial
shopkeeper, she couldn't spell properly and never read anything
except detective stories. She had a great respect for Tessa: he knew
everything, larded his conversation with poetry and Latin proverbs,
and talked of America as though it was just round the corner. She
also felt sorry for Tessa; he worked hard and had a sick wife and
unappreciative children. She tried to give him pleasure, doing her
hair the way he liked it, knitting scarves, and cooking pies for him.
Tessa spoiled her, and she was convinced that she was faithful to
him, although she had a second lover, Albert the jockey, whose
existence was not suspected by Tessa. Paulette did not look on this
as being unfaithful. Once a week she had a rendezvous with the
young jockey, who only knew the names of stud horses. He even
found detective stories tiring. Paulette did not talk to him, nor
did she knit scarves or cook pies for him. She just made love to him,
greedily and in silence, as very hungry people eat. And when she
left him, she felt neither sadness nor remorse.

She was sitting at home dressed in a blue kimono embroidered

with herons when the door-bell rang. She was surprised to see
Tessa, as she had not been expecting him. He greeted her in silence,
went into the room, sat down, and undid his collar. He was feeling
queer and could hardly breathe. Paulette was torn with pity. She
didn't know what to say, and the silence was unbearable. It was
Tessa who spoke first:

"When there was a fire in Marseille, they said it was a bad sign.
I don't believe in omens. Anyhow, you sometimes wonder. . . ."

Paulette was superstitious. She was afraid to pass under a ladder
and cried over a broken mirror. Tessa's words made her feel uncomfortable. Maybe there really was a higher power. But Tessa was
already talking about something else:

"It's dreadful it should have happened at a time like this! I'm
completely off the rails, but I've got to go on working. They're getting ready for a general strike. It'll be a catastrophe. We've only
just managed to avoid war by a hair's breadth. . . ."

Paulette got out a bottle of old Armagnac. Tessa warmed the
glass with his hands and drank the spirit. Weariness came over
him again, as at the graveside. His thoughts got all mixed up and
he said all of a sudden: "You know, I've bought two places."
Paulette turned away. He thought to himself: " The same as I did —
from Amalie." He put his hand uder his shirt and touched his chest.
The warmth of his body comforted him. He was alive! He poured
out some more Armagnac for himself and Paulette. They clinked
their glasses and he said:

"Here's to you! The doctor has given me some stuff to soothe
my nerves. He said she didn't suffer. All the same, it's a terrible
thing! I can't realize what has happened. It was easier for her; she
believed. She was afraid of going to hell. But I'm simply afraid.
It's next to Admiral Lepérier. . . ."

They had another drink. He looked at her kimono.

"What a silly dressing-gown. Why birds? "

He looked round the room as though he had never been there
before. There was an upright piano. The walls were hung with
actors' photographs signed with great flourishes. There was a divan
and a dozen or so bright-coloured cushions. The Armagnac was
good, very good.

"Where did you get this Armagnac? . . . She wanted to be
buried by a priest. I didn't mind. But I have my political position
to consider. Of course, Breteuil would have been delighted, but I

have to reckon with the Left wing as well. They're in a nasty mood at present. And it's all the same to her; she doesn't hear. And if you call her, she won't hear you. . . . I've thought it all over. Paulette, my child, sing me something sad."

"Lord! You haven't any heart! Ni-ni. . . ."

CHAPTER 20

THE NOVEMBER fogs were yellow, brown, and black. The ramshackle grimy houses of the suburbs dripped with moisture. That autumn a wave of despondency had come over the people. The workers had lost all the gains they had secured in the summer of 1936. Every new decree of the Government imposed fresh restrictions and privations. The hours of the working week had been increased, the rate of pay for overtime reduced, and the workers' miserable wages subjected to taxation. Strikes were breaking out in a haphazard way. The police cleared the strikers out of the factories. Pickets were arrested and put in the dock, and the judges imposed severe sentences on the "ringleaders." And who was ruling the country? Daladier, who but a short while ago had raised his fist in the Place de la Bastille and declared: "I'm the son of a baker, a friend of the people"; Tessa, for whom the Communists had voted at Poitiers. Disillusion lay heavily over the land. Newspaper circulation had declined. Meetings were being held in half-empty halls. A weary stillness came over the little cafés where the workers gathered. People watched the agony of Spain and said: "Now it's our turn."

Daladier suffered from persecution mania: he was afraid of disorder. He had no idea of the extent of the fatigue which had overtaken France. And his opponents were living on illusions. The trade unions decided to carry out a one-day strike. They announced the appointed day a long time beforehand. Tessa forgot all about Amalie and livened up: he was commander-in-chief. Once again the walls were plastered with white notices announcing mobilization: the railwaymen and workers in the armament factories and public-works enterprises were put on the same footing as soldiers.

The Government announced that strikers would be treated as deserters. Smiling with self-complacency, Tessa declared: "It's my own idea. Only it was difficult to make a start. But now everybody realizes that mobilization is a natural phenomenon, so to speak."

After having a talk with Tessa, Joliot wrote in his paper that the strike was playing into the hands of the Germans — "Frenchmen, beware the gifts of the Muscovite Greeks!"

Desser's defeat was the talk of the day. At a meeting of industrialists he suggested a compromise: the workers were to abandon the idea of the intended strike, and the Government was to reconsider some of the decrees. There was an outburst of indignation among the employers; were they to capitulate to the Communists? In vain Desser urged: "We're threatened with war. This is not the time to anger the workers." Montigny shouted angrily: "It's time to put a stop to all this. Hitler has shown us the way. Let them go on strike. At least we shall be able to clear the Communists out of the factories."

Looking at the thermometer which he had just taken from his mouth, Villard exclaimed with a feeling of relief: "Thirty-seven point eight." Influenza relieved him of responsibility. He was indignant at the policy of the Radicals and said: "They're driving the workers into the arms of the Communists. It will end in a revolt and the victory of Fascism." Before his attack of influenza he had written an obscurely worded leading article, in which he said: "It is our duty to warn the workers against the danger of provocation. If the proletariat, in their just indignation at the new decrees, fold their hands, it will be a national disaster." He neither supported the strike nor condemned it. But some of his friends appealed to the workers not to strike.

The citizens of Paris opened their shutters and anxiously wondered what the day would bring forth. They were sweeping the terraces of the cafés. It was a dull, foggy morning. But near the factories helmets flashed. Detachments of special police were keeping guard at railway stations, Government buildings, and post offices. A policeman sat beside the driver in the buses. Guardsmen with horse-tail plumes on their brass helmets looked up and down the streets. Everybody was talking about harsh sentences, gangs of convicts, penal servitude. . . .

The older workers were glum and sullen; they were afraid the strike would be broken. For Denise it was the day of her baptism of struggle. She was convinced the Government would be unable to stand up to the blow. Then there would be an end to the disgrace. The workers of Paris would save Spain, which, though weakened, was still alive.

Denise had long been preparing for this day. She wondered whether she would have the strength, versatility, and daring. She felt she would be able to shame the faint-hearted by reading Michaud's letter to them about the bravery of the Ebro fighters. And if any soldiers were sent against her, she would say: "You are our brothers!" Her dry, sparkling eyes revealed the tension of her mind.

The workers were holding a meeting. Nobody was working. Then somebody came and reported that part of the foundry staff had gone back to work. The crowd of workers tried to sing *The Young Guard,* but their voices soon flagged and died away in the mournful stillness. The chief engineer came into the workshop. He was surrounded by plain-clothes men, one of whom waved a revolver. The engineer said: "Messieurs, if you don't intend to do any work, I request you to leave the premises." He was answered by shouts of indignation. The engineer waved his hand and went away. But the police remained. The workers then began to discuss in low voices what they ought to do.

"They're working in the foundry."

"Nothing will come of all this."

Denise cried out: "Comrades!"

The plain-clothes men caught hold of her and dragged her away. One of them twisted her arm till it hurt.

Some of the workers started work. Others went away. About a dozen of the less submissive ones were taken out into the yard. A police van was standing in one of the side-streets. They shoved the arrested men into it, knocking out the teeth of one of them in the process. They tore Denise's dress. She said to her comrades: "Our men won't go away!" She looked upon her pain and arrest as a reward. Neither her comrades' depression nor the dark dirty room in the Prefecture where they were taken could quench her enthusiasm.

The police searched her. The whiskered gendarme, who smelt of rum, ran his big fat hand over her body and indulged in some obscene remarks. She gazed with empty eyes, as though she was not there. Her only thought was of how the strike would go on.

At Billancourt, at the other end of Paris, preparations were being made to storm the Seine factory. Desser sat at his table, gazing dully at one spot. He tried to light his pipe, but it kept going out. He found it difficult to breathe. His left arm and shoulder ached. He vaguely wondered whether he had got angina pectoris. For the first time in his life Desser felt a sense of helplessness. The employers' stupid lack of foresight amazed him. They were blind men. Where were they leading the country? He had done his utmost to prevent the strike. He had talked with Daladier, Tessa, Frossard, giving his reasons and trying to convince them. They listened to him politely and then said: "We must make an end of the Communists." And the industrialists demanded solidarity. They said to him: "You're a member of our confederation." Desser had thought of shutting down his factories for a day or two. In that way he would save the situation and there would be no need to have recourse to repression. But Tessa began to scream: "Sabotage! What will the Chamber say?" The engineers grumbled: "If the Government won't deal with the Communists, we'll form defence detachments." Montigny threatened to make a row. So Desser gave way. He became a mere spectator. Now he was sitting at his table, wearily waiting for what was going to happen.

Legrais was afraid the strike would fail. The men were tired and had lost faith. But the threats now stirred them to anger. They shouted: "You won't frighten us!" Even the opponents of the strike had little to say. The red flags fluttered in the grey fog. In the workshops and the yard the workers were getting ready for the struggle.

In the management building the engineers gathered round Pierre and called him a "demagogue," an "agent of Moscow"!

Wild with rage, he shouted back: "Fascists! Nazis!"

They nearly came to blows, but Pierre had to answer a call from Desser.

"You go home," Desser said. "This is a bad business. This isn't 1936. They wanted this strike. And you're breaking your head for nothing. They'll come down on you as an engineer. And I won't be able to defend you."

"I'm not thinking about myself at all at present."

"You're wrong. You've got a wife and child. As for ideas — give them up! You've already come to the conclusion that Villard is an old humbug. The others are no better. Now you've got to save your skin."

"That's what you're doing. Yes, yes, you're trying to save your skin. At Munich, and now here. And you won't succeed!"

When Pierre went out to the workers, thousands of fists were raised: "Engineer Dubois is with us!" All the warmth of those rough, angry people went out to him.

Seeing the crowd, the police superintendent grew alarmed and went to see Desser. Desser shrugged his shoulders with annoyance. "I'm powerless," he said. "And I advise you also not to insist."

"Unfortunately, I have instructions."

When they saw the police, the workers were silent. Some of them had stones or iron bars in their hands. The police got the hoses ready. Legrais was standing at the main gates.

Once again fate had intervened in the affairs of his heart. He had not told Josette about his sentiments. But a month ago his life had undergone a change. He had been to see Josette's father about the party funds. As he was going away, Josette asked him which way he was going. He said he was going to Suresnes. "So am I," Josette said. On the Seine embankment she said: "I haven't got to go to Suresnes." It was a damp autumn evening. For some reason they walked along the deserted embankment as far as the bridge and back. At last Josette said: "I feel very sad when you don't come." "Really?" he said. And then he added: "I'm too old for you, I'm —" She did not let him finish. She kissed him. And now there was the strike. Legrais had no time for sentiment. Only from time to time the thought passed through his mind: "I wonder what's happening to Josette."

Pierre was in the laboratory upstairs when he saw the police break open the gates. They rushed at Legrais. He was a strong fellow and defended himself, but they tumbled him to the ground. A shower of stones came flying from the windows. Pierre ran downstairs. Suddenly he felt a violent smarting in his eyes. He grabbed the door-post for support. People were rushing about the yard. Somebody cried out: "Gas!"

Desser was standing at the window. He saw everything and mournfully he asked himself: "Is this France?" Was this the country he loved? That country was no more. It was no longer the cosy amiable France where the workers kind-heartedly abused their employers and then clinked glasses with them, where people made fiery speeches and then sat down to dine, forgetting all about the "social revolution" over a tasty ragout, where people loved flowers and jokes. He wanted to save a fictitious France, memoirs, books, a myth. With gas. Well, let them! It couldn't be helped now. He had to think about saving his skin, smoking less, and looking after his health. He would ring up Jeannette, get away, go to Java or Chile.

The police took away about a hundred workers. At the Prefecture they were at a loss to know what to do with those who had been arrested; the trucks kept bringing in new ones every half-hour.

Denise listened eagerly to what the police had to say. They were angry. That meant the strike had succeeded. From time to time new prisoners were brought into the room. A telephone operator said everything had collapsed. They were afraid of the repressions. A Metro employee was brought in, his face covered with blood. When he had rested a little while, he began to shout: " Cowards! " The Metro was working. By evening Denise learned that only the big factories were on strike. When it was getting dark, the police thrust three more workers into the room.

" Everybody went on strike at the Seine," they said. " They stayed there. And the police used gas."

Everybody was alarmed at the word " gas." The telephone operator began to cry. But Denise stood up and began to sing. The others took up the song. Though the police threatened to beat them up, they went on singing. The song was heard by the others in the neighbouring cells. It floated along the wretched corridors that smelt of damp, leather, and mice. It expressed all the sentiments of courage, anger, and brotherhood. And the workers of the Seine, the Gnome, and Renaud's sang the song of the Siberian partisans.

In the evening Daladier broadcast a statement. He spoke from his own study, alone in front of the microphone. He gazed dully into empty space and the veins stood out on his forehead.

" The Government has won a victory."

After so many retreats and Munich he was able to utter at last the sweet word " victory."

They began to question the prisoners. On hearing the name Denise Tessa the superintendent smiled:

" You're not a relation, I suppose? "

No tortures would have been able to break Denise. But this man touched on what was most terrible to her. At first she was silent, then she thought it was even more humiliating to conceal the fact.

" I'm the daughter of your Minister. But it has nothing to do with the matter. I'm a Communist. You may continue. . . ."

The superintendent blinked, made a wry face, and went to the Chief. He informed the Prefect.

Tessa was asleep. He was awakened by the "urgent business" bell. It had been a very warm day. Tessa had taken the reports from his secretary as they came in and had been constantly on the telephone to the Prefecture. He was afraid the strike was spreading. Not until late at night had he ceased worrying. At three o'clock in the morning he had a bath. The white tiles gleamed and the water looked blue. He looked at his slender legs and began to hum an aria from *Rigoletto*. That would teach them not to strike! If only the Right didn't try to make too much capital out of it!

Half-awake, he heard the voice at the telephone: "It concerns your daughter." He realized everything at once. Now he was in the Prefect's hands! What guarantee was there that Breteuil wouldn't get to know? What a windfall for the papers! The damned little hussy!

Tessa was standing in the Prefect's study beside a plaster bust of the Republic when Denise was brought in. He was moved to pity at the sight of her. Her dress was torn. Her hair was dishevelled and her face was pale after a sleepless night. And this was his daughter, whose health he had been so anxious about, taking her to the spas and providing the best medical treatment that money could buy. He tried to overcome his displeasure and said gently, but with a tremor in his voice:

" Denise, I've come to release you."

He had his own plan: he would tell the Prefect that Denise wanted to write a novel about the life of the masses and had gone into a factory to study conditions at first hand. He would take her back with him, and his deserted home would come to life again. How he would pamper her!

Denise said: " In that case you must release all of them."

The words, Denise's tones, and her unexpected use of the plural "you" stunned him.

" Denise! "

She was silent. This man in front of her belonged to a different world. Yesterday had freed her from the past.

Tessa was beside himself. " Release those ruffians? Do you realize what you're saying? "

"Who are ruffians? With the Germans you behaved like cowards: 'We're not ready.' But this is what you needed gas for!"

"Your Communists are working for the Germans," said Tessa. "Yesterday while you were striking, the Italians put forward demands for Nice and Corsica. Those are the first results of the strike."

"It's you who're working for the Germans. Who closed the aircraft factories? And it's not for you to say what you did. When Fouget opened his mouth, you sent gangsters —"

"That's a lie! A malicious lie! You little idiot, you believe everything they tell you. Sheep!"

He went on shouting abuse for a long while. Then he suddenly became silent. What was the use? She was possessed by a crazy idea. It was impossible to open her eyes. The affair would have to be hushed up.

"We won't argue," he said. "We've both of us got our own convictions. But you must understand me. If this gets into the papers, it will delight our common enemies, the Fascists, Breteuil."

"What makes you any better than Breteuil?"

"You turn everything into politics. There are such things as feelings. After all, you're my daughter. Remember your dead mother. What a good heart she had! Denise, I implore you. Come back home! In your mother's name!"

Denise could bear it no longer. She cried out:

"Shut up! You're a vile man!"

Later on she blamed herself for having said this: she had given vent to her suffering.

Tessa went away having attained nothing. He was obliged to put pressure on the Prefect. The report of Denise's arrest was kept out of the newspapers, and no mention was made of the sentence. She was tried together with other workers of the Gnome factory, and all of them were sentenced to a month's imprisonment. Denise was happy; the president of the court muttered her name rapidly and did not ask about her origins. She did not suspect the amount of trouble this had caused her father.

From now on, Tessa took a violent personal dislike to the Communists. Formerly he had been without enemies. Of course he sometimes fell out with Breteuil or Villard, but they were partners in the game. He was even sorry for Fouget, even though the bearded fanatic had tried to blacken him. But the Communists had taken Denise away from him. They had turned a gentle, affectionate

girl into a virago and a firebrand. Women like that danced round
the guillotine in 1793. How could that be a political party? It was
the spiritual underworld. If they were not destroyed they would
torture, stab, and stifle. They looked upon Tessa as a bug. But
France was still on her feet! The strike had failed. That meant we'd
go on living. One could go to Paulette's for a little relaxation.

CHAPTER 21

DESSER was unwilling to part with Pierre. The sense of his own
impotence irked him; to think that he, to whom ministers had
toadied, should have to submit to a bunch of brawlers. Nevertheless, he could not make up his mind to let Pierre stay on at the
factory; the Right newspapers had written up the story of the
"Red engineer." He said to Pierre: "I'll send you to America. You'll
have to wait a year." Pierre declined; he thought this was a sop.

They were talking on the terrace of a big café. The evening was
unusually cold: twenty-eight degrees. The customers puffed and
snorted as they hurried inside to warm themselves with a glass of
grog. And on the empty terrace the lonely braziers shone with a
ruddy glow.

"Of course, you're quite right not to have any confidence in me,"
said Desser. "But it's like this: we're tied by our environment,
public opinion, and prejudices. For instance, there were probably
quite a lot of good men among the workers who were against the
strike, but they happened to be powerless. I'm obliged to consider
the opinions of Monsieur Montigny. In your language he's a Fascist.
In mine he's a fool and a lout. They accuse Cot of being responsible
for the lack of aircraft. But you yourself are one of the engineers
and I'm obliged to part with you. What do they care about bombers? What do they care about France?"

Although he had once been infinitely trusting, Pierre had now
become suspicious and brusque. He felt that Desser's complaints
were deceitful.

"Why do you blame them?" he said. "You too were in favour
of Munich."

"I wanted an armed peace, negotiations, and a compromise. But all they're thinking of is to put themselves at Hitler's mercy as quickly as they can. Only the rogues can make out what is happening, and they're in a hurry to grab what they can. But honest people are blinded."

"But there are others," said Pierre. "Have you had a talk with Legrais? He was beaten up by the police and now he's in hospital. There are many others like him. There are hundreds of thoughts and feelings in a man. Usually they find an outlet. People create art, comfort, a family. Why do I mention the Communists? Because they concentrate on one thing. And it isn't blindness. It's the ability to look in one direction."

Desser said: "You see those braziers? They give the illusion of warmth — as if one could warm a street! Which reminds me, I'm absolutely frozen. So for the last time — you still refuse?"

Pierre expected Agnès to reproach him. They would have to face unemployment and poverty, on top of which there was Doudou to think about. But Agnès said at once: "You're right." She did not agree with him when he talked about politics, but as soon as the question of independence and dignity was raised, she looked at him with admiration as she had looked at her father when she was a girl.

Three weeks went by, and the poverty which but a short while ago had seemed to be a spectre now became a reality. Agnès's salary went for the rent of the flat and the doctor's fees — Doudou was ill. By the end of the month they had no money left. In the past both of them had known respectable poverty, but now they were right up against it, in the grip of humiliating penury.

There appeared to be no factory that would take Pierre on. The Employers' Confederation had put his name on their black list. He tried in vain to get a job as a mechanic and even as a manual labourer, but was met with refusals everywhere.

He sold his watch to pay the milkman's bill. Agnès took her winter coat to the old-clothes man — she said: "It's too big for me" — and they had a dinner each day for a week. She tried to buoy Pierre up, telling him that she might get extra pay for the holiday. He went out early in the morning, wandered about all day, called at little workshops, and studied the advertisements for hours. In the evening he told Agnès he had met a friend who had stood him a meal. He was neatly dressed and shaved every day. Nobody would have taken the clean-looking grey-haired dreamer for a beggar. But when he passed a sausage shop, he averted his eyes.

One day he saw a notice: in the event of a snowfall, workers would be required for cleaning the streets. Application to be made at five o'clock in the morning. Snow began to fall in the evening in big flakes, which melted at first and then covered the pavements. At four o'clock in the morning Pierre crept quietly out of the flat for fear of waking Agnès. He felt chilly in the cold, but smiled at the thought that now at last he would bring home to Agnès twenty or perhaps even thirty francs. He got to the place at a quarter to five. A big gas lamp lit up the wilderness of white snow and the crowd of men waiting outside the dark brick building. All sorts of people were there: down-and-outs, hoboes, postmen dismissed for taking part in the strike, a starving artist, some German refugees, old men and young lads. Forty men were needed, and no less than three hundred had turned up. Pierre waited patiently. At last they called out: " No more! " He trudged back home. He felt weak and cold. His feet were sore and his head began to swim.

He passed Les Halles. It was an animated scene: restaurant-keepers, butchers, and greengrocers and owners of food stores jostled one another as they selected their goods. Everything in Paris seemed to have changed except its "belly," as Zola described it. And looking at the damp oozing arches and the piles of food-stuff, Pierre dimly recalled that half-forgotten novel about the hungry visionary and fugitive convict amid the well-fed, unfeeling dealers.

Enormous carcasses, purple, red, and unbearably pink, were hanging from the hooks. How many bullocks and lambs were needed by the gluttonous city? How many geese with artificially enlarged livers? How many speckled guinea-fowls and beautifully breasted pheasants?

In the fish market lay enormous tunnies looking as though they were modelled in Plasticine, tender turbots, mackerel, whiting, slippery flounders, fat Marennes oysters and the curly Portugaises, sea-urchins, and all kinds of sea food. The smell was unbearable. The fishwives' hands were red and rough with salt. The water streamed from the marble slabs.

Farther on were the vegetable-dealers: pale endives, carrots, turnips, asparagus. Mushrooms lay in dainty little baskets next to lettuces from Roussillon. Farther on were slabs of butter from Charente, cheeses, eggs, cream in tin cans, Messina and Jaffa oranges, apples, bunches of bananas with their spicy tropical smell, dates and pineapples.

The women dealers ate onion soup, warming their numbed fingers on the bowls. Tramps slouched about, picking up the scattered potatoes. Connoisseurs fingered the cheeses and asked the price of the game. Newsboys passed through the rows with grey papers smelling of fresh ink. Then the bells of the mediæval Church of St. Eustache began to ring. Butchers in purple aprons cut up the carcasses. Market gardeners unloaded turnips and leeks from battered old Citroens, and then drank coffee with a dash of cognac at the coffee counter. Red wine flowed like blood across the pavement. Pinks, carnations, and roses were piled up in enormous bunches. From Nice and Grasse trains had brought sweet-smelling loads of mimosa, primulas, hyacinths, lilies of the valley, and azaleas. There was no calendar season for Paris: flowers bloomed on the push-carts the whole year round.

And now the wet snow-flakes were falling from the sky. The lucky ones were sweeping the snow away. But not Pierre. He walked as though he had been wound up. He did not even feel hungry. The smells made him feel sick. The mountains of food seemed to crush him. It was not food to be thought of with delight, but a challenge, a whole philosophy — a hostile world of dealers, brokers, weights, and filthy pocketbooks. And a hundred thousand bouquets. What did Paris care about the tears of Vanek, the sorrow of Catalonia, the suffering of Legrais, the hunger of Pierre? Paris went on living. The sausage-man hummed "Paris is still Paris" as he sold forty pounds of sausage meat. There was so much pathos in this belief in life that Pierre felt pacified. He pretended to be in a hurry although he knew he had nowhere to hurry to. He began to feel cold and suddenly slowed down his pace. Turning back, he wandered about the narrow, crooked streets of the Bussy quarter, returning again and again to the cross-streets, where the slippery flat fish were dying on the carts.

Later on, Pierre sat down on a wet seat to read a newspaper he had picked up: "Tension in Europe relieved. . . . Tessa's speech. . . . Peace guarantees. . . ." Suddenly he became on the alert: there was a smell of fried potatoes. They were being boiled in large vats and served in paper bags, while the shopwoman cried out: "All hot! . . . Twenty sous!" Yes, there was a wonderful dream for twenty sous! Pierre suddenly jumped up and offered the crumpled newspaper to a passer-by, some official on his way to business. He stared with surprise at Pierre and hurried on. Pierre strolled back to the seat. Why had he done that, he asked himself. Once again he fell into a sort of listlessness. From the distance came the hooting of autos and the shouts of the market women. A man and a girl went past. The girl looked at Pierre and whispered something to her companion. An elderly dachshund trotted up, sniffed at Pierre's boots, dropped her tail between her legs, and waddled away. He was miserable; even a dog could feel that.

More trouble was waiting for him at home. Agnès whispered to him as he came in: "Father's come."

At any other time they would have been delighted. Agnès's father, who lived in a little town in southwest France, had long been meaning to visit his daughter and see his little grandson. From time to time he wrote her short letters in a large childlike hand.

Agnès often used to talk to Pierre about her father. Legendre was an old mechanic. Before the war he had spent ten months in prison for anti-military propaganda. Five years ago he had begun ailing. He left the factory and went to Dax, where his younger brother ran a small garage. He helped with the repairs and pottered about in the kitchen garden. He was sixty-four. Pierre had imagined him as a big man with grey hair, but now he saw a dried-up little old man with a fluffy down on his head like a newborn baby.

Pierre realized at once why Agnès had whispered anxiously: "Father's come." The old man thought his daughter had married an engineer and was living in comfort and that Doudou was getting everything he needed. Now he had chosen this of all times for his long-promised visit. If they told him the truth, the old man would worry. But what had they got to feed him on?

He looked Pierre all over with curiosity and said: "That's a good strong pair of boots you've got." Pierre remembered the dachshund, the newspaper, and the fried potatoes. Legendre inspected everything in the apartment, went into the kitchen and gave his approval; it was clean. "How's your work getting on?" he asked Pierre. He listened with rapt attention to Pierre's account of the new engines. Then they began to talk about politics. Legendre sighed: "I'm 'way behind. Dax is a sleepy hollow. My brother doesn't bother much. He subscribes to *Le Matin*." Legendre failed to understand the meaning of Munich and only livened up when Pierre mentioned

Spain. Then he began to shout: " They'll win! They're bound to win! " The conversation changed to the subject of what had happened in the past. Legendre beamed as he recalled the strikes and demonstrations. " In 1906," he said, " we went out on the streets with banners." He was proud of having known Jaurès. " Whenever he spoke at a meeting," he said, " he always took off his collar. They were stiff ones in those days. He used to get so worked up. And what a voice he had! "

Pierre lapsed into silence. The cheerful old man made him feel intensely conscious of his own helplessness. Legendre interpreted his son-in-law's silence in his own way. Perhaps he hadn't said the right thing. Was he a man of his own class? Pierre's manner rather intimidated him; after all, he was an engineer! Agnès was now living in a different world, and she had not chosen a working man. Legendre felt embarrassed and said: " I expect I'm in the way. I'll go and see Douai."

Agnès and Pierre glanced at each other. They must hold him back. But it was already dinner-time and what had they got to give him? Doudou's soup? Ought they to say they had been invited out? The old man would take offence. Agnès said to him: " Oh, don't go yet. Tell us all about Dax." The old man began to tell them. There had been a lot of tourists in the summer. His brother had made quite a bit of money. But now it was all very quiet. People were afraid there was going to be a war. They weren't building and they bought very few cars as they were afraid they would be requisitioned. The business in trucks was particularly bad. Unemployment was on the increase.

" Are there many unemployed in Paris? " he asked.

" A good many. In all branches, too. Today I saw the men who came to clean the streets. There was a compositor and a confectioner and even an artist. We waited for two hours."

At once Pierre realized his slip of the tongue. The old man wouldn't understand, but Agnès. . . . And he'd told her they were going to take him on as an engineer. And, indeed, Agnès glanced at him with a look of dread as though she now realized for the first time all the misery of destitution. But Legendre was on the alert. He suddenly understood everything: Agnès's embarrassment, Pierre's silences, and the empty kitchen.

" I'm just going to pop out to the corner for a moment," he said. " I want to ring up Douai."

Half an hour later he came back loaded with parcels — a quart of wine, sardines, a pie, cheese, and coffee. And he hadn't forgotten the sugar. He muttered to Agnès: " What about a little daughter? " He didn't ask any questions. At dinner Pierre told him about the strike, the gas, his talk with Desser, and the black list. Legendre beamed at the thought that Pierre was one of his own class. As for being in want — well, they were young; they'd come out all right.

Then he clinked glasses with Pierre: " To victory! "

Everything was clear to him — the Spaniards would soon smash the Fascists, and the workers would rise everywhere. There would be strikes and barricades.

Pierre felt dizzy with the food and wine. He was warm and snug, but somehow his depression did not seem to pass. So this was the old generation. They too had known what it was to suffer defeat and disillusionment. Why hadn't Pierre got the faith, the simplicity and gaiety of this old man?

They put Doudou to sleep. He was in one of his tantrums and did not want to go to bed, but of course he dropped off to sleep at once. Legendre gazed at him and said in a whisper: " He'll have a peaceful life, you'll see. Not the sort of thing we've had. We've been through the war. I was in Champagne. What misery it was! But there won't be any more wars now. The workers have got a little wiser. Besides, the Germans won't go to war. They've got workers in their country, too. Do you think they would allow it? "

He was accustomed to going to bed early and getting up at five o'clock. His eyes became motionless and glassy. He struggled to keep awake and then dozed off as he sat on Doudou's little bed. And his face was like that of a child.

CHAPTER 22

NEVER had time seemed to drag so slowly as during that winter. Paris was quiet and puzzling. The blue December twilight shrouded the monuments of past glory. In the shop windows the multi-coloured dolls and *marrons glacés* still gave the illusion of a peaceful Christmas. A few lonely revellers still roamed about the streets, pursuing the muse or some confiding midinette. But the spirit of oblivion seemed to have descended on the city.

Every morning the ministers regularly signed the decrees dismissing insubordinate telegraphers and stokers. The employers were dropping workers everywhere. Hunger gnawed hundreds of thousands of unemployed. Daladier spoke about national defence, but the benches of the armament factories stood silent as though under a spell.

With his readers' money, Joliot presented Mrs. Chamberlain with a gold toilet set. The little fat man whispered boastfully: "It's the very best on the market!" But when Chamberlain came to Paris, the workers gathered at the railway station and booed him. This was the last intervention of the people. Afterwards all was quiet. Judges and magistrates worked without ceasing. In the prisons mechanics, polishers, smelters, and other industrial workers varnished chocolate-boxes.

Legrais was taken to court from the hospital. Two gendarmes stood on either side of him. He began his defence with the words: "I accuse Daladier . . ." The president said quietly: "Take him away," and five minutes later he began droning the sentence: "In accordance with the law of the 19th of July . . . Legrais, Jacques . . . is sentenced to hard labour. . . ."

At a meeting of the Radical Party, Fouget's friends demanded the resignation of the Government. Smiling jauntily, Tessa answered: "The resignation of the Government would lead to war with our powerful neighbour." After spending the evening over an atlas, he had dinner with one of the deputies, and during that solemn interval between the cheese and the pear he said: "You'll see, the Germans will go east! There's oil there, my dear chap. And do you know what oil is? It's the blood of this age."

Ribbentrop came on a visit to Paris. As a precaution, the police cleared the streets and the visitor was presented with a fantastic picture: the red winter sun over the empty Place de la Concorde. He said politely: "Paris has particularly pleased me this time. . . ."

The Italian divisions were approaching Barcelona. The deputies held a meeting and decided to send Senator Bérard to General Franco. Tessa welcomed this decision and said: "It's time to dispel any misunderstandings!"

Villard spoke at a meeting. He deplored the fate of the Czech women and Catalonian children. He said the Government had attacked the working class unjustly, and then he exclaimed with a sob in his voice: "Our Republic is the last bulwark of liberty in enslaved Europe!" There was a round of half-hearted applause. Then Duchesne, the old watchman of the Seine factory, who was sitting in the front row, got up and said: "Who's going to die for this bulwark? Only the saints and the tarts. But the saints are in heaven and the tarts never die."

When Tessa was told about Duchesne's retort, he said with a smile: "Whatever you may say, the French are a witty people. I'm not afraid of Ducane's croaking. We're not Czechs."

Nevertheless, Tessa often had fits of despondency. He asked himself why he had loaded himself with this burden. The Communists were shouting: "Down with Tessa!" Ducane had taken up the story of the letter to Grandel and was yelling about "a German spy in the Chamber!" Even the parliamentary commissions were grumbling and demanding the lifting of the repressions.

Villard called on Tessa on behalf of the Commission for Labour.

"I defended you at a workers' meeting a few days ago," he said. "They interrupted me and wanted to lynch me. You've laid it on too thick. The Government is more unpopular than ever."

Tessa shrugged his shoulders. "But who is popular? You? Flandin? Breteuil? It's all nonsense! I'll tell you who is popular here — Hitler! Personally, I'm sorry I took your place. It's far more peaceful to be in the opposition at present. You say: 'Stop the repressions.' I'd be only too glad. What do you take me for? A wild beast? But let the Communists stop their campaign. We're doing our best to arrange peace, but they're upsetting everything. It's far better to send a few thousands to jail than to send millions to the slaughter. They want a preventive war, but my idea — ha ha! — my idea is preventive arrests!"

Villard whipped off his eyeglasses, wiped the lenses with his handkerchief, and said as he looked at Tessa with his mild, unseeing eyes: "Do you really believe in peace?"

"What shall I say? There's a chance that the Germans may go east. In that case we're safe for twenty years. One may miscalculate. I'm fond of a gamble myself, but at present we happen to be the cards; we're shuffled and dealt out. An atrocious profession! I envy the unemployed; they sleep under the bridge and have nothing to think about. Auguste, we don't live. We haven't time to concentrate. When Amalie died —"

His voice quavered. He remembered the two candles and the lilies. And Villard experienced a change of feeling towards him. He had never liked Tessa. He looked upon him as a business man. Now he saw in him a man who was dear to his own heart. They had grown up on the same books. They loved the same pictures. And both of them had sacrificed themselves for nothing and lost their spiritual fire in debating, voting, and playing the rough parliamentary game. He went up to Tessa and shook his hand warmly: "I understand. I, too, am lonely."

They forgot about the vote of the Commission and the fate of France. The two old men gave themselves up to their personal sorrows. Villard complained: "Once upon a time there were monasteries. People used to shut themselves up, read, think on the mysteries of the universe, and water their flowers. But now there's no place of refuge anywhere."

Tessa quickly changed the subject. What good to him were such dismal thoughts? "Don't say that," he said gaily. "The day before yesterday I went to the Folies Bergère. One must admit the girls are a marvellous invention! Of course, one can't have the same approach to it as to choreography. It isn't Pavlova . . . But when they leap about, well, really it honestly makes me feel I'm alive."

CHAPTER 23

TESSA was now looking to the Right for support. He tried to win over Breteuil, but Breteuil became daily more exacting and insisted on the resignation of Mandel. At a sport-club dinner Breteuil said: "Alas, the Jew Mandel is still a Minister! He is trying to make us quarrel with Germany." Tessa hastened to express his regrets to Mandel: "What can you expect? Breteuil is a fanatic. He has an Oriental mind. He wasn't born in Lorraine for nothing. But we are Cartesians. That sort of thing is quite alien to us." To Breteuil he said: "Yes, yes, there's a good deal of truth in your remarks about Mandel. The Jews remain an alien body."

Tessa was worried by the shadow of Grandel. The man went

about everywhere, smiling in his captivating way and murmuring:
"My dear friend." And Tessa said to himself: "Perhaps he wants
to ensnare me too?" Grandel became the darling of the Paris draw-
ing-rooms. He gave a lecture to a fashionable audience at L'Am-
bassadeur on the subject of "The German-Latin World and the
Struggle against Bolshevism." He was filmed by the news-reel
cameramen. He went about everywhere, smiling and casually
dropping the hint: "You know, the Ukraine is really worth studying. Yesterday I read the life of Mazeppa. It's most interesting and
instructive!" Tessa did not know who Mazeppa was, but he was
suspicious of everything Grandel said. From time to time he remembered Kilmann's letter, but more often he thought to himself:
"Grandel is aiming at becoming a minister. I must be more careful
with him!"

Breteuil continued to back Grandel. Nobody would have
dreamed there had been any misunderstanding between them.
Fouget's assertions were now taken up by Ducane. Everywhere he
was heard warning people to beware of Grandel. When they asked
him whether he had any evidence, he said: "No, but I feel it." He
no longer passed the time of day with Breteuil, and left the party.
The Right wing attacked him, calling him a "degenerate," a "re-
venge-monger," a "national Bolshevik." But his personal integrity
had given him the reputation of an honest patriot, and this was
not easily shattered. Many of Breteuil's friends continued to meet
Ducane, and disruption began to spread in what had hitherto been
a disciplined party.

General Picard became alarmed at Ducane's agitation and went
to see Breteuil. "I don't have any secrets from you," he said, "but
this man Grandel comes to me with questions about our armaments.
How can I trust him?"

"Grandel is working with me."

"Yes, but you know what's being said about him. We're not in
1936, with Blum at the head of France. If war breaks out, it's we
who'll have to be responsible for it."

Breteuil fumbled nervously with the tablecloth. "It's a very
complicated game," he said. "And a dangerous one; I don't deny
that. We're incapable of winning by ourselves. We've only got to
yield and then we'll have the Popular Front again. Of course, if I
could, I'd choose other allies. After all, I'm a Lorrainer. But we've
got no choice. The British are like gods on Olympus. We're just

pawns in their game; they'll pay with our Tunisia or Indo-China. Besides, it's easy for them to talk about a Tripartite Pact, when they've got only one Communist in Parliament. Yes, yes, only one! But look what we've got! I look at it from the national point of view. The Germans want to take advantage of us. That's quite understandable. But France is a single body. It can't be broken into pieces. The infection hasn't affected the framework. Therefore the very opposite will happen: it's we who'll take advantage of the Germans, not they of us. You understand me? The war menace will give us the chance to get rid of the Communists. Victory will be on the side of the one who says to the people: " Peace! " But Hitler won't dare to make war; after all, our Army is something to be reckoned with. However, you know that better than I do."

" I no longer know anything," said Picard. " I'm afraid our Army won't stand up to the blow. It's not a question of armaments, though even on that score I have my doubts. I've just been talking to our attaché who was in Spain. He's got a very high opinion of the German Air Force. But I repeat, it's not a question of that. The morale is low. The officers don't want to fight. And it's hardly likely they will want to even if the circumstances demand it. You reckon on retreating to a certain limit. But I don't know if we'll be able to hold out even there. The Army is a living thing. It's an organism."

Picard got excited; the Army was something very close to his heart. But Breteuil, having expounded his plan, remained quite calm. He had said everything he had to say. The only thing he failed to mention was the question of Grandel's contact with Kilmann. But that was a detail. Of course the game was complicated. How many times had Breteuil hesitated! But he was sustained by his belief in God — in Providence. He always remembered the Shepherdess of Lorraine, who was sent by God Almighty to save France. No, France would not perish.

Shortly after his talk with Picard, Breteuil insisted on Tessa's issuing a denial of the rumours about Grandel. " These rumours defaming Grandel can all be traced back to Ducane," he said. " He's an irresponsible fellow. But your name is constantly being mentioned. The question of that forgery has been dragged out into the open again. You've got to put a stop to it."

Tessa was obstinate. " I don't affirm anything," he said, " but I've no intention of denying anything either. What's it got to do with me? Besides, I've no feelings of sympathy towards Grandel.

I'll tell you candidly — he doesn't inspire me with confidence."

"And do you think I have any liking for Grandel? He's a money-grubbing adventurer, and a gigolo into the bargain. If I had a daughter, I certainly wouldn't give her to Grandel. But we're dealing with a question of politics, not what one likes. Who is it who is carrying on this campaign against Grandel — Fouget, Ducane; and the Communists are behind them. They want to revive the Popular Front. If you refute the slander, we'll upset their plans."

"That's all very well," said Tessa, "but I'm far from being convinced that the letter is a forgery. Between ourselves, I think Grandel is mixed up in a very unwholesome affair."

"Impossible. But have you got any evidence?"

"No."

"There you are, then. It's impossible for us to expel him. In that case all we can do is to examine the matter not from the moral but from the political viewpoint. If you remain silent, they'll devour you. Now look at this. Here's Ducane's latest stunt."

He showed Tessa a letter which Ducane had sent round to some of the Right deputies demanding an investigation of the financial resources not only of Grandel but also of everyone implicated in the "Kilmann affair," and among them — Tessa.

Tessa began to cough with indignation. "Good God, what villainy!"

After this it was easy for Breteuil to get Tessa's signature to a brief, emphatic denial.

That evening Tessa said to Paulette: "Breteuil had me with my back to the wall. The infernal blackmailer! Of course, we'll win another victory. The budget commission wanted to overthrow us. Not surprising, considering Fouget's friends are on it. But I presented them with a little surprise package in the form of the Franco-German declaration. They calmed down at once. You see what a hell of a lot of victories we've been winning: Munich, the collapse of the strike, Bérard's mission to Franco, and now the declaration. As they used to say in the old days, one more victory like that, and everything will go to the devil!"

"What will go to the devil?"

"What? Why, France."

Paulette took no interest in politics. The only things she ever read in the papers were the murder cases and the serials, but she had been brought up in the cult of Joan of Arc, Napoleon, Hugo,

and Verdun. She looked horrified at Tessa. But he was shaking with
laughter.

"What are you laughing for?"

"It's better than weeping," said Tessa meekly. "I'm tired. I've
got a right to a little recreation. Now, don't be annoyed, my little
kitten. I was only joking. It's impossible for France to collapse.
That won't happen before the world comes to an end."

CHAPTER 24

WISHING to influence the policy of Daladier and Tessa, the Spanish
Government refused to help the International Brigade. The Paris
Commune battalion was languishing in a tiny Catalonian village
near the frontier, as the men were not allowed to enter France. The
peasant women scrubbed their washing in the little stream and
gathered pale winter greens. Life seemed to be at peace. Suddenly,
like whirlwinds of dust before a storm, the refugees began to
pour in.

The people of Barcelona had taken to flight as the Moorish
troops approached the town. The peasants left the countryside,
driving their mules and goats before them or killing their cattle.
Sideboards and chicken-coops jolted on the carts, while the women
walked alongside carrying bundles. Then the soldiers began to
flee. Boxes of ammunition were left lying by the roadside. Artillery-
men dragged the guns. And all the while the Fascist planes bombed
the roads, and little children squatted in the craters, clasping to
their breasts the toys they had managed to save.

The terrified people streamed towards the distant dim blue
mountains, beyond which lay France. But Tessa told the French
press: "We can't admit the refugees. I don't like blackmail, and
the Communists are trying to blackmail us with compassion." So
the frontier was closed.

A few commanders still tried to organize resistance. They cheered
up the flagging spirits of the men and brought back the deserters
from the frontier and put them to shame. Tiny newspapers came out
with appeals for courage and calm. The Government ministries

and the General Staff led a nomadic life, moving every day from one frontier village to another. Underwood typewriters clattered in the sheds and barns. Italian bombers bombed Figueras, the last town of the Republic, shattering its old balconied houses and murdering the refugees. And the mutilated bodies lay among the dust and rubble.

The last meeting of the Cortes took place in a cellar. The deputies were covered with the dust of the roads, unshaven, and tired. Their eyes were red from sleepless nights. Negrin made a speech. He spoke of the holy war of the Spanish people, the barbarity of Hitler and Mussolini, and the heartlessness of France, which refused to allow the women and the wounded to enter the country. Several times during his speech he was obliged to cover his face with his hands. Some old man had laid a carpet on the stairs leading down into the cellar. "After all, it's the Cortes," he explained. And all around were burning villages that had been set on fire by the bombs.

When the sound of the cannonade reached the village where the French battalion was quartered, Michaud said: "They're coming, and how! Don't let them take us alive! Fall in!"

The battalion went out. They helped to evacuate munitions and beat off a tank attack. For an hour there was a lively interlude: it was war again. They were sustained by the spirit of Madrid, Teruel, and the Ebro, and for a few last hours the ghost of victory turned up again. But in the night a car drove up to battalion headquarters. The hood was riddled with bullet holes. A pale adjutant with his arm in a sling called out: "Tomorrow the last units must cross the frontier."

Michaud actually screamed with anger; he considered the fight had only just begun. Stifling their rage, the Frenchmen turned towards the north.

The frontier region was like a vast camp. For two weeks the refugees had been waiting for the frontier to be opened. They killed the last sheep and burned cupboards, archives, rags, boxes, and trunks of linen. Why had they brought all these goods and chattels with them? The night was cold, and the women warmed themselves around the campfires. The donkeys brayed. A trumpet sounded in the stillness.

The military authorities told Daladier that if the Spaniards were obliged to defend themselves right up to the frontier, the fighting might easily cross into French territory. So Daladier ordered the frontier to be opened. Chains of gendarmes and soldiers, for the most Senegalese, filtered the people through, searching them and taking away their arms, their cattle, and part of their belongings. In Perpignan the police did a brisk trade in " captured booty," especially revolvers, typewriters, and watches.

The Paris Commune battalion was far from looking like a defeated unit. The soldiers marched in step, with their rifles slung over their shoulders and with their flag fluttering in the breeze. Only their faces betrayed their bitter sense of defeat. Never had they dreamed they would come home like this. It was like an expulsion. And many of them, looking for the last time at the bomb-scarred soil of Spain with its litter of abandoned guns and chattels, could scarcely hold back their tears.

The Senegalese who were barring the way shouted something the Frenchmen could not understand. Michaud was in command, and the Paris Commune battalion saluted the faded, weather-beaten old flag. The soldiers of the regular French Army looked embarrassed, but the Senegalese grinned good-naturedly and showed their excessively white teeth.

A policeman tore the bandage from Michaud's friend Jules. " Maybe you've got some gold hidden there," he said. When he saw the fresh wound, he swore. They drove the Frenchmen into a camp and told them: " You'll be dealt with later on. You're deserters." Others were driven along with them — Spaniards and Swedes, British and Serbs, women with children at the breast, professors of Barcelona University, village children, poets, shepherds, and the gravely wounded. Those who lagged behind were driven on by the Senegalese, who used the butts of their rifles.

Behind the barbed-wire fences the people were jumbled together like sheep in a pen. The cold north wind blew the sand into their faces. Towards evening it began to rain. There was no shelter anywhere. They were told they were going to be given some bread, but nobody brought any. The camp was right on the seashore, and the breakers rumbled on the beach the whole night long. From time to time came the sound of shooting in the distance.

Tessa's friend Piroux, the deputy, arrived from Paris. He sat in the customs house waiting for the Spanish Fascists the whole day long. When through field-glasses he caught sight of the red and yellow flag his face beamed with pleasure. A quarter of an hour later he gave his visiting-card to the Spanish general and said: "I congratulate you on your magnificent victory." The general answered with a condescending smile.

Days went by. The prisoners in the camp were tortured with hunger. The water from the shallow well smelt of urine. Tourists began to arrive. They gazed at the Spaniards as though they were wild beasts in a menagerie. Every night the corpses of those who had died of dysentery or pneumonia were carted away.

Perpignan was a gay, happy-go-lucky town where people had eaten almond nougat, drunk strong "rancio" wine, listened enraptured to the military music in the squares, and voted for the Popular Front. Now they were hunting for people in Perpignan. The schools were turned into prisons. The police were looking for Spaniards. In vain the Spanish women, who were used to going bare-headed, spent their last pennies on the tiny hats which were the fashion that winter; their tear-stained eyes gave them away.

Many French men and women concealed the Spaniards in their attics, wine cellars, bathhouses and shepherds' shelters. Thousands of devoted people went up to the mountain passes and guided the refugees by unfamiliar paths.

It was a melancholy evening in the camp. A gendarme struck a young Spaniard in the face. He could not bear the insult and hanged himself. All the prisoners were in low spirits. Then the daily allowance of bread was reduced again. All they got now was an ounce and a half. Michaud gave his share to Fernandez, a Spanish drawing-teacher, who had commanded a battalion of sappers.

"It's a disgrace!" said Michaud. "It's not so bad for you. You aren't responsible for this. But I'm a Frenchman."

Fernandez said naïvely: "I was never abroad before. This is the first time. . . ."

"I'm only sorry you can't see other people, our comrades. It's the truth I'm telling you. There *are* other Frenchmen. But where are they? And how many of them are there? France was different once upon a time. We called our battalion Paris Commune. That's a fine name! They don't call their divisions the Munich Divisions. You know what our trouble is? We've got an easy life in France. People have forgotten all about the war of 1914. They say to themselves: 'The trouble's all over. It won't come back again. We're wiser now.' As if reason could save you from disaster! They live too well. They eat well, the girls are pretty, they've got the sea and the mountains, gardens and cafés everywhere, and the climate is neither too hot nor too cold. And so they've begun not only to be unafraid of trouble but to despise it. Twenty years ago they despised the Russians. I was a child at the time but I remember it quite well. They used to laugh and say: 'The Russians want to change the whole world, and they haven't got any trousers or bread themselves!' Now they despise the Spaniards and say: 'They talked about dignity and said they didn't want to "live on their knees," and now they've had to come and ask us to give them refuge.' What a base philosophy! And they don't see the danger. They don't set any store on the simple feelings of friendship and fidelity. It seems to me that only great suffering will save France. Great human suffering."

Thousands of stars twinkled above them, and a threatening murmur came from the sea. The time of the March gales was at hand.

CHAPTER 25

Joliot looked at the photograph and smiled. The young actress had had herself photographed wearing a gas-mask. Her low-cut dress afforded a good view of her feminine attraction, but her face in the mask looked like a pig's snout, and Joliot said to his secretary: "The star Honk-honk. We'll print that. By the way, today is Mardi Gras."

Once upon a time Mardi Gras was a holiday. Joliot remembered the crowds on the boulevards, the white robes of the pierrots and the glittering tights of the harlequins, the boleros, the plaits, the black velvet masks trimmed with lace, and the coloured confetti. Later on, the carnival began to die out. Nevertheless, there was still some semblance of masquerade on Mardi Gras; bands of mummers went round the cafés, children in masks with false noses and beards roamed about the streets. But what had it come to now? The gas-mask Honk-honk. Joliot heaved a heavy sigh — he did everything with pathos, and when people made fun of him, he always said: "In Paris people express their reason. In Marseille they express their feelings!"

Joliot's affairs were going splendidly; he was getting large sums from the Government's secret funds. He overwhelmed his wife with presents: a sapphire necklace, a casket which according to the experts had belonged to Mme. Récamier, a cairn which had won a first prize at Cruft's in London. Joliot supported a whole pack of parasites: out-of-work journalists, Marseille poets, and weary-souled sharpers, who for some reason called themselves Anarchists. Nobody now dared to sue Joliot for defamation of character. Deputies toadied to him. He dined with ambassadors and said disdainfully to his secretary: "Not a word about Rumania! The Hungarians are far more sympathetic; besides, they've got a broader outlook. . . ."

In spite of his success, he began to look older and rather faded. Even his new tie-pin — an emerald parrot with a ruby eye — failed to brighten his appearance. He was worried by the complicated game of his patrons. He said to himself: "I don't understand myself what I write."

Tessa said to him: "Write an article on the weakness of the Red Army. Make it agree with the statement of the Italian attaché." Two days later Tessa put forward another demand: "I want you to stress the point that the military resources of Russia are inexhaustible."

This morning he was again rung up by Tessa. "The international situation is becoming serious. These are the ides of March. It's important for us to maintain communications with the colonies. But central and eastern Europe is not our concern."

Joliot began: "As M. Marcel Déat has so well expressed it, we don't want to die for Danzig. . . ." What was he to write after that? Then he had an inspiration, screwed up his right eye and wrote furiously: "We don't want to die for Warsaw, for Belgrade, ·for Bucharest. . . ." He threw himself back exhausted. The main thing was to dish it up properly. The word "die" would have to be printed in big letters. And underneath the article he would put the photograph of Honk-honk.

He lunched with Gézier, the editor of *La République*. As a sweet they had pancakes soaked in maraschino. "It's all the most terrible nonsense," said Gézier gaily, with his mouth full. "Chamberlain is said to have offered Tunisia to the Italians. And Bonnet shouts: 'We'd better give them Malta!' It's a regular brothel! Daladier said to me yesterday: 'Not a word about collective security.' Tomorrow we're publishing a leading article on the Jewish menace. By the way, it was written by a Jew. I tell you, it's a regular brothel! "

They drank some armagnac. Gézier was in a hurry to get away, but Joliot walked back to the office in order to get a breath of air. He said to himself: "Gézier is a scoundrel and a fool! What has Malta got to do with it? Is Malta in Europe?" He walked along the boulevard Wagram as far as the Place de l'Étoile. The weather was fickle. Whenever the sun came out, everything brightened up. The buds of the chestnut trees opened and the women looked prettier. Then the cold wind blew up low clouds and a wintry rain began to fall. When he reached the square Joliot stopped by the Tomb of the Unknown Soldier. It was the same as always — a pale flame, wreaths, provincial visitors. Over the tomb rose the great arch. The place always had an emotional effect on Joliot. Sometimes he took off his hat, sometimes he whistled the *Marseillaise*. Like most people of his generation, he looked on the years of the war as the years of youth and spiritual integrity. He even recalled with warm affection the sergeant's bawling voice, the bunk in which he lay for two months with typhus, the sickening feeling and cold chill before going over the top, when the troops were given coffee with rum and how they eagerly clutched at the hot tin mug. He remembered all his comrades: dumpy little Dornier, short-sighted Deval, and jovial Clément — he was killed, poor chap.

Who was buried under the arch? Maybe Clément? Why not? And Clément was having flowers brought to him and being saluted by generals, ambassadors, Tessa. Poor Clément, couldn't he knock music out of a jew's-harp! And he wanted to marry a girl from Marseille.

Joliot remembered the words: " We don't want to die for Danzig." And what had Clément died for? They used to say: " For France." The girl from Marseille was probably married to somebody else. She might even be dead — a quarter of a century had gone by!

The usual hubbub reigned in the office. Joliot was comforted by it; he was tired of thinking. An article had been sent in by the Ministry. It was entitled: " Italy — the Bulwark of Latin Culture in the Near East." Honk-honk grimaced on the front page. Outside in the street the newspaper women were wailing with a nasal twang: " Fifth edition! We don't want to die."

After finishing work for the day, Joliot went to a cabaret. They had long been inviting and imploring him to come. A young male singer with a heavily painted face was singing:

> *If only we live till tomorrow,*
> *We don't care a damn what's ahead!*

The public took up the refrain: " We don't care a damn what's ahead! " Then another actor, remembering it was Shrove Tuesday, came on the stage wearing a mask — a white mask, with a sharp beak and black holes for the eyes. Somebody in the hall called out: " It's Death." Someone else said: " Nonsense! It's Tessa. That's his nose."

Joliot got bored with the ridiculous show and went home. His wife was sitting in the dining-room reading a newspaper. She never asked Joliot about his business, being far too preoccupied with her own affairs. She was always busy with dressmakers, sales, and fashions. But of late she couldn't help thinking to herself: " Good Lord! What do they really mean in the newspapers? " She ventured to say to her husband: " I don't understand."

Joliot waved his hands. " Do you think I know? They're up to some game. Maybe they're not even that, but only pretending to be. I used to admire their cleverness, but now I don't know. Sometimes I think they're out of their wits with fear."

His wife kept staring at him. Then she asked in a whisper: " You're not taking anything from the Germans? I'm worried. They can shoot people for that."

Joliot began to shout. " You're out of your mind! What on earth put that idea into your head? Who do you think gives me anything? Why, our own people, Frenchmen, the Government! "

And suddenly he started muttering: " To die for Paris. Poor Clément! "

Mme. Joliot could not understand what on earth he meant.

CHAPTER 26

" How are you? "

" Not too bad. And you? "

Desser passed on without listening to the rest. Suddenly he

thought: whatever would it be like if we all answered truthfully? There would be never-ending confessions of woe and fears. But it was just a formula, like Tessa's speeches, prayers in church, and lovers' vows. Probably there was a saving grace in it. If everything was stripped bare it would be impossible to live.

Nobody guessed that Desser was on the decline. All his business affairs were flourishing. Chicago and Liverpool waited as before for his orders. His quarrel with Daladier and his speeches before the strike remained casual episodes. Montigny thought that Desser was merely "trying to be original." And Tessa nodded his head admiringly and said: "That's a clever man! He'll dish them all. He's got the devil of an eye! . . ."

But Desser didn't see anything. He went on with the game, but the seat opposite him was empty — he was playing with a dummy. Events now seemed to him to be like a convulsion of nature. He was reading at night a long history of Byzantium, and it made him laugh, as everybody knew what was wrong but nobody was able to prevent disaster.

Of course Munich was the only way out. Of course it was necessary to come to an agreement by all means. But how? And with whom? With the hurricane? Marvels! Marvels!

Until he was fifty Desser had never had any serious illness. He drank a good deal, smoked incessantly, and never got enough sleep. He began to ail all of a sudden. He was very touchy about his health and listened attentively to what the doctors had to say, but he was too bored to carry out their prescriptions and went on living as before in his old haphazard, enervating way. He even took to drinking more than ever. He was afraid of dying. At night he would get into his sports car and drive on and on miles away from Paris; then he would stop at some little roadside café, drink white wine with the railway workers, and talk about the weather.

Like many other people Desser was saved by the very inertia of his thoughts, mental reactions, and behaviour. He went on with his financial operations, opened a couple of new factories, and took part in the negotiations with Rome. He did all this without any enthusiasm, but he found comfort in working. It was much easier than thinking about the decline and fall of Byzantium, angina pectoris, or loneliness.

In the hope of finding a few moments of forgetfulness he even went to see Jeannette. He did not admit he was in love with "that crack-brained girl." And after spending the evening with her, he felt even more lonely than before. " It's still not the right thing," he told himself on the way home. But he didn't even know himself what he really wanted.

They saw quite a lot of each other. They used to go to the little cafés on the outskirts of Paris. Sometimes he would take her in his car along the wet, deserted roads, rushing along at nearly ninety miles an hour and infecting her with his own restlessness. Then he would drive her back and kiss her hand ceremoniously when they parted. He was relieved whenever he found a tiresome telegram waiting for him or when the piles of urgent business kept him at his desk, stopping him from thinking about Jeannette. Even his emotions seemed like a convulsion of nature which no mental calculations were capable of suppressing.

Desser called for Jeannette at the studio. He had never listened to her on the radio. Somehow he felt it wasn't the right thing; she wouldn't question him about the Stock Exchange! He was asked to wait and was shown into an empty room with heavy red blinds. He heard Jennette's voice. She was reading some poetry. He thought he remembered having seen it in a school anthology of verse:

> Even Death admits thy mighty sway,
> And earth scarce holds the power of love.
> Together we'll find the ship of oblivion
> And roam about the Elysian fields.

He didn't hear any more; depression, like a thick fog, descended on him.

Jeannette came in. "You recited nicely," he said.

She laughed. " It was an advertisement. A dye for eyelashes."

They went out together. A light rain was beginning to fall. She asked: "What do you think about war?" She remembered the talk that had been going on in the studio. Desser would probably know. But all he said was: " I'm not an oracle."

A woman in a tattered old-fashioned cape was walking alongside them. She was carrying a lot of parcels and bags and muttering to herself: "I'd poke my finger into his gullet. There's a fine to-do! " Desser whispered: " She's mad." They felt embarrassed and hurried to the car. Desser did not press the self-starter at once; he sat for a moment as though dazed. Then they were off. Green and red lights flashed through the streaming windows. The head-lamps poured a jet of light into the darkness, picking out the rain-drenched trees. Desser drove Jeannette to his house in the suburbs. He didn't ask her if she wanted to go. He scarcely opened his mouth the whole way.

When they got there he offered her some brandy.

" Have a drop to warm yourself up," he said. " You recited very well indeed. You ought to go on the stage. You remember you said your manager had no money. That's a mere trifle."

She shook her head: " No. I can't act now. When you speak, you must believe every word. If you don't, then the audience doesn't believe it either. Then there's a silence in the theatre, and one's voice seems to get lost. You don't understand? I'm lost too. Once upon a time I believed. Then I was living with an actor. He used to snore and I lay beside him reciting speeches from Racine's *Phèdre.* . . ."

She went out into the garden. There was a smell of earth and wet leaves. Spring was coming on with a rush, and the patter of the raindrops sounded to her like hurrying steps. She breathed the fresh air eagerly. " You'll get a chill! " Desser called out. She didn't answer. She felt that for a few moments a great happiness had come within her reach, and once again, as at Fleury, she believed in the illusion. She went back into the room and smiled at Desser with her haunted eyes. He was embarrassed. But she said: " No, I won't catch a cold. I'm a lost soul, Desser. I'm a lost soul."

She began to kiss him in a sad, impulsive way without herself knowing why she did so.

Even afterwards she couldn't make out why she went with Desser. There was nothing in store for her but sorrow and insults. But that night, as she listened to the hissing of the rain, she re-peated the words of the poem:

> *In thé land where the golden spring is eternal,*
> *Where hearts are free from all care and woe,*
> *Where, fed by the hand of fertile nature,*
> *The fruit on the golden tree hangs low,*
> *There on the shore in gentle play*
> *Or roaming in the myrtle grove,*
> *Even in the tents of paradise*
> *We'll never forget the vow of love.*

Suddenly Desser asked: "Jeannette, why all this sadness?"

"It isn't sadness. The sadness is at Fleury — our tree. Or in the poetry. But this is despair. You remember the madwoman? You're lost too, Desser. I know now."

As she said this she kissed him.

They went back to Paris in the morning. Jeannette couldn't make out why the papers made so much fuss over Desser. They thought he was all-powerful. They called him the "uncrowned king." And in reality he was destitute. His heart was empty. And he had come to her. How ridiculous to think he could find salvation with her! She was sorry for him on account of his boyishness. And he was sorry for her too. But you couldn't build up love on pity. What about poetry? It was an advertisement for face-creams, vacuum cleaners, and oblivion. She would never be an actress. And she would never marry him either. When he suggested it, she laughed. No, she had no desire to become an "uncrowned queen." It was a good thing he had his own business to attend to. Presently he'd be going off to work, just like a workman. He'd sit down at his desk and reckon in millions. Why couldn't he see that she was just as much a beggar as himself? She had been plundered. She had given something of herself to Figet and Lucien. And now she was empty. Yesterday it wasn't herself that spoke — it was the rain, and Ronsard. It was only when she was with André that she was natural, free from guile and unconscious of pity. André lived like her — purposefully. No, that wasn't the right word. . . . He said "like a plant that drifts from field to field." Only they were drifting in different directions. No doubt there were many people like them. She had read somewhere about people who were "poisoned with art." But why did she think only of André? Simply because she was in love with him.

This was the first time she admitted it to herself. And she turned at once to Desser and said: "I'm in love with someone else. It doesn't make any difference. I don't see him and I don't think I shall ever see him again. But I want you to know it."

She spoke dryly, almost officially. He stopped the car and kissed her hands.

"You've touched me," he said. "You've touched me very deeply. It's a pity you don't want to go on the stage. Anyway, that isn't important."

He drove her to her apartment. They made arrangements to meet again in the evening and parted. Everything became clear at once. It was even banal — a liaison.

Desser read the cable: the German troops were in Prague. Suddenly he began to laugh out loud. Then he got the bottle from the bookcase. What was the good of paying attention to the doctor now? In a year it would be the end. What about Jeannette? Anyway, she was in love with somebody else. She was a good girl, but rather terrible; she had eyes like that old madwoman. But one thing was true — they would find the ship of oblivion together.

CHAPTER 27

" I OFTEN saw you there. The hills are red and there isn't even a bush. And the air is heavy and thick. It's so hot. And suddenly I felt you were next to me and I was putting my arms around you. Oh, Denise, why mustn't I talk about it? I'm talking about love! Don't you understand? "

Denise said nothing, but kissed him all the harder.

" I used to think it was terrible to die — according to what everybody says. No, it's quite simple. It's even wonderful. Like now. Everything was hard to understand, but it wasn't terrible. It was defeat that was terrible. You had a horrible feeling. You didn't want to talk to anyone. But death's another matter. That's your own affair inside yourself."

" I used to lie awake at night in prison," said Denise. " I could hear the shooting. But I knew they wouldn't kill you. It sounds silly, but I knew it. They couldn't kill you. I was with you all the time."

" Denise! "

" What? "

" Nothing."

There were red asters on the wallpaper. They must have been blooming for nearly a century already but still they hadn't faded. Why was that portrait of a mustachioed marshal hanging on the wall? And on the mantelpiece was a money-box — a dwarf in a red bonnet. It was a casual room with casual furniture. Others might live there all their lives. But for these two it was just a halting-place.

For an hour, for a week — it was all the same. But the asters wouldn't dare to fade. The marshal looked awkward and envious: he was biting his grey moustaches. Whom he conquered and where was forgotten with the school-books. The dwarf was empty; there wasn't even a sou in his little belly. If you flicked him on the nose he wouldn't mind. Perhaps she'd remember this dwarf when she was next in prison. The walls there were white and dull; you looked at the cracks and you thought you saw a tree, clouds, or the face of a viking. And Michaud in the trenches would suddenly see a red aster. He'd stretch out his hand to pluck it, and then a bullet. . . . But the bullet was sure to fly past him.

"Michaud, you're really here?"

She felt his breath on her cheek, but she wanted to hear his voice. She stroked his forehead and his crisp hair and tried all the time to realize that they were really together.

And then they began to run about the room like wanton children.

"Michaud, you've gone out of your head! What will they think below? And how are you going out into the street? Look at yourself in the glass."

Obediently he looked.

"Well?"

"But your eyes! Don't you see? Oh, you lunatic!"

At last he had to go: the meeting was fixed for nine o'clock. He frowned, trying to collect his thoughts.

"The party has grown stronger. Only the lovers of easy successes have fallen away. On the other hand, there are lots of new people. I understand why Villard writes about death; their outlook is empty. And everybody's laughing at the Government. I heard a man shout in the bus today: 'You traitor, Daladier! We'll smash them — I'll say we will, and how!'"

"Michaud, is it you? Tell me, is it really you?"

"Luc Michaud. I confirm it. You know where I heard they'd arrested you? In Perpignan. You were already released, but I didn't know it. I nearly went mad. I wanted to bash some damn police spy's head in. I was very proud of you. What fine people we've got! Thorez thinks they're going to suppress the party. That's Tessa's line. But we've got everything ready for underground work. The skeleton organization is really strong. The main thing is not to upset communications. They're sending me to Saint Étienne to arrange everything. . . ."

"When are you going?"

"I don't know yet. Maybe tomorrow or Saturday."

He put on his overcoat and cap and assumed a preoccupied air. Only his eyes still spoke of his happiness. They went out together and walked to the Metro. There were jostling crowds in the long dim tunnels. The air was warm and damp, and the trains thundered as they passed. On the tiled walls were enormous geese in ladies' bonnets, skull-caps, and fezzes — "The best *pâté de foie gras.*"

So tomorrow they would part again. It was impossible to talk now. There were too many people around. They could talk neither of love nor of underground political work. Everything was secret. But Denise was proud of Michaud's courage, of the battles that lay ahead, and of her love. Michaud was unable to restrain himself and whispered: "And how!"

"And how" — that would be their password. They said good-bye to each other. Michaud went off in the train. Another red light faded away into the darkness. Denise hurried along, down, up, and then down again. The underground passages were complicated and tortuous. Everywhere was bustle, noise, and indifference. Denise thought: "We've put up with one separation, but how many lie ahead?" Life was terrible when one had to wait all the time! Later on, people would say to them: "May you be happy!" But it might be too late. No, it wasn't really like that. They were young. They had only to wish and to wish strongly that everything would happen: their meeting, the revolution, and their happiness. And Denise wished. She stood on the platform among the people, automatic machines and advertisements and whispered to herself: "And how!" Michaud, Michaud! . . .

CHAPTER 28

ANDRÉ's studio was tidied up in the most unusual manner. The empty bottles had been taken away. The shabby old shoes were hidden in the cupboard. The canvases were arranged in decent order along the walls. The big table was bare except for a text-book on astronomy and a postcard with a view of Rügen with sand-dunes and white clouds. It had been sent to André by the German who had amused him by telling him that he was fond of landscape but was studying fish. The ichthyologist had only written the word "Greetings," but André immediately remembered their meeting in the Smoking Dog. The German had said to him: "I'm glad to have seen Paris while Paris still exists." More than two years had passed and Paris still stood on the same spot. But something had happened to André. He wondered whether the German could now take any interest in his fish. André had given up painting. The studio no longer smelt of turpentine. The easel lay on a shelf beside a rusty teapot. The tidiness astonished even the master of the studio. He walked about as carefully as a visitor. The concièrge gasped and asked if he was going away. No, he wasn't going anywhere. It is said that people put their house in order when they feel the approach of death. But André was strong and healthy, ate enough for three, roamed about all day, and dropped off to sleep as soon as he lay down. Where, then, was the cog in the wheel?

He spent the summer in Paris. People kept wailing: "There'll be a war," but went away for their vacations just the same. The same as last year. André was tired of it all: the waiting, the hullabaloo in the newspapers, and the arguments. The agony before death became part of life. Life had fallen to pieces, but life still went on. He had just received an invitation to the Autumn Salon. What strange people!

After a wretched six months Pierre got a job in a fountain-pen factory. He went to see André one day and said: "We must keep our courage up!" and looked away sadly. His hands shook like those of an old man.

André ran into Lucien on the Boulevards. Lucien shouted that there were traitors everywhere and life was only worth living for one's own pleasure. But when André said to him: "Then I suppose you're living well?" Lucien swore: "In the lavatory, my dear chap."

Then there was another alarm and again the papers were splashed with sensational headlines. This time it was Danzig. André did not read the papers and seldom listened to the radio. From time to time he remembered Jeannette, but it all seemed a very long time ago, another life. One rainy evening as he was looking out over the purple-coloured city, he heard some poetry mingled with the names of business firms. It was Jeannette on the radio:

O stay with me, I will not break my vow,
Revive once more my faith in happiness,
Inspire me with the life of your own soul
And soothe away the sorrow of the past!

He smiled convulsively: a dye for eyelashes, a good dye which allows beautiful women to weep! Everyone had broken his vow: himself, Jeannette, the whole world. And not a soul was alive. . . .

"How's business?" asked Josephine, all flushed with the heat of the kitchen. "So, so," Boileau said. The rue Cherche-Midi was still alive. Only the cobbler who used to sing about "roguish love" had died of inflammation of the kidneys. His successor was a man of thirty with a pretty wife and a couple of children. He too was a jolly fellow and said to his customers: "You won't wear these soles out till the war."

At the Smoking Dog the old fox-terrier continued to beg with a cigarette-holder clenched between its teeth. One day André said to it: "You look too much like Tardieu, my friend. I'm afraid you may start talking about Danzig!"

That summer all the women took to knitting. They said it soothed the nerves. André had picked up an old text-book on astronomy at a bookstall on the quay of the Seine; he couldn't knit. The stars became terra firma for him, and the earth slipped away from under his feet. He pored over the book for hours on end; he would read a few lines and then soar away on his thoughts. The figures, tables, and names all helped to soothe him.

In Nicæa two centuries before the present era Hipparchus measured the distance between the earth and the sun. And even then kingdoms were crumbling; people made gods of clay and burned heretics, soldiers died, and the clash of bronze resounded. Hipparchus spent the time compiling a catalogue of the stars.

Another time André envied the fate of Herschel. This son of a poor musician gazed into the sky at the time of the autumnal equinox. He had no money for a telescope, so he ground the lenses himself. He discovered the planet Uranus as one discovers a girl in the window opposite. Revolution was raging over Europe. Napoleon was threatening to conquer England. Pitt was weaving coalitions like a spider. But Herschel went on describing the variable stars and nebulæ.

André went over to the window. The newsboys were shouting:

" Rome expected to mediate! Repercussions of the Moscow Pact! Danzig! Danzig! " André went back to his beloved book. Once upon a time Hevelius lived in Danzig. He was engaged on making a map of the moon. Suddenly a fire broke out and consumed all his notes and drawings. He was then an old man, but he started the work all over again.

" And as for me," said André to himself, " I've forsaken my paints and betrayed my brushes." No doubt there were astronomers in Paris and they were going on with their work. Maybe the old physicist whom André had seen at the Maison de Culture was working too. Doctors were fighting cancer. André's father was gathering the first pale waxy apples of the season. Should he go and see his father? No, you couldn't get away from it. André was a rolling stone. In his unsettled mood he went out to the corner of the street and drank a bitter Calvados at the bar. Then he roamed across the city, which was wrapped in a white sultry haze.

It was a hot day. A storm had been threatening all the morning; then the clouds dispersed, but still the air got no fresher. André spent the whole day in the stifling studio. The people on the floor below were packing. They were nailing up boxes, and the constant tap, tap made André's temples throb. Towards evening he decided to go to the Smoking Dog — only spirits could soothe that dull ache. When he got out into the street he realized at once that some disaster had occurred. The florist was weeping over a bunch of crushed roses: " They'll be killed! They'll be killed! " The café-owner poured out a Calvados for André and himself and clinked glasses: " Here's to you! Now we shall have war! They waited long enough. May they perish! "

People were arguing with one another: " There's no war yet. It's only mobilization."

" No, it's war this time. We can't get out of it. Damn that Hitler! "

" Oh, it's nothing. They're sure to come to an agreement."

A workman in a cap gave the fox-terrier a lump of sugar.

" Come on! " he said. " Sit up and beg for the last time. Why did they come to an agreement last year? It's quite simple. They were afraid. They didn't want to be on the same side as the Russians. But now it's a different pair of shoes. Now they're howling. In their hearts they're for Hitler. They'll betray us. That's as clear as daylight. And who's got to go and die? We have! Sit up and beg, pup, sit up and beg! I'm a soldier of the second line too. . . ."

The cobbler pinned up a notice on the door of his shop: " Closed on account of annual mobilization." He didn't believe there would be any war and grumbled: "What next! I've got urgent orders on hand!" The florist went on weeping.

Once again the men trudged through the streets with suitcases and bags. Little blue lights gleamed in the darkness. Good-bye Herschel and the nebulæ! With an air of indifference André put shirts, soap and shaving kit into his large suitcase. He thought lazily: "It'll be the same as last time." Or were they really going to war? He didn't trouble to think any more about it. It bored him. Tomorrow he would have to go to Toul. That was certain. Did it matter what came after? Anyway, it wouldn't be this life.

There were neither songs nor shouts. Nobody vowed, nobody spoke of hatred, nobody raved of victory. There was a certain amount of commotion in the street and the florist was still sobbing. A small faint light gleamed through the leaves of a chestnut tree. Jeannette — that was his star! But he hadn't discovered her. He hadn't put her on the map. She had flashed past. Where was she — not the star, but the living girl with her slender, warm hands and unhappy fate? Probably she was weeping like the florist.

A trumpet whined mournfully along the boulevard. And the tipsy cobbler shouted out:

" Right! Left! To the right, to the grave! "

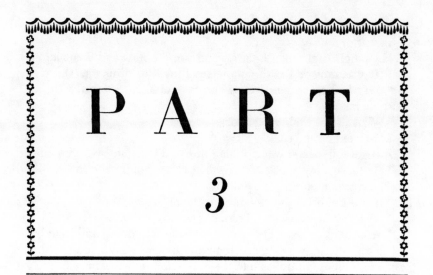

PART
3

CHAPTER 1

LUCIEN walked through the town in the blackout. He walked in an unusual way, as though he was groping for the unfriendly earth. A light rain was falling. The little blue lights gleamed mysteriously among the dark leaves of the plane trees. Lucien was in an angry mood. Only a day or two ago he had thought there would be no war; it was merely his father working up another ministerial crisis. And now what a surprise! It was rumoured they were already shooting on the Maginot Line. Tomorrow evening Lucien had got to present himself at the mobilization depot. What would he have to fight for? For M. Beck of Poland? For "human dignity," as Papa said? He might get killed. But there were worse things than that. What could be more unpleasant than the trenches, the corporal's vile language, and forty-mile marches? Besides, it was all so boring.

Lucien yawned loudly. A woman called after him: " Like a little bye-bye? " He smiled; they weren't losing any time! — prostitutes with gas-masks were standing at the corner. " So you're at your action station already? " Lucien said. One of the women let loose a torrent of abuse.

He caught sight of a light behind some blinds and went into a bar. It was crowded with people shouting and drinking. The proprietress had tear-stained eyes and was clinking glasses with her customers.

" What about your husband? "

" He went off today."

A vegetable-dealer was drinking rum and roaring: " No, you don't tell me there's any need for this war! Let the Poles go to the devil! "

There was a chorus of approval.

" If the English want to fight, let them! "

" It's an open secret that Tessa has received a million francs."

Lucien took no part in the conversation. He drank and raged in silence. Then he went to see Jenny, in order to say good-bye and get a few thousand francs into the bargain. Tomorrow he was going to drink the whole day long. Besides, he would have to have some money in his pocket in the Army. He couldn't exist on a soldier's pittance.

Jenny looked sad, but she greeted him enthusiastically. It all seemed so extraordinary to her; Lucien was going to fight in defence of liberty, but Paris would be destroyed and the Louvre would be blown to pieces. She flung her arms round his neck and said: " Everybody will have to do something. I've bought you some warm things. . . ."

When he saw the fur-lined jacket, he snorted: " My dear, this is for an officer, and I'm only a soldier of the second line. And besides, this is only September. It'll be all over before winter."

" Have you got a gas-mask, Lucien? The Germans will probably fly over Paris today. I went to get one, but they won't give them to foreigners. At the druggist's they gave me some sort of liquid and told me to sprinkle it on my handkerchief when there's a gas attack. Here it is."

" The bottle is charming. Why not use Coty's perfumes? 'Long live la vie élégante!' I say. I hope the lice in the trenches will also be elegant."

He began to sing in a cracked voice: " Paris is still Paris." Jenny covered her ears. Then her expression became serious.

" Tell me, Lucien, are you afraid? "

" No. It's merely disgusting."

" But truth is on our side? "

He hadn't drunk four glasses in the bar for nothing; he laughed uproariously. His usually pale face flushed red.

" Truth? Wait a minute and I'll explain it all to you."

He dragged the lace bed-spread off the bed and threw it round his shoulders. Then he put Jenny's hat on his head, folded his hands, and began to mutter:

" My children, the Holy Ghost has descended on Bonnet and Tessa. We are going to the aid of the great martyr Beck. That holy despiser of the goods of this world was vouchsafed a vision of the Virgin in the Czech town of Teschen. And in the Bialovezski Forest he fasted together with Saint Sebastian, who is known to the world as Marshal Göring. But now Beelzebub wants to deprive Beck of Danzig. Tremble, ye ungodly ones! Paul Tessa is setting forth to liberate the Tomb of the Lord! Amen! "

Jenny was at a loss to understand. Who was Beck? And where was Teschen? She never read the papers and had no idea of politics. But she felt that Lucien's buffoonery masked a deep sorrow. They drank coffee in silence. At last Jenny timidly asked:

" Then you don't think it's a war for freedom? "

" What freedom? "

" I don't know. Freedom in general. I mean being able to write what you like in the newspapers."

He yawned. " Yesterday Joliot was a Red, today he's a Snow-White, tomorrow he'll be dark purple. It's so boring."

She thought for a while and then said naïvely: " Then you must have a revolution."

Lucien got angry. What a lot of trouble he had taken over that word! He had attended the Maison de Culture, written articles and books, and quarrelled with his father. And now this idiotic American woman was telling him to have a revolution!

" Have one yourself. We've had one four times. I've done enough! All right, get undressed. I want to go to bed."

He was roused from sleep by the wailing of sirens. Jenny was trembling so hard she couldn't get her arms into the wide sleeves of her dressing-gown. He turned over on his other side; he didn't care a damn! In vain Jenny implored him to go down to the cellar. At last somebody knocked on the door: " Come out."

" Go to hell! " said Lucien.

" I'm the air-raid warden."

They had to go down. The cellar was stuffy, and crowded with men in striped pyjamas and dishevelled, half-naked women. The unshaved individual who called himself "air-raid warden" kept calling out: "Silence. Have your gas-masks ready!" At his command the little old concierge began to splash water on the walls. A woman sniffed as she clasped her children to her body. A rumour went round that a bomb had fallen in the next street. Jenny clutched her bottle of mysterious liquid and a lace handkerchief. One of the women had beautiful shoulders. Lucien stared at her and elbowed his way through the crowd in order to stand beside her. She moved away.

"It's war-time now, madame!" Lucien growled angrily.

Jenny's eyes were wet with jealousy, fear, and grief at the prospect of parting with Lucien. But Lucien kept on yawning and yawning.

The adventures of the night prevented him from having a good sleep. In the morning he came out feeling sleepy and irritable. A woman was making a row in the doorway. She had a wine-shop and they wanted to turn the cellar into an air-raid shelter.

"I'll go and see the Minister!" she shouted. "They keep telling us that France must be strong. Then why interfere with trade? I won't empty the cellar. You hear me? Not over my dead body!"

Lucien raised his crumpled hat.

"Splendid!" he said. "You're worthy of the best heroines of Racine. To arms, citizens! What a Punch and Judy show."

CHAPTER 2

EVERY night the Parisians were wakened by the howling of the sirens. Some people talked of having seen bombed houses. But Tessa said with a smile: "It's merely a precaution. The Germans have only to fly across the frontier and we sound the alarm. It helps to teach Paris the idea of self-sacrifice." A large number of people preferred to leave the capital. The rich quarters were deserted, but the seaside resorts of Normandy and Brittany were crowded. The soldiers were going to the east, while the discriminating bourgeoisie flocked to the west.

Montigny sent his family to Auvergne. "An ideal spot!" he said. "Not a single factory within a hundred miles!" After seeing to the comfort of his own *ménage*, he set about another and more complicated affair. He began transferring his capital to America. When Ducane got to hear about it, he wrote an article under the heading: "A Bad Frenchman." The article was refused publication by the censorship, and two white columns in the newspaper were adorned with the picture of a pair of scissors. When Montigny was told of Ducane's attack, he flamed with anger and cried out: "Does he think he's Danton? I want to save what belongs to me and to me alone. France isn't likely to gain anything if I'm ruined."

Paulette decided to go to her aunt at Morvan in central France, as she was terrified of gas raids. Tessa was upset. It was terrible to be deprived of the solace of feminine affection at such a time!

"You want to leave me all by myself," he protested.

"Paul, I'm not a heroine."

"You've got nothing to fear. They won't fly here. It's a silent agreement. If they touch Paris, we'll start bombing Berlin. And that wouldn't be to their advantage."

Paulette began to whine: "Why did you bring about this war?"

"Me?" said Tessa with a resentful tremor in his voice. "How can you say such a thing? You know I only wanted one thing, and that was to preserve peace. But what could we do? They've gone mad."

Paulette went on whining: "Why send people to their death?"

"Nobody is being sent to his death. It's the Poles who are fighting. After all, it's their affair. It's Danzig, not Strasbourg. Of course, there may be a few accidental victims on the Maginot Line. But think of the number of people who are killed on the roads in peacetime! You must realize, my little kitten, that everything has changed now. You mustn't look at things from an old-fashioned point of view. This isn't a war in the sense in which the word was formerly understood. We've got the Maginot Line and they've got the Siegfried Line. Neither side can advance a single mile. So we shall sit opposite each other and gape. 'Like china dogs on a whatnot,' as my dear Amalie used to say. The Poles are defending themselves magnificently. I always said they were a chivalrous people. They'll hold out till spring and perhaps longer. Meanwhile we shall have equipped ourselves very nicely. And then we shall be able to come to terms with the Germans. So, you see, you've nothing to be afraid of."

"All the same, it's dreadful. Especially in the blackout. And at night the sirens wail. . . ."

Her tear-stained eyes made her seem even more attractive to Tessa. He pressed his little birdlike head to her breast.

"My little kitten, don't go away! I'm absolutely done in. You can't imagine how much work I've got to do. The next few weeks will be decisive."

"But you said there wouldn't be anything."

He smiled. "Silly! Of course there won't be anything. I'm talking about home affairs. The majority in the Chamber is assured. But do you realize what it means to liquidate the Communists? It isn't a simple police operation. It's a real campaign on a big scale. One needs a Napoleon for it. But we'll root them out! "

His face stiffened. He thought he was setting an example of civic virtue. Did anyone know how much he loved Denise? Yet she had taken sides with the enemies of France and he had torn his paternal feelings from his breast.

Suddenly he began to snigger. "I'll tell you something very amusing! Guess what's in store for me tomorrow. You'll never guess. I've got to represent the Government at a solemn Mass. Can you see me on my knees? Now, isn't that amusing? "

But Paulette went on sniffling.

Tessa had not been to church since the days of his childhood. He hated everything connected with religion. Whenever he wanted to make fun of somebody, he would say: " He smells of incense." He called the priests " black crows " and had often wounded Amalie's feelings in this way.

He thought that only old women went to church and he was astonished when he saw men and even soldiers among the worshippers. Inside the church it was dim and there were lighted candles reminding him of those round Amalie's coffin. A sadness came over Tessa. The delicate voices of the singers and the sunbeams filtering through the coloured windows spoke of a lost paradise. Tessa now understood that language; he had lost Amalie, his children, and his peace. Of course these ceremonies were just a form of superstition, but sometimes it was pleasant to get away from the petty wranglings and forget oneself.

He looked at the fat bishop. There were red veins in his face, and his eyes were sad and intelligent. No doubt the bishop had his worries like everybody else. He had to keep on good terms with the Pope, the cardinals, and his flock. Life was a form of politics. And at the end there were wax candles.

A little bell rang. Everyone went down on his knees. Tessa smiled to himself. It was like a theatre. But he knelt submissively and then stood up with all the others.

He was bored with the ceremony and could hardly restrain himself from yawning convulsively. Suddenly he livened up; standing on his right was a young woman in a long black dress. She had a large prominent forehead and thin bright lips. Tessa thought she was like a Florentine, a Bronzino portrait. That type was passionate, very passionate indeed.

Suddenly he felt that Breteuil was staring at him. Tessa shuddered and began to move his lips as though he was praying. The fools thought that Breteuil's game was played out because he had been in favour of a rapprochement with Germany. But Tessa realized that the future belonged to Breteuil. Everybody was cursing the Popular Front. That meant the Government's majority would be transferred to the Right. Besides, the war wouldn't last for ever, and who except Breteuil could reach an agreement with Hitler? Yes, it was advisable to keep on good terms with that superstitious Breteuil.

The notes of the organ again filled Tessa with sadness. There was no doubt about it, the organist played beautifully. In 1917 there was a disaster; a shell from the German Big Bertha struck a church and many people were killed. What if a bomb suddenly dropped at this moment? No, it couldn't happen; they were afraid to begin. Nobody wanted to make war. Candidly speaking, the Poles were savages. The Germans were carrying on a colonial war in Poland. But they respected the French. What a pity they hadn't been able to reach an agreement! Mussolini would no doubt have reconciled everybody. People had panicked. And now there was war. Gamelin had got the idea of carrying out some sort of operation in a forest. But there were mines there. It was killing people for nothing. Lucien might get killed too. Of course, it would have been possible to get him a staff job, but the damned young ne'er-do-well had vanished and was nowhere to be found. It was very sad! Yes, it was all very sad! Would they never finish playing the organ?

He caught sight of General de Visset. How devoutly he was praying! And yet he was said to be a friend of Fouget, a Red. How funny! The general was in command of an army and yet he was praying just like a village wench. Could he really believe in the Immaculate Conception? Well, let him if he wanted to! It was better than having any truck with Fouget.

At last the service came to an end. After the dim light of church Tessa enjoyed the radiant glow of the autumn day. The chestnut trees were a shower of gold. In the Champs-Élysées patches of sunlight shimmered like rippling water. The women looked particularly smart. As a precaution against air raids the window-panes of the houses were covered with strips of paper that made ingenious designs. Tessa smiled and thought: "There's a new style of decoration for you!"

CHAPTER 3

OCTOBER came in with heavy rains. Tessa shouted in the lobbies of Parliament: "I said all along the Poles wouldn't hold out even a month! They're thieves and drunkards! But we haven't lost anything. On the contrary. Hitler has lulled the Germans with his victories in the east. Now they'll find something different in the Maginot Line. Next 14th of July we'll see dancing the whole night long in the streets — all lit up. You'll see!"

Leaflets were dropped from the sky instead of bombs. And the fashionable quarters began to wake up again. Montigny wrote and told his family to come back; what was the use of getting wet in the rain in a dull country place? His wife grumbled at the food restrictions.

"God knows what it's all about," she said. "What business has the Government to poke its nose into people's kitchens? One never knows what to order for dinner. On Monday it was impossible to get mutton, on Tuesday it was forbidden to sell beefsteak, and on Wednesday they weren't making any pies. It's an insult!"

For several days there was no coffee to be had anywhere. Mme Montigny was at her wits' end: "I've been to all the shops and

I couldn't find any coffee anywhere. And to think we've got to put up with all this on account of the Poles! I'm convinced the English are drinking their tea. They don't deny themselves anything. It's Daladier's fault. He's a nobody, a schoolteacher, not a Prime Minister! "

Coffee began to appear again in the shops, and Mme Montigny quieted down somewhat.

Business was flourishing. The nearness of death made even misers extravagant. The restaurants were crammed with people. The fashionable shops were doing a roaring trade. Women's hats were modelled on military lines. The shop windows displayed brooches in the shape of tanks, compacts with the Union Jack, amulets and silk handkerchiefs with the inscription: " He's somewhere in France."

" Somewhere in France " became a stock phrase in place of the tiresome letter N. The newspapers reported: " Yesterday, somewhere in France, General Sikorski inspected a parade." And under the windows the street-singers lifted up their twangy voices: " Somewhere in France remember my caresses! "

At a luncheon to the foreign press Tessa made a speech:

" Tell the whole world that we're living as before. Instead of the thunder of the guns we have the words of the song *Paris is Still Paris.*"

People said the troops were bored. All sorts of things were collected for them: phonograph records, footballs, playing-cards, dominoes, detective stories. Loving wives sent their officer husbands camel-hair waistcoats, Napoleon brandy, and preserves prepared by the best chefs of the capital.

It had been feared that the war would bring sorrow and privation. But the autumn season opened more brilliantly than ever: first nights, receptions, exhibitions, bazaars, and auctions for charities. And fortune's favourite, Grandel, was to be seen everywhere. No reception was complete without him.

In the early days of the war, Grandel demanded to be sent to the front. " I want to fight! " he repeated. His fellow deputies protested: " You're far more useful here." His popularity grew to such an extent that when Ducane attempted to bring up the subject of the lost document, they fairly hummed with indignation: " Don't shatter the national unity with personal squabbles! "

Grandel himself made no secret of the fact that he had been in

favour of a compromise right up to the last minute. " On the evening
of September 1 it was still possible to avert everything," he declared.
" Bonnet had a talk with Ciano on the telephone. I urged that the
four Premiers should get together. I was backed by the deputies
of our group. But events followed too quickly one on top of another.
History will show who was to blame. But this is not the time to
argue. Now war has been declared, we must go on with it till
victory."

The war released Grandel from his entanglements; the cards had
been reshuffled. He was ready to fight. When he spoke about the
necessity of winning the war, his voice had a note of sincere emotion.

The deputies were delighted with Grandel's patriotism. The industrialists called him " sober-minded," and society women were
in love with him; he was so handsome and spoke so beautifully it
made you feel you wanted to cry; you felt that underneath his
quiet manner there was hidden passion.

Even Breteuil began to doubt whether he might not have been
the victim of a hoax. He had believed Lucien, who adored cheap
romanticism. But Grandel was behaving irreproachably.

Breteuil looked on the war as a drama. He tried to think it all out
to the end, but failed. Sometimes he said to himself: " We've got
to win the war." And then he laughed, realizing that the war could
never be won while authority was in the hands of a gang of
deputies. How could France win the war unless Parliament was
dissolved and the windbags put under lock and key? Maybe the
enemy's fire would reforge France.

Grandel's temples turned white and his eyes became sad. Looking at him, Breteuil thought to himself: " He's worried the same
as myself." When they happened to be alone he shook hands with
Grandel and said: " Let's forget the past! "

Nobody knew of the quarrel between Breteuil and Grandel,
which had lasted over a year, nor was anyone aware of their recon-
ciliation. In the face of the deputies and the country they had
always remained friends and colleagues. Nobody was surprised
when Breteuil proposed that Grandel should be appointed to the
responsible post of Director of War Industries.

Breteuil remembered how difficult it had been for him to get
Tessa to rehabilitate Grandel. Even now he expected to meet with
opposition from Tessa. But Tessa was not in the mood to bring up

the past. He now regarded the affair of the document which Lucien
had stolen as something remote and uninteresting. Who had suspected Grandel? — Fouget and Ducane. Fouget had been expelled
from the Radical Party; during the Moscow negotiations he had
attacked Chamberlain and nearly embroiled Paris with London.
And Ducane was playing the orator. Despite his stutter, he imagined himself to be a Gambetta and set everybody against him.
Villard had called him " A chauvinist with a smell of moth-balls,"
and Breteuil was suing him for defamation of character. No,
Grandel's enemies were not the people to inspire confidence. Besides, one had to take a sober view of things. Grandel hated the
Communists; he had been among them and knew them inside out.
The public imagined him to be a " Leftist " because he was fond
of showing up the " Two Hundred Families " and had written a
pamphlet against the American plutocracy. As for the war industries, that was the very front where there would have to be a
general round-up of the Communists. So let Grandel pop them into
jail, extend the hours of the working week, and reduce wages. If
he laid it on too thick he could take the blame, and Tessa and the
Radicals would remain without a blemish.

Not very long ago Breteuil had said he wouldn't let Grandel
marry a daughter of his. Now both he and Tessa forgot all about
that conversation. One had to rise above party squabbles when
there was a war on! So Tessa said: " Well, I approve your choice."

All the big industrialists, with the exception of Desser, backed
Grandel. Montigny shouted: " At least he will restore order. How
is it possible to carry on the war with anarchy in the rear? The
workers don't want to give up anything. You won't convince them
with words. You need a firm hand."

Meuger, the chairman of the Employers' Confederation, also
gave his backing to Grandel. One day Ducane declared that Meuger
was still supplying the Germans with bauxite through Switzerland.
Meuger said: " It's a slander. But I've got my own program." His
program was quite simple; he thought the war ought to be fought
against Moscow, not Berlin. Meuger's hobby-horse was a " crusade
against the Third International." When Tessa tried to object: " Unfortunately, we're fighting against Germany," Meuger answered
significantly: " Wait. This is only the first act." After war was
declared, he had gone to Madrid, and it was rumoured that he had
talks with the German Ambassador.

Only Desser was angry when Grandel's appointment was announced. "It's a job for a technical expert, not a political intriguer," he said. But Desser's position was no longer what it used to be. His unsuccessful political speculations were the talk of financial circles. The deputies thought he had made a fool of himself; he had supported the Popular Front and wanted to prevent war with airy resolutions by the League of Nations. Breteuil cracked a joke: "He's a fireman with a scent-spray." Even Tessa now regarded Desser as a failure.

A month went by. Grandel proved to be an indefatigable worker. Not a day passed without his having a meeting with Breteuil in order to make a report and receive advice. "It's the Communists and Desser," he said. "It's worse than the Augean stables! We've got to clean them out before anything can be done."

Only a third of the workers remained at the Seine factory. Desser decided to have an explanation. He entered Grandel's study in a state of great indignation. He kept his hat in his hand and waved his walking-stick as he talked. Grandel smiled and kept turning over the papers on his desk. He was enjoying the situation; the once all-powerful Desser, the patron of Briand and Boncour, was sitting before him like a petitioner!

Desser struggled for breath. He was ill and knew that it was a serious illness, although he was taking no treatment and went on drinking. His personal life was neglected and depressed, like his business; his meetings with Jeannette were full of pity and anxiety, his nights in the suburban house were lonely, and his mind was racked with thoughts of death. He was afraid to die. He tried to overcome the fear, but failed. He saw how the country was going to ruin, and he was tormented by the sense of his own impotence. Only a short while ago he had felt all-powerful. Now he was left out of the game. They listened to what he had to say, but nobody took any notice of him. He had become a widowed empress, a Stock Exchange academician, a relic of idyllic times. People paid attention to bawling Montigny and Meuger, who would sell his own mother for a few millions, but nobody took any notice of Desser.

Now he said to Grandel: "How can you expect me to deliver the orders in November when I've got no workers left? The war hasn't begun yet, but all the skilled workers are at the front."

"It's very unfortunate," said Grandel, "but I don't see any other way out. We can't put the workers in a privileged position. Our

country is an agricultural one. What will the peasants say? Have
they got to die while the workers are earning double? It's impossible to win the war by neglecting the dictates of elementary
justice."

"What about the men in their forties? They're not at the front.
Mechanics are washing windows in the barracks."

"We can't make distinctions among the workers."

"I ask you: do you want engines or don't you? I'd like to know
how you're going to fight without aircraft. But if you want engines,
give us back the workers. Yesterday they arrested another two
hundred workers at the Seine factory."

"You can't cure a pest with soothing-ointment," said Grandel.
"We're now paying for the Popular Front."

"What's the Popular Front got to do with it?" Desser waved
his stick as though he were going to hit Grandel. "And besides, you
were elected to the Chamber as a Popular Front candidate yourself."

"As far as I remember, Monsieur Desser, you didn't spare any
money in order to secure the victory of the Popular Front."

Desser looked at Grandel's handsome face with those delicate
eyebrows, the chiselled nose, and the cool, hardly perceptible smile,
which infuriated him even more.

"I also remember," said Desser. "I remember everything. The
Fouget document . . ."

Grandel did not move a muscle. Still smiling, he said: "Duels
are out of place in war-time. For that reason I must ask you to
leave."

As he went out of the room, Desser dropped his hat and broke
into a fit of coughing. Grandel pretended to be reading a report.

In the evening Grandel gave a party. The invitation cards bore
the inscription: "Soldier's Supper." The guests were served with
salmis de faisan on pewter plates and drank excellent *Hospice de
Beaune* out of mugs. Mouche received the guests. After her break
with Lucien she had been in a bad state of health for a long time
and had gone to stay in the Alps. She was still pretty, but one
could see she was already beginning to fade. Sorrow and suffering
showed themselves in all her movements.

When all the guests had left, Grandel took off his dinner-jacket
and waistcoat. His thin black suspenders showed up against the
dazzling white shirt. He said to his wife: "Colonel Moreau seems

to be dangling after you. He's an outstanding figure. I shouldn't be surprised if he ended up as Chief of the General Staff."

He yawned. It had been a tiring day. He carefully took off his trousers. "All the same, we'll win," he said suddenly.

Mouche never interfered with his business. She had even forgotten all about the unfortunate letter. Her last encounter with Lucien had devastated her completely. The war, the talk about the Maginot Line and bombing, and her husband's career were like a vague projection on a tiny screen. But now she suddenly asked: "Whom do you mean by 'we'?"

She realized at once that she had said something tactless. She turned away, expecting to be reviled. Grandel quietly answered: "We Frenchmen."

He was a gambler. His whole life somehow reminded one of the bated whispers and muffled cries around the green cloth. It had been just the same in those terrible months when he had done so many stupid things and nearly came to grief. He had lost eighty thousand francs. Vernon had come to his rescue. He had been obliged to meet Kilmann and had been engaged to get documents for the Germans. But why remember all that? He was after big game. He said to himself: "We'll win," but he was quite sure what victory he was referring to. Aloud he said — as much to himself as to Mouche: "A stupid question! The fools want to argue with fate. It's the same as at roulette: they keep backing the same number. But one should change, try to get the feeling of where the luck's going and go out to meet it. . . . The whole trick is in that."

CHAPTER 4

Even Montigny was grumbling: "It's one thing to arrest the Communists, but it's quite another to send old men to the barracks. I haven't got enough workmen." The problem of the war industries had become the fashion in the lobbies of the Chamber since the secret opposition had taken it up.

In his conversation with Desser about "the dictates of justice,"

Grandel had merely repeated Breteuil's words. Grandel hated the French peasantry and was afraid of them. He said they were not human beings, but turnips. On the other hand, Breteuil firmly believed that the troubles of France lay in the excessive growth of industry and the towns. Life in the villages was dull. There were no movies, the work was hard, and the young people were flocking to the towns. How many deserted villages there were throughout France! The houses were tumbling down, the barns were rotting, and the orchards were running wild. Hence Communism, the Popular Front, irreligion, and disintegration. Breteuil thought that the war would bring the peasants to the fore, and suggested to Grandel "not to pander to the workers."

However, he was obliged to yield. At the end of October the Government decided to release the forty-year-old workers who were needed for the war industries.

One of them was Legrais. At the beginning of the war he had been sent to the south. He was stationed near Toulouse, where he guarded a bridge over which a narrow-gauge railway used to pass once upon a time. The branch line had long been done away with and the bridge was overgrown with yellow shrubs. But it still figured in the lists of the army command, and for two months Legrais gazed at the meadow and the dappled cows.

He had plenty of time to think about things. He remembered the last war, the Forest of Argonne, the trenches, and the hospitals. It seemed only yesterday, while more recent events now appeared to him hazy and ghost-like, as if there was only a single day between the two wars. In those days they thought people had grown wiser and would make short work of the war-mongers. Some believed in Wilson; others repeated: "Lenin . . . Lenin. . . ." What if they had been told then that it would all start again in twenty years?

Legrais pined for Josette. He seemed fated never to know happiness. Back in the summer they had decided to get married and started looking for an apartment. The war put a stop to all that. Josette's father was arrested. She went away to her sister at Besançon. She wrote brief mournful letters. Gazing at night at the myriad stars of the southern sky, Legrais thought of Josette's tenderness and yawned wearily.

He found none of his old friends at the factory when he got back. Michaud and Pierre were at the front. In the evening he went out in search of familiar faces. He called at the cafés where his comrades used to gather, roamed around the shut library, went out to Montrouge and then to Villejuive. He met nobody; some had been arrested and others were in hiding.

Legrais was lonely and unsettled. He had no idea what the party was doing, and this to him was like blindness. He angrily tossed aside the newspapers which said that the Communists were traitors, that the Russians were fighting on the Siegfried Line, and that Maurice Thorez had fled to Germany. In Toulouse he had been told that *L'Humanité* was being printed in secret and distributed, but how was he to get hold of it? The men he worked with were strangers to him. They looked at him suspiciously as though wondering whether he had been sent by the police.

He felt lost in his loneliness and enforced idleness. This went on for four days. On the fifth he was arrested.

He spent the night in a tiny cell. All sorts of people were there: political prisoners and pimps, German refugees and Polish Jews, wits who had been taken into custody for repeating an anecdote about Daladier's apéritifs or Tessa's amorous adventures, citizens who were pounced on for daring to sigh pathetically: " There won't be any milk," or " They're going to call up the seventeen-year-olds."

In the morning Legrais was taken to be examined. Neuville, the police superintendent, was a Freemason and was not afraid to say that he preferred Édouard Herriot to Édouard Daladier. This, coming from a policeman, amounted to free-thought. He knew that Legrais was one of the leaders of the Communist organization at the Seine factory. If Legrais recanted, it would make an impression. The newspapers would write: " Another one sees the light." Tessa would appreciate Neuville's efforts; one penitent was worth a thousand sinners.

Neuville was exceedingly polite and offered Legrais a cigarette.

" I'm an official," he began, " and I'm not entitled to express my convictions, but, believe me, I'm no Fascist. I was sincerely pleased by the Popular Front victory. We thought at the time that it was going to be a settled alliance. It has turned out otherwise. But this is not the time for party struggles. All Frenchmen must be united. You're a Communist, but you're a Frenchman. You were wounded in the war. I can't look upon you as a traitor."

He waited to see what Legrais would say. But Legrais crumpled his cap in silence and gazed at the table littered with blue files.

" Why don't you say something? "

"I don't really know what to say. You've said it yourself. I was a Communist and I remain one."

"I understand your obstinacy. It is dictated by considerations of a noble character. You don't want to betray your comrades. But, my friend, this is not the time to be fastidious. You've been a pawn in the hands of others. They've deceived you. They talked about patriotism and called on you to fight the Fascists. And now what has happened? Maurice Thorez is a deserter."

"We're not the deserters. You'd better leave that subject alone. I don't know where Maurice Thorez is at present. Only he's not in Germany, as your papers say. I think he is publishing *L'Humanité*. That's a genuine business. But I know where the deserters are. I seem to remember Munich. *And* what happened with regard to Spain. Our men were fighting against the Fascists there, but Bonnet was helping the enemies of France. Even the children know that. I listen to you and I'm astonished. You talk about 'Fascists.' You've always defended them with clubs. And now the Fascists are in power."

Neuville smiled a condescending smile.

"You're forty-three years of age," he said, "and you've got the ardour of a youth. That's very praiseworthy. Only it's a pity you don't want to part with your blinders. Your party has betrayed you. It is working for the victory of Germany."

"I'll never believe that!"

"Then what is it they do want?"

Legrais knit his brows. "I don't know what the party slogans are at present," he said. "That's all thanks to you. You've suppressed *L'Humanité* and arrested all the honest people. And you're trying to throw dust in my eyes. But I can see through some of it myself. Who is it that's hounding the Communists? Daladier, Tessa, Blum, Villard, Breteuil, Laval — in a word, the whole gang. No, it isn't the Communists who are traitors. It's their old enemies. If Laval was to begin shouting: 'Bravo, Communists!' I'd think twice. But now we know where we are."

Neuville threw away his cigarette and rang the bell.

"Take him away," he ordered.

Legrais was sent, together with other Communists, to a concentration camp. The train with the prisoners stopped for over an hour at the junction of Noisy-le-Sec. The police refused to allow the public to come near them and explained that they were deserters.

Soldiers and women threw angry glances at the railway cars and muttered: " Rotters! They can let other people die for them! " Somebody called out: " Cowards! " Whereupon Legrais began singing the *Internationale*. The people on the platform listened astonished. And from the cars the prisoners shouted: "We're not deserters! We're workers, Communists." After the *Internationale* they sang the *Marseillaise*. The soldiers on the platform took up the refrain. In vain the police tried to press the crowd back. Leaning out of the window, Legrais shouted:

" I was wounded in the last war. I've got the mark on my face. They can't rub that off. They've taken me from an aircraft factory. They're taking me to clean out lavatories. Bonnet, Tessa, Flandin — that's who the traitors are! But we'd give our lives for France! "

He raised his fist — a half-forgotten, threatening gesture that recalled the great hopes of the year 1936 which were destined not to be fulfilled. The police dragged him away. As the train moved off, hundreds of fists were raised in farewell greetings by the soldiers and women on the platform.

CHAPTER 5

THE ARRESTS were carried out according to lists, denunciations, and simple inspiration. One criminal had raised his fist, another had been caught whistling the *Internationale*, a third had hung up a picture of the Kremlin in his home. When he read the police reports, Tessa fluttered his hand; the Communists had penetrated everywhere! the Nièvre Amateur Anglers' Association, the Chess Circle of the Department of Var, the Grenoble Mountaineers' Society all turned out to be branches of the Communist Party. Tessa said to himself: " Yes, it shows how strong they are! Now I begin to understand how it was they managed to sweep Denise off her feet. Poor naïve little girl! "

Breteuil demanded that the Communist deputies be shot. Tessa put him off with the answer: " Be careful, my friend. Whatever else they may be, remember they're the elected representatives of the people." Tessa was afraid of creating a precedent. He had a feeling of professional *esprit de corps* towards the arrested deputies and wanted to save them. He told them that if they signed a document declaring that they renounced the Third International they would be allowed to retain their seats in the Chamber. When he heard that the arrested deputies refused to yield, he was furious and shouted: " The fanatics! I've done everything I could for them! "

Fouget now began to renew his attacks. The Marseille gangsters had failed to knock any sense into the hare-brained creature. He came out with the statement: " The persecution of the Communists is demoralizing the Army." Tessa retorted: " Then you are for Hitler? " The deputies applauded him, and Fouget left the tribune to the accompaniment of good-natured jeers.

Never in his life had Tessa been called upon to work so hard. He was seldom able to snatch an hour off for Paulette. He began to feel so exhausted that he asked himself whether it wouldn't be better to throw it all up. Why pretend? He was old. How much longer had he got to live? He dismissed the thought at once. Didn't Clemenceau save France when he was well advanced in years? Tessa imagined he was Clemenceau's successor. His statues would adorn the squares. He once said to Paulette: " *La rue Tessa* — that doesn't sound so bad."

He was obliged to deal with strategy, economics, even engineering, and to talk about cotton supplies, new bombers, and a trade agreement with Venezuela. Everybody came to him with various claims and everybody complained of chaos. Formerly he had had to do with deputies and financiers. Now he had to listen to army men without understanding the meaning of the military terms, not knowing what to promise or how to put them off. " The Army is another world," he said aloud, and to himself he added: " An inferior one."

When he heard that General de Visset intended to call on him, Tessa frowned. He was going to have a tough job to keep on the right side of this renowned grumbler.

General de Visset had come to the fore in 1915. He was then in command at Chemin-des-Dames. Though wounded in the foot, he refused to leave his command. At sixty-four he still retained his vigour and had lost none of his ardour. His round weather-beaten face with its stiff yellow moustache looked like a bulldog's. He was a kind-hearted man but with a fiery temper. He shouted at his wife and swore at his adjutant. His two passions were the Army and gardening. He spent his free time pottering about with a watering-can, tying up rose bushes, pruning and grafting.

He never talked about politics; whenever he was asked what he thought of this or that minister, he would reply: "The Army is a great dumb being." Some said he was a Monarchist and hobnobbed with the emissaries of the Pretender. Others — including General Picard — said that de Visset was practically a Communist. He listened to Fouget without contradicting him and had a good word for the Soviet Air Force. When Tessa saw de Visset praying in church, he was genuinely surprised and thought to himself: "And yet he's a friend of Fouget's!"

What was he coming to see him for now? Perhaps he wanted to complain about Picard, who had forbidden the troops to read the Left newspapers. Or perhaps he was going to demand that the institution of Army chaplains should be confirmed! God alone knew what he was coming for!

Tessa settled the general in a comfortable armchair and held out a box of cigars.

"Partagas," he said, "and they seem to be in really good condition. I'm afraid it'll be a long time before we get another consignment. The ships are loaded with other stuff. Now what brings you to see me, my dear general?"

De Visset had long been preparing himself for this conversation. At home he had composed an elaborate introduction dealing with patriotism, the lessons of the last war, and the duty of a soldier. But now everything slipped his memory. He bit off the end of the cigar, spat it out, and blurted out straightway:

"The situation is atrocious! There's a shortage of everything! Do you know how many machine-guns there are to a battalion? Not to mention aircraft. For instance, I have ten bombers at my disposal. Yes, yes, ten, you didn't mishear the number. Ten! And no boots, no blankets! And the winter right on top of us!"

Tessa shook his head regretfully. "I know, I know," he said. "It's the outcome of the Popular Front, vacations with pay and so forth. But the situation will soon change. We'll buy stuff from America."

"You'll have to buy as quickly as you can!"

"One can see that you're not an economist, general." Tessa smiled patronizingly. "It's exceedingly expensive to buy aircraft in America. It's far more intelligent to buy equipment. We'll economize on every engine. Besides, the industrialists are up in arms.

Meuger is opposed to it; he says we mustn't prejudice our national industries. But I repeat, we'll buy stuff from America. We've already placed a few orders in Italy. By the spring of 1941 — "

The general interrupted: " But what if they start fighting in the spring of 1940? "

" You know better than I do that it's impossible to take the Maginot Line."

" Nothing is impossible. It all depends on how many men they're prepared to sacrifice. Besides, the Maginot Line doesn't protect us from the north."

" What about the forts of Liége and the Albert Canal? If the Belgians start, they'll fight like lions. They're a chivalrous people."

" That may be. But one can't rely on others. We must fortify the northern frontier."

" It would take years to do that. And we're obliged to husband our resources. It's the one who has the most gold who will win this war."

Tessa glanced condescendingly at his visitor and thought to himself: " What a child! " The general's face went purple. The ribbons on his chest began to heave.

" I'm a military man," he said. " My business is to obey orders. But I can't keep silent. General Picard says that heavy artillery is necessary for 1942 in order to take the Siegfried Line. But you saw what happened in Poland? You saw what mechanized units the Germans have? They may try to break through the front, on a small sector. And yet I'm told the production of anti-tank guns has not only not been increased, it has even decreased. Why? Because the workers have been sent to concentration camps. I've seen them with my own eyes. They're making sacks. It's a good thing it's not choco-late-boxes. I've been to see Grandel. He says: " Not before 1942." Monsieur le Ministre, this is a disaster! Why take away the skilled workers? . . ."

Tessa said angrily: " It's very wrong of you to listen to Fouget. Only the Communists are being sent to the camps. I don't interfere in matters of strategy. Please don't interfere in politics! "

" What have politics got to do with it? I'm talking about guns and aircraft."

Tessa rose and took a turn round the room. Then he held out his hand and said in a strident voice as though he was addressing a jury: " I saw you saying your prayers the other day, general. I must admit I was astonished. I was brought up in a non-religious family myself, but I respect religion and I understand the feelings of a believer. Tell me: how can you, a Catholic, stand up for the Communists? "

" I'm not standing up for the Communists. I'm entrusted with the Army. Religion has nothing to do with the matter. Who will be held responsible? We, the military. I detest the Germans. You understand that? They may come here to Paris. Yes, I'm ready to put into the factories not only the Communists but the Devil himself if only we can have the armaments! "

" You're getting excited over nothing," Tessa said. " You forget this war is unlike any other. It's more like an armed peace. I don't know why Gamelin has sacrificed so many lives in the Forest of Warndt. France is a country with a low birth-rate. We must be doubly economical. Fine gestures are too expensive for us. Besides, the war will be decided in a different way. The blockade — that's our weapon! Moreover, the British will bear the brunt of it. It's the British who are being sunk by the Germans. That's all to our advantage; let England come to the peace conference well bruised and battered. The blockade is an enormous press which we're going to screw tight. Not too tight, though. It would be a mistake to drive the Germans to despair. In that case they might really attack the Maginot Line. They've got to be frightened a little and then they'll be more tractable. Why are we fighting Germany? It's a fatal misunderstanding and nothing more. You will excuse me, but I'm accustomed to speaking my mind. The military must keep in the background. It's not the generals but the diplomats who will win this war."

Afterwards, when he described his conversation with the Minister, de Visset shouted: " He showed me out like a servant and told me it was none of my business! They don't want to buy in America. It's too dear. They don't do anything here: the workers are Communists. And they're not even preparing to fight; the soldiers have got to sit still. What is it they want? Can anyone make anything of it? "

That evening Tessa broadcast to the nation. He disliked talking into the microphone. He missed the visible presence of an audience — the eyes that lit up or became moist with emotion. When the broadcasting staff arrived he sent for his old messenger:

"Maurice, sit down here while I read my speech. Your face inspires me."

Maurice smiled and sat down. Then Tessa began with a jaunty smile:

"We have crossed the Rubicon! Our war is the crusade of the twentieth century. We have drawn the sword on behalf of the supreme moral values, Christian humanism and the humanizing of brute mechanical force. Our sword is a terrible sword. I shall not be giving away any secrets to the enemy when I say that never before have the skies of France seen such a powerful air force. Never before has the soil of our country known such thundering hordes of tanks. We are working day and night without ceasing in order to increase our gigantic armaments. We are being helped by our noble allies, the British, and the great transatlantic democracy. But our principal strength is our spirit, the fraternal feeling that binds together people of all parties, all classes, the unity of the nation and its will to win. Frenchmen, we will not sheathe the sword until we have defeated the accursed enemy of civilization!"

Maurice was afraid to stir. He remained sitting on the edge of the chair and smiling with the same artificial smile one wears when being photographed.

CHAPTER 6

THE ARMY STAFF H.Q. was stationed in the country house of a rich Alsatian industrialist. It was a spacious house with a conservatory and a billiard-room, where the officers played in the evening. In the library the officers studied the maps. In the secretaries' room, which had formerly been the nursery, the typewriters clattered ceaselessly. Underneath a picture of Mickey Mouse which still hung on the wall, sat Lucie, the stenographer secretary. She had straw-coloured hair and long, violet-tinted eyelashes. Major Leroy, the general's favourite, dangled after her.

The owner of the house was fond of knick-knacks, and on the writing-table where General Leridot worked stood an ink-pot in the shape of the tower of Pisa, a penguin of Copenhagen porcelain, and a clock with a dial indicating the time of Paris, San Francisco, and Tokyo. When the general sat down to work, he invariably moved the penguin aside. He was terrified of breaking it. He couldn't bear the sight of any damage. He was furious if a drop of ink was spilt on the parquet floor or the soldiers trampled the lawn with their boots.

One might have thought that a man with such a temperament would have chosen a different career, but all the men in Leridot's family were in the Army. In 1914 Leridot had commanded a regiment. He had shown himself to be efficient and was promoted to the rank of general. He knew how to get on with both heads and underlings. He never pushed himself forward. He called himself a disciple of Foch and said: "What we need most of all in our jobs is calm and a sense of proportion." Always polite, clean-shaven, and smelling of toilet water, he was a general favourite and had a soothing effect on everybody. His one drawback was his small stature. He never allowed photographers to take pictures of him if there was anyone standing beside him.

His success was largely due to his tact. He hated deputies, but whenever civilians began to talk about politics in his presence he would reply: "I trust the elected representatives of the nation." Breteuil, Ducane, and Villard were all on good terms with him. He willingly discussed with them the part which the 75 mm. guns played in the victory of the Marne, or about the beauty of classical poetry. He adored literature, bought de-luxe editions of Racine and Corneille, and thirty years ago had even published in a provincial journal an article on " Some Errors of Stendhal," which dealt with the *Chartreuse de Parme* from the point of view of military science.

Leridot loved his profession, but the chaos of the war filled him with dismay. Everything that had been perfect on manœuvres was now spoilt by a thousand accidental factors. And in the last three months he had grown thinner and older. He complained of pains. The doctor said it was his liver, but Leridot put it all down to worry. Everything irritated him: the front was a short one and he didn't know how to dispose his troops. He kept repeating: "The trouble is we've got too many." The men were sleeping under the open sky and in November there was an outbreak of influenza. The officers pampered their men and neglected to give them any orders, and the men were bored to death and took to drinking.

When Leridot was told that Gamelin was massing heavy artillery for an attack on the Siegfried Line, he said with a sigh: " The officers haven't even got revolvers."

He kept a strict watch over the daily routine at H.Q. Everybody rose at six o'clock in the morning. Colonel Moreau received reports. Major Leroy read boring newspapers and tried to look in at the secretaries' room, where Lucie was tapping on her machine. Major Giset gingered up the commissariat officers. Colonel Javotte studied maps. Dreamy bald-headed Captain Sanger sighed for the cafés of Paris and reported to the general: " Two soldiers were wounded at Zwincker. . . . A movement has been observed opposite the 16th Division. The Germans have brought up the 186th Regiment. . . . Yesterday no enemy aircraft operations were observed. . . . A hospital for venereal diseases has been opened at Tanville. . . ." The general moved the penguin aside and muttered: " That's that! " At twelve o'clock they sat down to lunch.

That day there was Strasbourg *pâté de foie gras*. Colonel Moreau said it was the gift of the local gods. The general sighed; the doctor had put him on a diet. By way of consoling himself he remarked: " Salad is better for you than anything. When a man gets on in years he becomes a grass-eating animal. It's one of the laws of nature."

Captain Sanger guiltily swallowed a delicious morsel of the *pâté*. " Of course it is, *mon général*," he said.

They talked about Hitler being a vegetarian. The general was surprised. He kept repeating: " There, now! A very interesting trait." Then Major Leroy began to give the current views of the newspapers.

Finland was the main topic of the day. Everybody wondered what the Russians would do.

The general livened up and said: " That's very interesting! Of course they may begin an encircling movement and try to come out on the Gulf of Bothnia in order to cut off Helsinki from Sweden. They may even make a frontal attack on the Mannerheim Line. We'll see, we shall see." The war in Finland provided him with a strategical problem. Somehow it took him back to the comfort of his study in Paris and he heaved a melancholy sigh. " And what do they say about our own affairs? "

" Very little. The censorship has suppressed two columns of *L'Époque*."

" And quite right too. It was probably an article by Kérillis or Ducane. I can't understand how they allow them to write."

Colonel Moreau was a close friend of General Picard, and both of them hated Ducane.

" They write to me from Paris that Ducane intends to come here," said the colonel. " As if we couldn't do without him! "

Whenever he felt angry the general always licked his lips. He performed this operation now and said: " Never! Daladier can spare us surprises of that sort. Ducane is capable of infecting everybody with his panic. I myself heard him shouting: ' The Germans are going to launch decisive operations in the spring.' What can you expect? The man was an airman once upon a time, but he's an ignoramus as far as strategy is concerned. He's behind the times and can't see anything. He looks upon the Maginot Line as though it were the same as field fortifications on the Aisne or the Somme."

He carefully selected a pear, feeling it all over to make sure that it wasn't rotting. Then he peeled it with a fruit-knife and wiped the juice off his fingers. " Aha, when the knife goes in as though it was butter, the pear is sure to be a good one. . . . Taste it, major." He passed half the pear to Sanger. " General de Gaulle's influence shows itself in Ducane's chattering. I've read de Gaulle's report. Gamelin is right: the man's a fantastic. He doesn't wish to realize that the Germans are bluffing. He mixes up everything, Poland and Spain, where anarchists fought against the regular Army, and our front. Anyway, it's a bad thing when people feed their minds on newspaper sensations instead of the classical science of warfare. This fellow de Gaulle thinks he's got an inventive mind. In reality he's hidebound. He's got his mind fixed on Sedan or the Napoleonic Wars. He's forgotten the experience of the World War. He imagines tanks are going to rush across Europe where once upon a time the cavalry dashed. But the age of lightning wars is past. We've returned to long sieges. This is a Trojan War; that's what it is! "

He carefully folded up his napkin, slipped it into the ring, and got up. Coffee was served in the drawing-room.

" General Monet has been ringing up," said Colonel Moreau. " They want to carry out some sort of manœuvres in order to accustom the troops to the action of dive-bombers."

The word " manœuvres " reminded Leridot of peace-time, but he frowned at once; that Monet was up to something again. An upstart. He was always wanting to get ahead of everybody else.

"The Prefect is against it," Moreau went on, "for the reason that the population beyond Munster hasn't been evacuated, and the peasants are afraid the vineyards will suffer."

The general nodded his head. "I entirely agree with the Prefect," he said. "We must be particularly nice to the Alsatians. It's a ridiculous idea all together. Dive-bombers indeed! Yes, in Poland or in Spain when there are no anti-aircraft guns. These silly people snap at every bait the Germans throw out to them. They get into a panic at every rumour. So let General Monet know: the usual exercises and nothing more. Besides, we must give the men a rest."

After lunch the general and Captain Sanger set out for the positions. Leridot's chauffeur was the son of Meuger, the industrialist. He was a sporting type of young man, who had been given a job at Headquarters owing to his father's influence. He drove the car at top speed and Leridot kept saying to him: "Not so fast, my friend, not so fast!"

Leridot liked talking to his chauffeur. Young Meuger knew all that was going on in the neighbourhood.

"What's the news, my friend?"

"All quiet, *mon général.* I had a talk with a lawyer at Munster. He'd come from Périgueux to get his belongings. He says the Rosset affair has made a bad impression on the Alsatians."

"That's just what I expected." Leridot turned to Sanger. "They're quite blind in Paris. Even if Rosset was connected with the German secret service, this is hardly the time to drag out the affair. Why intensify political dissensions?" The general turned his head slightly towards the chauffeur. "Did you drive the colonel to the positions?"

"We were at Erstein, *mon général.* Major Lesage complained the men there were getting out of hand."

Meuger would have liked to tell how the men had rubbed Major Lesage all over with cow-dung, but he managed to restrain himself: it would have made the general furious. Meuger only grinned at the thought of how the poor major had shrieked.

"What can you do?" said Leridot. "The men are bored to death. Reasonable distractions must be organized."

They drove into Strasbourg. The town was empty. Newspapers dating from the end of August were still hanging behind the windows of the kiosks. Marble tables and wicker chairs stood on the café terraces with an air of waiting for customers. The cathedral porch was piled up with sandbags. The clocks in the square all told different times. On catching sight of a lilac-coloured dressing-gown in a shop window, the general sighed: Sophie had a dressing-gown like that. Four years ago he had married his second wife, the young daughter of an Army doctor. At twenty-six Sophie was discriminating and considerate. When Leridot was working, everybody in the house went about on tiptoe. Sophie prepared his favourite dish: calf's head *à la vinaigrette*. Her favourite scent was Corsican Jasmine, and plenty of it.

The observation post was at the top of a slope in a nook camouflaged with branches. Leridot looked through his field-glasses and saw some men standing near a pillbox. Automatically he thought to himself: " That's the enemy." Then he noticed a large sheet on which was written: " Frenchmen, our common enemy is England! " It was flanked by pictures of Hitler and Joan of Arc. Leridot frowned and thought: " How vulgar it all is! Instead of military operations they indulge in propaganda. As though war were an election campaign." Farther on he saw houses with brown roofs, wisps of blue smoke, and vineyards. There was no word to express it! It was indeed a strange war. You might imagine you were on manœuvres and the Blues were trying to force the river. It had been altogether different in 1916. He remembered the ruins of Péronne, the rubble, the craters, and dead men's bones. Nothing like that would happen now. In those days we went into war with songs and the red trousers of the poilus. Now we had the Maginot Line.

Leridot walked along a muddy path. There was a smell of damp earth. A pale winter sun struggled through the clouds. Suddenly he heard the sound of music: Schubert. It was a piece that Sophie was fond of playing.

" What's that? " he asked.

The regimental commander replied: " It's a loud-speaker. We're drowning the German propaganda. The enemy hears familiar music. We're showing them we've got nothing against the Germans."

" That's an excellent idea," said Leridot.

" It has been suggested that we should make short appeals in the German language in between the music. They're already doing that in the 27th Division. But I didn't think it was suitable."

" You're quite right. Wars were meant to be fought. We can

leave politics to the politicians. Do you have a concert going on all day long? "

" This morning there was an artillery duel from seven a.m. till seven forty. Their batteries are — "

" I know, I know. Were there any casualties? "

" Three men killed and one sergeant severely wounded."

All was quiet for a few moments. Then from the other side of the Rhine came the words of a song in French:

> And so behind your backs
> They sold you well and good:
> England agreed to send the guns,
> And France — to shed her blood.

They proceeded to the headquarters of the 27th Division. Leridot was anxious to find out whether it was true that they were indulging in political propaganda there. But he forgot all about the loudspeaker when he was informed that a German fighter plane had crashed near Erstein that morning. The pilot was killed and according to documents found on the body his name was Lieutenant Karl von Schirau.

Leridot gave orders to stage a grandiose funeral.

" That's real propaganda! " he explained. " We'll show them that we know how to respect the enemy. I'll send Colonel Moreau." He thought for a moment. " You say it was von Schirau? . . . Von. . . . No doubt he belonged to an aristocratic family. It will have a tremendous impression in Germany. I'll try to come myself."

He inspected the hospital and went into the barracks. As soon as the men saw him they hurriedly threw their coats over the playing-cards.

" Well, my lads, are you having a good rest? "

" Oui, mon général."

Leridot didn't know what else to say and went out. As he was going through the doorway he overheard someone remark: " General Tom Thumb! " Once before he had heard that offensive nickname in the street in Paris, but he had never dreamed that anybody at the front would dare to make fun of him. Doubtless it was a Communist. He licked his lips, and Captain Sanger sighed; he had just been on the point of suggesting a three-day leave.

Throughout the drive back Leridot sat nursing the insult. In the hall of the château there was a large mirror. As he passed it, the general turned back. He sent for Colonel Moreau.

" The 27th Division are getting out of hand," he said. " The men made an abominable impression. Instead of smartening up his men, General Monet is spending his time on propaganda. He's passing on some sort of political speeches to the Germans. Probably speeches by refugees or Communists. We must draw up a report at once to the commander-in-chief and a copy for Daladier immediately."

The colonel heaved a sigh. He had intended playing billiards — a return match with Major Giset — two games of a hundred up. The captain said to Leroy: " He's licking his lips. Somebody called him Tom Thumb. And I thought yesterday he was going away to Paris. What a life! "

Six o'clock struck. The secretaries' room was empty except for Lucie, who still went on working. At last she finished typing: " Dubois, Pierre, sergeant," folded up the copies, pulled the cover over the machine. Then, looking cautiously around her, she went upstairs. Major Leroy was waiting for her.

" My child, let's imagine we're in Venice, in a gondola."

CHAPTER 7

IT had been pouring rain since dawn, the cold dreary rain of winter. The yellowish-grey sky was enough to give you the blues. Pierre gazed at his sodden brown boots. He often gazed at one spot now as though he was looking for something. But he didn't see anything. He wasn't even thinking. Everything going on around him seemed to be vague and unreal. He wanted to pinch himself and cry out to make sure that he wasn't asleep. Nothing ever happened; as a private of the 39th Regiment he got drenched in the rain and listened to the rhapsodies of Liszt or the sergeant's abuse, occasionally interrupted by the thunder of gunfire. There was something horrible in it all, but Pierre didn't dare think about it.

It had begun one hot day back in August. When he woke up that morning he had stretched his limbs with pleasure. Agnès was making coffee; Doudou was playing on the floor, and his little

brown horse was rocking in the bright sunlight. Now all that was
a memory.

Since then he had lived in a sort of torpor. He could no longer
move about at will and he scarcely spoke. His nature demanded
a life of noise and bustle.

In his own part of the country the weather was warm at this
time of year; the December roses were in bloom, and the naked
brown peaks of Mount Canigou were visible in the distance. He
had once climbed right to the summit. But here the rain would
go on the whole day long and tomorrow and the day after as well.
And soon the angels would be singing like a loud-speaker *Gloria
in excelsis* in the sky that looked like dirty cotton wool.

Before he had left home, Pierre had wandered about like a condemned man. Agnès had seen that he was going to pieces, and
tried to find a way of escape.

"Pierre," she said, "let's go away somewhere. Let's go to America.
We'll find work."

He shook his head. "It's bad for everybody. Do you think I want
to save myself? We can never bring back the days that are gone."

He was thinking about the days of the Popular Front.

In the past he had felt that he was taking part in events and had
a share of the general responsibility. Even after Villard's betrayal
he could say: "I'm sending aircraft." But now he was like a tree
marked by the woodcutter's axe, and even his death would make
no difference to the course of events.

On the day of his departure he nearly had a quarrel with Agnès.
She had frowned in perplexity and said: "But you wanted it. . . ."

He had answered indignantly: "Not this war! It isn't ours."

Agnès saw no distinction. To her, war was war — shells, mud,
blood, and death. How could he try to make out that September
1939 was any different from September 1938? She objected that
his attempt to draw a distinction was "mere twisting, politics, a
game." But to him it was the truth. There was something different
in the sound of the marching steps of the conscripts. Nobody sang.
Their faces had the look of men who were being sent to their doom.
And Pierre saw no prospect of relief.

He now began to realize what it was that separated him from
Michaud. Their former arguments were not accidental. Michaud
was a strong character. He could be broken and then he would
fall, as Jules had fallen yesterday. But Michaud could not be bent;

he would smile, exclaim: "And how!" and survive the attack. Where was he now? Was he being drenched in the rain? Had they put him in jail? How Pierre would have liked to have a talk with him! And yet even Michaud wouldn't be able to help him. Michaud was sure to say: "You must look ahead. The logic of events. . . ."

Pierre felt the burden of loneliness. He found himself in a company consisting almost entirely of pious and timid Breton peasants. They had been told that he was an anarchist infidel who had burned down churches in Spain. Lieutenant Esterel, an ugly dwarf, was one of Breteuil's "Ironclads." He adored poetry, said that poverty was romantic and that there was a "mystical quality" in Fascism. He despised his men: they smelt of sweat, spoke French badly, and wore scapulars with an image of St. Gwenolé. He was afraid of Pierre and warned the other officers against him: "A man like that is capable of shooting you in the back." It annoyed him to think that Pierre was an engineer, went to the Atelier theatre, and read the poems of Eluard.

Pierre chummed with Jules, the only other Parisian in the company. Before being called up, Jules used to work in a gas-works. He was an incorrigible jester and said to Pierre: "You mustn't take it so hard, chum. It won't do you any good. No doubt Maurice Thorez is thinking up something at present. But I'm off to do a bit of pilfering. There's a whiff of chicken dung around here. I've not had a mouthful of omelet for a long time." He made Pierre laugh when he said: "I'm an optimist. Let's look at events from the pig's point of view. Before the war they killed pigs seven days a week. But now it's forbidden to sell pork on Mondays and Tuesdays. At that rate it won't be a hundred years before the pigs obtain personal inviolability. You'll see!" For a moment Pierre came out of his daze and laughed. And now Jules has been killed.

Pierre's letters were very short: he didn't know what to say to Agnès. The rain? Jules's jokes? Or how he kept saying "Turnip" when he was dying? About Lieutenant Esterel, who read Valéry's poems and was afraid of touching a soldier's coat as he passed by? Agnès's letters were full of questions about his health or stories of Doudou's pranks. They had so much to tell each other, but they were both dumb. Pierre often thought of Agnès. She was like a straight road leading into bright July sunlight. If he went along it he was bound to get somewhere. But now he had come to the crossroads and he couldn't make out which was the right one. He had gone astray.

Lieutenant Esterel sent for him.

"Take this to Captain Gémier."

"At your service, *mon lieutenant*."

He took the book. The lieutenant wanted to humiliate Pierre. He was a Communist and probably only read proletarian poets. So let him take a walk! It was four miles to the farm where the gunners were stationed. Captain Gémier was also an æsthete and had asked for something to read; he was compiling a rhyming dictionary out of boredom.

Pierre took shelter in a shed and opened the book. It was a book of poems. He didn't look to see who the author was, but opened it at random and read the lines:

> Some day he'll get a glimpse of joy.
> He will not bloom, but he will live.

Pierre shut the book with a snap. He felt as though Agnès had called to him and touched his wet cheek with her hand. It was a warm hand, but drops of rain were trickling down his face.

He went farther along the steep path between the vineyards. The farm was hidden by a little copse. On his right was a church. The weathercock had been knocked off the steeple. Pierre skirted a shell-crater and thought automatically: "They've been firing pretty close." Then he turned off the road.

He delivered the book to the bashful, short-sighted captain, drank a mug of sour new wine with the gunners, and set off on the way back. The rain stopped. The loud-speakers were shut off an hour earlier than usual. There was a rattle of machine-gun fire somewhere down below, but nobody replied to it. It was all quiet at the front. Pierre kept repeating drearily to himself: "Some day he'll get a glimpse of joy." In the evening there would be a letter from Agnès. Then he would go to the hayloft, where it would be stuffy and warm and red-haired Yves would fill the place with happy snoring.

Suddenly the stillness was shattered by a thundering explosion. This happened about twice a day, but Pierre was unable to get accustomed to it. All of a sudden the whole world seemed to change and the air was rent. Our men would reply presently. Pierre crossed to the side of the road and squatted down in the wet. He would have to stay there an hour. But in the evening there would be the letter from Agnès.

He was hardly aware of the second explosion. He fell forward: the fragment had struck him in the groin. Half an hour later he was picked up by some of the gunners.

He opened his eyes and saw the bright light of an unshaded lamp and immediately closed his eyes again. Gradually he remembered the book, gunners, the wine, and the shell. Then he must have been wounded. . . . Maybe he was dying. No. Was he sleeping? . . . He wanted to turn over on his right side — he always slept like that — but he cried out. Then he must be dying. There was something important he must remember. He tried his utmost to remember, but he couldn't think what it was. He wanted to see Agnès as he had seen her under the shed, but he could not — there was no face. All he could do was to repeat her name in order to soothe himself. The nurse came and straightened his pillow. She had a long face, like a straight line, and he thought to himself: " She's not one of us." Then he saw a bright plaything on the bedcover. It was a red sand-box with bright green stripes. He was sitting on a heap of sand. Little pies were coming out of the sand-box. No, they were fish. Or was it a dwarf with a long beard? . . . The sand was dry. The shapes all crumbled away. He cried out: " Why is it dry? " The nurse came up with a wet towel and laid it on his forehead. He did not feel anything and lapsed into unconsciousness again.

The music of a band could be heard coming from outside, the third battalion, which was saluting the dead German pilot. General Leridot made a speech: " We bow our heads before the remains of a gallant fighter. The love of one's native country. . . . The sentiment of duty . . ."

Then the rain came down again in still greater torrents than the day before, as though trying to make up for lost time.

Agnès's letter came in the evening, as Pierre had expected. It lay in the office for three days. Then they sent it back with the inscription: " Addressee dead."

CHAPTER 8

THE CENSORSHIP was known as "Aunt Anastasia," and Joliot complained that she was driving him to the grave. *La Voie Nouvelle* came out with white spaces all over the place. It was forbidden to write that the weather was bitterly cold in the Vosges, or that the Italians had greeted the German Ambassador with enormous enthusiasm, or that the Chinese Government was giving shelter to the Spanish refugees. Joliot waved his hand and exclaimed: "There's only one subject, and that's bromide! "

It was rumoured that the authorities were mixing bromide with the soldiers' coffee so that they shouldn't yearn for their wives. And Joliot published in his newspaper the following jingle:

> *Outside your house, Gretchen, I patiently wait;*
> *Please don't think I've taken my bromide of late!*

The eclipse of Desser obliged Joliot to look for a new patron. Breteuil put him in touch with Montigny. It was not the first time that *La Voie Nouvelle* had changed its policy, but this time Joliot was really sad. Desser had known how to live, he had smoothed over any unpleasantness with a joke and handed over his cheque as easily as a cigarette. But Montigny shouted at him as if he were a servant. He interfered in the business of editing the paper and flew into a rage if Joliot dared so much as mention the marriage of some Radical or Socialist. But how could Joliot get himself in wrong with everybody? After all, Montigny wasn't going to last for ever.

When one of the contributors used the word "Boches" in an article, Montigny was livid with rage. "Outrageous! " he shouted. "You're pandering to the basest instincts. Of course we're fighting Germany, but it's a chivalrous duel. If you like, it's a historical tragedy. Hitler is a great statesman! "

It was not surprising, therefore, that Joliot was delighted when he heard of the grand funeral of the German airman. A whole column was devoted to the description of the ceremony and Leridot's speech. But next day Joliot was once again racking his brains over what he was going to write about. The war had already been going on for four months, yet there was no sign of it. It was a phony war. Soldiers were dying of influenza. Yesterday in the Chamber they had announced a treaty with Germany regarding railway communications across the Rhine. Only when it was put to the vote did somebody point out that the bill had been introduced in Parliament in the summer and that the bridges over the Rhine had already been blown up. The war was nicknamed "the phony war," and people said: "How do you like this phony war?" Everybody liked it all right. Only there was nothing to write about.

The enemy seemed to be unknown. German airmen dropped leaflets, and people picked them up and said: "How well got up they are!" They listened to the broadcasts in French from Stuttgart. The speaker was a Frenchman. Joliot dubbed him "the Stuttgart Traitor." The name caught on. But the "Stuttgart Traitor" became a popular character. The deputies asked one another: "What did the Stuttgart Traitor say about the secret session of the Chamber?"

And then a miracle happened. Late one evening Montigny sent for Joliot. He was cheerful and even polite and gave Joliot all he had asked for. Then he added eagerly: "Hand the political side over to Breteuil. And let's have more military anecdotes, heroic stunts and exploits. Send out the best war correspondents."

The enemy had been found at last. Two days later the war correspondents set out for Helsinki.

Tessa invited the Italian Ambassador to lunch. He praised Italian cooking, Piedmontese wine, the art of Veronese, and the statesmanlike genius of Mussolini.

"You can't imagine," he said, "how distressed I was when war was declared in spite of the Duce's intervention. These months have been a nightmare to me. So they have to all cultured Europeans. But here's the first gleam of light; the reactions to Moscow's war on Finland show that all is far from being lost. In particular, I'm greatly encouraged by Italy's position. I've always stood for the alliance of the Latin countries. We are the friends of great Rome. What does Danzig signify, or the whole of Poland for that matter, in comparison with the fate of civilization? Let's be quite frank: our common enemy is Moscow. The future of Paris and Rome, and of Berlin as well, depends on the result of the struggle in the Karelian isthmus."

Everybody livened up. Mme Montigny organized "Northern Tuesdays"; society women knitted socks and scarves for the Finnish soldiers to the strains of Sibelius. Meuger gave a million and a half francs for Mannerheim's cause, and the cheque was ceremoniously handed over to the Finnish marshal's daughter. The Marseille gangster Billet demanded that the rue Moscou should be renamed rue Helsingfors.

A service was held in the Madeleine for the victory of Finland. Breteuil prayed devoutly. When he came out of the church, he went straight to the offices of *La Voie Nouvelle*. He astonished Joliot, who was seldom astonished at anything, by saying to him: "Go at once to Villard. Get him to write a few articles on Finland."

Montigny disliked Villard intensely and shouted: "He's the man who corrupted the workers and taught them to lounge about on bathing beaches!" Joliot had been obliged to respect the whims of his new patron and avoided Villard. Once they met in the Marius restaurant near the Palais Bourbon. Villard gave a melancholy sigh and said: "You've forgotten me."

"Do you take me for Zeus?" Joliot protested. "I'm only the messenger of the gods. I'm Mercury. You know what a swine Montigny is. It's a misfortune that Desser gave in, not only for me, but for France as well. Now I'm writing at Breteuil's dictation. He's a dry stick and as savage as a wildcat. We've got nobody like that in Marseille. He's a mixture of the Gallic cock and a German wolfhound. I've said to him several times: 'What about Villard?' Alas, national unity exists only in words! Personally I appreciate and respect you, and what's more, I like you!"

Villard smiled sadly and chose a quiet corner table. He was going to have a hard job ordering lunch in accordance with his doctor's instructions. He carried a list of forbidden dishes about with him and always consulted it: "Sorrel? No. Tomatoes? No. Carrots? Permissible."

And now Breteuil was sending Joliot to Villard. The tubby little editor was so taken aback that he talked to himself all the way there. What times we were living in! Nothing was ever the same two days running. It was quite bewildering. One never knew from one moment to the next whom one had got to smile at or whom one had got to run down.

Villard was now living in retirement among his books and pictures. He watched events with disgust, like a spectator who is obliged to sit out a bad play. " I don't see any sense in it," he said. And to himself he thought complacently: " Anyway, I was lucky. Tessa took over from me in good time. They made the mess. Now let them clear it up! " Of course he continued to vote for the Government in the Chamber and on two occasions made patriotic speeches, but he spoke in a dull tone as though repeating an uninteresting quotation. The " phony " war seemed to him to be a lot of unnecessary fuss. There was already enough killing being done in China.

He livened up a little when they started attacking the Communists. His old resentment came to life again. He regarded the Communists as the cause of his defeat. It was they who had engineered the seizure of the factories, upset the shopkeepers, and driven Daladier into Breteuil's arms. They shouted about patriotism and hummed like hornets at the shame of Munich, but when it came to war they wriggled out. Now the workers were saying that only the Communists were against war. He thought this was a cunning election manœuvre and said to himself: " They'll get millions of votes." Of course he supported the proposal to arrest the Communist deputies, and said: " It's impossible to make any objection. It's only right." And when he heard that Senator Cachin had remained at large, he was grieved. He detested Cachin. Once upon a time they had belonged to the same party and addressed meetings together. He regarded the young Communists as people from another planet and considered Cachin as a renegade. To think that a man of culture, a humanist and a democrat, could throw in his lot with the Communists!

Hundreds of people were being arrested every day. In some provinces even Socialists were being pulled in. Villard got alarmed. This was the thin edge of reaction! He felt he was the guardian of tradition, a venerable high priest. He asked himself whether he ought not to make a stand, but very quickly dropped the idea: it would only be playing into the Communists' hands.

He retired into his shell again. He had recently acquired a still life of Cézanne's: a couple of apples on a lacquer tray. He spent hours gazing at the canvas. The apples were worlds in themselves, complete and infinitely heavy, like the essence of matter.

Villard had thought that nothing could awaken any enthusiasm in him, but now he hardly recognized himself: the events in Finland had restored his youth. He made an indignant speech in the Cham-

ber and his eye-glasses bobbed up and down as they had twenty
years ago. The war immediately acquired significance. " The Communists," he said, " are the secret army of Russian imperialism! "

When Joliot explained Breteuil's request, Villard answered:
" Willingly, my friend, willingly, and in spite of my age and indis-
position. The doctor has forbidden me to work. But when it's a case
of helping the weak, I'm on the spot. It's a good thing that Breteuil
has forgotten party squabbles. Now we can bring about national
unity in reality and not only in words."

He dictated the first article in a voice that trembled with emotion: " I seethe with indignation. Once upon a time the soldiers
of von Goltz fought for a righteous cause. Marshal Mannerheim
is fighting for justice."

Afterwards he said to Joliot: " We've got a mighty ally: General
Frost."

Joliot waved his hands. " To tell you the truth," he said, " I don't
even know exactly where Finland is. But they say it's damned cold
up there. If our men are sent there, they'll freeze to death. I'll
take my oath on that! But what do you think about the attitude of
Italy? You see, I'm a Marseille patriot. They may attack Marseille."

" Never! They're as indignant with Moscow as we are. The Italian
menace is now averted."

On the following day Villard's daughter Louise came to see him.
Her husband had been called up.

" Gaston writes that there's the most frightful chaos in the Army,"
she said. " There are no anti-tank guns and the men haven't any
boots. They're in a very bad mood. Gaston is afraid to say anything
to them. Papa, what's going to happen to France? "

Villard listened with a distracted air.

" It's terrible! " he exclaimed. " I've always said this war wouldn't
lead to anything. There's no sense in it. Now, Finland — that's a
different matter."

He began talking excitedly about the operations in Karelia, the
ski troops, and the collections for Mannerheim. Louise interrupted
him: " I can't get to sleep now till four or five in the morning. I keep
thinking and thinking. . . . What would happen if the Germans
were to win? "

" It might happen."

He said this so naturally that Louise was taken aback.

" Papa! " she cried out. " What are you saying? "

He saw that her lips were trembling and that she was on the verge of tears. He tried to soothe her: "Don't be afraid. We've got the Maginot Line."

When the papers were brought in, Villard saw that *La Voie Nouvelle* contained his article. He read it through attentively, nodding his head and approving his own words. Then he looked at a photograph. It showed a wilderness of snow and a couple of dead soldiers standing upright and frozen stiff. They had rifles in their hands. They looked as though they were going into battle and continuing in death the gestures of life. Villard thought it was repulsive: there was no appeasement, no way out.

Louise left. Sitting in his armchair, he wallowed in the sense of restfulness. He now realized that it was a matter of indifference to him who won. And even in Finland. What did it matter? Some people or other were running about, falling and freezing. Life was like that. But he was above it: he was a world in himself like the apples. He'd had enough of excitement, words, and worries. It was time to take a rest.

He was disturbed by a photographer from *La Voie Nouvelle*, a fellow townsman of Joliot, a bustling but rather pathetic little man.

"Excuse me for intruding," he said. "We must have your photograph for the front page in connection with the events in Finland. 'The indefatigable fighter for freedom and justice.'"

Villard adjusted his glasses and tried to give his face an expression of courage.

CHAPTER 9

TESSA would hardly have recognized his daughter in the dainty modiste who was delivering dresses to fashionable women. Her hair was cut short and elaborately waved; her lips were scarlet; she wore a hat like a miniature chef's cap and carried a cardboard box tied up with lilac ribbon.

Denise was working at a dressmaker's on the boulevard Malesherbes. The girls modelled evening dresses. There were long mirrors in the show-room. Customers were few, and the proprietor complained that business was bad. He was a middle-aged man with a short grey moustache and mournful eyes. From time to time he looked through the pages of *Le Jardin des modes* or *Vogue*. In the dim light the mannequins looked like customers. There was a hum of sewing-machines, a constant waving of electric irons, and the rippling of long fingernails over lengths of silk. The noise was beyond endurance. But in the back room a lame man called Eugène was fixing a sheet of paper in a small printing press. This was the illegal printing office of the Communist Party. The proprietor took little interest in fashions. He wrote political leaflets, and Denise carried them away in the smart cardboard box for distribution in the various quarters of the city.

Today was a holiday for Denise. She was hurrying to Belleville. She'd got the address. She was going to meet Michaud there. It was their first meeting after four months of separation.

Michaud had been sent to Brest at first, as he was in the naval reserve. After reading his service record, Headquarters wondered how they could best get rid of this "firebrand." Two weeks later they sent him to an infantry regiment at Arras. His job was to wash the floors of the barracks. Major Fabre, the battalion commander, was a crank and a drunkard who despised politics and had no faith in the authorities. His favourite saying was: "There are two pleasant phenomena of life — taxis and cactuses." At first he took Michaud for a thief, but after discovering that the "criminal" had fought in Spain, he dubbed him Don Quixote and showed him various marks of favour. Now he had given Michaud a couple of days' leave in Paris.

Denise was excited. She had difficulty in finding the narrow gloomy street, which had nothing to distinguish it from scores of others. An old woman opened the door. Michaud had not yet arrived.

"Sit down, my dear. I'll make you some coffee. Are you frozen? Michaud will soon be here."

But Michaud was a long time coming. "You never knew my Jeannot?" the old woman asked. "The Fascists killed him at the factory."

Denise remembered Michaud's stories of Clémence.

"Is it you?" she exclaimed.

Clémence wiped her eyes with her apron. Jeannot! Denise now began to understand the meaning of the things in the room. The portrait of a boy with big ears hung on the wall. Books and exercise-books lay on the chest of drawers. An old cap hung on a peg. Clémence refused to part with the things that had belonged to her son. She looked after his comrades, gave them meals, and sewed on their buttons. When the war broke out, she used to sit alone all the evening and cry. They were all taken away from her! But in November a stranger had called on her.

"I've come from Michaud," he said. "Could I stay the night here? I'm on the run. . . ."

She was now hiding the Communists. She never asked them their names or any questions at all. She got the bed ready and prepared a meal. They talked to her about events and she was proud of their confidence in her.

"The papers have made it all up about Finland in order to distract attention," she said to Denise.

Then she looked at Denise attentively and smiled. "I've been telling Michaud all along that it wasn't good for him to be all alone. It's a good thing you've noticed him. He's shy, but he's got a wonderful heart. And he's a clever fellow too. He'll soon be like Maurice Thorez. Only he wants a woman behind him. Jeannot had me."

Although Denise was usually reserved, she did not feel embarrassed. It was as though a close relation was talking to her.

At last Michaud came. How funny he looked in uniform!

"You!"

He embraced Clémence, and the old woman immediately served him coffee.

"I've got to go to work," she said. "If you go away before I get back, lock the door and put the key under the mat. Take care they don't kill you, Michaud. They say there's no war yet, but they're killing people all the same. We shall want you later on. I've been telling her you're going to be like Maurice Thorez."

When she was gone, Michaud took Denise in his arms and murmured: "I've been pining to see you, I'll say I have, and how!"

The short January day drew to a close. The twilight in the room was like a blue haze. Clémence would soon be coming back, but they still had a lot more to say to each other.

"Everything's in a mess. We're stationed on the Belgian frontier. They wanted to dig fortifications and then they changed their minds. I heard the colonel shouting: 'Only defeatists can say the

Germans will come here!' That's their favourite word. But who are the defeatists? Themselves. They're doing everything so that the Germans can smash us. Of course, if there was a different government, it would be another matter. The front can be held. Only I'm afraid they'll smash us to begin with, and then we'll be asked to save the situation. The men keep asking about the Communists. When I got some leaflets, they made a rush for them. The officers are Fascists. They're pro-Nazi too. The only exception is my man, who's crazy on cactuses. But the rest keep saying it's all due to the Popular Front, the treachery of the Communists, and so on. They're afraid of the men. And the men are waiting. They don't know what for themselves. There's plenty of powder, but there's nothing to set fire to it with. But if it starts in Paris, they'll back it up."

"It's just the same here," said Denise. "The people in the factories are angry, but they don't say anything. Only the Finnish affair has given them a jolt. They say they won't make planes for the Finnish Fascists on any account. They may go out on strike. And then the fat will be in the fire."

He asked her about the news from abroad and what was the news from the U.S.S.R. Denise explained everything.

Michaud smiled. "See how important you've become," he said. "You remember how I took you to your first meeting?"

They recalled the first days of their love, the hesitations and embarrassment. Neither their lips, hands, nor their eyes could express the strength of their emotion. And soon they would have to part again.

"I read in the papers about an English captain on board a ship," said Denise. "It was about New Year's. They were having dinner. Suddenly there was an explosion. A German submarine. His young wife was with him. He fastened a lifebelt round her and dragged her to the side of the ship. She struggled to get away. She thought he'd gone mad. He threw her into the water. She was saved. What self-control. What strength of feeling! Now we need courage in order to live, Michaud. You must tell me that and shout it at me so that I become strong. I'm not talking about danger. I'm not threatened with anything. But when we part, I always wonder whether it's the last time and for ever!"

"We're all on a raft now. They've sunk the ship. But we'll hold on. And we'll get there, Denise. You'll see!"

They parted at the corner of two dark streets that were broad and quiet as rivers at night. Michaud had a bundle of leaflets and two issues of *L'Humanité* tucked inside his jacket. There was still three hours before the train left. He walked to the station. Paris in the blackout was like a strange new city. From time to time the bare branches of the trees thrust themselves out of the darkness. But the houses were invisible. You were vaguely conscious of them, like distant mountains. A child laughed. A woman's voice said: "I've dropped my glove." A bus hooted. A cigarette glowed. . . . And everywhere in the darkness was a moist blue haze, and the vague murmur of the city, which sounded like the surging of the sea.

Michaud thought of Denise and their hurried good-bye — they were both afraid to reveal their pain. She had told him: "I've put some cigarettes in your pocket." He had said: "Cover up your neck. You'll catch cold." When would they meet again? And would they ever meet?

The broad streets rolled on like rivers. Now there was someone coming towards him with a flashlight. The faint light seemed strong in the darkness. It lit up the pavement, the railings round a tree, and the person's feet. Had there ever been any bright lamps in the streets? The light disappeared as the stranger turned a corner. Oh, to carry love through all these dark years, like the gleam of a torch in the blackout!

CHAPTER 10

ANDRÉ was sent to Poitiers. Every day it was rumoured that the regiment was going to be sent to the Maginot Line, but the rumours were not confirmed. Four months went by. The colonel was a frequent visitor in the drawing-room of the Marquise de Nior. He had served with old General Grandmaison in the campaign against Baku, and the local archæologists were always asking him whether Poitiers was in danger of being attacked from the air. The officers had installed their mistresses in the town. The soldiers were in debt in all the bars and had gone the rounds of all the brothels. Every evening André crossed off another day in his diary.

His friend Laurier said to him: "It would be interesting to know whether we've lost a day or won it."

Life was dull and monotonous as in a prison. They went on route marches, swept out the yard, ate turnip soup. Then they wandered about the town, struck up acquaintance with the shopgirls, looked at old movies, and drank apéritifs. Then they went back to the barracks and sat round the iron stove, belching and dozing. André looked at their faces. They gradually lost their expression of anxiety and cunning and reminded him of a landscape. He often thought of man's likeness to the earth and the link between the potter and the clay. In moments like this André felt the urge to work. He poked fun at himself: "When I was in Paris I didn't want to paint, and now I'm here I crave for my paints." Laurier said: "We're going to the front in a week." André had visions of enormous columns of smoke, cold dawns, barbed wire, and pale empty death, like those intolerable sunless but dazzling days when objects lose their form and colour.

André made friends easily. In Paris he had lived alone in his studio with his canvases. But here he was with other people, laughing, telling stories, and joking. He chummed with Laurier especially. Laurier was a café musician from Avignon, a boyish, carefree southerner, who sang *Tout va bien, Madame la Marquise* one moment and the next said: "This war's going to last a hundred years." Then he laughed: "The colonel has presented wax hands and feet to the Virgin Mary in advance so that he won't get wounded."

Yves, the Breton, remarked with a sigh: "The soil is good here. And there are lots of goats. We don't have goats where I come from. Anyway, whose idea was it to go to war?" At every tree he stopped as though he had met a fellow countryman. André had long talks with him about manures and rye. Sometimes at night Yves cried quietly to himself. He pined for his wife and children and home.

Nivelle had been a waiter in a café. He had spent two months in a hospital before he was passed as fit. His wife brought him a geranium. He had been told that geranium would give him a weak heart and then he would be released from the Army. Nothing happened. "Why do they keep me here?" he asked. "I was earning eighty francs a day. Multiply that by thirty. And business is ever so much better now. The waiter at the Café de Paris told me yesterday he was earning twice as much as before. Work it out for your-self: multiply two thousand four hundred by two. I know they don't care a damn about my business, and I don't care a damn about them either. And how many are there like me? Three million at least. So work it out: multiply four thousand eight hundred by three million." He fished out a gnawed stump of pencil. " It works out at fourteen million four hundred thousand. Multiply by twelve."

Labonne, the book-keeper, was afraid of planes. " I wouldn't mind if it was ordinary gunfire," he said. " But when it comes to being shot at from above — well, I ask you! " He consoled himself with the thought that his wife was a long way off. He was always in the brothels. " I shall get killed anyway," he said. " I might as well enjoy a free life while I can."

Then there was Givert, a youngish, weak-chested fellow, who wrote poems about the dark night street and a mad organ-grinder.

All these men lived together, shared the same boredom, and got drunk. Somebody would rush up and shout: " We're off tomorrow! " Then whole barracks began to hum with excitement. The men wrote letters home and embraced the local girls. Then would come the announcement: " False alarm." And Yves began to sigh again and ask: " What's it all for? "

One day André said to Laurier: " It's no use trying to understand! It's all a mix-up. You don't know who's fighting whom. It's like being caught in a crowd; only nobody stirs from the spot. What's the use of listening to what they say? They won't tell the truth, anyway. They're cheating and trying to outwit one another. It's just as though I were painting a picture and squeezing the colours out of the tubes. You squeeze the vermilion and out comes black. You squeeze the white and out comes madder. No, it's better not to think at all! "

When the radio stopped playing dance music and started giving the announcements, everybody shouted: " Switch that damn thing off! " They were fed up with hearing that Daladier was defending the cause of culture, that nothing of importance had taken place at the front, and that the Germans had sunk another seventeen thousand tons of shipping.

The town had forgotten all about the war. For a few weeks its life had been disturbed by the mobilization; then it sank back into its usual rut. Chardonnet, the hairdresser, won two hundred thou-sand francs in a lottery. The current number of the *Archæological*

Journal was published with long accounts of the excavations in Afghanistan. The Marquise de Nior complained of the rise in the cost of living; she had been obliged to dismiss her gardener and saddle her chauffeur with the job of looking after the garden. The gardener took his revenge by stealing the Marquise's gold watch and the family plate. He was caught in a brothel. The local papers were far more concerned with this affair than with the naval battle off the coast of Uruguay. A circus pitched its tent in the big square. Three tormented leopards kept springing from armchair to armchair.

One day in January the colonel bellowed at Yves: "You're no more like a soldier than a village fireman!" The barracks were made spick and span, and Tricolour streamers were hung out across the main street in readiness for the arrival of the deputy for Poitiers, who had become a Minister. The Mayor made a speech of welcome, in which he compared Tessa to the great men of old and Clemenceau. Tessa complacently nodded his head. After the Mayor's speech he got up and said: "I thought I would like, in these historic days, to visit the town which has honoured me with its confidence. I know that the sacred fire still burns in the breasts of the sons of Poitiers. In the olden days it inspired St. Hilarion, the patron saint of Poitiers. Today it inspires the defenders of the Maginot Line. All our thoughts are devoted to one thing — victory."

Tessa had come to buy some land in the Department of Vienne. In the past he had spent every penny he earned, but now he was at a loss to know what to do with his money. The various companies with which he was connected were in a flourishing condition. Of course, he could transfer the money to America, but in that case it would become a mere figure, a sort of abstraction. And besides, you could never be quite sure. He no longer had any faith either in stocks or in dollars. Land was the only thing which didn't change. It would be nice to buy a charming country estate. He could bring Paulette there for Easter and, strolling among the flowers, forget all about the war, Breteuil, and the generals. Recently he had been making fun of Laval, whom he called "an Auvergnat, a skinflint, who only knows one thing — he buys land." In a lawyer's office Tessa inspected a host of plans and photographs. There was one that took his fancy. The house had an eighteenth-century façade, and a garden laid out in the style of the Petit Trianon; inside it was fitted with all modern conveniences.

Next day he drove out to Pré-des-Daims, as the estate was called. He took the precaution of putting on woollen underclothes and two knitted waistcoats, as the weather was bitterly cold. He kept wondering what had become of Lucien and pictured his son frozen to death.

"It's as bad as in Finland," he said to the lawyer. "By the way, have you read today's papers? That marshal with the German name is a wonderful fellow! I'm convinced he'll win."

In front of the house stood a naked nymph holding a bronze basin. Icicles hung in spikes from the rim. Even the nymph seemed frozen.

"It's a beautiful house," said Tessa. "I like the combination of feudal Louis XV ceilings and central heating."

He got back to the town towards evening. He remembered having bought a box of chocolates for Denise at the confectioner's, and the memory of it made him feel sad. Nearly four years had gone by since then. If it hadn't been for the war, he would soon have had to face his constituents again. But now he had other worries. What a wonderful time that was! He was the only candidate. All the others had given way before him. Amalie and his children were waiting for him at home. Denise was smiling and even Lucien tried to be nice. How pleased Amalie would have been to know that he was buying Pré-des-Daims! She loved country life, chickens, and vegetables. And whom was he to buy the estate for now? Paulette? But she'd throw him over as soon as some rich young chap like Meuger's son turned up. No, the land was for him, and for him alone. Suddenly he began to think of that other land in the cemetery of Père Lachaise next to Amalie's grave. He was on the verge of tears, but fortunately he remembered the Marquise de Nior was giving a reception in his honour that evening, and this was enough to console him.

The Marquise received him with animated chatter.

"We're delighted to welcome you as a neighbour," she said. "It's nice of you to have chosen Poitou."

In the salon he found the local aristocrats, archæologists, a number of Army officers and his old rival Grandmaison, who was shouting: "They've got to be taught a lesson! I can't understand the delicacy of the English. Go into the Black Sea and put an end to it!"

The visitors surrounded Tessa. He sipped weak tea and explained: "Everything is going according to plan. It would be a mistake to regard Germany as completely united. This winter has taught them a good deal. The flight of Thyssen is far more important than a military victory. The Reichswehr is furious. I foresee the possibility of our having a serious talk with the Germans. A man like Göring fully realizes the situation. As for Hess! "

He made inquiries about the fate of his opponents at the elections. Breteuil's protégé, Dugard, had been called up and was now in charge of oil supplies. Didier, the locksmith, had been sent to a concentration camp in the Isle of Ré. Tessa exclaimed with a sigh: " It's terrible to have to resort to such measures! But one can't do anything else: the enemy is at the gates of France."

Next morning Tessa left by car for Paris. The battalion provided him with a guard of honour. André had often heard Lucien talk about his father, but he had never seen Tessa in the flesh. He was surprised when he saw him now: he looked like a little bird. Tessa inspected the guard of honour and then wiped his long nose with his kid glove. The strains of the *Marseillaise* resounded in the wintry air.

The troops talked about Tessa's visit. They all knew that he had bought an estate. Yves said with a sigh: " The son of a bitch has poked his nose around. He smelt the land was good! And he hasn't spared his money. They tell me the land around here has gone up from three francs to twelve."

" It makes no difference to him," growled Nivelle. " He makes a bit on every shell. Just the same as I used to do on every glass of beer. But he wouldn't even think of releasing me."

" He's got a solemn face," said Laurier. " They only go to funerals with a face like that. And yet he shouts: ' Victory! ' Let's go to the circus. Coming? "

The circus smelt of powder and animals' urine. The glass beads glittered on the skirts of the equestrienne. The performing monkey sneezed, and the enormous hurdy-gurdy roared. André recalled the 14th of July, the merry-go-round, and the shiny blue elephant. Where was Jeannette now? Was she still advertising pills? Was she weeping? Nobody had had any luck. He used to think he was unlucky. Now he knew that everybody was the same. Laurier was right: they would never live to see peace. Even if it were signed, it would only last a year or two and then the trouble would start all over again.

Yves had his own thoughts. " The land here is remarkable," he said to himself. " But the peasants are crafty. They've mixed millet with the corn so as not to give it all up. They're killing the cattle. They say: ' What's the good of paper money to us? ' They don't trust anybody. And look how the price of land has gone up! Who's behind all this? "

The leopards blinked their eyes in the bright light and lowered their ears. The puny little tamer in a purple frock coat cracked his whip without ceasing.

" Those armchairs are too small for them," said Givert.

Then the hurdy-gurdy started to roar again.

André went out with Laurier. " The worst thing of all is the indifference," he said. " They go to the circus. All the cafés are full. Tessa's buying up land. The peasants are hiding the wheat. And what's going to happen tomorrow? In the last war it was all different. Perhaps it was sillier but it was more human. They shouted: ' To Berlin! ' looted the shops owned by Germans, and hated the Boches. And they fought. They were full of spirit. Clemenceau got his back up and said: ' We'll defend ourselves in front of Paris, in Paris, and behind Paris! ' Then there were proclamations: ' Lenin said so and so. . . .' And everything seethed. But now it's all so quiet you feel you want to howl. I feel like those leopards. They're advertised as ' ferocious beasts of prey,' and they're no fiercer than a mangy old cat. I don't like it, Laurier."

" Neither do I," Laurier said.

CHAPTER 11

THE MEN jokingly asked Lucien if he was a relation of Tessa's. He said: " A namesake." Nevertheless, the name was something to be reckoned with, and the cautious major made Lucien a hospital orderly so as to keep him as far away as possible from a stray bullet.

The former monastery was being used as a mental hospital. Lucien had to restrain the maniacs, and feed melancholics through the nose with rubber tubes. A sergeant lay tied up in his bunk: he wanted to bayonet people. A young soldier called Bérand screamed at the top of his voice; he was terrified of everything, a hairbrush, a spittoon, or the doctor's spectacles. Another patient kept drawing naked soldiers with female breasts, and a demented man from Marseille repeated from morning to night the formula of the war communiqués: "Nothing of importance. . . . Nothing of importance. . . ."

Another man frankly admitted to Lucien: "I'm doing it on purpose. First of all I thought the liver would do the trick. I swallowed fifteen eggs at Limoges. It's horrible to think of it. It didn't come off. They sent me to the front. Then I thought I'd moo like a cow. Only don't give me away." Lucien shrugged his shoulders and said: "What does it matter to me? Moo as much as you like."

The orderlies played cards and zealously visited the brothels. In their quarters in the hospital the niches in which the images of the saints had once stood were filled with wine-bottles. Lucien liked to sit by the stove. It was his only pleasure, and he thought: "I can understand the fire-worshippers." Today he felt inspired by the fire. It had died down, but now it was burning again and devouring the wood. And Lucien's hair looked like the continuation of the flames.

Jenny had written that she was going back to America. She gave as an excuse that the American Consul insisted on her leaving. She said they must meet again in Paris or New York. Lucien threw the letter into the fire. It was only now that he realized he loved Jeannette. People said that time was an enemy. It wasn't true. Time wore away the husk; the insincere sorrows and artificial passions disappeared, but the genuine sentiments remained. He was alien to Jenny, as she was to him. It was like a jig-saw puzzle: the picture had to be put together, but one piece didn't fit in with another.

The radio was barking: "Nothing of importance took place at the front," and the man from Marseille howled at the top of his voice: "Nothing of importance."

After New Year's Lucien applied to be sent to the front. He thought the nearness of death would enliven his weary mood. He found the life there primitive, cold, and full of curses. The shells were always killing somebody, but the troops were used to this by now and yawned: "It's a gamble."

He found a companion for conversation — a Norman with a jaw like a horse and glaring eyes. He was an archæologist by profession. His name was Alfred. He told Lucien about the excavations in the Sahara, the relics of a vanished world. And Lucien recalled the ice and the penguins. One day they talked about the war. Alfred was confident that Daladier stood for freedom and that after victory the arts would flourish again and there would be a new Athens, a new Renaissance. Lucien didn't care to disillusion him. Only occasionally he interrupted Alfred with the remark: "It's a good thing you don't know them."

A soldier was carried away with frost-bitten feet. Warm socks seemed like an unobtainable dream. Rumours went round that the troops were to be sent to Finland.

One cold February morning when the world looked like a white field with a red sun over it, the positions were inspected by a parliamentary delegation accompanied by General Picard.

Recently there had been a rumour that Picard was being sent to Syria. Weygand called himself a "fireman," and said that he had been called in to put out the fire in the Near East. Picard objected: "In war a fire-bomb is more useful than a hose."

Picard had worked out the plan of operations. He called the army in Syria the "Baku Army." But the events in Finland obliged him to turn to the north. He said to Tessa: "We must send a strong expeditionary force. We can't fight the Germans. Besides, we don't want to. And it's dangerous to keep the men unoccupied. The Communists are hard at work. There'll be disorders in the spring. Only a decisive victory in Finland will get us out of the impasse."

In the parliamentary lobbies there was a good deal of talk about the ore in Lapland, the "colossus with feet of clay," and the sympathy of Rome. The deputies were visiting the front to reassure themselves as to the solidity of the Maginot Line. Before they could approve a serious expedition, they had to make sure that all the doors were properly shut. The delegates consisted of three Radicals, two members of the Right, and one Socialist. With the exception of Breteuil they were all people who knew absolutely nothing about warfare. They were like spectators who had accidentally found themselves on the stage; they felt secretly ashamed of their hats and trousers. One of them, a cheery fat fellow, asked to be given a tin hat to protect his head.

They asked all sorts of stupid questions, inspected the fortifications, exclaiming "Oh!" and "Ah!" like tourists looking at a mediæval castle, and shrank nervously away from the heavy guns.

General Picard walked with Breteuil. They talked about the

prospects of the campaign in the north. Breteuil was in high spirits.

"We've reached a turning-point," he said. "I was afraid the Socialists would stand in the way, but Blum keeps mum and Villard rushes into battle. The question of sending the Chasseurs Alpins will be settled in a day or two."

They passed a military post. Lucien saluted. He had a few anxious moments wondering whether Breteuil would recognize him. But Breteuil was deep in conversation, and besides, it wasn't his style to take any notice of privates.

Lucien could not help reviving painful memories of the past. Even the sight of the deputies hunching their backs as though bullets were flying over them failed to amuse him. He realized what it meant to "burn with shame." Yes, his past was shameful. How could he ever have had any confidence in that heartless man? It was easy to guess what Breteuil was talking about with Picard; they wanted to put France on her knees. They were taking their revenge for 1936. They would send troops to Syria and Finland, no matter where. And they would let Hitler in. Lucien remembered how his father used to say, when he was furious at the strikes: "Even the Germans would be better!" They were all alike. Perhaps Grandel was in a way the least harmful of the lot. But meanwhile people were getting killed. Yesterday it was Charles. He was a mountain shepherd and played the bagpipes. Why had they sent him to his death? The blackguards.

In the evening Lucien and Alfred squatted round a little camp-fire. They were frozen and silent. Then Alfred began to talk: " After the resolutions of the League of Nations . . ."

Lucien interrupted him. "Rubbish!" he said. "It's all empty words which they use to cover up all sorts of treachery, personal interests, and petty spites. You saw Breteuil? He's holy. He's aiming at heaven. And, of course, he's a 'patriot.' You should hear the sob in his voice when he starts talking about Lorraine. But he knows all the time that Grandel is a German spy. He's been shielding him. Do you think that Picard is getting ready for war? Of course not! He has been busy with something else. He's been hard at work preparing the Fascist revolution. Where did the machine-guns come from? From Düsseldorf. And who gave him the money? A German named Kilmann! It's a sordid story. Don't talk to me about the League of Nations. You'd do better to tell me what it is that Charles has been killed for."

For a long time Lucien talked about Breteuil's "Faithful," the meetings at Montigny's house, and the betrayal of the country. He only neglected to say how he had got Kilmann's letter. He didn't like to admit that he was Tessa's son; he felt that was even more shameful. Alfred sat with a look of the deepest depression on his face. He kept saying "But —" and failed to go on. At last he got it out: "But if it's like that, we must let everybody know. They must be kicked out. We must save France."

Lucien smiled maliciously. "Just the same as Jenny!" he said. "She was an American. I used to live with her, or rather with her dollars. She said exactly the same thing to me: 'Then you must have a revolution.' It's too late, old chap. What did we do in 1936? It's no use trying it now. They'll crush us and set up Breteuil as *Gauleiter*. Or perhaps they'll simply send everything to the devil. You and me included. It'll all be like your excavations. Twenty centuries from now they'll dig up a Dunhill lighter, a Messerschmitt engine, the skull of the noble Villard, and then they'll exclaim: 'It was a wonderful civilization!' One consolation, we won't be there to say it! Ugh! It's damned cold! To tell the truth, it's boring."

CHAPTER 12

JOLIOT celebrated the New Year with his wife and her brother Alfred, an Army doctor who had got three days' leave from the front. They went out to a restaurant and drank two bottles of champagne. Some girls threw little pink and blue paper balls at them. Alfred blinked bashfully and said: "They're bombs." Joliot proclaimed a toast: "To victory! I can see our soldiers greeting the new year in Berlin."

Then in a fit of superstition he hastily touched wood on the side of the table. Alfred turned away. Joliot's expansive manners made him feel uncomfortable. But Marie looked fondly at her brother and murmured: "If only you don't get killed!"

Joliot began to give his reasons: "It's absolutely logical. By the end of the year we'll have five heavy guns to every German one."

"I don't know," said Alfred. "I'm not up on those things. But we're in a bad way as regards serums. I'm afraid they'll take us unawares. There was tetanus in the last war. . . ."

Joliot cut him short; he couldn't bear to hear about diseases or death.

Alfred left the next day. Joliot never referred to him. He looked on him as a nice chap but rather colourless. But Marie often shed tears; she was afraid her brother would get killed. In vain Joliot kept telling her that doctors were in the rear and away from danger. She kept saying: "But what if all of a sudden — ? "

Joliot's life was full of the usual feverish bustle. His head was now crammed with difficult Finnish names. At night as he dozed off into an uneasy sleep he was haunted by strange visions of frozen men hanging like stalactites from the sky. It made him feel cold and he drew the blanket over his head.

He was not a greedy man and he wanted everybody to have a share of the pie. He dispatched a dozen of his friends to Finland and Stockholm. To his cousin Marius, a nimble Marseillais, he said: " Get up a gala *soirée*. Say something about Mannerheim. It can be in aid of the Finnish ' Lottas.' It's a gold mine! "

Two weeks later Marius appeared before an elegant audience and, keeping his eye on Josephine Montigny, piped: " One day the marshal was sitting under a tree. The terrible revolution had only just begun. An impudent ragged soldier, a Bolshevik, came up to him and asked him for a light. I forgot to say that the marshal was smoking a cigar. He looked indignantly at the soldier and, at the risk of his life, replied: 'I would sooner swallow this burning cigar.' "

The ladies clapped their hands. Of course, the collection went into Marius's pockets, not to the Finns.

Joliot had long wanted to do a good turn to Poirier, the printer, who had never once pressed him for payment. The opportunity now presented itself. The General Staff needed maps of Finland. Joliot recommended Poirier. Joliot rang him up and said: " My dear chap, it's as simple as picking up four hundred thousand francs in the street. Only don't look at the map. It's enough to send you off your head. When I try to pronounce the names I feel I've got putty instead of a tongue in my mouth."

The paper was doing good business, but Joliot continued to feel depressed. He was afraid of something, he didn't know what. Twice a day he received the communiqués from the front: " Nothing of importance. . . ." Paris was getting rich and enjoying itself.

"Just take a look," said Joliot. "They're buying houses and cars like plush curtains."

Side by side with photographs of Finnish soldiers, the *Voie Nouvelle* published accounts of the skiing competitions at Chamonix and the winter sports resorts; the fashionable ladies of Paris did not want to lag behind Mannerheim's soldiers. But Joliot believed neither the pretty skiers nor the military communiqués. Something terrible had happened to the world. The weather was cold as never before. There was snow in Seville, and in the Argentine hundreds of people were dying of sunstroke. There was an earthquake in Turkey. It all showed that something was wrong. Joliot became even more superstitious and always had a piece of wood handy. At night he kept wondering whether he had walked under a ladder during the day. When Marie said anxiously: "We've had no letter from Alfred for a long time," he replied: "I expect he's on a spree," but gripped the chip of wood in his pocket as a precaution against bad luck.

Thyssen, the Ruhr magnate, arrived in Paris. He was pestered by the photographers, and all the smart women smiled at him. A photograph of his little dog appeared in *La Voie Nouvelle*. Joliot knew that Breteuil was hobnobbing with him.

The matter did not end with the photograph. Breteuil rang up; the newspaper must publish Thyssen's memoirs.

"It's just the thing we want. It points the way to a mutual understanding."

Joliot set off to the Crillon, where Thyssen was staying. He waited a long time in the ornate lounge. Then a man with a contemptuous expression came out to him. Joliot jauntily bowed his head and smiled and began to talk about freedom and the fraternity of nations. Thyssen said dryly:

"Excuse me. I'm busy."

He gave Joliot the manuscript and went away. When Joliot looked at it, he read: "That spring I elaborated together with Hitler the plan of the campaign against the Communists. . . ."

He arrived home tired out. When he found Marie crying, he said: "You needn't worry about Alfred. There isn't any war and there's not going to be any. You ought to have seen that German! His place is in a concentration camp. But he has just this moment gone to see Tessa, word of honour! Tomorrow we're going to publish his memoirs. Montigny said to me: 'Contact is being restored.' You realize what that means? Don't cry, Marie. Nothing will happen to Alfred. There's no war — except in Finland."

His wife took the handkerchief away from her mouth and said softly: "Alfred has been killed."

Only then Joliot noticed the big yellow envelope lying on the table.

CHAPTER 13

MICHAUD's regiment was sent to Le Havre. Michaud was alarmed; he thought they were going to be sent to Finland.

He looked on Moscow as the pledge that his life was not in vain and that happiness was not an empty word. Everything that was being done in Moscow seemed to him mysterious, but at the same time it was something which he felt to be familiar and part of himself. His face would light up with a blissful smile when he listened to the radio stories of the citron groves of Abkhasia. He followed every detail of the construction of the Moscow subway as though they were building his own home. "In Brussels," he said, "our pianists have won the first prize in the competition." The word "our" came to him quite naturally. Once he said to Denise: "Even the flowers out there are on our side. Yes, yes, the ordinary flowers, the daisies and buttercups." Whenever he felt he could bear it no longer, he would look at the map of the Soviet Union: the enormous green space soothed his nerves. Even at his last meeting with Denise he asked: "How's the exhibition in Moscow?" He saw the far-off city in his imagination as though he had lived there for years. He was ready to die for it. And he was not the only one. He was sustained by the knowledge that hundreds of soldiers around him shared his belief. And in other regiments as well. It was a secret fellowship of millions.

And now the wind was rushing down the broad streets of Le Havre, tearing the curtains, overturning the billboards, and whirling the pedestrians. The harbour sirens were hooting. The cranes were grating their teeth. Work was going on day and night. There was talk of an expeditionary force.

Michaud kept taking aside first one soldier and then another. He didn't know which were Communists, but there were a good many signs: one man might say he missed *L'Humanité,* another might sneer at Villard's noble mind or talk of Thorez as "our Maurice." Michaud whispered: "If they send us against the Russians, we must refuse to go. They can't keep it hushed up. The whole country will know about it."

"I don't know," came the answer. "What will the others say? You've got to remember it isn't an election affair. You might get shot."

The men liked Michaud for his bold language and cheerful spirit. They backed him up when he made fun of the sergeant. But to revolt was a different matter. Michaud himself didn't know what the men would say. He tried to persuade and explain, telling them enthusiastically about Leningrad, which the Russians were fighting to defend. There was a big river there and the workers were in the palaces. Lenin used to live there. He abused the traitors who were prepared to strip the front. He talked to each man in a different way, getting excited and making haste, as they might be sent off tomorrow.

When Colonel Quérier heard that his regiment was included in the expeditionary force he was unable to sleep. He spent the nights playing solitaire. He was a man of fiery temperament and weak character. He had given proof of his courage in the last war and had been decorated twice. He was indifferent to death but was afraid of life, the authorities, the crafty web of politics, denunciations, and street demonstrations.

The regiment had been stationed in Picardy all the winter. Quérier had decided to dig fortifications, as it was impossible to let the men be without some occupation. But General Picard snubbed him: "Who asked you to create a panic? They're not likely to come here. You've been listening to the defeatists."

Quérier was scared. Who could understand them? It was all politics. He ordered the work to be stopped and declared: "It's no use building any fortifications. Only the defeatists think they're necessary. The Germans won't come here."

Now they were talking about Finland. Nobody knew what the troops would say. But out there they might start fraternizing with the Russians. Whose idea was it, anyway? It had always been said that one enemy was better than two. How could Russia be con-

quered? Even Napoleon was bogged down there. Would Gamelin
really allow it? But then, even Gamelin was powerless; it was the
politicians who would decide everything.

In despair the colonel swept the cards aside; again the solitaire
wouldn't come out. He wanted two jacks. That was the sixth time
it wouldn't come out! Well — enough for tonight!

Michaud was saying to his comrades: "Have you seen the frontier? No fortifications. They're taking men away. They want to fight
the Russians. And they'll let Hitler's army come in here! That's
their game!"

The dim lamp shed a faint light on the men's faces. Long shadows
flickered on the whitewashed wall. Michaud tried in vain to guess
the meaning of their silence. They were men of various types. One
was a locksmith from Asnières and seemed to be a Communist.
Another was a peasant and talked about the good home he had
left. A third was a travelling salesman who sold sewing-machines.
There was also a porter, a butcher, and a postman. What were they
thinking about?

The dénouement came suddenly. Picard arrived to inspect the
troops. Two platoons were drawn up. Quérier stood with a gloomy,
preoccupied air and did not look at the men. Suddenly some men
behind him shouted: "Where are they taking us to?"

The colonel went red in the face. He mopped his forehead with
his handkerchief and said: "Who's that shouting?"

"All of us!" came the reply.

Quérier was at his wits' end. He made no threats and used no
persuasion. The men's rifles were taken away. The rumour went
round that they were going to be court-martialled. At night the
men were unable to sleep. They remembered their childhood, their
life in the days of peace, and their families.

They were asked: "Who's the ringleader?" Everybody had
Michaud in mind, but nobody gave him away. And all the while
the March gale roared over the town.

Next day Picard said to the colonel: "We'll have to shoot three
or four of them as an example to the rest."

Then Quérier began to exclaim: "Do you realize what it would
lead to? They'll kill us!"

He recovered himself at once and hung his head. He expected a
court martial; it looked as though he was the ringleader.

Picard turned aside and drummed on the dirty window-pane.

He forgot that a subordinate was standing beside him. He kept saying to himself: " Marne, Verdun. . . . A thing of the past. Do you call this an army? It's a horde, a bunch of rabble! " He recalled how many times he had said to Breteuil: " Be careful. We may have to pay for this." Of course, a campaign in Finland might be a good thing for the men's morale. But the Radicals were hesitating as usual. And there were a good many Communists among the troops. What was going to happen? The officers wouldn't go against the Germans. It would be more honest to say: " I surrender." The pawns in the game were still safe, but the game itself was already lost.

He looked out of the window. The men were surrounding a newspaper-seller. The wind caught the papers and blew them along the wide street.

" *La Voie Nouvelle*! Latest edition! Rumoured negotiations between Helsinki and Moscow! "

CHAPTER 14

TESSA was eating a boiled egg when a telegram was brought to him. The words danced before his eyes: " Peace negotiations . . . Stockholm . . . Finnish delegation." He frowned as though he felt a physical pain. After he had recovered himself he rang up Daladier.

" What a misfortune! " he exclaimed.

Daladier replied that he was going to make a speech on the radio. He would suggest to the Finns that they should go on fighting: an expeditionary force was ready to go to their aid.

Tessa shook his head. " It's too late, my friend. They won't believe you. We must think of something else."

Daladier began talking about the " tragedy of little nations." Tessa interrupted him in a tone of annoyance: " Of course it's a tragedy! And not only for the Finns. You can trust my instincts. The Cabinet won't last a week."

Tessa began to reckon up the votes. There would be a majority against. There was no justice in the world. He would have to pay

for the mistakes of an individual called Mannerheim. Tessa cursed
the Finns. They were savages!

It turned out as he had foreseen: only a minority voted for the
Government. Reynaud came to the fore. Tessa hated him: he was
a gnome, a youthful prodigy, an ape! Reynard proposed to Tessa
that he should retain his ministerial portfolio.

"I'll think it over," Tessa said. "I'll have a word with my friends."

He went to see Daladier at once. Daladier was drinking an apéritif. He looked from underneath his brows and said: "Reynaud is a
disaster. But I've decided to remain at my post. Right to the end."

Tessa could get no more out of him, so he decided to go and see
Breteuil; he was the coming man! If Breteuil advised him to go
over to the opposition he would give up his portfolio. He would
have to know how to wait and show civic courage.

In Breteuil's study Tessa met a tall blue-eyed man, who said
to him at once: "I had the pleasure of making your acquaintance
just before the Marseille congress."

Tessa vaguely recollected the delegate for Colmar who had prevented Fouget from speaking. "Of course I remember you," he said
with a friendly smile.

When Weiss went away, Breteuil said to Tessa: "Don't be surprised at the Radicals coming to me. We're carrying out national
unity. Weiss is working with Grandel. In general I consider things
are not working out at all badly."

His bold tone of voice puzzled Tessa. "In my opinion," he said,
"things are going very badly indeed. The Finns have let us down.
As for Reynaud, he's capable of anything."

"I'm not one of his admirers either," said Breteuil. "He's a tool
of England. He wants us to become a dominion. But Reynaud's
a butterfly. He won't last till summer. In the meantime we can make
use of him. He'll get rid of Gamelin, and that will be an advantage.
We must put forward Picard. Besides, the dwarf has climbed up
onto stilts. He's got to do something to make an impression. And the
first leap he takes will bring him down."

"He has offered me a portfolio. But I want to refuse."

"On no account! You must consider the interests of the nation.
We've got to have one of our men in the Cabinet."

Tessa did not require to be persuaded. Very well, he would work
with Reynaud. The Left would forgive him a good deal on that
account. He had had misgivings with regard to the Right, but now

Breteuil had given him his blessing. Of course he would remain in the Government! It was very pleasant to be a Minister. And more honourable into the bargain; future historians would point out that Tessa did not desert his post during the war.

When Joliot received the list of names of the new Government he began to shout: " What do you think of this? Out of thirty Ministers sixteen are lawyers. And they call it a ' War Cabinet '! "

Agency cables were brought in. Joliot turned pale. " Dreadful omens! " he exclaimed. " Etna has started belching fire again. That's a bad sign! They're complaining they missed the bus in Finland. But I'm afraid the Moors may come to Marseille."

The General Staff were astonished when Poirier, the printer, delivered the maps that had been ordered. " What do we want maps of Finland for? " they asked. However, the maps were paid for.

Three weeks went by. Early one morning Joliot heard of the laying of the mine-fields off the coast of Norway. He immediately telephoned to Poirier: " I congratulate you on getting another order. Reynaud also wants to have a crack at the polar bears. Now they'll want maps of Norway, you'll see! Only don't knock your price down."

Montigny held a grand reception — the first ever given by the Right in honour of Tessa. Among the guests were Breteuil, Laval, Flandin, Grandel, Meuger, and General Picard.

The women discussed the problem of where was the best place to go for a vacation. Mme Picard was in favour of Briançon.

" I know it's near the Italian frontier," she said, " but my husband tells me Mussolini is not going to declare war on any account. I want to have a good rest from this dreadful war. It's so marvellously quiet and peaceful down there."

Mme Meuger announced her intention of spending a few weeks at Biarritz. One always met such charming people there. Besides, she adored the Atlantic.

They asked Mouche where she was going. " My husband wants me to take a rest in Switzerland," she said. " But I don't know. . . ." She remembered the neat Swiss hotel, the loud laughter of the tourists, the back of Kilmann's neck, the jingling cow-bells, and all that she had suffered afterwards — Lucien's wild behaviour and his furious face.

Mme Montigny, her heavily powdered shoulders emerging from an incredibly low-cut dress, did the honours to her guests. " Tuesday is a dreadful day — no meat, no pastries, no liqueurs. But thank heaven the French aren't fussy. My dear general, I really can recommend this armagnac. It comes from my brother's cellars. You seem rather preoccupied."

"Oh, not at all. Yes indeed, this armagnac is excellent."

"Have you any news?"

"Nothing cheerful. I'm referring to the war." The general sighed. "They said they were going to hold the Bergen-Oslo road, but the Germans are sweeping all before them. There's nothing left except the north. The situation . . ."

Tessa heard only the last word and immediately chimed in: "The situation has undoubtedly improved. I was expecting a big majority, but I'll tell you frankly, the unanimous vote of the Chamber astonished me. What maturity of political thought! We really express the will of the whole of France today. Isn't that so, general?"

Picard began to talk about Bergen and the fjords. Airily Tessa waved his hand. "Those are details," he said.

Picard annoyed him; the man showed all the typical blindness of a soldier. After all, where had the Germans gone? A wild, poverty-stricken country. It was only cranks who went up the fjords and admired the midnight sun. It was a good thing the Germans had nibbled at the bait. Anyway, it drew them away from the frontiers of France.

"It was the British who thought up the Norwegian stunt," he said. "We've got nothing to do with it. Admiral Darlan is indignant. He says quite frankly that Hitler would be better."

Breteuil grinned. "The British, eh?" he said. "I saw them on the Somme in '16. They used to shave in the trenches every morning. We'll see what they'll do in the wild tundra of the north."

There was a general chorus of approval from the guests: "They'll eat the codfish they're so fond of." "Or the codfish will eat them." "I can imagine how scared Reynaud was." "Yes, the gnome is not having a pleasant time. I think even the Australian Government enjoys more independence." "Ha ha! We're on the same footing as the kangaroos."

Tessa felt bound to stand up for the Government. "Of course," he said, "Reynaud is an Anglophil and a snob. But Countess Hélène de Portes is a clever woman. She's a sort of Egeria. But I work through the Countess's friend, Baudouin."

Someone snorted: "The lover of another man's mistress!"

" It's a pity," Tessa went on, " that our friends Breteuil and Laval
didn't enter the Cabinet. But you may rest assured that we're not
standing for any wild adventure in Norway. I was the first to insist
on helping Finland. France has always stretched out a helping
hand to the weak. But we're not interested in the fate of Norway.
That's a quarrel between the British and the Germans. Let Churchill
clear up the mess. As far as our own territory is concerned, we're
guaranteed against surprises. The Germans can't go by way of
Holland; the Dutch will open the dikes. They've carried out tests
which passed off brilliantly. And the Belgian fortifications are
almost as good as the Maginot Line. Of course, the Germans have
a certain superiority in aeroplanes and tanks, but that isn't enough.
General Leridot says that for a real attack the Germans must put
up six guns to every one of ours. So, you see, their game is lost."

" Our weak spot is the rear," said Meuger. " The Communists are
raising their heads again. The strike at Courneuve may spread.
Look at their leaflets. Here, take a look at these."

" Outrageous! "

" It would have been far better to have shot the deputies."

" They've been given a cheap advertisement. Everybody is talking about Greuze's speech at the trial."

" The whole trial was a mistake. I said so to Daladier. They
should have been kept in prison without trial and charged with
treason against the State."

" We're bound by the laws," said Tessa with a sigh. " Look at the
sentences: two or three years' imprisonment. Who can put a stop
to it? Reynaud is a bungler. And Mandel has a blind hatred of
Hitler. He's a most dangerous demagogue. He's aiming at becoming
the emissary of the Commune. I'm counting on the support of
Sérol. He's a Socialist, but a decent chap. It's fortunate they've
given him the post of Minister of Justice. He says quite frankly
that the Moscow plague must be burned out with iron."

Tessa drank a glass of armagnac and felt depressed. He was
thinking they might shoot Denise. But he quickly mastered his
feelings and once again became intransigent and courageous. The
guests encouraged him with their approving chatter. He stood beside the round table holding the sugar-tongs in his hand. He felt
he was standing at the helm of the State.

Then Picard became the centre of attraction. He was telling
anecdotes about General Gort.

Josephine Montigny came up to Tessa and said softly: "Where's Lucien?"

Tessa was embarrassed. It was the first time anyone had spoken to him about his son. He answered without thinking: "He's disappeared." He realized at once that this sounded ambiguous and corrected himself. "Perhaps he's dead. Poor Lucien!" His voice trembled.

Josephine Montigny was so moved that she began to cry. Tessa also felt the tears gathering and hurriedly drew a finger across his eyes and blew his birdlike nose.

Montigny came over to them. Tessa pulled himself together: one ought not to give way to one's feelings. He must be strong, like Clemenceau.

"Hitler has made another mistake," he said. "He's going to fight the walruses. In the meantime we can go on working. Daladier has decided to demobilize half a million peasants. We've got to plough and sow. We can't live without bread. Let Ducane and Fouget go into epileptic fits. We'll show the world what French staying-power means."

Montigny nodded his head. Yes, that was quite right. Then he embraced Tessa and began shouting for all the drawing-room to hear: "You did well to buy a bit of land in Poitou. It's the navel of France, right away from the frontiers. My estate is in Savoy, and, frankly speaking, I'm rather afraid. The Italians are a fantastic race, you know. But you can sleep in peace, my dear fellow. Nobody will ever come to Poitou. I've always told Breteuil that you had the mind of a statesman."

CHAPTER 15

WHEN Meuger heard that Reynaud had taken Daladier's place, he said to Grandel: "I was to have delivered one hundred and eighty bombers by the first of May. But now the situation has changed. You may tell the Minister that further tests are necessary."

"I understand," said Grandel with a smile. "Reynaud is an adventurer. He's quite capable of dragging us into a real war. What did he want to send the Chasseurs Alpins to Narvik for? I hope he'll soon be kicked out. One good defeat would be enough. The Germans are doing their best. It's rumoured that he has congratulated Desser. That's an excellent omen: his friendship with Desser won't do him any good."

Desser, who until recently had been all-powerful, had now become a laughing-stock. The caricaturists made their living out of him. And Breteuil gave instructions to Joliot. "Keep rubbing it in about Desser," he said. "Say that he's an international trader, a cannon-merchant, and a plutocrat. Of course, he wants the war to go on to a victorious end. You can defame him as much as you like. Tessa has promised me that the censorship won't interfere."

Montigny also ordered Joliot to begin the campaign against Desser.

The little editor protested. "The political trend can be changed," he said. "That's quite in order. But Desser saved me when I was on my beam ends. You know what it means to betray an old friend? And besides, Desser's an honest man. Of course, he's not a Marseillais, but he's fond of Marseille. I've heard about how he talked to the fishermen down there. He's a real Frenchman. And I've got to write that he's an Austrian Jew and bought by the Americans."

In the past Desser had occupied too high a position. No sooner did he begin to totter than everybody jumped to the conclusion that he was falling. They kept saying: "He's broke," although he still owned factories and stocks. Nobody took the trouble to inquire how his affairs were going. The engineers of the Seine works said: "He'll have a job to scrape along till the annual meeting." Even the old gardener doubted his master's solvency and asked for his wages in advance.

More and more Desser took to drink. He held aloof from people and said nothing to Jeannette about his attacks of angina pectoris. When he met his friends he said jokingly: "Allow me to introduce myself — an Austrian-Jewish plutocrat whose gardener demands his wages in advance." People he spoke to turned away; it was dreadful to look at him. Disease and anxiety had blurred his face until it had become flabby and shapeless.

Jeannette felt an acute and almost unbearable pity for him. It was a feeling which humiliated them both, and more than once she tried to force herself to get angry and said hard things to him in the hope that he would have the spirit to lose his temper. But

Desser only hunched himself up and gazed at her with the gentle, dim eyes of an old dog. Then she would throw her arms around him and murmur tender things to him. He would whisper: "Jeannette!" like the words of an incantation, as though Jeannette could save him. He knew that she was the only thing that attached him to life. He feared death more than ever — not the pain, but the emptiness. There would be nothing, neither good nor bad, and the very idea of it was enough to make you want to howl. He often told himself that he was ruining Jeannette. He made up his mind to break with her, and kept his resolution for a few weeks. Then he suddenly rang her up late at night and came running round to her with a distracted look. "May I?" he asked. She stroked his stiff grey hair, and tears welled up in her large frightened eyes and trickled down her cheeks.

On the 1st of May Desser ran into Meuger in the Carlton bar.

"They told me you weren't feeling well," Meuger said.

"Oh, no, I'm feeling quite all right."

"Health is the main thing, especially at our age. Do you know what today is? It's the 1st of May. And nobody's thinking about it. You remember how anxious we were last year? We expected strikes and demonstrations. Now it's an ordinary day of the week. There's never an evil without some good. Don't you agree with me?" Meuger had got so used to calling Desser a "Red" that he himself began to believe in the myth he had created. But Desser said indifferently: "It's all very quiet. I think it's a bit too quiet myself."

A young flower-girl stopped him in the street. "Buy some lilies of the valley," she said. "Twenty sous. They'll bring you luck."

She had teeth like a rodent's and a hunted look in her eyes. Desser took the bunch of half-opened flowers. Would they bring him luck? No, not they! He recalled Meuger's smile, the flower-girl's eyes, Jeannette. There was no escape. They would all be killed. Who? Jeannette, himself, everybody. . . . He went into the nearest bar and eagerly gulped down a glass of cognac. The radio was blaring:

> Down by the brook there is happiness,
> But swift is the current that bears it away.

A week later Desser met Jeannette. She walked past without noticing him. She was smiling as she walked. He realized that she was livening up without him. It was time to end it!

He had often tried to persuade her to change her lodgings, but she refused. She was still living in the same little old hotel off the rue Bonaparte. He well knew the stout, powdered landlady and the dark, winding stairs he had so often climbed, panting and doubting on every step. The passages smelt of the lavatory, cheap scent and cooking. Jeannette's room was long and narrow. A tarnished bronze Daphnis had been kissing a bronze Chloe on the mantelshelf for half a century. Who had lived there before? An artist who dreamed of glory? A book-keeper in love with a beauty from the Folies Bergère? An ugly fellow with plastered hair and gaudy ties? Or a German refugee without a permit? In that stuffy, poky room loneliness seemed to increase and weigh heavily on the soul.

Desser said quietly to Jeannette: " We mustn't meet any more." He had come armed with those very words; he was afraid she'd ask: " Why? " or look at him, and then he'd be unable to stand it. But Jeannette turned away and said: " Yes." She thought to herself: " There's nothing left, not even deception." So much the better! And Desser was surprised at his own calm: this was death and it wasn't so terrible.

It was a warm May night. The stars were shining above the darkened city. There was a murmur in the leaves of the chestnut trees. The chimes of the neighbouring church clock accurately struck the quarters of the hour.

" A night for lovers." Desser smiled. He was standing at the window.

" There aren't any lovers," she said. " There are stars, trees, poems. You and I have grown old, Desser! "

" You haven't begun to live. I've stood in your way. I won't do it any longer. I'm not going to stand in your way — and I'm not going to live. . . ."

The last words escaped his lips against his will. He was angry with himself: she would pity him. She'd think he was entreating her. He had always known that love couldn't be bought with money, and she wasn't to be bought even with tears. Without noticing his emotion, Jeannette said: " I don't want to live. I did once upon a time, but it didn't come off. And how about you? "

" I'm afraid of death. That is, I can't understand what it is to die."

He was turning to go when the anti-aircraft guns began to roar. It was as though a pack of hounds had broken loose and were barking and barking. The searchlights were stretched up into the soft velvety sky. And the sirens raised their mad voices with something alive and ferocious in their wailing.

" What's that? " Jeannette asked.

" It's very likely the beginning. It's spring. I told you it was a night for lovers. They thought the Germans would sit and wait. Meuger was delighted when he said to me: ' How quiet it is! ' Miserable creatures! No, they're worse than that. They're traitors. Anyhow, what does it matter? . . . Jeannette, do you mean to say you really aren't afraid of death at all? "

She said firmly, almost dryly: " No, I'm not."

And the guns still went on roaring.

The air-raid warning came to an end at last. Desser sat in the armchair by the window; he had asked if he could stay till morning. The birds began to chirp their simple little sounds. There were slanting sunbeams and long shadows, and the air was cool. Trucks went by with vegetables for the market. Then a milkwoman passed. Desser felt as though nothing had happened — no air-raid warning in the night, no mutual explanations. He looked at Jeannette. She was asleep. Her face was peaceful and indifferent. He thought: " She looks quite ordinary when her eyes are closed." She seemed to have guessed his thoughts in her sleep. She woke up and looked towards him. He turned away.

" Good morning, Desser! " she said cheerfully.

Perhaps she, too, had forgotten everything. The sound of schoolchildren's laughter came from the street.

" If the Behemoth calls me out, there'll be a row," said one.

" I've got a problem about a reservoir," said another. " We went to the movie to see *The Kiss of Death.* . . ."

Then, from the radio came the twangy voice of the announcer: " At the third stroke it will be exactly one minute after seven o'clock. We will now give the morning news. Last night German troops entered Holland and Belgium. . . ."

Jeannette gave a cry and ran to the window. A woman in the street was standing still and listening to the news: " Parachute troops were dropped on Dutch territory. . . ." The woman dropped the basket she was holding and pale, rosy strawberries rolled all over the pavement.

Desser turned to Jeannette. " I told you it was the beginning," he said.

The news-stand in the street was surrounded by a crowd of

people — workers, shopkeepers, and women — all discussing the news.

"The same as in 1914. . . . They may come here. . . ."

"They'll get stuck there. Let's suppose they even take Holland, but what will happen after that? This is all to our advantage."

"They said in the papers the Dutch would flood everything. . . ."

"What they write in the papers is nothing! They get paid for it. But the Germans may land in parachutes right on the Champs-de-Mars. . . ."

Desser closed the window with a bang. "How many of these people have been deceived!" He sat down in the armchair. His breathing was heavy and his arms and shoulders ached. "Jeannette, look at me. I'm afraid of your eyes. . . . Pay attention! Pay attention carefully! I, too, have been deceiving. Perhaps more than the others. I wanted to preserve — What did I want to preserve? Tessa? This is the punishment! I don't know what will happen to us. Hitler will come. Then it will be the end of France. Pierre was right. He said to me: 'Chuck it!' I'm dead. But they killed Pierre instead of me. If only they don't kill you, Jeannette! Well, good-bye. You see what our parting has coincided with? It's quite as effective as at the theatre, but in reality it's quite simple. . . . And terrible."

He spoke dryly, haltingly. Then he put on his hat and, bending suddenly as he stood in the doorway, he kissed Jeannette's hand. The strength of his sentiment, his illness and despair were all conveyed in that kiss, the bent back, and the trembling of his hand.

"Jeannette, I'll get a passport and a visa for you. Go right away! Go to America."

She shook her head. No, she was tired. And now she experienced a wave of pity almost beyond endurance. She was sorry for everybody — the Dutch, the people who were still clamouring outside in the street, and Desser. She felt sorry for Desser most of all. People thought he could do everything, but he was even more unfortunate than herself. He was a slave, a puppet, a shadow. And for the first time she addressed him as *tu*.

"Don't wear yourself out with worry. It will all come to an end. My dear, dear Desser, good-bye!"

CHAPTER 16

MAJOR LEROY went green in the face. His jaw trembled as though he were talking to himself.

"I don't understand," said General Leridot. "What have bridges got to do with it? "

"General Moquet said so — I've been in communication on the telephone."

"General Moquet ought to be court-martialled for such conversation. The enemy is sixty miles from the bridges. I'm convinced it's only a feint, in view of the fact that our main forces have penetrated into Belgium from the direction of Cateau-Vervins. But let's suppose even the very worst happens — a blow directed against us. It will take the Germans a month to reach the Maas; and that's allowing for a good rate of advance. But what about our counter-attacks? The 7th Army has got as far as Antwerp. What do you think that is: defence or attack? When the general operations are in the nature of an offensive, only ignoramuses can talk of blowing up bridges. You understand me, major? And stop muttering under your breath."

"But I — "

"You? It's quite obvious that you sat through the whole of the last war in Paris. The first rule is calm. The war has entered an acute phase. That's to be expected. But we've got to go on working as before. That's the secret of victory. And now be so good as to tell me the contents of today's newspapers."

Leroy tried to keep himself in hand. "In *Le Figaro*," he began, "the military expert considers it will be possible to hold the enemy on the line Namur-Antwerp." His jaw began to tremble again. "*Mon général*," he said, "the Germans are forty miles away, not sixty. They've occupied Marche."

"Anyone would think you were a deputy instead of an officer. In the first place, this report is not confirmed. In the second place, even if enemy patrols have reached Marche, it proves absolutely nothing. You may go. And send the colonel."

Leridot unfolded a large map. Moreau came in, impassive as

ever. "It's a wonderful day," he said. "I've just come back from having a look at the tanks. It's a very lovely spot all around here — woods and little hills."

Leridot was deep in thought. "The locality is strongly intersected," he said. "Therefore it would be foolish to get into a panic. Look here — I've marked the line of the front with a blue pencil. Does this coincide with your information? "

The colonel looked like a giant beside the dwarfish Leridot. He regarded the general complacently and with a tinge of condescension. "This isn't the front," he said. "You've marked off Marche-Libramont. But that was in the morning, and it's now four o'clock in the afternoon."

"You mean to say they're continuing to advance? "

"They're simply driving forward."

For a moment Leridot was embarrassed and closed his eyes. His cheeks were purple and fleshy. Quickly he regained his composure. "So much the worse for them," he said. "The bulge is being extended, but our troops are on both sides of it. It remains for us to find out their weak spot. I must have a talk with General Picard. It's a good thing you are with me. Our major has lost his head. And so has Moquet. There is nothing menacing in the situation. What's your opinion, colonel? "

"General Picard is hardly likely to want to put the reserves on the map. You know his attitude to this war? "

"Yes, but the situation has altered. They're advancing now. We're obliged to act."

"I'm afraid there's nothing we can do. They've thrown in no less than seven hundred tanks. And the defence is weak. There are no shells for the 47-mm. guns."

"That's a detail. They can use the field guns. I see you've become a victim of the general psychosis. Remember August 1914. It was worse then. I shall never forget the flight from Charleroi to Meaux. The gunners abandoned the guns and jumped on the horses. But a couple of weeks later we drove the Germans back to the Aisne. Von Kluck had failed to cover his right flank and had to pay for it. But now they're advancing in a narrow column. It's sheer madness! Their communications are exposed wide open to our attacks."

He went on talking for hours about the laws of strategy, the fickleness of military fortune and the qualities of the French infantry. The colonel stood at the window and gazed at the sloping

hills with their chessboard pattern of fields. His face wore a perplexed smile. Then he went off to inspect the positions of the anti-
aircraft guns. Leridot was left alone. He wiped his brow with his
handkerchief and began to think. Moreau was a cool-headed man.
If he was getting panicky, it was a bad sign. One had to admit that
the enemy was advancing with unheard-of speed. Either the Germans were mad or they were devilishly strong. Instead of military
operations according to plan, there was some sort of chaos. Who
could make it all out? It was much quieter on the Maginot Line.
No surprises like this were likely to happen there. Was this what
they called modern warfare? It was nothing but a vulgar brawl!

The regrouping had taken place in April. At that time the Sedan
sector was in the peaceful rear. The troops were delighted — they
smoked contraband Belgian tobacco. But Leridot was bored. He
was convinced that the Germans would not go into Belgium. " What
do they want to repeat Wilhelm's mistakes for? " he asked. He followed closely the operations in Norway and abused the British:
" A nation of shopkeepers, but they're not soldiers! " In the evenings
he played chess with the colonel or wrote long letters to Sophie:

My darling songster:
     It's three days since I had a letter from you. I'm dread-
fully worried. Sanger says there is an epidemic of gastric illnesses
in Paris. My dear child, don't eat raw fruit or salads. I'm hale and
hearty, although the last few days have been very exhausting. You
probably know from the papers that the enemy has started operations on a large scale. He cannot fail to exhaust himself very soon.
The weather is quite good and I go for a walk for a couple of hours
every day. Yesterday we had a visit from Major de Graves, who is
General Picard's adjutant. He is a young man with musical talents.
He played Grieg to us. I congratulated him, but I thought to myself
that he was far below the standard of my darling Sophie. How I
long for you, my treasure! I dream of the day when I shall see your
little hands that fly like seagulls over the piano keys. Stendhal was
right when he said that real love . . .

Leridot was startled by the roar of an explosion. He made a blot
on the paper and snorted with anger. Moreau came into the room
without knocking.
    "We'll have to go down below," he said.

It was cool in the cellar. The dusty bottles on the shelves gleamed mysteriously. There was a smell of wine. The officers yawned and stretched themselves. Moreau sat on a barrel and smiled. The general was sulky because he hadn't been allowed to finish his letter, so they brought him a stool.

"They're aiming here," said Major Leroy.

Moreau nodded. "They've got an excellent intelligence service. We no sooner get settled in a place than they immediately send us their congratulations as a house-warming. We'll have to move somewhere else in the morning. And I sleep so badly in a new place."

"There's nothing to be done," said the general. "This is war, not manœuvres. But I must say people have become savages. In the last war nobody touched the army staffs. One must have some mutual respect. But now they try to get us as though we were a battery. We've gone a long way from the spirit of chivalry! They stoop to anything. You remember *Pompée*, colonel? It's one of Corneille's masterpieces — especially the scene in which Cornelia learns of the conspiracy while she is bewailing Pompey. She says to Cæsar: 'You are an enemy. You cast a shadow over my country. And now the slaves have conspired to smite you down. But I will not accept the help of slaves.' There's character for you! What noble lines!"

He went on declaiming Cornelia's speech without paying any attention to the explosions. Then he got tired and gave it up. He could scarcely keep from yawning. The major wanted to light a cigarette. His hand shook as he raised it to his lips. But Sanger began to whistle: "*Tout va bien, Madame la Marquise.*"

"Shut up!" shouted the major.

"I'm sorry. It's these surroundings — the bottles, the barrels, and the poetry. I almost thought I was in a Montmartre cabaret."

When the bombardment was over, Leridot wanted to finish writing his letter. But he was interrupted again. Moreau came into the room.

"The performance continues," he said. "The German tanks are at Palizel."

Leridot glanced at the map and began to pace up and down the room. He was anxious, but he did not want to let Moreau see that he had made a mistake.

"I told you, colonel, that it was nothing but madness," he said. "They're not even trying to widen the bulge." He was silent for a while. Then he went on: "In any case I consider it necessary to blow up the bridges between Monthermé and Nouzon. Are you in touch with Moquet?"

"Contact was all right this morning. But I think they've left Nouzon."

"Then you'd better send Captain Sanger. At the same time arrange to have the bridges demolished from the air if the sappers are too late."

At last he finished writing his letter: "The situation has become rather complicated. But I still hope to see you again in May. With so much waste of men and gas they'll soon be obliged to come to a stop. Take care of yourself."

Sanger poured some brandy into a coffee cup, gulped it down, and took leave of Leridot. "Not exactly a pleasant excursion," he said.

An hour later the major heard that Sanger and the driver had been shot dead soon after leaving the house. Peasants came running up shouting: "It's the Germans!"

Leridot exclaimed: "Nonsense! I'll go at once and see for myself."

Who killed Sanger remained a mystery. When Leridot saw the bodies in the car, he saluted. He was quite calm.

"Do you order me to go?" Colonel Moreau asked.

"No."

They all stood waiting to see who Leridot would send. But he climbed back into the car and said: "Nobody's going. After all, General Moquet isn't a child. He knows himself what to do. They'll demolish the bridges from the air. Get in, colonel."

"Are we going back?"

"No. We're going to Rettel. We haven't the right to risk our lives. That's as simple as A B C." He recalled the dead captain's gaping mouth and licked his lips. "We've got an abominable rear, I can tell you that!"

They drove slowly, as the roads were blocked with tanks, trucks, and horses, all coming towards them. Leridot was somewhat pacified.

"At last," he said, "they've realized it's impossible to liquidate the break-through without reinforcements."

As they approached Charleville they were stopped by some soldiers who shouted something. When they caught sight of the general they held their tongues.

"What's happened?" Leridot asked.

Somebody at the back said: "The Germans."

Then all of them began yelling together: "Parachute landing. . . . They've killed the station-master! . . . Parachutists! . . . They shot two officers. . . ."

Leridot leaned forward. "Be quiet," he snapped. "Where are you going?"

The soldiers were silent.

"It's obvious," said Moreau with a smile. "Deserters."

Whereupon from the background came a cry like a yelp: "Hey! Are you running away, general?"

Leridot did not lose his self-control. "Be silent!" he ordered. He glanced at the man who had insulted him and saw that he was a wounded soldier. The ground all around him was covered with blood. Leridot gave orders immediately. "Meuger," he said to the driver, "we'll take him to the ambulance station."

They put the wounded man next to the driver. He did not speak and his eyes were closed.

In vain Meuger sounded the horn. Refugees were flocking in crowds along the road. Many of them were driving their cattle, and the car had to thread its way among them. Peasants' carts were rumbling along in double rows.

Leridot began to lose patience. "We'll never get through like this! It's panic. That's what it is!"

Meuger stopped the car and listened. The general looked out of the window. There were bombers overhead. The refugees and soldiers scattered and ran into the fields and woods. It was impossible to drive any farther. The road was completely blocked with carts and cattle. The general's car pulled in to the side. The colonel lay down on the ground and Meuger followed his example. Leridot thought this was too degrading; he stood, small but majestic, and looked up at the sky. There were nine aeroplanes overhead.

"They're flying in good formation," he said.

One of the bombs fell in a little wood near by. When they got back into the car, the general saw a girl of six or seven on a stretcher; a bomb splinter had torn off her legs. Leridot blew his nose and said softly to the colonel: "How terrible!"

Then he turned to the wounded soldier. "Well, and how goes it with our hero?" The soldier said nothing. Shortly afterwards Meuger said: "Will you permit me to chuck him out? He keeps leaning on me. He gets in my way."

"But you're mad! How can we throw out a wounded man?"

"He's dead. He's cold."

The soldier's body swayed to and fro, and from behind, it looked as though he was dozing. They stopped outside a railway station — Meuger wanted to fill up the radiator with water. Shells were lying about on the platform. Leridot got out of the car and looked at them. "Shells for 47's," he said. "And you told me there weren't any. Why are they here? Unheard-of muddle!"

They went all over the station, but didn't see a soul. In the telegraph office a barefooted private was sitting on the floor chewing something. Catching sight of the general, he looked scared and began putting on his boots.

"What's your regiment?" Leridot asked.

"The 173rd. I've blistered my foot and fallen out."

"Where's your rifle?"

The private did not answer.

"Where's the station-master?"

"They've all run away. They say the Germans are close by. They're on motorcycles. It's terrible!"

He snivelled like a child. Leridot frowned disdainfully.

They filled up with water and drove on. The general did not say a word. Only when they were about to enter Rettel, he suddenly said to Moreau: "The war is lost! I don't know what the deputies are thinking of. They're a pack of adventurers and ignoramuses, with Reynaud at the head of them. But we can now wash our hands of it all. We've done all we could. As the Romans used to say: 'Let others do better.'"

CHAPTER 17

THE VILLAGE where the battalion was stationed was remote from the restless world. The peasants used juniper for fuel and smoked hams in the chimney. The fat cows gazed like ancient goddesses at the army trucks. Alfalfa and clover flourished in the fields and purple crocuses bloomed at the foot of the trees.

When the newspapers arrived, the soldiers turned eagerly to the back page. They were not interested in the amount of tonnage sunk by the Germans or in the battle for Trondheim. They read every line about what was happening in Paris and devoured the advertisements. Somewhere far away they had left behind the theatres, cafés, and women, so many gay, smartly dressed women.

André did not worry about Paris. The son of a Norman peasant, he somehow felt at home in the slow, dragging life of the country. Even his memories of the past were only vague, spectral images: Jeannette's smile, or canvases he had failed to paint — ash-coloured houses or the dove-coloured Seine.

The troops settled down and got on well with the peasants. Givert wrote poems to a green-eyed wench, whom he compared to a Gorgon. Laurier got hold of a flute and played at weddings. Nivelle, as a knowledgeable man, proved to the owner of the village café that Crucifix vermouth was more profitable than Cinzano. Yves said: "The land here is good." He gaped with surprise to find that the land was good everywhere. André was a general favourite. With the same awkward smile he gave Yves his last pinch of tobacco and did a drawing of Givert "for his bride."

The company commander, Lieutenant Fressinet, was a photographer in peace-time, who used to take pictures of young married couples, new-born babies, and local celebrities. He was easy-going, though inclined to grumble and exceedingly sensitive. He was fond of telling the men about Verdun. "The men were different then," he said. "They were more stupid, but they were more decent." The soldiers smiled politely. They did not believe in heroism, nor did they want glory. They did not connect their fate with the war, which they did not understand and did not feel was their own. And Fressinet thought at night: "Is this an army? They'll smash us to pulp. But Daladier doesn't see anything."

The wheat was beginning to swell. The young calves became more reflective and their eyes revealed an early melancholy. The hot days were beginning. In the café the soldiers ordered beer instead of grog. They played the phonograph to their heart's content. There were only a few records, and the nasal tenor kept moaning: "No, no, no, it will never end, you know. . . ." Every soldier joined in the chorus. Yves thought of his little white house in Brittany, while André gazed up at the starry skies and remembered Herschel's nebulæ.

And now war had come all of a sudden and caught everybody unawares, the Staff as well as the men. In the autumn of 1938 the soldiers had been better prepared for battle and death. But now the long months of stagnation had taken the guts out of them. And when Laurier came running up and shouted: " It's started! " nobody believed him. Yves swore and shuffled the cards. Nivelle said: " Baloney! The devil knows what sort of hand you've dealt me this time! "

Four days went by and everything remained as before. The radio announced that French troops had reached the borders of Holland, Roosevelt was indignant at the German aggression, and the King of the Belgians — they called him " Le Roi Chevalier " — had sent his congratulations to the brave defenders of Liége. But on the fifth day from dawn onwards cars and motorcycles began rushing to and fro. The gentle quiet of the green morning was broken by the sound of distant gunfire. Fressinet said gloomily: " There's Holland for you! "

At midday German bombers flew over and bombed the church and a number of houses. A woman was killed. Refugees began to stream down the narrow cross-country road, shouting excitedly: " The Germans are killing people! " The villagers had not been scared by the bombing, but when they saw the refugees they flew into a panic. The women cried and began loading their belongings onto the creaking carts, while the men killed the pigs and drove the cattle. A peasant set fire to his house, and the soldiers were scarcely able to cope with the flames. In vain Fressinet tried to calm the people. " Where are you going? " he asked. " You'll get killed on the road." Nobody paid any attention to him. They all looked at him with dim, bewildered eyes. By evening nobody was left in the village. André entered a house; the stove was still warm and a pot containing a stew stood on the hob.

Interspersed with the refugees were soldiers who had thrown away their rifles. People said the Germans were only five miles away.

" The tanks are coming! " was the general cry.

" Why aren't our men firing? "

" They are firing, only our shells are no good. The German tanks are as big as mountains! "

Nivelle turned to his comrades. "Shall we go too?" he asked.

Yves spat angrily. "Go if you want to," he said.

Nivelle boiled with rage. "Do you take me for a coward?" he snapped. "If you're staying, I'm staying too."

André looked at Yves with surprise. Who would have thought it? This was the man who could only say: "The land here is good." André then realized how close was his own attachment to the land and the deserted village. Only an hour ago he had looked on the war as something alien to himself, little flags on the map and Tessa's policy. But now he was in the very thick of war. He had no desire to think and argue. He lay on the brow of the bare hill and waited. Was he to give up these fields, the poplar-lined road, and the little house nestling under the hill? Never! All his thoughts were brushed aside, leaving only the obscure, burning sentiment: "I won't go away!" And next to him lay Givert, a frail lad with chronic laryngitis, who wrote verse about a Gorgon, and he was saying the same as Yves: "We mustn't quit. . . ." And jaunty Laurier was trying to joke: "Keep your mouth shut, Yves! The tanks will get a fright. They'll think it's a trap!" But Yves went on standing there with his enormous mouth wide open.

Lieutenant Fressinet said gloomily: "It was worse at Douaumont. But the men were different."

"Are you referring to us?" André asked him.

"No, but Paris. . . ." Fressinet waved his hand.

Night came on. It was the same as usual in other villages: the dogs barked, the old folk snored in the alcoves, babies cried. But in this village there were no dogs, no children, no old folk. The village had died out. The soldiers lay silently on the dry ground. The night was short. Dawn came about four o'clock, and the sun's first rays had hardly begun to shine before the aeroplanes appeared. The battalion lost 109 men.

Again soldiers were running down below. "No shells!" they shouted. "They haven't brought any up since Thursday. They say there's no gas. . . . What have they been thinking about? . . . They've sold us for a couple of sous!"

Nivelle felt he wanted to quit, but he didn't want to go alone, and the others would only wave their hands and say: "Go if you want to!" To quiet himself he started reckoning up: the losses were big, almost two thirds of their strength. That meant out of 166, let's say, 67. . . And one killed to every three wounded.

That meant 17 killed out of every hundred. It was possible to remain alive. . . .

The German tanks rumbled on past the brickworks to the railway
station. They had gone round the hill. Now the sound of firing came
from all sides. Why had they remained intact on that hill? There
were Germans to the right of them, Germans in front of them, and
Germans in the rear. On the left? Who the hell knew what was on
the left? They ought to be our own men, the third battalion. But
even on the left they were running away. . . . What about quit-
ting? No! This hill was now more precious than anything. It was
not something alien, a "position," as the newspapers would say.
It was all that remained of life. André felt as though he had been
born where he lay beside the machine-gun. And all the others felt
the same. Givert was muttering something under his breath; not
poetry, but curses. He was boiling over.

Once more the bombers came over. This time they killed Nivelle.
The cheerful waiter was no more! Now nobody would talk about
bitter-sweet apéritifs. Nobody would say: "How many stars do you
think there are? I read somewhere that there were 18,000 to which
they had given names. Multiply that by a hundred. . . ."

Another night came down with its named and nameless stars.
The men gnawed dry rusks. Weary and exhausted, they waited for
the dawn, for battle and death as a relief.

At half past four Fressinet called out: "Machine-guns into
action!"

Laurier noticed that the light silvery haze at the back of the road
shuddered and began to stir.

"Machine-gun number one, field 97!"

"Fire!"

The Germans had not expected any opposition. They thought the
French had run away long ago. André felt an extraordinary ex-
hilaration. It rushed like wine to his head. Beside him Yves shouted
out: "They're bolting back!"

The Germans took cover in a hollow beside the road. Twenty
minutes later they opened artillery fire at the crest of the hill.
The first shells flew wide.

"Right into the village! The Boches are firing at their own men."

Then the shells began to fall on the hill. Clouds of earth flew
up. In the intervals between the explosions the men shouted. They
uttered desperate cries that sounded unreal. The sun glared in their

eyes; their only thought was not to quit; they would clutch and grow into this shuddering, flying soil and blow up with it, but they would never yield.

And then came silence. There seemed to be nobody left. André looked and saw with surprise that Givert was blinking his eyelids. So he must be alive. Laurier was laughing. And Laurier was alive. A silly bird was crying in the grass. Fressinet was smoking. But where was Yves? Probably killed. All these thoughts passed rapidly through André's mind and he felt neither pity nor fear. " I shall be killed myself presently," he thought. What did it matter? The one thing was not to let the Germans get near. Never had André loved anyone so passionately as he now loved that machine-gun.

" Six hundred and fifty! "

Aeroplanes again. The bombs were dropping from above like stones.

André felt a sharp pain just above his knee. He wanted to look and see what had happened. He rubbed his eyes a long time; he was falling asleep. When he opened them he saw Laurier's face. It was covered with blood. Never mind! Don't let them come near!

They dragged him aside. " Givert, take Corneau's place! "

André lay with his face thrust into the prickly grass. Again the Germans went into attack.

Lying half-unconscious, André heard the rattle of the machine-gun. Its detailed circumstantial story soothed him. Suddenly the machine-gun stopped. " The drum's come off! " Givert shouted.

André gathered all his strength and crawled towards the gun. He wanted to speak, to explain, but his tongue refused to obey. He raised his hand and struck the drum a sweeping blow with his palm. " There! " he gasped. Again his head fell to the ground.

When he woke up it was night. There was straw all around him. At first he thought he had fallen asleep in a field. He was asking his father: " Why are they reaping so early? " Then he remembered — he was wounded. Laurier was lying next to him. He couldn't see his face, but it was Laurier's voice: " It is you? "

" Yes, it's me."

André frowned with pain. There was so much he wanted to say.

" Laurier, can you hear me? The machine-gun saved us. But you remember what a snotty nose Tessa had? He's been buying land. I'm afraid they've killed Yves. 'The land here is good.' It's really funny! No, no, no, it'll never end, you know."

"Never!" Laurier said softly.

When André next opened his eyes he was lying on a bed. Somebody came and stood beside him. Slowly André turned his head.

"Yves! I thought they'd killed you!"

"Me?" said Yves indignantly. "To hell with that! But you mustn't talk. The nurse said so. She didn't want to let me in."

"Nonsense! Tell me, Yves, did they hold out?"

"They did. Our tanks captured the village again. Four tanks. At seven o'clock. Then a dispatch rider came from H.Q. He brought the order to withdraw."

"What do you mean?"

"It was General Picard's order. Fressinet read it and then whipped out his revolver and, bang! right through his brains! Word of honour! He was a good chap, only a bit nervous. I'll light a candle for him. And for Nivelle too. I'm sorry they gave up the hill."

André was sorry too. He thought of the road with its lines of poplars, the little house nestling under the hill and the prickly grass. "The land here is good. . . ." The land . . . Jeannette. . . .

"Yves, don't go away. You mustn't. You hear me? You mustn't."

CHAPTER 18

THE PAPERS said the Germans were marking time. But soldiers of the defeated 9th Army began to arrive in the eastern suburbs of Paris. Montigny sent his family to Biarritz. The luxurious cars, the Cadillacs, Hispano-Suizas, and Buicks, streamed out of the city. Trenches were being dug in the Bois de Boulogne. People were talking about mysterious parachutists and the fifth column. Breteuil declared the fifth column was made up of foreigners and refugees. On his orders the police arrested several thousands of German Jews, workers who had escaped from Fascist Italy, and Spanish Republicans. Rifles were dealt out to the police and they stood at the street crossings directing the traffic. The life of the great city went on as before. The cafés were crowded, the ships did a brisk trade; autographs of Marie Antoinette and Directoire furniture were put up for auction. The fashion workrooms were already getting ready for the winter season. The Bourse was particularly animated. In spite of everything, prices had risen a few points. The buses disappeared; they had been requisitioned for the troops. This had a soothing effect on the Parisians. They recalled the days before the Battle of the Marne, when General Gallieni requisitioned the taxis and smashed the Germans.

On the morning of the 16th of May, Tessa's secretary informed him that the German tanks had reached Laon. He added significantly: " They've covered 85 miles in five days. And the distance from Laon to Paris is 80."

Tessa was furious. " How dare you spread such panicky rumours! " he shouted. " I shall have to take stern measures! "

When the secretary went out, Tessa rang up Reynaud. " Listen, apropos of the Germans, I hope this is all nonsense? "

" They're in the neighbourhood of Laon."

" In other words, you think they're making for Paris? "

" There can be no doubt about it."

" In that case, they'll be here in four days at the latest. They're covering nearly twenty miles a day. I've reckoned it out."

" Gamelin says they may be in the suburbs of Paris this evening. I've given orders to burn the archives. We must be ready to leave. I'll call you back in an hour."

Tessa called his secretary. " I was a little sharp just now," he said. " But you realize yourself that the news is enough to make anybody lose his head. Speaking for myself, I'm perfectly calm. But emergency measures have got to be taken. In the first place, destroy the archives. Secondly, make a list of the employees who are to be evacuated. And tell the chauffeur to look over the car. Don't let him go away even for a moment. I may be leaving after lunch."

He remembered Paulette. It was impossible to take her with him. The crowd was worked up. And everybody knew Paulette. There might be incidents. The Socialists would make capital out of the scandal. But how could he explain it to her? She was not of this world. She would only start to weep. It was far simpler to tell her on the phone.

" My child, you must go away at once. . . . I can't tell you. . . . The news is terrible. . . . They'll be here this evening. There's no doubt about it. But the public doesn't know yet and, whatever you

do, don't breathe a word. Why create a panic? Go to the Gare de
Lyon and take the first train. . . . Me? . . . I can't. I must stay at
my post right to the very end. We're not asked. We're obliged to
be heroes. . . . Good-bye, my little kitten! "

Tessa put down the receiver and suddenly dropped his head on
the table and began to cry. What an appalling misfortune! To think
that only a week ago everything was so nice and quiet! They had
been discussing the operations in Norway. He had been thinking of
taking Paulette with him to Pré-des-Daims. Eighty-five miles in five
days! It was monstrous! Obviously the troops had simply run away!
Perhaps they were not even to blame. Who wanted to die for nothing? Poor France!

He shuddered and glanced hurriedly at the clock. Why didn't
Reynaud ring up? They'd all run away and forget all about him.

He rang again for his secretary. " Tell Bernard to get the car
ready, and put in some extra cans of gas. One can't tell what it's
going to be like on the roads."

The secretary nodded. " Excuse me," he said. " Monsieur Desser
wishes to see you on an urgent matter."

" Desser? . . . What an odd man he is! What business can there
be now? Very well, show him in."

They shook hands in silence and tried not to look at each other.
Tessa's eyes were red. Desser looked like an old man; the dim pupils
of his eyes were scarcely visible under his shaggy grey brows. He
smoothed out his gloves and took out his cigar-case, but did not
light up. He kept moving the paper-weight backwards and forwards. Tessa found the silence unbearable.

" What have you got to say, Jules? " he asked.

Desser stared straight in front of him. He didn't know himself
why he had come to see Tessa. He had been rushing everywhere
like a maniac. He had been to the Army staffs and the ministries.
He had called on Reynaud, Mandel, and General Georges, trying
to persuade, threatening and proving. Politely they had shown him
out.

At last he began to speak. " The Germans may occupy Paris tomorrow," he said. " The remaining minutes are numbered. Clear
out! Or say you're going to make a stand, but say it honestly and
in earnest. There are spies everywhere. You must arrest them and
shoot them. Not the workers, but Laval, Grandel, Breteuil, Picard."

" Do you realize what you're saying? Of course we're old friends, but I occupy a responsible post. I'm a Minister and you're suggesting I should carry out a State revolution."

" I'm suggesting you should go away. Or fight. Paris can be defended, street by street."

" Thank you very much! So that messieurs the workers may set up the Commune? No, I prefer to retain my honour."

" But France . . ."

" France recovered after 1871, and she'll recover now."

" In those days Belfort held out, and they fought on the Loire. Gambetta raised a militia, Paris sustained a siege, and there were partisans. But now the Germans have only to show themselves and everybody runs away."

" What do you propose? "

" To resist. If it's impossible to hold Paris, make a stand on the Loire. If they break through there, go to Algiers. I'm ready to sacrifice everything, not only money but my life as well. And there are plenty like me. You've got to realize that nobody believes you ministers any longer."

Tessa took umbrage. " We don't need your confidence," he said. " We have the support of the Chamber, and that means of the country. Tomorrow you'll be saying we ought to go to Madagascar."

Desser realized how far he had gone; he had tried exhortation; now he changed his tone.

" Paul," he said, " think of yourself. If the Germans win, there won't be any parliament. They'll set up a *Gauleiter* — Breteuil or Laval. You're compromised enough as it is. What will you do? "

" I'll come through somehow. Anyway, Breteuil is better than the Commune. You're a bad adviser. I'm not superstitious, but thirteen is my lucky number. Amalie died on the 14th. But everyone has his own omens. I've noticed that you always bring bad luck. Just like the British. You supported Breteuil. The result was the Popular Front. You began to be friends with Villard, and Villard was overthrown. If you advise resistance it means we must capitulate."

Desser rose and made for the door. Tessa felt sorry for him. " Jules," he said, " why don't you go to America? You've got plenty of money. America is a paradise. I can't go there, because I'm tied. By the way, that's all on account of you. . . . Wait a minute, this isn't the time to quarrel. Listen to me now — go away somewhere."

Desser drew himself up. His eyes brightened and he smiled.

"Go away?" he said. "I knov' I'm a bad Frenchman. It wouldn't surprise me if the first man I met insulted me. But all the same, by God, I am a Frenchman!"

Tessa shrugged his shoulders and closed the door behind him. Immediately he dismissed the conversation from his mind. He made out a list of all the things he must take with him: a General Staff map, post-office forms, the latest edition of *La Revue des Deux Mondes*, a supply of liver extract, a bottle of old armagnac, a road guide. He was just on the point of setting out when Reynaud rang up.

"The situation in the Laon district has improved," said Reynaud. "The main attack is directed against the 1st Army — the Saint-Quentin-Péronne sector. Apparently they're trying to break through to the coast. I'm going to speak in the Chamber today."

Tessa beamed with pleasure. Smiling with self-satisfaction, he sent for his secretary. "I told you there was no need to get in a panic. Old as I am, I'm called upon to teach you courage, although courage is a virtue that belongs to youth."

He rang up Paulette, but it was too late; she had already left. Then he asked Joliot to come and see him. The tubby little editor flew round frantic with agitation. He blurted everything out at once: "There's a panic in the city. Montigny has fled. All I've got in the cash-box is a hundred francs. All the papers are leaving. But where can I go? Marseille? But I heard what Rome is saying. In my opinion, the Italians will attack us tomorrow."

"We'll arrange the money question," Tessa said. "I can't understand why you're so anxious. The situation has not been so stable for a long time. You think the Germans are coming to Paris? Nothing of the sort! They're going to London." Tessa smiled with satisfaction.

Joliot tried to object: "They must know quite well what's happening here. And who can know what their plans are?"

However, when Tessa said that he would hand over three hundred thousand francs from the secret funds, Joliot calmed down. Back in the editor's office he dictated the leading article: "The enemy's manœuvre is now apparent. The Germans want to seize Great Britain, which is the weak spot in the Allied front. We are assured that our friends across the Channel will not be taken unawares." When he got home, he shouted to his wife: "Marie, you can unpack the trunks. The Germans have turned off to London.

Tessa has given me three hundred thousand francs. I can imagine what's happening in England now! But they've given us a month, and that's something to be thankful for!"

After reading Joliot's article the Parisians sighed with relief. The press announced two measures which the Government had taken. Tomorrow there was to be a service in the cathedral of Notre Dame at which Reynaud would be present. The Minister of the Interior and the Minister of Justice had been requested to clear out the remnants of the Communist organizations in Paris. Eight workers who were found with copies of *L'Humanité* were sentenced to five years' imprisonment. The newspapers also reported that the German troops in Belgium were suffering heavy losses and that many units were refusing to go into battle. Business had been a brisk one on the Bourse.

Reynaud spoke in the Chamber about firmness and courage. When he finished his speech, Tessa congratulated him. "You were in good form today. It's a good thing the Government didn't go away in the morning. When you told me the Germans were going to London . . ."

Reynaud puckered up his brow in surprise. "To London?" he said. "I told you they wanted to break through to the coast. They're going to Amiens in order to encircle the Army. Understand?"

Tessa nodded his head, but did not believe it. Five minutes later he whispered to Breteuil: "Reynaud is anxious on account of his masters. What can you expect? He's just an English groom! But he's on his last legs now. If the Germans get as far as Amiens, Reynaud is finished. And the sooner that happens, the better it will be for France."

CHAPTER 19

IT was difficult to hear anything. The old cracked voice scarcely reached the general's ears. De Visset shouted: "I can't hear!" The roar drowned his words. Suddenly it became quiet, and Picard's voice sounded as though in the next room: "The enemy is pressing on Laon. This will put the capital in danger."

De Visset was furious. "Nonsense! They're making a feint at Laon. The blow is in the direction of Amiens. The situation here can be re-established if you send reinforcements. Send de Gaulle's tank brigade. . . . Do you hear me?"

The roar began again. A woman's tired, unhappy voice kept repeating: "Paris . . . Paris. . . ." At last de Visset was able to hear: "The tank brigade . . . will not . . . be sent."

It was insufferably hot in the room. The heated telephone receiver gave off an unpleasant smell. De Visset unfastened his collar and drank a glass of warm water. Streams of sweat poured down his unshaven face. His red eyes were almost falling out of their sockets. He had not slept for three nights.

The Chief of Staff came in. "General Gort has just communicated that they're going to attack at six o'clock in the morning."

"Have you contacted the 11th Division?"

"General Vignot has lost his head. He told me that the division was actually withdrawn from the line. Moreover, they had to beat off an attack on their left flank."

"Tanks?"

"Infantry. On motor trucks."

"Yes." The general went red and drank another glass of water. "What a muddle! But all the same, we've got to support the British. Although General Gort might have consulted me, before making a decision. Where is the staff of the 11th Division now?"

"At Granget."

"How far is it from here?"

"Ten and a half miles. I don't know if you'll get there. It's difficult to say for certain where the enemy is. It's like a Neapolitan ice: we, they, we, they."

The road was blocked. A tank had got stuck. Little boys were driving goats. Smashed cars were scattered along the road. The refugees, who were mostly Belgians, looked with horror at the ruined houses.

The general's car was stuck for half an hour; a tire had gone flat and there was no spare wheel. An old peasant woman came up to the general. Her dark-brown, wrinkled face looked like the soil. She was crying and wiping her eyes with her apron.

"Why are the soldiers going away?" she asked. "They're forsaking us."

De Visset replied: "Calm yourself! I'm an old man and an old soldier. I can't tell a lie. We're not going to leave here. And don't you leave."

Just before they reached Granget, the general told the chauffeur to stop. He leaned his head out of the window.

"Hey, Monsieur le Préfet, where are you going?"

The tall man in an elegant suit with a red rosette in his button-hole looked embarrassed. He got out of the car and dropped one of his gloves. Inside sat a young woman surrounded with trunks and cardboard boxes: the Prefect was running away and trying to get in front of the refugees.

"I . . ." he stammered.

"I'll tell you straight what you are!" shouted de Visset. "You're a coward!"

The Prefect picked up his glove from the ground. Trying to appear calm and even indifferent, he said: "I happen to be carrying out the instructions of the Minister of the Interior. As regards your insult, in view of your glorious past —"

He didn't finish — de Visset slapped his face. The woman in the car began to yell: "Gaston!" Then she turned to the general and shouted: "Butcher!"

De Visset immediately forgot all about the unpleasant incident and began weighing the chances of tomorrow's operations. It was easier for the Germans — they had a single Command. Why hadn't General Gort consulted him? The Belgians were also said to be acting independently. Sheer anarchy! But there was no choice. The British would draw off eight divisions at least. If only the air force didn't let us down!

He explained the plan of attack to General Vignot, who listened without saying a word. De Visset decided to shake him up a little: "Above all, don't pay any attention to Paris," he said. "They've messed their trousers. They thought war was simply a matter of debates — three speeches by Hitler and six by Daladier. Everything they've done has been sheer stupidity. The 'campaign' in Holland, for instance. . . . The Germans knew perfectly well that our weak spot was the 9th Army. As for Leridot, he's nothing but a wedding-breakfast general! But there's some sign of a change now. The Royal Air Force is doing excellent work. The prisoners confirm that the German losses are serious. Their tanks have got cut off from the infantry in the region of Arras. I hope they'll send us de Gaulle's brigade. Much depends on the result of tomorrow's operation. If we can get as far as . . ."

Vignot interrupted him. He was a handsome old man with a rosy, girlish face and a neat white moustache.

" I told General Ramillet that without reinforcements my division wasn't even capable of defence," he said. " We haven't seen our air force for three days. You say their tanks have got cut off. But what of that? Our guns can't penetrate their armour-plate. You know that as well as I do. Yesterday we lost 3,200 men. The men are demoralized. The officers don't carry out orders. When you see how quickly the Germans are advancing . . ."

De Visset banged his fist on the table. An ash-tray tumbled to the floor.

" We're not at a meeting! " he roared. " What sort of talk is this? They're advancing. . . . Of course they'll advance so long as they don't meet with any resistance. And you tell me the officers are not carrying out orders! It's obvious. Who's setting them the example? You are! I tell you about the plan of attack, and you snivel. I'll have you court-martialled. It's a disgrace. With a career like yours, and yet you behave like a little boy! "

De Visset explained once again the tasks of the 11th Division and went off. General Vignot said to his adjutant: " We can't attack. And we'll see who's going to be court-martialled. . . ."

The staff of the 11th Army was accommodated in a big farm. The owners had left. The hens were roaming about the yard in search of grains of corn. A youngish lieutenant in spectacles was standing among the hens. When he saw de Visset, he saluted and began speaking very fast: " *Mon général!* Give the order to attack. Otherwise the men will disperse. *Mon général* . . ."

De Visset nodded his head and turned away, but he was visibly perturbed. He ordered his chauffeur to drive to the 42nd Division.

They turned off along the road to Péronne. The general switched on the radio. Paris was broadcasting foxtrots. He switched over to the French wave-band from Stuttgart: " The remnants of the Dutch Army that were still offering resistance capitulated yesterday. Our troops have occupied the town of Saint-Quentin and are moving forward on a broad front between Lille and Péronne. Since the beginning of the advance, we have taken 110,000 prisoners, not counting the Dutch, and a great quantity of ammunition. According to the reports of Swiss journalists, Paris is in a panic. Many ministers have already left the capital. Count Ciano, in a speech devoted to the anniversary of the Pact, stated: ' Italy can no longer stand aside.' "

De Visset began to reflect. Perhaps the Germans would be in Péronne tomorrow. It was all leading up to the dénouement. Was Weygand any better than Gamelin? They were different persons, but their set-up was the same — they clung to the past and refused to realize that times had changed. And the country was being ruled by ignorant mountebanks. He remembered Tessa's words: " The military must remain in the background." The Germans might already be able to take Paris. They wanted to annihilate the living strength of France. He wondered whether tomorrow's operation would be of any avail. There were cowards like Vignot everywhere — and how many traitors among them?

He switched the radio back again to Paris. The announcer declared in a high-pitched voice: " Today Churchill made the following statement: 'The rulers of France have given me their solemn assurance that whatever happens the French will fight on to the end.' " De Visset smiled. He wondered who had made that promise to Churchill. Tessa perhaps? Of course; hadn't he said with such feeling: " We'll fight to the end "? But he himself had run away with his little lady, just like that Prefect. Only one thing was true: the Army must fight to the end. But they didn't want to fight. What were Picard and Vignot dreaming of? Capitulation! It was necessary to set the example and die at one's post. Our grandchildren would know that there were some real Frenchmen in this terrible year. De Visset thought of the young lieutenant in spectacles and he felt a lump in his throat. All de Visset desired for himself was a worthy death. Automatically he repeated the words of a prayer, as he used to do when a boy before taking his examinations. He did not notice that they had arrived in Péronne.

The adjutant got out of the car. A few minutes later he came back shrugging his shoulders. "This is a tough show," he said. "They said they had established their H.Q. in the school."

There was no one to ask — the town had practically died out. The people were probably afraid of bombing. The scattered debris and smashed furniture of the ruined houses made it impossible to drive any farther. The general got out and looked around. An old woman came out of a doorway.

" Granny, do you happen to know where the military are living here? "

The old woman pointed to the town hall and began to cry. De Visset went through the empty rooms. The floor was littered with papers, tin hats, haversacks. He sent the adjutant to make inquiries and sat down at the big table while he waited. He looked distractedly at the paper lying in front of him. It was somebody's birth certificate. Thoughts assailed him once again; he saw his little house at Valence. His little granddaughter, his favourite, was playing with the kitten. He would never see them again. . . . All that was left was to die worthily.

He found it hard to open his eyes — he had been so tired he had dozed off. In front of him was standing a German officer and some soldiers. The officer had a scar on his cheek. His monocle flashed. Impudently showing his teeth, he said in broken French: " If I'm not mistaken, it's General de Visset? I have the honour to express my deep respect. . . ."

CHAPTER 20

" THERE has been treachery. . . . Death is hardly a sufficient punishment for the mistakes that have been committed. Remember, our soldiers are dying on the field of battle. We will destroy the cowards and traitors! If only a miracle can save France, I believe in a miracle! "

When Reynaud finished his speech, the senators applauded politely. They were old, experienced politicians. They realized that the Cabinet would soon fall. In the deputies gallery Fouget was in tears. The journalists laughed as they looked at the bearded dreamer, wiping his eyes with a bandanna handkerchief.

Tessa had just got into his car when Fouget caught him by the hand. " I must have a talk with you at once," he said. " Reynaud was right when he said: ' There has been treachery.' It was bold and frank, a lash with the whip. Now it's necessary to act. . . ."

Throughout the last few days Tessa had been living in a kind of fever, tossing between unconcern and black despair. The news was contradictory. Some reports mentioned successful counter-attacks; others foretold the fall of Paris. Pétain declared there was no longer any army. All that was left were unconnected detachments. Mandel was proving that it was possible to resist. The Ministers alternately decided to leave Paris, and then declared there was no threat to the capital. Tessa could neither sleep nor eat. He felt he was becoming ill. He looked at Fouget with horror — the last man in the world he wanted to see. But Fouget climbed into the car and started to exclaim immediately: "We must raise a people's militia!"

"It's too late," said Tessa, wearily blowing his nose. "I'm not a mystic. I don't believe in miracles. Yesterday the Germans occupied Arras and Amiens. Today they have reached the coast. The Army is surrounded."

"There are forty divisions there. The ring can be broken."

"Who's going to break it? Don't count on the Belgians. King Leopold is pro-German, as everybody knows. Today the British have withdrawn two divisions from Bapaume to Dunkirk. It's quite understandable that Weygand didn't want to meet General Gort. In a word, it's all over except the shouting."

"How can you talk like that? Reynaud said only a few minutes ago: 'Cowardice will be punished with death.' You're the first who ought to be shot!"

Fouget shouted, spluttering saliva all over Tessa; his beard bobbed up and down.

"Shouting won't help," said Tessa quietly. "Reynaud was talking for the benefit of the public. You should hear him at home. . . . You're an honest man, but you're a dreamer. You know you detest me. You're quite wrong. When you were attacked in Marseille I was really shocked."

"What on earth are you thinking about?" said Fouget. "I implore you to forget all about petty politics. France is dying. Rise above faction and parties!"

"Dreamer! More than that, you're a man of the past. Seventy-ton tanks. And who is there against them? Citizen Fouget. Perhaps you'll annihilate General von Kleist with a Declaration of the Rights of Man and the Citizen."

"This is no time for joking."

"I'm not joking. I've seldom talked so seriously. We've lived out our time, you understand? Perhaps Breteuil will survive. But he's old-fashioned too. He goes to church and prays. Grandel, Laval, and Meuger will survive. You think I'm a villain, although we're both Radicals. But you respect Ducane. And Cachin. So allow me to tell you they are heroes of a departed age. In other countries the nineteenth century died in good time with the last war. But in France it lingered on. Our old men are in no hurry to die. Pétain is over eighty, but you ought to hear him; he's full of plans and ambitions. As I said, the past age is finished. Like your Desser. By the way, he came to see me. What do you think he suggested? We should defend Paris."

"And he's quite right. They said Madrid wouldn't hold out even two days, and it held out for two years. Arm the workers and you'll see wonders."

Tessa shrugged his shoulders. "How can one talk to you?" he said. "You live in the world of the past. Do you think seventy divisions and three thousand tanks are going to stop at the barricades? And besides, it would be madness to arm the Communists with rifles. Of course, you'd be delighted. But you're the exception. All the Radicals would raise a howl, to say nothing of the Socialists. As for the Right — well, Picard once told me that if the workers attempted to seize power he'd open the front."

"You ought to arrest him. And Breteuil as well. Did Reynaud speak about treachery or didn't he? I want you to carry out your civic duty. You should realize that these people hate you. If Breteuil gets into power he won't have any consideration for you. He looks on you as a Radical, a Mason, a puppet of the Popular Front. Look what they're writing."

He held out a leaflet. Tessa at once caught sight of his own name. His hands were trembling violently. "It's difficult to read," he said, "it shakes so." But he managed to read the words: "We'll hang them on the lamp-posts." The leaflet was signed "H.Q. of the 'Faithful.'"

The car drew up at the Ministry. "Forgive me if I offended you," said Tessa in a weak voice. "But it's very hard for me, very hard."

When he got to his room he read the leaflet through with close attention. Suddenly he realized that Fouget was right; Breteuil's friends would never forgive him the gesture of the clenched fist, his friendship with Villard, or his intervention on behalf of Denise.

He took a nap for about half an hour and dreamed of refugees, tanks, and gallows. When he woke up, he sat on the sofa, clasped his knees, and said aloud: "It's not a question of myself. One has

got to think about France." A week ago he had given way to panic
and wanted to flee. Now he would calmly go to meet his death.
Nevertheless, he had a responsibility — he was a Minister. He must
endeavour to save the country. It was all very well for Ducane!
That madman thought only of himself. He went into the Army
merely to advertise himself. What a sorry figure he cut — a deputy
in the uniform of a lieutenant! What could he do like that? As if
there were not enough lieutenants without him!

No, what was needed now was some trick, some invention, some
unusual manœuvre! Mandel was of the opinion that France ought
to make friends with Moscow. The Germans had long realized that
Russia was a power to be reckoned with. But that fool Daladier
had caused the French to fall out definitely with the Russians (by
now Tessa had convinced himself that he had been opposed to
aiding Mannerheim). De Visset said the Air Force had very few
planes. But it would be possible to buy or barter for a thousand
bombers from Russia.

Tessa became enthusiastic; a lofty mission was incumbent upon
him. All around were weak-willed fools, Reynaud the peacock,
Daladier the dolt. But Tessa would begin a bold game; he would
come to terms with Moscow. Then Italy wouldn't dare come in.
Yes, and even the Germans would take fright. In France there would
be a change. The people would at once believe in victory. Everybody would recognize that Tessa had saved the country, like
Clemenceau in 1917.

He sent for Fouget. " Thank you, old chap, for coming to see me,"
he said. " Our conversation has opened my eyes to a lot. You see,
we're stewing in our own juice. But you take a broader view. I'll
explain my plan to you at once. We're going to send either you or
Cot to Moscow."

" To Moscow? What for? "

" They've got great respect for you. But if you don't want to go,
we can send Cot."

" I ask you again — what for? "

" What for? It will make an enormous impression. It will influence Italy. It will improve our morale. Finally, the Russians may
give us munitions — aeroplanes to start with."

Fouget got angry. " Have you gone mad? " he shouted. " Why
should the Russians let you have aeroplanes? A couple of months
ago you were shouting that Baku ought to be destroyed."

"Nothing of the kind. Personally I was against the idea. It was Daladier's stubbornness. It's quite wrong of people to call him the 'Bull of Vaucluse.' He's simply an ass. But why bring up the past? At present we want to establish friendly relations with Moscow. You can help me."

"The Russians will send you to the devil, and they'll be quite right. The first question will be: whom do you represent? There's nothing behind you. The workers are still being arrested. The papers report another trial today — eight Communists. Your 'Ass of Vaucluse' is Minister of Foreign Affairs. The French people may come to terms with Moscow, but not·you. There's only one thing I can advise you to do — write to the President and send in your resignation. We need a Committee of Public Safety! "

Fouget went out, banging the door behind him. Tessa began to think what else he could do. It might be a good idea to appeal to the Communists. What a pity he had fallen out with Denise!

He decided to approach Ferronet, the lawyer who had often defended the Communists, and ask him to come and see him at once.

" I know you've got a good number of acquaintances among the Communists," he said. " Please don't refuse to transmit this letter."

" To whom?"

Tessa blushed. " To my daughter," he muttered. " It's very important. As quickly as possible — it's a question of the life of someone very dear to me."

" Very well," said Ferronet. Then, with a faint smile, he added: " If your policemen don't shadow me, I'll deliver the letter this evening."

Tessa had written:

Denise,

I must have a talk with you. It is not a personal matter, but one of exceptional public importance. I beg you to come tomorrow morning at nine o'clock. I repeat, it is not a question of myself or private interests. I promise that nobody will know of your visit. Your unhappy father,

Paul Tessa

In the evening he had to go to a Cabinet meeting. He listened distractedly to Reynaud's report: " Weygand has returned. Of course, the situation is critical, but we are nevertheless preparing to counter-attack. The British have already begun the attack. The

5th Division is approaching Arras." Tessa was busy with his own thoughts. When the meeting came to an end he took Reynaud aside.

"What do you think of a rapprochement with Moscow?" he asked.

"Well," said Reynaud, "the situation has become so acute in the last few days that I've been exclusively occupied with military matters. I've handed over diplomacy to Baudouin."

Tessa went home and took a sleeping-draught. He woke up at eight. He was having breakfast when he was told that a lady was waiting to see him on a personal matter. He cried out: "Bring her in here."

He was so carried away with the game that he forgot all about his paternal sentiments. He felt as if he was receiving an ambassadress.

Denise said in a dry voice: "If this is a piece of provocation it won't succeed. I've come with the knowledge of the party."

"With the knowledge of the party?" said Tessa. "That's excellent! You know, Denise, the situation is very grave. We're on the eve of defeat. At a time like this we must put aside all questions of self-esteem. The salvation of France is at stake. But it is impossible to save the country without enthusiasm. I'll be the first to hold out my hand to the Communists. We'll cancel the repressions. They must cancel their propaganda. You understand? Their civic duty is to influence Moscow. I think we're going to send Cot there. I thought of Fouget, but he's an old man and a pedant. Of course, this is between ourselves. You must transmit my proposal to Thorez, or Duclos, or Cachin — in a word, to your bosses. If necessary, I'll meet them. I'm ready to do anything."

"I don't think anyone would treat your words seriously," Denise said. "There are thirty-four thousand Communists in the prisons. First of all, release the prisoners. And clear out. Hand over the power to the people."

"Power is not handed over like a package!" said Tessa, flaring up. But he quickly mastered himself. "We submit to the Constitution. So long as we're not deprived of the confidence of Parliament, we can't clear out. As regards the release of the arrested persons, personally I have no objection. Only I'm afraid it can't be done. The Socialists are against it. Sérol told me yesterday that he refuses to put the Communists under civil law. And when I hinted to him that we now needed national unity, he said: 'Let the Communists disarm first.' You see how complicated the situation is! Oh, the Right is only waiting for the opportunity to rush in. If we release the Communists, the Government will fall at the first ballot."

Denise was very worried. Throughout the last few days she had been talking with soldiers and had heard terrible stories of treachery and cowardice. Human sorrow overwhelmed Paris together with the streams of refugees. But the police continued to round up the Communists. Yesterday they had arrested Lucie, who always used to be laughing when Denise worked with her at the factory. They arrested her in the street. She had left her baby at home and wanted to go back for it. The police said: "That's none of your business." Michaud was in the encircled army in the north. Denise had had no letters from him since the battles in May. And now her nerves could stand it no longer. She began to cry.

Tessa was deeply moved. He forgot all about Fouget and his own plans. This was his daughter, Denise! How thin she had grown! It was obvious she was having a bad time. She was probably in hiding, expecting every night to be arrested.

"My poor little girl!" he said gently.

It brought Denise to her senses. She looked at him in amazement.

"You'll never be able to understand why I'm crying. It's dreadful to think that you're my father, that we both talk French, that the same bomb may kill us! You don't understand? It's more than I can bear to feel that I'm connected with you. . . ."

"But I've never ceased to feel that you're my daughter." He walked to the end of the room. He remembered he'd got to persuade her. "Denise, let's put party dissensions aside. You must help me. I want to save France, and so for the sake of France . . ."

"Shut up! Before it used to be 'for Mother's sake.' But France is France."

She stopped speaking. She thought of the refugees and the soldiers and felt a lump in her throat. And fearing that Tessa would again see her weakness, she ran out of the room.

Tessa thought resentfully: "She's a fanatic!" No doubt Lucien was a rotter, but he was more human. That girl wasn't living herself and didn't want other people to live! Hysterical little creature!

He went to see Baudouin to have a talk with him about Cot's mission. Baudouin answered evasively and switched the conversation over to Italy. He thought it was time to make concessions, give up Djibuti or perhaps a bit of Tunisia, and bring pressure to bear on the British; let them part with something too — Malta, for instance. Mussolini was ready to negotiate; but they would have to send a suitable man to Rome — Laval or Breteuil.

Back again in his own room, Tessa rang up Fouget. "I'm afraid you didn't quite understand me," he said. "We can send you or Cot with some sort of vague commission. For instance, to negotiate regarding compensation for the Galician industries, or the purchase of timber. Then you can put out feelers. The effect abroad will be the same. At the same time we're not taking any obligations on ourselves. We'll say to the Right: 'We haven't even got an ambassador in Moscow.' Breteuil won't be able to pick a quarrel with us — especially as we're opening serious negotiations with Mussolini. The British have promised to exempt Italian ships from control. That's already a victory! Do you hear me?"

There was no reply. Fouget had banged down the receiver in a rage.

Tessa's plan was a failure. He went out of town to console himself. It was a wonderful day. The lilac, jasmine, and wistaria were in bloom and there was a delicious fragrant smell everywhere. Tessa felt quite consoled; spring was here again in spite of everything.

On his way back he saw some soldiers in the Bois de Vincennes. They were digging anti-tank trenches. Tessa stopped to chat with them for a moment and said confidently: "Yes, they won't get a chance to see Paris! Paris will defend itself like a lion."

CHAPTER 21

IT was a tiny town like all the towns of Picardy: there was a square and a long street with low brick houses leading out of it. The square was adorned with a sixteenth-century town hall, which had a tower with a golden lion on top of it. Next to the town hall were two cafés, a department store, and a hotel, the Cheval Blanc.

The population was mainly composed of the employees of the bicycle works that stood about a mile outside the town. Many of the women were skilled lace-makers. They sat at their open windows manipulating the bobbins. Tourists sometimes came in the summer. They inspected the old town hall and drank beer in the square. In the winter the workers sat in the cafés, smoking long clay pipes and arguing about politics. Before the war the Mayor had been a Communist, and two flags, the Tricolour and the red flag, had flown over the town hall. The walls were still covered with inscriptions: " Down with Fascism! " " Long live the Popular Front! " together with a clumsily drawn hammer and sickle. On Sundays the people drank gin and watched cock-fights. That day the movie theatre had been showing a film called *The Kiss of Death*. Lovers had wandered along beside the canal, plucking water-lilies. The town went to bed early; at eleven o'clock there was not a soul in the streets. Only the chimes of the town-hall clock melodiously sounded the hours, or some woman softly lulled her baby to sleep in one of the little houses: " Little kitten, do not cry. Slumber, darling, lullaby! "

The first bomb fell on two houses near the railway station. It killed an old blacksmith and wounded two women. The second bomb demolished the town hall. The square was littered with rubble. The golden lion lay among the debris. The inhabitants took to flight. Out of eighteen thousand only one hundred remained.

A woman brought a blue enamel coffee-pot and poured out some coffee for Michaud. " Are you going away? " she asked quietly.

" We've only just arrived."

" They say you're going away. Everybody has left. I had to stay. My mother's ill. I keep telling her they won't go away."

" Of course we won't go away." Michaud smiled. " It's heartbreaking to see what's being done. People just rush off and blindly follow their noses. And nobody stops them. A fine lot! They wanted to send us to Finland, but as soon as the Germans show themselves they run away. It's a disgrace! If only we had a different lot! But don't get frightened. We won't go away. Have you got a good cellar? Take everything down there and sit quiet. We'll manage somehow."

Fabre, the commander of the battalion, had been given orders to defend the town at all costs. Everybody looked on him as a harmless crank; he drank apéritifs from morning to night and was always talking about the beauty of cactuses. But in the last few days he had shown himself to be brave and versatile. The battalion put up a good fight during its retreat from Cambrai. Twice it counter-attacked and recaptured from the Germans twenty men who had been left behind and taken prisoner. When the dive-bombers first began to attack, Fabre seized a rifle from a soldier and began shooting at them. This had the effect of calming the men and there was no panic. One of the bombers was shot down. Even so, in eight days the battalion had lost a third of its strength. When Fabre was given his orders, he was embarrassed; it was easy for them to say: " Defend the town at all costs! " How would they be able to hold out if the Germans sent tanks against them? "

Fabre knew that Michaud was very popular with the men. When Colonel Quérier took fright and wanted to disband two companies, Fabre protested. And the matter of the " mutiny " at Le Havre was hushed up. Whenever he had to make a decision, Fabre would say to Michaud: "What does Monsieur Don Quixote think about it? " He did the same on this occasion.

" We must hold out," Michaud said.

Michaud did not know what the party directives were; he had been out of touch with Paris for a long time, so he had to decide for himself. He did not hesitate. No, the Communists were not cowards! They would show they could fight. It was now no longer a question of Reynaud, or Tessa, or Daladier, but a question of fighting for France.

There were enemies everywhere. Some were proffering handcuffs, others were dropping bombs. The Nazis had come: the executioners of Thälmann, the people who had crucified Spain, the knights of death. And in the rear there were also Fascists — Hitler's friends, Breteuil, Grandel, Picard.

Peaceful, carefree France was no more. The country had been given over to the mercy of the enemy, and even here there were ruins and weeping women. " Are you really going to abandon us? " Michaud looked at the ruins of the town hall. Professor Malet had once called the building a " pearl of the Renaissance." On one of the walls Michaud read the words: " Bread, peace, freedom." He thought of 1936, the strike, the flags, the songs.

His love for his country grew even stronger now that misfortune had overtaken her. So many things were mingled in that sentiment — the mountains of Savoy, where he had lived as a boy, with their murmuring streams and bright meadows; Paris, his own Paris, the city of grey houses and smiles, the city where Jeannot had died and where Clémence still lived, Paris and Denise. He knew that he was defending a frail girl with blue eyes like Alpine flowers. He repeated automatically: " France . . . Denise. . . ."

All day long they were digging trenches, filling sandbags, and camouflaging the anti-tank guns and machine-guns. In the evening Fabre got into touch with divisional H.Q. " We're pressing on the enemy everywhere," they told him. " We'll send reinforcements. If you withdraw, use the second battalion for rear-guard action."

Michaud looked in at the factory. They had installed machine-guns. It had been bombed the day before. That morning it had rained and the water was gleaming in a large crater in one of the workshops. Bits of machinery were sticking out of the pool. In another workshop he saw a milling machine that had remained intact. He was delighted and felt as though he had met a friend of his childhood. He loved material and instruments. He endowed them with life, scolding and nursing them as though they were his children. He began to wonder what had come over people. They all wanted work, affection, and happiness. But the sea had got rough and one had to struggle to keep afloat. He would not reach the haven; he would be killed. But others would get there. Pierre, Legrais, old Duchesne, would remain. The children would remain, and Denise. . . . They would build huge factories like Magnitogorsk. He remembered the photographs of it. Yesterday they had marched over fields. The grain was trampled and destroyed. In any case, there would be no one to reap it. But they would sow again in the spring. Life would triumph. But at present it was hard. . . .

Michaud went to the town barrier. His comrades could hardly keep awake and were discussing how they could hold out. There were only three hundred men. And the Germans had tanks. Michaud cheered them up and told them about the fighting in Spain:

" Sometimes we had only thirty of us against a whole battalion. As for their tanks, we tackled them with hand grenades. We hadn't got anything else. One of the boys, Pepe, blew up eight of them."

" Those tanks were different. But the Germans' are armour-plated — like nothing on earth! "

" They can be knocked out too. But you want guys like the ones in Spain for that. Chaps like iron."

" You knew what you were fighting for there. I wanted to join up myself. But what are we dying for here? Whom are we defending — Tessa? "

Michaud did not reply at once. He himself was worried and felt the responsibility that rested on him.

"No!" he said firmly. "We'll settle accounts with those people later on. But this is our own country here. Have you seen the women? Their husbands are at the front the same as us. We can't quit! The Communists must set an example. And besides, honestly, is it easy to give all this up? I saw a milling machine today . . ."

Before he could finish speaking there was a loud explosion. The first shells had arrived before dawn. The little melting stars were still visible in the pale sky. The explosions were particularly terrifying; nobody had thought it would start before sunrise. Michaud felt chilled and thought it was the dew; but the chill came from within. He gripped his machine-gun and felt calm at once.

A quarter of an hour later there was a pause. The sun rose gently in the sky, in the fields the birds began to twitter, and the water took on a rosy hue. The men were silent. Michaud was thinking about Denise. Just as when he was in Spain, he felt the warmth of her breasts and the salt taste of her lips. He was conscious of a smell of pine needles. "My darling!" he said to himself. "This is the end!" Of course, this wasn't the time for joking; this was something great and serious. But it wasn't terrible. It was only sad that he would never see Denise again. . . .

The tanks were approaching the canal. Everything began to roar; it seemed as though the earth itself were shrieking. Michaud glanced round and saw Fabre, who waved his hands.

"Give them a burst! . . ."

Then there was another pause.

"They'll start soon. They know where we are now."

"That doesn't matter," Michaud laughed. "I saw them in Spain. They like to see people running away. But the Fascists don't like this sort of stuff."

"Do you think we'll hold out, Michaud?"

"I'll say we will. And how!"

About nine o'clock the Germans renewed the attack. The shells blew the unfortunate houses to pieces. A burning tank stood three yards away from Michaud.

"On the left coming out of the potato field . . ."

They were German motorcyclists. They halted. Then the tanks began to move forward again. The tanks were driving forward

over the wounded. Fabre cried out: "The swine! The beasts!
They're driving over their own men!"

A shell killed the company commander. The sergeant couldn't
stand it any longer and went down into a cellar. Fabre crawled up
to Michaud and said: "Don't listen to anyone. Go on. Give it to 'em
hot!"

How long was it since that moment — a few minutes or an hour?
There was a continuous roar of explosions. Michaud shook his left
hand; it was covered with blood.

"Crawl over here! . . ."

But Michaud did not stir. He did not even hear.

"Give me another belt! . . . Now, you Boches, take that! . . ."

At noon a high brilliant sun shone over the quiet world. Not a
shot, not a cry. Even the wounded had ceased to groan, as though
stifled by the stillness. Later they were put into trucks. Michaud got
his comrades to bandage his hand, but he refused to go away. They
buried the dead. They drank warm water that tasted of tin cans.
Everybody felt exhausted as after a serious illness. They wanted to
smile but couldn't. Gradually they became aware of a simple and
marvellous thing — they had beaten off the attack on the town.

Fabre went up to Michaud and muttered: "Bravo, Don Quixote!
What were you in Spain?"

"A lieutenant."

"The colonel wanted to lock you up for that. But today I'd make
you a general if I had my way. They say you're a Communist. What
a ridiculous tale! . . . Now we know what you're like! . . ."

He wiped his eyes and took a draught of rum from his flask.

"I'll try to get into touch with H.Q.," he said. "We must let them
know the good news."

When he got them on the wire, he heard the same indifferent
voice. Yesterday they had said to him: "Hold out at all costs."
Today they listened to what he had to say and said: "Leave the
town under cover of darkness." He cried out: "Why?" "We're regrouping," came the answer.

Fabre banged down the receiver and shouted: "A general? He's
not a general. He's a bag of tripe!"

"The traitors!" said Michaud to his comrades. "They're sur-
rendering the country!"

Everybody realized the truth and stood silent.

Good-bye, milling machine! Good-bye, golden lion of the town hall! Good-bye, kind woman with the blue coffee-pot, sick mother and hunted, crazy eyes! Michaud strode gloomily along the dusty road; it was a long road, the road of retreat. At noon amid the heat and quiet he had had a glimpse of victory. And the eyes of victory were like those of the woman with the coffee-pot. . . . Good-bye, fond dream! . . .

CHAPTER 22

PARIS in the evening was like a lonely forest; even the little blue lamps were extinguished. Passers-by were being stopped and asked for their papers. There was talk of spies and parachutists. A lame milkman in the rue Cherche-Midi was arrested; he was said to have been signalling to aeroplanes. People swore there were forty thousand disguised German soldiers in Paris. Mandel ordered three of the " Faithful " to be arrested. They were found to be in possession of a list of Italian addresses and a map of Paris marked with the locations of the A.A. guns. Breteuil was furious. " Why arrest honest Frenchmen? " he asked. Next morning the " Faithful " were released. Breteuil's wife kept crying: " The Germans will come here! " Breteuil said to her: " Pray! Who knows? Perhaps Marshal Pétain will save France. . . ."

Refugees began to appear in the streets. They roamed absent-mindedly around the railway stations and gazed at Paris with empty, unseeing eyes. The noise of the great city did not seem to reach them. In vain the chauffeurs sounded their horns and shouted abuse; the refugees did not hear; it was as though their ears were filled with other terrible voices.

Exhausted women sat down on the pavements. People crowded around them and asked them where they had come from. The Parisians still thought of the war as almost infinitely remote; the papers were still writing about the fighting in northern Norway. Only the refugees disturbed the calm as they muttered: " The Germans are killing people. We barely managed to get away." The police dispersed the crowd who stopped to listen. Why want to hear terrible stories?

The more cautious people went away to their relations in the provinces. Others went on working, trading, and amusing themselves. The press was discussing the question whether or not to open the cabarets which had been closed in the first days of the alarm. The old men calmed the young, saying: " They'll drive them off the same as they did in 1914."

Villard believed neither in Pétain's genius nor in Weygand's line, nor in miracles. He was busy packing up his treasures. From early in the morning the pounding of hammers resounded in his flat. Workmen kept coming and going. Villard now had no interest except in the fate of his pictures. He stood by and watched anxiously as each canvas was placed in the dark box. Then he glanced with indifference at the newspapers. He realized that all was lost, and it bored him to wait for the epilogue.

His boredom was not unmixed with anger. An angry gleam now began to flash in his usually affable and melancholy eyes. Why hadn't they let him end his hard life quietly? He didn't know whom to blame and hated all of them: the Germans and Daladier, Tessa and the Communists, the British and the incompetent generals.

As he looked at the nailed-up boxes, he thought of the future. What was going to become of his little house at Avignon? He saw the little bower covered with wistaria and the play of the sunbeams on the light brown sand. Paris was lost. But what if the Germans were to go on farther? No, that could never happen. They would surrender Paris, let the Germans in for two or three days in order to satisfy Prussian vainglory, and then they would sign peace. After all, Alsace-Lorraine was a shuttlecock, tossed backwards and forwards. Strasbourg would become German for twenty or forty years. On the other hand there would be peace. But there was no end to his anxiety. What if Churchill forced Reynaud to go on with the war even after the fall of Paris? France was now a British dominion. At this point, Villard coughed and looked angrily at his manservant and the workmen. What did it matter to them? They worked, thieved, and made merry.

There was a ring at the door and Tessa was shown in. Villard cheered up at the sight of Tessa. It pleased him to see Tessa worn out and unshaven. So Tessa was having a bad time, eh! Well, let him clear up the mess!

Tessa began with a sensation. "When we took Marshal Pétain into the Cabinet," he said, "we thought that by doing so we would settle all the disputed questions. But the situation gets more and more complicated each day. I've got some terrible news to tell you. The King of Belgium has capitulated." Tessa stared at Villard, who wiped the lenses of his glasses without showing any interest. "He didn't even give General Blanchard any warning. The position of the Army is tragic. You realize the depth of his villainy? They called his father Albert 'le Roi Chevalier,' but Leopold will go down in history as the personification of cunning."

"The King is right according to his lights," said Villard quietly. "What else could he do? In certain circumstances capitulation is an act of heroism."

"But have you thought what terms Hitler will dictate to us if we also display such 'heroism'? He may demand Alsace. He may even occupy Lille."

"You ought to have thought about that before. I don't want to be captious, but you've done nothing to prevent defeat. You surrendered all the positions without a fight. Defeat was prepared already at Munich. But you entered the Cabinet then."

"And you supported it, by the way. Besides, if we're going to talk about the causes of defeat, you've got to remember the strikes in 1936 and the forty-hour week. Who disorganized industry? And what about Spain? Blum set Mussolini against us. You enraged Franco and then helped him to win. It would be difficult to imagine anything more senseless."

Tessa's voice had risen to a shout, revealing all the excitement of the last few weeks. Villard spoke disjointedly; his hollow voice sounded like a bark. They went on a long time accusing each other and dragging up old parliamentary intrigues, ill-considered declarations, and divisions in the Chamber.

Tessa was the first to check himself. "It's no use our abusing each other," he said. "This is all nerves. But we're living in terrible times and we ought to stand together. I came to suggest that you should enter the Cabinet. Reynaud is preparing a surprise. A ministerial crisis would create a bad impression abroad, so we've decided to do everything in a family way. First of all, we must get rid of Daladier. That ass has very nearly ruined France. We also have other changes in view. Sarraut is to go. Baudouin and Prouvost are to be invited. They're business-like men. But you are dear to us as the conscience of the nation. Besides, you are the guarantee that the working classes will be with us."

Villard smiled ironically. Did they take him for a simpleton? Was he to enter the Government on the eve of capitulation? That would mean compromising himself and wiping out fifty years of struggle for his ideals. And for what? So that Tessa could say: "Villard too has signed." No, he wasn't going to stoop to that!

" I'm grateful to you and Reynaud," he said. " I'm deeply touched. But I won't enter the Cabinet. My party is already represented in the Cabinet. Nobody will dare to say that the Socialists shirk responsibility. But the Right won't stand me. Even in England they'd prefer somebody younger. I would only be ballast."

Tessa argued and tried to persuade him: " Auguste, you can't refuse! We're on the verge of the abyss. Everything we hold dear will perish — France, the parliamentary system, the ideas we imbibed with our mother's milk. . . ."

Tessa was moved by his own words; he thought of Amalie's death, his recent meeting with Denise, the refugees, the croaking of Pétain, whose reply to everything was: " Too late." There was a hint of tears in his voice.

Villard felt relieved. But he was not satisfied. He wanted to give Tessa the *coup de grâce*: " What ideas are you talking about? " he said. " We've got different points of view. Of course, so far as your attachment to economic liberalism is concerned, your ideas are bankrupt. But I'm keeping in step with the age. What is Hitler bringing? Socialism! No doubt it's somewhat distorted — cut to suit the German pattern, so to speak. But if we take National-Socialism and supplement it with the moral teachings of Saint-Simon, Proudhon, and our trade unions, we'll get something real and at the same time intensely French."

Tessa was no longer listening: he had no desire to argue about doctrines. Suddenly he became aware of the disorder in the study, with the trunks and packing-cases lying around.

" Are you going away? " he asked.

Villard looked embarrassed. " Yes," he said. " That is, personally I'm remaining. I'm going to drain the cup to the dregs. But I'm sending my pictures away. I've got no right to risk my collection. It represents the very cream of the French spirit. Political systems may perish, but one can't allow the masterpieces of art to be destroyed by a stupid bomb."

He accompanied Tessa to the hall. As he was saying good-bye, Tessa suddenly felt resentful: " I really intend to stay in Paris, whatever danger may threaten me! " he said. " I've got no collections. And I've got to think about France. . . ."

CHAPTER 23

MEUGER showed no signs of panic and went on working as usual, only he took a dose of veronal at night in order to sleep through the roar of the anti-aircraft guns. His cold face — he was more like a German or a Swede than a native of Lyon — retained its smile. He was a strong, handsome man who took great care of his personal appearance. He played tennis in order not to get fat. A solemn quiet reigned in his luxurious apartment. There were no pictures or knick-knacks in his study. A bronze bust of Napoleon stood opposite his writing-table. The bookcase was empty except for a number of reference books. Meuger wasn't fond of reading. On the other hand, he appreciated music, especially Bach. He was fond of saying: " It's my substitute for religion."

He had brought up two children. His son had recently finished his training as an engineer. Wishing to avoid misunderstandings, Meuger sent him into the Army and got him appointed to Leridot's staff. His daughter was married to a big financier who had quickly bought up all the nickel shares; they lived in Switzerland.

Meuger knew six languages and was a great traveller. He felt at home everywhere and said he was equally fond of chicken with bamboo shoots in a Shanghai restaurant, Californian fruit, and Algerian couscous. He took no interest in technical matters, leaving all that to the engineers. But he kept a close watch on the price of raw materials and the state of the various markets. He had business dealings everywhere. He was interested in the chemical industry of Germany, Norwegian nitrates, and Chaco platinum. He regarded Desser as an ignoramus and a dilettante: " A man like that could only come to the fore in the decadence of the post-war years." He used to smile disdainfully at Desser's careless personal appearance and rough manners.

Desser's decline gave Meuger a certain amount of pleasure. Events were not without their own kind of logic! But these were hard times, he reflected. No doubt business was good, but what was going to happen later on? The exhaustion of the warring countries was not a pleasant prospect. In the event of defeat there would be trouble and quite possibly a revolution. In the event of victory people like Desser would come to the fore, caliphs for an hour. Meuger was proud of his origins; his grandfather had owned three quarters of the railway system, and his great-grandfather, a banker, had been described by Balzac.

Meuger looked on war as a relic of ancient times. His attitude towards patriotic sentiments was one of irony. Of course, he knew how to hide his smile in order not to offend people; just as he never made fun of his wife, who believed in the miracles of Lourdes. He merely shrugged his shoulders at what he considered to be mediæ-valism, but gave his wife money which she devoted to the support of various chapels. Meuger held that war was right when the nations lived their own narrow life. But now the interests of the nations were intertwined. The Americans were unable to live without British rubber. The Germans needed oil: they were dependent on Deterding or the Bolsheviks. The French were dependent on everybody. Then what was the use of fighting? If Europe was governed by business people like Meuger instead of by idiots, it would be quite possible to come to an arrangement.

When the war broke out, Meuger did not believe in the victory of the Allies. He even doubted a German victory and said to himself that the winner would be a third party. He tried to stop the machine, went to Madrid, and talked to the Germans. In the winter he thought that common sense was getting the upper hand, but events turned out otherwise. Chamberlain went, and Bonnet was hounded down. And then came May 1940.

It was necessary to think and to save what could still be saved before it was too late. France had lost the war. Once upon a time those words would have shaken everybody; to Frenchmen France was the universe. But now . . . No doubt Hitler would have to reckon with the attitude of the Germans; they were taking their revenge for the Treaty of Versailles. But Hitler was a clever man. And besides, all this was a sentimental question for snivellers. Fortunately the sort of people who like Paul Déroulède and his patriotic songs had died out. France had lost her place long before the war. The snivellers would howl for a while and then calm down. And the country would heal its wounds.

So when General Picard said with a gasp: " But what you propose is capitulation," Meuger answered: " Don't let's be afraid of words. I'm proposing the only thing possible under the circumstances."

And then a most remarkable thing happened. Standing beside the bust of Napoleon, General Picard began to weep. Midinettes wept as a matter of course, but Picard was not a child. He knew what was being arranged. He was a friend of Breteuil's. He had said a good number of times: " The Germans will defeat us." Why, then, did the word " capitulation " scare him?

" I repeat," said Meuger, " this is the only way out. The fate of the northern army is a foregone conclusion. The Belgians are out of the game. The British are still playing the role of inaccessible virgins. But their virtue will come to an end when the Germans fly over London. It's more to our advantage to be one ahead of the British — at least in a separate peace. If we go on with the war, Hitler will occupy Paris, and the Italians will take Marseille. And the Commune will be set up at Lyon. Which is it more important to preserve: the old frontiers or civilization? In a couple of weeks the Communists will rise. . . ."

For the last few months Picard's thoughts had been in a whirl. He changed his views ten times a day. At one time he said: " We'll be defeated, and quite right too. It's time to bring this disgraceful regime to an end." At other times he recalled the glory of the French Army and thought: " Perhaps we may win? " He respected Hitler, feeling no animosity towards him and despising the German refugees, whom he contemptuously called " renegades." When the German advance began, Picard was scared. He gave orders and immediately countermanded them. He shouted that it was necessary to keep a cool head, but he himself was mortally afraid of paratroops: what if they attacked the Staff? He got mixed up in the political game. He took all his questions to Breteuil, who said to him: " Try to hold the enemy at least for a month. We'll get rid of Reynaud and come to terms with the Germans." Picard issued pathetic orders: " Soldiers, defend every inch! " " Not a step backwards! " The Germans were advancing at the rate of twenty miles a day. Picard shouted at Breteuil: " We can't hold on! " And Breteuil quietly answered: " I didn't even think you'd hold on."

However, nobody had ever spoken to Picard about capitulation until now. When Meuger said to him straight out: "We must follow the example of Belgium," it was too much for Picard. He began to weep. After he had quieted down a little, he mumbled: "They won't leave us the Army. . . ."

"I realize it's a hard blow to you," Meuger said. "But one must keep one's presence of mind. In 1936 I thought everything was lost. My factories were in the hands of the strikers. But I went on working all the same. Perhaps they'll leave us a small army. You'll be able to train the young officers. Your knowledge won't be lost. At the present moment you can save Paris. I'm not referring to resistance. No doubt there are sober-minded men among the ministers. Yesterday de Monzie began negotiations. But Reynaud has taken fright. And also one mustn't forget about the role of Mandel. That man is France's evil genius. He wants to defend Paris. That would lead to the destruction of the capital and unheard-of slaughter. You enjoy great authority. You must inform the Government that from the military point of view the defence of Paris is quite utopian. In that way you'll render a great service to France."

Picard remembered that bright July day, the clenched fists near the Arc de Triomphe and the red flags.

"Very well," he said. "I'll fulfil my duty. We'll try to hold the enemy. But if they break through Weygand's line, I'll recommend withdrawal from Paris. The city must be handed over to the enemy in proper order with the police at their posts, in order to preserve Paris for our children and grandchildren."

CHAPTER 24

At Grandel's suggestion the security of the war factories was entrusted to Weiss, the Alsatian. Weiss acted energetically. At his suggestion the Prefect sent detectives into the factories in order to keep a look-out for sabotage. The detectives knew nothing about production and merely irritated the workers with their stupid remarks, wranglings, and threats.

The agents were particularly aggressive at Meuger's aircraft works. They arrested a woman worker, who shouted angrily: "Brave heroes! You'd do better to go and fight. The Germans are

at Beauvais. Can't you see you're hindering people from working?"
The police report stated that she had attempted to damage a bench.

It was a sultry day that foretold a storm. The white light was
dazzling and people were gasping for breath. There was great
excitement among the workers of Meuger's factory. The Germans
were nearing Paris! The soldiers were saying there were no aeroplanes. The rich were all scuttling. But who was to clear up the
mess?

In the lunch hour the workers held a meeting on the wasteland
behind the works, where the slag was overgrown with chickweed.
The workers spoke of Hitler, police spies, and the approaching
dénouement.

The leading spirit in the illegal Communist organization was a
young locksmith named Claude. He had only been working at the
factory since January, but the workers had taken to him at once.
He was exempt from military service on account of tuberculosis.
The brightness of his eyes might have been mistaken for mental
tenseness. He was burning indeed, but his loud, fitful breathing
betrayed his illness.

Claude was a dreamer who spent his nights devouring books:
Tolstoy and Flaubert, Sholokhov and Malraux. Five years before,
he frequented the Maison de Culture, where he had met Lucien.
One day they had a long conversation. Lucien kept talking about
"eternal storm." Claude meekly replied: "I respect you. You know
everything. But that's not enough. In my opinion, a poet ought to
be an honest man. Don't you think so?" Lucien thought to himself:
"A middle-class mind!" Vaillant took a fancy to Claude and said
to him: "Surely you write poetry! I feel that you write." Claude
said nothing. It was true that he wrote, but he was too shy to
acknowledge it. His poetry turned out rather odd, and he didn't
know himself why he wrote like that. He began by describing a
strike, but suddenly found himself writing about the flaming
bracken in a damp wood or the rigging of a ship. He would say to
himself: "I must be playing pranks!"

Two years before, he had tried to get into Spain, but was detained
at the frontier and sent back to Paris. He was then working at the
Seine factory. "You're our principal agitator," Legrais told him.
Claude knew how to convince people although he seemed to be
irresolute and infinitely meek. He never laid down the law when
he was talking to people, and seemed always to be asking what

was to be done. There was something childish and deeply sincere in his manner of talking, with the unexpected pauses and painful searching after words, and people believed what he said.

Claude was arrested at the beginning of the war and spent four months in prison. He was released after a medical inspection. He had not expected to be able to get any work, but he had a stroke of luck. Turners were being engaged at Meuger's factory. The applicants' papers were inspected in the office. They saw the name "Claude Duval." There were plenty of Duvals in the world. He was taken on. He soon got together a secret group.

The workers now surrounded him. They wanted to hear what he had to say. "Is Reynaud any better than Daladier? " he began. " They'll betray us. . . ." He started to cough.

"The papers say they're going to defend themselves," said one of the workers. " They say the Army mustn't retreat any more. And they're digging trenches outside of Paris. I saw them myself."

"If they want to defend themselves we'll work," said Claude. "We'll work like devils. Isn't that so? It's all the same to Meuger. He'll go on making money whether it's with Reynaud or with Hitler. But I look on these aeroplanes in a different light. We can save Paris from being bombed. We can save France. I've been talking to the soldiers. They keep asking: 'Where's our Air Force?' The Germans are machine-gunning the refugees, but we haven't got any fighter planes. We must give all the help we can to the soldiers. Only let them take away the police spies. It's impossible to work with those dirty scoundrels about. Isn't that so? "

The workers decided to appoint a delegation. They would declare their willingness to increase production, but insisted on the removal of the police spies from the workshops.

When the delegation was ushered in, Weiss glanced at Claude and smiled politely. "I thank you," he said. "I know all about the patriotism of the Paris workers. Every extra aeroplane helps to bring the hour of victory nearer. As regards the 'disguised policemen,' as you call them, they've been sent into the workshops to ferret out the disguised Communists. I hope you've understood me? "

Weiss's blue eyes met the eyes of Claude. Claude turned away.

When the workers of the Meuger factory left, others arrived. All the big factories declared their willingness to increase their working hours and demanded the cessation of the police activities.

Weiss went to see Meuger in order to give him warning of the dismissal of a hundred and fourteen workers. Meuger glanced indifferently at the list and said: " Skilled workers. However, it doesn't matter now. By the way, tell me, how are you going to carry out the evacuation? "

" We'll have to send the workers away. The less there are during the interregnum period, the better."

" Of course. But I don't want you to evacuate the equipment. It's an awkward business and serves no purpose."

" It's very pleasant, Monsieur Meuger, to see that you've not caught the general panic," said Weiss with a smile. " I keep coming across people who've simply lost their heads. You may rest assured we won't touch the equipment."

Claude's friends succeeded in warning him. The factory gates were shut. His mates helped him to climb over the high fence. Suddenly he heard whistles. He took to flight and managed to reach a hovel inhabited by old-clothes dealers. An old woman was sitting among the heaps of rags. She cried out: "Parachutist! " Claude said softly: " Be quiet! I'm a Frenchman, a worker." And the woman agreed to hide him. The storm was still waiting to break. Claude felt suffocated among the dusty piles of rags in the tiny hovel. He would have to warn his mates. He took a look outside. There was no one about. He got as far as the Père Eugène café, where his mates were accustomed to gather.

The café consisted of two rooms. In the outer room was a zinc counter. It was here that casual customers drank beer and chatted with the proprietor, Père Eugène. He was a fat, good-natured man with a thick black moustache and wore no coat. The two passions of his life were his fat, moustached wife and Maurice Thorez. He was proud of being able to say: " In 1937 after the meeting at the cycle-track I went up to Maurice and he shook my hand." Père Eugène knew that Communists met in his back room. He never let any strangers go into it. He used to say: " The billiard-room is engaged." Meanwhile around the billiard table the representatives of the various districts discussed the party directives and held the billiard cues in their hands in case of surprise.

When Claude came in, he found Jules, from the Gnome factory. Later on, other men arrived. All of them talked about the arrests; the police had pulled in seven hundred workers.

Soon afterwards Denise came in and told them about the trial of four men. " They were sentenced to be shot for sabotage," she said. " The youngest was only eighteen. Ferronet defended them. I've just been talking to him. He says it's an obvious frame-up. It came out in court. Ferronet suspects Weiss."

" He's a terrible man," said Claude. " When we went to see him, he looked very hard at me. He must have guessed who I was. And I guessed who he was. What things they're doing, Denise! It's Hitler's spies who are in power."

Denise wanted to back him up, but she didn't know what to say. " But the people . . ." she whispered.

Claude didn't understand what she meant, but he refrained from asking her any questions.

Presently Denise went out. After a few minutes she came rushing back. " Claude," she said, " I've taken a room for you. Nobody will touch you there."

It was hot and quiet in the dim little café. Everybody had stopped talking. For a moment they thought the distant roar of the anti-aircraft guns was thunder and they were pleased. Then the sirens began to wail. Nobody stirred. They sat exhausted on the narrow sofa and thought about the dénouement. Were the Germans really coming?

Half an hour later the rain began to pour down with a deafening swish. Claude looked out into the street to get a breath of air. The woods of Meudon and Saint-Cloud seemed to have migrated to Paris. The leaves of the plane trees looked like a flock of sheep. There was a smell of the country.

Denise came up behind him. " Claude," she said, " when will France — " Once again she failed to finish her sentence. Eugène brought some beer.

" Have you heard from Michaud at all? " Denise asked.

" I haven't had any letters for a long time. He's somewhere in the north."

Eugène gave a sigh. " Damn it all! " he said. " They're fighting and dying up there. But what are they doing here? Arresting decent people! And who's doing it? German spies! If Maurice was minister, the Germans wouldn't get within sight of Paris! "

Later that evening Weiss went to see Grandel and reported to him about the day's events.

" On the whole," he said, " everything has turned out quite well.

I think we've now got rid of the most troublesome elements in the factories. Of course, the sooner we begin the evacuation, the better. It's a good thing the trial went off smoothly. It will act like a cold douche on them."

"Provided they don't get the sentence annulled. Ferronet went to see President Lebrun today. Lebrun listened to him and of course started to cry. As Breteuil says, he's the most snivelling President the Third Republic has ever known. But on the whole he behaves decently."

"What do you mean?"

"I mean Lebrun does everything that's necessary. He does nothing at all except cry."

They both burst out laughing.

When he was alone, Grandel loosened his tie and stretched himself out on a sofa. He was tired, but his affairs were going marvellously well. How could he have guessed what was in store for him? It was a mere chance that had put him in touch with Kilmann. It had started with his gambling losses and thoughts of suicide. He had thought it was a mistake, a fatal slip, a blot on his escutcheon. But it had turned out to be the beginning of his success. Of course, he was some time in finding the right road. He had been obliged to put up with a lot of set-backs, insults, and humiliations. Tessa, that petty bribe-taker Tessa, regarded him as a respectable woman looks at a streetwalker. Never mind, he'd get even with them yet! When the Germans took Paris, Grandel would be over everybody. They would all start toadying to him. The most important thing in gambling was to get the feeling of which number would turn up. He had backed the right number. All that remained now was to hold on for the last quarter of an hour. After that there would be power, honour, and recognition. He would be able to look everybody in the face. Kilmann? German marks? Nonsense! Subjective motives were nobody's concern. But objectively he would save France. He would secure a mitigation of the capitulation terms and give millions the possibility of a peaceful existence. That was real patriotism, not the hysterical ravings of a Ducane!

He wanted to humble somebody and to prove his superiority. He went into the bedroom. Mouche was lying on the wide bed. Her lengthy illness had ravaged her. Grandel said to himself: "How could I ever have embraced her?" He thought she looked half-dead. The smell of medicine nauseated him.

"Three years ago you took it into your head to be unfaithful to me," he said. "I didn't say anything at the time. Why? You might have thought I was jealous. But now we can talk frankly. I hope you've stopped thinking about lovers now. It's time for you to think about heaven. So you preferred a wretched ne'er-do-well to me? He's even worse, by the way, than his papa. Apparently, madame, you were fascinated by his curls and noble gestures. But your Romeo turned out to be a petty thief and a pimp. You thought I was a failure, a suspicious character, a spy. You made a mistake, Princess! I am the only man who can still save France."

Mouche lay, as before, without stirring. Her head was hanging off the pillow.

"Why is the Princess silent? Say something, you little tart."

He saw the little bubbles on her white lips — like those which appear on the lips of new-born babes. He frowned disdainfully and went out.

CHAPTER 25

Towards evening the sun came out and the milky haze over the sea turned pale orange. The sand-dunes looked like the map of the moon. The sand rolled on in gentle waves like hair. The dry creeping grasses, clinging to the tops of the sand-hills here and there, looked as though they were petrified. Close by foamed the sea — the tide had only just begun to go out. Explosions sent showers of water into the air; the bursting shells made the water seethe. In spite of the thunder of the bombardment, this world of sand and water seemed to be spectral and lifeless.

Lucien felt he wanted to tear the haze asunder, blow the dunes away, and let in the sea. He was stumbling along in the soft sand. British machine-gunners were somewhere close by, but he did not know where. He had fired all his ammunition. One hand-grenade was all that was left of his recent agitated life. He looked at it lovingly; it was as dear to him as the last drop of water.

The battle had been going on for eleven days. He hadn't even given a glance at the map. Here was the sea — that meant the end!

His comrades were calling him; out there beyond the haze were English ships and life beyond the Channel. He did not want to go. He had spent the day with the British and then got away. Now he was alone amid this cursed sand.

From the day the battle began he had tried to find death. He had sought it out insistently. He had passed under machine-gun fire, crawled up to tanks with a grenade in his hand, and fired at a German patrol from the attic of a Belgian farmhouse. But death as though purposely had given him a wide berth.

He never read the newspapers. One day he glanced at a sheet of paper in which some tomatoes were wrapped. He read the words: "Mechanized Joan of Arc will help us." He tossed the rag away and did not even swear. His comrades shouted about " treason." Some of them abused the Germans, others the British, and others the French generals. Lucien said nothing. Sometimes he sang in an unnaturally loud voice:

> *Here's your bunk and here's your bed.*
> *There's a buzz and a bomb and you're pretty soon dead.*

So the Belgians had surrendered? To hell with them! Lucien did not believe in victory; he remembered how he had taken secret papers to Breteuil and knew that his father and General Picard were capable of anything. The whole gang was hand in glove with Hitler. That meant it was the end. He longed for death in order to get away from his past. He had touched bottom and wanted to swim away. But for a soldier of a devoted and defeated army there was no other way out except foolhardy daring. Danger had freed Lucien from the toils of Breteuil and cleansed him of the taint of dollars and his youth, which bore the marks of sorry buffoonery.

In all the last ten days only one episode had stirred him. That was when he ran across Genteuil, the actor. Who didn't know Genteuil in Paris? He was the darling of the gods, a man of no great talent who knew how to make everybody laugh, handsome, fond of good living and flinging his money about as though life were the green meadow of a card-table — running through the dowries of girls and the savings of widows as gracefully as a little bird picking up grains of seed. Now he turned out to be a tankman. Eight French tanks had got as far as the enemy's position, where they were obliged to stop as they had run out of gas. They beat off the enemy till evening.

Help came in the morning. Five tanks were burned out. Genteuil somehow got out alive. He seemed to have turned black. When he was questioned about it he said nothing. When Lucien looked at him, he was reminded of Henri — how a few minutes could alter a man!

Lucien found life more tolerable and became attached to his comrades. He went to their rescue a number of times, acting quite spontaneously without stopping to think. He was delighted when he caught sight of the sea. His first reaction was: " Now Alfred will be saved! " But what had he got to do with Alfred? He was an archæologist, a ghoul-bug, a simpleton who believed in justice. " No," he said to himself. " that's not the right way to look at it. Alfred is a good chap." Never before could such simple words have entered Lucien's head; then he judged people by their wit, their brilliance, and their talent. And now he talked about a " good chap." Suddenly he blushed; he remembered Jeannette's eyes outside the druggist's, Mouche's tormented tears, and the enormous bed in Jenny's bedroom, which looked like a gilded catafalque.

Small detachments near the coast were keeping the enemy at bay. It was the last day of the evacuation. There were minor skirmishes going on among the dunes; the fighters crawled over the sand, came close to one another, and attacked with grenade, bullet, and bayonet. Meanwhile the opalescent columns of mist were shot through with sunlight and appeared to hover in the air.

Lucien scrambled to the top of a sand-hill and lay down. In the distance he could see the wet sand of the seashore. Half-naked men were crawling along and plunging into the water. Many of them were struck by bullets. The water foamed as though an enormous fish were disporting itself. Farther on were spouting fountains thrown up by the shells. Only a desperate courage saved the men. Others with even greater daring and desperation stood on the last ridge of the dunes and met the enemy with the fire of their rifles. Then German aeroplanes flew over and plastered the shore and the water with bombs. It began to get dark and the sea looked muddy and cold.

Lucien saw a helmet move among the dry grass; German troops were creeping in forward down below. Without thinking, Lucien jumped up and shouted as he hurled his grenade. The sand-dunes roared, and the echo rolled away till it was covered by the thunder of the batteries. Then one of the Germans ran towards Lucien.

Lucien also ran, stumbling in the sand. They fell on top of each other as though they were embracing.

Afterwards Lucien did not remember how he got the better of the German. All he knew was that he had had a tough job to tear himself away — the German's hand was gripping his throat. It was a slender strong hand with swollen veins. Lucien vaguely thought: "He hasn't cut his nails." But he did not look at the man's face. The devil take him!

And now there was not even the last grenade. Lucien ran across the cold wet sand — the sea had also retreated. He felt he would never get there. Then he plunged into the water and began to swim. He was not saving himself; he was hurrying towards the bullets and shells. His mouth was half open with the painful strain of his efforts. And his chestnut hair shone like fire.

Again death turned away from him; he swam till he reached an English motor-boat. They gave him a pair of trousers and a flask of whisky. He drank it and swore — the dream was over. An Englishman with a boyish smile said to him in broken French: "Now we've got to win the war."

Lucien nodded his head. To himself he added: "One must live. It's easier. It's easier and more painful."

CHAPTER 26

THE NEIGHBOURS whispered in astonishment. They could not make out why Agnès was so calm. Some of them admired her and said: "Now there's a strong character for you!" Others preferred a bit of backbiting: "She doesn't care a damn about her husband." Agnès went on correcting mistakes in the exercise-books, drawing leaves and stamens, carefully tidying up her room, and knitting little pants for Doudou. Nothing seemed to have changed in her life since the day when she received the yellow official envelope. They gave her six hundred francs (the sum due to her for her lost bread-winner) and said to her: "Sign the receipt." The pen did not scratch, and Agnès's eyes were dry. Doudou kept asking where his daddy was. " He'll soon be coming," she would tell him. In the morning she took Doudou round to old Mélanie, who looked after him while she was at the school. Mélanie often began to cry when she looked at Doudou. " What are you crying for? " he asked. " I've got the toothache," she said. Agnès never cried. In the past Pierre had been the only one to realize her strength of character; he used to say: " She'd even face the bullets." Sorrow and loneliness had even changed her personal appearance: her kind, short-sighted eyes had become hard, and whereas formerly she used to stoop, now she held herself erect. The old women gossiped: " She's blooming like a daisy in spring. You'll see; she'll soon get another husband."

Agnès did not even weep at night. She lay with wide-open eyes and hoped in vain for sleep; she wanted to grasp what had happened, but she couldn't. What had Pierre died for? The thought gave her no peace. She went over again in her mind their infrequent but heated arguments. Pierre had been enthusiastic about politics. He had believed in revolution and had felt the fall of every Spanish town as though it were his own suffering. She did not agree with him, but she realized that he had an ardent nature and sometimes she envied him. When he left for Spain, she was worried to the point of distraction, waiting for a knock at the door and saying to herself: " He may get killed." Then came the war and he went off without words and without hope, like a doomed man. At the station he had said to her: " This is not our war." And now he had been killed in another people's war. She wondered what his last thoughts had been. Agnès and Doudou? Or the other war, the " real " one? In vain Agnès desired to make peace with him, to understand and hear where the truth was. She would get up and go over to Doudou's cot and stand a long time listening to his breathing. What if they killed Doudou as well? He was all that was left to her from that other life, the spring that was.

But every morning she would turn up brave and bright at her class, and nobody guessed what her nights were like.

Her courage was inherent in her. It had been handed down to her by generations accustomed to hard toil, the struggle for life, and the loss of dear ones, generations that were like the houses of the Parisian suburbs which had imbibed the smoke of the street fighting. Her father used to tell her that he worked the whole time during the war, patching trousers, making lighters, mending window-frames in the peasants' cottages, and loading the hay. And he would say with a smile: " And you see I managed to survive." That was how Agnès went on living now.

When refugees began to appear in the streets and Agnès saw a bullet-riddled car with a load of children, she shuddered. She did not think of Pierre's death or the fate which might be waiting for Doudou, but she could not help feeling alarmed; the mutilated machine was like a continuation of her tortured nights.

Once again the windows of the houses were covered with narrow strips of paper. Agnès invented a complicated design. Her window looked as though it were covered with hoar frost — roses, stars, and palms. " What's that? " Doudou asked. " Aeroplanes," she said, and then added: " It's a garden." She suddenly remembered the verses which Pierre had written as a boy and which he had once recited to her:

> Before his death man sees the web of fate,
> Where winter weaves away the sins of youth.

The days went by. More and more refugees poured into Paris. Among them were the inhabitants of Lille, the weavers of Valenciennes, the miners of Lens, and the peasants of Picardy. The school where Agnès taught was put at their disposal, and she threw herself heart and soul into this new work. She moved into the school together with Doudou, looked after the sick, got food and medicine, and did the cooking. She had a large family on her hands. She had to soothe them and listen patiently to their long, incoherent stories. A woman from Fourmies told her adventures: " It was seven o'clock. I didn't know the German aeroplanes were coming." She had a child's bib covered with brown blood which she refused to part with. " He was eating his porridge," she said. " The beasts! " A Belgian woman, a miner's wife, told Agnès how she had lost her five-year-old daughter on the way. An old man from Roubaix was looking for his daughter-in-law and grandchildren. " Why did you leave? " Agnès asked. Some replied: " It was terrible! They flew low, the bombs dropped right near us." Others said: " Live under the Germans? No, we've had that experience before. We lived four years under them in the last war. Here in Paris they don't know what it's like, but we do. In the last war the Germans shot the hostages at Roubaix. In our place they arrested two of our men and told them to dig their own graves. And they killed them. They had no pity on children, the damned Boches! " Some of the refugees frankly admitted: "We saw everybody bolting, so we went too." One of the working women said: "Berger came to the town. We all knew that he was a Fascist. He shouted: 'Get away as fast as you can! You'll get killed if you don't!' But he stayed there himself to meet the Germans. The traitor! "

The refugees were constantly changing. As soon as one batch was sent off to the south, a new lot arrived. Old Riquet was the only one who stayed on. He was ill and had scarcely been able to reach Paris.

"My old woman died a long time ago," he told Agnès. "My son was called up to the Army. I don't know if he's alive. I was living all alone. The neighbours came in and said: 'The Boches are coming. Let's go.' I had such fine rabbits. I had to leave them behind. But my dog came with me, a wonderful dog; she's called Follette. I've had her twelve years and I've got used to her. At Compiègne they made us get out of the train. We had to go on foot. The Boches dropped bombs right on us. They did that in the last war. Everybody scattered. When I looked round, there was no Follette."

Agnès often noticed that, when the old man was dozing, he would move his lips and call Follette.

It was a fine summer day when the bombers flew over Paris. The whole sky was filled with a roar. The window-panes rattled. Doudou shouted: "Boom-boom!" Agnès was peeling potatoes. She put down the knife for a moment and then went on with her work again. Presently people came running in. "Two thousand killed!" they said. Agnès got alarmed and took Doudou by the hand. She was afraid they might kill him. Then she felt ashamed. "What have I got to be afraid of now?" she said to herself.

In the evening she went for a walk along the embankment of the river. A crowd of people were standing by the ruins of a large house, gazing, venting their anger, and joking. Someone said gloomily: "In any case, it's very accurate work." Life seemed to have broken up into its component parts — stones, iron, boards, and bars. Agnès saw a book with a leather binding and someone's initials. On a wall that had remained standing there was a picture of a woman in a wedding dress. Suddenly Agnès noticed a child's cot. It was hanging on the railings of a balcony. Agnès didn't stop to look any more. She rushed home. But next door to the ruins people were laughing on the café terraces, and hundreds of siphons gleamed blue like the sky.

That night Agnès saw Pierre again. She realized he was not thinking about anything; he felt ill, cold, and empty. She wanted to warm him, but couldn't; she tossed about in her bed and raved. Before dawn the anti-aircraft guns began to roar. And Doudou murmured simple childish words in his sleep.

CHAPTER 27

TESSA woke up in high spirits.

He had a talk with Joliot and said quite jauntily: "They'll smash their heads against Weygand's line. You may write that the gigantic battle is only just beginning."

"That's quite easy to write," said Joliot, "but that isn't the question. You may laugh at me, but I've never made a secret of the fact that I'm superstitious. They've called in the Germans, I give you my word! How many times have they kept on saying: 'They'll come! They'll come!' And now they have come."

"Old women's talk! Let's begin with the fact that they haven't come. Battles are taking place on the Somme."

"That may be. I haven't been there. But one thing I do know quite well: yesterday they dropped bombs on Marseille. You realize what that means? Marseille is at the other end of France. Who ever thought they would dare? Now it's all up. You may be quite sure the Italians will start today or tomorrow. And Weygand has taken the troops away from the Italian frontier. What do we want the silly Somme for?"

Tessa waved his hand in a careless don't-worry gesture. Then he asked distractedly: "Did you listen in to the Italian radio?"

"An hour ago. They're silent. That is, they were giving a talk on the paintings at Pompeii. That's a bad sign."

"Paintings?" Tessa smiled. "Just the thing for Villard. By the bye, I can tell you that our 'splendid warrior' has packed his trunks. He's probably going to bolt. Well, *au revoir!* Come and see me this evening, I shall be able to tell you something cheerful."

Tessa had in mind a partial reorganization of the Cabinet.

He had just begun to whistle an aria from *Rigoletto* when he was interrupted by the arrival of Picard, who came without being invited. Tessa glanced at him and realized at once that things were going badly. Picard said the Germans had forced the Somme. Their tank units were approaching Rouen. Everything would be decided in two or three days.

" Only madmen can talk seriously of defending Paris," he added.

Tessa nodded his head. His face assumed a sad and solemn air. It was with such an expression that he attended the funerals of ministers or senators. He shook Picard's hand in silence. When the general was gone, Tessa said to himself: " These are fatal moments! We've talked and worried and hoped, and now we're witnessing the dénouement!" He felt he would like to share this idea with somebody, but remembered that it was inadvisable to raise a panic.

When he arrived at the Cabinet meeting, he at once forgot all about the fate of France. The Cabinet had been reorganized at last. He found some of the appointments quite successful. He thought it was a good thing that foreign policy had been entrusted to Baudouin. Tessa's friend Prouvost had been appointed Minister of Information. On the other hand, Tessa was not at all pleased with the choice of Delbos. It was a plot — everybody knew that Delbos was a friend of Fouget's. He was even more indignant at the appointment of de Gaulle to the Under-Secretaryship for National Defence. It was madness! The idea of putting an adventurer in such a responsible position!

Tessa was so taken up with his own thoughts that he did not hear all that was being said. They were talking about the situation at the front. Then he remembered Picard's words and said to Reynaud: " What is it you're actually relying on? "

Reynaud replied that reinforcements were on their way from the Maginot Line and the Italian frontier. The British had promised to send some Canadian divisions. Yesterday he had appealed to President Roosevelt for help.

Tessa felt annoyed and frowned. " What interests me," he said, " is what are you going to do when the Germans get near Paris? "

Reynaud said the Government would go to Tours; if necessary, to Bordeaux.

" And after that? "

" If circumstances compel us we'll go to Algiers. We've got the fleet and the colonies."

Tessa said no more; why argue with a madman? This wasn't a government. It was a suicide club. Only Breteuil could save Tessa. But Breteuil would not save him. Tessa remembered the leaflet of the " Faithful " and closed his eyes — he was afraid.

Nevertheless he went to see Breteuil; death was better than such anxiety. If Breteuil left him in the lurch, then he would have to come to an arrangement with Fouget — or go off to America.

Breteuil was sitting motionless at his desk. Upright and arrogant, he looked as though he were posing.

That morning he had had an unfortunate scene with his wife. She had burst into tears and said: " The Germans will take Paris. You monster! You wanted it! " Attacks by political enemies never affected Breteuil; he realized that Ducane or Fouget wanted to put all the blame on others. As if Breteuil had not warned them that war against Germany would be a crime! But what could he reply to his wife, who, remembering her son, had cried out: " You killed him! You'll kill everybody! "

As he gazed at the map, he began to think. Capitulation, peace. . . . But after that? Would the enemies of yesterday realize that France was not Albania nor even Czechoslovakia? It was quite possible they would not realize; they were people of different blood and a different cast of mind. Then it would be the end. Lorraine, his own Lorraine, would be handed over to Germany! The future generations would curse the name of Breteuil. They would look upon that clown Ducane as a hero.

Breteuil had lived many years without looking ahead. The one feeling that swayed him was his hatred of the Popular Front. The victories of Hitler, Mussolini, and Franco appeared to him as his own victories. He was delighted that Beneš was no longer in Prague. When, recently, he had heard of the decision of the Danish Government, he smiled with satisfaction at the thought that the Social Democrats were once more on their backs.

Why, then, did he suddenly lose his composure? It was nerves. He would have to control himself. Now he would get the reins of government in his hands. He would dissolve Parliament; he would restore order. It would have to be paid for with humiliation, sorrow, and tears. Nevertheless, the new France, a widow in mourning, a poor little nun, would be infinitely more beautiful than Marianne the Mocker.

When Tessa arrived, Breteuil had already forgotten his wife's reproaches and his own cowardice. He was cold and impassive.

"They've gone mad!" Tessa shouted. "The ape proposes going to Madagascar — he's hankering after the virgin forests. But the Germans are on the way to Rouen. We've got to do something! These are the very last minutes."

"Didn't I warn you?"

"Warn me? How? Who advised me to remain in the Cabinet? You did. And now you're washing your hands of the whole thing, eh?" Tessa hopped around gesticulating. "I know your 'Faithful' are hostile towards me. But that's all due to a misunderstanding. You must explain to them. I was elected to the Chamber with your support. You can't chuck your friends in critical moments!"

"You're getting excited about nothing," said Breteuil. "I wanted to say that I warned you of the futility of resistance. But the nationalist circles esteem you very highly. In this house you're at home. Don't worry. We must discuss the situation and see about the composition of the Government."

"The Cabinet was reorganized today."

"That's like putting a patch on a patch. I'm talking about the new Government. The question of peace negotiations will come up in a few days. The country mustn't be left without a firm government. The Communists may take advantage of any weakness. The marshal will guarantee the transfer of authority. Moreover, it's an excellent name — the 'hero of Verdun.' Everything can be fixed up in half an hour."

"What about Reynaud?"

"He'll run away. Or we'll send him to America as ambassador. So we'll have the old man at the head. Then, of course, there'll be Laval. Myself. We'll take one or two of the former ministers."

"I think we ought to leave Baudouin."

"Quite right. He's popular with the Italians. Then we have Prouvost. He's the representative of the industrialists. Meuger thinks him very capable. I've also included you in the list."

Tessa could not hide his satisfaction, but for the sake of appearances he began to object: "I'm too old. It would be better to take one of the younger men."

"No, you will be very useful. It's not advisable that the country should take the reshuffle of the Cabinet for a change of regime. It's a great thing to put the brakes on. But everybody has got accustomed to you. One may say that to the average Frenchman you are the guarantee that nothing will be changed. At a time like this the most important thing is to pacify the country."

Tessa beamed. That rogue Fouget had made it all up! And that leaflet was a silly piece of bluff. Breteuil realized that Tessa was an honest Frenchman. And forgetting all about his recent anxieties, Tessa sat down to discuss the program of the new Government.

"If we declare in the Cabinet statement that we're prepared to open peace negotiations, a majority is assured," he said. "I'm only afraid the Germans will put forward excessively heavy conditions. Such brilliant successes may go to their head! It would be a good thing to get them to listen to reason. There's one name missing on your list, you know. No doubt what I'm going to propose is a bold step. Many people may consider is rather risky. But in times like these one has got to be tolerant."

"You're referring to Villard?"

"Villard?" Tessa looked at Breteuil in astonishment. "That old jade! By the way, he has probably bolted. No, I was thinking of Grandel. You and I are old friends and we can talk frankly. Of course you remember the story of the document . . ."

Breteuil looked annoyed and rapped the table with a ruler.

"I've already told you it is a forgery," he said. "How can you think of such vile things at a time like this?"

"You don't understand me. I didn't say that because I wanted to blacken him. On the contrary. But Grandel undoubtedly has a good many friends in Berlin. At the present time a man like that is invaluable. . . ."

"I consider supposition is out of place," said Breteuil in a dry, formal voice. "Of course Grandel is known abroad. He's an orator and a man of erudition. He'll be very useful to our Government. But someone must be left in Paris. The capital mustn't be left without a big politician. Laval and I have got to follow Reynaud in order to take over authority. I won't ask you to stay on in Paris. With your knowledge of parliamentary circles you are more necessary to us. Besides, I don't want to expose you to such a difficult situation; it's not easy for a Frenchman to see foreign troops in Paris. And lastly, so far as I know, the Germans are not particularly sorry for you. It's difficult for them to understand our subtleties. They look upon you as a puppet of the Popular Front, a man with a clenched fist. . . ."

Tessa was put out of countenance. They were silent for a long time. Breteuil's wife was crying in the next room, and he frowned as he listened to her sobbing. At last Tessa spoke. "What do you think?" he asked. "Will they be here soon?"

"It's a question of days, perhaps hours. . . ."

Tessa was in a state of perplexity when he left Breteuil. He no longer had any pleasure in the knowledge that he was to have a place in the new Cabinet. The world seemed to him to be unintelligible and hostile. What if Reynaud got to know that he had come to an arrangement with Breteuil? Mandel was capable of anything; he might order his arrest and have him shot. They would look upon him as a traitor. And the Germans considered him to be almost a Red. What a sordid business politics were! Happy were the soldiers — they at least knew where the enemy was. But as for himself, he had enemies everywhere. . . .

Tessa hunched his shoulders. His secretary poked his head round the door. "I've arranged for a reception on Thursday," he said.

Tessa thought: "Wretched people! They don't know that the Germans will be here on Thursday. Nobody knows anything. . . ." He decided to go out for a walk. Perhaps he would get rid of his nausea in the fresh air.

The dark city was unbearable. It was full of cries, hoots, and incomprehensible noises. People were crowding in the doorways. Tessa heard a variety of comments:

"They say Gamelin has shot himself."

"Reynaud has bolted to America."

"They'll all run away, but we'll have to stay and clear up the mess."

"I'm not afraid of the Germans. What does it matter to me? I'm nobody. The Germans won't touch me. But I'm afraid of bombs."

"The Germans are horrible swine. My father told me how they buried my uncle Jacques alive in 1915."

"Tessa has already come to a secret agreement with Hitler."

The voices died down. Tessa stood leaning against a lamp-post in the darkness. His heart was beating fast. He fancied he heard soldiers marching down the street. He closed his eyes and tried to prevent himself from crying out. Whose steps were they? But it was only heavy drops of rain beating on the café awnings.

He had never felt such fear before in all his life. He hardly man-

aged to run to the gates of the Ministry. He was as delighted as a
child to see the bright light in his study.

Then the anti-aircraft guns began to thunder. He ran to the window and turned back at once. The Germans were advancing on
Paris. They regarded him as a Red. Yet the workers were saying
that he had come to a secret agreement with Hitler. Everybody was
against him. They would shoot him. Or torture him. What was that
explosion? It must have been a bomb quite near. They were aiming
right at the Ministry. A five-hundred-pounder. Nobody would be
able to recognize whose body it was if he got killed. Something had
got to be done! He must make a bid for safety!

He rushed up and down the room, not knowing what to decide.
He sat down and then jumped up again. He felt a chill come over
him. At last he rang for his secretary. "Get the car ready," he
ordered. "And see that there's plenty of gas. I'm going to retire
into the country."

When Joliot arrived at half past eight for the cheerful news Tessa
had promised him, he was informed: "The Minister has retired
into the country." Joliot did not stop to ask any questions. He rushed
home. "Marie!" he called out to his wife. "We're going away at
once. That crook has already bolted. Ah, the son of a bitch! This
morning he was telling me everything in the garden was lovely.
Once upon a time they used to say: 'The rats are leaving the ship.'
Nothing of the sort — it's the captains who are leaving. They leave
the rat to look out for himself. But even a rat isn't a fool. Get a
move on, my dear, hurry up!"

CHAPTER 28

DURING the last few weeks Jeannette had been looking care-worn
and distracted. And in fact she took no interest in anything and
did not care to think at all. Her life resembled the semi-oblivion
of a patient in a serious illness. The emptiness which she had felt
after her break with Desser was overwhelming and stifling.

She went on with her work at the studio. The people around her
talked about the war and snatched the latest editions of the papers

out of one another's hands. She did not listen to their conversation. She continued as before to sing the praises of pills and liqueurs in her deceptively significant voice, and then repeated before the microphone the high-sounding words which nobody heeded about the trees, the quiet, and the wind. She had long ceased to distinguish the poetry from the advertisements. And even the things which the announcers said before her turn came on seemed to her like the advertisements of some strange firm: " So many registered tons of shipping have been sunk. . . . Patches of oil were observed on the surface."

On Sunday she roamed about the streets until evening, trying to forget herself in the noise and bustle. It was a wonderful day, and the Parisians, forgetting all about the gloomy rumours, thronged the Bois de Boulogne, played tennis, rowed boats on the stretches of water, or sat drinking green peppermint liqueurs or golden orangeades on the shady terraces of the cafés. Little children made ingenious pies in the sand. Jeannette noticed a smart blackbird. It was preening itself with its beak. She called to it wearily: " Blackbird," and the bird flew away. In one of the dark avenues she overtook a young couple — a soldier and a freckled, confiding girl in a pink frock. The soldier had a childishly serious face and a black moustache. He was holding his tin hat in his hand, and the girl was crying. " It'll end all right, you'll see," he said to her. And Jeannette felt a twinge of envy; what happiness it was to say good-bye like that! For she had been left without hopes, without tears and even without sorrow.

On Monday Jeannette stayed at home all the morning with the shutters closed. She did not want to see the light. But when she went out in the afternoon, she was astonished. Paris was quite unrecognizable. The shops and cafés were shut. Little white notices with the word " Closed " written in a trembling hand were stuck on the doors. People were bustling about near some of the houses, boarding up the windows and bringing out trunks, bundles, and hastily wrapped parcels. It was difficult to cross the street; cars moved along in an endless chain. The tops were loaded with mattresses, and frightened, tear-stained faces looked out of the windows.

Only yesterday the Parisians had been asking the refugees: " Why didn't you wait a little? What about the Weygand Line? " But now the Parisians were on the move. They rushed to the railway stations, climbed onto the tops of trucks, and implored the drivers to save them. The city became emptier and emptier with every hour; it was like a tattered sack that was spilling the flour.

Trucks were standing outside the Ministry of Pensions. The furniture was being taken out for some reason; tables, cupboards, and desks stood on the pavement. An old woman kept on repeating like a wheezy phonograph record: " Take me too! Take me too! "

Terrified, Jeannette asked: " Good heavens! What's it all about? "

The old woman gave her a blank look and replied: " Don't you know? The Germans are at Rouen." She dropped her bag and the contents scattered over the road — a ball of wool, a towel, candles, oranges. The old woman began to cry. And Jeannette began to cry too. Something had got to be done. The Germans would soon be here. They would drop bombs and shoot. Jeannette rushed away. She was no longer herself; she was just another wisp of straw blown along the dim streets of despair.

Suddenly she stopped — where was she to go to? She thought of dismal Lyon and saw her father's snarling old face. Then she remembered Fleury, the blue foliage of the vineyards, the hot day, and the quiet, when only the flies buzzed. And she wanted to live as never before. Life, which had been so cruel, now seemed sweet to her. Yes, she must go away.   ·

She went to the Gare de Lyon. Long before she reached the railway station she saw the long street packed with people. It was impossible to get through to the station yard. Chains of police were scarcely able to hold back the huge crowd. People were shouting and gesticulating: " The wretches! They've run away themselves and left us behind! Traitors! We're caught like rats in a trap! "

The policemen answered vaguely that there would be trains by evening. The people waited until dinner-time, getting hungrier and weaker. They began to look for shops that were still open, or sat down on the pavement and ate their snacks. An old workman cut off a neat piece of bread and a few slices of sausage and offered them to Jeannette. She wanted to thank him, but could not speak. She merely moved her lips. She could not have eaten anything; she felt as if she were on fire.

Night came sooner than usual; a dark pall hung over the city. People said it was Rouen burning. Somebody tried to pacify them by saying it was a smoke-screen. Women shouted wildly in the darkness. Jeannette felt she was being suffocated. In the morning, by the first dim light of the dawn, fresh crowds began to flock to the station. But there were no trains.

Jeannette wandered along the street and came out by the river. Her scared, unseeing eyes no longer caused anyone to stare at her; everybody's eyes were now like hers. People kept stopping passers-by and asking where they could get a suitcase or a wheelbarrow. Scraps of news were bandied to and fro: "The Germans are at Mantes" — "They're at Chantilly" — "Paratroops have landed in the Champs-Élysées" — "The trains are running from the Gare d'Austerlitz" — "No, they're not" — "They've betrayed us, they've betrayed us!"

A girl was greedily licking an ice-cream cone and crying. A general went by. An old man looked at him and called out in a quavering voice: "Your game's up!" And in a side-street a little girl cuddled an enormous headless doll and yelled.

There was a baker's shop open at the corner of the rue Saint-Jacques. Jeannette smelt the odour of fresh bread and seemed to wake up — she felt once more that she wanted to live. Feverish thoughts flew through her mind: what was she to do? She hurried along to the studio. The gates were closed. Even the porter had gone away. Then she remembered Maréchal. When she arrived at his apartment, she found him packing a suitcase with books, a thermos bottle, and a Negro idol. The idol wouldn't go in. It kept popping out and grinning craftily.

"The latest news is the Italians have declared war," muttered Maréchal. "You see, they've waited till today. The damned jackals! And the Government has bolted. That's your 'fight to the victorious end'! Plenty of motor-cars to be had! We've clubbed together and bought one. Grandet's looking for gas. If he gets any, we'll take you with us."

Jeannette was delighted. "Will you take me to Fleury?" she asked.

There was no gas to be had. Grandet came back with the dawn, looking quite gloomy.

"Charles drove away yesterday and had to come back on foot," he said. "There's no gas anywhere, blast them! If we could only get a horse! You could be certain to get away then. They've put guns in the Père Lachaise cemetery. I saw them myself. The soldiers are going away somewhere. I can't make it out. They say America has declared war. I don't believe it."

Maréchal began to shout: "No papers! No radio! They've all skipped! You realize what it means? They've abandoned Paris!"

When he recovered his breath he said to Jeannette: "We'll have to go on foot."

Jeannette livened up for a moment. She had a kind of childish idea that it would be a good thing to go to Fleury on foot. She hurried back to her room and said to herself: "I must put on some other shoes, I'll never get there in these."

Her animation soon passed. The dreadful bustle in the street, where the cars were tooting and the people were jostling one another, shouting, and crying, made her feel sad and weary. Where could she flee to? And what was the use? Her plight would be the same everywhere.

The hotel landlady greeted her as though she were a near relation. "It's a good thing you haven't left," she said. "There's hardly a soul in the place. It's a panic. It makes you feel ashamed to see it. What are they running away for? Tell me that, please! In 1914 the Germans were at Meaux. And the people ran away in those days too. But the Germans didn't get to Paris. The milkwoman told me they're going to bring in forty divisions today. That means they'll drive the Germans away."

Jeannette nodded her head in silence. She sat without stirring for an hour or more. The sun was now warming the landlady's little room that served as the hotel's office. A kitten was playing on the flagstones, trying to catch a sunbeam. Jeannette looked at it and jumped up. If only she could live!

She hurried back to Maréchal's flat. On the door was a note: "Jeannette, I'll wait for you till four o'clock outside the Denfert-Rochereau Metro station." She looked anxiously at the clock. It was already three. There was time. She went into a shop that happened to be open and bought a bottle of eau-de-Cologne. The man was a long time doing it up and she implored him to be quicker.

How did she come to mix up the stations? She waited till five o'clock outside the Alésia station. Then she took the note out of her handbag, and everything went dizzy before her eyes. But when she got to Denfert-Rochereau there was nobody there. She ran to the post office. It was shut. She did not think of telephoning until she got back to the hotel. She rang up Desser. It was no question of sentiment now. He would take her away. There was no answer. She took out her engagement book and rang up all the numbers, without even thinking whom she was ringing. She heard nothing but monotonous buzzings. Terrified, she said to herself: " There's nobody! "

Meanwhile the landlady had managed to see her brother-in-law, who had said to her: " There are no divisions. Only the police and the firemen have stayed on in the city. The general has gone to see the Germans at Chantilly." From the north the sound of gunfire came. When the landlady heard Jeannette exclaim: " Nobody! " she waved her hands and began to pack like a madwoman.

Jeannette went up to her room. She stood a long time at the window. Streams of people were passing down the long street. Some were pushing wheelbarrows loaded with furniture. And sometimes an old woman was sitting in a barrow or a little dog yapped. All the shutters were closed tight. And Jeannette exclaimed once again: " There's nobody! "

There was a man carrying an armchair on his back, and a little boy held a wooden horse which he refused to part with. An old woman went along swinging a bird-cage. Then there was a man wearing glasses, with a bag containing a cat. The cat was struggling and screaming. An old grandmother was being pushed along in a wheelbarrow, and a woman was carrying two little children in her arms. The last cyclists were rushing along. How terrible it was in the empty city!

Jeannette ran downstairs. The landlady had already gone. She had left everything. She had not warned Jeannette and had not even locked up her room. Jeannette walked in the middle of the road. There was a smell of burning and it was difficult to breathe. The oil tanks were on fire. Then it began to rain, and the raindrops were black with smoke. Black tears trickled down Jeannette's cheeks. And with a blank mind and wide-open eyes she joined the crowd and fled from the smoke-ridden city.

CHAPTER 29

AGNÈS spent the whole morning looking for a newspaper. A few old weeklies lay in the kiosks that were still open; then the kiosks were closed. People said there would not be any more newspapers, but

towards evening Agnès heard the cry of a news-vender and snatched
a paper from his hands. On the front page she saw a picture of the
Seine embankment with a woman bathing a dog and the caption:
" Paris is still Paris." Agnès was angry; they'd planted an old newspaper on her! No, the date was the 10th of June. . . . She ran to
the school and turned on the radio. They were broadcasting High
Mass. Then the American Ambassador Bullitt placed a bunch of
red roses at the foot of Joan of Arc's statue and exclaimed in a
marked Anglo-Saxon accent: " Save them, Joan! " Then the strains
of a tango resounded:

> *Oh la la, you dudes and dandies,*
> *What do you want pineapples for?*

And finally the announcer, with emphasis: " Our brave Chasseurs
Alpins are advancing east of Narvik. . . ."

" What do they say on the radio? " Riquet asked anxiously.

" Nothing," Agnès replied. " They're probably waiting for reports. They'll tell us tomorrow."

But next morning the radio was silent. Agnès was in despair. Her
first thought was to go away to her father at Dax. The Germans
would never come there.

She went through the empty rooms. There were rags and empty
tin cans everywhere. The refugees had been living there up to yesterday. Only Riquet had stayed on. " I can't move," he groaned. He
did not ask Agnès what she intended to do. He realized that she
would go away. Nevertheless, his anxious eyes followed every
movement she made, as though he hoped she might not go after
all. He feared nothing so much as to remain alone.

" Everybody's gone," he said. " What's going on in town? "

" They're going away."

Then after a pause she said: " I'm not going away."

He wanted to smile, but his face was seized with a convulsion.
Clasping Doudou to her, Agnès wondered why she had decided to
stay on. Was it because she was sorry for Riquet? But she had also
Doudou to think of. She must take him to safety. Of course he
might easily get lost on the way. The Belgian woman had lost her
daughter. But here there was sure to be bombing. Another two
thousand would be killed. It would be even more terrible. Why
didn't she go away? It was all a fit of pride. An hour ago she had
been bewildered when she had heard nothing but an empty noise

coming from the radio. She felt the general flight was shameful. Her strength of will asserted itself, and she thought she was doing something by remaining in the forsaken city.

Mélanie came running in and tried to persuade Agnès to go away with her. "We can go with the workers," she said. "They've got four trucks. In any case, we shall be among our own kind."

Agnès told her she had decided to stay on. Mélanie lost her temper. So it was quite true what they said: Agnès had no feeling; it was all the same to her who killed her husband. The idea of remaining with the Germans!

"That's your business," she said.

After giving Riquet something to eat, Agnès went out into the street. People were still moving along. And how she longed to go with them! She kept saying stubbornly to herself: "I mustn't." On the wall of the Mairie she saw a little notice. It was headed with the words: "French Republic. Liberty. Equality. Fraternity." Underneath was written: "Paris has been declared an open town. General Dentz, Military Governor." A little old man in a straw hat stood reading it.

"What does 'open town' mean?" Agnès asked.

The little old man shrugged his shoulders. "I don't know," he said. "Perhaps it means it isn't a fortress. Or perhaps it's at the Pope's request. In any case, madame, it's not at all gay."

A workman came up, read the notice, and shouted: "The blackguards! They've made a deal!"

One of his eyes was weeping. The other one looked with indifference at Agnès; it was a glass eye.

A fat policeman with a big moustache said with a grin: "They've left us to keep order. 'Open town' means they mustn't kill. Now they'll soon make peace."

People were still going away. Agnès looked at them with envy — when you're walking, you're not obliged to think.

In the evening she tried to soothe Riquet. "They've posted a notice that Paris is an open town," she told him. "That means they won't shoot and they won't drop bombs."

"I'm not afraid of the bombs. They kept dropping them all the time we were on the road. I'm afraid they'll come here."

She turned away. And for the first time she began to cry. She realized that, like Riquet, all she feared was that the Germans would come. Until that moment she had remained aloof from all that was happening and had thought to herself: "What does it matter?" The Germans were people like everybody else, only dressed differently. And now she felt a pang at her heart — would they really come? The Germans in Paris! . . . She repeated the words, and tears began to stream down her cheeks.

She couldn't sit still. She ran out into the street. Dirty, tired soldiers were slouching down the sloping street. They gazed wearily at the boarded windows as they hastened to get out of the town. Agnès gave one of them some bread and chocolate. He looked at her and said quietly: "Thank you. Good-bye."

She couldn't forget his eyes. And why did he say such an unusual thing as "Good-bye"?

When she got home she rushed to the radio. Toulouse was broadcasting Reynaud's speech. He said he had made a last appeal to Roosevelt. His voice could scarcely be heard. Then a bishop called the people to repentance — "This is a divine punishment." This was followed by a roaring jumble of sounds. And suddenly a voice resounded as though in the next room: "Radio station National Awakening. Surrender! We have organized secret detachments. The 16th Detachment has shot all the Masons and Marxists at Arles. At Grenoble the 47th Detachment . . ."

"Switch it off!" Riquet implored. "I can't bear to hear them!"

Agnès did not go to bed. All night long she sat at the dark window listening to the drone of the engines and the thunder of the guns. She grieved over Paris as over a dead person. In the morning she went out with Doudou in the hope of finding some milk for him and Riquet. No, all the shops were shut. And there was nobody about except a woman who was pushing a little car with a load of children. So people were still going away.

A soldier ran out from behind a corner. He reminded Agnès of Pierre — he had a swarthy complexion and large whites to his eyes.

"How do I get to the Porte d'Orléans? Quick!" he shouted.

She told him the way and asked: "Where are the Germans?"

The soldier flapped his hands and ran off. Agnès walked on. All the shutters were closed. There was not a soul to be seen. The clock in the square had stopped. It pointed to three o'clock. There was a dead stillness everywhere.

Then the sky began to rumble with a droning sound. Aeroplanes came flying very low; the black swastikas on their wings were clearly visible. "Now they're going to drop bombs," thought Agnès.

And she was amazed at her own calm — they might kill Doudou, but what did it matter to her? She thought she must have gone out of her head; she could no longer understand anything.

She went with Doudou as far as the boulevard and then she stopped suddenly: the Germans were coming towards her. Soldiers with rifles were sitting in an open car. Without thinking of anything, Agnès covered Doudou's eyes with her hand so that he might not see. She had no clear perception of what she wanted to do; she did not want to look, and yet she gazed eagerly at the alien faces. And all the while her mind kept repeating: "They've come!"

Agnès was standing by the gates of a house. An old woman in a black kerchief looked out, saw the Germans, began to cry, and hurried back. Two prostitutes sauntered by, rouged to the eyebrows. They laughed and waved their handkerchiefs to an officer.

Suddenly Doudou said in a bright voice: "Mamma, what a lot of soldiers! Is Papa coming?"

"Hold your tongue!" cried Agnès. "They're Germans!"

She was surprised at her own voice. And Doudou began to cry. She gripped his hand, turned into a narrow street, and rushed home as quickly as she could.

The midday sun was unbearable, and the refuse was rotting in the sun. There was an ash-can outside every house. They had been put out three days ago when there were still people in town. A carcass was lying near the gates of the school. A sickly smell of rotting meat filled the street. Abandoned dogs roamed about with their tails between their legs. They sniffed the pavement sadly and then lifted up their noses to the sky and whined.

In the corridor Agnès saw Riquet. He was lying flat on the floor. His hands were grasping the side of the half-open door. His tongue was sticking out of his open mouth.

"What's the matter with Uncle?" Doudou asked.

Agnès was silent. And from the street came the rousing strains of a march.

CHAPTER 30

ANDRÉ had got left behind. By the time he realized that the Germans were approaching Paris it was too late to get either train or car. He was unable to get away on foot, as he could hardly drag his wounded leg. The house where he was living was empty. For two days he had to listen to German military marches and the tramp of soldiers' boots. There was nothing to eat, but he did not feel hungry. He made no attempt to understand what had happened; he lay on the sofa like a felled tree and sometimes dozed off. He had never dreamed so many dreams before. They were a jumble of everything. He dreamed he was lying beside a machine-gun in an apple orchard and his father was handing him the ammunition belt. Suddenly the scene changed to a wedding. Nivelle passed him the cider and Jeannette said: "I've just got married." But whom was she married to? André woke up and look around the dim studio in bewilderment. He was in Paris. And the Germans were in Paris.

He heard the guttural voices of German soldiers coming from the street. He did not see them, as he kept away from the window. He said to himself: "What a pity it is I wasn't killed!"

On the third day there was a knock at the door. André got up and tidied himself a bit. Who could it be? Of course, it could only be the Germans. He was on his guard. But when he opened the door, he saw Laurier with a black bandage over one of his eyes.

"So you've stayed too?" André said.

"I couldn't get away," Laurier said. "I offered everything I had — money and my watch. One man with a car was just going to take me, but then he changed his mind. My mother's an old woman. I couldn't go away and leave her. André, do you realize what has happened?"

"No. And I don't want to either."

"We defended a little hill. But what have the others done? They've let Paris go."

André said nothing.

"Are you living here all alone?" Laurier said.

"Yes, I am. I haven't been out since the Germans came. But I shall have to go out — I've run out of tobacco."

There was not a living soul in the rue Cherche-Midi. The tobacco shop turned out to be closed. André suddenly stopped and thought: "How beautiful it all is!" The city seemed to have been cleansed. He had never seen these old streets like that before except in the pale light of dawn. But now it was midday, with bright light and short shadows. And such a stillness everywhere! . . . It must be like that when tourists walk through the streets of Pompeii. It was all right for the tourists, but he and Laurier were inhabitants.

"We're living in a sort of Pompeii," he said to Laurier, and smiled wearily.

They passed the dairy and the shop where André had admired the pipes. There was the antique shop where old Boileau used to blow the dust off the porcelain shepherdesses, and farther on was the restaurant where Josephine served her ragouts. But what was that up there? He had never before noticed the pelican feeding its young with its blood on the front of the corner house. The pelican was five hundred years old and must have seen a good many things. Or perhaps it had not seen — it was feeding its young and had no time to look.

Laurier was talking about his mother. "She keeps asking me what I'm going to do with my guitar," he said. "I can't do anything. Unless I play at German weddings."

He wanted to cheer André up and tried to smile. His face with its bandaged eye looked like a house after an air raid, and André turned away.

They were standing outside a patisserie. André suddenly felt hungry. They went inside. It was a smart patisserie that used to serve embassies and the mansions of the Saint-Germain district. The proprietress, a fifty-year-old woman with rouged cheeks and an opulent figure, was talking to a woman customer.

"Everybody said the savages were coming," she declared. "But they're very polite and they pay for everything."

"My mistress says they'll restore order and teach the workers to work. And quite right too!"

André was eating a bun and said with his mouth full: "You've got a fine mistress!"

The cashier whispered to him: "That's Madame Meuger's housekeeper. What are you going to pay with, francs or marks?"

"I haven't got any francs," said André with a smile. "I haven't earned any. You see, I'm not Monsieur Meuger."

The cashier failed to understand his irony and said in a business-like way: "They say the marks are not real ones. They're not valid in Germany. But I think it's all nonsense. They're quite decent people and they wouldn't think of paying with counterfeit money."

André clapped Laurier on the back. "You heard that? Madame Meuger. Our Lieutenant Fressinet realized what they were up to. No wonder he shot himself. He's well off now, but what are you and I going to do?"

He walked down the street, in which he knew every house and every lamp-post, but now he felt like a foreigner in his own city.

The bun had given him an appetite. They went into a restaurant. Germans were sitting at all the tables. They were eating voraciously, gobbling up enormous dishes of food and drinking beer and champagne. The victors were feasting. The atmosphere was that of a celebration, not with flags and fanfares, but with this gourmandizing and belching of men who were replete with power. Omelets made with ten eggs. A whole chicken for each man. Five bottles of champagne. The new mark notes rustled in the hand of the obsequious, oily proprietor with shifty eyes.

André and Laurier tried not to look at their neighbours. They ate their food in silence with a look of concentration, as though they were carrying out a difficult job.

Suddenly Laurier pushed his plate aside and went pale.

"What's the matter with you?" André asked.

"Do you see that?"

He pointed to a big mirror at the top of which was written: "No Jews served here."

"What about it?" André muttered. "They're decorating the place in honour of the new masters."

"Yes, but I'm —" For a moment Laurier was too agitated to speak. "I'm a Jew. I never thought of it before."

André got up without finishing his meal and paid the bill. The proprietor hurried forward. "Have you dined well, monsieur?" he inquired obsequiously.

André looked at him with disgust. "Why have you stuck up that notice?" he said.

"I can't do anything," the man whispered. "We've got to consider our clientele. Don't think that I — It's for them."

Then Laurier looked at him with his one excessively bright eye. "And what's this for?" he shouted, pointing to his bandaged eye. "For them or for us?"

They walked back in silence. What could they talk about? When they had been beside the machine-gun on the hill they were free men, but now they had to submit to the Germans. They had got to put their clocks and watches on Berlin time — such was the order displayed on the walls. They had got to adapt their thoughts and feelings. And what could they do after that? Play the guitar at German weddings? Take the brushes and paint the Rubens-like banquets of Berlin book-keepers? "No," André thought. "Now there are no brushes, no nebulæ, no Jeannette!"

A tipsy tramp with cunning eyes was sitting on a bench. A bottle was standing beside him.

"Peace?" he muttered drunkenly. "Give me a scrap of paper and I'll sign it. Why shouldn't I sign it? My throat's parched and I want to have a drink."

Young German soldiers were now marching down the rue Cherche-Midi. Their eyes were very bright and empty. They were singing loudly and the old grey houses heard a song they could not understand. One of the soldiers stopped and looked at a narrow street that seemed like a chink.

"A filthy town!" he laughed. "And they call it Paris! It's a place for Negroes!"

Then he marched on.

"And we were still wondering what we were going to do," said André. "It's very simple — we're going to clean up Paris; it's not for Negroes now, and it's not for Frenchmen."

The milkwoman was standing with a couple of children near the house where André lived. She was looking at the Germans and sobbing. She greeted André through her tears. "Just think of it," she said. "I can't get used to it."

One of the soldiers, a middle-aged, tired-looking man, went up to her and began to say something, as though trying to console her. She did not understand his language. Then he took a photograph out of his pocket. It showed him dressed in his Sunday best and surrounded by four children. In an attempt to make her understand he held up four fingers. He began to pat the milkwoman's children, but they shrank away in fear and hid behind their mother. She thanked him and even tried to smile, but when the soldier went away she said to André: " The most terrible thing was that for a moment I began to feel sorry for him. We mustn't feel sorry now. Now we've got to . . ." She burst into tears again and André couldn't understand what she was saying.

Slowly, with a heavy tread, André mounted the winding stairs.

" Well, here we are in our eyrie," he said. " Let's have a smoke. I don't know what we can do. I understood something in 1936, or I thought I did. I had a friend called Pierre. He was killed near Strasbourg. No, I didn't even understand Pierre, but he had an ardent spirit and he believed. And so did the people in those days. They talked and argued and laughed. But now you and I are alone. If you only knew how bewildered I am! Everybody's bewildered. I really don't know if it's possible to go on living. And the Germans are in Paris."

Laurier did not reply. For a long time they sat facing each other and smoking in silence. From outside came the sound of loud singing that rose to a shout.

CHAPTER 31

JEANNETTE went on walking till dawn. Footsteps, children's cries, and distant shots resounded in the darkness. In the morning Jeannette sank on the trampled grass together with the others. She slept for a few hours and was roused by the roar of an explosion. She jumped up and saw a cloud of smoke in the distance. People were lying flat as though they wanted to grow into the earth. Later a little girl with her belly torn open was carried past. Weary and footsore, Jeannette walked another twenty miles. Her legs ached and she was tortured with hunger. When she arrived at a village with her companions, they found the place deserted. All the inhabitants had fled. The people gathered outside a closed shop and somebody shouted: " What does it matter? My children haven't had anything to eat for two days."

They looted the shop. Bottles and tins were seized. An old woman plastered herself with jam. A workman gave Jeannette a tin of preserves and some crackers. She was afraid of lagging behind the people with whom she had walked so far. She was afraid not only of getting separated from the people but even from the various things — the old woman's white hair, the little boy's sailor suit, and the wheelbarrow with the rattling teapot. She ran to catch up with the people and ate as she ran.

There were still a few peasants left in the next village. A man and his wife were standing at the door of one of the houses. Jeannette asked for a glass of water.

"This is not Paris!" the woman answered angrily. "I have to get it from the well. Give me a franc."

The husband looked at his wife in amazement as though he had never seen her before. "You bastard!" he shouted.

Then the sky was filled with the drone of engines. The people scattered and lay flat on the ground. Jeannette was covered with warm dust. When she walked on, she could still hear the woman's wild shrieks. Her husband had been killed.

They came across some soldiers who were standing by the roadside. "Where are the Germans?" the refugees asked. "Are we going to defend the left bank of the Loire?"

"To hell with that!" said the soldiers. "Who knows what they're going to do? The colonel's gone away. They say the Germans are on the left bank. And that'll be the end of us. It's very simple. Daladier has got five million francs for it. They've worked it all out according to plan. Hanging's too good for them, the blackguards!"

One of the soldiers was a little fellow with an enormous bandage round his head. He ran up to Jeannette and began shouting: "First it was Spain. Then it was the Czechs. And who's paying for it? Me. I'm paying for it. They've gone off to Bordeaux. Can you tell me how much more a man can stand?"

Jeannette looked at him and answered quietly: "Quite a lot."

At night the refugees took shelter in a church. There was a smell of incense and dried flowers. A mother crouching next to Jeannette carefully fed her child at the breast. An old woman moaned near the altar. When morning came she was silent. The purple rays of the sun streamed through the stained glass. She was lying still with her sharp nose pointing up at the dome. Nobody knew whether she was asleep or dead.

Jeannette dozed where she sat. Snatches of memories passed

through her mind: most of all, she saw the night in July when she walked down the narrow street with André, the shiny blue elephant of the merry-go-round, the lantern, and the kiss under the spreading chestnut tree.

The people began to stir and went on their way groaning. Only the old woman stayed behind in the sunlit, whitewashed church.

About midday Jeannette caught sight of Fleury from the top of a hill. She could see the flashing water. " I'm saved! " she thought to herself. Like all the others, she imagined that she had only to cross the Loire and life would be waiting for her on the other side.

All around were burnt-out or abandoned motor-cars. The trees were ravaged and splintered. The telegraph wires trailed in fragments. Jeannette stumbled across the carcass of a horse. Its big yellow teeth were sticking out and it looked as though it were smiling. A wounded woman was sitting by the roadside. Another woman was sitting beside her and holding her hand over her face. The town of Gien had been destroyed. Saucepans, books, and soldiers' haversacks were lying about among the rubble. On a wall that happened to remain intact there was a bright placard: " The castles of the Loire — the pearl of France."

Jeannette could scarcely pick her way across the ruins. The sun was scorching. A mephitic smell came from the jumble of stones; victims were lying beneath them. Here and there a head protruded; feet in women's shoes or old people's hands stuck out. Jeannette went on, like a lunatic. She did not see anything, but she was going towards the river.

Suddenly she stopped and screamed. The bridge was blown up. She sat down on a stone and began to wait for death, just as a few days ago she had waited for the train, with a dull intensity, seeing nothing and thinking of nothing. And when the German aeroplanes flew over and raked the road where the refugees were lying with machine-gun fire, Jeannette did not stir from the spot. She would very likely have stayed there until morning, if the others had not come up to her. Their common misfortune had left them to care for one another. They shared their food, helped carry the wounded, and even brought back an old woman's dog that had lagged behind.

Someone said to Jeannette: " There are some boats down there." She got up and followed the people.

On the other side of the river she began to laugh. She wanted to say to the trees: " Here I am, alive! "

She began to climb a hill, although she had barely the strength to put one foot after the other.

"Jeannette!" someone called out to her.

It took her some time before she realized that the dirty-looking soldier with a scrubby face was Lucien. He shook her by the hand and laughed. It was four years since they had last seen each other. Only once Lucien had caught sight of her in the foyer of a theatre and tried to get away unnoticed. Now he was laughing for joy; it was such tremendous happiness to meet Jeannette at a time like this! What an extraordinary piece of luck to run across her among so many thousands. He felt he had never ceased to love her. All that had happened since — the conspiracy game, Jenny, the sand-dunes — was only a long, bad dream. And now she was talking and he heard her voice!

"Lucien!" she said. "What's happened? It's frightful. Over the other side of the river. They've killed women and children, and just now a boy. I can't understand anything."

Lucien grinned. "Twenty thousand refugees have perished on this road alone," he said. "And how many roads there are like this! I saw what it was like up north. We couldn't move for the refugees. And the Germans were in front of them. You don't understand? It's what the plotters wanted all along. They led the Army into a trap and ran away. They wanted to smash us. And my father is among them. How many times he used to say: 'The Germans would be better!' Now they've got their 'better'!"

He stroked Jeannette's hand mournfully. "You'll have to get going," he said. "They're going to bomb. You see what a lot of soldiers there are. And how many officers are there? Three. The rest have bolted. They say we're going to defend this hill. I can hardly believe it. It's been like that the whole time. We dig trenches and wait. Then we get the order to retreat. And they come and bomb us. Get going, Jeannette."

"Lucien, are you going to stay here?"

"Me? I was at Dunkirk. It might be better if I got killed."

"But I'm afraid. I want to live, Lucien."

She gave him a warm kiss and went on her way. At the top of the hill she stopped. The setting sun was very large and red. None of the ruins were visible from the hill-top and the world seemed to be peaceful and full of green and freshness. The broad shallow Loire gleamed lazily in the distance. The sandy islets were covered with bushes. Two trees near Jeannette stood calmly like sentinels on guard; the pattern of their dark leaves was etched against the sky. The trees looked blue in the distance. Swallows were skimming the unmown grass. Far away a dog was barking with a bass note. A little white house, probably forsaken by its owners, beckoned to her with its offer of peaceful shelter. " How lovely it is here! " she thought as she took a cracker out of her bag. The simple joy of life filled her with its charm.

Then the familiar droning began again. She lay down submissively on the grass. As the others had done before, she tried to lie flat and unnoticed, to bury herself in the grass. And the grass smelt wonderful — it seemed to smell of her childhood and her first delight in spring. Her heart was beating fast. The droning grew louder. She still had time to think: " There must be some thyme growing about here. There's a smell of thyme. . . ."

Her death agony did not last long. Her clothes and the surrounding grass were red with blood. Her face was peaceful. The wind sprang up and tossed her long wavy hair. And her big dreamy eyes gazed at the first pale stars.

CHAPTER 32

TESSA was to lunch with the Spanish Ambassador at the Coq d'Or restaurant. The conversation promised to be a laborious one, but the dainty Bordeaux cuisine and the restaurant's famous wine-cellar mitigated the unpleasantness of the situation.

Tessa had been through a terrible week. He had arrived in Tours a couple of days before his fellow members of the Cabinet. It was only on account of this that he managed to get decent accommodation. The other ministers had to rush about like homeless tramps. The town was bombed. Reynaud could do nothing but write telegrams to Roosevelt. Tessa came out with a witticism: " Our Premier has become the special correspondent of the United Press." The muddle was so great that one of the telegrams to Roosevelt lay in the telegraph office all night long. And the Germans were advancing at the rate of thirty miles a day.

Tessa tried to see Breteuil as often as he could, but Breteuil was gloomy and unforthcoming. He said his wife was suffering from a nervous breakdown. A lame excuse! Tessa could not understand why he had not broken down himself. Only Laval was beaming; his white tie looked like the adornment of a young bridegroom. But Laval paid no attention to Tessa. As for the Cabinet ministers, they fluttered foolishly from the château where Reynaud was living to the town, where they looked for their lost pieces of luggage and waved aside their secretaries, who kept pestering them with the question: "Where are we going?"

At the Cabinet meeting Tessa proposed the opening of peace negotiations. Reynaud interrupted him with the question: "What about our obligations? We must wait and see what Roosevelt replies." Mandel looked fixedly at Tessa, and Tessa turned away. That man was capable of anything. He regarded Tessa as a traitor. Even the children knew that when Mandel was bent on ruining a man, you might just as well write his obituary. A horrible face — not a drop of blood in it! An inquisitor!

Help came unexpectedly; General Picard demanded admittance to the meeting, as he had very important news. Usually restrained, Picard was now in a terrible state. He mumbled, and Tessa suddenly noticed that he had no teeth. How did he come to lose his jaw? Tessa did not realize at first that the general was speaking. Picard kept on repeating: "Yes, yes, a Communist revolution! The rabble is besieging the Élysée Palace. Big fires have broken out. . . ."

Tessa closed his eyes in horror. He was not afraid of bombs or shells. He had even accustomed himself to the idea of being taken prisoner. That was terrible, of course, but the Germans were cultured people; they wouldn't treat a minister like a criminal. The only people he was afraid of were the Communists. He had realized after his conversation with Denise that the Communists hated him. If they seized power, they would put him to death. And besides, what a misfortune it would be for France! When the Germans entered Paris, it would be a day of national mourning. But in any case, the Germans were better than the Communists. The Germans would hoist their flag over the Élysée Palace, but they would not touch the palace itself. But the Communists would burn down everything as they had done in 1871. Even now they had already started setting fire to places. They were fanatics and wild beasts!

Mandel got in touch with Paris, and half an hour later he an-

nounced: "There is perfect order in Paris." Picard tried to dispute
the statement, but finally he said with a self-satisfied smile: "Of
course! General Dentz is a friend of mine. He's one of the best
Army leaders. He has ordered the police to fire on the provocateurs
who attempt to offer armed resistance to the enemy."

Tessa kept saying: "It's time to leave Tours!" Another day went
by. The Germans had advanced another thirty miles. It was a horrid
day — the 14th of July. Tessa had always thought that fourteen
was his fatal number. Amalie had died on the 14th. He was at the
barber's when he was told that the Germans had taken Paris. He
had been prepared for the event, but it was too much for him and
he exclaimed: "What a misfortune!" But the barber started shouting: "Go away! I can't work!" The man must be a Communist!

In the evening Tessa went to Bordeaux.

It was only the day before yesterday, but it seemed to him to be
a hundred years ago. What a lot he had gone through! He had given
up distinguishing one day from the other. The Germans continued
to advance and had reached the Loire. How fortunate were the
people who had stayed on in Paris — for them it was all over! But
here it was necessary to do something and make decisions. Churchill was blackmailing. It was rumoured that de Gaulle had arrived
in Bordeaux. Who knew, he might be connected with the Communists? There were a great many dockers in the town; the Prefect
had said they were a "dangerous element." Reynaud must be got
rid of, but Lebrun was still hesitating. He simply sat and wept.
Tears were out of place. What was needed at the present time was
a firm hand!

Breteuil asked Tessa to have a talk with the Spanish Ambassador;
Berlin was to be asked to state the terms. Breteuil added that a lot
depended on the talk. Tessa was proud of his mission and depressed
at the same time. He tried to humour the Spaniard. When the Ambassador began to praise the wine of Bordeaux, Tessa diplomati-
cally retorted: "I've tasted your Rioja. It's in no way inferior to our
best vintages."

Then he added with a sigh: "My son was Consul at Salamanca at
the time of the epic events in your country. He was a great friend
of many of the Falangists and gave his active support to General
Franco."

"Where is he now?"

"He's lost. He was killed by the Communists."

After the roast chicken *à la broche,* Tessa got down to the business at last. What were Berlin's terms? The Spaniard answered vaguely at first — it was not worth while bothering about details; there must be mutual understanding, the victors had no desire to humiliate France. When he started to talk about what he called the "details," Tessa felt a cold shudder run down his spine.

"But this is out of the question!" he exclaimed.

"Of course, some of the points can be modified. As I've just said, the main thing is to establish contact. Much depends on the fate of your Navy. Berlin doubts whether the marshal will be able to get everybody to submit to his orders when he is in power. In particular, the Germans are anxious about certain unwholesome attitudes in Morocco and Syria."

"That's a misunderstanding. Nobody in France commands more authority than the hero of Verdun."

"So much the better. . . . You're quite right. The armagnac here is really enchanting."

After the lunch with the Spaniard, Tessa went to see Breteuil.

"The Germans are quite mad!" he said. "The terms are unheard-of. I'll say frankly — they're degrading! I'm afraid Reynaud is right — we shall have to slip away to Madagascar."

When he saw that Breteuil was not astonished at the German demands, Tessa calmed down. "Of course," he said, "we must look at the matter in a sober light. On the whole it's not so ghastly as it seemed to be at first sight. Only I think it would be better not to divulge the terms immediately. First of all we'll sign and then we can publish. Otherwise the Communists will try to make capital out of it. Or de Gaulle. By the way, he's in Bordeaux. I'd like to know what he's doing here. Yes, the next few days will be critical for us. But afterwards everything will go back to normal."

In the evening Reynaud resigned. Tessa warmly congratulated Pétain. "You have the prestige of a victor," he said. The marshal replied in a hollow, aged voice: "I thank you."

Late at night Tessa dictated to Joliot the names of the new Government. The tubby little editor had already managed to bring out a tiny edition of *La Voie Nouvelle* in Bordeaux.

"Of course the ministerial crisis did not pass off quite according to the rules. But the marshal had his list ready. It won't be possible to announce the declaration in the Chamber. We can't help that — we're in the position of refugees at present."

"What are the German terms?" Joliot asked.

"I can't say anything about that — it's a State secret. I can say one thing — the terms are entirely compatible with our dignity. The marshal would have refused to consider any other."

Joliot screwed up one eye distrustfully. "Dignity is an elastic commodity," he said. "What I want to know is, are the Germans going to be allowed to come here or not? I've just found a tolerable printing-press. And besides, I can't live in a motor-car!"

"You can settle here. Bordeaux will become the second capital."

The hours dragged on like months. The Germans were in no hurry to reply; they were continuing to advance. Twice a day Tessa marked on the map the towns occupied by the enemy: Orléans, Cherbourg, Rennes, Dijon, Belfort. On the fourth day he ordered the map to be taken away. "You'd better tell me what towns we still have left," he said wearily to Pomaret.

Chautemps suddenly protested to Tessa: "They want to knock us out completely. The terms are such that no Frenchman would put his signature to them." Then he added with a smile: "Unless it's your Grandel, but he has stayed behind in Paris."

"Since when has Grandel been 'mine'?" Tessa asked resentfully. "Besides, I am by no means insisting on capitulation. I wanted peace with honour. That's only natural. If necessary, we'll go away to Algiers. Perhaps to Perpignan to start with — it will be easy to get a boat from Port-Vendres."

Tessa even began to think about resistance. He pored a long time over the map, had a talk with General Leridot, and broadcast to the country: "Soldiers and sailors! The armistice has not been signed. The struggle goes on. Hand in hand with the Allies, defend our honour on land and sea and in the air!"

In the evening he went out for a walk, as he had a headache and wanted to get some fresh air. On the quayside he was recognized by some dockers, who began to shout: "What about ducking the traitors? Or swinging them from a lamp-post?"

Tessa caught sight of a taxi and hopped into it for safety. He pulled up the windows in spite of the heat and stuffiness; he thought he was being pursued. He drove at once to Breteuil's.

"Chautemps is intriguing again," he said. "He wants us to go to Perpignan and then to Africa. This is Churchill up to his tricks again. Chautemps could never say no to money. You've only got to remember the Stavisky affair. I consider the German terms should be accepted. We're being swept into revolution and anarchy."

The Germans were still in no hurry to give their reply. They were advancing on Bordeaux.

In the early hours of the morning Tessa was awakened by the thunder of explosions. German bombers were flying low over the town. An hour later he was informed that the victims numbered seven hundred. He was obliged to visit the hospital. The sight of the wounded children and the smell of ether overwhelmed him. "We send them telegrams," he wailed, "and they answer us with bombs!" Marquet, the Mayor of Bordeaux, came in at the double and demanded the withdrawal of the Government in order to save the town. Then the panic began. Tessa spent the whole day with the Spanish Ambassador. In the evening he said proudly to Joliot: "You may pacify the population. The Germans have promised the marshal not to touch the town."

On the following day he was sorry he had spoken to Joliot. Crowds of frantic refugees were pouring into the town from all parts. It was impossible to get through the streets. There was not even a scrap of bread in the bakers' shops. People were sleeping out in the squares. And still they came flocking into the town.

Tessa sent for the Prefect. "Don't let anybody into the town," he ordered. "Otherwise we'll be done for. Put the police on duty with automatics. It's impossible to rely on the Army — the troops are demoralized. They will let in anybody — refugees, Germans, and Communists."

When Tessa was informed that the town of Tours was resisting, he was furious. What madness! What was the good of enraging Hitler? And so at his suggestion the Government declared all the towns of France "open."

Tessa made another speech on the radio. His voice shook with emotion: "We hope that our enemies will show magnanimity. The French have always been a realistic people. We are able to look truth in the face. If we are obliged to sheathe the sword, we can say: the spirit is invincible! But at the present moment, alas, tanks are stronger than the spirit!"

He sat down worn out; the sweat poured down his face. Suddenly Weiss came in. Tessa was surprised — why had Weiss been allowed in without being announced? They seemed to have forgotten that Tessa was a Minister and that Bordeaux was now the capital.

Weiss held out a scrap of paper. " Sign! " he said.

" What is it? "

Weiss explained: a considerable number of airmen were anxious to fly to England. They must be prevented. The gas must be rendered unserviceable.

" But it's not my department," said Tessa. " Go and see the general."

A malicious smile flitted across Weiss's face. " The general can never be found when he's wanted," he explained. " And the matter is urgent. I advise you not to stand on formalities. The ministerial labels are of no interest to anybody now. And you'll have to answer to the Germans for every aeroplane that gets away. You understand me? "

Tessa wanted to shout out: " Blackguard! Spy! " but he refrained. He gazed at Weiss in bewilderment. Then he took out his fountain-pen, screwed up his eyes, and signed the paper. Weiss politely thanked him.

CHAPTER 33

TOURS was holding out. The defenders of the town had twice destroyed the pontoons. The Germans looked with amazement at the grey island of houses with the gleaming River Loire in front of it. The road to Poitiers and farther on to the south passed through Tours, and the unexpected hold-up irritated the advancing Army. One of the German generals who was fond of showing off his erudition said to the officers: " What can you expect? These Froggies are defending Balzac's birthplace."

How did it come about that Tours was not declared an open town? It was said that the Mayor had appealed to the population to defend the town, and the courage of the inhabitants had so shamed the soldiers that they decided not to retreat. The first attacks were said to have been repelled by the wounded in the local hospital. All sorts of legends were born in the cellars where the inhabitants were hiding among the barrels of wine. Battalions were magnified to divisions. People talked of mysterious shells that were destroying the German tanks. Nobody could understand why Tours held out. Apparently, even in the days of panic, there were brave people and brave towns. Tours was defended by two battalions together with a few hundred wounded soldiers and a certain number of volunteers — elderly men who had been through the last war and young lads who were not liable for military service.

Among the defenders was the parliamentary deputy Lieutenant Ducane. The soldiers called him "the old chap" — he had aged considerably in the last year. The things he had lived for had turned out to be elusive. He was not blind; he saw his mistake, but secretly he hoped that the blood of self-sacrificing people would resurrect the old France, which he knew from books. He looked upon the defence of Tours as the last gift of fate.

Thirty-five years ago Ducane had been to a party given by some of his literary friends. He was then an ill-favoured youth, with big ears sticking out, who dreamed of becoming an aviator. Charles Péguy, the poet, had recited some verses:

> *Blessed are they who die in righteous battle*
> *For the four corners of their native land.*

Péguy was killed on the first day of the battle which was afterwards known as the Battle of the Marne. He did not know that the battle would end in victory; he died with defeat, panic, and flight all around him; he died defending Paris. And France was victorious. Ducane often repeated his favourite lines to himself in these dark days. Péguy's poetry sustained him in his moments of despair. He tried not to think about what was happening in Bordeaux. Though he was worn out and had not slept for nights on end amid the roar of the shells and the groans of the wounded, he still believed in victory: he looked on the defence of this small town as a battle for France.

The German batteries on the right bank of the Loire were assiduously blowing Tours to pieces. And the bombers were helping them. The heavy bombs shattered the old houses with mediæval façades, pillars, and turrets. The defenders were without provisions, medical supplies, or shells. The French guns ceased to fire; only the machine-guns kept the enemy at a distance.

At the end of the second day there was a short pause. Ducane and Sergeant Maillot were having supper in one of the houses overlooking the quay. The soldiers had brought them some bread and a scrap of sausage. They munched heartily and the noise sounded like an echo of comfort in the unusual stillness. The windows were blocked up with sandbags and the room was dark. The furniture reminded one of old times: there was a sideboard with china cups painted with pink cockerels. The floor was littered with cigarette ends, empty cans, and torn-up letters. The soldiers were resting in the next room.

Somebody switched on the radio. Tessa was making a speech from Bordeaux. The Minister of the new Government was talking about tanks and the " immortal soul."

" Shut his mouth, the blackguard! " shouted Ducane.

The soldiers burst out laughing. " He won't let the ' old chap ' get on with his grub! "

They switched off the radio. Sergeant Maillot, with thick grey stubble on his face and inflamed red eyes, suddenly said to Ducane: " Why did you help them — in 1936? You're an honest man. It looks as if we're not going to get out of here. I'd like to understand. . . ."

" Understand? " Ducane smiled. " I can't understand anything myself. White has turned out to be black, and black white. And so we've gone blind. Or, on the contrary, we've begun to see something. I don't know. There are some honest people — de Gaulle, for instance. The British won't give in. But our fate — " He waved his hand.

" I was up north at Arras in the last war," said Maillot. " The town was literally wiped off the face of the earth. This time I was at Arras again at the beginning of the war. Funny, wasn't it? I saw the people had built up the town again in the last twenty years. It was quiet there. It was the Belgian rear. Nobody ever dreamed it was coming there. And then they got it again. When we left Arras there was nothing left, only dust and rubble. They'll build it all up again. Nonsense! Is it possible to go on living like that? Something has got to be changed, and properly. . . ."

" Are you a Communist? "

" No. I was a teacher. I voted for the Popular Front and against you. I never bothered about politics. But now I'm almost driven to despair. Yesterday Captain Grémy told me I was a bad Frenchman. Is it always going to remain like this? "

" If we survive," shouted Ducane, " I'll be the first to say no! But this is not the time. Tell me, do you mean to say you're not going — " he stuttered and could hardly get his words out — " to defend the town? "

The answer was the roar of a shell — the pause was over.

The third day settled everything. The Germans burst into Tours. The library was set on fire. Fighting went on in the narrow streets between the quay and the boulevards. The sun looked murky red through the smoke and there was a heavy smell of burning.

Ducane stood at the window of an attic. Tiled roofs and a long winding street stretched before him. He was not a bad shot. There used to be a Whitsuntide fair in the little town where he grew up. He was no good at flirting with the girls, as he stuttered and was ashamed of his ugliness, but he used to shine at the shooting range. The onlookers stood and gasped: " Can't he shoot! " That was a young lad's conceit. Now it was his last hope. He would not let his life go cheaply.

He noticed some Germans in the distance. They were advancing in file, keeping close to the grey wall. Across the street was a barricade of barrels, furniture, and mattresses.

Suddenly Ducane saw a French soldier. It was Sergeant Maillot. What was he doing? He must be mad. He rushed towards the Germans, then stopped and hurled a hand-grenade. Three Germans lay on the pavement. The rest took to their heels.

Ducane was beside himself with delight. " Bravo, sergeant! " he roared. Maillot stood motionless, as though petrified. A shot rang out; he threw up his arms and fell.

Germans began to appear again. Ducane fired without missing. The Germans could not stand it. They ran back to the quay.

Ducane wiped his steaming forehead with his handkerchief and took out his flask — he had been tortured with thirst for some time. Then he looked out of the window and grabbed his rifle. The Germans were crawling along the roofs of the houses. He saw a tall red-haired soldier in front of him. They fought for a long time and Ducane brought the German down.

There was a moment of quiet. A bumble-bee that had flown into the room buzzed monotonously. Ducane picked up his rifle and took aim — the Germans were crawling over the roofs. He fired two more shots. He had time to think: " That's the ninth. . . ." Then he staggered and fell with a crash like a tree.

CHAPTER 34

TESSA was lying exhausted on the sofa. The flies gave him no peace, settling on his nose and the crown of his head and tickling his ears. He was unable to move; he was longing to go to sleep, but sleep refused to come. He felt every minute was a weary desert of time. But once upon a time the days and months had simply flown. He thought anxiously of Denise. Where was she now? She was in the hands of the Germans. And Paulette was dead, no doubt. Otherwise she would have found him — it was an easy matter to find a minister. Everybody said the roads were strewn with the corpses of refugees. As for Lucien, he could hardly have survived. He was such a hare-brained fellow. People of that type were always the first to go under.

What was going to happen now? Laval was wearing a smile. Marquet was feeling proud of the wines of Bordeaux. Breteuil merely answered curtly: "It'll pass off." There was not a single gleam of light. The Germans continued to advance and had occupied Brest and Lyon. They were at La Rochelle, not so far from Bordeaux. Envoys with an armistice had left, together with Picard. But who knew what the Germans would say to them? Perhaps they were delaying on purpose. The country was seething. Pomaret said the Communists in Marseille were shouting in all the squares. And here in Bordeaux the people's mood was absolutely abominable. He remembered his encounter with the dockers and gave a deep sigh. De Gaulle was openly urging disobedience: "Destroy aeroplanes and war supplies, so that they may not fall into the hands of the enemy! . . ." No doubt Weiss was an insolent creature, but he was right — the aircraft would have to be accounted for. Some of the Radicals were thinking of bolting to Africa. Not at all a bad idea! They had offered him a berth on board the *Massilia*. He had been on the point of accepting it, but Breteuil said: "We'll put the passengers of the *Massilia* up against the wall." And Tessa hastily exclaimed: "Quite right! One can't leave one's country at a time like this!"

The telephone bell rang; Tessa was summoned to a meeting of the Cabinet.

As soon as he caught sight of Lebrun blowing his nose, Tessa realized that the news was bad. Breteuil read out monotonously like a funeral prayer the German terms which Picard had telegraphed.

"Shameful terms!" cried out Tessa indignantly.

Breteuil gave him a stern look and said: "It must not be forgotten that we're beaten."

"I understand," Tessa nodded. "Personally I'm in favour of signing."

Half dead with exhaustion, he went to the microphone, cleared his throat, and began his speech " to the nation " with all the jauntiness of old times : " Let us not lose heart! The terms of the armistice signed by our delegates are severe, but they are not shameful. They are honourable terms. All my life is the guarantee of that! "

But afterwards, having drunk a glass of mineral water, he said to Breteuil in a weak voice: " Only take care it doesn't get into print. At least before the troops have laid down their arms. Why play with fire? There are plenty of hotheads among them."

Picard returned to Bordeaux. Tessa went to see him at once. He was devoured with curiosity.

"What was it like? " he asked. " I mean the atmosphere."

The general looked at him with his dull empty eyes. " I was ashamed of my uniform," he said.

"Is that all? I'm interested in the details."

"Details? By all means. There was a table with a jug of water, an inkstand and some pens. The officer said to me: ' We're receiving you magnanimously, are we not? ' — and he pointed to the jug. Then he turned to his colleagues and said: ' I'm not Marshal Foch.' "

"But what about him? How did he behave? "

"He was like some film actor. He strutted about and fussed and made a speech — he's got a hoarse voice. He stood on the turf and stamped the grass with his foot, as though he wanted to say: 'I'm trampling the soil of France.' That was all. As for the rest, I won't even tell it to myself — it's too shameful."

Three more days went by. Tessa was loaded with work. The cares of the day distracted him from his own thoughts. He was obliged to do all sorts of things — receive the press, check up on the police cordons, see to the supply of flour, and wheedle the

Spanish Ambassador. And then there was also the reorganization of the Cabinet; two new Ministers were introduced.

The armistice envoys now set out for Rome. Everybody waited for the final solution. The Germans went on bombing the towns.

"I no longer believe anybody," Joliot croaked. "You'll see, they'll come to Bordeaux."

At last the terms of the armistice were made public. Breteuil proposed that a "national day of mourning" should be observed.

"He has got only one idea," Tessa laughed, "and that is to say his prayers. He likes the smell of incense."

It was decided to hold a solemn Requiem Mass. Pétain and all the ministers were present at the service. Tessa put on a black tie as when he attended funerals. A few people near the doors of the cathedral shouted: "Long live the marshal!" Tessa was annoyed; they were again singling out the Premier!

He was very bored during the ceremony and all kinds of foolish thoughts kept coming into his head. What if Paulette was still alive and had joined up with somebody? No doubt Villard was glad he hadn't joined the Cabinet. Later on he would say: "My hands are clean. I didn't sign." In a couple of days they would have to move on somewhere else. Oh, how farcical was the outcome of it all! And Hitler had got a little moustache like Charlie Chaplin's. How hot it was in the church!

When Tessa came out of the cathedral he was approached by a good-looking elderly man who wore a ribbon in his buttonhole.

"What can I do for you, monsieur?" Tessa asked politely.

Instead of answering, the stranger gave him a slap in the face. Tessa put his hand to his cheek and merely shouted: "What's that for?"

The man stared at him with dark, angry eyes and replied: "I've lost two sons."

He was not allowed to say any more as he was led away by the police. A crowd began to gather. An old woman in mourning was crying. Somebody was sniggering: "They've socked him on the jaw." Tessa quickly hopped into the car.

He still had not recovered from his shake-up when Joliot came bustling in.

"You've fooled me again," he cried. "It turns out they're going to occupy Bordeaux in accordance with the treaty. It beats me why you didn't give them Marseille."

In vain Tessa tried to soothe him. He told him there were excellent printing-presses at Clermont-Ferrand and that the newspaper would flourish there — he would arrange a subsidy for it.

"As if I wanted your help!" yelled Joliot. "It's not worth a sou! One can be a lackey to gentlemen, but not a lackey to lackeys! I'd rather sell winkles in Marseille."

Joliot went on raging for a long time. Then he strolled back to his hotel, where Marie was waiting for him. It took him some time to calm down; he drank a whole siphon. At last he got his breath back. "Tessa's going to Clermont-Farrand," he told his wife. "That makes the fourth capital. Then there'll be a fifth. But I'm fed up with it! Full stop. Anyway, the Germans are ruling France, so we might just as well go back to Paris. At least we've got our own flat there."

"But what are you going to do in Paris?"

"What I did before. I'll carry on with *La Voie Nouvelle*. As if the Germans don't need newspapers! And who's going to throw stones at me? Tessa? He's just had a sock on the jaw. His cheek's all swollen. That's some satisfaction."

A few days later the Government moved to Clermont-Farrand. Tessa put his documents in a large portfolio and examined the locks of the trunks. Then he looked out of the window and started back. The Germans were marching along the street. A smart lieutenant was looking with a condescending air at the few passers-by. Tessa was indignant; they had not been able to wait till evening. In any case, it was most inconvenient; here was a sovereign Government and a foreign power in occupation. What would they think abroad? He drew the velvet curtains, as though he wanted to fence himself off from the Germans.

The secretary said the car would be ready in an hour. The engine was being repaired. Tessa lay down for a while before starting on the journey. Golden sunbeams streamed through the curtains and danced on the wall. Suddenly he thought he saw the hard metallic eyes of the man who had insulted him. He wondered what had become of him. One must realize that he had a father's feelings. . . . What about Denise? And Lucien?

After these reflections Tessa rang up the Prefect. "I've got a request to make to you," he said. "I was attacked by a man today. Thank you, thank you, quite well. I want to ask you to set the man free. He told me his sons were killed at the front. You're the father of a family. You'll understand what a misfortune it is. It's enough to turn a man's brain. I also have got two children. Yes, yes, they've perished."

Tessa could hardly finish speaking; he was choked with tears.

The secretary came in and announced: "The car's ready."

Tessa pulled himself together. A few minutes later there sat in the car a man who realized that he was endowed with the confidence of the nation.

CHAPTER 35

THE GOVERNMENT settled in Clermont-Farrand because the neighbourhood abounded in mineral springs, and all around were spas with comfortable hotels. Laval stayed in Clermont-Farrand. The other ministers took a fancy to Vichy, or Mont-Dore, or La Bourboule. Tessa considered Royat to be the most suitable place — rooms had been reserved for the President of the Republic.

The big confectioner's La Marquise de Sévigny was chock-full of customers. Crowds were waiting outside for a table to become vacant. The refugees were attracted not so much by the thick chocolate for which Royat was famous as by the society — it was so nice after all the horrors to meet your friends again and to find yourself in your own circle. All the cafés of the Champs-Élysées seemed to have migrated here — the Marigny, the Carlton bar, and Lucien's favourite Fouquette's.

Panting with the heat and her load of sorrow, Mme Montigny was telling her tale: "I had to return to Paris a week before the disaster — my husband was ill with angina. And then we barely managed to get away. It was a terrible journey! We had to leave our Cadillac near Nevers — there was no gas to be had. We were brought to Vichy by some ruffian or other. I hope the car is still intact. . . ."

At another table a fashionable playwright was pouring out his woes: "The first night was to have been on the 16th. But it all started on the 10th, and now nobody knows when the theatre season is going to open. . . ."

A stockbroker was shouting to his deaf companion, who had an apparatus near his ear: "It's impossible to say anything definite without having the New York quotations. But I wouldn't risk it. When everything calms down, those stocks will go up."

Listening to the stories, complaints, and prophecies which reached his ears, Desser smiled mournfully. They still did not realize what had happened. They had the idea that the old life would start again in a week or a month.

Why had Desser come here? He had no liking for fashionable places and preferred wine to chocolate. And the chatter of the perplexed and worried ladies, the lamentations of men with their dusty travelling bags, the yelping of the Pekinese and toy terriers, the sighs ("I lost my suitcase at Moulins"), the triumphs ("I gave the porter three thousand francs and got a room"), all the bustle of agitated society and its hangers-on were now doubly repulsive to him. But he wanted to surfeit himself. When he saw Tessa go into the confectioner's, he got out of the car.

He listened to the chatter and felt stifled. All the baseness, all the dirt was here! He still saw blood before his eyes. He had come by the route known as the "Blue Route," which leads from Paris to Nice. The people who used to drive along it before were rich smarties, women in shorts, snobs, lovers of the south or roulette. It was along this road that the refugees had swarmed. German aeroplanes had flown low over them; smiling, the pilots let one another pass. Desser saw the communal graves. He saw thousands of homeless people. The Paris buses were turned into dwellings and those who lived in them thought themselves lucky. Starving soldiers roamed about the fields looking for beets or turnips. Women shouted as though demented; they were calling their lost children. Where towns had stood, there were ruins. The unmilked cows lowed frantically. There was a smell of burning and dead bodies.

Remembering the "Blue Route," Desser closed his eyes. It was Tessa's laughter that made him look up.

"So you're here too?" said Tessa. "The world's a small place indeed! Who'd have thought we'd meet at La Marquise de Sévigny after all we've been through!"

Desser said nothing. "You don't look well," Tessa went on. "That's bad, Jules. You must take yourself in hand. Personally I expected it to be worse. But everything has passed off all right. You know, our fools — Mandel and company — wanted to bolt to

Africa. But we didn't let them. In times like these the whole nation must be united. It will soon be all over. The Germans will go for London. It's only a matter of two or three months. We're out of the game and that's to our advantage. What do you intend to do? You can lend us a hand — we're now going to undertake the economic reconstruction of the country. What are you laughing for? I'm talking perfectly seriously."

Desser's smile faded. "It's a good thing you don't understand anything," he said pensively. "Drink your chocolate and don't think. You see, you're a bug. Don't be angry with me, but you're an old, respectable bug. And you lived in an old, respectable house. Now the house is burned down. But the bug is still alive. But what has it got left? I'm sorry for you as you are."

"You'd do better to be sorry for yourself!" Tessa shouted resentfully. "I don't want your pity. I'm not Fouget! I'm a man with up-to-date ideas. It was you who clung to the past — the Popular Front, liberalism, America. I tell you we're going to clean up the country. I'm preparing the text of the new constitution. We shall take from Hitler everything that is most valuable — the idea of the co-operation of all classes, hierarchy, discipline, and we shall add our own traditions, the cult of the family, French good sense, and then . . ."

Desser was not listening. He kept repeating thoughtfully: "Poor old bug."

Tessa went off. Desser still remained sitting. He no longer listened to the conversations or looked at his neighbours. At last he got up and walked with uncertain steps to the door. Somebody said aloud: "Desser's here too! That means everything's all right."

He did not turn round; perhaps he didn't hear. Again he saw Paris wrapped in a dark mist, the refugees with their carts, and the mountains of rubble. This was the France he had wanted to defend and save — the France of his childhood, the anglers, the Chinese lanterns, and the "Cafés de Commerce." Once he had pointed out to Pierre the lighted windows in a quiet deserted street where people were eating soup, preparing their lessons, knitting body belts, making love and kissing. Now there was nothing: dark windows, like the sockets of eyes, bomb-scarred walls, and Germans in the Place de la Concorde. He'd got to think and draw his conclusions. He had wanted to save so many things. And he had fed bugs, hundreds of bugs. He had loved humble taverns and financial millions.

It was all false! And that was why Jeannette had been worried. Yes, in all his long life he had loved one hare-brained, insignificant, good woman. What had become of Jeannette? Perhaps she was wandering about somewhere in the neighbourhood in search of a night's lodging. Or had she perished on the way? Or had she stayed on in Paris, standing at the long window and gazing? Grey-green soldiers were now marching down the old street. He could not help her. He had sunk everybody.

The hotels, shops, and cars had long since been left behind. The fresh smell of pastureland was wafted about him as he drive along. The dark green grass gladdened his eyes, which were fatigued by the turmoil of life. He drove on without knowing where he was going. For some unknown reason he turned to the right, where the road went uphill. The air was cool and fresh. And how pleasant it was! He stopped the car and got out. The place was deserted. For the first time in many months he was alone. He gazed with admiration at the meadows and the yellow, pink, and purple flowers. Those over there were called snapdragons. What a childish name! And farther on were the dark-blue mountains. The clouds on them were sheep.

The air was so pure that Desser stood and breathed in amazement. It had seemed to him of late that he was being suffocated. But here his heart beat fast, his temples throbbed, and his ears were filled with a rumble.

He thought of Bernard, his friend of long ago. Everybody knew Bernard as an experienced surgeon. Yesterday Desser had been told that Bernard had shot himself. He had a face like an Ibsen pastor, dry and stern. But he was fond of life, cultivated his garden, and played with his little daughter. And now Bernard had shot himself — he had seen the Germans pass by his window and had written on a sheet of paper torn from a scratch-pad: " I can't bear it. I prefer to die."

At one time the idea of death used to terrify Desser. It was strange and incomprehensible. Now he thought of Bernard's end as something wise and related to the business of life. He had suddenly realized that death was a part of life; and death ceased to frighten him.

He walked across the meadow as far as a tree. He walked in a funny way — he did not want to crush the flowers. The tree reminded him of Fleury and his meeting with Jeannette.

Together we'll find the ship of oblivion
And roam about the Elysian fields. . . .

Here were the fields of oblivion, Elysium!

It must have been a strange sight — an elderly man, podgy and slow in his movements, dressed in a long overcoat, walking about the meadow, waving his arms and muttering: "The grain . . . love . . . cold. . . ." But there was nobody there to see him. Only on the mountain-side the shepherds were lighting a fire; neither the blare of the radio nor the agony of the refugees had reached them. They lived in the peace of the past.

The sun went down behind the mountain. And death at once came near in the shape of a light mist. The mist was alive, quivering and moving like the sheep. Desser smiled absentmindedly, drew a large revolver from his hip pocket, and pressed his lips eagerly to the muzzle as though it was the mouth of a bottle and he was dying of thirst on a hot day.

The echo repeated the shot. The shepherds stood on their guard, thinking that the wicked war was coming even to them!

CHAPTER 36

It was already the end of July, but the fields of Limousin were bright green as in the month of May. Lucien gazed for hours at the green. It was so soothing. Then he got up from the ground and went on his way. He had no idea where he was going. He would have stretched himself out and gone to sleep under the big ash tree long ago, only hunger made him get up. It was the last human feeling — he smiled to himself. He had been living on carrots and beets. Sometimes a soldier whom he happened to meet, as dirty and unshaved as himself, shared his bread with him. Sometimes in a village he would get a bowl of fresh milk, and the warm smell of bread — which formerly used to make him feel sick — now seemed to him marvellous, a relic of his bygone youth, and the very smell of life.

He had cut himself a stick. Only a week ago he was still a soldier of the 87th Regiment of the Line. But there was no longer any army and Lucien looked on himself as a tramp. In a little village he heard his father speak on the radio and announce the armistice. An old woman standing next to Lucien exclaimed: " It's all over? That's a good thing! " and drove on her pig, which was pink as a painter's nude. The soldiers swore, but Lucien went on listening to the timbre of his father's voice. Yes, it was his father's voice. Memories of his distant childhood awoke in his mind. He remembered his father standing at his bedside when he was ill, and saying: " Amalie, my darling, don't worry. Science is all-powerful." Now his father was saying: " The soul is immortal." But Jeannette wanted to live. Lucien had seen a great number who wanted to live. The German pilots must have devilishly strong nerves — they fired point-blank at women and children. . . . What was the meaning of the speech? Apparently his father had been granted an indulgence by Breteuil and would very likely get an Iron Cross from Hitler. Lucien yawned heavily. Would somebody give him a drink of milk or not? But thousands of soldiers had already passed that way before him. The terrified peasants fastened the doors of their houses, and the old woman whom he overtook on the road protected her rosy pig with her arms and wailed: " I've got nothing, nothing! "

That evening Lucien was ravenously hungry. He threatened the old woman with his rifle. She stopped wailing, but clung all the more to the cord to which the pig was attached. " I've nothing to give," she muttered. " A lot of fuss! " Lucien growled, spitting at the ground. He was thinking of the pig.

He went on his way. A short distance from the road there was a farm. The shutters were tightly closed. The peasants were afraid to look out at night. There was no sound except the incessant barking of the dogs. Lucien shouted: " Give me something to eat, you rascals! " Nobody answered, and the dogs went on barking furiously. Lucien waited for a while and then went towards a little stream at the side of the track. He took a drink of the warm water that smelt of slime. Then he lay down under a cattle-shed. He was waked by a woman's voice calling softly: " Soldier! Soldier! " A girl was standing beside him. She was wearing a man's overcoat over her nightdress. It was a moonlight night, and Lucien took a good look at the girl. He even thought to himself: " She's not at all bad." Her lively eyes and snub nose gave her a merry look, although she had nothing to be merry about. She kept repeating anxiously:

"Soldier! Are you sleeping, soldier?" She had brought him a large hunk of bread and a piece of fat.

"I waited till the mistress went to sleep," she explained. "She left the fat out, but locked all the rest up in the storeroom. I saw you when you were standing in the yard. The master isn't a bad man, but there are so many of you coming now. He says we'll die of hunger ourselves. I came out and I saw you go down to the brook. As soon as they went to bed, I got the food and ran down to you."

Lucien said nothing, took out his knife, and began to eat voraciously. The girl stood watching him. He was a long time eating — he was satisfied, but he couldn't stop. Still half-dazed with fatigue and sleep, he looked up at her and asked: "Are you the daughter?"

"I'm the servant."

He finished eating at last, wiped his knife on the grass, and glanced silently at the girl. He realized she was gazing at him with a look of pleasure. He was surprised — he thought he looked wild enough to frighten everybody now. His face was covered with a stiff brown stubble. But his green eyes sparkled. His uniform was permeated with dust and sweat. He beckoned to her with his hand to sit down. The girl obeyed him. She turned out to be shorter than Lucien by a head. Quietly, and as it were thoughtfully, he put his left arm round her neck, carefully tilted back her head, and kissed her. He felt he was drinking water. She kissed him affectionately and often, and when they lay down together on the grass she murmured: "Soldier! Oh, soldier! . . ."

It began to get light. The girl grew anxious. "The mistress will wake up," she whispered.

"What's your name?" he asked.

"Jeanne Prélys."

Lucien felt his heart flutter. He gently stroked the girl's red scruffy hand and moved his lips — he wanted to say something kind, but failed. At last he said: "Jeannette. . . ."

"And what's your name?"

"Lucien."

"What else?"

"Lucien Duval."

He shook the soil from his uniform and went on his way without looking back. The night he had spent beside the brook seemed to him like a gift of fate, the dream of a doomed man. Now he was awake. Duval, Durand, Prélys — anything you like except Tessa!

They could put him on the rack, but he would never admit it! Of course, he had only to say that he was Tessa's son and they would feed and clothe him at once and take him in a car to Vichy. But he would rather kill the old woman, the one with the pig. . . .

He came across an unknown soldier, who was also tramping with a stick. They looked at each other and winked.

"The marshal seems to have lost his army," the soldier jested.

"Like a pin," said Lucien.

They went their separate ways. A new day had begun and they had to hunt for food.

Marshal Pétain, however, was not concerned about the Army. The day before, he had made a great speech to the French nation. He said he did not want to deceive anyone. Querulously he repeated: "Don't rely on the State. The State can give you nothing. Rely on your children. Bring them up in the spirit of religion and the principle of the family. They will sustain you." When Tessa heard the marshal's speech, he was depressed at first. Nobody would sustain him — neither that wastrel Lucien nor that hot-headed girl Denise. But a few minutes later he whispered ironically to Laval: "It's quite logical at eighty-five, especially as he's not being maintained by his children, but by the State."

Nobody remembered the soldiers; the ministers were busy allocating the various ambassadors and representatives, sending delegations to Paris with Breteuil at their head, drawing up the new constitution, handing war material over to the Germans, and combating the partisans of de Gaulle. The Army went to pieces of its own accord. There were no trains. The inhabitants of the unoccupied zone made their way to the south by road. The Parisians and the people of the north were turned into tramps, and the peasants implored the police to protect them from the soldiers.

Lucien climbed to the top of a hill. All day long he lay in a meadow and did not want to stir. The day was cool and the sun kept disappearing behind the big bulging clouds, which were sailing towards the two grey towers of the neighbouring town in the east. The movement of the clouds intrigued Lucien. He did not remember anything clearly, nor did he try to conjure up the picture of the past, but the movement of the clouds gave him the sense of time. He seemed to live once again his short, rackety life. Everything was blended together: Henri's death, Jeannette's eyes when she stood outside the druggist's, the sea beyond the dunes, and the light haze above the two towers. And so, when the sun went down and the clouds vanished in the quickly falling dusk, life seemed to him to be over. He even shivered — partly with cold and partly with fear. He had never before been afraid of death. Why, then, was he afraid in this damp evening on the hill under the dim misty stars? He was surprised himself and suddenly exclaimed: "Grub!" Of course! He'd had nothing to eat all day. He would have to go and look for some bread.

He plunged into the valley. He saw the light of a little square window glimmering among the trees. He knocked on the door and called out: "Some bread for a soldier!" Nobody answered. The house belonged to an old pig-headed man called Serget, who had starved his wife to death because she went to confession. He was strong as a lion and could bend copper coins in his hand. He was like a bear lurking in his den. He lived alone with a young cowed servant-girl, who always got hiccups as soon as her master began to scold her. His elder son had left for Canada years ago, but the younger lived with his father-in-law in a neighbouring village. He had been called up a month ago, although, being left-handed, he had previously been exempt from military service. Fate brought Lucien to Serget's house.

He banged on the door and shouted: "Give me some bread!" A smell of cabbage and onions came from another window: the servant was cooking soup. The smell of it made Lucien furious. A savage feeling was roused in him. The lighted window was silent, and this was more than Lucien could bear. Let them abuse and drive him away, but how could they dare to keep silent? Damn it all, whom had he been fighting for?

He put his face to the window. He saw behind the net curtain the face of an old man which reminded him of Breteuil. Serget was unlike the leader of the "Faithful," but Lucien was so enraged that he imagined he saw the resemblance. He stepped back from the house and began to yell: "Open the door, you scoundrel! I'll shoot!"

He would have fired at the odious bright window, but a shot rang out, and, swinging his leg round as though he was dancing, he fell to the ground.

He fell without a word. It was Serget who shouted, and he shouted terribly. If there had been houses in the neighbourhood, the people would have run out; but the house stood in a lonely valley and only the echo answered: "A-a-ai!" And the servant-girl hiccuped, half dead with fear in the kitchen.

Serget threw away the rifle he had once upon a time used for boar-hunting and ran up to Lucien. He was at his last gasp. Death had been almost instantaneous. The misty moon bathed Lucien's cheeks with a green light. His eyes sparkled like a cat's and his hair seemed to glow as though it was on fire. He looked like a handsome brigand in some popular picture, and in the light of Serget's lantern the blood on his uniform seemed like thick fresh paint.

Serget put the lantern on the ground and sat down next to the body. He sat like that till midnight; he wanted to smoke and even took out his pouch, but then he forgot about it. He sat without stirring; only his large head with its mop of dishevelled grey hair moved slightly to and fro.

The servant-girl came out. She went timidly up to the body and screamed. "Oh! he's beautiful!" — then the hiccups began to choke her again. "Be quiet!" growled Serget. She wanted to go away, but he ordered her to stay. Then he got up and said in a strange, unfeeling voice: "Bandits! But who is he? A soldier. A Frenchman. . . ."

And then the girl went white as a sheet with terror, for her master suddenly fell down beside the dead man and began to wail:

"Pierrot! Little son!"

A report was drawn up in the morning. Serget signed it and said: "Now take me." But the police had enough already on their hands without any more trouble. "The matter will be investigated," the sergeant said. "They'll call you, if necessary." They searched Lucien's pockets but found no papers. They put down in the report: "An unknown person, dressed in a soldier's uniform." Suddenly the girl cried out: "I've found it!" She showed a scrap of paper which she had found in a little inside pocket in Lucien's coat. The sergeant unfolded the paper. It contained three words carefully written in large letters: "France. Jeannette. *Merde.*"

The sergeant spat. "Bandits!" he exclaimed.

CHAPTER 37

DENISE was hiding at Clémence's flat. That was the only reason why the old woman had stayed on in Paris. Neither the rattle of the drums nor the sound of the songs reached the crooked street. The stillness seemed almost unbearable. Denise tried many times to go away, but the old woman persuaded her to stay.

"Wait," she said. "The place is empty. They'll spot you at once."

Clémence went out every morning with a bag and came back with bread and vegetables and sometimes with meat. It gave her pleasure to prepare the meal; she felt she was pampering Jeannot.

She reported all the news: "The Devilles are back, and so are Rousseau and his wife. They say a lot of people are coming back. Deville was upset and asked me where the Communists were. I told him the Communists were in hiding. It's not so easy to find out. But they're not the sort of people to give themselves up. What else could I say? That wasn't enough for him. People are saying: 'What have we got to hope for now?' Nobody wants to live under the Germans. Have a bit of sausage. There's no meat. Soon there won't be anything. The Germans are exporting everything. They've got as many marks as you like; they print them and give them to their soldiers. I saw the orderlies carrying out crates of stuff! They're grabbing everything — coffee, stockings, boots. Eat as much as you can. Who knows, we may soon be starving. But you've got to keep your strength up. Deville was right when he said: 'Now all our hope is in them.'"

When the panic started, Denise was given her instructions. "You'll stay on," she was told. "You'll carry on the work in Paris. Keep in touch through Gaston." The day before the Germans arrived, Denise went to the address she had been given. The door was opened by a woman with tear-stained eyes who said: "They've taken Gaston, and I'm going away on foot." Denise went round to all the comrades; the houses were boarded up. Had they gone away? Or were they hiding?

She found inactivity the most terrible thing of all. Time dragged slowly. At night she was almost driven to smash the clock — it kept ticking, ticking. And the water kept dripping in the wash-basin — drip, drip, drip.

What had become of Michaud? She might die without knowing whether he was still alive or hearing him say once again: " And how! " They could have been together; they might have been happy. Now there would be nothing — no meetings, no life. And the Germans were in Paris. You had to say those words over and over again to believe them. And there was no Michaud. Perhaps he had been killed, or taken prisoner. How terrible it was to fall alive into the hands of the Germans! They had captured whole armies.

The June night seemed interminably long, and Denise kept repeating: " Michaud! Michaud! " till she was almost stupefied.

Suddenly she remembered Claude having told her that he was to remain in Paris. She would have to find him. She remembered his address; she had taken a room for him after the trouble in May. Perhaps he was still there.

Clémence embraced her as though she was setting out on a long journey.

" Put more rouge on your lips," she said. " They don't touch that class of women."

Denise had to go across the centre of Paris. When she caught sight of the first German, she drew back and very nearly ran away. What a repulsive face he had! And there was a swastika on his sleeve. She told herself she mustn't be so nervous. She had got to hide everything now. She went on her way, thinking only of whether she would find Claude and be able to start the work.

She reached the Boulevards. She tried not to look, but looked all the same. German officers were sitting with prostitutes on the terraces of the big cafés. The women were dressed as at the seaside with bare legs and sandals and their fingernails enamelled like rubies. They were laughing, drinking champagne, and clinking glasses. In the shop windows there were dictionaries and guides to Paris in German. The shopkeepers were offering souvenirs to the soldiers — little models of the Eiffel Tower, brooches, picture postcards, and obscene photographs. They were doing a brisk trade. They exchanged francs for marks. The news-venders were shouting: " Le Matin," " La Victoire."

Denise bought a newspaper and glanced at it. " Our amiable guests," she read, " no doubt appreciate the delicacy of French cooking." Then there was an advertisement: " I have been educated at two universities. I speak German. I am looking for a waiter's job." She threw the paper away.

The obscure unwholesome life of maggots and ghoul-bugs went on in the deserted occupied city. People were selling their pictures, shirts, smiles, and the remnants of their honour. Denise asked herself with loathing: " Can this be Paris? "

She crossed over to the left bank of the river and wandered a long time about the empty streets. Without people they seemed longer than ever.

An enchanted city! The usual things were displayed in the abandoned shops: ties, toys, tankards with inscriptions. A forgotten umbrella was leaning like an old man against a boarded-up door. A withered geranium stood in a pot on a balcony. There was a cage hanging in a window with a dead canary in it. "The sleeping beauty," thought Denise. She remembered the picture in the book of fairy-tales.

She had never noticed before in such detail the ornate façades, the Renaissance statues, the eighteenth-century columns; the people had worn the stone and now the stone was celebrating its victory over the people.

In the boulevard Port-Royal a hunchback was gazing up at the trees. A blind man went by, tapping the pavement with his stick. A lame youth hobbled past. All the cripples, all the monsters had crept out of their holes; they had not been able to get away and now they alone populated the city.

The limes were in flower. The air smelt like the far-off country. The frightened birds rushed hither and thither; they could not get used to the roar of the engines in the sky. German aeroplanes flew over the conquered city from morning to night, flying so low that they seemed about to strike the roofs.

The place was empty. Then suddenly people appeared! Refugees were walking along the pavement with tired, sleepy children in their arms. They had left the city a week ago. At that time fear and hope were expressed in their faces. They had asked the way they were to take, railed at the traitors, and rushed hither and thither in an effort to reach safety. And now they were plodding back like cattle to the slaughter-house. What terrible things they had seen in those few days! They had lain down under machine-gun fire, looted trains, and wept over the poisoned wells. Many of them had lost their dear ones, and all of them had lost hope. When they left they

were unaware that Paris was surrounded. When they reached
Chartres, Orléans, Gien, they saw the Germans. They were stopped
and driven back. They returned to their native city like captured
fugitives returning to jail. And looking in terror at the Germans, a
mother whispered to her wailing child: " Be quiet."

Denise saw a placard on a wall. It showed a German soldier holding a child while a woman stood by smiling. Underneath was
written: " Behold the protector of the French population! " And
next to it hung the faded tatters of a theatrical announcement:
" Odéon . . . First Performance . . . *The Taming of the Shrew.*"
The German's eyes were blue and bright. Eyes like that were now
looking at Denise on all sides. She turned away, but the eyes appeared again; she crossed to the other side of the street — the same
bright blue enamel appeared there. And unable to bear it any
longer, she cried out — the eyes came towards her from off the wall.
She didn't realize at first that it was a live man. But the lieutenant
smacked his lips playfully.

She came out into the avenue des Gobelins. A queue of twenty or
thirty women were standing in the broiling sun. Then there was
a fluttering of handkerchiefs, hair, and bags. Somebody called out:
" They're rounding up the soldiers! "

The women rushed to the house near by, and some bluish milk
was spilt on the asphalt. The policemen brought a youth out of the
house. He was wearing a pair of army trousers and a workman's
blue blouse. Somebody shouted: " Let his mother come! "

An old woman — for a moment Denise thought it was Clémence
— went up to the soldier and embraced him passionately. " Good-
bye, Mother! " he whispered.

The police shoved him into the van. The mother looked at the
embarrassed policemen and said sternly: " So that's who you're
working for! "

And again the blue enamel eyes — drinking cognac, eating
sausage, and grunting.

Denise turned the corner of the street. It was a poor quarter behind the Place d'Italie. The houses looked as though they were
stripped. There was dirt and ugliness everywhere. Nothing adorned
them any longer — neither the noisy crowds nor the bright shop
windows. Some old men were sitting on a seat playing cards.
Women were standing in the doorways, ready to vanish as soon as
any soldiers appeared. But the Germans did not go there.

Denise rang the bell. Nobody answered. Who could tell? In the last hours people had left against their will, carried away by the tramping rhythm of the huge crowd on the move and the mad desire of the others to get out and away. Besides, Claude might have been arrested. The Germans were going into the houses. Denise put her ear to the door and listened. Not a sound.

But inside Claude, with his hand on the bolt, thought anxiously: "Now they've come!" For several minutes he did not open the door — he wanted to have another moment of freedom.

"You!"

For a long time they could not say anything. Then Claude began to speak: "Look what we've come to! I never thought I'd see this! You know what I mean — the Germans in Paris!"

Denise looked at him. His cheeks were grey, but his eyes sparkled. It was a miserable room. On the table lay a hunk of bread, a copy-book with verses, and a book entitled *How the Steel was Tempered.*

"We must do something," said Denise. "Have you any contacts?"

"No. Out of all our people only Julien has stayed on. But I don't know his whereabouts. I thought he would come. But I don't suppose he'll walk about the streets. We're marked men now. They're looking for us. Chiappe didn't stay on for nothing — he's working with the Germans."

"We must do something, Claude! The refugees are coming back and the first thing they ask is what about the Communists? We can't wait. It would be criminal!"

"We've got a hectograph, ink, and paper — everything's still here. Only it's all to no purpose. Do we know what to write about now?"

He began to cough painfully. Denise said nothing. She realized there was no sense in the idea. No doubt Claude was a good comrade, bold and ready for anything. But he did not know — as she knew. And there was nobody to get in touch with.

She sat slumped by the window. In front of her stretched the lifeless street. And suddenly she remembered everything. The demonstration had passed down this street. She saw the red shawls on the balconies and heard the people singing. Little boys like sparrows were shouting in the trees. The women were holding up their clenched fists. Everything was colourful, resonant, and vibrating. Michaud was striding at the head of the column. Denise straightened her back. Michaud, are you there? He did not answer. He went on marching and looking straight in front of him. He was very tall and cheerful. He was striding over the trenches and over the Germans — Michaud knew, he wouldn't make a mistake, he wouldn't stop. Michaud was marching.

Smiling vaguely, Denise moved her lips.

" Claude, give me some paper."

He thought she was writing poetry; he tiptoed to the corner, but Denise was searching for the words. She felt they were quite near, but could not find them. She thought once again of the phrase which had come to her in the Boulevards: " And this is Paris? " And again the phrases came one after another: " The cradle of the Revolution. . . . The city of the Commune. . . . The heart of France. . . ."

She thought she heard the voices of the soldiers who were wandering about, forsaken by everybody; the voices of the prisoners of war who were breaking stones on the roads, while the Nazis made fun of them; the voices of the refugees wandering down the long, long roads. It was the voice of the French people. And farther on were other voices. And the girl alone in the empty city heard the cries, the silence, the words of anger and hope. She wrote without stopping as though someone was dictating to her.

Claude read the manuscript through and quietly wiped his eyes. He dirtied his face — his hand was stained with purple ink.

" How did you manage to write it, Denise? "

" Be quiet! "

She had heard the heavy footsteps of the patrol. Then the loud-speaker on the roof of a car called out:

" Go into your houses! It's time! Go into your houses! It's time! "

CHAPTER 38

THE NATIONAL ASSEMBLY convoked by Marshal Pétain was to hold its meetings at Vichy. The hall of the Casino was got ready for the occasion. It was here that Montigny had been playing poker until quite recently, and Josephine did her best to forget Lucien's charms by dancing the tango with the Venezuelan press attaché.

The catastrophe had come while several thousand visitors were at Vichy taking the waters for their liver. During the winter several hotels had been turned into military hospitals. The sick and wounded soldiers now gazed wearily at a motley crowd. Vichy was changed beyond recognition. The place was invaded not only by deputies and senators, but by the whole of Paris society as well: industrialists, speculators, high officials, journalists, and cocottes. You couldn't move a step without hearing: " Ah, it's you, Count! " " Well, so you managed to get away too, Jules? " " But where's the little girl friend? "

Everybody was excited; today was the great event of this extraordinary season, the high spot of which was the meeting of the National Assembly. Laval wanted to do without ceremonies, but Breteuil was fond of ritual, so they had decided to bury the Third Republic with great pomp.

Tessa had long been preparing for this event. As always, he remained an optimist; after recovering from the excitements of the journey, he now felt quite well and wanted to live. He kept telling himself that the marshal's scheme was to his advantage, as he would be appointed instead of elected, and that was much more peaceful. Nevertheless, in the depth of his heart he felt anxious. He could not help remembering Desser's remark: " Poor old bug." Of course, Desser was out of his mind, but there was a grain of truth in the offensive remark. People had made use of him, Tessa, had sheltered behind his resounding name, and now they wanted to squeeze him out. Who could guarantee that they would not throw him out tomorrow? The Right regarded him as a radical. At Bordeaux everybody had smiled at him, but here Laval had passed him by almost without saying how-d'you-do. When the lemonade is ready, nobody bothers about the squeezed-out lemon.

Tessa was on the verge of tears; everybody was insulting him. Had he not helped Laval? Who had made up to that horrible Spaniard when it was necessary to come to terms with the Germans? Who had shown that the Compiègne terms were quite acceptable? Everyone had a very short memory! And even his own family had not understood him. Take proud little Denise, for instance. How he had loved and pampered her! Now the Germans would cut off her head. It was terrible to think of it! Hitler wasn't joking. That's why he had conquered. What would become of Denise? Tessa blew his nose twice; the tears trickled down it. Then he remembered Lucien's chestnut hair and shuddered. Lucien was sure to soil the name of Tessa. It was in his blood: he took after his uncle Robert. Only Robert had got off with four years' imprisonment, whereas Lucien was a crook by nature. But perhaps he had been killed. That would be the end of the house of Tessa. And France would come to an end as well. Tessa waved his hand. Suddenly his face took on an angry look; he was thinking of Paulette. The base creature was probably singing her songs to the Germans. She would not care about national mourning so long as she could find somebody younger and livelier.

An hour later Tessa was in a different mood altogether. A mere trifle was the cause of the change. Breteuil had rung up to ask him how he was feeling. Tessa then realized that he was still needed. Although he had refused to undertake the task of showing up the Masons at the meeting of the Assembly, he proposed to make a short telling speech. He had succeeded in discovering that *L'Humanité* had published the advertisements of a furniture firm owned by an Alsatian Jew. He would be able to exclaim: "Invisible golden chains link Jewish capital with the Communists. That is the origin of this criminal war."

At the last moment Breteuil took Tessa on one side. "It will be better if you don't speak," he said. Tessa blinked his eyelids resentfully. Breteuil explained to him that it was a question of tact. The nerves of the country were raw and the gallery had to be taken into consideration. They would drag up all the past: Stavisky, the Popular Front, and so on. . . . Tessa agreed to the suggestion, but felt depressed once again; he wanted to live, but the earth was trembling beneath him.

Grandel, who had just arrived from Paris, brought him a little comfort. Catching sight of Tessa in the foyer of the Casino, Grandel hurried across to him and amiably told him all about Paris. "There were very few people there at first," he said, "but now the place is gradually filling up. They want to reopen the opera. On the whole, the Germans have restored order. They're behaving very well. You'd hardly think they were conquerors. They're more like guardians. . . ."

Some deputies who had come up listened to Grandel in silence.

A senator exclaimed: "Oho!" But it was impossible to make out whether he was delighted or dissatisfied.

Bergery shook Tessa warmly by the hand. "It's a good thing to see you here at your post. I was convinced you wouldn't leave France in her hour of difficulty."

Tessa gave a slight inclination of his birdlike head by way of acknowledgment. Tiny beads of sweat gleamed on his sharp nose. He was quite touched by Bergery's remark; it showed that at least some people realized that he had taken a heavy cross upon himself. Was it an easy matter to sign a shameful armistice and to come here to take part in the liquidation of the past?

"I serve France," he replied. "By the way, Blum's here, and so is Fouget. I wonder what they'll do when it comes to the voting? Especially Fouget. It's no joke to lie down and scourge oneself. Ha! That's what it comes to. He won't dare to vote against. It's a pity Ducane isn't here. That war-monger. . . ."

"Where is he?"

"In the Army, I suppose."

"Probably he was the first to give himself up," Grandel put in; "I know these 'last-ditchers.'"

"But where is Villard?"

"Nobody knows. He disappeared after we left Tours."

"I heard he bolted to Lisbon through Spain."

"Surely the Spaniards wouldn't let him through?"

"What a story that would make — Villard asking Franco for a visa!"

"They say the Spaniards have mounted machine-guns on the frontier. And they're putting everybody who gets across into a concentration camp."

Tessa smiled. What, after all, was history, he thought. A set of quadrilles — backwards and forwards and gentlemen change partners. . . . The Spaniards had probably put Villard into a concentration camp. It was easy to picture his indignation with his glasses bobbing up and down on his nose. And what about his pictures? Had he really left his pictures at Avignon?

"There's something ludicrous in every tragedy," Tessa said. "Villard's fate amuses me. What a fright he must have had to make him leave his collection! Can you imagine his face?"

From behind Tessa came an injured voice: "If you can't imagine it, you can see it. I think your irony is out of place, Paul."

Tessa was astonished. "Is it you, Auguste? But where have you come from?"

"Avignon. Why are you so surprised at my presence? I'm at my post, as always."

Then Villard began to explain that he was a warm adherent of the new order. "Defeat will cure us," he said. "We must take a lesson from our conquerors. Why is Hitler in Paris? Because he dared. Marshal Pétain has shown himself to be a pioneer. He's over eighty, but he dares. I'm the first to acclaim him."

Even Grandel was embarrassed. And Tessa said to himself: "The old fox! He'll outwit everybody yet."

At last the president of the Assembly rattled his bell. Tessa paid no attention to the speakers. It was easy for Laval to talk now. Why was he silent in September? And Villard was getting all the applause. Blum was looking furious. Of course Blum would vote against; anyway his day was over.

During the intermission the deputies gathered round Grandel. Everybody was toadying to him. "Very well," he would say nonchalantly, "I'll have a talk with Abetz about your affair." Tessa remembered the document that Lucien had stolen. He frowned. It was unpleasant to think that a petty spy had become the saviour of France.

After the intermission Breteuil made a speech. He dwelt on the immorality that had weakened the country and spoke of the " great redemption " that was to restore it. Then he slandered the British, and finally announced in solemn tones as he held out his hand: "The victors have shown themselves to be magnanimous." Tessa yawned — what an old hypocrite! His Lorraine, incidentally, had been given over to the Germans. What a mountebank! And a dull one into the bargain!

Suddenly everybody livened up. Fouget mounted the platform. He started roaring at once: "When the enemies of the fatherland and the petty-minded lift up their hands . . ." He was prevented from saying any more. Then the voting began. Half an hour later the president announced: "569 — for. 80 — against."

Tessa felt exceedingly tired, as though he had made a very long speech. Ladies in the garden were shouting: "Long live Laval!" Tessa did not even feel envious. His head was aching. He strolled wearily back to his hotel.

Fate was merciful to him. In the lounge he saw a very pretty young woman with high breasts and bright vermilion lips. She reminded him of Paulette. He cheered up and went over to her. It was only then that he saw there were tears in her eyes.

Weeping women had always struck him as being particularly attractive. He began to talk excitedly about the sufferings of France. The pretty stranger nodded her head. Then he modestly added: "As a Minister, I . . ." The stranger smiled and began to tell him about her troubles. She had lost a trunk at Nevers. She had left her old mother behind in Paris and was now looking for her uncle; he was employed in the Ministry of Commerce, but apparently had stayed on in Clermont-Ferrand. She didn't know what to do — all she had got in her bag was a hundred francs.

Tessa consoled her and felt consoled himself. They had supper together and he was gay and witty. They drank champagne — first to "eternal France" and then to "eternal love."

In the night he said gaily: "You'd never guess how old I am, *petite poupée.*"

"Fifty?"

He smiled and wagged his finger at her.

"No, *petite poupée!* I'm eighteen in love. But not to the public. In any case, the marshal could very well be my father."

Suddenly he remembered all the events of that historic day — Breteuil's hard look, Villard's craftiness, Fouget's beard, and the disgusting figure 80. Only eighty had come clean! It was sure to be written down in history that they had protested against the "capitulation." In the eyes of posterity the tiresome day would look like a State revolution. And all through the session he had been suffering from heartburn. He ought not to have eaten that snipe *à l'Indienne.* He had not felt well ever since and his head was splitting. Perhaps it was the champagne. He raised himself a little and took a peep at his sleepy *petite poupée.* He felt a lump rise in his throat.

"Do you know what took place at the Casino today?" he murmured.

"The porter told me. Some important session or other."

"It was hara-kiri. You don't understand. I'll explain it to you. The deputies and senators came together. Laval made a speech. He always wears a white tie, *petite poupée.* And then — then we committed suicide. You don't believe it? I give you my word. We declared ourselves dead and then applauded. There were 569 corpses and 80 impudent ones. That's all. Now all you've got beside you is Tessa's ghost, his shadow." He hiccuped and then added apologetically: "I ought not to have drunk so much champagne. Anyway, it doesn't matter now. The death certificate has already been made out."

The woman wanted to go to sleep, but overcame her sleepiness and said politely: "Why worry? When the Germans clear out of Paris, we'll start living as we did before. You said yourself you were young in spirit. You're — " she yawned into her hand and whispered: "you're — a real lover."

Tessa shook his head. "No," he said. "That's a thing of the past. And now? I like clearness and logic. I'll tell you frankly who I am. I'm a bug. An old bug in a crack."

He got up and walked unsteadily to the bathroom.

Fouget came out of the Casino in a state of excitement. He was waving his arms and muttering as though he was talking to invisible listeners. The contemptible cowards had buried the Republic. What had the heroes of Valmy died for? What had the soldiers of Verdun fought for? Shame, citizens, shame! The whole world would turn away with contempt from a France that licked the boots of Hitler.

Of course Fouget had protested, but they had not allowed him to declare the truth. He was now going back to his hotel. The waiter would bring in the soup. Then Fouget would have to go to bed. After all that had happened a peaceful life seemed to him beyond endurance. He thirsted for martyrdom, the whistle of bombs, the guillotine. And look at them! There they all were, sitting on the café terraces and drinking vermouth!

All night long he paced up and down the room. He thought neither of Marie-Louise nor of his sons. He was choking with indignation. He was in Coblenz. Yes, Vichy was Coblenz, the town where the émigrés had organized the counter-revolution in 1792. And who was at the head of the traitors? If it had been Laval, nobody would have been surprised. Everybody knew Laval was a creature who would sell his soul to the devil. He was a greedy Auvergnat with the face of a horse-thief. And Fouget would not have been surprised at Tessa even; he was no better than a streetwalker provided he got his living. But at the head of the traitors was a soldier of the Republic, the old marshal. The Army was dishonoured for all

eternity. Even the grey hair of the aged was dishonoured. Who
was to be trusted any longer? Everybody had been defamed, squan-
dered, and drunk away — on the café terraces — both glory and
common decency.

Tomorrow they would be shouting: " Long live the saviours of
France, the magnanimous Boches! " They would cringe before the
Prussians. They might even declare Göring to be Joan of Arc. It
was not ludicrous — it was disgusting.

Who was Fouget talking to? The butterflies on the wall? His
dim reflection in the mirror? The pale dawn?

At nine o'clock in the morning there was a knock at the door.
The policemen were wearing alpaca coats. One of them said: " We
have an order to arrest you for an inquiry."

" Show me," said Fouget, smiling. " But why isn't it in German?
Learn the German language, messieurs! Enough of translations!
I like the originals. Anyway, don't be embarrassed. You were not
among the defenders of Verdun." He combed his beard and put on
his hat. " I'm ready. And long live the Republic! "

On the staircase landing he saw Tessa, who had managed to get
shaved and have breakfast. He was hurrying to a meeting of the
lawyers' council. When he saw the arrested man, he turned away.
His face was stern and solemn as at funerals. But Fouget passed
downstairs and swore: " *Merde, messieurs, merde!* "

CHAPTER 39

While still in Paris, General Leridot had said: " When a war is lost
there's no sense in going on with it. I will even say it's a sign of
ignorance."

Breteuil wanted to include Leridot in the delegation that was to
sign the armistice, but Leridot had taken to his bed with liver
attack. He thought this was a stroke of luck. He had no desire to
commit his name to history on such a lamentable document.

In the reorganization of the Government General Leridot was
appointed Minister of Armaments. The Ministry was situated in the

small spa of La Bourboule. He was quite grieved when he heard that La Bourboule specialized in the treatment of asthma. He had hoped to find himself at Vichy, where he could have looked after his liver. He was not suffering from asthma. Nevertheless, he went every morning to the inhaling-room. " The war is over," he said. " The period of reconstruction has begun. Treatment can never do any harm."

He sent for his wife, and when he saw her lilac-coloured dressing-gown he beamed with pleasure. They lived in a hotel, but she at once gave the uncomfortable room a domestic atmosphere with her knitting, electric iron, and conversations about the high cost of living. Leridot was happy. The only thing that worried him was the responsibility of his work — he was obliged to hand over war material to the Germans in accordance with the terms of the armistice. " I used to think that rearming was a hard job," he said. " But it's far more difficult to disarm, Sophie."

He considered that it was part of his duty to conceal as much as he possibly could from the Germans. His assistant was Colonel Moreau. Leridot said to him: " We must already start preparing for 1960. Yes, yes! The Germans started to prepare their revenge immediately after they were defeated. It's the law of nature." But Moreau smiled condescendingly: " You needn't worry. The moon can't fight against the sun."

In the morning Leridot was drinking coffee after returning from the inhaling-room. There was a knock at the door. Thinking it was his aide-de-camp or a waiter, the general shouted: " Come in!" Weiss entered.

The former Radical from Comar had now become the bosom friend of Laval and a member of the mixed Franco-German Commission.

The general was still wearing his dressing-gown for the inhaling-room and looked like a carnival puppet. Weiss could not help smiling. Leridot felt embarrassed: a general ought to give a proper impression.

" We're camping out," he said, " and my A.D.C. is inexperienced."

" If you please, general. Excuse my early visit. I've got urgent business for you."

A quarter of an hour later the general came out to Weiss in full uniform with six ribbons on his chest.

Weiss asked him point-blank: " Tell me, general, there were

forty-two medium tanks at Montpellier? But you've handed over sixteen?"

Leridot nodded his head and replied complacently: "Of course. The Germans indicated sixteen."

"But what about our signature?"

"It seems to me, Monsieur Weiss, that we'll be fulfilling our duty to posterity if we start —"

Weiss interrupted him: "What have high-sounding words got to do with it? Sixteen is sixteen. But forty-two is forty-two. What reasons can we have to conceal twenty-six tanks?"

"What do you mean?" Leridot now began to shout. "I've carried out my duty. I will not be spoken to as if I were a schoolboy. I'm a French soldier, monsieur!"

He drew himself up, and in spite of his small stature he thought he was looking down on Weiss.

"You're getting nervous, general," said Weiss, shrugging his shoulders. "You're not fighting a battle. This is a serious business. I'll ask your chief to explain arithmetic to you."

Whereupon Weiss left the room. Leridot was a long time getting over the upset.

"I can't understand," he said to Sophie, "why we've got to present our former enemy with twenty-six tanks. I get a visit from a Frenchman, a friend of Laval's, a man who enjoys the confidence of Breteuil, and he talks to me as though he were a German officer. It's most abnormal, I must say."

Next day Leridot went to see General Picard. He had prepared a report regarding interference in military matters by politicians like Weiss. It was against the marshal's instructions.

Picard greeted him dryly and said: "You seem to have been listening to de Gaulle's chatter. You're wasting your time. The Germans will be in London not later than the middle of August. You're not a young man. You've got experience. Your military past puts you under an obligation. You can't consort with traitors."

Leridot felt embarrassed. He was scarcely able to say: "I don't think I've deserved this."

Picard realized that he had said a little too much. They parted friends. When he got back to La Bourboule, Leridot began to set everything in order. He shouted at his entourage: "You're responsible for the machine-guns, major! You mustn't think they're brooches! We've got to show our former enemy that we're carrying

out our obligations even in trifles. To the very last button, captain!
Do you understand me?"

After supper he had a political talk with Moreau. "That adventurer de Gaulle has backed the wrong horse," he said. "I foresaw
it. The Germans have assembled a strong force on the coast. What
about the Channel, you say? Nonsense! They upset all ideas about
landing-operations at Narvik. In a month Hitler will be in London.
That's as simple as A B C. I consider Laval's line is right. Of course,
we Army men have no right to interfere in politics. But we're not
concerned with parliamentary intrigues now, but with the fate of
France. I tell you frankly, the victory of Germany is to our advantage. We'll be able to occupy a prominent position in the new
Europe on a level with Italy. When Hitler has finished with England, he'll deal with Russia. Of course, there's the Red Army, but
it's not worth much. Only there's all that vast country, my friend,
all that vast country, remember. I'm convinced Hitler will be
obliged to have recourse to our assistance. We'll be able to demand
some concessions. General Picard considers that once Hitler has
got hold of Kiev, he'll give us back Lille. Now just imagine for a
moment that England wins. It would be disastrous. Churchill would
never forgive us for making a separate armistice. And de Gaulle is
connected with obscure elements. I wouldn't be surprised if he
entered into negotiations with the Communists. Yes, yes, anything
can be expected of those people! Personally I prefer the Germans.
They're our former enemies, but they're honest people. Perhaps
Peyrouton or the ex-deputies may hesitate. My choice is made.
We really must help the Germans, not formally, but with all our
heart and soul! What's your opinion, colonel?"

Moreau replied indolently: "I've already told you that the moon
shines with a reflected light. It's difficult to go against facts. Of
course, if they beat the Germans, they won't treat us with any
delicacy. I also think that it's better to live even at La Bourboule
than to hang from a tree."

A few days later General Leridot arranged a picnic. He went
with Sophie and the colonel to a mountain lake. They drove out in
the car to a village and then walked along a little path to the lake.
Leridot was much interested by the landscape; the grey rocks were
piled up in disorder as though intentionally. There were no trees
or flowers to soften the wild aspect. Only a rough prickly bush
grew here and there among the rocks, as grey as everything around

it. The water of the lake was grey. It reminded Leridot of the world after capitulation. For some reason he remembered a green forest in the Ardennes and a legless girl. . . .

They had taken a cold lunch with them. Moreau presented the general's wife with a box of *marrons glacés*. "The local specialty," he said. The shrewd Sophie gasped and thought to herself: "He must be mad to spend eighty francs on sweets at a time like this!"

The sun came out and the lake became rosy. Leridot felt calm and even mellow. "Nature," he said, "nature is the absolute equilibrium of the emotions."

Sophie began to sing an aria from *Mignon*. Moreau thought, looking at her with tenderness and irony: "You'll be mine, you little chicken." Leridot was dozing: the air was like a strong infusion that cheered you up and weakened you at the same time.

Hearing the excited voice of the adjutant, Leridot did not come to his senses immediately. When he was fully awake, he began to shout: "Who gave you permission? Today is Sunday. In any case, we're not at the front!"

"*Monsieur le Général,* there has been a disaster."

The cause of the event which had disturbed the general's Sunday rest was a corporal of the 287th Regiment of the Line, who had formerly been a worker at the Seine factory. His name was Legrais.

Till the month of May, Legrais had been kept a prisoner in a concentration camp near Briançon, where with his fellow prisoners he was obliged to drag stones up a mountain. Nobody knew what they were intended for. The piles of stones lay beside the road in a lonely mountain pass. Legrais did not give way to indignation or quarrel with the soldiers who were guarding the prisoners. Something inside him had broken down. He became taciturn. His eyes looked bored and empty; his face was covered with stiff grey stubble.

In May the prisoners were unexpectedly released. The colonel made a speech to them, in which he repeated several times: "France is sick." The released men were sent to the Italian frontier. Legrais was even given back his corporal's stripes. He treated the change in his fate as an event of little interest. But when he read that the Germans had entered Belgium, he came out of his lethargy and began to look more like his former self, the agitator and fighter.

He now gripped his rifle in a different way and only complained that his regiment was not being sent to the north.

He wanted to get to the front, although he did not believe in the victorious outcome of the struggle. All that winter he had thought of nothing except that France had been blinded, put under a spell, bamboozled, and turned from a great country into a little Monaco! And the sense of this wrong bruised his spirit so deeply that he no longer believed in the possibility of resurrection. He did not have long to wait for his fears to be confirmed. A month later the Italians attacked France. His regiment was stationed near the Petit Saint-Bernard. Legrais defended a strong point.

The Italians kept up a hurricane fire for four days, but the defenders held on. Then came a day of breathing-space. Hot food was brought, but there were no newspapers. A lieutenant who had come from Chambéry said the Germans had occupied Paris. Nobody knew where the French Government was.

The soldiers began to buzz:

" Perhaps there isn't one."

" The Fascists have probably seized power — Laval, Doriot, the whole gang."

" Does that mean we've got to die for Laval? Not me! "

Legrais flared up. " Are you afraid? " he shouted. " Nobody wants to die for Laval. But how do you know it's Laval's Government now? People say so? People say lots of things. Laval won't fight. He's in Mussolini's pocket. We don't know who's there." He pointed to the west. " But we know who's here in front of us. There can't be any mistake here. Think what you like, but I'm not going to let the Fascists in."

For a moment his empty eyes flashed with grief and anger.

His comrades backed him up. Next day the Italians asked the French to surrender. They refused. Cut off from the world, they held out for another five days.

Legrais thought he was dreaming when he heard the words: " An armistice has been signed." Then he could not help swearing: " That's Laval now! " They went out and saw a couple of Italians with a French colonel. Someone growled: " Macaronis! " Legrais became dull and grim once again.

His battalion happened to be one of those that did not break up. They were stationed at Clermont-Ferrand. There was a big arsenal with war supplies near the town. Legrais heard the major say to Lieutenant Brézier: "We're handing over to the Germans on Wednesday." The words penetrated vaguely to Legrais's consciousness, like a ray of light passing through water.

It was a warm night after a downpour of rain that had not freshened the world. Legrais was standing on sentry duty. He was thinking of Josette. She had not written to him even once. Perhaps she had written and the letters had not arrived. And now there was no mail at all. The trains were not running. Everything had gone to pieces like his own life. Where was Michaud? Where was the party? Perhaps it was close at hand — in a neighbour's heart. Perhaps it was far away. Everything had happened as they had foretold: the Nazis had come and found friends, helpers, and lackeys in France. It was terrible to think how precisely *L'Humanité* had foretold it all a couple of years ago. And how vast was the sorrow into which the country had been plunged! The Germans were taking away everything — work-benches, sugar, boots. They were not allowing the prisoners of war to return. What if Michaud had fallen into their hands? Now they would go for the British. And after that for the Russians. They were rats, hungry rats! Was it possible that everything would perish — work, heroism, and even simple human life?

And so the night began with long, weary thoughts. It was not the first weary night that Legrais had passed. In the daytime he tried to talk, asking questions in a hollow, cracked voice and gazing with empty eyes. People had little to say. They were crushed and bruised by all that had happened. They were looking for their relations or hunting for food and shelter. Nobody had time to think about the tragedy; they were all living it.

But when the dawn brought out the trees from the darkness, a decision formed itself in Legrais's mind. It came to him of its own accord. It was neither weighed up nor verified. It was dictated to him by his heart. It was the conclusion that he had drawn from all those mad weeks, the unavailing defence of the strong point, the complaints of the refugees, the stories of the homeless and hungry soldiers wandering about the town, and the impudent, but cowardly remark of the major: "We're handing over on Wednesday." No! They would not hand over, and the Germans would not receive!

Legrais sent the three soldiers into the town. Lieutenant Brézier was asleep in his room. There was not a soul about. Legrais perished alone. His end was simple, humble, and sincere, as his life had been. The explosion shook the entire neighbourhood. The birds flew out of the trees. The windows rattled in a brickworks two miles away from the arsenal.

When General Leridot was informed of what had occurred, he buried his face in his hands. He thought the explosion was a greater disaster than the defeat of France. He would be held responsible for it. The Germans would never believe that it was the act of a miscreant. And Picard would put all the blame on him. Leridot suddenly remembered the grey unfriendly lake and the waste of rocks. "Everything has been blown up," he said to Sophie. "Everything has been bombed. Even nature. Even one's heart."

CHAPTER 40

JOLIOT was fixed up in Paris and *La Voie Nouvelle* was being published there again. He was getting francs from Vichy and marks from the Germans. But the tubby little man complained that Sieburg of the German Embassy was stingy and stank. "Put him in the same cage with a skunk," he said, "and the skunk would be suffocated."

General von Schaumberg was well disposed towards Joliot. He liked the frivolous and sparkling flights of fancy of the little chap from Marseille. But Joliot was depressed and sad. He seldom joked and was not at all sociable. On arriving home from the office he would sit on the bed without taking off his clothes and gaze in silence at the carpet. If his wife asked him what was the matter, he would shake his head as if to say: "Nothing."

The day before, Breteuil had come to the office with an article. Joliot did not read it, but just wrote: "Set" on it. But Breteuil said: "Things are so bad that I shall soon have to start praying." Joliot no longer thought about sensational headlines. What was the use? Nobody would read the paper anyway. The Parisians disdained it, and the Germans had their own newspapers. Joliot often received articles that had been clumsily translated from the German. He would change the word "we" to "the Germans"; *La Voie Nouvelle* had got at least to look like a French organ. On the other hand, Joliot was getting paid for it. What about Breteuil? He was probably getting paid too. But who wanted Breteuil now? It was terrible to think of the past — the 6th of February, the "Faithful," the speeches in the Chamber. All those were things of the past. Then France existed. But now Oberleutnant Francke with pink eyes like a rabbit's was sitting in the *Voie Nouvelle* office, precise and nasty.

"Breteuil has arrived," Joliot said to his wife. "Let 'em all come! We shall soon see Laval and Tessa."

"We shan't be any the better for that," his wife moaned. "I've been all over the place today. There's not a bit of soap to be found. You can't get anything. They've taken everything out of the country."

"That's obvious. But where can we go? It's just the same at Marseille. These damned rats have eaten up all Europe like a cheese. Breteuil told me that Desser had shot himself. Somewhere in Auvergne. There's a heroic act for you — instead of the Marne and Verdun! It's funny! Do you know what came into my head? What if " — he shut the window and lowered his voice — "what if they get beaten after all? You can imagine what an incredible sensation it would be! Five million extra specials would be sold out in one evening. And they'd put a rope round Breteuil's neck. . . ."

"What are you talking about? If the British win, they'll kill you too."

Joliot jauntily nodded his head. "Of course!" he said. "And a damned good thing, anyway! Good Lord alive, how they'll cut the devils' throats! It's worth while being hanged on a lamp-post for the sake of it!"

He went off to the office. On the way he decided to drink an apéritif — "Before they guzzle everything up." He chose a little café in a side-street, where he thought there would be no Germans.

The young girl who served him had tear-stained eyes. Joliot picked up a newspaper. He did not read it, nor did he think about anything. He often sank into this sort of torpor now; he felt he was sailing away to somewhere. The door creaked and a German officer with a heavy jaw and dull eyes came in. He said: "*Bon jour*" politely. Nobody answered him. The waitress brought him a tankard of beer. The German asked her to sit down, but she silently refused. He drank another tankard of beer and then said to the girl: " My beauty, you mustn't be so silent. Why don't you speak? "

She covered her face with the tray and replied: " Monsieur, I'm a Frenchwoman."

The officer flew into a temper. He got up and shouted as he went out: " Look at yourself in a mirror. Your mother slept with a Negro."

The waitress sobbed for a long time: " Oh, why didn't we have any tanks? "

" We did have tanks," Joliot said to her. " Tessa had them. But it's no good crying. You won't get rid of them with tears. They're rats. You've got to kill them. That's not my business. No, I get money from them. Like everybody. But what can I do? Even Marseille is no more. There's practically nothing left — only the Boches and sorrow. Stop crying like a calf! You'd better take the money for the two drinks. Everything may turn out all right in the end — I shall be swinging on the lamp-post, and you'll be dancing with some chap from Marseille. We dance like the devil in Marseille."

CHAPTER 41

BRETEUIL tried to give his reasons and appealed to justice and logic. General von Schaumberg was impenetrable. He looked at Breteuil with his round blue eyes, puffed clouds of pungent cigar smoke, and kept repeating: " No, no! " from time to time. It seemed to be the only word left in his vocabulary.

General von Schaumberg considered it was impossible to take Frenchmen seriously. He liked Joliot. He entertained a music-hall actress at lunch. He was fond of saying: " France is a beautiful holiday resort and Paris is a wonderful *café chantant*." He looked on Breteuil as a " serious Frenchman " — in other words, a fool.

Breteuil had already been nonplussed at Bordeaux when he heard the German demands. He had thought he was going to play a game of poker, hiding the cards and using his cunning. Instead, they shouted at him. Breteuil was particularly amazed at the German demand that all broadcasting should cease after the armistice. He

shrugged his shoulders and said: "They want France to be dumb."
Yet, even at Bordeaux, Breteuil still went on hoping. Hitler loved
outward display, and the shameful scene at Compiègne was necessary to him. In the past blood was wiped out with blood, but Hitler
wanted to wipe out tears with tears. However, the fumes of jubila-
tion would pass, the bells of Germany would stop ringing, the
bonfires lit upon the hilltops in honour of victory would die down,
and then perhaps it would be possible to have a talk. France was
beaten, but France was, and would continue to be, a great power.
She had colonies and a Navy. And Hitler had got England on his
hands. He would have to pay court to France.

Pétain had sent Breteuil to Paris to settle a number of urgent
matters. Millions of homeless people were starving in the unoccupied zone. But the Germans were unwilling to let the refugees enter
the occupied area. They were forcing the prisoners to carry on heavy
labour and keeping the wounded out in the open.

Breteuil explained all this to General von Schaumberg, who
listened attentively. But when Breteuil asked: "Do you agree with
me?" the general replied quite indifferently: "No."

Breteuil mentioned the fact that the occupation authorities in
Lorraine were removing all signs in the French language. At this
the general livened up a little and said: "There are no occupation
authorities in Lorraine. It is part of Germany."

Breteuil could stand it no longer. For the first time he permitted
himself to abandon the language of diplomacy. "I'm a Lorrainer,"
he said.

Von Schaumberg carefully knocked the ash off the end of his
cigar into an ash-tray and said nothing. Then Breteuil returned to
the subject of the refugees. Looking bored, the general cleaned his
fingernails with a file and yawned; finally he decided to put an end
to the useless conversation.

"I can't enter into a discussion of the details," he said.

"They're not details to us. It's a question of life or death for
millions of Frenchmen. The refusal of the German authorities
hinders co-operation between the two nations. I hope . . ."

"No."

Breteuil stood up. Tall and dry, he looked like a German officer,
and von Schaumberg felt a twinge of embarrassment.

"I'm sorry I've not been able to give you any satisfaction," he
said. "We have different points of view. You reason like a diplomat.

But I'm a military man first of all. To me France is a vanquished country. Of course, we can be magnanimous. But I find nothing worthy of sympathy in your requests." He glanced at Breteuil and added in a tone of annoyance: " No, sir, no! "

Not until he was outside did Breteuil recover his senses. Von Schaumberg's headquarters were in a fashionable hotel in the Place de la Concorde. Breteuil glanced round the wide, empty square. German flags were everywhere. There were no passers-by. German soldiers were marching along the quay: right-left, right-left. Grey-green uniforms . . . And all around was blue — the sky, the Seine, and the houses.

Breteuil remembered von Schaumberg and frowned: " What a villain! " Yes; these Germans realized they were the conquerors. They were drunk with victory and it would be ten years before they got sober again. " No! No! " . . . What was the use of talking to such a man about collaboration? He had not been brought to his knees before and now he was forcing the French to crawl on their bellies.

Breteuil turned into the rue Royale. He walked along wrapped in thought and did not hear the sentry call out to him. The German ran after him and swore at him: " Get out in the road, you old fool! " Obediently Breteuil left the pavement. Then he stopped and began to laugh. He very seldom laughed, and the sound of his own squeaky laughter scared him. Everything made him laugh — the fact that they had driven him off the pavement, that he had once killed Grisnez, that Lorraine was a province of Germany, and that the general had answered: " No! " in and out of season. What was particularly funny was the fact that there was no longer any France. There was Paris — streets, houses, shop-signs, there was the aged marshal, and there were forty million wretched people. But there was no France. That, he thought, is where one can say like von Schaumberg: " No! No! "

But what was there left? Breteuil was scared by his own question. In the empty street he moved his lips, muttering a prayer he had known from childhood. The prayer brought him no consolation. The words slipped out and left nothing behind them. He came to the Church of St. Augustin and went inside. It was cool and restful; there were no refugees and no Germans. By the vestry door he saw a priest whom he knew. The abbé gave him his blessing. " How are you, *monsieur l'abbé*? " Breteuil asked.

"It's difficult," he said. "I stayed on in Paris all the time. We've seen so much suffering. I pray God to forgive our blind rulers. They've forsaken the people. As for the Germans, they've got no conscience at all."

Breteuil closed his eyes. The abbé could not make out why he had upset him.

"God knows it wasn't what I wanted!" Breteuil said. "But it's too late to justify oneself now. My son will rise again in the flesh. But I shan't. What I mean to say is I no longer exist. Probably I never did exist — in the image and likeness . . ."

"Here's another one," thought the abbé. Events had turned people's brains, and day after day the abbé had to listen to incoherent, raving confessions.

Breteuil went out of the church. He walked like a wound-up robot — a tall, bony man in a black hat, the leader of the "Faithful," who more than once had sent people to an inglorious death and had lived in the hope of seeing his son again in the next world, a Lorrainer without Lorraine. It was all over and done with now — there were no longer any "Faithful," there was no longer any faith, not even a handful of French earth. And the streets were filled with Prussians, talking their guttural language and doing up packages of sausages, boots, stockings, dolls, presents for brides, feasting for Germany, supplies for a rainy day — the body and blood of France. Breteuil whispered to himself: "They have eaten the body and drunk the blood."

A husky-voiced woman was crying out: "La Voie Nouvelle! Latest edition!" At least one could still buy a newspaper. Breteuil unfolded it and read: "The principles of collaboration are triumphing." He had dictated the article yesterday, before his visit to von Schaumberg. Anyway, tomorrow he would write: "The principles of collaboration have triumphed." All was well with the refugees on the roads, the prisoners were having a wonderful time in their camps. France was snug under the German boot. Joliot was the editor. And Breteuil was the writer.

He wandered on till the loud-speakers began to yell: "Go into your houses! It's time!"

Looking at the dress suits and ribbons scattered over the sofa in his uninhabited house, Breteuil yawned aloud. Then he decided to do some work. He made a little cross at the top of a sheet of paper and then wrote: "The weariness of the human spirit." He laid down the pen and walked about the house. He stopped in front of the baby's chair and stood there without thinking or praying. Then he went back and sat down at the table again.

He wrote rapidly:

To His Excellency, Herr General von Schaumberg.

In view of the disruptive activities of the partisans of England and de Gaulle, I consider it necessary that the German Command should make a gesture conducive to the pacification of the country, if only by allowing the mothers of large families to enter Paris.

For my own part, I am prepared to work with you in exterminating British agents, Communists, and adherents of de Gaulle. I am forwarding to the Commandant's office a list of bad Frenchmen. . . .

He wrote for a long time. His shadow fell motionless across the table — long and sharp like the shadow of a pole.

CHAPTER 42

ALL this time the Parisians had been staying indoors. They could not get used to the German soldiers in the streets. In the morning Agnès went shopping. The long queue was silent. The people tried not to think about anything. Searching for a pound of potatoes or a bottle of milk helped to distract their minds. If they talked at all it was about relations who had disappeared — one had lost a husband, another a son.

Once an old man in a queue exclaimed: " What about France? " Nobody answered, but everybody thought: " France is also lost."

The monuments of Paris, like the relics on the table of a dead person, brought tears into people's eyes. The poets grasped their muted lyres. The marshals rode on dead horses. The orators spoke to the pigeons. People remembered the days of the past: " It was by the statue of Danton that I used to wait for Madeleine."

They did not want to go on with this illusory life, but all the same they went on living, stood in the queues, cooked beans, and wrote letters. They addressed them with the old addresses that no longer existed. There was no mail. The lonely city only heard the unintelligible songs of the German soldiers and the chatter of the birds in the shady squares.

Not far from the school where Agnès lived was a square with a few plane trees in it. Doudou played under the spreading trees and scooped up handfuls of the warm golden sand. A swarthy little boy, impulsive and impatient like Pierre, he was Agnès's salvation.

At first Agnès had wanted to get away from Paris. She kept thinking of Dax, where her father lived. But when she heard that the Germans were also at Dax, she scowled. The last loop-hole of escape was closed. So she said to herself: " That means I've got to live with the Germans! "

She sold clothes, books, and knick-knacks to the second-hand dealer and lived on the proceeds. Her dull dreamy existence was like the winter sleep of a wild animal. She was not the only one who lived like that. All Paris did the same. People talked about it everywhere, making fun of Paris or feeling sorry for it. But in Paris itself nobody felt anything. It was like a sick man on the operating-table who was incapable of throwing off the chloroform mask.

On a sultry evening Agnès was sitting at the window after putting Doudou to bed. Time dragged slowly. She was half asleep when there was a knock at the door. Who could it be at that hour? Only them. . . . She never thought of the Germans except as " them." What had they come for? And she thought quite clearly: " If it's death, I'm not prepared for it."

Opening the door, she saw three youths.

" They're after us," they said.

Agnès took them into the empty, untidy sitting-room.

" I'm a soldier, a gunner," said the eldest boy. " This is my brother and that's his pal. We're from Beauvais. We got as far as here safely, but they stopped us at the Metro, so we made a bolt for it. We knocked and rang, but nobody came to the door. They've probably all gone away."

Suddenly there was a loud insistent knocking down below. Agnès was in a panic: what was to be done? Then in a flash she remembered — there were some big trunks in the storeroom. She quickly shoved the boys inside and covered the boxes with the rags left behind by the refugees. Then, obeying some instinctive prompting, she picked up sleepy little Doudou and ran to the door.

Two Germans and a Frenchman came in.

"Who lives here?"

"I do. And my son, aged four."

"Nobody else?"

"Have a look. . . ."

The Frenchman went into the first room, looked in the cupboard, and for some reason picked up a book that was lying on the table. One of the Germans said politely: "We apologize, madame. There has been a mistake."

When they had left, Agnès put Doudou, who was in one of his tantrums, back to bed; then she went to the storeroom. The youngest, whose name was Jacques, climbed out first.

"I was afraid of sneezing," he laughed. "The dust was enough to choke a chimneysweep!"

"I must give you something to eat," Agnès said.

Fortunately there was still some soup in the pot, a little bread, and some salad.

"We haven't had anything to eat since yesterday," said the soldier, munching a piece of bread.

"Now you must have a good rest," she said.

"No. We'll wait an hour or so till everything's quiet and then we must get going. We only want to get as far as Chartres. There's a man there. He'll get us out."

"But where are you going from Chartres? The Germans are everywhere."

They glanced at one another. Their eyes were asking whether they ought to tell her.

"We mustn't talk about it," said the soldier. "But you're a Frenchwoman. You'll understand. We want to get to London, to the general, to fight."

"To fight?" said Agnès naïvely. "But the armistice has been signed."

Jacques cried out with indignation: "Who by? Traitors!"

"Not so loud!" snapped the soldier. Then, turning to Agnès he said: "The war isn't over. I was at Dunkirk. My brother and Jacques were still waiting to be called up. But now all decent people have got to fight. Look what they've done to France! At Beauvais — No, I don't want to talk about it. . . . No, the war isn't finished yet.

General de Gaulle is calling everybody. We heard him on the radio. We've got to get from Chartres to Brittany. It's easy from there — the fishermen will take us over. The main thing is to get out of Paris. I've got a jacket and a cloak, but look at these."

He pointed to his army trousers. Agnès got busy. "Right away!" In a few minutes she produced some trousers from among the clutter left by the refugees. The soldier tried them on. Everybody laughed. They were a bit short, but they would do.

Suddenly Agnès said: "My husband was killed at the front. What do we want victory for?" She thought she was arguing with Pierre and flared up for a moment. "The important thing is something else: what's in the soul. But people think about frontiers and the map. . . ."

"The soul is just what we're thinking of!" Jacques cried. (And again the soldier snapped: "Not so loud!") "Yes, yes, the soul! Isn't France on the map? It's right here. If there's no France, I can't live. And I'm eighteen and I want to live, very much so. . . . What if we do get killed? Somebody will be saved. You've got a son. And he's France. Isn't that so?"

She shook her head; again she wasn't convinced. But when she said good-bye to the three youngsters, she kissed them all warmly and her eyes were wet.

Then she sat down beside Doudou and cried. Her tears lasted only a few minutes, but it seemed to her a long time. Suddenly she screamed and rushed to the window. Two shots rang out quite close. Doudou woke up and began to cry. The door flew open with a crash and German soldiers rushed into the room.

Agnès recognized the French policeman who had come before. He shouted: "That's her!" The German officer said something and a couple of soldiers grabbed hold of her. The officer said to the Frenchman: "How did you let them get away?" Doudou was crying. The soldiers took Agnès away to the car. They wrenched her arms, but she felt neither pain nor fear. The thought flashed through her mind: "What about Doudou?" Then she gave a feeble scream. "This isn't a lover's embraces," the German said to her roughly.

The night was particularly dark. Agnès thought she saw a forest — she mistook the houses for trees. Then she was taken down a long corridor which smelt of leather, cabbage, and urine. She was pushed into an empty room. "I'm not in a prison," she thought. But what had it been before? There were ink stains on the floor. Perhaps it was a school. . . . She thought she saw Pierre's swarthy face. He was looking over her shoulder at the exercise-book and kissing her. What a bright little lamp! It was close up against the ceiling. She sat down on the floor against the wall. She remembered that Doudou was all alone. She was overcome with despair, insidious and heavy like a fainting fit. Suddenly she shuddered; she read on the wall some words that had been scratched there with a nail or a pin: " Good-bye, Mother! Good-bye, France! Robert." Why did Agnès want to write next to them: " Good-bye, Doudou "? Why did it seem to her like a relief? But she had no pin. She looked at her short nails and began to cry. Then she thought: " They said they'd let the boys get away. Then they must have escaped. They'll get to their general. Jacques was such a nice boy." Of all the events of her life this now seemed to her to be the most important — they had escaped.

She was taken out to be questioned. The German officer, who spoke French well, sent the interpreter away. Irrelevantly he said to Agnès: " I spent two years at Grenoble. It's a beautiful town." He was quite amiable and tried to calm her: " Your son is being taken care of." Then he tried to persuade her to speak: " Tell me who these people are and we'll let you go."

Agnès's silence annoyed him. " Madame," he said. " I've got no time to waste. You're silent? Therefore you're an English spy."

She nodded her head. " Yes," she said. Her eyes became soft and tender, just as they had been under the attic window at Belleville when Pierre had raved and stormed. " Yes, I'm a spy," she said. " Why have you come to our country? Everybody is against you. Even the children, I'll not tell you who these people are. Thank God, you didn't catch them. That's the main thing. And you can kill me. I'm not necessary. I don't even know how to shoot."

Now she felt she was ready to die. The feeling raised her spirits and made her cheerful. Only a short while ago she had argued with the three boys. Now she wanted to repeat what they had said over and over again without stopping in front of this pink, well-dressed officer. How neatly his hair was parted!

The German nervously pushed back the ink-stand. " Enough of this posturing! " he said. " You're not here to make speeches. You're here to give information. Be so good as to answer. Do you know these people? "

" I know them."

"Who are they?"

"Frenchmen."

The officer was beside himself with rage. Usually well-behaved, only a year ago he had charmed the ladies at Swinemünde with his good manners, but now he ran up to Agnès and struck her in the face. She did not cry out. She automatically raised her hand to her mouth and was surprised at the blood. She was now beyond the feelings inherent in man and felt no pain, nor was she indignant at the brutality of the smart, scented officer. It was as though she were intoxicated with a feeling of self-renunciation and ecstasy. "I love," she kept repeating to herself. "I love Doudou, and Pierre, and Father, and Jacques, and Robert, and those who in the last days of Paris went down the crooked street tired and unhappy." One of them had said to her: "Good-bye!" "No," she said to herself, "not good-bye, but how do you do, my dear? Now we're together again! With Pierre. With Paris."

She said these things aloud as she sat on the seat in the corridor. They took her to the colonel. He had a scar on his cheek, and his fishlike eyes were goggling. He asked Agnès to sit down.

"I want to save you," he said. "Tell me, who are these people? Aren't you sorry for your little son? I speak to you as a father — I've got two daughters."

Agnès looked at him in amazement. He had brought her back from another world. She answered in a muffled voice as though she was talking to herself: "Am I sorry for my son? No. Today I've understood everything. If one man dies, he saves somebody, he's certain to save somebody. . . . The people — my people . . ." She remembered that she was being questioned. Usually round-shouldered, she now stood up with a back as straight as a ramrod and began to speak in a different tone. "You say you're a father? That's not true! Do you know who you are? You're a Boche! A Boche!"

The colonel called the sentry. "Take her away!" he ordered.

Then he turned to Agnès and said: "This is the end of you, madame."

She looked past him and replied: "Not of France. And it is not the end. There is no end."

CHAPTER 43

DENISE didn't rush towards him, didn't embrace him, didn't say anything. Only she did not take her tear-filled eyes off him, and in those eyes was something of fear and something of delight.

Michaud was smiling. Then he felt awkward and said: "What's the matter with you, Denise? "

He had longed so much for this meeting! Nine days ago he had hit a sentry on the head with a rock. The rock was hot with the sun's rays. The German's short shadow had disappeared. Then Michaud lay in a gulley till nightfall.

An old woman gave him some clothes and said he could stay in her house until morning. He sat gazing at the white wall while the woman altered the buttons on the jacket. It had belonged to her late husband, the director of the Catholic Guild of St. Just. Michaud asked her what was in the papers. She told him she no longer read them, as they had now become German. The clock on the wall struck the hour with long pauses between the strokes. Neither of them thought about going to sleep. They talked from time to time, and their conversation was disjointed and rather strange.

"His name was Legrais," Michaud said. "He was a Communist, too."

"I live in another world. I'm a believer. But Hitler . . ."

"I loathe him! "

"That's why I let you in. They've put up notices at St. Just. Anyone who helps prisoners will be shot."

"They led me out. They put it off for a day. It was morning. The birds . . ."

"I'm fifty-eight — getting on, but it's still life. Everything is all mixed up. My husband thought we'd all be ruined through you Communists. I thought so, too. Perhaps it was true — yesterday. But now — I used to take *L'Ordre*. Ducane wrote that the Communists were patriots."

"Ducane realized that too late."

"But all of you were too late. And the Germans came. Now I

wonder wnere the truth is — not the truth for one year, but the real abiding truth."

Her dim eyes rested on the plaster figure of the Crucifix. The grey dawn peeped in through the chinks in the window. Michaud thought of Denise, warm and alive. He picked up his cap and said good-bye.

And now Denise was at his side. But she was not laughing. He kissed her and her lips were cold.

"Denise! What's the matter with you? See, I've got away. I've escaped."

She burst into tears and wept noisily like a child. Michaud tried to soothe her. "I've escaped!" he kept saying. "Don't cry, Denise!"

"Michaud," she said through her tears. "When you kissed me, I felt so terrible. I don't believe I'm alive. You don't understand? I can't tell you what I mean. I feel as though we're all dead and we're only pretending to be alive because the Germans have ordered us to live."

He did not reply at once. He did not want to admit that he had felt like that himself more than once after Arras. He had said to himself he must not be pusillanimous. The thought of Denise sustained him. He imagined for some reason or other that Denise would meet him with a smile, a warm hand, and life. Her despondency perplexed him. He stroked her hand in silence.

They were in the little ironmonger's near the Porte de Versailles. It was here that Denise and Claude printed the leaflets. Denise had been calm until the moment she met Michaud. She had talked to Claude about the struggle, strength, and victory. Now she was alone with Michaud.

"Don't cry, Denise," Michaud said.

Claude came in. He did not notice Michaud at once and began to chatter excitedly: "We'll have the type tomorrow. Understand?" Suddenly he cried out: "Michaud! You! Now we're saved! Denise, we're saved! Understand?"

For Claude, Michaud's arrival was a victory for the cause. His joy helped Michaud to revive his strength. He realized they had been waiting for him. He had been beginning to feel ashamed of himself. Denise had thought he was ashamed on her account.

"We'll get to work," he said. "It's a good thing Claude is with us. Claude, it's remarkable that you've been able to find the type. Now we can print leaflets."

" Five hundred at the most," Denise said with a sigh.

" That's just to begin with, and it's a good thing too! We've got to begin all over again. *L'Humanité* ran into half a million. But we were beaten all the same. We've got to get over this period. All the decent people are bewildered at present. And the rotters are triumphant. I saw Doriot's paper today. He's as proud as a peacock. You'd think he'd taken Paris. We must live through all this. Do you realize what it means to live through Fascism? Thousands of books will be written about it as an era in history. In a hundred years . . . But we'll live through it in our day and we'll win. I'll say we will, and how, Denise! "

Denise clutched his hand. " Michaud! " she said.

Michaud now appeared to her as she had known him before. That meant that she too was alive. And Paris was alive. And it was possible to live through all this and to win. . . .

" They've got enormous strength," said Claude. " Troops are passing through every night. Now they're going from the south to the sea. They want to take England."

" They want," Michaud smiled. " It has got to be seen whether they will. Did they take Paris? It was simply dropped into their mouths. Anyhow, Churchill isn't Pétain. I don't say the Germans haven't great forces. I've seen what a lot of tanks they've got. And they've got organization. Everything's run in the German way. But they'll meet their match, they're bound to meet their match. Maybe in England, maybe in some other place. I don't know, but they'll meet their match. We're stronger."

Denise raised her eyebrows. " How are we stronger? "

" Reckon it up. England — that is, the Navy, the Royal Air Force, the people. America. Then look at the conquered countries. All the nations: Norway, Holland, Denmark, Belgium, France, Poland, Czechoslovakia — seven, I'm counting them on my fingers. They've got no army, but the people are also a force. And do you think we haven't our own people in Germany? We have. You wait. But the principal force is Russia."

" But they've got the pact," sighed Claude.

" What of it? Hitler is bound to attack them. Do you think he can put up with the idea that such a power exists? Even a child can understand that. The Russians will show him something. We'll see the Red Army, Denise. We're bound to see it."

" Say: ' and how! ' " Denise laughed.

"I will — and how!"

Claude went out to get some paper. As he went along he thought over Michaud's words. If Michaud said a thing it was sure to be true. Claude was smiling — in a dirty, forsaken street in half-dead Paris. He looked at the German soldiers and smiled. He did not see them; he saw something else — a tiny red star amid the white mist. Thin, worn-out with his advancing illness and all the privations he had suffered, he beamed like a child. He took a piece of chalk out of his pocket and after glancing about him, wrote upon a grey patch of wall: "Hitler began it. Stalin will finish it" — and winked at the blackbird on the blue asphalt.

All was quiet in the workshop. Michaud and Denise sat silent with their arms round each other. Then Denise freed herself and said: "You don't know what it's like in Paris now. Yesterday I saw a German club a workman on the head with a revolver. The man fell down, but the German didn't even look back. They arrested Gémier for listening to the London radio. They tortured him two days running. A German officer said to Marie: 'Your father's jacket is blood-stained. Bring a new one.' She brought it. The officer took the jacket and went away with it. Then he came back and said: 'You're still here? What are you waiting for? Your father is already in the English heaven.' Michaud, are they human beings?"

"No. They're Fascists. I've seen just the same. They killed a child. No, I won't talk about it. But there's going to be happiness, Denise, a great happiness! Don't you believe it? You must realize we're going to win. It's as simple as day after night or spring after winter. It can't be otherwise. What fine people we've got! They're ready to lay down their lives. But whom have the others got? Robbers. Or degenerates. We're bound to win! And then there will be happiness. How the people have longed for it! Big, simple happiness, the simplest happiness even — to live and breathe, not to fear the sound of footsteps, not to hear the wail of sirens, and to fondle children, and to love, just as you and I. . . . It will be happiness. . . ."

She answered gravely, like an Amen: "So it will."

CHAPTER 44

It was a hot morning. For a long time André stayed in his studio.
He was afraid to go out. Yesterday he had heard that Laurier had
been killed. They had shouted: "Jew! " and torn the black bandage
from his dead eye.

André paced up and down the studio all night long, asking himself what was the use of defending that hill, what was the good of
that friendship? They had left him, but had taken Laurier away
somewhere. He had looked at the terrible city with one eye. It was
a treacherous city.

Why did André leave his refuge? Why was he walking about the
odious streets?

Again the beauty of his beloved city took hold of him in spite
of everything. Paris was still as beautiful as ever in spite of its
shame. His fists were clenched, but his eyes could not help admiring
what they saw. The grimy houses of the Île St. Louis, the waters
of the Seine, mysterious as Lethe, the dimly perceived, pale sky —
all this fascinated and soothed him. He thought: "We have seen
many other things besides this; we were, we shall be, we are
Lutetia, the ship, the city of Paris."

He walked as far as Châtelet. He was amazed; he still could not
get used to the quiet. Motor-cars had disappeared. The people
never laughed, and talked in low tones. Under the arcades of the
rue de Rivoli there was a dull thudding as the German soldiers
entered the shops and restaurants, stamping their feet as though
on parade. The women looked paler than before. Either they had
stopped making up their faces or they were feeling ill. Everybody
tried to look plainer, less noticeable, more insignificant. Like insects,
André thought. It was a body without a soul — the architecture and
bones of Paris. But it was not Paris; it was another and an alien city.

The sound of trumpets made him shudder. He had not noticed
that he had reached the Place de l'Opéra. Grey-green German
bandsmen were sitting on the steps of the opera-house, blowing
trumpets. There was something painfully pauperish in the German

march, something akin to the tramping under the arches: life was marking time to the soldiers' boots. German officers were lounging on the café terraces, surrounded by gaudy girls. But the sky was the same — the high sky of Paris.

André leaned against a wall. He tried hard to realize what was going on in front of him, but he was unable to think. A dull torpor took possession of him again. Individual pictures came and went incoherently — an officer with a monocle in his eye, a fountain with a nymph and a dried-up bowl, the tall grass on the paths of the Tuileries, and a hill, that hill . . .

It was a girl who roused him. She was selling the evening paper. He waved it aside disdainfully. She whispered like a conspirator: "I know. I have a little sister."

He gave her a coin and glanced casually at the date. He could not help smiling. It was the 14th of July. Perhaps that was why the Germans were blowing the trumpets? Nobody remembered that today was a holiday. Everybody was standing in the milk queues or shrinking in the doorways.

Once upon a time Paris had stormed the Bastille. . . .

He saw the night with the merry-go-round and the shiny blue elephant, the chestnut tree and the Chinese lanterns. Where was Jeannette now? Could she possibly be wandering about this accursed town, not recognizing the familiar houses and meeting grey-green Germans instead of friends? Or had she gone away to safety? But where could one escape from all this sorrow? Where could one be safe? "Deceived, I go to meet my death." They were only the words of an advertisement in those days. Nobody wanted to understand that a lonely woman was crying out in the night and that France was crying out with her, dead and covered with the dust of the road and blood.

He was saying all this to himself after he had climbed the stairs to his studio and was standing at the window. The rue Cherche-Midi lay before him. German soldiers were marching down the street. Today Josephine had said: "I'm going to open the restaurant. I've got to live." She had looked at André with an air of humiliation, as though his silence insulted her. Yes, she would make ragout for the Germans. The cobblers would sole their boots. The florist would die. Another would take her place and hand a bouquet to a monocled German officer. The street was like Paris: nobody could get out of the circle. No, there was no way out. One might as well hang oneself on that hook.

And André could no longer take his eyes off the dark spot on the grey wall.

When he heard a knock at the door he was embarrassed, as though he had been discovered doing something wrong. It was only when he got to the door that he wondered who it could be. If it was the Germans . . . but he did not finish the thought.

A German came into the studio. Seeing the grey-green uniform, André smiled.

"Anyhow, it will be much better," he said. "You can take me along. I won't bring anything with me."

"Don't you recognize me?" the German said. "I used to live at Madame Coad's. I liked your landscapes very much. We got acquainted with each other in the Smoking Dog."

The German wanted to shake hands, but André did not offer his hand.

"I remember," he said. "You were interested in fishes. It was called — I've forgotten the word."

"Ichthyologist."

"Yes, that's it. You told me that Paris would be destroyed. Probably you were more interested in espionage than in fish when you were here. You knew all the secrets of Berlin. Well, are you satisfied? It's true, you haven't destroyed Paris." He went close up to the German. "But do you think you have taken Paris? Nonsense, monsieur, it's your diseased imagination. Paris has gone away. You'll tell me it will return. I deny it. Josephine has opened her restaurant. People are coming back, but not Paris. Paris will not return. It no longer exists. Not anywhere. And now enough of talk! Take me along."

"Where to?"

"I don't know. You know better. To the Commandant's office, to the wall, to the pit, damn it all!"

The German said nothing. André went on shouting abuse. At last the German said: "Why be offensive?"

"It's impossible to be offensive to you. First, you've got tanks; second, bombers; third, machine-guns; fourth, tommy guns; and fifth, your dull-witted head. As for me, there's that hook. Take me along or I'll strangle you."

"It's not for me to take you anywhere. I don't even know why I came to see you. I suppose I remembered you and felt I'd like to see you. Today the lieutenant told me I was a bad German. It's very odd — maybe tomorrow they'll shoot me."

"Is that so?" There was neither surprise nor sympathy in André's voice. He shrugged his shoulders angrily. He had expected death and it turned out to be the ichthyologist with his own private dissatisfactions. "What is it you don't like?" André asked. "The food? Or are you afraid your fish will eat you in the Channel?"

"I don't know how to explain it. What is it I don't like? My fellow countrymen in Paris. I don't like the fact that I'm in your studio with this uniform on."

"Ho-ho! So you're an æsthete. Ash-grey tones and so on. But do you realize, monsieur, that I'm a Frenchman?"

"I do realize it. It's the very thing that hinders me from speaking. I thought we were people of the same culture. But there is a gulf between us. I don't know how it can be filled up."

"Neither do I." André's voice became more gentle. "It will have to be filled up with blood. It won't be able to be done without blood here."

"Isn't there enough of it already?"

"Plenty. But not the right sort. And now go away."

"I know I must go. This is all very much out of place. It was a foolish idea, my coming here. I'm now going to ask you a foolish question. I don't know why, but it's been worrying me quite a lot. It's a question of grammar. This street is known as Cherche-Midi; that means: 'I look for midday.' Why?"

"That was what the lodgers were called once upon a time. They had to look for where they could get a meal for nothing. Just like your Hitler. But it's a good name. 'I look for midday.' Only the street didn't seek it. People used to sleep soundly here with the shutters shut and coverlets on the beds. As for the street, it was looking for the night. And now your people have come."

"Do you think I feel easy about it?" the German said. "We can't go on living as we do. Everybody hates us. I was walking down the rue Monge yesterday. A woman came along. She caught sight of me and bolted as if I was death himself. Personally I've never killed anyone, but that's of no significance. I might say Hitler is to blame. That would be the easiest. But it isn't true. I'm to blame as well. One must draw conclusions. I'll try. *Au revoir.*"

" Good-bye. Perhaps you'll turn out to be a decent fellow tomorrow, but then I shan't see you. Decency has now got to be proved with blood. That's the low sort of times we're living in. And it's impossible to understand anything. Why have you come here? It's all nonsense. If you were a Communist, it would be a different matter. They may be able to do something. They very nearly won here before. But now we've got Tessa and your lieutenant. But what are you going to do? You're alone in the field. And so am I. And together we don't make two, we make nought. Life is against us. If you're a decent fellow you won't misjudge me for giving you a bad reception. You were a German from Lübeck, a bit of a crank. You drank Calvados. And now you're a grey-green soldier. It's all a question of Paris."

The German went out, and André forgot him at once, as though nobody had ever come in. He walked up and down the studio several times. The blue dusk floated in at the window. A landscape hung opposite the window. André stopped and peered at it: a merry-go-round, a chestnut tree, a lantern, shade in the distance. That was also the 14th of July. Jeannette was still smiling then. Paris was still dancing, marching with flags, and hoping. It was another life. That picture was well painted. It was his best work. And it was Paris. Paris remained. They would burn the museums, they would destroy the pictures — but Paris would remain all the same.

André was smiling. He went over to the window. The rue Cherche-Midi was there with its shutters shut tight and black streaks on the front of the houses, as always. A dead flower drooped in an attic window. Starving cats were wandering about; the florist was weeping; a new-born child was crying. Rue Cherche-Midi . . . " I look for midday " . . . " And I will look for midday," he thought. " I'm bound to find it — light and carnival in the sky — honey, poppies, azure — Paris by day. . . ."

He did not hear the roar of the loud-speaker: "Go into your houses. It's time! It's time! "

August 1940–July 1941

A NOTE ON THE TYPE

The text of this book is set in Caledonia, a Linotype face designed by W. A. Dwiggins. Caledonia belongs to the family of printing types called " modern face " by printers — a term used to mark the change in style of type-letters that occurred about 1800. Caledonia borders on the general design of Scotch Modern, but is more freely drawn than that letter.

The book was composed, printed, and bound by The Plimpton Press, Norwood, Massachusetts.

Printed in the United States
121233LV00004B/58/A